AWAKENED DESIRE

It was deep in the night, and Philippa was dreaming that she felt a warm hand stroking her hair and it felt wonderful. Then a man's mouth was touching her cheek, her jaw, nipping at her throat, licking over her lips. She sighed and stretched onto her back. She loved the dream, cherished it, held it tightly. She could even feel the dream man's fingers caressing her breasts, his callused fingertips stroking her.

Philippa opened her eyes and saw him above her. It wasn't a dream. It was Dienwald and he was breathing hard as he stared down at her. "It wasn't a dream," she said.

Earth Song

CATHERINE COULTER
EARTH Song

AN ONYX BOOK

ONYX
Published by the Penguin Group
Penguin Books USA Inc., 375 Hudson Street,
New York, New York 10014, U.S.A.
Penguin Books Ltd, 27 Wrights Lane,
London W8 5TZ, England
Penguin Books Australia Ltd, Ringwood,
Victoria, Australia
Penguin Books Canada Ltd, 2801 John Street,
Markham, Ontario, Canada L3R 1B4
Penguin Books (N.Z.) Ltd, 182-190 Wairau Road,
Auckland 10, New Zealand

Penguin Books Ltd, Registered Offices:
Harmondsworth, Middlesex, England

First published by Onyx, an imprint of New American Library,
a division of Penguin Books USA Inc.

First Printing, September, 1990
10 9 8 7 6 5 4 3 2 1

 REGISTERED TRADEMARK—MARCA REGISTRADA

PRINTED IN THE UNITED STATES OF AMERICA

To Carol Steffens Woodrum
Bright and beautiful and loved very very much by
her auntie Catherine.

1

Beauchamp Castle
Cornwall, England
April 1275

"You must wed me, you must!"

Philippa looked at Ivo de Vescy's intense young face with its errant reddish whiskers that would never form the neat forked mustache he hoped for. "No, Ivo," she said again, her palms pressed against his chest. "You are here for Bernice, not for me. Please, I don't want you for a husband. Go now, before someone comes upon us."

"There's someone else! You love another!"

"Nay, I do not. There is no other for me right now, but it cannot be you, Ivo, please believe me."

Philippa really did expect him to leave. She had told him the truth: she didn't love him and didn't wish to marry him. Instead of leaving her chamber, instead of releasing her, he simply stood there staring at her, his arms loose now around her back.

"Please leave my chamber, Ivo," she said again. "You shouldn't have come. I shouldn't have let you in."

But Ivo de Vescy wasn't about to leave. "You will wed with me," he said, and attacked.

Philippa thought, even as he lifted her off her feet and tossed her onto her back on her narrow bed, that a man bent on winning a lady was not best served using rape as an argument. She jerked her face back as he wetly kissed her cheek, her jaw, her nose. "Please, this is absurd! Stop, now."

But Ivo de Vescy, newly knighted, newly pronounced a man by his stringent sire, saw his goal and dismissed the obstacles to his goal as more pleasurable then risky. Philippa would want him soon, he told himself, when he pressed his manhood hard against her, very soon now she would be begging him to take her. He finally found her mouth, open because she was primed to yell at him, and thrust his tongue inside.

It was like putting flame to dry sticks. He was breathing heavily, wanting her desperately, pinning her now-struggling body under his full weight. He got his hand under her long woolen gown, shoved aside her thin linen shift, and the feel of her smooth flesh relieved him of his few remaining wits.

Philippa twisted her head until his tongue was out of her mouth—not a pleasant experience, and one she didn't care to repeat. She wasn't worried until Ivo managed to slither his hand over her knee. His fingers on her bare thigh turned him into a heaving, gasping creature whose body had become rigid and heavy on top of her.

"Stop it, Ivo!" She wriggled beneath him, realized quickly that this would gain her naught—indeed, would gain her even more of a ravening monster—and held perfectly still. "Listen to me, Ivo de Vescy," she whispered into his ear. "Get off me this minute or I will see to the destruction of your precious manhood. I mean it, Ivo. You will be a eunuch and I will tell my father and he will tell yours why it happened. You cannot ravish a lady, you fool. Besides, I have as much strength as you, and—"

Ivo groaned in his dazed ardor; he unwisely thrust his tongue into her mouth again. Philippa bit him hard. He yowled and raised his head to stare down at the girl he wanted so desperately. She didn't yet look as if she wanted him, as if she was ready to beg him for his ardor, but it didn't matter. He decided he would try a bit of reason even as he thrust his member against her in a parody of the sex act.

"No, Philippa, don't try to hurt me. Listen, 'tis you I want, not Bernice. 'Tis you and only you who will bear my sons, and I will take you now so that you will want to be my wife. Aye, 'twill happen. Don't move, sweeting."

His eyes were glazed anew, but Philippa tried again, speaking slowly, very distinctly. "I won't marry you, Ivo. I don't want you. Listen to me, you must stop this, you—"

He moaned and jerked his belly repeatedly against hers. They were of a height, and every male part of him fitted against her perfectly, at least in his mind. Philippa decided it was time to

do something. She was loath to harm him; he
was, after all, Bernice's suitor and perhaps future
husband. Her sister wouldn't want him to be a
eunuch. But he was in her chamber, pinning her
to her narrow bed, breathing into her face, and
planning to force her.

When his fingers eased higher on her thigh,
she yelled into his ear, and he winced, his eyes
nearly crossing, and moaned again—whether from
passion or from the pain of her shrill cry, Philippa
didn't know.

"Stop it!" she yelled once again, and pounded
his back with her fists. Ivo touched her female
flesh, warm and incredibly soft, and thought that
finally she wanted him, would soon be begging
him. Her legs were so long he'd begun to wonder
if he would ever reach his goal. Ah, but he'd
arrived, finally. He pressed his fingers inward
and nearly spilled his seed at the excitement of
touching her. He was panting now, beyond himself. He would take her and then he would marry
her, and he would have her every night, he
would . . .

"You bloody little whoreson! Devil's toes and
St. Andrew's shins, get off my daughter, you stupid whelp!"

Lord Henry de Beauchamp was shorter than his
daughter, blessed with a full head of hair that he
was at this moment vigorously tugging. His belly
well-fed, but when aroused to fury, he was still
formidable. He was nearly apoplectic at this
point. He clutched Ivo's surcoat at his neck, ripping the precious silk, and dragged him off Philippa. But Ivo didn't let go. He held tightly to
Philippa's waist, his other hand, the one that had
touched her intimately, dragging slowly back

down her thigh. She pushed and shoved at him and her father tugged and cursed. Ivo howled as he fell on the floor beside her bed, rolled onto his back, and stared blankly up at Lord Henry's convulsed face.

"My lord, I love Philippa, and you must—" He shut his mouth, belated wisdom quieting his tongue.

Lord Henry turned to his daughter. "Did the little worm harm you, Philippa?"

"Nay, Papa. He was lively, but I would have stopped him soon. He lost his head."

"Better his head than your maidenhead, my girl. How comes he to be in your chamber?"

Philippa stared down at her erstwhile attacker. "He claimed to want only to speak to me. I didn't think it would become so serious. Ivo forgot himself."

Ivo de Vescy had more than forgotten himself, Lord Henry thought, but he merely stared down at the young man, still sprawled on his back, his eyes now closed, his Adam's apple bobbing wildly. Lord Henry had nearly succumbed to a seizure when he'd seen Ivo de Vescy atop his daughter. The shock of it still made the blood pound in his head. He shook himself, becoming calmer. "You stay here, Philippa. Straighten yourself, and, I might add, you will keep silent about this debacle. I will speak to our enthusiastic puppy here. Mayhap I'll show him how we geld frisky stallions at Beauchamp."

Lord Henry grabbed Ivo's arm and jerked him to his feet. "You will come with me, you randy young goat. I have much to say to you."

Ivo deserved any curse her father chose to heap on his head, Philippa thought, straightening her

clothing, and her father had an impressive reper-
toire of the most revolting curses known in Cornwall. She thought of Ivo's hand creeping up her
leg and frowned. She should have sent her fist
into his moaning mouth, should have kicked him
in his spirited manhood, should have . . . Philippa paused, wondering exactly what her father
would say to Ivo. Would he tell him to forget
about Bernice? Would he order Ivo out of Beauchamp Castle? This was the *third* man who'd
acted foolishly . . . well, not so foolishly as Ivo,
and it wasn't amusing, not anymore. Bernice
didn't think so, and neither did their mother,
Lady Maude. Lord Henry wouldn't order Ivo
away from Beauchamp; he couldn't. Bernice
wanted Ivo Vescy very much. Lady Maude wanted
him for Bernice. Philippa wanted him for Bernice
as well.

Philippa felt a thick curl of hair fall over her
forehead and slapped it away, then sighed and
tried to weave it back into its braid. Life wasn't
always reasonable; one couldn't expect it to be.
But there had been five suitors for Bernice's well-
dowered hand. Two of the men had swooned
over Bernice, but she hadn't shared their enthusi-
asms. The other two had preferred Philippa, and
Bernice, unaccountably to her sister, had decided
it was Philippa's fault. And now Ivo de Vescy,
the young man most profoundly desired by Bernice, the one with the sweetest smile, the clever-
est way of arching only one eyebrow, and the
most manly of bodies, had turned coat.

What was Lord Henry saying to him? Philippa
couldn't allow Ivo to be turned out of Beauchamp.
Neither Bernice nor Lady Maude would ever forgive her. They would both accuse her of trying

to gain Ivo's affections for herself. Bernice would probably try to scratch her face and pull out her hair, which would make life excessively unpleasant.

Philippa didn't hesitate a moment. She hurried quietly down the deeply indented stone stairs from the Beauchamps' living quarters into the great hall with its monstrous fireplace and a beam-arched ceiling so high it couldn't be seen in the winter for all the smoke gushing upward. She didn't stop, but speeded up, slipping out of the great hall into the inner ward and running toward the eastern tower. She climbed the damp stone stairs, slowing down only when she reached the second floor and the door to her father's private chamber. His war room, it was called, but Philippa knew that her father frolicked away long winter nights in that room with willing local women. Without hesitation she eased the door open a crack, just enough for her to see her father standing near one of the narrow arrow slits that gave out over the moat to the Dunroyal Forest beyond. Ivo de Vescy, his shoulders attempting arrogance, stood straight as a rod in front of him. She heard her father say sharply, "Have you no sense, you half-witted puppy? You cannot have Philippa! Bernice is the daughter who is to be wed, not Philippa. I will not tell you this again."

Ivo, sullen yet striving with all his might to be manly, squared his shoulders until his back hurt and said, "My lord, I must beg you to reconsider. 'Tis Philippa I wish to have. I beg your pardon for trying to . . . convince her of my devotion in such . . ." He faltered, understandably, Philippa thought, easing her ear even closer.

"You were ravishing her, you cretin!"

"Mayhap, my lord, but I wouldn't have hurt her. Never would I harm a hair on her little head!"

"Hellfire, boy, her *little* head is the same height as yours!"

That was true, but Ivo didn't turn a hair at the idea of having a wife who could stare him right in the eye. "Lord Henry, you must give her to me, you must let me take her to wive. My father will cherish her, as will all my family. Please, my lord, I wouldn't have hurt her."

Lord Henry smiled at that. "True enough, young de Vescy. She wouldn't have allowed you to ravish her, you callow clattermouth. Little you know her. She would have destroyed you, for she is strong of limb, strong as my hulking squire, not a mincing little bauble like other ladies." There was sudden silence, and Lord Henry stared at the young man. There came a glimmer of softening in his rheumy eyes and a touch of understanding in his voice. "Ah, forget your desire, young Ivo, do you hear me?" But Ivo shook his head.

All softening and understanding fled Lord Henry's face. His fearsome dark brows drew together. He looked malevolent, and even Philippa, well used to her sire's rages, shrank back. Surely Ivo would back down very soon; no man faced her father in that mood. To her shock and Lord Henry's, Ivo made another push, his voice nearly cracking as he said, "I love her, my lord! Only Philippa!"

Lord Henry crossed his meaty arms over his chest. He studied Ivo silently, then seemed to come to a decision. Frowning, he said, "Philippa is already betrothed. She is to wed on her eigh-

teenth birthday, which is only two months from
now."

"Wed! Nay!"

"Aye. So be off with you, Ivo de Vescy. 'Tis
either my lovely Bernice or—"

"But, my lord, who would claim her? Whom
would you prefer over me?"

Philippa, whose curiosity was by far greater
than her erstwhile ravisher's, pressed her face
even closer, her eyes on her father's face.

"She is to wed William de Bridgport."

De Bridgport!

Philippa whipped about, her mouth agape, not
believing what she'd heard. Then she caught the
sound of her mother's soft footfall and quickly
slithered behind a tapestry her grandmother had
woven some thirty years before, where only her
pointed slippers could be seen. She held her
breath. Her mother passed into the chamber without knocking. Philippa heard some muttered
words but could not make them out. She quickly
resumed her post by the open door.

Philippa heard her mother laugh aloud, a rusty
sound, for Lady Maude had not been favored
with a humorous nature. "Aye, Ivo de Vescy, 'tis
William de Bridgport who will wed her, not you."

Ivo stared from one to the other, then took a
step back. "William de Bridgport! Why, my lord,
my lady, 'tis an old man he is, a fat old man with
no teeth, and a paunch that . . ." Words failed
Ivo, and he demonstrated, holding his hands out
three feet in front of his stomach. "He's a terror,
my lord, a man of my father's years, a—"

"Devil's teeth! Hold your tongue, you impudent little stick! You know less than aught about
anything!"

Lady Maude took her turn, her voice virulent. "Aye, 'tis none of your affair! 'Tis Bernice we offer, and Bernice you accept, or get you gone from Beauchamp."

Philippa eased back, her face pale, images, not words, flooding her brain. De Bridgport! Ivo was right, except that de Bridgport was even worse than he had said. The man was also the father of three repellent offspring older than her—two daughters, shrill and demanding, and a son who had no chin and a leering eye. Philippa closed her eyes. This had to be some sort of jest. Her father wouldn't . . . There was no need to give her in marriage to de Bridgport. It made no sense, unless her father was simply making it up, trying to get Ivo to leave off. Aye, that had to be it. Ivo had caught him off-guard and he'd spit out the first name that had come to mind in order to make Ivo switch his ardor to the other sister.

But then Lady Maude said, her voice high and officious, "Listen you, Ivo de Vescy. That giant of a girl has no dowry from Lord Henry, not a farthing, hear you? She goes to de Bridgport because he'll take her with naught but her shift. Be glad de Bridgport will have her, because her shift is nearly all Lord Henry will provide her. Ah, didn't you know all call her the Giant? 'Tis because she's such a lanky, graceless creature, unlike her sweet-natured sister."

Lord Henry stared in some consternation at his pallid-faced wife whose pale gray eyes hadn't shone with this much passion since their first wedded night, a very short wedded night, and slowly nodded, adding, "Now, young pup, 'tis either you return to York and your father or you'll take my pretty Bernice, as her mother says, and you'll sign the betrothal contract, eh?"

But Ivo wasn't quite through, and Philippa, for a moment at least, was proud of him, for he mouthed her own questions. "But, my lord, why? You don't care for your daughter, my lady? I mean no disrespect, my lord, but . . ."

Lord Henry eyed the young man. He watched his wife eye de Vescy as well, no passion in either eye now, just cold fury. Even her thin cheeks sported two red anger spots. Ivo was being impertinent, but then again, Lord Henry had been a fool to mention de Bridgport, but his had been the only name to pop into his mind. And Maude had quickly affirmed the man, and so he'd been caught, unable to back down. De Bridgport! The man was a mangy article.

"Why, my lord?"

There was not only desperation but also honest puzzlement in the young man's voice, and Lord Henry sighed. But it was Maude who spoke, astonishing him with the venom of her voice. "Philippa has no hold on Lord Henry. Thus she will have no dowry. She is naught to us, a burden, a vexation. Make up your mind, Ivo, and quickly, for you sorely tax me with your impertinence."

"Will you now accept Bernice?" Lord Henry asked. "She, dulcet child, tells me she wants you and none other."

Ivo wanted to say that he'd take Philippa without a dowry, even without a shift, but sanity stilled his impetuosity. He wasn't stupid; he was aware of his duty as his father's eldest son. The de Vescy holdings near York were a drain at present, given the poor crops that had plagued the area for the past several years. He must wed an heiress; it was his duty. He had no choice, none at all. And, his thinking continued, Philippa wasn't small and soft and cuddly like her sister. She was too tall, too strong, too self-willed—by all the saints, she could read and cipher like a bloody priest or clerk—ah, but her rich dark blond hair was so full of colors, curling wildly around her face and making an unruly fall down her back, free and soft. And her eyes were a glorious clear blue, bright and vivid with laughter, and her breasts were so wondrously full and round and . . . Ivo cleared his throat. "I'll take Bernice, my lord," he said, and Lord Henry prayed that the young man wouldn't burst into tears.

Maude walked to him, and even smiled as she touched his tunic sleeve. " 'Tis right and proper," she said. "You will not regret your choice."

Philippa felt like Lot's wife. She couldn't seem to move, even when her father waved toward the door, telling Ivo to repose himself before seeking out Bernice. In an instant of time her life had changed. She didn't understand why both her parents had turned on her—if turn they had. She'd always assumed that her father loved her; he worked her like a horse, that was true, but she enjoyed her chores as Beauchamp's steward. She reveled in keeping the accounts, in dealing with the merchants of Beauchamp, with settling disputes amongst the peasants.

As for her mother, she'd learned to keep clear of Lady Maude some years before. She'd been told not to call her "Mother," but as a small child she'd accepted that and not worried unduly about it. Nor had she sought affection from that thin-lipped lady since she'd gained her tenth year and Lady Maude had slapped her so hard she'd heard

ringing in her ears for three days. Her transgres-
sion, she remembered now, was to accuse Bernice
of stealing her small pile of pennies. Her father
had done nothing. He hadn't taken her side, but
merely waved her away and muttered that he was
too busy for such female foolishness. She'd forgotten until now that her father hadn't defended
her—probably because it had hurt too much to
remember.

And now they planned to marry her to William
de Bridgport. They wouldn't even provide her
with a dowry. Nor had anyone mentioned it to
her. Philippa couldn't take it all in. From a
beloved younger daughter—at least by her father—
to a cast-off daughter who wasn't loved by anyone, who had no hold on her parents, who was
of no account, who had only her shift and nothing more . . . What had she done? How had she
offended them so deeply as to find herself thus
discarded?

Even as Ivo turned, his young face set, she
couldn't make herself move. Finally, when Ivo
was close enough to see her, she did move,
turned on the toes of her soft leather slippers,
and raced away. The toes of the slippers were
long and pointed, the latest fashion from Queen
Eleanor's court, and they weren't meant for running. Philippa tripped twice before she reached
the seclusion of her chamber. She slid the bolt
across the thick oak door and leaned against it,
breathing harshly.

It wasn't just that they didn't want her. Nor
was it that they simply wanted her away from
them and from Beauchamp. They wanted to punish her. They wanted to give her to that profane
old man, de Bridgport. Why? There was no

answer that came to mind. She could, she supposed, simply go ask her father why he and her mother were doing this. She could ask him how she had offended them so much that they wanted to repulse her and chastise her.

Philippa looked out the narrow window onto the inner ward of Beauchamp Castle. Comforting smells drifted upward with the stiff eastern breeze, smells of dogs and cattle and pigs and the lathered horses of Lord Henry's men-at-arms. The jakes were set in the outer wall in the western side of the castle, and the wind, fortunately, wafted away the smell of human excrement today.

This was her home; she'd never questioned that she belonged; such thoughts would never have occurred to her. She knew that Lady Maude cared not for her, not as she cared for Bernice, but Philippa had ignored the hurt she'd felt as a child, coming not to care over the years, and she'd tried instead to win her father, to make him proud of her, to make him love her. But now even her father had sided with Lady Maude. She was to be exiled to William de Bridgport's keep and company and bed. She felt a moment of deep resentment toward her sister. Bernice, who'd been the only one to garner the stingy affections Lady Maud had doled out as if a hug or a kiss were something to be hoarded.

Was it because Philippa was taller than her father, a veritable tower of a girl who had not the soft sweet look of Bernice? Lady Maude had told Ivo that she was called the Giant. Philippa hadn't known; she'd never heard that, even from Bernice in moments of anger.

Was it because she'd been born a girl and not a boy?

Philippa shook her head at that thought. If true, then Bernice wouldn't be exempt from displeasure, surely.

Philippa wasn't really a giant, just tall for a female, that was all. She turned from the window and looked blankly around her small chamber.

It was a comfortable room with strewn herbs and rushes covering the cold stone floor. She had to do something. She could not simply wait here for William de Bridgport to come and claim her.

It occurred to Philippa at that moment to wonder why Lord Henry had gone to such pains to educate her if his intention were simply to marry her off to William de Bridgport. It seemed a mighty waste unless de Bridgport wanted a steward and a wife and a brood mare all in one. Philippa had been Lord Henry's steward for the past two years, since old Master Davie had died of the flux, and she was becoming more skilled by the day. What use was it all now? she wondered as she unfastened her soft leather belt, stripped off her loose-fitting sleeveless overtunic of soft pale blue linen and then her long fitted woolen gown, nearly ripping the tight sleeves in her haste. She stood for a moment clothed only in her white linen shift that came to mid-thigh. Then she jerked the shift over her head. She realized in that instant that she'd seen something else in the inner ward of the castle. She'd seen several wagons loaded high with raw wool bound for the St. Ives April Fair. Two wagons belonged to the demesne farmers and one to Lord Henry.

She stood tall and naked and shivering, not with cold, but with the realization that she couldn't stay here and be forced to wed de Bridgport. She couldn't remain here at Beauchamp and pretend that nothing had happened. She couldn't remain here like a helpless foundling awaiting her fate. She could hear Bernice taunting her now: . . . *an evil old man for you, a handsome young man for me. I'm the favorite and now you'll pay, pay* . . .

She wasn't helpless. In another minute Philippa had pulled a very old shapeless gown over an equally old shift and topped the lot with an overtunice that had been washed so many times its color was now an indeterminate gray. She replaced her fashionable pointed slippers with sturdy boots that came to her calves. She quickly took strips of linen and cross-gartered the boots to keep them up. She braided her thick hair anew, wound it around her head, and shoved a woolen càp over it. The cap was too small, having last been worn when she was but nine years old, but it would do.

Now she simply had to wait until it grew dark. Her cousin Sir Walter de Grasse, Lady Maude's nephew, lived near St. Ives. He was the castellan of Crandall, a holding of the powerful Graelam de Moreton of Wolffeton. Philippa had met Walter only twice in her life, but she remembered him as being kind. It was to her cousin she'd go. Surely he would protect her, surely. And then . . . To her consternation, she saw the farmers and three of her father's men-at-arms fall in beside the three wagons. They were leaving now!

Philippa was confounded, but only for a minute. Beauchamp had been her home for nearly eighteen years. She knew every niche and cavity of it. She slipped quietly from her chamber, crept down the deep stairs into the great hall, saw that no one noticed her, and escaped through the great open oak doors into the inner ward.

Quickly, she thought, she must move quickly.
She ran to the hidden postern gate, cleared it
enough to open it, and slipped through. She
clamped her fingers over her nostrils, shuddered
with loathing, and waded into the stinking moat.
The moat suddenly deepened, and her feet sank
into thick mud, bringing the slimy water to her
eyebrows. She coughed and choked and gagged,
then swam to the other side, crawled up the slippery bank, and raced toward the Dunroyal Forest
beyond. The odor of the moat was now part of
her.

Well, she wasn't on her way to London to meet
the king. She was bent on escape. She wiped off
her face as best she could and stared down the
pitted narrow road. The wagons would come this
way. They had to come this way.

And they did, some twenty minutes later. She
pulled her cap down and hid, positioning herself.
The wagons came slowly. The three men-at-arms
accompanying the wagons to the fair were jesting
about one of the local village women who could
exercise a man better than a day of working in
the fields.

Philippa didn't hear anything else. From the
protection of her hiding place she flung several
small rocks across the road. They ripped into the
thick underbrush, thudding loudly, and the men-
at-arms reacted immediately. They whipped their
horses about, drawing the craning attention of the
farmers who drove the wagons. As quickly as she
could move, Philippa slipped to the second
wagon and burrowed under the piles of dirty gray
wool. She couldn't smell the foul odor of the raw
wool because she'd become used to the smell of
the moat that engulfed her. The wool was coarse

and scratchy, and any exposed flesh was instantly miserable. She would ignore it; she had to. She relaxed a bit when she heard one of the men-at-arms yell, " 'Tis naught!"

"Aye, a rabbit or a grouse."

"I was hoping it was a hungry wench wanting to ride me and my horse."

"Ha! 'Tis only the meanest harlot who'd take you on!"

The men-at-arms continued their coarse jesting until they heard one of the peasants snicker behind his hand. One of them yelled, "Get thee forward, you lazy lout, else you'll feel the flat of my sword!"

2

St. Erth Castle, Near St. Ives Bay
Cornwall, England

The sheep were dead. Every last miserable one of them was dead. Every one of them had belonged to him, and now they were all dead, all forty-four of them, and all because the shepherd, Robin, had suffered with watery bowels from eating hawthorn berries until he'd fallen over in a dead faint and the sheep had wandered off, gotten caught in a ferocious storm, and bleated themselves over a sheer cliff into the Irish Sea.

Forty-four sheep! By Christ, it wasn't fair. What was he to do now? He had no coin—at least not enough to take to the St. Ives Fair and purchase more sheep, and sheep that hadn't already been spring-shorn. He couldn't get much wool off a spring-shorn sheep. He needed clothes, his son needed clothes, his men needed clothes, not to mention all the servants who toiled in his keep. He had a weaver, Prink, who was eating his head off, and content to sit on his fat backside with nary a thing to do. And Old Agnes, who told everyone what to do, including Prink, was also doing nothing but carping and complaining and driving him berserk.

Dienwald de Fortenberry cursed, sending his fist against his thigh, and felt the wool tunic he wore split from his elbow to his armpit. The harsh winter had done him in. At least his people were planting crops—wheat and barley—enough for St. Erth and all the villeins who spent their lives working for him and depending on him to keep them from starving. Many lords didn't care if their serfs starved in ditches, but Dienwald thought such an attitude foolhardy. Dead men couldn't plant crops or shoe horses or defend St. Erth.

On the other hand, dead men didn't need clothes.

Dienwald was deep in thought, tossing about for something to do, when Crooky, his fool, who'd been struck by a falling tree as a boy and grown up with a twisted back, shuffled into view and began to twitch violently. Dienwald wasn't in a mood to enjoy his contortions at the moment and waved him away. Then Crooky hopped on one foot, and Dienwald realized he was miming something. He watched the hops and the hand movements, then bellowed, "Get thee gone, meddlesome dunce! You disturb my brain."

Crooky curtsied in a grotesque parody of a lady and then threaded a needle, sat down on the floor, and mimed sewing. He began singing:

My sweet Lord of St. Erth
Ye need not ponder bare-arsed or
Fret yer brain for revelations
For you come three wagons and full they be
Ready, my sweet lord, for yer preservations.

"That has no sensible rhyme, lackwit, and you waste my energies! Get out out of my sight!"

My sweet lord of St. Erth
Ye need not go a-begging
In yer humble holey lin-en
There come three wagons full of wool and
But a clutch of knaves to guard them-in.

"Enough of your twaddle!" Dienwald jumped to his feet and advanced on Crooky, who lay on the rush-strewn floor smiling beautifully up at his master. "Get to your feet and tell me about this wool."

Crooky began another mime, still crouched on the floor. He was driving a wagon, looking over his shoulder; then fright screwed up his homely features. Dienwald kicked him in the ribs. "Cease this!" he bellowed. "You've less ability than the bloody sheep that slaughtered themselves."

Crooky, exquisitely sensitive to his master's moods, and more wily than he was brain-full, guessed from the pain in his ribs that his lord was serious. He quickly rolled to his knees and told Dienwald what he'd heard.

Dienwald stroked his hand over his jaw. He hesitated. He sat down in the lord's chair and stretched out his legs in front of him. There was a hole in his hose at the ankle. So there were three wagons of raw wool coming from Beau-

champ. Long he'd wanted to tangle with that
overfed Lord Henry. But the man was powerful
and had many men in his service. From the corner of his eye Dienwald saw his son, Edmund,
dash into the great hall. His short tunic was
patched and worn and remarkably filthy. His
hose were long disintegrated, and the boy's legs
were bare. He looked like a serf.

Edmund, unconcerned with his frayed appearance, looked from his father to Crooky, who gave
him a wink and a wave. " 'Tis true, Father? Wool
for the taking?"

Dienwald looked again at the patches that were
quick wearing through on his son's elbows. He
shouted for his master-at-arms, Eldwin. The man
appeared in an instant and Dienwald knew he'd
heard all. "We'll take eight men—our most fero-
cious-looking fighters—and those wagons will
soon be ours. Don't forget Gorkel the Hideous.
One look at him and those wagon drivers will
faint with terror. Tell that useless cur Prink and
Old Agnes that we'll soon have enough work for
every able-bodied servant in the keep."

"Can I come with you, Papa?"

Dienwald shook his head, buffeted the boy
fondly on the shoulder, a loving gesture that
nearly knocked him down into the stale rushes.
"Nay, Edmund. You will guard the castle in my
absence. You can bear Old Agnes' advice and
endless counsel whilst I'm gone."

The stench was awful. By the evening of that
first day, when the wagons and men camped near
a stream close to St. Hilary, Philippa was very
nearly ready to announce her presence and beg
mercy, a bath, and some of the roasting rabbit

she smelled. But she didn't; she endured, she had to. They would reach St. Ives Fair late on the morrow. She could bear it. It wasn't just the raw, bur-filled wool, but the smell of moat dried against her skin and clothes and mingled with the odor of the raw wool. It didn't get better. Philippa had managed to burrow through the thick piles of wool to form a small breathing hole, but she dared not make the hole larger. One of the men might notice, and it would be all over. They would sympathize with her plight rightly enough, and let her bathe and doubtless feed her, but then they would return her to Beauchamp. Their loyalty and their very lives were bound up with Lord Henry.

She pictured her cousin Sir Walter de Grasse and tried to imagine his reaction when she suddenly appeared at Crandall looking and smelling like a nightmare hag from Burgotha's Swamp. She could imagine his thin long nose twitching, imagine his eyes closing tightly at the sight of her. But he couldn't turn her away. He wouldn't. She prayed that she would find a stream before arriving at Crandall.

To make matters worse, the day was hot and the night remained uncomfortably warm. Under the scratchy thick wool, adding sweat to the stench, the hell described by Lord Henry's priest began to seem like naught more than a cool summer's afternoon.

Philippa itched but couldn't reach all the places that were making her more desperate by the minute. Had it been imperative that she jump into the moat? Wasn't there another way to get to the forest? She'd acted without thinking, not used her brain and planned. "You think with your feet,

Philippa," Lord Henry was wont to tell her, watching her dash hither and yon in search of something. And she'd done it again. She'd certainly jumped into the moat with her feet.

How many more hours now before she could slip away? She had to wait until they reached the St. Ives Fair or her father's men would likely see her and it would have all been for naught. All the stench, all the itches, all the hunger, all for naught. She would wait it out; her sheer investment in misery wouldn't allow her to back down now. Her stomach grumbled loudly and she was so thirsty her tongue was swollen.

Her father's guards unknowingly shared their amorous secrets with her that evening. "Aye," said Alfred, a man who weighed more than Lord Henry's prize bull, "they pretend it pains them to take ye—then, jist when ye spill yer seed and want to rest a bit, they whine about a little bauble. Bah!"

Philippa could just imagine Alfred lying on her, and the thought made her ribs hurt. Ivo had been heavy enough; Alfred was three times his size. There were offerings of consolation and advice, followed by tall tales of conquest—none of it in the service of her father against his enemies—and Philippa wanted to scream that a young lady was in the wool wagon and her ears were burning, but instead she fell asleep in her misery and slept the whole night through.

The next day continued as the first, except that she was so hungry and thirsty she forgot for whole minutes at a time the fiery itching of her flesh and her own stink. She'd sunk into a kind of apathy when she suddenly heard a shout from one of Lord Henry's guards. She stuck her nose up into the small air passage. Another shout; then: "Attack! Attack! Flank the last wagon! No, over there!"

Good God! Thieves!

The wagon that held Philippa lurched to a stop, leaned precariously to the left, then righted itself. She heard more shouting, the sound of horses' hooves pounding nearer, until they seemed right on top of her, and then the clash of steel against steel. There were several loud moans and the sound of running feet. She wanted to help but knew that the only thing she could possibly do was show herself and pray that the thieves died of fright. No, she had to hold still and pray that her father's men would vanquish the attackers. She heard a loud gurgling sound, quite close, and felt a bolt of terror.

There came another loud shout, then the loud twang of an arrow being released. She heard a loud thump—the sound of a man falling from his horse. And then she heard one voice, raised over all the others, and that voice was giving orders. It was a voice that was oddly calm, yet at the same time deep in its intensity, and she felt her blood run cold. It wasn't the voice of a common thief. No, the voice . . . Her thinking stopped. There was only silence now. The brief fighting was over. And she knew her father's men hadn't won. They would tell no tall tales about this day. She waited, frozen deep in her nest of wool.

The man's voice came again. "You, fellow, listen to me. Your guards are such cowards they've fled with but slight wounds to nag at them. I have no desire to slit any of your throats for you. What say you?"

Osbert wasn't amused; he was terrified, and his

mouth was as dry as the dirty wool in the wagon, for he'd swallowed all his spit and could scarce form words. But self-interest moistened his tongue, and he managed to fawn, saying, "My lord, please allow this one wagon to pass. Thass ours, my lord, my brother's and mine, and thass all we own. We'll starve if ye take it. The other two wagons are the property of my lord Henry de Beauchamp. He's fat and needs not the profits. Have pity on us, my lord."

Philippa wanted to rise from her bed of wool and shriek at Osbert, the scurvy liar. Starve indeed. The fellow owned the most prosperous of Lord Henry's demesne farms. He was a free-man and his duty to Lord Henry lightened his purse not overly much. She waited for the man with the mean voice to cut out Osbert's tongue for his effrontery. To her chagrin and relief, the man said, " 'Tis fair. I will take the two wagons and you may keep yours. Say nothing, fellow," the man added, and Philippa knew he said those words only to hear himself give the order. Her father's farmers would race back to Beauchamp to tell of this thievery, and likely bray about their bravery against overwhelming forces—and take her with them, if, that is, she was in the right wagon.

Suddenly the wagon moved. She heard the man's voice say, "Easy on the reins, Peter. That mangy horse looks ready to crumple in his tracks. 'Twould appear that Lord Henry is stingy and mean."

Philippa wasn't in the right wagon. She was in one of the stolen wagons and she had no idea where she was going. For that matter, when the farmers returned to Beauchamp they wouldn't have any idea who'd attacked them.

Dienwald sat back on his destrier, Philbo, and looked upon the two wagons filled with fine raw wool, now his. He rubbed his hands together, then patted Philbo's neck. The guards had fled into Treywen Forest. They would be fools to ride back to Beauchamp. If they did, Lord Henry would have their ears cut off for cowardice. Other parts of their anatomy would doubtless follow the ears. The farmers would travel to St. Ives. He knew their sort. Greedy but not stupid, and liars of superb ability when their lives were at stake. He imagined them playing the terrified and guiltless victims very well. He imagined them carrying on about this monster at least seven feet tall whose face was nearly purple with scars, who'd threatened to eat them and spit them out in the dirt. And they wouldn't be far off the mark. That was the beauty of Gorkel; he hadn't said a word to the terrified peasants; he didn't have to. Perhaps Lord Henry would even let them keep the proceeds from the sale of their wool—well, not all, but enough for their efforts. And St. Erth now had enough wool for Old Agnes to weave her gnarly fingers to the bone; and in addition, he had two new horses. Not that the nags were anything wonderful, but they were free, and that made them special. It wasn't a bad outcome. Dienwald was content with his day's work. He would remember to give Crooky an extra tunic for his information.

"Don't dawdle," he called out. "To St. Erth! I want to reach home before nightfall."

"Aye, my lord," Eldwin called out, and the wagon lurched and careened wildly as the poor

nag broke into a shuffling canter. Philippa fell
back, bringing piles of the filthy wool over her
face. She couldn't breathe anything save her own
stench until she managed to burrow another
breathing hole. Where was St. Erth? She'd heard
of the place but didn't know its location. Then
her stomach soured and she thought only to keep
herself from retching. The nausea overpowered
her and she clawed through the layers of wool
until her head was clear and the hot sun was sear-
ing her face from overhead.

Philippa kept drawing deep gulping breaths,
and when her stomach eased, she grew brave
enough to look around. The man driving the
wagon had his back to her. She craned her neck
and saw the other wagon ahead, and beyond the
first wagon rode six men. All were facing away
from her. Which one was the leader, the lord?
They were all poorly garbed, which was odd, but
their horses seemed well-fed and well-muscled.
Philippa, her stomach snarling even more loudly,
tried to ignore it and take stock of her surroundings. She had no idea where she was. Gnarled
oak trees, older than the Celtic witches, grew in
clumps on either side of the pitted dirt road. She
fancied she would get an occasional sniff of the
sea from the north. Mayhap they were traveling
directly toward St. Ives. Mayhap all was not lost.

Philippa continued thinking optimistically for
another hour. They passed through two small villages—clumped-together huts, really, nothing
more. Then she saw a castle loom up before them.
Set on a high rocky hill, stunted pine trees clus-
tered about its base, was a large Norman-style
castle. Its walls were crenellated and there were
arrow loops, narrow windows in the four thin

towers and walls at least eight feet thick. It was
gray and cold, an excellent fortress that looked
like it would stand for a thousand years. It stood
guard like a grim sentinel over mile upon mile of
countryside in all directions. As the wagons drew
nearer, Philippa saw there was no moat, since the
castle was elevated, but there was a series of
obstacles—rusted pikes buried in the ground at
irregular intervals, their sharp teeth at a level to
rip open a horse's belly or a man's throat if he
fell on them. Then came the holes covered with
grass and reeds, holding, she imagined, vertical
spears. The wagons negotiated the obstacles without hesitation or difficulty.

Philippa heard a loud creaking sound and saw
twenty-foot gates made of thick oak slowly part
to reveal a narrow inner passage some thirty feet
long, with withdrawn iron teeth of a portcullis
ready to be lowered onto an enemy. The wagons
rolled into an inner ward filled with men, women,
children, and animals. It was pandemonium, with
everyone talking at once, children shrieking, pigs
squealing, chickens squawking. There were more
people and animals here than in the inner ward
at Beauchamp, and Beauchamp was twice as big.
Even the chickens sounded demented.

Philippa barely had time to duck under the
wool again before the wagons were surrounded
by dozens of people cheering and shouting con-
gratulations. She heard the thick outer gates grind
close again, and it seemed a great distance away.

Philippa felt her first complete shock of fear.
Her optimism crumbled. She'd done it this time.
She'd truly acted with her feet and not with her
brain. She'd jumped into a slimy moat and then
into a wagon of filthy raw wool. And now she

was alone at a stranger's castle—a prisoner, or worse. She was so hungry she was ready to gnaw at her fingers.

The wagon lurched to a sudden jolting halt. Dozens of hands rocked the wagon. Philippa felt them grabbing at the wool, felt their hands sifting through the layers, nearer and nearer to where she was buried.

Then she heard the leader's voice, closer now, saying something about Gorkel the Hideous and his magnificent visage, and then her stomach announced its rebellion in no uncertain terms and she fought her way up through the wool until she flew out the top, gasping, gulping the clean air.

"God's glory," Dienwald said, and stared.

A little boy bellowed, "What is it, Papa? A witch? A druid ghost? Thass hideous!"

Gorkel shuddered at the apparition and yelled, " 'Tis more hideous than I! God gi' us his mercy! Deliver us from this snare of the devil's!"

Dienwald continued to stare at the daunting creature lurching about, its arms flapping, trying to keep its balance in the shifting wool. The creature was tall, that much was obvious, its head covered with wool, thick and wild and sticking straight out. Then the great wigged hag gained its footing and turned toward him downwind, and he gagged. The noxious odor surpassed that of his many villeins who didn't bathe from their birth until their death.

The creature suddenly began to shake itself, jerking away clumps of wool with its grubby fingers, until its face was cleared and he saw it was a female sort of creature staring back at him with frightened eyes as blue as the April sky that was just beginning to mellow into late afternoon.

His people were as silent as mourners at a pope's tomb—an achievement even St. Erth's priest, Cramdle, had never accomplished in his holiest of moments—all of them staring gape-mouthed and bug-eyed. Then slowly they began to speak in frightened whispers. "Aye, Master Edmund has the right of it: thass a witch from the swamp."

" 'Tis most likely a crone tossed out for thievery!"

"Nay, 'tis as Gorkel says: thass not human, thass an evil monster, a punishment from the devil."

Edmund yelled, " 'Tis a witch, Papa, and she's here to curse us!"

"Be quiet," Dienwald told his son and his people. He dug his heels gently into Philbo's sleek sides. He got within five feet of the ghastly female and could not bear to bring himself closer. He fought the urge to hold his nose.

"I'm no witch!" the female shouted in a clear loud voice.

"Then who are you?" Dienwald asked.

Philippa turned to stare at the man. She wasn't blind. She saw the distaste on his face, and in truth, she couldn't blame him. She touched her fingers to her hair and found that her cap was long gone and the thick curls had worked free of the braid and were covered with slime from the Beauchamp moat and crowned with clumps of the squalid wool. She could just imagine what she looked like. She felt totally miserable. People were making the sign of the cross as they stared at her, horror and revulsion on their faces, calling upon a dizzying array of saints to protect them.

And she was Philippa de Beauchamp, such a

wondrous and beauteous girl that Ivo de Vescy
had tried to force her so she would wed him. It
was too much. By all the saints, even William de
Bridgport wouldn't want her now. She imagined
herself standing before him covered with slime
and wool, her smell overwhelming. Surely he
would shriek like the little boy had. She pictured
de Bridgport turning and running, his fat stomach
bouncing up and down. She couldn't help herself.
She laughed.

"I am in obvious disarray, sirrah. Forgive me,
but if you would allow me to quit your very nice
castle, I will be on my way and you won't have to
bear my noxious smell or my company further."

"Don't move," Dienwald said, raising his hand
as she moved to climb over the side of the wagon.
"Now, answer me. Who are you?"

It was the man with the mean deep voice, and
her brief bout of laughter died a quick death. She
was in a very dangerous situation. It didn't occur
to her to lie. She was of high birth. No one with
any chivalry would hurt a lady of high birth. She
threw back her wild bushy head, straightened her
shoulders, and shouted, "I am Philippa de Beauchamp, daughter of Lord Henry de Beauchamp."

"A witch! A lying crone!"

"I am not!" Philippa shouted, furious now. "I
might look like a witch, but I'm not!"

Dienwald gazed at the hideous apparition, and
it was his turn to laugh. "Philippa de Beauchamp,
you say? From my vantage, 'tis barely female you
appear, and such an unappetizing female that my
dogs would cringe away from you. In addition,
you have likely spoiled some of my wool."

"She will curse us, Papa!"

"*Your* wool? Ha! 'Tis my father's wool and you

are nothing more than a common thief. As for you, you loud crude boy, I am mightily tempted to curse you."

Edmund shrieked, and Dienwald began to laugh. His people looked at him, then at the female creature, and they began to laugh as well, their chuckles swelling into a great noise. Philippa saw a misshapen fellow standing near the steps to the great hall, and even he was cackling wildly.

She wished now she'd lied. If she'd claimed to be a wench from a village, perhaps he'd simply have let her leave. But no, she'd told the truth— like a fool. How could she have imagined chivalry from a man who'd stolen two wagons of wool? Well, there was no hope for it. Up went her wool-clumped chin. "I am Philippa de Beauchamp. I demand that you give me respect."

The moment the creature had opened her mouth, Dienwald realized she wasn't an escaped serf or a girl from the village of St. Erth. She spoke like a gentlewoman—all arrogant, and loud, and haughty—like a queen caught in the jakes with her skirts up, yelling at the person who'd seen her. What the devil was this damned female doing hidden in a wool wagon, stinking like a hog's entrails, and covered with slime?

"I have long thought Lord Henry to be a red-nosed glutton whose girth makes his horses neigh in dread of carrying his bulk, but even he couldn't have been cursed with such as you. Now, get you down from the wagon." Dienwald watched her weave about, gain her balance, and climb down. She was very tall, and his villeins moved away from her, especially those unfortunate enough to be downwind of her. She stood on the ground, watching him, looking so awful it would curdle

the blood of the unwary. He let Philbo back away
from the fright and shouted at her, "Don't move!"

Dienwald dismounted, tossed the reins to his
master-at-arms, Eldwin, and strode over to the
well. He filled a bucket, then returned to the
wagon. Without hesitation, he threw the bucket
of water over her head. She wheezed and
shrieked and jerked about, and some of the wool
rolled off her body and tunic. He could see her
face now, and it wasn't hideous, just filthy.
"More water, Egbert!"

"Water alone won't get me clean," Philippa
said, gasping from the shock of the cold water.
But she was grateful; she could now sniff herself
without wanting to gag. She licked her lips and
gratefully swallowed the drops of water that
remained.

"I can't very well strip you naked here in my
inner ward and hand you a chunk of lye soap. I
mean, I could, but since you claim to be a lady,
you would no doubt shriek were your modesty
defiled."

A howl of laughter met this jest, and Philippa
tried not to react. She said, calm as a snake sun-
ning itself on a warm rock, "Couldn't I have the
soap and perhaps go behind one of your
outbuildings?"

"I don't know. My cat has just had kittens back
there, and I hesitate to have her so frightened that
her milk dries up." Dienwald felt the laughter bil-
lowing up again. He yelled for lye soap; then
added, "Egbert, take the creature behind the
cookhouse and leave her be. Look first for Eleanor. If she and her kittens are there, take the creature behind the barracks. Agnes, fetch clean
clothes for her and attend her. Then bring her

to me—but only when she no longer offends the nose."

"But, Papa, she's a witch!"

"Officious little boy," Philippa said as she turned on her bare heel—her boots were buried somewhere in the wool—and followed the man with the wonderful bucket of water.

"Careful what you call the creature, young Edmund," Crooky said, hobbling up. "It might cast a foul spell on you. Thass a relic from Hades, master." He threw back his head and cleared his throat. Dienwald, recognizing all too well the signs, yelled, "Keep your lips stitched, fool! No, not a word, Crooky, not a single foul rhyme out of your twitching mouth.

"As for you, Edmund," he continued to his son, "the creature isn't a relic. Relics don't turn your stomach with their stench, nor have I ever seen a relic that talked back to me. Now, let's have our wool begin its progress into cloth and into tunics. Prink! Get your fat arse out here!"

3

"The well will go dry before the creature is clean enough for mortal viewing and smelling," Dienwald said, rubbing his jaw as he spoke.

"Aye, thass the truth," said Northbert, who was sniffing the wool. " 'Tis not a virtuous smell, my lord," he added, picking up a clump of wool and bringing it to his nose, an appendage flattened some ten years before by a well-aimed stone.

"We'll let Old Agnes deal with it," Dienwald said.

"There she comes!" Edmund shouted.

Dienwald looked up at his son's yell. Indeed, he thought, staring at the female vision striding toward him, barefoot, the rough gown nearly threadbare and loose everywhere except her breasts. Her hair was a damp wild halo around her head, hair the color of dark honey and fall leaves and rich brown dirt, and growing curlier by the minute as it dried.

She walked up to him, stopped, looked him squarely in the eye, and said, "I am Philippa de Beauchamp. You are a thief, but you also appear to be master of this castle and thus my host. What is your name?"

"Dienwald de Fortenberry. Aye, I am lord of this castle and master of all those herein, including you. Now, I have much to say to you, and I don't wish to speak in front of all my people. Follow me."

He turned without another word and strode across the dusty inner bailey toward the great hall. He was tall, she saw, following in his wake, some three or four inches taller than she was, and straight as a lance and just as solid. She couldn't see a patch of fat on him. He was also tough-looking and younger than she'd first thought when she heard him giving orders after his theft of the wool wagons. He wasn't all that much older than she, but he was treacherous—he'd already proved that. He was naught but a thief without remorse. She had still to see if he had the slightest bit of chivalry.

Dienwald de Fortenberry. She turned pale with sudden memory and was grateful he wasn't looking at her to see her face. She'd heard tales of him since she was ten years old. He was known variously as the Rogue of Cornwall, the Scourge, and the Devil's Blight. When de Fortenberry chanced to plunder or rob or pillage close to Beauchamp lands, Lord Henry would shake his fist in the air, spit in the rushes, and scream, "That damnable bastard should be cleaved into three parts!" Why *three* parts, no one at Beauchamp had ever dared to ask. She should never have told him who she was. She'd been ten times a fool. Now it was too late. He was master of this castle.

The great hall was shadowed and gloomy, with smoke-blackened beams supporting the high ceiling, and only a half-dozen narrow windows covered with hides. The floor rushes snapped and crackled beneath her bare feet, and several times she felt one of the twigs dig into her sole—a twig or mayhap a discarded bone. There wasn't much of an odor, just a stale smell. She watched the man wave away poorly garbed servants, several men-at-arms, the crooked-backed fellow, and the small boy whom she assumed was his son. Where was his wife? He had a son; surely he had a wife. On the other hand, what woman would want to be wedded to a scourge or a blight or a bastard? Philippa watched him sit down in the lord's chair, a high-backed affair of goodly proportions that had been made by a carpenter with some skill and a love of ornamentation. "Come here," the Scourge of Cornwall said, and crooked his finger at her.

No one had ever crooked a finger at her in such a peremptory way. Not even Lord Henry in his most officious moments.

Philippa forgot for a moment where she was and who it was who'd commanded her. She straightened her shoulders with alarming force. Her breasts nearly split the center seam of her gown. She nearly wailed with humiliation as she quickly hunched forward.

Dienwald de Fortenberry laughed.

"Come here," he said again.

Philippa walked forward, keeping her eyes on his face. It wasn't a bad face. She would have thought a scourge's face would be pitted by the pox, that he'd be wild-eyed and black-toothed, not hard and well-muscled and with eyes of light brown ringed with gold, with hair and brows the identical shade. There was a deep dimple in the center of his chin. Mayhap that was a mark of the devil. But if it were a devil's mark, why didn't he wear a beard to hide it? Instead he was clean-shaven, his hair worn longer than was the current fashion, with tight curls at his nape. He didn't look like a rogue or a devil's blight, but hadn't he stolen her father's wool without a by-your-leave?

"Who are you?"

"I am Dienwald de Fortenberry—"

"I know that. I mean, are you truly a devil's tool? Or perhaps one of his familiars?"

"Ah, you have realized my identity. Have you heard mind-boggling tales of me? Tales that have me flying over treetops with my arms spread like great wings to escape Christian soldiers? Tales that have me traveling a hundred miles from Cornwall in the flash of an eye to kill and butcher and maim in the wilds of Scotland?"

"No, I have heard my father curse you mightily when you have raided near Beauchamp, but you are always just a man to him, even though he roars about scourges and blights and such."

" 'Tis true. I am of this earth, not above it or below it. I am but a simple man. Do you, Philippa de Beauchamp, consider this earthbound man of sufficient prominence to sit in your august presence?"

"I don't think you care at all what I think. Moreover, I'm lost."

Dienwald sat forward in his chair. "You are in my castle, St. Erth by name. As to your exact whereabouts, I believe I shall keep that to myself for a time. Sit you down. I have questions for you, and you will answer them promptly and truthfully."

Philippa gazed about. There was no other chair.

He pointed downward at his feet. "On the floor."

"Don't be absurd! Of course I won't sit on the floor."

Dienwald stood up, still pointing to his feet. "Sit, now, or I will have my men fling you down. Perhaps I shall plant my foot on your neck to keep you down."

Philippa sat down on the floor, folding her long legs beneath her. She tried to straighten the skirt of her borrowed gown, but it was too narrow and too short and left her knees bare.

Dienwald resumed his seat, crossing his arms over his chest, negligently stretching his long legs in front of him. She noticed for the first time that his tunic and hose were in shameful condition.

She looked up at him. "May I please have something to drink? I am very thirsty."

Dienwald frowned at her. "You aren't a guest," he said, then in his next breath bellowed, "Margot!"

A thin young girl scurried into the hall, managed a curtsy, and waited, her eyes on the now-clean creature barely covered by a tattered garment of dull green belonging to one of the cookhouse wenches.

"Ale and . . ." He eyed the seated female, whose knees were showing. Nice knees connected to very nice legs. "Are you hungry as well?"

Her stomach growled loudly.

"Bread and cheese as well, Margot. Be speedy, we don't want our guest to collapse in the rushes."

Philippa could have hugged him at that moment. Food, at last. *Food!*

"Now, wench—"

"I am not a wench. I am Philippa de Beauchamp. I demand that you treat me according to my rank. I demand that you . . . well, you could begin by getting me a chair and then a gown that isn't so very rough and worn and old."

"Yes? What else? That isn't all you wish, is it?"

She ignored his sarcasm. "I know I am tall, but perhaps one of your wife's gowns would fit me."

"I have no wife. I had a wife once, but I don't have one now, nor have I had one for many a year, thank the saints. The gown Old Agnes found for you is doubtless precious. There isn't a single hole in it. It deserves your thanks, not your disdain."

"I meant no insult and I do thank you and the gown's owner. May I please borrow a horse? A nag, it matters not. I will see that it is returned to you."

"Why?"

To lie or to speak more foolish truths? Philippa settled for the middle ground. "I was traveling to see my cousin, who lives near St. Ives. I was riding in the wool wagon to the fair and then I planned to walk the rest of the way to my cousin's keep. Now, of course, I am here, and 'tis probably still too far away for me to walk."

Dienwald looked at the female and realized she was quite young. The wild hair and the ill-fitting gown had deceived him. The hair was now dry and a full glorious fall down her back. There were more shades than he could count, from the palest flaxen to dark ash to deepest brown. He frowned at himself. "All right, I believe you are Philippa de Beauchamp. Why were you hiding in a wool wagon?"

Margot appeared with a wooden tray that held ale, bread, and a chunk of yellow cheese. Philippa's mouth began to water. She stared at the food, unable to tear her eyes away, until Dienwald, shrugging, rose and pointed her toward the long row of trestle tables that lined the eastern side of the great hall.

He kept further questions to himself and merely watched her eat. She tried to be dainty and restrained, but her hunger overcame her refined manners for a few minutes. When she chanced to look up, her mouth full of bread, to see him watching her, she quickly ducked her head, swallowed, and fell into a paroxysm of coughing.

Dienwald rose and leaned over the trestle table, and pounded her back. He handed her a cup of ale. "Drink."

Once she'd gotten her breath back, he was sitting again, silently watching her. If she'd been in that damned wool wagon all the way from Beauchamp, she hadn't eaten or drunk anything for nearly two days. It also seemed to Dienwald that she'd acted without much thought to any consequences, a usual feminine failing.

"You have a lot of hair."

She unconsciously touched her fingers to the tumbled curls. "Aye."

"Who is this cousin you were traveling to see?"

"I can't tell you that. Besides, it isn't important."

"How old are you?"

"Nearly eighteen."

"A great age. At first I had believed you older. Why were you running away from Beauchamp?"

"Because my father wanted me to marry a—" Philippa stopped cold. She dropped a piece of cheese onto the trestle table, then jumped to retrieve it. She fought with all her better instincts not to stuff it into her mouth. She bit off a big chunk.

"You were so against this marriage that you jumped into the moat, then buried yourself in my wool, making both it and you stink like a marsh hog?"

She nodded vigorously, her mouth full of the wonderful cheese. "Truly, I had to. If you don't mind, I should like to keep running."

"It won't work, you know. A lady of your tender years and wealth doesn't go against her father." He paused, giving her a long, brooding look, a look Philippa didn't like a bit. "A daughter should never go against her sire. As for marriage, 'tis to increase the family's wealth and lands and political influence. Surely you know that. Weren't you raised properly? What is wrong with you? Have you taken the minstrels' silly songs to heart? Did you fall in love with some silly fellow's eyebrows? Some clerk who read you romantic tales?"

She shook her head, thinking about her family gaining lands and wealth. Marrying her to William de Bridgport wouldn't bring any of those benefits. "Truly, sir, I can walk, if you'll just tell me the direction to St. Ives."

Dienwald continued brooding and looking. Finally he rose and returned to his chair, saying over his shoulder, "Well, come along. Sit on the floor."

Philippa grabbed the last piece of bread and the last morsel of cheese and followed. When she sat, the tunic slid up above her knees. She chewed on the bread, watching him, praying he wouldn't ask anything until she'd swallowed the rest of her food. But his next words nearly made her choke again.

"There are many things to consider here. I could ransom you. Your father is very wealthy, from what I've heard. Beauchamp is a formidable holding, and has been since William gave it to Rolfe de Beauchamp two hundred years ago. And your father has some influence at court, or so I heard some years ago." He paused, looking away, and Philippa's gaze followed his. He said, "Ah, I believed myself too lucky to be alone. Come here, Crooky, and join in my musings. What do you think the wench would bring in ransom?"

Crooky hobbled up, looked Philippa up and down, and said. "Thass a tall wench, master, even sitting, a strapping big wench. Those legs of hers just don't stop. By Saint Andrew's nose, 'tis yer height she be, or nearly, I'll wager ye."

"No, no," Philippa said, "he is taller than I, by at least four inches."

"Yes, that's true," Dienwald said, ignoring her. "This is Crooky," he added after a moment to Philippa, "my fool, my ears, and a great piece of impertinence a good deal of the time. But I suffer his presence." He saw her nose go up. It was a nice narrow nose. It was also an arrogant and supercilious nose.

Fitting for a Philippa de Beauchamp.

To Philippa's surprise, Crooky suddenly broke into song.

What be she worth?
This wooly-haired wench?
Jewels for a ransom?
Not with her stench.
She looks like a hag
She brays and she brags—

"You're blind, clattermouth," Dienwald inter-rupted. "She's clean and wholesome and I've even fed her so her ribs are no longer clanking together. Come here so I can kick you in the ribs."

Crooky cackled and backed quickly away. "A bath did her good, sweet lord. Aye, ransom the wench. She'll bring you coin, much-needed coin. Mayhap we'll need more weavers for all that wool. Let de Beauchamp pay dear to fetch the little partridge back into his fold. God gi' ye grace, madam." And the strange little man who bel-lowed off-key gave her a crooked-toothed grin.

"That was a horrid rhyme," Philippa said. "You've no talent at all. My mare neighs more agreeably than you sing."

"Slit her throat," Crooky said to his master. "She's got a bold tongue and she's naught but a pesky female. Of what earthly good is she?"

"You're right, Crooky. A deadly combination, surely, and of no use." Dienwald reached for the dagger at his belt.

Philippa gasped, sudden fear causing her to jump to her feet and back away. With her hunger and thirst slaked, she'd let herself forget who this man was, had let down her guard and behaved as she would have at home, and now look what her tongue had gotten her into.

Dienwald drew his dagger and fingered the

sharp edge. He rose slowly. "Have a care, lady. This is not your domain. You have no power here, no authority. Moreover, you are naught but a female, a big strapping female with more wit than most, but nonetheless you are to keep your mouth closed and your tongue behind your teeth. Aye, I will ransom your hide, now that it is white again and sweet-smelling. I will have my steward write to your father telling him of your status. Have you an idea of what he'll pay for your return? A clean and hearty wench he'll get, I will promise it, a wench ready for him to flail with his tongue and his belt. Both of which you deserve."

Philippa shook her head. Fear clogged her throat. Fear of this unpredictable man and fear of the truth. Perchance the truth in this instance would serve her well. On the other hand, perhaps it wouldn't. She didn't know what to do. She said finally, "My father doesn't want me back. He won't pay you anything. He will be pleased never to see my face again in this life. He didn't want me. That's why I ran away."

"That's not hard to believe, what with the face you had when I first beheld you. He would have believed himself in hell, faced by the devil's mistress."

"I told you that I jumped into our moat and that I ran away. It was foolish, I admit, but I did it and I can't now undo it."

Philippa heard a gasp and saw a plump big-breasted girl staring at them, her face pale. Then she saw the direction of the girl's eyes, and saw the girl was staring at the man's dagger. He was still holding it, caressing the blade with the pad of his thumb. Philippa had forgotten the dagger. Would he slit her throat? Wasn't he possessed of any chivalrous instincts? She very quickly returned to the floor, folding her legs under her as far as she could manage.

"It begins to rain, my sweet lord," Crooky said. "I'll see the wool is kept dry. Come along, Alice, the master is busy counting coins in his head. He'll make you happy later, once he's rid himself of this extra wench."

"Aye," Dienwald said, not looking toward the big-breasted girl. "Go. Leave me. I will make you happy tonight."

Philippa stared. Her father had mistresses; she and all at Beauchamp knew it. But he pretended otherwise; he was discreet. Of course this man had no wife to shriek at him. She turned back and saw that Dienwald was speaking to an old woman.

"Aye, master, that old fool Prink has sickened suddenly, taken to his bed, he has, yelling that he's dying."

Dienwald cursed, then said, "I'll wager Father Cramdle is at his bedside even now, just in case. His list of sins is long enough for three days."

Then the little boy strode up and bellowed, "Hers a witch, kill her, Papa, stick your dagger in her gullet!"

Philippa looked at the boy standing out of her reach, legs apart, an expression on his face that was remarkably like his father's.

"Not *hers* a witch," Philippa said. "Can't you speak properly? It's *she's* a witch." Of the boy's father she asked, "Have you no privacy here? And I'm not a witch."

"Very little privacy," Dienwald said, and waved Edmund away. "Go see to our wool. And keep out of mischief. Aye, and speak properly!"

Philippa added her coin. "Why don't you go visit the water and the lye soap?"

"I shan't. You're a lanky spear with a wooly head!"

"Officious little clodpole!"

"Enough! Edmund, get thee gone now. You, lady, keep your tongue behind your teeth or you will surely regret it." Again he pointedly fingered his dagger, and Philippa, not liking the sharpness of that blade, nor the tone of his voice, lowered her head and shut her mouth. She'd been a fool, but she didn't have to continue being one.

"I had great need of the wool," Dienwald said, looking down at his frayed hose. "I lost forty-four sheep before shearing, and all of us are ragged. That's why I took the two wagons." He glanced up, straight at her, and seemed startled that he'd explained his theft.

"Your need is quite evident. But thievery will bring you only retribution from my father, doubt you not."

"Ah, you think so? Let me tell you something, Lady Lackwit. Those dauntless farmers with the other wagon will continue to the fair at St. Ives. They will sell the wool and hide well their profits. Then they will go bleating to Lord Henry about the theft of all three wagons. Moreover, they have no idea who robbed them. Now, in addition, you are my prisoner, as of this minute. If I decide to ransom you, I can always say I found you creeping along a road. And if you, wench, tell your sire the truth, think you those brave farmers will say they lied and robbed your father and were cowards? Now, I was considering treating you like a guest, but I think that isn't what you need. You are too bold, too brazen for a female. You want mastering and proper manners. Perhaps I shall take on the chore. You will remain at St. Erth until I decide what to do with you. You will leave me now."

"I would like to leave you forever! My father will discover the truth and crush you like the pestilence you are!"

Dienwald smiled. "It will make a jongleur's tale that will cause the beams of the hall to creak with mirth."

"You are the only lackwit here. I told you, my father wants nothing more to do with me."

"Then perhaps I can instead discover the name of the man he wished you to marry. I can send a message to the clothhead and *he* can ransom you."

"Nay!"

She'd actually turned white, Dienwald observed. Let her skin creep with the thought. He wondered who the man was.

"Arrogant fool," Philippa said as she looked out the narrow window of her cell down into the inner ward. The sky was leaden in the late afternoon, and fog rolled over the castle walls. It had stopped raining some minutes before.

Dienwald de Fortenberry was striding across the now-muddy ward toward the stables, three dogs at his heels, followed by two small children and a chicken with sodden feathers. He'd ordered her taken by Northbert, a man with a very flat nose, to a tower chamber and locked in. Chamber, ha! 'Twas a cell, nothing more. At least he hadn't locked her down in the granary. Philippa watched him until he disappeared into the stables. Only the chicken followed him inside. The children and dogs were stopped by a yelling stable hand with the blackest hair Philippa had ever seen. Although he spoke loudly, calling the children little crackbrains, she could barely hear him over all the other people in the inner bailey. So many people, and so noisy, each with an opinion and a loud voice. The men yelled and shouted, the women yelled and shouted, and the children and chickens squawked and shrieked. It was a cacophony of head-splitting noise and Philippa turned away from the window slit and surveyed her room. It was narrow and long and held only a low bed with a rank-smelling straw-stuffed mattress and a coarse blanket. There was no pillow, no water to drink; there was a cracked pot under the cot in which to relieve herself, but nothing more.

It was heaven-sent compared to her residence in the wool wagon, but it still wasn't at all what she was used to. She'd always taken Beauchamp and all the luxuries it had afforded her for granted. It had been her home, and all the people there were known to her and trusted. Now she was nothing more than a prisoner. All her wondrous escape had netted her was a dank cheerless room in the keep tower of a man more unpredictable than the Cornish weather and, by reputation, a thoroughly bad lot.

"Thass good quality, master," Old Agnes was saying to the thoroughly bad lot, her gnarled fingers caressing the wool. "Jes' lovely."

"Aye," Dienwald agreed. "Pick what wenches you need to help you clean and weave the wool and tell Ellis. I'll have Alain hire weavers immediately. The first new tunic is for Master Edmund—aye, a new tunic and new hose."

Old Agnes looked sour at that order but didn't say anything. "What about the creature, master?"

"The what? Oh, her. She'll be gone before you can give her a new gown. Let her return home in what we gave her. 'Tis a gift."

"Thass a lady, master, not a scullion."

Old Agnes sometimes forgot herself, Dienwald bluntly informed her. Old Agnes gave him a toothless grin and a mirthless cackle and returned to picking filth from the wool. Dienwald left the stables, nearly stumbling over a chicken. The bird squawked, deftly avoiding the kick of a foot.

Dienwald sniffed the heavy air. White fog hung over his head in patches. It would shower again soon. There was time enough to practice with the quintains, since today was Tuesday, but he felt unsettled and restless. He made his way to the solar, where there were three small rooms, one used for St. Erth's priest and Edmund's tutor, Father Cramdle. He eased open the door to the sound of his son's penetrating voice: "Thass naught but silly tripe for peasants!"

4

Father Cramdle's voice, normally the model of patience and tolerance, was a bit frayed. "Master Edmund, peasants can't read, much less cipher. Listen, now, 'tis what your father wants. If I add eleven apples from this barrel to the seven bunches of grapes in this barrel, what is the result?"

"Purple apples!"

Dienwald's first response was to laugh at his son's wit, but he saw the pained look on Father Cramdle's homely face. Edmund not only looked like a villein's child, he was as ignorant as any of them.

"Answer Father Cramdle, Edmund. Now."

"But, Papa, thass a foolish problem, and—"

"*That is*, not *thass*. I don't want to hear that from you again. Answer the problem. Speak properly." He remembered Philippa's correction, made without thought. Had his son become so ill-managed? He wanted Edmund to read at least enough so he wouldn't be cheated by merchants or his own steward in the future. He wanted him to cipher so that he would know if he'd gotten the correct measure of flour from the miller. Dienwald could sign his name and make out words if he spoke them aloud slowly, but little more. It wasn't something he regretted very often, just at times like this when he saw the proof of ignorance in his son.

It required all of Edmund's fingers and toes and painstaking counting, but finally the correct answer came from his mouth.

"Excellent," Dienwald said. "Father, if the boy needs the birch rod, tell me. He will learn."

"Papa!"

"Nay, little gamecock. You will remain here studying with Father Cramdle until he sees fit to release you. It is what I wish of you, and you will obey me."

Dienwald left the room knowing that the kindly and very weak-willed Father Cramdle didn't have the spirit to control a nine-year-old boy. Dienwald would have to involve himself more. As for Alain, the steward, he could control the boy, but Edmund hated Alain. Though he would never say why, he avoided him, slinking away whenever Alain came into the vicinity.

As Dienwald left the solar, he glanced over to the east tower. He saw Philippa de Beauchamp at the narrow window, looking down. He hoped she was scared out of her wits wondering what he was going to do to her. He would give her until the following afternoon to become appropriately submissive. She was too proud. She was also too big, too tall, too curly-haired. He had no complaint about her legs, which seemed to go on until they reached her throat, just as Crooky had pointed out. Her breasts seemed more than ample as well. But she wasn't . . . He forced his thinking away from that channel. Kassia de Moreton was delicate and small and sweetly soft. And she would never belong to him. It wasn't fated to be. Pity that he liked her hulking warrior husband nearly as much as he cared for her, else he would be tempted to slit Graelam's throat some dark night and relieve him of his wife.

Dienwald sighed. He admired everything about Kassia—her gentleness, her shy humor and guile-less candor, her fierce loyalty to her husband, her daintiness, even the smallness of her bones and her delicate wrists . . . Ah, well, it was hopeless. At least she was his friend, delighting in his com-pany, though now she was determined to find him an heiress—to save him from mold and damp and ruin, she'd say, and pour him some of her father's precious wine from Aquitaine. She wanted Dienwald to become respectable, a concept that thoroughly irritated and frightened him. But not for long. After all, what family would want to be allied with a rogue like him? It was just as well. The Scourge of Cornwall liked life just as it was. With the acquisition of the wool, the days would continue to be as entertaining as they'd been before the mindless sheep had plunged off that cliff.

It occurred to him a few moments later why he was so restless. He needed a woman. He didn't delay, simply asked to have Alice sent to his chamber. When she arrived, plump and smiling, her arms held forward a bit to further push out her breasts, Dienwald waved her closer. When she stood in front of him, he started to sweep her onto his lap. But her smell stopped him cold. "When did you last bathe?"

Alice flushed. "I forgot, master," she said, eyes cast down. She knew to avert her eyes, because if she looked at him, he just might see the amazement on her face. All this insistence upon rubbing her body with water and soap! It was beyond foolish.

Dienwald wanted her, but even her breath smelled of the stuffed cabbage she'd eaten the previous night.

"I won't have you again in my bed until you wash yourself—all of you, do you understand, Alice? With soap. Even between your legs and under your arms. And cleanse your teeth."

He sent her away, calling out, "Use the soap!" He'd first herded her into his bed only two weeks before. She'd learn, he hoped, that he liked a woman's body to be free of odor and her breath sweeter than that of his wolfhounds.

He waited, tapping his fingertips impatiently on the arms of the single chair in his chamber. When Alice appeared thirty minutes later, her hair wet from its washing but smooth from a good combing, and her breath pure as a spring breeze, he smiled and patted his thighs.

She came to him willingly, and when he brought her to stand between his thighs, she again pressed her breasts forward. He wondered who'd taught her to do this. Normally it amused him. Now, however, he wanted only release, and quickly. He slipped her coarse gown over her head, to find her naked beneath. She hadn't dried

herself completely, and his hands slid over her
moist flesh.

He clasped her hands down to her sides and
looked at her. She was white and plump and
smooth as an egg. She would also be quite fat in
no more than five years, but that didn't disturb
him one whit. She was merely pleasingly bountiful now, the flesh between her legs soft and
damp, and she was nearly the same age as his
long-legged prisoner in the east tower.

He kissed Alice's mouth, tentatively at first,
until he knew that she'd cleansed her teeth; then
he became more enthusiastic. When at last he
eased her down onto his manhood, groaning at
the feel of sinking deep into her body, he leaned
back his head, closing his eyes. Finally he played
with her hot woman's flesh until she squirmed
and arched her back and cried out. Then he
allowed himself relief, and it was sweet and long
and good.

He left her asleep on his bed and quit his solar,
stretching and contented, every restless feeling
stilled. Night had fallen and the evening meal was
late, as usual. Dienwald thought about his prisoner, alone and probably so hungry she was
ready to gnaw on the cot in her chamber. He
decided he was feeling benevolent and told
Northbert to have her fetched. She would doubtless be grateful to him for feeding her.

When she appeared beside Northbert, he motioned her to the chair beside his.

"Thass the witch," Edmund said, waving a
handful of bread toward the approaching Philippa.

"She's not a witch. And it's *that is*, not *thass*.
Mind your manners, Edmund. She's a lady, and
you will treat her politely."

Edmund grumbled, and Dienwald, giving him a very pointed look, added, "One insult, and you will spend your evening with Father Cramdle reading the holy writ."

The threat brought instant obedience. Dienwald studied his prisoner again. She didn't look like a lady, of course, in that shapeless coarse gown, bare feet, and thick curling hair loose around her head.

"God's greetings to you, lady," he said easily to Philippa. "Sit thee here and take your fill."

"What? The master offers me a chair rather than the dank floor?"

He eyed her. Some show of gratitude. He should have guessed. She wasn't one whit broken; not a shadow of submissivenes. She was still insolent. He should have held to his original plan and left her in that chamber alone for twenty-four hours. He continued, still tolerant, lounging back in his chair, "There are no females at St. Erth as great-sized as you, lady, so moderate your appetite accordingly, for there are no more gowns for you."

"God bless your sweet kindness, sir," Philippa said with all the gratitude of a nun who'd just been made an abbess. "You have the charitable soul of Saint Orkney and the pious spirit of a zealot."

"There is no Saint Orkney."

"Is there not? Why, with your example, kind lord, there should be. Yes, indeed."

Philippa smiled at him, her dimples deep, so pleased with herself that she couldn't help it. Then she smelled the food. Her stomach growled loudly. She forgot Dienwald de Fortenberry, forgot that her situation was fraught with uncertainty, and looked down at her trencher, on which lay a thick slab of bread soggy with rich gravy and decorated with large chunks of beef.

Dienwald watched her attack the meal. A bold wench with a ready tongue. No wonder she thought her father didn't want to ransom her. Who would want such a needle-witted wench in his keeping? Unaccountably, he smiled. When she mopped up the trencher with her last chunk of bread, he said, "Will you eat all my mutton and pigeon as well? Every one of my boiled capons, with ginger and cinnamon, and all of my jellied eggs?"

"I don't see the jellied eggs." There was stark disappointment in her voice.

"Perhaps you ate them without seeing them. Your hands and your mouth toiled very diligently."

She turned to him. "And surely you wouldn't have mutton, would you? Didn't you lose all your sheep?"

Dienwald had to pause a moment on that one. He saw her dimples deepen again, and realized she was enjoying herself mightily at his expense. One could not allow a woman to have the last word. It was against the laws of man and God. It was as intolerable as a kick to the groin.

He shook himself. "What wear you beneath that gown?"

A man, Philippa thought, used whatever weapons available to him. Her father was a master at bluster. His nose turned red, his eyes bulged, and he raged long and loud. Her cousin Sir Walter de Grasse, if she remembered aright, turned sarcastic and cold when he was in a foul temper. Her father's master-at-arms never thought, just struck out with his huge fists. As for this man, at least his dagger still lay snug in its sheath at his belt, so a show of violence wasn't on his mind. It relieved her that he wished to best her with words, even though they were meant to shrivel her with embarrassment. Unfortunately, she'd taken a sip of the strong ale when he'd spoken, and now she choked on it. He slapped her on the back, nearly sending her face into a wooden platter of boiled capon.

"I can feel nothing," Dienwald said as he leaned down close to her. His fingers splayed wide over her back. "No shift? No pretense at modesty?"

Philippa felt the urge to violence—after all, she was her father's daughter—and she acted instantly. Quick as a snake, she reached for his dagger. She felt his hand lock around her wrist until her fingers turned white from lack of blood.

"You dare?"

She'd thought with her feet again, and the result had brought his anger on her head. She shook her head.

"You *don't* dare?"

But there was no anger in his tone, not now. He seemed amused. That was surprising, and vastly relieving as well. He loosened his grip on her wrist and pressed her hand palm-down against his thigh. Her eyes flew to his face, but she didn't move.

"I have decided to give you a choice, lady," Dienwald said.

Philippa wasn't at all certain she wanted to hear of any choices from him.

"Not a word? I don't believe it." He paused a moment, cocking a brow at her. She remained silent.

"You tell me your father won't ransom you. You also refuse to tell me the name of your unpleasant suitor. You balk at telling me the name of this cousin you were running to. Very well, if you aren't able to bring me pounds and shillings and pence, the very least you can do is repay my hospitality on your back. It is doubtful, but perhaps I'll find you acceptable in that role, at least for a limited time."

She'd been right: she *hadn't* wanted to hear his choices.

"You don't care for the thought of me covering you?"

Surely a man who allowed children, dogs, and a chicken to follow him about couldn't be all that bad. There were still no words in her mind.

"Wrapping those long white legs of yours around my flanks? They're so long, mayhap they'll go around me twice. And plucking your virginity? Doesn't that give you visions of delirious pleasure?"

"Actually," she said, looking out over the noisy great hall at all the men and women who sat at the trestle tables eating their fill, laughing, jesting, arguing, "no."

"No, what?"

Philippa reached for a capon wing with her left hand and took a thoughtful bite. She couldn't let him see that he'd stunned her, demolished her confidence, and made her nearly frantic with consternation. Wrapping her legs around his flanks? Plucking her . . . Philippa wanted to gasp, but she didn't; she took another bite of her capon wing. Dienwald was so surprised at her nonchalance, her utter indifference, that he released her wrist. She shook her hand to get the feeling back, then reached for another piece of capon. Before she brought it to her mouth, she dipped it deep in the ginger-and-cinnamon sauce.

Dienwald stared at her profile. More thick tendrils had worked loose from her braid, a braid as thick as Edmund's ankle, and curled around her face.

She turned back to him finally, dipping her fingers into the small wooden bowl of water between their places. " 'Tis very good, the capon. I like the ginger. No, my father won't ransom me. I should have lied and told you he would, but again, I didn't think, I just spoke."

"True. Your point, lady?"

"I don't want to be your mistress. I don't want to be any man's mistress."

"That won't be up to you to decide. You are a woman."

"That is a problem I share with half the world. What will you decide, then?"

"Must you persist in your picking and harping? Must you nag me with questions until I am forced to put my dagger point to your white neck?"

"Nay, but—"

"Swallow your tongue! I shall have the name of your betrothed, and I shall have it soon. I will even demand less ransom if he will have you back."

"No!"

Dienwald picked up her long braid and wrapped it around his hand, drawing her face close to his. "Listen, wench—"

"I am not a wench. My name is Philippa de—"

"You will do my bidding in all things, no matter you're the Queen of France. Now, what is the poor crackbrain's name?"

Philippa swallowed. She smelled the tart ale on his breath, felt its warmth on her temple. His eyes were darker, the flecks of gold more prominent. "I won't tell you."

"I think you will. You lack proper submissiveness and obedience. You need training, as I told you earlier. I think I should begin your lessons right now." He looked quite wicked as he said, "Take off your gown and dance for my people."

She stared at him. "Your priest would not approve."

Dienwald took his turn at staring. " 'Tis true," he said. "Father Cramdle would flee to meet his maker."

"Very well. If my choices are between being your mistress and telling you the name of that awful man my father wished me to wed, and if you then plan to ransom me to that horrid old man and make me suffer his presence for the rest of my life, then my answer is obvious. I will be your mistress until you don't want me anymore."

It took a moment for her flow of words to make sense. When they did, he refused to let her see how stunned he was. Was her intended husband that repulsive? Or had she simply no womanly delicacy? No, she was just toying with him, first telling him nay, then changing her tune.

"I could give you over to my men," he continued thoughtfully. "You are really not to my taste, with your big bones and your legs as long as a man's. Have you also feet the size of a man's?"

Philippa was frightened; she didn't understand this man. Unlike her father, who would have been purple-faced with rage and yelling his head off by now, this man's agile tongue cavorted hither and yon, leaving her mind in disarray. She didn't want to have to prance atop the trestle table naked. She didn't want Father Cramdle to clutch his heart with shock. All the power she'd felt whilst they fenced with words had been an illusion at best. The fact that this man didn't kick children or dogs or chickens didn't automatically endow him with an honorable nature. Now he was showing his true colors. Now he was get ting down to serious business. She opened her mouth, but what came out was unbidden and unsanctioned.

"You make me sound like an ugly girl."

She was appalled that such errant vanity could come from her brain, much less from her mouth. But his insults, piled up now as high as the stale and matted rushes on the cold stone floor, had cut deep.

He laughed, an evil laugh. "Nay, but a gentle soft lady you are not. Now, let me see. There must be something about you that is . . . You do have very nice eyes. The blue is beyond anything I have ever seen, even beyond the blue speckles on robins' eggs. There, does that placate your female vanity?"

Philippa managed to say nothing. To her surprise, she saw the fool, Crooky, who'd been crouched beside Dienwald on the floor beside her chair, leap to his feet and sing out a coarse lyric about the effect a woman's blue eyes could have on a man's body.

Dienwald burst into loud laughter, and at the sound, the remaining fifty people in the great hall guffawed and thumped their fists on the tables until the beams seemed to shake with their raucous mirth.

"Come here, Crooky, you witless fool," Philippa called out over the din, caution again tossed to the four winds, "I want to kick your ribs."

Dienwald looked at the girl beside him. She was laughing, and she'd mimicked him perfectly.

Philippa, basking in her temporary wit, failed to notice that utter silence had fallen. She further failed to notice how everyone was gazing from her to Dienwald with ill-disguised consternation.

Then she noticed. If he didn't cut her throat, he'd throw her to his men. She didn't doubt it. He hadn't a shred of honor, and she'd crossed the line. Without a word, she quickly slipped out of the chair, jumped back, and ran as fast as she could toward the huge oak doors of the great hall.

5

Windsor Castle

Robert Burnell, Chancellor of England and King
Edward's trusted secretary, rubbed a hand over
his wide forehead, leaving a black ink stain.

" 'Tis time to take your rest," King Edward
said, stretching as he rose. He was a large man,
lean and fit, and one of the tallest man Robert
Burnell had ever seen. Longshanks, he was called
fondly by his subjects. A Plantagenet through and
through, Burnell thought, but without the slyness
and deceit of his sire, Henry, or the evil of his
grandfather, John I, who'd maimed and tortured
with joyous abandon anyone who chanced to displease him. Nor was he a pederast like his great
uncle, Richard Coeur de Lion—thus the string of
children he and his queen, Eleanor, had assembled to date. And that brought up the matter at

hand. Robert wondered if his broaching the topic would call forth the Plantagenet temper. Unlike his grandfather, Edward wouldn't fall to the floor and bash his fists and his heels in bellowing rage. No, his anger was like a fire, perilous one moment, cold ashes the next, a smile in its place.

"I work you too hard, Robbie, much too hard," Edward said fondly, and Burnell silently agreed. But he knew the king would continue to use him as a workhorse until he met his maker, thanks be to that maker.

"Just one more small matter, your highness," Burnell said, holding up a piece of parchment. "A matter of your . . . er, illegitimate daughter, Philippa de Beauchamp by name."

"Good God," Edward said, "I'd forgotten about the girl. She survived, did she? Bless her sweet face, she must be a woman grown by now. Philippa, a pretty name—given to her by her mother, as I recall. Her mother's name was Constance and she was but fifteen, if I remember aright. A bonny girl." The king paused and his face went soft with his memories. "My father married her off to Mortimer of Bledsoe and the babe went to Lord Henry de Beauchamp to be raised as his own."

"Aye, sire. 'Tis nearly eighteen she is, and according to Lord Henry, a Plantagenet in looks and temperament, healthy as a stoat, and he's had her educated as you instructed all those years ago. He reminds us 'tis time to see her wedded. He also writes that he's already been beleaguered for her hand."

The king muttered under his breath as he strode back and forth in front of his secretary's table.

"I'd forgotten . . . ah, Constance, her flesh was

soft as a babe's . . ." The king cleared his throat. "That was, naturally, before I became a husband to my dear Eleanor . . . she was still a child . . . also, my daughter is a Plantagenet in looks . . . not a hag then . . . excellent, but still . . ." He paused and looked at his secretary with bright Plantagenet blue eyes, eyes the same color as his illegitimate daughter's. He snapped his fingers and smiled.

"My dear Uncle Richard is dead, God rest his loyal soul, and we miss the stability he provided us in Cornwall. For a son-in-law, Robbie, we must have a man who will give us unquestioning loyalty, a man with strength of fist and character and heart, but not a man who will try to empty my coffers or trade on my royal generosity to enrich himself and all his brothers and cousins."

Burnell nodded, saying nothing. He wouldn't remind the king that he, his faithful secretary, hadn't received an increase in compensation for a good five years now. Not that he'd ever expected one. He sighed, waiting.

"Such a man is probably a saint and in residence in heaven," the king continued, giving Burnell another Plantagenet gift—a smile of genuine warmth and humor that rendered all those in his service weak-kneed with the pleasure of serving him. "I don't suppose Lord Henry has a suggestion?"

"No, sire. He does write that suitors for his other daughter tend to look upon Philippa instead, as likely as not. He tires of the situation, sire. Indeed, he sounds a bit frantic. He writes that Philippa's true identity becomes more difficult to keep a secret as the days pass, what with all the young pups wanting her hand in marriage."

"A beauty." Edward rubbed his large hands together. "A beauty, and I spawned her. All Plantagenet ladies are wondrous fair. Does she have golden hair? Skin as white as a sow's underbelly? Find me that man, Robbie, a man of strength and good heart. In all of Cornwall there must be a man we can trust with our daughter and our honor and our purse."

Robert Burnell, a devout and unstinting laborer, toiled well into the dark hours of the night, burning three candles to their stumps, examining names of men in Cornwall to fit the king's requirements. The following morning, he was bleary-eyed and stymied.

The king, on the other hand, was blazing with energy and thwacked his secretary on the shoulders. "I know what we'll do about that little matter, Robbie. 'Tis my sweet queen who gave me the answer."

Was this another little matter he didn't know about yet? Burnell wondered, wishing only for his bed.

"Yes, sire?"

"The queen reminded me of our very loyal and good subject in Cornwall—Lord Graelam de Moreton of Wolffeton."

"Lord Graelam," Burnell repeated. "What is this matter, sire?"

"Lackwit," Edward said, his good humor unimpaired. " 'Tis about my little Philippa and a husband for her fair hand and a sainted son-in-law for me."

Burnell gaped at the king. He'd discussed his illegitimate daughter with the queen, with his *wife*?

He swallowed, saying, "Lord Graelam's wed-

ded, sire. He was atop my list until I remembered
he'd married Kassia of Belleterre, from Brittany."

"Certainly he'd wedded, Robbie. Have you lost
your wits? You really should get more rest at
night. 'Tis needful, sleep, for a sprightly brain.
Now, Lord Graelam is the one to ferret out my
ideal son-in-law. You will readily enough wring a
list of likely candidates out of him."

"I, sire?"

"Aye, Robbie, certainly you. Whom else can I
trust? Get you gone after you've had some good
brown ale and bread and cheese. You must eat,
Robbie—'tis needful to keep up your strength.
Ah, and write to Lord Henry and tell him what's
afoot. Now, I must needs speak to you about the
special levy against those cockscomb Scots. I think
that we must—"

"Forgive me, sire, but do you not wish me to
leave for Cornwall very soon? To Wolffeton? To
see Lord Graelam?"

"Eh? Aye, certainly, Robbie. This afternoon.
Nay, better by the end of the week. Now,
sharpen your wits and recall for me the names of
those Scottish lords who blacken the Cheviot Hills
with their knavery."

6

St. Erth Castle

Philippa heard shouts behind her. One great bearded man grabbed at her, ripping the sleeve from her tunic, but she broke free. She heard a bellow of laughter and a man shouting, "Ye should have grabbed her skirt, rotbrain! Better a pretty bare ass than an arm!"

It was as dark as the interior of a well outside the great hall. Philippa dashed full-tilt across the inner bailey toward the stables, hoping to get to a horse and . . . And what? The gates were closed. There were guards posted on the ramparts, surely. The night was cold and she was shivering in nothing but a ragged one-sleeved gown to cover her.

Still, her fear kept her going. The stables were dark and warm and smelled of fresh hay, dung, and horses. They were also deserted, the keepers, she supposed, in the great hall, eating their evening meal with all the rest of the denizens of this keep. She stopped, pressing her fingers to the stitch in her side. She was breathing hard, and froze in her tracks when she heard her captor say from nearby, "You are but a female. I accept that as a flaw you can't remedy—God's error, if you will—yet it would seem that you never think before you act. What were you planning to do if you managed to get a horse?"

Philippa slowly turned to face him. Dienwald de Fortenberry was standing in the open doorway of the stable, holding a lantern in his right hand. He wasn't even breathing hard. How had he found the time to light a lantern?

"I don't know," she said, her shoulders slumping. "You have so many people within the keep, I hoped mayhap the gates would be open, with people milling in and out, that mayhap the guards and porters wouldn't notice me, but they all appear to be in the great hall eating, and—"

"And mayhap the moon would make an appearance and guide you to London to court, eh? And thieves would salute you and blow you sweet kisses as you rode past them, your gown up about your thighs. Stupid wench, I would not have gained my twenty-sixth year if I'd been so heedless of myself and my castle. We are quite snug within these walls." He leaned down and set the lantern on the ground. Philippa backed up against a stall door as he straightened to look at her.

"If you don't begin to think before you act, I doubt you will gain your twentieth year. You ripped off a sleeve."

"Nay, one of your clumsy men did that." She remembered another man's coarse jest and felt suddenly quite exposed, standing here alone with him, her right arm hanging naked from her shoulder. "Please, my lord, may I leave? I'm thinking clearly now. I should be most grateful."

"Leave? Tread softly, lady. Your position at present is not passing sweet. I think it more fitting that I should beat you. Tie you down and beat you soundly for your audacity and disrespect—something your father never did, I suspect. Do you prefer a whip or my hand?"

"Stay away!"

"I haven't moved. Now, you told me that you didn't want to be my mistress. Then, like a female, you danced away to a different tune and said you would prefer my using you as my mistress rather than wedding the man your father selected for you. Have I the sequence aright?"

She nodded, her back now flat against the stall door. "I should prefer Satan's smiles, but that doesn't seem to be an available choice. You told me you would give me choices but you didn't."

"Don't keep pushing against that stall door, wench. Philbo, my destrier, is within. He isn't pleased with people who disturb him, and is likely to take a bite of your soft shoulder."

Philippa quickly slid away from the stall door and looked back at the black-faced destrier. He had mean eyes and looked as dangerous as his master.

"Are you a shrew?"

"Certainly not! 'Tis just that de Bridg—" She broke off, stuffed her fist in her open mouth, and gazed at Dienwald in horror.

"William de Bridgport?" Interest stirred in

Dienwald's eyes. He got no response but he saw
that she'd terrified herself just by saying the
man's name. He imagined anyone could eventually get everything out of this girl. She spoke
without thinking, acted without considering consequences. She was a danger to herself, a quite
remarkable danger. He wondered if she would
yell in passion without thinking. "He is a repulsive sort," Dienwald said. "Fat and rotten-toothed,
not possessed of an agreeable disposition."

"Nay, 'tis someone else! I just said his name
because he looks like . . . your horse!"

"My poor Philbo, insulted by a wench with
threadbare wits." He became silent, watching her,
then said, "You would prefer my using your fair
body to wedding him. I know not whether to be
flattered or simply amazed. Are you certain Lord
Henry won't ransom you? I really do need the
money. I would prefer money to your doubtless
soft and fair—but large—body."

Philippa shook her head. "I'm sorry, but he
won't. You must believe me, for I don't lie, not
this time. I overheard him tell my mother and a
suitor for my sister's hand who tried to ravish me
that I would have no dowry at all."

"Your sister's suitor tried to ravish you? How
was this accomplished?"

" 'Twas Ivo de Vescy. He's a sweet boy, but he
fancied me and not my sister. My father pulled
him off me before I hurt him, which I would have
done, for I am quite strong."

Dienwald laughed; he couldn't help it. He'd
come after her with violence in mind, but she'd
disarmed him, first with her pale-faced fear, then
with her artless candor. He looked at the long
naked white arm. She was so young . . . Nay, not

so young. Many girls were married with a babe suckling at their breast by her age.

"Your father told de Vescy that he was marrying you to de Bridgport?"

She nodded. "I didn't know—he'd never said a word to me about de Bridgport. At first I couldn't believe it, wouldn't believe it, but then . . ."

"And then you didn't think, just acted, and jumped in the moat, then into the wool wagon. Well, 'tis done. Come along, now. You've gooseflesh on your naked arm, and it's powerfully unappetizing. I think I'll take you to my chamber and tie you to my bed. I will be careful not to rip your gown further, since it is the only piece of clothing you have."

Beauchamp Castle

"She's a deceitful bitch and I hope she falls into a ditch! I hope she's been set upon by pillaging soldiers. I hope she's imprisoned in a convent. At least dear Ivo doesn't want her—at least, he'd better not."

"Bernice, quiet!" Lord Henry roared. "I must write to the king immediately . . . again. God's nails, I will lose Beauchamp, he will tear my limbs from my body."

Lady Maude quickly ordered Bernice from the solar. Her daughter whined and balked, for her curiosity was at high tide, but her mother's hand was strong and she was determined. Bernice would not find out her supposed sister's true parentage, not if Lady Maude had any say about it, which she did.

"My lord," she said upon returning to her

spouse, "you must moderate your speech. Aye, you must write to the king again, but don't tell him the girl is missing. Nay, a moment." Lady Maude stared toward the ornate *prie-dieu* in the corner of the chamber. "We must think. We mustn't act precipitately. Philippa must have overheard our talk of marrying her off to de Bridgport."

Lord Henry groaned. "And she fled Beauchamp. Why did I think of that whoreson's name, much less spew it out to de Vescy like that? God's eyebrows, the man's a braying ass, and I've proved myself a fool."

Lady Maude didn't disagree with his assessment of himself, but said loudly, "I think William de Bridgport a man to make a girl a fine husband."

Lord Henry stared at his thin-lipped wife. When, he wondered, had her lips disappeared into her face? He seemed to remember years before that she'd had full, pouting lips that curved into sweet smiles. He stared down her body and wondered where her breasts had gone. They'd disappeared just like her lips. Through her endless prayers? No, that would just make her bony knees bonier. He thought of little Giselle, his sixteen-year-old mistress. She had magnificent breasts, and *her* lips hadn't disappeared. She also had all her teeth, which nipped him delightfully.

He groaned again, recalling his current problem. The king's daughter was gone; he had no idea where, and he was terrified that she would be killed or ravaged. His mind boggled at the possible fates that could befall a young, beautiful girl like Philippa. More than that, Lord Henry was quite fond of her. For a girl, she was all a father could wish. Nay, she was more, for she was also his steward.

She wasn't filled with nonsense like her sister. She wasn't particularly vain. She could read and write and cipher, and she could think. The problem with Philippa was that she didn't think when things were critical. Oh, aye, set her to solving a dispute between two peasants and she'd come up with a solution worthy of Solomon. But face her with a crisis and she turned into a whirling dervish without a sensible thought in her head. And she'd heard de Bridgport's name and panicked.

Where had she run?

Suddenly Lord Henry's eyes widened. He'd been stupid not to think of it before. The wool wagons bound for the St. Ives Fair. Philippa wasn't altogether stupid; she hadn't merely thrown herself out on the road and started walking to God only knew where. He grinned at his wife, whose nostrils had even grown pinched over the years. Would they eventually close and she'd suffocate?

"I know where Philippa went," he said. "I'll find her."

St. Erth Castle

Dienwald hadn't completely lost his wits. Unlike Philippa de Beauchamp, he tended to think things through thoroughly before acting—if he had the chance, that is—and in this matter he had all the time he wanted. And he did want to punish the wench for dashing out of the great hall the way she had, making him look the fool in front of all his people. He held firmly to her

naked white arm as he walked her back across
the inner bailey. A donkey brayed from the animal pen behind the barracks; two pigs were rut-
ting happily in refuse, from the sound of their
squeals; and a hen gave a final squawk before
tucking in her feathers and going to sleep.

Philippa was frightened now, and he felt her
resistance with every step. It was a chilly night
and she was shivering. "Hurry up," he said, and
quickened his pace, then slowed, realizing her
feet were bare. She was going to try to escape
him on bare feet and in a flimsy torn gown? She
was an immense danger to herself.

Silence fell when he strode into the great hall
with her at his side. He yelled for his squire, Tancrid. Tancrid, a boy of Philippa's years, was
skinny and fair, with soft brown eyes and a very
stubborn jaw. He ran to his master and listened
to his low words, nodding continuously. Dienwald then turned on his heel and left. He pulled
Philippa up the outside stairs to the solar.

"You're not taking me back to that tower cell?"

"No. I told you, I'm taking you to my bed and
tying you down."

"I would wish that you wouldn't. Cannot you
give me another choice?"

"You have played your games with me,
wench—"

"Philippa. I'm not a wench."

Dienwald hissed between his teeth. "You begin
to irk me, you wench, harpy, nag, shrew . . . The
list of seemly names for you is endless. No, keep
quiet or I will make you very sorry."

As a threat it seemed to lack unique menace,
but Philippa hadn't known him long enough to
judge. She bit her lip, kept walking beside him

up the solar stairs, and shivered from the cold. His fingers were tight about her upper arm, but he hadn't hurt her. At least not yet.

They passed three serving maids and two well-armed men, bound, evidently, for guard duty. Dienwald paused, speaking low to them, then dismissed them. He took Philippa to a large bedchamber that hadn't seen a woman's gentling touch in a long time. There was a large bed with a thick straw mattress and a dark brown woolen spread atop it. There were no hangings to draw around it. There were two rough chairs, a scarred table, a large trunk, a single wool carpet in ugly shades of green, and nothing else. No tapestries, no wall hangings of any sort, no bright ewers or softening cushions for the chair seats. It was a man's chamber, a man who wasn't dirty or slovenly, but a man to whom comforts, even the smallest luxuries, weren't necessary. Or perhaps he simply hadn't the funds to furnish the room properly. Still, whatever the reason, Philippa didn't like the starkness of the chamber at all.

She wished now that there weren't any privacy. She wished there was an army camping throughout the solar. She wished there was a chapel in the chamber next to this one filled with praying priests and nuns. But the chamber was empty save for the two of them. He released her arm, turned, and closed the chamber door. He slid the key into the lock, then pocketed the key in his tunic. He lit the two tallow candles that sat atop the table. They illuminated the chamber and had a sour smell. Didn't the lord of St. Erth merit candles that were honey-scented or perhaps lavender-scented?

"There is little moonlight," he said, looking

toward the row of narrow windows, "as you'd
have noted if you'd paused to do any planning at
all in your mad dash for escape."

Philippa said nothing, for she was staring.
There was glass in the windows, and that surprised her. Lord Henry had glass windows in the
Beauchamp solar, but he'd carped and complained at the cost, until her mother had threatened to cave in his head with a mace.

Dienwald smiled at her then and strode toward
her. "No," Philippa said, backing away.

He stopped, as if changing his mind. "I asked
Tancrid to bring us wine and more food. I assume
you're yet hungry? Your appetite seems endless."

To her own surprise, Philippa shook her head.

"You dashed out of the hall before you ate any
boiled raisins. My cook does them quite nicely, as
well as honey and almond pastes." He was prat-
tling on and on about food, and all she could do
was stand there looking petrified. He smiled at
her, and if possible she looked even more
alarmed.

There came a knock on the door. She nearly
collapsed with relief, and Dienwald frowned.
"You like having someone besides my exalted self
with you? Well, 'tis just Tancrid with wine and
food. Don't move."

The boy entered bearing a tray that was dented
and bent but of surprisingly good craftsmanship.
He set it upon the table and fiddled with the
flagons.

"Go," Dienwald said, and Tancrid, with a curious look at Philippa, took himself off.

"They all wonder if I'm going to ravish you,"
Dienwald said with little show of interest, and sat
at the table. "That, or poor Tancrid is afraid you'll

stick a knife between my ribs." He didn't sound at all concerned. He poured himself wine, sat back in his chair, and sipped it.

"Are you?" She swallowed convulsively. "Are you going to ravish me?"

Dienwald stretched. "I think not . . . tonight. I have already lain with a very comely wench, and have not the urge to do it again, particularly with a girl of such noble proportions and such—"

"I'm not ugly! Nor am I oversized or ungainly! I have had three very fitting men want my hand in marriage. How dare you say that I'm not worth your energy or that I am not to your taste or to your—"

Dienwald burst out laughing. Here she was, heedless as a squeaking hen, taking exception to his refusal to ravish her. He continued to laugh, watching her face turn alarmingly pale when she realized finally what she was doing.

Very suddenly she sat down on his bed, covered her face with her hands, and started crying. Not dainty feminine tears, but deep tearing sobs that racked her body and made her shoulders jerk.

"By god! I have done nothing to you! Stop your tears, wench, or I'll—"

She jerked up at his words and said through hiccups, "I am not a wench, I'm Philippa de—"

"I know, you're Goddess Philippa, Queen Philippa, Grand Templar Philippa. Be quiet. You'll sour my stomach. Now, no more crying. You have no reason to cry. I have done nothing to harm you. Indeed, I saved you from death. Thank me, Empress Philippa."

"Thank you."

Dienwald hadn't expected that. Perhaps she

wasn't such a little tartar after all. He rose and watched her jump from the bed and scurry back against the far wall. He smiled and leaned down to unwrap the stout cross garters that wrapped securely about his calves.

When he rose to face her again, he waved the long cross garters. "Come here and let me tie you down. I won't tie you tightly."

"Nay!" she whispered.

Dienwald merely smiled and reached for her, a length of cross garter in his hand. She ducked away from him, stumbled and fell to her hands and knees on the floor. He winced for her, knowing that the rough stones were hard as a witch's kettle.

He grabbed her around her waist, realizing as he hauled her up that he liked the feel of her. Her waist was narrow and . . . He had no more time for female appraisal because Philippa turned on him. She screamed, making his ears ring, and her fist caught his jaw, sending his head snapping backward with the force of her blow.

He released her and she fell onto her back. He came over her, ready to thrash her, but her dirty foot caught him squarely in the belly, kicking him a good three feet back. He grunted and landed in a heap on the bed. Dienwald had blood in his eyes. He managed to stop himself, managed to remind himself that he, unlike this raving wench, thought before he acted. Slowly, very slowly, he sat up on the bed and looked at her.

Philippa scurried up to her knees, jerking the gown back into place. She stared back at him, her breath hitching, her breasts heaving deeply.

"Come here."

"Nay."

Dienwald sighed and smiled an evil smile at her. "Come to me now or I will tell Tancrid, who is doubtless outside my chamber door, his ear pressed against the oak, to fetch me three of my most foul men. They, wench, will strip you and have their sport with you. In front of me, I think. I should enjoy watching."

His threat this time was quite specific, and Philippa, without another contrary thought or word, struggled to her feet. She stiffly walked over to him, afraid, but still wanting to smash her fist into his face. He motioned her closer, and she stood between his spread legs, her head down.

"Put your hands together."

She shook her head, but at his look she slapped her palms together, watching as he wrapped the long narrow leather cross garter around her wrists.

"I can't take the chance you will be stupid enough to try to escape me again. Now, don't struggle."

He clasped his hands beneath her hips and lifted her onto the bed, dropping her on her back. He wrapped the other cross garter through the knot at her tied wrists and tethered her to a post at the top of the bed. Her arms were pulled above her head, but not tightly. She stared up at him, and he saw that she was very afraid. He didn't blame her; she was completely helpless.

Her gown had tangled up about her thighs, and the expanse of white flesh was annoying his groin. He pulled a blanket over her, bringing it to her chin. "Now, keep quiet."

It was an unnecessary command. She was silent as a tomb.

Within moments the bedchamber was as silent

as she was. Dienwald snuffed out the single candle, then quickly undressed. He stretched out
naked beside her. She could hear his breathing.
He'd made no move to touch her. She gave the
leather strap a tentative tug; nothing happened.
She lay there trying to decide what she could do.

Dienwald said, "Were William de Bridgport
here, he would have tied you down as well. The
difference is, he would have pulled your white
legs wide apart and pinched you with his dirty
fingers and leered at you, whereas I, wench, will
stroke your white flesh with clean fingers and a
warm mouth and—"

"I have to relieve myself!"

"I'm powerfully comfortable and you've quite
tired me out. Do you really have to relieve yourself or are you again lying to me?"

"Nay, please."

He cursed, lit the single candle again, then
released her wrists. "The pot is beneath the window, yon. I will leave you for a minute or two.
Don't dally." He pulled on his bedrobe as he
spoke.

Philippa didn't look at him. She didn't move
until he'd closed the chamber door behind him.
She raced from the bed to the chamber pot without bothering to light the tallow candle. She could
see well enough.

The chamber door opened some minutes later,
and for a moment Dienwald was silhouetted in
faint light. He closed the door behind him. "Get
back into bed and stretch your hands above your
head so I can tie you again."

He heard a deep hitching breath close to him,
far too close, but he wasn't fast enough. The

chamber pot hit him squarely atop the head and he dropped like a stone.

Philippa stared down at him. He looked dead, and she felt the shock of fear and guilt. She dropped to her knees and pressed her palm against his chest. "Don't you dare die, you scoundrel!" His heartbeat was steady and slow. She got to her feet and stood over him. Her mind began to function again as she stared down at the unconscious man.

Now what was she to do?

She'd thought with her feet again, only this time her actions could well prove to be worse than jumping into the Beauchamp moat.

Tancrid. She had to get the squire out of the way. Perhaps she could take him as a hostage. Yes, that's what she'd do. And she could take his clothes and his shoes and . . . Her mind squirreled madly about.

A hand curled around her ankle and pulled hard. Philippa's legs went out from under her and she went down hard on her bottom. Dienwald, his head spinning, threw himself on top of her, pinning her down with his weight.

She was larger than most women, but she couldn't push him off her. His eyes accustomed themselves to the dim candlelight and he stared down into her face.

"I didn't hit you hard enough."

"Aye, you did. I'm seeing four of you, and believe me, wench, even one of your sort is too many."

Dienwald became suddenly aware of her full breasts and her soft body beneath him. His lust sprang full-blown into life, and with it his manhood. Without thinking, he pressed himself against her.

"You're a menace," he said, hating the fact that he wanted to jerk up her gown and ride her until she was yelling with the pleasure of it and his own pleasure was washing over him. Instead he said, "You're a foolish girl who hasn't a thought for consequences, and I'm tired of it."

"What are you going to do to me?"

Dienwald didn't answer. His vision cleared, as did his lust. Cleansing anger took its place. He pulled himself off her and hauled her up with him. He strode to the bed, dragging her behind him, then pulled her down over his thighs. He held her down with one arm and lit the candle with the other. Then he yanked up her gown, baring a very lovely bottom. And brought the flat of his hand down as hard as he could on the white flesh.

For an instant, Philippa froze. No, he couldn't be spanking her, not like this, with her buttocks as bare as the day she'd come from her mother's womb. He struck her again, and she shrieked in rage and pain and tried to rear up.

He smacked her again, harder this time, then again and again. She was sobbing with pain and impotent fury, struggling with all her strength, when she felt his fingers pressing inward, pushing her legs more widely apart, touching her. She let out a small terrified cry.

Just as quickly, Dienwald flung her off him, onto her back on the bed. He wrapped her wrists again, tying her more securely this time.

She gave a pitiful sob.

"Don't you dare accuse me of hurting you. Edmund would laugh at a hiding that tender."

He hated that word the moment it came from his mouth. It brought to mind the violent lust he'd felt for her moments before.

Her sobs died in her throat. "Your hand is hard and callused. You did hurt me."

"You can't even lie convincingly. Would you prefer a chamber pot on your head, you stupid wench? Thank St. George's lance you hadn't relieved yourself in it first!"

"Of course I hadn't used it! I'm not a—"

"Quiet! You will drive me to lunacy and back! Enough. Go to sleep."

Philippa's bottom felt hot and her flesh was stinging. Her tears were drying on her cheeks and itching. There was nothing she could do about it.

Dienwald was so irritated he couldn't remain silent. "I don't know why I don't simply take you. Why don't—"

"My father would see to it that you were sent as a eunuch to Jerusalem if you forced me."

"What know you of eunuchs and the Holy Land?"

"I am not an ignorant girl. I have learned much. I've had lessons since my eighth year."

"Why would your father waste good coin to educate you, a silly female? That makes no sense at all."

"I don't know why," Philippa said, having wondered the same thing herself. Bernice fluttered about with her ribbons and clothes and her extravagantly pointed slippers, given no opportunity for learning with Father Boise—not, of course, that she'd ever desired to read the *Chanson de Roland*. "Perhaps he thought I could be of use to him. And I have been of use to him. Our steward died nearly two years ago, and I have taken his place."

"You're telling me that you, a female, did the duties of your father's steward?"

"Aye. But my mother also insisted that I learn to manage the household. She didn't enjoy my instruction, but she did it—as an abbess would with an indigent nun."

This entire evening was odd in the extreme, Dienwald decided, exhausted by her nonsense, her violence, her female softness. He snuffed out the candle beside him, and turned onto his back.

"What am I going to do with you, wench?"

"I'm not a wench, I'm—"

Dienwald turned on his side away from her and began snoring very loudly.

"I'm Philippa de Beauchamp and—"

Philippa got no further. He rolled over atop her and kissed her hard. She felt his manhood swell against her belly, felt the heat of him, and opened her mouth to protest. His tongue was her reward, and without thought, she bit him.

He yelped, drawing back.

"I should have known you'd try to make me into a mute. Damned stupid wench, I . . . No, don't you dare say it, lady, else I'll pull up your gown and—"

"You already did! And you looked at me and you hit me!"

He stopped, and even though she couldn't see his face clearly, she knew his expression was filled with evil intent.

He rolled off her and pulled up her gown: She was naked to the waist, her hands tied above her head, as helpless as could be.

"Now," Dienwald said, sounding quite pleased,

"let's continue this conversation. What is it you wanted to say to me, *wench*?"

She shook her head, but he couldn't see it, and that infuriated him. All he'd done this night was to light and snuff candles, protect himself, curse her, and have his rod swell with lust.

He lurched over to the far side of the bed and lit the tallow candle again. It had nearly burned down to the mottled brass holder. He rested on his knees, the candle held high, and looked down at her. For a very long time Dienwald didn't say anything. He was pleasantly surprised, that was all, nothing more. This was to be her punishment, not his, damn her. He stared at her flat belly, then lower, at the profusion of curls that covered her woman's flesh. Curls the color of her head hair, rich and dark, with gleaming browns mingling with strands of the palest blond and . . .

". . . dirt, rich dark dirt."

His words took her so much by surprise that she forgot her terror of him, forgot he was staring at her, seeing her as no man had ever seen her before.

"What is like dirt?"

"Your woman's hair," he said, and cupped his hand over her, pressing his fingers inward.

She yelped like a wounded dog, and he lifted his hand and sat back.

He reached out and splayed his fingers over her flat belly. He stretched out his fingers, watching them nearly touch her pelvic bones. "You're made for birthing babes." He felt something within him move, and lifted his hand as if from a scalding pot. He looked at her face and schooled his expression into a cruel mask. "Remember what I can do to you, wench. Are you such an

innocent that I must explain it to you? No? Good.
Now, have you anything more to say to me? Any
more carping? Any more nagging?"

She shook her head.

"You finally show some wisdom. Good night,
wench."

He snuffed the candle yet again, burning his
fingers, since the candle had burned down to a
wax puddle, then rolled onto his back. He forgot
his burning fingers, still seeing her lying there,
naked to the waist, those long white legs spread;
he could still feel the softness of her flesh, feel
the tensing of the muscles in her belly beneath
his splayed fingers.

He cursed, grabbed the blanket, and pulled it
over her.

When he was nearing the edge of sleep, he
heard her whisper, "I'm Philippa de Beauchamp
and I will awaken and this won't really be
happening."

He grinned into the darkness. The wench had
spirit and fire. A bit of it was interesting; too
much, painful. He rubbed the back of his head.
He hoped it hadn't cracked the chamber pot. It
was the only one he owned.

7

The next morning, Dienwald wasn't grinning. His weaver, Prink, was very seriously ill with the ague, and much of the wool had already been cleaned and prepared and spun ready for weaving. Dienwald stomped about, cursing, until Old Agnes plucked at his worn sleeve.

"Master, listen. What of the fine young lady ye've tied to yer bed, eh? Be she really a lady or jest enouther of yer trollops?"

Dienwald ceased his ranting. He'd left Philippa asleep, but he'd untied her wrists, frowning at himself as he brought her arms down to her sides and rubbed the feeling back into her wrists. She'd never even moved. He imagined her bottom was still soft and white, without the mark of his palm, whereas his head ached abominably from her blow with the chamber pot.

"You mean, old hag, that she could weave, mayhap? Direct the women, instruct them?"

Old Agnes nodded wisely. "Aye, master, she looks a good girl. Thass what I mean."

Dienwald remembered Philippa's words about her household instruction. He took the solar stairs two at a time. When he opened his bedchamber door it was to see Philippa standing in the middle of the room staring around her.

"What's the matter?"

She pointed toward the corner of the bedchamber. "The chamber pot. I broke it when I struck your head with it. I need to . . ." She winced, then burst out, "I must relieve myself! You locked me in and—"

His only chamber pot, and she'd destroyed it. "Satan's earlobes! Get you here, wench." He directed her to a much smaller chamber, waving her inside. " 'Tis Edmund's room. Use his pot, then come down to the hall. 'Tis not a lovely hand-painted pot, merely a pottery pot, but it will do. After this, use the jakes. They're in the north tower; you won't get lost, you'll smell them. Don't tarry."

Why did he want her in the great hall? She dreaded it, knowing there would be snickering servants looking at her and knowing that she was now their master's mistress. When he'd burst into the chamber she'd momentarily forgotten what he'd done to her the previous night—smacking her, toying with her, stripping her, *looking* at her. She didn't understand him and was both relieved and afraid because she didn't. It was a good thing that she wasn't to his liking; otherwise she would no longer be a maid and no longer worth much to her father. That thought brought forth the

vision of William de Bridgport, and she prayed
that all her maneuvers and ill-fated stratagems
wouldn't lead to marriage to him. When she left
Edmund's small chamber and made her way
down the outside solar stairs, her ears were
nearly overcome by the noise. There were men
and women and children and animals everywhere. All were shouting and squawking and carrying on. It seemed louder than the day before;
it was, oddly, comforting.

"Come wi' me, lady."

She turned to see Gorkel the Hideous, the
fiercest-looking and ugliest man she'd ever
beheld, obviously waiting for her. Odd, though,
he didn't seem quite so gruesome of mien as he
had yesterday.

"I'm Gorkel, iffen ye remember. Come wi' me.
The master wants ye."

She nodded, wishing she had shoes on her feet
and cloth covering her naked right arm. She'd
combed her fingers through her hair, but she had
no idea of the result. Gorkel could have told her
that she was as delicious a morsel as a man could
pray for, if she'd asked. The master was lucky,
he was, and about time, too. A hard winter, but
they'd outlasted it, and now it was spring and
there was wool and the master had this lovely girl
to share his bed. Gorkel left her at the entrance
to the great hall, his task completed.

Dienwald saw Philippa, nodded briefly in her
direction, and went back to his conversation with
Alain, his steward. The man who'd given her
dirty looks the evening before. He looked at her
now, and there was contemptuous dismissal in
his eyes.

Philippa waited patiently, although her stomach was growling with hunger.

It was as if Dienwald had heard her. "Eat," he called out, waving toward the trestle table. "Margot, fetch her milk and bread and cheese."

Philippa ate. She wondered what was going on between Dienwald and the steward Alain. They seemed to be arguing. As she studied the master of St. Erth, she wondered at herself and her reaction to him. She felt no particular embarrassment upon seeing him this morning. In fact, truth be told, she'd rather been looking forward to seeing him again, to crossing verbal swords with him again. She felt a tug on her one sleeve and turned to see the serving maid, Margot, looking at her with worry.

She lifted an eyebrow.

" 'Tis the master," Margot said as low as she could.

"He's a lout," Philippa said, and took a big bite of goat cheese.

"Mayhap," Dienwald said agreeably, dismissing Margot with a wave of his hand. "But I'm the lout who's in charge of you, wench."

That was true, but it didn't frighten her. He hadn't ravished her last night, and he could have. She'd been completely helpless. She thrust her chin two inches into the air and fetched forth her most goading look. "Why do you want me here?"

Dienwald sat in his chair, noted her look, sprawled out to take his ease, and watched her eat, saying nothing for some time.

"You told me your mother taught you household matters. Is this true?"

"Certainly. I'm not a liar. Well, not usually."

Dienwald had a flash of memory of another lady speaking to him candidly, without guile. Kassia. That was absurd. This girl was no more like the gentle, loyal Kassia de Moreton than was a thorn on an apple tree.

"Can you weave?"

Philippa very nearly choked on the cheese in her mouth. No ravisher or ravening beast here. "You want me to weave my father's wool that you stole?"

"Yes. I want you to oversee the weaving and train the women, although several of them already know a bit about it, so Old Agnes told me."

Philippa grew crafty, and he saw it in her eyes and was amused by it. He was also impatient and on tenterhooks. He needed her help, but he couldn't afford to let her see that. She said with the eye of a bargainer at the St. Ives Fair, "What will you do for me if I help you with the wool?"

"I will allow you the first gown, or an overtunic, or hose. Just one, not all three, though."

Philippa looked down at the wrinkled, stained woolen gown that hung about her body like an empty flour bag. The bargain seemed like an excellent one to her. "Will you let me go if I do it for you?"

"Let you go where? Back to your father's household? Back into the repulsive arms of de Bridgport?"

She shook her head.

"Ah, to this other person, this alleged cousin of yours. Who is it, Philippa?"

She shook her head again.

"The gown or the overtunic or the hose. That's all I offer. For the moment, at least."

"Why?"

"Yea or nay, wench."

"I'm not a—"

"Answer me!"

She nodded. "I will do it." She looked him straight in the eye. "How will you behave toward me?"

He knew exactly what she wanted him to say, but he was perverse and she irritated him and amused him and she'd nearly felled him with a chamber pot.

"I will keep you in my bed until I tire of you." He spoke loudly, and Alain looked up, his contempt now magnified.

Philippa grabbed Dienwald's arm and pinched him, hissing, "You make it sound as if I'm already your mistress, damn you!"

"Aye, I know. In any case, you will remain in my bed. I can't trust you out of my sight. Now, 'tis time for you to earn your keep."

He yelled for Old Agnes and brought her over to Philippa. Old Agnes was older than the stunted oak trees to the north of the castle, and mean as the dung beetles that roamed about the stables. He stood back, crossing his arms over his chest.

Philippa ate another piece of cheese, slowly, as she looked the old woman over.

To Dienwald's amazement, Old Agnes fidgeted.

Philippa drained her flagon of milk, then said, "I shall see the wool after I've finished my meal. If it isn't thoroughly cleaned and treated, I shan't be pleased. The thread must be pure before it's woven. See to it now. Where is your weaving room?"

Old Agnes drew up her scrawny back, then

sagged under Philippa's militant eye. " 'Tis in the outbuilding by the men's barracks . . . mistress."

"I will need you to pick at least five women with nimble fingers and with minds that rise above the thoughts of useless men and, can learn quickly. You will assist me, naturally. Go now and see to the quality of the thread. I will come shortly."

Old Agnes stared at this young lady who knew her way quite well, and said, "It will be as you say, mistress."

She shuffled out, her step lighter and quicker than it had been in two decades. Dienwald stared after her. This damned girl had wrought a miracle—and she'd not been nice, she'd been imperious and arrogant and haughty and . . .

He became aware that Philippa was looking at him, and she was smiling. "She needs a strong hand, and more, she wants a sense of worth. She now has both." Then Philippa began whistling.

Dienwald turned on his heel and strode from the great hall, bested again by a girl who'd already smashed his head. He cursed.

Philippa silently thanked her mother, whose tongue was sharper than an adder's when it suited her purpose. But, Philippa remembered, her mother's tongue was also sweet with praise when it served her ends. Old Agnes would do more work than all the others combined, and she'd drive them in turn. Philippa turned back to her place, only to see a slight shadow hovering over her.

"Philippa de Beauchamp. I am Alain, Lord Dienwald's steward."

He was speaking to her. She hadn't expected it, given the dislike she'd felt coming from him. She raised her head and kept her face expressionless.

"If you will but tell me this cousin's name, I will see that you are quickly on your way out of this keep and away from Dienwald de Fortenberry."

"Why?"

His good humor slipped. "You don't belong here," he said, his voice loud and vicious. He immediately got hold of himself. "You are an innocent young lady. Dienwald de Fortenberry is a villain, if you will, a rogue, a blackguard, a man who owes loyalty to few men on this earth. He makes his own rules and doesn't abide by others'. He raids and steals and enjoys it. He will continue to hurt you, he will continue to use you until you are with child, and then he will cast you out. He has no scruples, no conscience, and no liking for women. He abused his first wife until she died. He enjoys abusing women, lady or serf. He cares not. He will see that you are cast out, both by him and by your family."

His venom shocked her. She'd smashed a chamber pot over the lord's head the previous night, but that had been different. That was between the two of them. Dienwald hadn't ravished her, and he could have. He hadn't abused her, even when she'd angered him to the point of insensibility. She'd hurt *him.* She thought suddenly of the thrashing he'd given her, but then again, what would she have done to him had he smacked her over the head with a chamber pot? But this steward of his, who should be praising his master, not maligning him—it was beyond anything she'd ever seen.

"Why do you hate him, sirrah?"

Alain drew back as if she'd struck him. "Hate my master? Certainly I don't hate him. But I know what he is and how he thinks. He's a savage, ruthless, and a renegade. Leave, lady, leave before you die or wish to. Tell me this cousin's name and I will get you away from here."

"Yes," she said slowly. "I will tell you."

She watched him closely, and saw immense relief flood his face. His eyes positively glowed and his breath came out in a whoosh. "Who?"

"I shan't tell you today. First of all I must earn a new gown for myself. That was my bargain with your master. I cannot go to my cousin as I am now. You must understand that, sir."

"I think you are a stupid girl," he said. "He will grunt over you and plow your belly until you carry a bastard, then will kick you out of here and you will die in a ditch." He turned on his heel with those magnificent words and strode away, anger in every taut line of his body.

Philippa brooded a moment. This was a peculiar household, and the lord and master was the oddest of them all. She rose from the wooden bench, replete with cheese and bread, and made her way to the weaving building.

Old Agnes had assembled six women, and silence immediately fell when Philippa entered the long, narrow, totally airless room. There were three old spinning wheels and three looms, each of them more decrepit-looking than its neighbor. Philippa looked at each of the women, then nodded. She spoke to each of the women, learned their names and their level of skill, which in all cases but two was nil. Then she tackled the looms. A shuttle had cracked on one; a harness had come loose on another; the treadle had slipped out of its moorings on yet another. She sighed and spoke to Old Agnes.

"You say that Gorkel knows how to solve these problems?"

"Aye, 'tis a monster he is to look at, but he has known how to repair things since he was a little sprat."

"Fetch Gorkel, then."

In the meanwhile Philippa inspected the spinning wheels and the quality of thread the women had produced from the wool. Given the precarious balance of two of the spindles and the wobbling of the huge wheels, the results were more than satisfactory. She smiled and praised the women, seeing her mother's face in her mind's eye.

Two hours later, the women were at their looms weaving interlacing threads into soft wool. They worked slowly and carefully, but that was to the good. As they gained confidence and skill, the weaving would quicken. Old Agnes was chirping over their shoulders, carping and scolding, then turning to Philippa and giving her a wide toothless grin. "Prink—he were the weaver, ye know, milady—well, a purty sod he were, wot with his proud ways. Said, he did, that females couldn't do it right, the weaving part, only the spinning. Ha!" Old Agnes looked toward the busy looms and cackled. "I hope the old bugger corks it. Thass why none of the females knew aught—the old cockshead was afraid to teach them. Make him look the fool, they would have done."

Philippa wanted very much to meet Prink before he corked it.

All was going well. Philippa de Beauchamp, lately of Beauchamp, was busy directing the weaving of her father's wool into cloth for the man who'd stolen it. She laughed aloud at the irony of it.

"Why do you laugh? You can't see me!"

"I should have known—how long have you been watching, Edmund?"

"I don't watch women working," Edmund said, planting his fists on his hips. "I was watching the maypole!"

"Nasty little boy," she remarked toward one of the looms, and turned her back on him.

"I'll tell my papa, and he won't let you use my chamber pot again!"

Philippa whipped around, pleading in her eyes and in her voice as she clasped her hands in front of her. "Ah, no, Master Edmund! I must use your chamber pot. Don't make me use the jakes, please, Master Edmund!"

Edmund drew up and stared. He was stymied, and he didn't like it. He assumed a crafty expression, and Philippa recognized it instantly as his father's. She whimpered now, wringing her clasped hands.

"My papa will make you sorry, and thass the truth!"

"*That's*, not *thass*."

She'd spoken without thinking, and watched the little boy puff up with fury like a courting cock. "I'll speak the way I want! No one tells me how to say things, and thass—"

"*That's*, not *thass*."

"You're big and ugly and my papa doesn't like

you. I hope you get back into a wagon and leave." He whirled about, tossing back over his shoulder, "You're not a girl, you're a silly may-pole!"—and ran straight into his father.

"I should expire with such an insult," Dienwald said, staring down at his son. "Why did you say such a thing to her, Edmund?"

"I don't like her," the boy said, and scuffed at the dirt with a very dirty foot.

"Why aren't you wearing shoes?"

"There's holes in them."

"Isn't there a cobbler here in the castle?" Philippa asked, wishing she could have shoes on her own very dirty feet.

Dienwald shook his head. "Grimson died six months ago. He was very old, and the apprentice died a week after, curse his selfish heart. I haven't hired another."

Philippa started to tell him to send his precious steward to St. Ives and hire a cobbler, when she remembered he didn't have any coin. She searched for a solution. "You know," she said at last, "it's possible to stitch leather if your armorer could but cut it to size for the boy. Also, I'll need very sturdy thick needles."

Dienwald frowned. Meddlesome, female. Edmund was right: she didn't belong here. He looked again at his son's filthy feet and saw a small scabbing sore on his little toe. He cursed, and Edmund smiled in anticipation of his father's wrath.

Philippa said nothing, merely waited.

"I'll speak to my armorer," Dienwald said, and took Edmund by the arm. " 'Tis time for your lessons, Edmund, and don't carp!"

Edmund looked at Philippa over his shoulder as his father dragged him from the room. His look was one of astonishment, fury, and utter bewilderment.

8

Philippa was sweating in the airless outbuilding. All the weavers were sweating as well, their fingers less nimble, their grumbling louder now than an hour before. Swirls of dust from the floor hung in the hot air, kicked up by the many feet. Even Old Agnes looked ready to drop in the corner and hang her scraggly head.

The master had demanded too much too quickly, a habit, Philippa learned from one of the main grumblers, that was one of his foremost traits. Philippa finally called out, "Enough! Agnes, send someone for water and food. 'Tis the afternoon. We all deserve it."

There were tired smiles from the women as they flexed their cramping fingers. The morning couldn't have gone much worse, Philippa was thinking as she walked around praising the cloth that had been woven. If Philippa had believed in divine retribution for sins she might have been convinced that the morning's calamities stemmed from some mortal act of heinous proportions on her part. The wretched looms, ill-cared-for by the infamous Prink, kept breaking, their parts were so old and worn. She'd become closer to Gorkel the Hideous than to anyone else during the long morning. He'd worked harder than she had, tinkering with the ancient treadle, tying together the spindle whose wood kept cracking from dry rot, balancing the loom when it kept teetering. Even Gorkel now looked ready to tumble to the ground. But even at his worst scowls, Philippa was no longer afraid of him or repelled by his face.

Excellent quality wool, though, Philippa thought as she examined the cloth woven by Mordrid, the only woman Prink had taught anything. Mordrid, Old Agnes had whispered to Philippa, had let the old cootshead into her bed, and thus he'd had to teach her something as payment.

Philippa could see that the woven wool was stout and strong enough to last through winters of wear, and would have fetched a good price at the St. Ives Fair. She didn't want to wait for the wool to be dyed before she set other servants to making a gown for herself. Perhaps an overtunic as well, one with soft full sleeves and a fitted waist. Dienwald wouldn't have to know.

Then she saw Edmund in her mind's eyes. The little ruffian dressed and spoke like the lowest villein. She sighed. His tunic was a rag.

Then she saw Dienwald, the elbow poking out of his sleeve, and sighed again.

It occurred to her only then that he was her captor and that she owed him nothing. He could

rot in the worn tunic he was wearing. Her clothing came first. Then she would escape and make
her way to Walter, her cousin.

After everyone had eaten bread, goat cheese,
and some cold slices of beef, Philippa reluctantly
herded the women back to the looms. Nothing
improved. The fates were still against her. The
remainder of the day passed with agonizing slowness and heat. The looms continued to break, one
part after another. Gorkel was taxed to his limits
and was looking more bleak-browed as the afternoon wore on. The lord and master didn't show
himself again. He'd set her the task and the
responsibility and then proceeded to absent himself, curse him.

It was late, and Philippa was so tired she could
barely stand. She rose from the loom where she
was working, told the women to be back on the
morrow, nodded to Old Agnes, then simply
walked out of the weaving building. Long shadows were slicing across one-third of the inner bailey. She spoke to no one, merely walked toward
the thick gates that led to the outer bailey. She
weaved her way through squawking chickens,
several pigs, three goats and a score of children.
She just looked straight ahead, as if she had an
important errand, and didn't stop.

She'd nearly reached the inner gates when she
heard his voice from behind her. "Do my eyes
deceive me? Does my slave wish to flee me again?
Shall I tether you to my wrist, wench?"

So, now she knew. He must have set up a sys-
tem whereby he would be told immediately if she
did something out of the ordinary. Walking to the
inner-bailey gates must meet that requirement.
Well, she'd tried. She didn't turn around, merely

stood there staring at the gates. She said over her shoulder, still not turning, "If you tether yourself to me, then you must needs sweat until you want to die in that dreadful weaving room. I doubt you wish to do that."

"True," Dienwald said, regarding her thoughtfully. Her face was flushed, but not, he thought, from his threat, but from the heat in the weaving room.

"And I'm not your slave."

He smiled at her defiance. Her hair was bound loosely with a piece of leather and lay thick and curling between her shoulder blades almost to her waist. Her shoulders weren't straight and high, but slumped. She looked weary and defeated. He didn't like it, and frowned, then said, "I will have the pieces of leather for you soon. My armorer is cutting them. He will measure your feet as well."

"I doubt he has so much leather in single pieces."

"I did ask him to be certain. I wouldn't want him to measure your feet, only to discover that he couldn't cover them after all. I don't wish you to be humiliated."

"My feet aren't that large!"

"But they are dirty, nearly as dirty as my son's. Should you like to bathe now? The day is nearly done. Actually, I was on my way to the outbuilding to see to your progress. How goes it? Prink is trying his best to overcome his ague. He's furious that *women* are doing the weaving and that a woman is directing the proceedings. He is accusing poor Mordrid of base treachery."

"Old Agnes said he was about to cork it," Philippa said, so diverted that she turned to face him, smiling despite herself.

He was garbed in the same clothes as yesterday, and he looked hot and tired. His hair was standing a bit on end. Perhaps he'd had reason not to see to the work during the day. Then she happened to look at his long fingers, and she closed her eyes over the vision of his hands on her body.

This was absurd. He'd looked at her but hadn't wanted her. If he had tried to ravish her, she would have brought him low—naturally, she would have fought him to her dying breath. "You don't need me anymore. Old Agnes is adept at battering the women. Mordrid is capable of teaching them. Gorkel can repair the looms, even when they break every other breath. Your wonderful Prink is a sluggard and a fool. The looms should have been burned and new ones made ten years ago, and . . . Oh, what do you care?" Philippa threw up her hands, for he was simply looking at her with casual interest, the sort of look one would give a precocious dog. "Truly, all the women can weave passably now. I want my gown, and then I want to leave and go to my cousin."

"What did you say his name was, this so-called cousin of yours?"

"His name is Father Ralth. He's a dour Benedictine and will garb me as a choirboy and let me have a small cell of my own. I plan to meditate the rest of my days, thanking God for saving me from de Bridgport and villains like you."

"You will be known as Philippa the castrato?"

"What's a castrato?"

"A man who isn't a man, who's had his manhood nipped in the bud, so to speak."

"That sounds awful." Her eyes went inadvertently to his crotch, and he laughed.

"I would imagine it isn't a fate to be devoutly sought. Now, wench, come with me to my bedchamber. The both of us can bathe. I tire of my own stench, not to mention yours. I shall consider letting you scrub my back."

Philippa, as much as she wanted to exercise an acid tongue on his head, couldn't find the energy to do it. A bath sounded wonderful. Then she looked down at the old gown, dirty and sweat-stained, and sighed. Dienwald said nothing. He turned on his heel, firmly expecting her to follow after him like a faithful hound, which she did, curse his eyes.

They passed Alain. Philippa saw the steward give Dienwald an approving nod and wondered at it. Why had he so openly attacked his master to her just this morning? Something was decidedly wrong. Philippa had never before considered herself to be of an overly curious nature, even though her parents had accused her of it frequently, but now she wanted very much to shake Master Alain and see what fell out of his mouth.

It didn't occur to her to wonder how the bathing ritual would take place until Dienwald had locked the bedchamber door, tossed the key into the pocket of his outer tunic, and turned to say, "I'll exercise some knightly virtue and let you bathe first. You see, chivalry still abounds in Cornwall."

"I'm so dirty you'll need another tub. Also, you can't stay in here. Will you wait outside?"

"No." Frank enjoyment removed the tiredness from Dienwald's eyes. "No, I want to see you naked. Again. Only this time, all of you at one time, not just parts."

Philippa sat on the floor. She eyed the copper-bound wooden tub with steam rising from it and felt a nearly murderous desire to jump in, but she didn't move. She wouldn't move, even if she had to rot here. She wouldn't allow him to humiliate her anymore. She wouldn't play the partial trollop. To her surprise, Dienwald didn't say anything, didn't threaten her with dire punishments. He rose from the bed and calmly stripped off his clothes.

She didn't look at him, but after several minutes had passed and she heard no further sound, no movement, she couldn't stand it anymore. When she raised her head, it was to see him standing by the tub, not three feet away from her. She'd seen naked men before; only girls who had been raised by nuns in convents hadn't. But this was different; *he* was different. He was hard and lean and hairy, his legs long and muscled, his belly flat and sculptured. She looked—and couldn't look away. His manhood swelled from the thick bush of hair at his groin, and she stared with open fascination as it grew thicker and longer.

She felt something quite odd and quite warm low in her belly. Philippa knew this wasn't right; she also knew she was losing control of a situation she somehow no longer wanted to control. She swiveled about and faced away from him.

Dienwald laughed and climbed into the tub. He'd seen her stare at him, felt his sex rise in concert with her interest, seen her interest rise as well and her confusion. He reveled in her reactions—when they didn't irritate him.

He lathered himself, feeling the grime soak off,

and said, "Wench, tell me of your progress. And
don't whine to me about all your problems or of
the heat in the outbuilding or of Old Agnes' carping. What did you accomplish?"

Philippa turned back, knowing the height of the
tub would keep her from further inappropriate
perusal of his man's body. His hair was white
with lather, as were his face and shoulders. She
couldn't see any more of him.

"It has been nearly nothing *but* problems, and
I'm not whining. I may skin Prink alive if the
ague doesn't bring him to his grave first. Oh, we
now have wool, curse you. I was thinking, mayhap the first tunic should be for Edmund. He
looks ragged as a villein's child."

Dienwald opened his eyes, and soap seeped in.
He cursed, ducking his head under the water.
When he'd cleansed his eyes of the soap he
turned to her and nearly yelled, "Nay, 'tis for
you, foolish girl. That was our bargain. I am an
honorable man, and though you, as a woman,
can't understand bargains or honor, I suggest you
simply keep your ignorance behind your tongue.
I dislike martyrs, so don't enact touching gestures
for me. And you simply haven't looked at the
villeins' children. They're nearly naked."

"You're taking your anger out on me because
you were clumsy with the soap! You're naught
but a tyrant and a stupid cockshead!"

"Not bad for a maiden of tender years. Should I
improve upon your insults? Teach you ones more
spiteful and less civil?"

He saw her jump to her feet and knew what
was in her mind. He said very calmly, even
though his eyes still burned from the soap and
he wasn't through with her, "Don't, Philippa.

Leave the key where it is. You're not using your brain. Tancrid is outside the door. If you managed to trip him up and smash his head with something, there would still be all my men to be gotten through. Sit down on the bed and tell me more of your day. If you must, you may whine."

She sat down on the bed and folded her hands in her lap. He resumed his scrubbing. She looked at his discarded outer tunic, the one that held the bedchamber key. She sighed. He was right.

"We will begin dyeing the wool tomorrow."

He nodded.

"If there are skilled people, then the first of the cloth will be ready for sewing into garments the next day."

He was washing his belly. Philippa knew it was his belly—or flesh even more southerly—and she was looking, she couldn't help herself. She wondered what it would feel like to touch him, to rub soap over him . . . He looked at her then and smiled. "I will order clean water for you. I have blackened this."

"Will you stay to watch me?"

Dienwald imagined that she'd choose to remain dirty if he said yes. He shook his head. "Nay, I'll leave you in peace. But if you try anything stupid I will do things to you that you will dislike intensely."

"What?"

"You irritate me. Close that silly mouth of yours and hand me that towel. 'Tis the only one, so I will use only half of it. Thank me, wench."

"Thank you."

Wolffeton Castle, near St. Agnes

"That damned whoreson! He *knew*, damn him,
the scoundrel *knew* full well that wine was bound
for Wolffeton from your father. I'll break all his
fingers and both his arms, then I'll smash his
nose, stomp his toes into the ground—"

Graelam de Moreton, Lord of Wolffeton,
stopped short at the laughter from his wife. He
eyed her, then tried again. "We have but two
casks left, Kassia. 'Tis a present from your sire. It
costs him dear to have the wine brought to Brittany from Aquitaine, then shipped here to us.
Care you not that the damned whoreson had the
gall to wreck the ship and steal all the goods?"

"You don't now that Dienwald is responsible,"
Kassia de Moreton said, still gasping with laughter. "And you just discovered today that the ship
had been wrecked. It must have happened over
a sennight ago. Mayhap it was the captain's mis-
judgment and he struck the rocks; mayhap the
peasants stole the goods once the ship was sinking; mayhap everything went down."

"You're full of mayhaps! Aye, but I know 'twas
he," Graelam said, bitterness filling his voice as
he paced away from her. "If you would know the
truth, I made a wager with him some months ago.
If you would know more of the truth, our wager
involved who could drink the most Aquitaine
wine at one time without passing out under the
trestle table. I told him about the wine your father
was sending us. When we'd gotten the wine,
Dienwald and I would have our contest. He knew
he would lose, and that's why he lured the captain to his doom, I know it. And so do you
beneath all that giggling. Now he has all the wine

and can drink it at his leisure, rot his liver! Nay, don't defend him, Kassia! Who else has his skill and his boldness? Rot his heathen eyes, he's won because he stole the damned wine!"

Kassia looked at her fierce husband and began to laugh again. "So, this is what it is all about. Dienwald has bested you through sheer cunning, and you can't bear being the loser."

Graelam gave his wife a look that would curdle milk. It didn't move her noticeably. "He's no longer a friend; he's no longer welcome at Wolffeton. I denounce him. I shall notch his ears for him at the next tourney. I shall carve out his gullet for his insolence—"

Kassia patted her hair and rose, shaking the skirts of her full gown. "Dienwald is to come next month to visit, once the spring planting is undertaken. He will stay a week with us. I will write to him and beg him to bring some of his delicious Aquitaine wine, since we are neighbors and good friends."

"He's a treacherous knave and I forbid it!"

"Good friends are important, don't you agree, my lord? Good friends find wagers to amuse each other. I look forward to seeing Dienwald and hearing what he has to say to you when you accuse him of treachery."

"Kassia . . ." Graelam said, advancing on his wife. She laughed up at him and he lifted her beneath the arms, high over his head, and felt her warm laughter rain down upon his head. She was still too thin, he thought, but her pregnancy was filling her out, finally. He lowered her, kissing her mouth. She tasted sweet and soft and ever so willing, and he smiled. Then he hardened.

"Dienwald," Graelam said slowly, evil in his eyes, "must needs be taught a lesson."

"You have one in mind, my lord?"

"Not yet, but I shall soon. Aye, a lesson for the rogue, one that he shan't soon forget."

St. Erth Castle

At least she was clean, Philippa thought, staring about the great hall, a stringy beef rib in her right hand. The dirty tunic itched, but she would bear it. She wouldn't be a martyr; Dienwald was right about that. She wanted clean soft wool against her flesh; it was all she asked. She didn't even consider praying for silk. It was as beyond her as the moon. Her eyes met Alain's at that moment and she nearly cringed at the malice she saw in his expression. She didn't react, merely chewed on her rib.

She heard Crooky singing in a high falsetto about a man who'd sired thirty children and whose women all turned on him when they discovered he'd been unfaithful to them, all nine of them. Dienwald was roaring with laughter, as were most of the men in the hall. The women, however, were howling the loudest as Crooky graphically described what the women did to the faithless fellow.

"That's awful," Philippa said once the loud laughter had died down. "Crooky's rhymes are a fright and his words are disgusting."

"He's but angry because Margot refused to let him fondle her and the men saw and laughed at him."

Philippa chewed on some bread, saying finally

to Dienwald, "Your steward, Alain. Who is he? Has he been your steward long?"

"I saved his life some three years ago. He is beholden to me, thus gives me excellent service and his loyalty."

"Saved his life? How?"

"A landless knight had taken a dislike to him and was pounding his head in. I came upon them and killed the knight. He was a lout and a fool, a local bully I had no liking for in any case. Alain came to St. Erth with me and became my steward."

Dienwald paused a moment, gazing thoughtfully at her profile. "Has he insulted you?"

She quickly shook her head. "Nay, 'tis just that . . . I don't trust him."

She regretted her hasty words the moment they'd escaped her mouth. Dienwald was staring at her as if she had two heads and no sense at all.

"Don't be foolish," he said, then added, "Why do you say that?"

"He offered to help me get away from you."

"Lies don't become you, wench. Tell me no more of them. Don't ever again attack a man who's given me his complete fealty for three years. Do you understand?"

Philippa looked at Dienwald, saw the banked fury in his eyes, making his irises more gold than brown, and read his thought: A woman couldn't be trusted to give a clear accounting, nor could she be trusted to be honest. She calmly picked up another rib from her trencher and chewed on it.

Dienwald was reminding himself at that moment that only one woman in all his life hadn't been filled with treachery and guile, and that was Kassia de Moreton. For a while he'd been unsure

about Philippa. She had seemed so open, so
blunt, so straightforward. He shook his head;
even a woman as young as Philippa de Beauchamp was filled with deceit. He should simply
take her maidenhead, use her until he wearied of
her, then discard her. It mattered not if she was
ruined; it mattered not if her father kicked her
into a convent for the remainder of her days. It
mattered not if . . . "Perhaps Alain distrusts you,
perhaps he fears you'll try to harm me. That is
why he wishes you gone from St. Erth, if, of
course, he truly said that to you."

Philippa found she couldn't tell him of the
steward's venom. Perhaps he was right about
Alain's motives. But she didn't think so. She
merely shook her head, then turned to Edmund.

"What color would you like your new tunic to
be?"

"I don't want a new tunic."

"No one asked you that. Only whether you
wish a certain color."

"Aye, black! You're a witch, so you can give
me a black tunic."

"You are such an officious little boy."

"You're a girl, and thass much worse."

"*That's*, not *thass*."

Dienwald overheard this exchange, smiling
until he heard her correct Edmund. He frowned.
Meddlesome wench. But even so, he didn't want
his son speaking like the butcher's boy.

"You will not have a black tunic. Do you like
green?"

"Aye, he'll have green, a dark green, to show
less dirt."

His father's voice kept Edmund quiet, but he
stuck his tongue out at Philippa.

She looked at him with a wondering smile. " 'Tis odd, Edmund, but you remind me of one of my suitors. His name was Simon and he was twenty-one years old but acted as if he were no more than six, just like you."

"I'm nine years old!"

"Are you truly? My, I was certain you were no more than a precocious five, you know, the way you act, the way you speak, the—"

"Do you want more ale, wench?"

So Dienwald had some protective instincts toward his son. She turned and smiled at him. "Aye, thank you."

She sipped at the tart ale. It was better than her father's ale, made by the fattest man at Beauchamp, Rolly, who, Philippa suspected, drank most of his own brew.

"How much more ale do you need?"

She took another sip before asking, "Why do you think I need more? For what?"

"I think, wench, that I will take your precious maidenhead tonight. It taunts me, wench, that maidenhead of yours, just being there. And you do belong to me, at least until I tire of you. But who knows? If you please me—though I doubt you have the skill to do so—I will let you stay and see to the sewing of all the woolen cloth into clothing. What say you to that?"

Philippa, without a thought to the precariousness of her position, tossed the remaining ale from her flagon into his face.

She heard a gasp; then the hall suddenly fell silent as one by one the men and women realized something had happened. Oh, dear, Philippa thought, closing her eyes a moment. She'd thought with her feet again.

Dienwald knew he'd taunted her to violence, and actually, the ale in his face was a minor violence—nothing more or less than he'd expected of her. He supposed he should have waited until he had her in his bedchamber to mock her. Now he would have to act; he couldn't be thought weak in front of his villeins and his men. He cursed softly, wiped his palm over his face, then shoved back the heavy master's chair. He grabbed her arm and dragged her to her feet.

He saw the fear in her eyes, saw her chin go up at the same time, and wondered what the devil he should do to her for her insolence. For now, he needed a show worthy of Crooky. He turned to his fool, who'd come to his feet and was staring avidly at his master like all the others in the great hall.

"What, Crooky, is to be her fate for throwing ale in her master's face?"

Crooky stroked his stubbled jaw. He opened his mouth, looking ready to burst into song, when Dienwald changed his mind. "Nay, do not say it or sing it."

" 'Tis not a song, master, not even a rhyme. I just wanted to ask the wench if she would make me a new tunic as well."

"Aye, I will sew it myself," Philippa said. "Any color you wish, Crooky."

"Give her another flagon of ale, master. Aye, 'tis a good wench she be. Don't flog her just yet."

"You're not to be trusted," Dienwald said close to her ear. "You'd promise the devil a new tunic, wouldn't you, to keep me from your precious maidenhead?"

"Where *is* the devil tonight?" Philippa asked,

looking around. "In residence here? There are so many likely candidates for his services, after all."

"Come along, wench. I have plans for you this long and warm night."

"No," she said, and grabbed the thick arm of his chair with her left hand. She held on tight, her fingers white with the strain, and Dienwald saw that he'd set himself a problem. He looked at the white arm he held, then at the hand holding the chair arm for dear life. "Will you release it now?"

She shook her head.

Dienwald smiled, and she knew at once that she wasn't going to like what followed.

"I will give you one more chance to obey me."

She stared up at him, knowing all the people in the hall were watching. "I can't."

She didn't have to wait long. He smiled again, then lifted his hand, grasped the front of her gown, and ripped it open all the way to the hem.

Philippa yelled, released the chair arm, and jerked at the ragged pieces, trying to draw them over her body.

Dienwald locked his hands together beneath her buttocks and heaved her over his shoulder. He smacked her bottom with the flat of his hand and strode from the great hall laughing like the devil himself.

9

"You note, wench, I'm not breathing hard, even carrying you up these steep stairs."

Philippa held her tongue.

She felt his hands on her buttocks, caressing her, and felt him press his cheek for a moment against her side.

"You smell nice. A big girl isn't such a bad thing—there's a lot of you for me to enjoy. You're all soft and smooth and sweet-smelling."

She reared up at that, but he smacked her buttocks with the flat of his hand.

"Hold still or I'll take you back into the great hall and finish stripping off that gown of yours."

She held still, but thought that his priest would surely die of shock were he to do that. When Dienwald reached his bedchamber, he carried her inside and dropped her onto the bed, then strode across the room and locked the thick door.

When he turned, Philippa was already sitting on the side of the bed, clutching the frayed material together over her breasts.

She fretted with the jagged edges, not looking at him. "I must sew it. I have nothing else to wear."

"You shouldn't have thwarted me. You forced me to retaliate. It was a stupid thing to do, wench."

"I was supposed to let you tread on me like rushes on the floor? I'm not a wen—"

"Shut your annoying mouth!"

"All right. What are you going to do?"

He kicked a low stool across the bedchamber. One of its three legs shuddered against the wall and broke off. He cursed. "Get into bed. No, wait. I must tie you up first. I'll wager you'd even try to escape nearly naked, wouldn't you?"

Philippa didn't move. "I want to sew my gown."

"On the morrow. Hold out your hands." When she didn't, he merely stripped off his clothes. He shrugged into his bedrobe, and when he turned back to her, he was holding a leather cross garter in his right hand.

"No, I won't do it. It's like demanding a chicken to willingly lay its neck on the chopping block. I'm not witless."

"I'm not at all certain of that, but you're right about one thing. Remove the torn gown first."

"Please . . ." she said, and swallowed. "I've never done anything like that before. Please don't make me do it."

"I've already seen you," he said slowly, the man of patience and reason. "I don't suppose you've perchance grown a new part to interest me?"

She shook her head.

He stared down at her bent head. He wanted her very much, but he wasn't about to give in to his appetite for her. It would do him in, mayhap irreparably. It would be stupid—and extremely pleasant. As much as Dienwald hated the notion of denying himself something because an outside authority would disapprove, he wasn't completely witless. If he ravished her, her father would sooner or later hear of it and come to St. Erth and besiege him until there was nothing left but rubble. Also, Dienwald didn't want to get a bastard on her. There were some things he simply couldn't bring himself to do. He wouldn't dishonor her and he wouldn't end up ruined. What he felt was only lust. Lust, he understood. Lust, like a thirst, could be quenched from any available flagon. He said nothing more. He wanted no more than to simply lock her in, but that would allow her to believe she'd gained the upper hand.

He took her off-guard, knocking her backward on the bed. He was fast and he was determined. Within moments the torn gown was on the floor and Philippa was naked beneath him. He saw that she was terrified and, oddly, seemingly curious. He saw it in her eyes. She was curious because she was a maid and he was the first man to treat her in this way. He knew she could feel his increasing interest. Well, let her feel it. It didn't matter. He rolled off, grabbed her wrists, and bound them together.

After he'd tethered the other cross garter to the bed, he stood beside her and looked down at her dispassionately. "You're quite beautiful," he said after a long study, and it was the truth. "You have large breasts, full and round, and your nipples are pale pink. Aye, I like that." He looked down at the curling triangle at the base of her belly. He'd like to sift his fingers through that hair and hear her cry out for him . . . He forced his eyes downward to those magnificently long legs, sleek with muscle and white as pale snow and of a shape to make a man groan with pleasure. Even her arched feet were elegant and graceful. He leaned down and lightly flicked a finger over her nipple. She tried to jerk away but couldn't move out of his reach. "Has a man ever looked at you this way before, wench?"

Philippa was beyond words. She'd watched him look at her, watched his eyes narrow. She could only shake her head, staring at him like a trapped animal, a trapped animal nearly incoherent from the strange sensations flooding its body.

"Have you ever had a man suckle your breast?"

She shook her head again, but he could see in her eyes not only the shock of his words but also the possible effect of the action.

He leaned down and took her nipple in his mouth. She tasted sweet and female and he felt her nipple tighten as he caressed her with his tongue, then suckled her more deeply. He felt his sex throbbing and pressing against his bedrobe. He had to stop this, or . . . "Do you like that?"

He expected a vehement denial—an obvious lie—mayhap a hysterical denial, but to his surprise, she said nothing. He felt a quiver go through her before he forced himself to rise. He tried desperately to keep his look dispassionate. "Has no man ever before touched his fingers to the soft woman's flesh between your thighs?"

"Please," she whispered, then closed her eyes, turning her head away from him.

He frowned. Please *what*? He didn't ask, but merely grabbed a blanket and covered her. He'd tortured himself quite enough.

"I will go relieve myself now with a willing woman," he said, and strode toward the door of the bedchamber.

"You make a woman sound like a chamber pot!"

"Nay, but she is a vessel for my seed." To his surprise, his own words made him all the randier. He was aching, his groin heavy. He wanted Margot or Alice—it didn't matter which—and he wanted her within the next three minutes.

"I hope your male parts rot off!"

He paused, not turning, and grinned. "I will find out soon enough if your curses carry more than the air from your mouth," he said, and strode back down the solar stairs and into the great hall. He saw Margot sitting close to Northbert. He frowned at the same moment she saw him, for he realized he was wearing naught but his bedrobe. A wondrous smile spread over her round face, making her almost pretty. She jumped to her feet and hurried over to him.

"I want you now," he said, and Margot smiled a siren's smile. She followed him outside, then bumped into his back when he came to an abrupt halt. Dienwald didn't know where to take her. Philippa was bound to his bed. He quivered. Damned female. Where, then?

"'Come," he said, grabbed her hand, and nearly ran to the stables. He took her in the warm hay in a far empty stall. And when she cried out her pleasure, her fingers digging into his back, he

let his seed spill into her, and in that moment he
saw Philippa, and could nearly feel her long white
legs clutching his flanks, drawing him deeper and
deeper. "Curse you, wench," he said, and fell
asleep on Margot's breast.

She woke him nearly three hours later. She was
stiff and sore, bits of hay sticking into her back
and bottom, and he'd sprawled his full weight on
top of her, flattening her.

Dienwald straightened his clothes and took
himself to his bedchamber after giving Margot a
perfunctory pat on the bottom. He'd left the single candle lit and it had burned itself out. He
could make out Philippa's form on the far side of
the bed as he stripped off his bedrobe and eased
in beside her. He untied the cross garter that tethered her to the bed and lowered her arms and
pulled her to him. With a soft sigh, she nestled
against him. Fortunately for his peace of mind
and Philippa's continued state of innocence, he
fell asleep.

When Philippa awoke the following morning,
she was alone, which was a relief, and her wrists
were free. Her ripped gown was gone, and in its
place she found a long flowing gown of faded
scarlet, the style from her childhood, its waist
loose and its sleeves tight-fitting to the wrists.
With it was an equally faded overtunic with wide
elbow-length sleeves and a fitted waist. She felt a
jolt when she realized that the faded clothing
must have belonged to Dienwald's long dead
wife.

The gown was too short and far too tight in the
bosom, but the material was sturdy despite its
age, and well-sewn, so she needn't fear the seams
splitting.

Her ankles and feet were bare, and she imagined that she looked passably strange in her faded too-small clothes, the skirt swishing above her ankles.

It was thoughtful of Dienwald to have had the clothes fetched for her, she thought, until she remembered that it was he who had ripped the other gown up the front, rendering it an instant rag. She hardened her heart toward him with ease, though the rest of her still felt the faint tremors of the previous night, when he'd looked down at her, then kissed her breast. Those feelings had been odd in the extreme, more than pleasant, truth be told, but now, alone, in the light of day, Philippa couldn't seem to grasp them as being real.

She made her way to the great hall, drank a flagon of fresh milk, and ate some gritty goat's cheese and soft black bread. It didn't occur to her not to go to the weaving shed to see to the work. Old Agnes, bless her tartar's soul, was berating Gorkel the Hideous for being slow to repair one of the looms. Philippa watched, saying nothing, until Old Agnes saw her and exclaimed as she shuffled toward her, "Gorkel's complaining of wood mold, but I got him at it again. Prink is threatening to come upon us today and whip off our hides. He didn't cork it! Mordrid said he ate this morning and was up on his own to relieve his bowels. May God shrivel his eyeballs! He'll ruin everything."

"No, he won't," Philippa said. She wanted a fight, and Prink sounded like a wonderful offering to her dark mood. She discovered when she called a halt for the noonday meal that Dienwald and a half-dozen men had left St. Erth early that

morning, bound for no-one-knew-where. That, or
no one would tell her.

Now was the time to escape.

"Ye look like a princess who's too big fer her
gown," said Old Agnes as she gummed a piece
of chicken. "That gown belonged to the former
mistress, Lady Anne. Small she were, small in
her body and in her heart. Aye, she weren't a
sweetling, that one weren't. Master Edmund's
lucky to have ye here, and not that one who
birthed him. She made the master miserable with
her mean-spirited ways. When she died of the
bloody flux, he was relieved, I knew it, even
though he pretended to grieve."

Old Agnes then nodded as Philippa stared
openmouthed. "The master'll fill yer belly quick
enough. Then he'll wed ye, as he should. Yer
father's a lord, and that makes ye a lady—and all
will be well, aye, it will." Old Agnes nodded,
pleased at her own conclusions, and shuffled
away to where Gorkel squatted eating his food.

Philippa walked outside the shed, Old Agnes'
words whirling about in her mind. Wed with the
master of St. Erth? The rogue who'd stolen her
father's wool and her with it? Well, it hadn't quite
been that way, but still . . . Philippa shook her
head, gazing up at the darkening skies. Evidently
he had to get her with child first before such
notions as marriage would come to him. She
didn't want him; she didn't want his child. She
wanted to leave, to go to . . . Where? To Walter's
keep, Crandall? To a virtual stranger? More of a
stranger than Dienwald was to her?

"It'll rain and we'll have to rot inside."

She turned to see Edmund, his hands on his
hips, looking disgruntled.

"Rain makes the crops grow. The rain won't last long, you'll see. We'll survive it." She grinned down at him. "And aren't you supposed to be at your lessons?"

He looked guilty for only an instant, but Philippa saw it. "Come along and let's find Father Cramdle. I haven't yet met him, you know."

"He won't want to see you. He'll go all stiff like a tree branch. My father ripped off your gown last night and carried you off. You're only my father's mis—"

"I don't think you'd better say it, Edmund. I am not your father's mistress. Do you understand me? I'm a lady, and your father doesn't dare to . . . harm me."

Edmund seemed to think this over for a half-dozen steps before finally nodding. "Aye," he said, "you're a big lady. And I don't need lessons."

"Of course you do. You must know how to read and to cipher and to write, else you'll be cheated by your steward and by anyone else who gets the chance."

"Thass what my father says. *That's!*" he said before she could.

Philippa smiled. "Tomorrow you'll have a new tunic. Also study new shoes and hose. You'll look like Master Edmund of St. Erth. What do you think of that?"

Edmund didn't think much of it. He scuffed his filthy toes against a rock. "Father went a-raiding. He's angry at a man who hates him and who struck last night and burned all our wheat crop near the south edge of St. Erth land."

"Who is this man?"

Edmund shrugged.

"How long will your father be away?"

"He said mayhap a week, longer or shorter."

"How did your father find out about the burned crops?"

"Crooky. He sang it to him at dawn. Father nearly kicked his ribs into his back."

"I can imagine. How does Crooky find out things so quickly?"

"He won't tell anyone how he does it."

"If he provides useful information, I suppose one can forgive his miserable rhymes."

"Aye, but Father said that only he could kick Crooky because Crooky was *his* fool and no one else's and had his protection. So no one touches Crooky." Edmund shrugged. "Crooky always finds out everything first. I think mayhap he's a witch, like you, except he's not a silly girl."

So much for a little peace talk, Philippa thought.

"There's Father Cramdle," Edmund said as they came in sight of the priest.

Philippa made his acquaintance, and was pleased when he looked her squarely in the eye and was polite to her. She gave him Edmund with the admonition, "You will do as Father Cramdle tells you, Edmund, or you will answer to me."

"Maypole! Woolly head! Witch!"

Philippa didn't turn around when she heard Edmund's fierce whispers; she merely smiled and kept on going. She met with the armorer, a ferocious old man whose name was Proctor and who had only one eye and that one rheumy. He'd cut leather for many pairs of shoes, including a pair for her. She delivered the leather to Old Agnes, and she, in turn, set others to stitching the leather into shoes.

It was late afternoon when Philippa thought again of escape. Why not? She stopped cold. She'd acted all through the day, she realized suddenly, as if she were chatelaine here at St. Erth, and that was absurd. She was a prisoner; she was as good as a serf; she was a *wench*.

She stopped her ruminations at the sight of Alain. He was speaking with a man she hadn't noticed before. The conversation looked furtive to her sharp eyes, and the steward gave something to the man. She watched silently until the man melted away behind the soldiers' barracks. Alain then mounted a horse and rode out of St. Erth. Most curious, she thought. Without hesitation Philippa went into the great hall, through the side chambers, until she found the steward's small accounting room.

There were wooden shelves built against the walls, and in the small cubicles were rolled parchments tied with bits of string. There were also larger sections in which bound ledgers were kept. Quills and ink pots and a thick pile of foolscap lay atop the table, as well as large dust particles. There were books stacked on the floor in front of the shelves, a narrow cot against one wall, and a low trunk at the foot of the cot. Nothing more. Evidently Alain both worked and slept in this room.

Philippa took one of the large ledgers from a shelf, moved to his desk, and opened it. It was a record of the past three years' crops—what was planted in which section of land, the price of the grain, the sale of the product, and a log of the villeins who'd worked each section, including the number of hours and days. Another bound book contained birth and marriage records of St. Erth.

Philippa returned to the first book and read it through. She sought out another book that held all the records of building and repairs done at St. Erth in the past three years—the tenure of Alain's stewardship.

It took Philippa only an hour and a half to discover that Alain was a thief. No wonder Dienwald had had to steal the wool: there was no coin available because Alain had stolen it all. Why didn't Dienwald know this? Didn't he go over his steward's records?

Philippa rose and rearranged all the steward's materials the way she'd found them and left the small airless room. He still hadn't returned. Where had he gone? Who was the man to whom he'd been speaking? What had he given the man? She had no answers.

Philippa went back to the weaving shed, saw that all work was progressing satisfactorily, then went in search of Crooky. She found him curled up in a corner of the great hall—sleeping off a huge meal, Margot told her, glaring down at the snoring fool.

Philippa walked over to him and lightly stuck a toe in his ribs. He jerked up, his mouth opened, and he started singing:

> Ah, my sweet lord,
> don't cuff your loving slave;
> He slumbers rarely in your service,
> like a toothsome wench who—

"Don't finish that atrocious rhyme," Philippa said. "Stand up, fool. I'll have words with you."

Crooky blinked and staggered to his feet, scratching his armpit. "What want you, mistress?"

"I suppose 'mistress' is better than 'wench.' "

"My sweet lord isn't here, mistress."

"I know it. I need your help, Crooky. I want to ask you several questions, but please don't sing your answers, just speak them like sensible people."

Crooky rubbed his ribs. "You've a sharp toe, mistress."

"It'll be sharper if you don't attend me."

"Oh, aye, I'm whetted."

Ten minutes later Philippa left the fool to resume his sleep. He'd given her more food for thought than she wished to consume. The greatest shock of all was the fact that the Lord of St. Erth could make out written words, but only slowly and with difficulty. He could write only his name and cipher only the most simple of problems. Not that all that many men could, and no more than a handful of women. She was foolish to be so surprised. She'd just thought that Dienwald, who, despite his stubbornness, his arrogance, was intelligent and seemingly learned . . . No wonder he was firm about Edmund's lessons with Father Cramdle. He knew it was important; he felt the lack in himself.

Philippa was very angry. She also realized when she saw Alain ride back into the inner bailey that she had less than no power at all. She was a prisoner, not the mistress of St. Erth.

She had to bide her time.

Unfortunately, Alain sought her out at the evening meal. He, she quickly discovered, played the master in Dienwald's absence, with Dienwald's permission, evidently. She knew she must tread

warily. He sat beside her in the master's high-
backed chair, ignored her for a good long while,
then turned and gave her a leer a man would give
a worn-out trollop of no account at all. She said
nothing, didn't change her expression, merely
sank her white teeth into a piece of pigeon pie,
a delicious concoction that included carrots and
turnips and potatoes.

"I see you stole the dead mistress's clothes."

So, Philippa thought, the steward wanted to
bait her. He couldn't keep his dislike of her to
himself. He really wasn't very good at the game.
Not nearly so accomplished as his master. She
smiled. "Do you see that, really? I'd thought you
here only three years, *Master* Alain. The mistress,
I'd heard, died shortly after Edmund's birth."

His right hand crushed a piece of bread. "Don't
think you to insult me, whore. Dienwald will
plow your belly, but he will show you no favors.
You are but one of many, as I told you before.
He will toss you to his men when he's through
with you. You look a fool in the gown—'tis far
too small for you. Your breasts look absurd, flattened like that. And your legs stick out like two
poles, it is so short."

" 'Tis better than wearing nothing."

"Aye, all of us saw him rip your clothing off
you, then carry you to his bed. You must have
angered him mightily. Did he ravish you until
you screamed? Or did you enjoy his plunging
member inside you?"

"Nay," Philippa replied, as if considering the
matter.

Alain laughed, sopped up some gravy from his
trencher with the large piece of bread he'd

crushed in his hand, and stuffed it into his mouth.

"You really don't look good in his chair," Philippa said, looking at his bulging cheeks. "It is too large for you, too substantial, too important. Or perhaps 'tis you who are just too meager, too paltry, for Dienwald's place." She thought he would spit out the bread in his anger at her, but he managed to keep chewing and swallow.

It was then she saw the shift in his expression. He'd realized that what he was doing wouldn't get him what he wanted. He was prepared to retrench. She waited. "We argue to no account," he said finally, and he sounded the reasonable man, not the furious brute who wanted to strike her. "Truly, Philippa de Beauchamp, you must leave St. Erth while there is still time. I will help you return to your father. You must go before Dienwald returns."

He wanted her gone, and very badly. Why? She was a threat to him now that she knew him for a thief, but he couldn't know that she'd discovered the truth about him. Why, then? "I've a notion to stay here and wed the Lord of St. Erth. He is a man of worth, and comely. What think you, steward?" The moment the words were out, Philippa was appalled at herself. But she wouldn't take them back. She watched, fascinated, as his face mottled with rage—and something else, something sly and frightening. His hand shook.

"I'll have you whipped, whore," he said very quietly. "I've a fancy to wield the whip myself. God, how I'd enjoy it. I'd see those breasts of yours heave up and down when you scream and try to escape the whip, and I'd mark that back of yours with bloody welts."

Edmund suddenly slipped out of his place at the trestle table and quickly moved to her side even as Philippa said, "No you won't, Master Alain. You have no power here either. If Dienwald only knew that you—" She bit her lower lip until she felt the sting of her own blood. She'd very nearly spit at him that he was a liar and a thief and a scoundrel and probably even worse.

At that moment Crooky rose from the floor beside Alain's chair and moved to stand on Philippa's other side. He yawned deeply, stared blankly at the steward, then sprawled back onto the rushes.

Alain didn't look pleased. He eyed Edmund, who looked for all the world like a mangy little gamecock. "The boy can't protect you, whore, nor can the fool, who's an idiot, a half-wit. He's naught of anything, and Dienwald keeps him here only because he finds it amusing to endure him. Now, what were you going to say, whore? You were going to accuse me of something? Make up lies about me?"

"My name is Philippa de Beauchamp. I am a lady. You're naught but offal."

"You're no more a lady than the fool is a poet. You're a silly vain trollop." Without warning, the steward raised his hand and struck her hard across the face. Her head snapped back from the force of it and she felt tears burn her eyes. Oddly, she noticed ink stains on his fingers, and wondered when he'd last bathed.

"Damned slut!" He raised his hand to strike her again, but suddenly, to Philippa's bewilderment, his chair began to shake, tip backward, then go crashing to the floor, the steward with it, landing on his back, his head striking the carved chair back.

Philippa, her hand pressed to her flaming cheek, could only stare at the fallen steward. Edmund stood over him, rubbing his hands together and crowing with laughter. The hall had fallen silent.

Alain scrambled to his feet, his face blotchy with rage, his thin body trembling. He waved his fists toward Edmund, yelling, "You damned little cockscomb! I'll hide you for that!"

Philippa was out of her chair and standing in front of Edmund in a flash. "You touch the boy and I'll kill you. Doubt me not."

The steward drew up short, looking at the woman who was at eye level with him. She was strong, but she wasn't strong enough to do him damage. Her words meant nothing; she'd cringe away at the first threat of violence, like every other woman he'd known. He wanted to spit on her, he wanted to wring her neck. No, he had to keep control. "Stand aside, whore."

He raised his hand when Philippa didn't move. There came a deep grumbling sound from behind the steward. Slowly, very slowly, Alain lowered his arm, turning toward the sound as he did so. Philippa stared at Gorkel the Hideous. He was the most terrifying sight she'd ever seen. His bony face, with its pocked surface and puckered scars, its stubbled jaw and thick beetle eyebrows that met over his nose, looked like a vision from hell. And there was that low growl coming from his throat, like an animal warning its prey.

"Get ye gone, little man," Gorkel said finally, and his lips barely opened.

Alain wanted to tell the codshead take himself

to hell, but he was afraid of Gorkel; the man could easily break his spine with but little effort of his huge hands. He looked at Philippa, then at the boy, who was standing there with his hands on his hips, his chin thrust forward. He'd get her; then he'd punish the boy. The steward turned on his heel and strode from the hall.

Crooky suddenly jumped to his feet and burst into wild song, the words following the enraged steward from the hall:

> A varlet he'll be to the end
> A stench that rots in the walls
> Next time he'll not have the gall
> When the master's back in the hall.

Philippa looked down at Edmund. "Thank you."

"He's a bully. Father doesn't see it because Alain's always careful around him. Why does he hate you? You're naught but a girl. You've never done anything to him, have you?"

"No, I haven't. I truly don't know why he hates me, Edmund."

"You will stay away from him. I can't always be around to protect you."

"I know." She looked up and met Gorkel's eyes. She smiled at him and he nodded, a deep rumbling sound in his throat. He scratched his belly, turned, and strode back to his place below the salt.

Noise filled the hall again. Crooky sprawled once more to the rushes. Edmund crammed bread into his mouth, and Philippa, her cheek still stinging, merely sat back into her chair, wondering what she was to do now.

For the next three days she kept close to Gorkel. He didn't seem to mind, and his presence kept Alain well away from her. He even disdained to sit beside her at the lord's trestle table. Gorkel didn't tell her that it was the master's order that he keep close to her. It would be Gorkel's head were the wench to escape St. Erth. In those three days Philippa learned more about St. Erth, met all its inhabitants, sewed Edmund a tunic of forest-green wool, and began one for Dienwald. Hers could wait a bit longer. Philippa became so used to all the noise that she could even identify what squawks came from what chicken. One pig in particular chose her as its mother and followed her everywhere, making Gorkel laugh. Philippa named the pig Tupper.

On the morning of the third day, Philippa, her step buoyant and carefree, entered the weaving shed to be greeted by pandemonium. A gaunt middle-aged man with tufts of gray hair sticking straight up on his head was screaming at Mordrid. He was quaking with rage, shaking so violently that his clothes, hanging loosely around him, were in danger of leaving his body.

He yelled, "Bitch! Slut! Treacherous cow! I lie on my deathbed and ye take my job. I'll kill ye!"

10

Philippa stared at the man, then shouted, "Hold! Who are you? What do you do here?"

The man whirled about. He looked Philippa up and down and sneered, and his eyes seemed to turn red. "Aye, so ye're t' witch who's beleaguered t' master. Ye're t' one who's made him think of naught but plungin' into yer belly and givin' ye wot's mine!"

"Ah," Philippa said, crossing her arms over her breasts. "You must be Prink. Fresh from your deathbed. I see you are still with us."

Her bright, very polite voice stalled Prink, but only for a moment. He felt ill-used, betrayed, and he wanted to leap on the wench and tear the hair from her head. It was her size that held him back. He didn't have his full strength back yet. He drew himself up. "I'm here t' do my work. Ye're not welcome, wench. Out wi' ye, and take all these

145

stupid women wi' ye." He grabbed Mordrid's arm
and twisted it. "I'll keep this one—she deserves
a hidin', she does, and I'll gi' it to her."

"Prink," Philippa said very slowly, "you will
release Mordrid, now."

The weaver looked fit to spit. His hold tightened on Mordrid's arm until the woman moaned
with pain.

Philippa wondered where Gorkel was. During
the past three days he'd been where she'd been.
Well, he wasn't here and she had no one but herself to handle this predicament. Even mouthy Old
Agnes was hiding behind a huge woven piece of
cloth newly dyed a bright yellow. Philippa
stepped up to the furious weaver, saw his pallor,
saw the spasms that shook his muscles, and knew
him still to be very ill. She said calmly, her voice
pitched low, "You aren't well, Prink. Here, allow
me to help you back to your bed."

He squealed like Philippa's worshipful pig,
Tupper, but he did drop Mordrid's arm. He gave
Philippa his full attention. "Ye're naught but t'
master's slut, and ye've taken wot's mine and—"

"Your face is gray as the sky this morning,
Prink, and sweat drips off your forehead. Do you
wish to remain here and fall on your face in a
faint, in front of all the women?"

Prink didn't know what to do. He'd exhausted
himself with his rightful indignation. He wanted
to wring the wench's neck, but he hadn't the
strength. He mumbled curses at Mordrid and
walked slowly, his muscles cramping, toward the
door of the outbuilding. At that moment Gorkel
appeared, looking from the weaver to Philippa.

"Do help him back to his bed, Gorkel, and see

that he remains there until he's completely well again. I will speak to you later, Prink."

The instant the weaver disappeared, Old Agnes bounded out of her hidey-hole, squawking with fury. "Old codshead! How dare he try to ruin everything, the stinking poltroon!"

Philippa ignored Old Agnes. "Mordrid, are you all right? Did he hurt your arm?"

The woman shook her head. "Thank you, mistress." She fretted a moment, then said, "Prink's a good man, he is, a proud man. The cramping illness makes him feel less than a man."

Would a woman forgive a man absolutely anything? Philippa wondered as she watched the work settle back into its placid routine. When Gorkel reappeared, he merely nodded to Philippa and took his post by the door.

The following afternoon, Philippa was hot and tired and feeling lonely. She was walking across the inner bailey, the pig, Tupper, squealing at her bare feet in hot pursuit, when the porter, Hood, called out to her that a tinker was coming. Did she want him to enter? Excitement flowed through Philippa as she yelled back that, yes, she wanted him to come. A tinker meant trinkets and ribbons and thread and items the keep sorely needed. Perhaps the tinker even had gowns, sold or bartered to him on his travels. She didn't stop to think that it was odd for her to be asked permission by the porter.

Men and women were gathering in the inner bailey, buzzing with excited conversation. Children, feeling their parents' anticipation, stayed close. Even the animals quieted as the stranger came through the huge gates. Philippa greeted the tinker and her eyes glistened with enthusiasm

at the sight of the two pack mules he led, each
one carrying more packages than she'd ever seen.

It was when she was fingering two long lengths
of pink ribbon that she realized she had no coin.

She had nothing, either, with which to trade.

She wanted to cry.

A soft voice sounded in her ear. "You agree
to leave St. Erth, and I'll buy you all the ribbons
you want. Mayhap even a gown and some shoes.
The tinker has everything. Ah, yes, you silly girl,
those ribbons would go very nicely with your
hair. Do you want them?"

She expelled her breath, turning to see the
steward standing close beside her, his leer as pronounced as ever.

Anger filled her and she very nearly screamed
that she knew he was a thief and that was why
the master had no coin. She stopped herself in
the nick of time. She had to keep quiet. She had
to wait until Dienwald returned. She tilted her
head back so that she was looking down her nose
at him. "Nay, sir steward, there is nothing I
wish."

"Liar."

She stepped back then and watched the people
of St. Erth buy and trade goods with the tinker.

She wanted to weep when she handed him
back the ribbons. It was foolish, but she wanted
them desperately. They were as pale a pink as
the sunrise in early May, and matched a gown
she owned back at Beauchamp.

The tinker remained the night and Crooky
proved to be in fine fettle, singing until he was
hoarse, the words of his songs so colorfully crude
that Father Cramdle was forced to clear his throat

several times. When Philippa finally left the great hall, Gorkel beside her, she was still smiling.

"I told the tinker to circle back this way when the master is here," Gorkel said as he left her beside her bedchamber door.

"It truly doesn't matter," Philippa said, and swallowed a bit hard.

"Keep the door locked," Gorkel said as he'd said each preceding night. She did as he'd said, then turned with her candle to set it down. Standing in front of her was Alain, holding a knife.

Philippa rushed back to the door and turned the large brass key in the lock, yelling, "Gorkel! Gorkel! *A moi! A moi!*"

The steward was on her in a second, his arm closing around her throat as he jerked her back against him. His right hand rose and the sharp point of the knife pointed down at her breast. Philippa couldn't scream now; his arm was cutting off her breath. She clawed at his arm with her nails, but he was strong—and strong with purpose.

He didn't slam the knife into her breast. She realized that he didn't want to kill her here. It would be far too dangerous for him. The knife was to ensure her obedience. His arm tightened and she felt the chamber spinning as white lights burst before her eyes. She jerked at his arm and felt the tip of the knife prick into her throat. She felt a cold numbing followed by the slick wetness of her own blood.

"Hold still, whore, or I'll gullet you now. As for Gorkel, that cretinous idiot can't hear you. The doors are thick. But you'll keep quiet or all that will come from your mouth is a bloody gurgle."

Philippa held still as a stone, dropping her arms
to her sides.

"Good. Now, come here."

He half-dragged her over to Dienwald's bed
and shoved her down onto her back. He came
down next to her, holding the knife over her
throat. She swallowed, looking up at him.

" 'Tis past time for you to escape from St. Erth.
Aye, you'll be long gone by the time the master
returns. And he'll blame Gorkel, the hulking
fright. Not me. He'll never even think about me."

She said nothing, letting her brain work rather
than her mouth. It was a novel approach.

"You wonder why I want you gone so badly
from St. Erth—I can see it in your silly female's
eyes. Those eyes of yours . . . they're familiar,
the shape and the color, aye, that shade of blue
has bothered me . . . I have seem them before,
somewhere . . . but no, I have no time for such
nonsense. I wouldn't have killed you had you left
before, but now you give me no choice. Stupid
sow, you should have left when I first offered you
the chance.

"But you didn't, did you? You wanted the master, wanted to believe his lies. Did he tell you that
he wanted you more than any other female? He
deceives women well. You should have left. But
now 'tis too late, far too late."

He was rambling on and on, bragging and
insulting Dienwald, and it seemed to Philippa
that he must be mad.

"Why?" she whispered, not moving because
the knife was still pressed so deep, its tip already
bathed in her blood.

"Why? Should I tell you, I wonder? Well, soon

you'll be dead and gone, so it matters not. I know who you are."

That made no sense. She said slowly, "I'm Philippa de Beauchamp. Everyone knows that."

"Aye, but you see, I sent my two men after the third wagon of wool, the one my foolish master left to the farmers because he felt pity for them. Aye, my men got them, and before they killed the luggards, they found out all about you. The farmers didn't know you'd been hiding in one of their wagons, but they were ready to talk all about you once knives were at their hearts. My men found out you were your father's favorite, that you were his steward in fact and in deed, that it was you who had set the price of the wool and sent them to the St. Ives Fair to get that price. Which means that you can read and write and cipher, unlike my master, who believes whatever I tell him.

"So you must die. You wonder why Dienwald trusts me, don't you? Aye, I can see it in your eyes. Dienwald saved me from a knight I'd swindled, and then he killed my master, who'd sided with the knight, after I told him how I'd been cheated and beaten. Then he brought me to St. Erth, where I've become a rich man. He believed he had earned my gratitude, the pathetic fool.

"Dienwald believes himself a rogue, a scoundrel, a rebel who can wave his fist in the face of higher authority, but deep in his soul he holds beliefs that can and will do him in. So you see, I can't let you remain, for I also know you visited my chamber. You left papers and documents just the way you found them, but one of my spies saw you. Aye, he saw you leaving, looking furtive and wary. So you found out the truth, did you, and were just waiting for the proper moment to tell Dienwald.

"And he set Gorkel to keep you from escaping, not realizing that he was at the same time protecting you from me. You didn't know that, did you? Gorkel has stayed close, and I didn't know how to get you until tonight. Then it came to me, and I knew I must be bold. You know, Philippa de Beauchamp, I hated you the moment I first saw you. I knew your purpose to be contrary to mine."

Before she could say a word, before she could draw another breath, Alain brought the bone handle of the knife down against her temple, hard. She saw a burst of lights, felt a sharp pain, and then there was blackness.

Philippa awoke with the earthy smells of the stables filling her nostrils. Her hands were bound tightly behind her, but her legs were free. She lay perfectly still, waiting for the dizziness to clear. When it did, she realized she couldn't breathe easily. A blanket covered her. She gripped an edge with her teeth and pulled it off her face. She seemed to be alone, but it was very dark in the stables and she couldn't be certain. She couldn't hear anyone moving about or speaking. Where was Alain?

Now, she thought, now was the time to think. Not with her feet, though they were the only free part of her, but with her brain. What to do? Alain had nothing to lose; he had to remove her from St. Erth. Snatches of songs sung by the jongleurs paraded through her mind in those moments, songs about mighty heroes rescuing fair maids from degrading and frightful situations. There

wasn't a mighty hero anywhere to be found. The
fair maid would have to save herself.

She tried to loosen the ropes at her wrists, but
the effort did nothing but shred her skin. She
rolled over and managed to rise to her feet, peering from the stall where she'd been left unconscious. She nearly fainted from the pain in her
temple where the knife handle had struck, but
she held on. She had no choice but to hold on.
She couldn't have much time left now. Alain
would be coming back for her soon. And he'd kill
her; she didn't doubt it for an instant.

Philippa managed to free the latch on the stall
and push the door open. It squealed on its rusted
hinges, and she froze. Where was the steward?

It was at that moment that she heard two men
speaking in low voices in the stableyard. The
steward's men. Standing guard until he returned.
From where?

Philippa drew a deep breath of relief. She'd
been on the point of rushing out of the stables at
full tilt, screaming for help. She'd been fully ready
to think with her feet again. She looked around
carefully, her eyes now used to the darkness, and
saw an old scythe, sharp and deadly, hanging
from a hook on the wall.

Her bonds didn't take long to cut through, but
the edge of the scythe was sharp and she felt
her own blood, sticky and slippery, covering her
palms before she was free. Once she was loose,
she stooped down and eased back to the stable
door. The two men were still there, still speaking
in low voices.

Now, she decided, she could take them by surprise and run as far as the great hall before they
caught up with her.

"Well? Heard you aught out of the whore? Is she still unconscious?"

Alain had returned. Philippa shrank back, her heart pounding so loudly they must hear it. No matter. Let them come. She pulled the scythe from the wall and clutched it to her breast.

She heard one of the men say, "Nay, t' wench is still quiet. T' blow will keep her unconscious until we cut her throat. Can we split her afore we kill her?"

Philippa swallowed convulsively. She realized suddenly that her bloody hands were making the scythe handle slick. She picked up some hay at her feet and rubbed it over the handle and over her palms. The pain was fierce, but she welcomed it. As long as she felt pain, she was alive. And as long as she had the scythe, she had a chance.

"You can do whatever you wish to her. But you must kill her afterward, make no mistake about it, and make certain her body's never found. The wench is conniving, so take care if she comes to herself again. Now, I've spoken to Hood, the porter, and told him that I'm sending some supplies to the master. The man's not stupid, so be careful. You'll load the girl on a pack mule and take her away from St. Erth. When you return, you'll be paid. Now, go."

Then Alain was leaving; she heard his retreating footsteps. Only his two accomplices remained, then.

All she had on her side was surprise.

She raised the scythe over her head and waited. One of the men was coming into the stables, saying to the other, "Wait here and I'll fetch t' wench."

The other man protested, "Nay, ye'll take her in t' stall, ye bastid!"

They were fighting over who was going to ravish her first. Her hold on the scythe handle tightened. Filthy villains. One appeared in the doorway, moonlight framing his head. Philippa drew a sharp breath and brought the scythe down hard. It was only the blunted, curved edge of the blade that hit him, but the force of her blow cracked the man's head open and he didn't even cry out, but fell, blood spewing everywhere, to the hay-strewn floor.

The man behind him cried out, but Philippa, like a blood-spewed vision from hell, screamed and came at him, the scythe raised over her head.

The man bellowed in fear, his eyes rolling in his head, and turned on his heel. Philippa drew up for an instant, her mouth gaping in surprise. The man had run from her, terrified. She quickly ran across the inner bailey and up the steps of the great hall. She flung the doors open and rushed in. As always, there was the loud noise of general conversation. Then a few people noticed her standing there, the scythe in her hands, covered with blood, her hair wild about her pale face.

There was an awesome silence. Then Alain jumped to his feet and yelled, "Kill the whore! By the devil's knees, she's butchered our people! Look at her, covered with blood! Murderess! She's stolen the master's jewels! Kill her! Strike her down quickly!"

Philippa looked around her and raised the scythe. The silence was deafening and paralyzing. No one was moving yet. Everyone was staring as if at a mummers' scene. "Gorkel," she said, her voice just above a croak, "help me."

Alain, seeing that no one had moved, bounded to his feet, screaming as he ran toward her, "Kill the damned witch! That's what she is, a cursed witch!"

He grabbed one of the men-at-arms' swords and ran straight toward her.

"Kill her!" another man's voice roared with the steward's. "Aye, she's a witch who steals men's jobs!" It was Prink, still pale and sweaty but ready to do her in. "Slay her where she stands!"

Eerily, Philippa now heard each voice separately. Every sound came singly and loudly and obscenely. She heard Father Cramdle praying loudly, she heard Edmund screech like one of her mother's peacocks as he dashed toward her. "No, Edmund, stay back!" But her words were just an echo in her mind. Northbert, Proctor, the armorer, Margot, Crooky, Alice—all of them were rushing at her. To aid her? To kill her?

She shuddered and backed away. She knew Alain's other henchman was out there in the inner bailey somewhere, just waiting to kill her if she came out. And here was Alain, fury and hatred burning him, ready to kill her even as she stood here in a hall filled with people.

She wasn't a coward. She raised the scythe.

"Nay, mistress."

It was Gorkel and he was moving slowly toward her, a look of abandoned joy on his terrifying face. His teeth were bared in a smile, and in that instant Philippa felt a bolt of pity for Alain.

Gorkel caught the steward's arm just above the elbow and simply squeezed. Alain's sword clanked harmlessly to the floor.

Then the steward was screaming and begging and pleading. Philippa saw that Gorkel was twisting the steward's elbow back and up, even as Alain's screams grew louder and louder.

Finally, seemingly without emotion, Gorkel closed the thick fingers of his other hand about the steward's neck. He raised him with one arm, the fingers tightening, and the steward dangled above the floor. He couldn't scream now; his voice was a mere liquid gurgle in his throat, as Gorkel shook him until his neck snapped—an indecently loud noise in the silent hall.

Gorkel grunted and flung the quite-dead steward to the rushes.

Philippa dropped the scythe, covered her face with her bloody hands, fell to her knees, and burst into tears.

She heard voices, felt hands touching her gently.

Then she heard a little boy's voice, Edmund's voice, and it brought her face out of her hands, for he said, "Stop those silly female tears."

She looked at him, and, surprising herself, smiled. "You are a mean little boy, with no more sympathy than a bug, but the sight of you right this moment pleases me."

"Aye," Edmund said. "That's because you're a female and need to be protected. You're filthy and covered with blood. Come along."

"Go with the boy," Gorkel said. "You did well, mistress, very well."

"There's another man, Gorkel. I killed his partner—he's in the stables—but the other man ran. I don't know who he was, but I would recognize his voice."

"It was probably the cistern keeper, a scurvy ruffian," Gorkel said. "He's been hanging about the steward. Aye, I'll have him fetched, and the master can see to his punishment when he returns."

"What about him?" Old Agnes screeched, pointing at Prink. "He's a filthy traitor!"

The weaver was swaying on his feet, looking sick and afraid as Gorkel advanced on him.

"Leave him be," Philippa called. "Don't kill him, Gorkel. He's just stupid and foolish from his illness. Leave him be."

"I'll give him a taste of pain," Gorkel said. "Just a little taste of pain so he'll remember not to make another mistake like this one."

Philippa watched him lift the weaver high above the floor and shake him like a mongrel. Then he sent his fist into the weaver's stomach, dropping him, kicking his ribs, and saying softly, "Ye touch the mistress again, ye say one word out of the side of yer mouth to her, and I'll kick ye until yer ass comes out yer ears."

Philippa turned away. Edmund took her hand. "Come along, Philippa. I'll take you to your chamber."

Edmund was whistling as he walked beside her up the solar stairs.

Wolffeton Castle, Cornwall

Graelam de Moreton wiped the sweat from his brow and greeted his visitor. "Aye, Burnell, 'tis a pleasure to see you again. Is our king well? And Eleanor? Is our kingdom healthy?"

The two men spoke as Burnell, weary to the tips of his worn leather boots, trudged beside the lord of Wolffeton Castle. He was met by Graelam's wife, Lady Kassia, a charming, slight lady with large eyes and a laughing mouth. He found her delightful but wondered how such a small female dealt with the huge warrior that was her husband.

"What brings you here, Burnell?" Graelam asked finally, waiting for their guest to refresh himself with a bit of the remaining excellent Aquitaine wine.

"Actually, my lord, 'tis a mission for the king. He wishes your advice."

Graelam's dark brows shot upward. "Edward wants *me* to advise *him*? Come, Burnell, 'tis nearly May and the king must want to march against the Welsh or the Scots, and I imagine he wants more men and more money for a campaign. Come, now, and tell me the truth—"

" 'Tis true, my lord. The king has a daughter and he wants to find her a husband, one here in Cornwall."

"But Edward's daughters are far too young, and the king couldn't want an alliance with only a baron," Lady Kassia protested.

"His daughter isn't a princess, my lady," Burnell said to Kassia, who was sitting in her husband's vast chair. Graelam was standing beside her. It was then that Burnell noticed that she was heavy with child.

"What is she, then?"

"Kassia, my love," Graelam said, grinning down at her, "methinks I scent a royal indiscretion. Edward must have been quite young, Burnell."

" 'Tis true. Her name is Philippa de Beauchamp. She's nearly eighteen and 'tis past time for her to be wedded."

"De Beauchamp! But Lord Henry's daughter—"

"She's the king's illegitimate daughter, my lord, raised by Lord Henry as his own."

Both Graelam and Kassia were staring with fascinated eyes at the king's secretary. Slowly Robert Burnell gave them all the facts and the king's request. ". . . So you see, my lord, the king wants a man who won't try to bleed him, but also a man of honor and strength here in Cornwall."

Graelam was frowning. He said nothing.

Burnell, hot and tired, said with some desperation, "He wants you to give him a man who would be worthy of his daughter's hand, my lord, so—"

"I may know the man the king seeks," Graelam said with his first spark of enthusiasm, and Kassia saw the evil intent in her husband's eyes.

"You do?" she asked, staring at him.

"Aye, mayhap I do."

"His present rank isn't important, my lord. The king will make him an earl."

"An earl, you say? 'Tis something to think about. You will remain until tomorrow, Burnell?"

Robert Burnell would have happily remained in a soft feather mattress for a week. After visiting Lord Graelam, he would have to stop at Beauchamp and speak to Lord Henry and tell him, hopefully, that there would be a groom for Philippa shortly.

"Good. I will tell you my opinion on the morrow. Aye, advice for the king."

That night, Graelam was laughing heartily in bed beside his wife. Kassia was chiding him sharply. "You cannot, Graelam! Truly, you cannot!"

"I told you I would bring that whoreson down, Kassia. This will do it." And Graelam continued to laugh, finally holding his belly.

"But Dienwald despises authority—you know that. His father-in-law would be the King of England! Dienwald wouldn't accept it. He'd travel to the Pope to plead for his freedom, or escape to the Tartars, or even pray to the devil if need be. And to be made an earl. Dienwald disdains such trappings. He hates respectability and responsibility and tending to his name and his holdings and his *worth*. Oh, my lord, he bested you, but this revenge would make him miserable forever. He could no longer raid when it pleased him. He could no longer brag about being a rogue and a scoundrel. He is proud of his reputation! And what if the girl is a hag? What then?"

Graelam laughed harder.

Kassia just looked at her husband and thought about the casks of Aquitaine wine that Dienwald had probably stolen from the wrecked ship. She thought of Dienwald as an earl, his father-in-law the King of England himself. Hadn't Burnell mentioned that the girl, Philippa, looked every inch a Plantagenet?

Kassia started laughing herself. "He'll murder the both of us," she said, "if Edward takes your advice."

St. Erth Castle

It was the middle of the night and Philippa was dreaming that she felt a warm hand lightly stroking through her hair, rubbing her scalp, and it felt wonderful. Then a man's mouth was touching her cheek, her jaw, nipping at her throat, licking over her lips; then a man's tongue was stroking rhythmically over her lower lip. She sighed and

stretched onto her back. She loved the dream,
cherished it, held it tightly, now feeling the man's
fingers caressing her breasts, his callused fingertips stroking her nipples.

When the man's fingers rubbed over her ribs,
curved in with her waist, then stroked her belly,
her muscles contracted with pleasure. Then he
was pressing her legs open and delving through
her hair to find her, and she sighed, then moaned
deeply, wanting more, lifting her hips, and wanting, wanting . . .

She opened her eyes to see the man wasn't a
dream. It was Dienwald, and she looked at him
until she could make out his features in the darkness. He looked tired and intent and he was
breathing hard as he stared down at her.

"It wasn't a dream," she said.

"No, wench, it wasn't a dream. You feel like
the softest of God's creatures." She felt his fingers
caressing her flesh and knew she was wet
beneath his fingers and swelling, her flesh heating. Then he eased his middle finger inside her,
and she cried out, jerking up, feelings she'd never
before imagined welling up inside her.

"Hush," he said, and pressed his palm against
her belly to push her down again, and then his
finger eased more deeply within her, and more
deeply still. "Does that pain you, wench? I can
feel you stretching for my finger. Ah, there it is,
your badge of innocence. Your precious maidenhead. Intact, ready for my assault." He shuddered, his whole body heaving, and for a moment
he laid his face against her, his finger still inside
her, not moving now, soothing and warm. "You
almost died tonight, Gorkel told me. I'm sorry,
Philippa. I thought you well-protected—from

yourself, truth be told—yet my trusted man was an enemy of the worst sort. I'm so sorry." He kissed her belly, licked her soft flesh, and his finger pressed more deeply into her, testing the strength of her maidenhead. He moaned, a jagged raw sound, and withdrew his finger.

He came over her and his mouth covered her, and Philippa, excited and quiescent in the dark of the night, yielded completely to him.

His tongue was inside her mouth, tasting her, savoring her, and she touched the tip of his tongue with hers. Then, once again, without warning, he rolled off her, leaving her abruptly.

"Please," Philippa whispered, holding her hand toward him. She felt nearly frantic with longing—for what, she knew not.

"Nay, wench," he said, sounding as though he'd been running hard. "Nay, 'tis just that I've been without a woman for a week and my loins are fit to burst with lust. Get you back to sleep."

She cried out at his words, hating them, hating him for making her realize yet again that she was nothing to him, nothing but a vessel, nothing more. She heard him leave the chamber and slam the door.

She turned onto her side and wept, her sobs a faint sound in the quiet darkness.

When Dienwald returned some time later, she pretended to be asleep. He made no move to touch her when he climbed into the bed beside her. She listened to his breathing even into sleep and knew she had to leave him and St. Erth.

As soon as she could find a way.

11

The next morning, Philippa awoke to the slap of a hand on her naked buttocks and lurched up.

"You're awake. 'Tis time I had some answers from you, wench. I leave my castle in fine fettle, only to return and find my steward dead and everything in an uproar. Get you up and come into the great hall."

Dienwald smacked her bottom one more time and left her alone. She lay there wondering what would happen to her if she cracked his head open with a scythe. The cockscomb.

She rolled onto her side and tried to go back to sleep, but it was impossible.

In the great hall, Dienwald was staring at his fool, stretched on his side on the floor. "Tell me again what happened, Crooky, and say it in words that make sense. No rhymes, no songs."

Crooky looked at Dienwald. His master was

tired, ill-tempered, and had obviously ridden back to St. Erth in haste. Why? To see the mistress? He'd missed the girl? Crooky hadn't seen him the previous evening when he'd stormed into the hall yelling his head off because the porter had screeched about Philippa being covered with blood and dead bodies everywhere.

Crooky grinned at his master. "Methinks you grow cockhard, master."

"I grow what? Listen, you damnable mule offal, I don't—"

"You caught the bastards who burned the crops?"

Dienwald tore into a piece of bread with his strong teeth. "Aye, three of them, but curse their tongues, they were already dead and couldn't tell me who'd sent them."

" 'Twas Walter de Grasse, the slimy serpent."

"Aye, in all likelihood." Dienwald chewed another piece of bread, not speaking again until he'd swallowed. Then he bellowed, "Margot! Bring me ale!"

"Let the mistress tell you of her adventures, master. 'Twill make your hair stand up in fright."

"You dare to call the wench 'mistress'? It's mad! I should kick you—"

Crooky quickly rolled away from his master's foot and came up onto his knees. "She's good for St. Erth," he said. "And stouthearted. She saved herself."

Margot brought the ale, giving Dienwald a wary look as she served him. "What's the matter with you?" he demanded, then waved an irritable hand when she paled at his words.

He turned back to the hapless fool. "You were

here, damn your ears! I want to hear what happened."

"Oh, leave him alone," came Philippa's irritated voice from behind him. "The last thing I want to listen to is Crooky singing at dawn."

Dienwald turned about and eyed her. It required all his will not to smile at her. It took him only a few moments more to tamp down on the wild relief he felt upon seeing her whole and ill-tempered. " 'Tis about time you deign to come to me," he said. "You look like a snabbly hag."

Actually, she looked tousled and soft and very, very sweet. He eased back into his chair, stretching out his legs in front of him, folding his hands over his chest. He'd fetched her another old gown worn by his first wife, this one a pale gray, frayed and baggy. It stopped a good three inches above her ankles.

"Thank you for the gown. There is no overtunic?"

"I didn't even have the chance to see you in the other gown I gave you. This one doesn't fit you at all, but there was nothing else. And don't whine. Why haven't you yet sewn yourself a new gown and overtunic?"

"I should have," she said, wanting to kick him. He'd touched her and caressed her and kissed her, then left her to find himself another female vessel. And now he was baiting her and insulting her. But she also remembered how he'd laid his head on her stomach and told her how he'd been afraid when he'd heard what had happened. Had she dreamed that? He didn't seem at all concerned about her this morning, just bad-tempered. She raised her chin. "I think I shall begin immediately." She picked up a piece of bread and begin to chew it with enraging indifference.

"Tell me what happened, wench. Now."

She chanced to look down at her wrists. They were bruised and raw but there wasn't much pain now.

Dienwald hadn't yet noticed her wrists; now he did, and sucked in his breath. His irritation rose to alarming heights. "I don't believe this," he bellowed at her. "I leave my keep, and look what happens. Have Margot wrap up your wrists." He added several lurid curses, then sat back, closing his eyes. "Tell me what happened whilst I was gone."

Philippa looked at him closely, decided he'd calmed himself sufficiently, and said, "Not all that much happened at the beginning. We spun nearly all the wool into cloth, and now we've gotten most of it dyed. The sewing has begun, just yesterday. Oh, just one small happening out of the ordinary—Gorkel had to break your steward's neck, but Alain deserved it. I have determined that you are the most pious of saints when compared to the loathsome departed Alain."

"I see. Now, before I take you to my chamber and thrash you, you will tell me why my loathsome steward wanted you dead."

Philippa just shrugged. She knew it infuriated him, and, unable to stop herself, she shrugged again.

He rose swiftly from his chair, walked to her and grabbed her beneath the arms, and lifted her off the bench. He held her eye-to-eye. "Tell me what happened, else you'll be very sorry."

"What will you do? Will you continue what you did to me in my sleep during the night?"

A spasm of some emotion Philippa couldn't identify crossed his face; then his expression was closed again. "Give over, Philippa, give over. I am weary and wish to know what happened."

His serious voice, empty of amusement, brought her eyes open. "I'll tell you. Put me down."

Dienwald very slowly lowered her to her bare feet. He walked back to his chair, pressing his hand against the small of his back. "Your weight strains even my strength," he remarked to the black-beamed ceiling, and sat down again, waving his hand at her.

She told him of what she'd found in the steward's chamber. "I didn't trust him, even from that first day I was here. He hated me, and there was no reason I could see. Well, my lord, he's been cheating you all the time he's been here, and when he held the knife to my throat in your chamber, he admitted it and insulted you and me and said he was going to kill me."

He made a strangled sound but said nothing. Philippa, swallowing against the remembered fear, spoke in a clipped and precise voice, emotionlessly telling him of coming to in the stables, of killing one of the men with the scythe, of running into the great hall, and of Gorkel's killing of the steward. "Alain also sent his men out to take the other wool wagon. He had the farmers killed. It was from them that he learned that I could read and write and that I'd acted as my father's steward."

Dienwald said nothing for a very long time. He merely looked beyond her, over her right shoulder, she thought, as she waited tensely for him to say something, anything. To show concern per-

haps for her safety, as he had in the dark of the
night. To tell her of his undying gratitude. To tell
her that he was glad she wasn't hurt, to tell her
he was sorry it had happened. To exclaim over
the perfidy of his steward. To thank her for her
diligence, her concern for him and for St. Erth.
To tell . . .

He exploded into her thoughts, nearly yelling,
"What in the name of St. Andrew am I to do
now? I have no steward because you ensured that
he'd die, curse you! Poor Gorkel had no choice
but to dispatch him, and 'tis all your fault!"

Philippa stared at him, nearly choking on the
piece of buttered bread in her mouth. "He was
cheating you! Didn't you attend me? He was a
filthy knave! Didn't you hear me? Don't you
care?"

Dienwald merely shrugged, causing her to leap
to her feet and throw the remaining bread at his
head. He ducked, but some of the sweet butter
hit his cheek in a yellow streak.

"You ungrateful fool! You—"

"Enough!" Dienwald rose from his chair, wiping the butter from his face with his hand.

"I repeat, wench, what will I do for a steward?"

She stuck out her chin, squared her shoulders,
and readied herself for his insults. "I will be your
steward."

It didn't take him long to produce the insults
she expected at her announcement. "You? A
female? A female who has no more sense than to
spy on a man and be caught and nearly butchered
for her stupidity? Ha, wench, ha!"

"That's not true. I was careful when I searched
through his chamber. I saw him ride away before
I went into the room. It was just bad fortune that

he had spies and one of them saw me. And what about his dishonesty? You, so astute, such a keen and intelligent male, didn't even begin to realize he was robbing you down to your last tunic, to your last hay straw, to your last . . . You, a brave male, didn't realize anything at all. You might even now give a thought to the fact that Alain's spies are very likely still here. Ha!"

"Females don't have the brains to resolve problems and keep correct records of things."

Philippa just stared at him, her bile spent, her rage simmering down to weary resentment.

"Females," Dienwald continued, waxing fluent now, "don't know the first thing about organizing facts and making decisions. Females have one useful role only, and that is—"

"Don't you dare say it!"

"They should see to the weaving and the sewing and the cooking. They are useful for the soft things, the things a man needs to ease him after he's toiled a long day with both his body and his brain."

"You're a fool," Philippa said, and without another word, for she'd spent even her anger now, turned on her bare heel and strode toward the oak doors.

"Don't you dare leave, wench!"

She speeded up, and was through the door within moments. She raced across the inner bailey, dodging chickens and Tupper, who squealed with berserk joy at the sight of her. She felt his wet snout against her ankle as she ran. Children called to her, women stared, and men just shook their heads, particularly when the master emerged from the great hall, his face a storm, his temper there for all to see.

"Come back here, you stupid wench!"

Philippa turned to see him striding toward her. "By the saints, you are a miserable clod!" She ran now, holding the frayed gown to her knees. Her legs were long and strong and she ran quickly—right into Gorkel.

"Mistress," Gorkel said. "What goes?"

"I go," she said, and jerked away from his huge hands. "Release me, Gorkel!"

"Hold her, Gorkel. Then, if you wish, you can watch me thrash her hide."

Gorkel gave a mournful sigh and shook his ugly head. "Ye shouldn't prick t' master."

"He's a fool and I'd like to kick him hard."

Dienwald winced at that mental imagine. At the same time, he felt an unwanted sting of distress at her words, but shook it off. "Come with me," he said, and grabbed her arm.

"Nay."

He stopped, looked from Gorkel back to Philippa, who was pale with fury. "You'll but hurt my back if you force me to carry you again."

Philippa drew back her right arm and swung with all her strength. Her fist struck his jaw so sharply that his head snapped back. He lost his balance and would have gone down in humiliation into the dirt had not Gorkel grabbed him and held him until he regained his balance.

Dienwald looked at Philippa as he stroked his sore jaw. "You're strong," he said at last. "You're really very strong."

She raised her fist and shook it at him. "Aye, and I'll bring you down again if you try anything."

Dienwald looked beyond her, his eyes widening. He shook his head, and Philippa snapped about to see what or who was behind her. In the next instant, she was flung over his shoulder, head down, her hair nearly trailing the ground as she yelled and screeched like hens caught in a rainstorm.

He laughed, and strode back toward the great hall. He took the solar stairs, aware that all his people were watching and talking about them and laughing, and the men, ah, they were shouting the most explicit and wondrous advice to him.

When he reached the solar he tossed her on her back onto his bed. "Now," he said. "Now."

"Now what?"

"I suppose you expect me to give you wages?"

She stared at him, her brain fuzzy from hanging upside down.

"Well?"

"Wages for what?"

"For being my steward, of course. Have you no brain, wench?" Suddenly he smacked his palm to his forehead. "I cannot believe what I'm saying. A female who has so little sense that she escapes in a gown reeking of a moat in a wagon of wool. And this female wants to control all that happens at St. Erth."

"My father trusted me." Philippa came up onto her elbows. She looked wistfully toward the empty chamber pot on the floor beside the bed. Old Agnes had seen that it was mended.

Dienwald said absently, "Don't do it, wench, else you'll regret it. Now, just be quiet. I must think."

"The pain it must cause you!"

He ignored her remark, saying finally, "I suppose you will demand to sleep in the steward's chamber as well as do the work there."

"Aye, of course. Certainly. To be free of you is—"

He grabbed her arms and kissed her hard. She didn't fight him. It didn't occur to her to do anything but ask him to kiss her again.

"Did you not beg me last night, wench?" he said when he raised his head. "Beg me to take you? You wanted me to relieve you of your maidenhead, didn't you? Well, sleep in your cold bed by yourself. You'll miss me, you'll want my hands and mouth on you, you know it. But enough. I won't miss you. I will sleep sweetly as a babe. Now, straighten yourself and sew yourself something to wear. I can't abide the way you look." He dropped her back onto the bed and strode from his bedchamber.

Nearly an hour later, her hair combed and fastened at the nape of her neck with a piece of cloth, bathed and sweet-smelling, Philippa visited the steward's chamber—now her chamber, she amended to herself. She arranged papers and moved the table some inches to the right. She asked Margot to bring fresh rushes for the floor, then returned to Dienwald's bedchamber. He was in bed, asleep, snoring loudly. On the floor beside the bed were her blood-stained clothes. She'd looked at them briefly, hoping they could be saved, but saw now that it was impossible.

Then she looked at Dienwald. He was sprawled on his stomach, one arm hanging over the side of the bed. Clutched in his hand was the nearly finished tunic she'd sewn for him. Philippa slowly eased it out of his fingers and shook out the wrinkles.

"I should burn it," she said, and left the chamber, needle and thread in her other hand.

Crandall Keep, near Badger's Cross,
Cornwall

Lord Henry wiped his hand across his sweating brow and listened to his destrier blow loudly. The trip had been long and hot and wet and altogether miserable. Three days to get to this damned keep, and what if he were wrong? What if Philippa hadn't run here to her cousin? He took a deep drink from the water skin and handed it back to his servant. His men had just spotted Crandall Keep, where his nephew Sir Walter de Grasse was castellan. All appeared calm. Lord Henry motioned his men forward again.

Crandall was a prosperous keep, he saw, noting the green fields that surrounded the low thick walls. But its defenses were meager, the reason being that Crandall paid obeisance to Lord Graelam de Moreton of Wolffeton. An attack on Crandall would mean swift and awful retribution from Lord Graelam.

Philippa had to be here, she simply had to be. Lord Henry wiped his brow again. There was no other place for her to escape to. She was either here or she was dead. His farmers had been found dead, all the wool wagons disappeared, the guards gone—fled or dead, he didn't know. No sign of his daughter. He'd put off Burnell, the king's tenacious chancellor and secretary, but the man wasn't stupid and would want to see Philippa. He would want to give a personal report to the king. He would want to tell Lord Henry the name of the man the king had selected to be Philippa's husband. Lord Henry raised his eyes to the heavens. Philippa had to be here with her cousin, she had to be.

Sir Walter de Grasse was playing draughts in the hall with his mistress, Britta. She knew the game well, as well as she knew him. She always managed to lose just when he became frustrated, a ploy that pleased Sir Walter. He was informed that his uncle, Lord Henry de Beauchamp, was approaching Crandall. What was his uncle doing here? He thanked the powers that he'd returned two days before from the raid on the southern lands of that whoreson Dienwald de Fortenberry. He'd lost three men, curse the luck. But he'd burned the crops and razed peasants' huts and killed the villeins. All in all it had been worth the price the three men had paid. De Fortenberry must be grinding his teeth by now. The bastard was helpless; he would know who was behind the attack. Oh, he could guess, but Lord Graelam wouldn't act against him, Walter, unless there was proof, and Walter was too smart for that. Luckily the three men had died before Dienwald could question them.

Sir Walter frowned and lightly patted Britta's cheek in dismissal. She removed the draught board and herself, giving him a look over her shoulder designed to excite him. Walter frowned after her. He wished he'd had some warning of his uncle's visit. The keep could be in better condition, fresh rushes strewn on the floor and the like, but it was well enough. It wasn't his overlord, Lord Graelam, thank the saints.

The two men greeted each other. Lord Henry had never been particularly fond of his wife's nephew. Walter was thin and tall and his nose was very long and narrow. His eyes were shrewd and cold and he had no sense of humor. He hated well, but to Lord Henry's knowledge, he'd never loved well.

As for Walter, he thought his uncle by marriage a fat buffoon with more wealth than he deserved. He should have been Lord Henry's heir, but there were the two stupid girls instead. When they were finally alone, Lord Henry wasted no more time. "Your cousin Philippa has run away from Beauchamp. Is she here?"

Now, this was a surprise, Walter thought, staring at his uncle. Slowly he shook his head. "Nay, I haven't seen Philippa since she was a gangly girl with hair hanging to her knees."

"She's no longer gangly. She's nearly eighteen, long since ready to be wedded."

Suddenly, to Walter's surprise, Lord Henry lowered his face into his hands and began to sob. Not knowing what to do, Walter merely stared at his uncle's bowed head, saying nothing.

"I fear she's dead," Lord Henry said once he'd regained control.

"Tell me what happened."

Lord Henry saw no reason not to tell Walter the entire truth. After all, it hardly mattered now. He spoke slowly, sorrow filling his voice.

"She's *what*?"

"I said that Philippa is the king's illegitimate daughter. He is at this moment selecting a husband for her."

Walter could only stare. Damn! What had happened to the girl?

Lord Henry soon enlightened him about the rest of it.

"I know not who killed the farmers or who stole the wool, but Philippa is now likely as dead as the farmers."

Lord Henry wiped his eyes. His sweet Philippa, his stubborn-as-a-mule Philippa. Dead. He couldn't bear it. He'd lost a daughter, a steward, and, most terrifying, he'd lost the king's illegitimate progeny. It wasn't to be borne.

"I shouldn't be too certain, Uncle," Walter said, stroking his rather pointed chin gently. "I hear things, you know. I can find out things too. Return to Beauchamp and let me try to discover what happened to my dear little cousin. I will send you word immediately, of course, if I find her."

Lord Henry left Crandall the following day, Sir Walter's assurances ringing hollow in his ears. Walter had already dispatched men to scout out information. Empty words, Lord Henry thought, but they had lightened his burden, if just for a little while.

As for Sir Walter, he was rubbing his hands together by the following afternoon. The cistern keeper of St. Erth had escaped to Crandall, arriving just that morning with news that Walter's steward, Alain, was dead, unmasked by a big female with lavish tits and bountiful hair whose name was Philippa. Walter nearly swallowed his tongue when he realized how very close Philippa had been to dying by the steward's order.

Now he knew where his dear cousin was, his dearest cousin, the girl he would wed as soon as he got his hands on her. Oh, aye, she'd want him. After all, in all likelihood she'd been on her way to him when she'd been captured by that miserable Dienwald de Fortenberry. Walter could just imagine how Dienwald had treated the gently bred girl—ravishing her, humiliating her, shaming her . . . But why and how had she uncovered the steward's perfidy if she'd been thus shamed?

It didn't matter. The cistern keeper had probably confused things. Walter would marry the king's illegitimate daughter. She was his gift horse and he would have her. He prayed she wasn't carrying de Fortenberry's bastard in her womb. Perhaps he could rid her of the brat—if there was one—when he got his hands on her.

Walter sighed with the pleasure of his contemplations. At last he would be somebody to reckon with. He would starve out de Fortenberry and have him torn limb from limb. He would regain St. Erth, the inheritance he should have had, the inheritance his father had lost to Dienwald's father so many years before. He would spit on Lord Graelam—behind his back, of course—and leave this pigsty Crandall. He would be overlord of all Cornwall and Lord Graelam would be his vassal, with his father-in-law's agreement and assistance. He would almost be a royal duke! He would then look south to Brittany. Aye, his grandfather had held lands there, now stolen away by that whoreson de Bracy of Brittany. Aye, with the king's help, with the king's money, with the king's men, he would take back what was his, all of what should have been his in the first place. And he could add to it if he were wily and cunning.

Sir Walter hummed as he made his plans. He wondered briefly what Philippa looked like. If she were a true Plantagenet, he thought, she must be beautiful. The cistern keeper spoke of her tits and hair. What color? he wondered. He liked big breasts on a woman. He couldn't let himself forget, though, that she was a bastard, after all, and

.thus tainted, despite her royal blood. He wouldn't forget that, nor would he allow her to forget it. Aye, she would welcome him, her dear cousin. After her doubtless brutal treatment at de Fortenberry's hands, she'd come leaping into his waiting arms.

St. Erth Castle

Philippa sat in the steward's chamber, her head bowed, entering inventories of the crops in a ledger. Her back hurt from sitting so long, but there was much to be done, much to be corrected and adjusted. Alain had created fiction, and it must be set aright, and quickly.

Dienwald's new tunic of deep blue, so soft that it slithered over the flesh, was finished and lay spread smooth over the back of the only other chair in the small chamber. She was a fine needlewoman, and the thread, thankfully, was stout.

She looked up then and smiled upon the tunic. He would look very nice wearing it, very nice indeed, fit to meet the king thus garbed. She hoped she'd made the shoulders big enough and tapered the waist inward enough, for he was lean. She hoped he thought the color nice and . . .

She stopped herself in mid-thought. Here she was thinking like the mistress of St. Erth again. As if this were her home, as if this were where she belonged. She'd entertained no thought of escape in more hours than she cared to reckon.

She laid down the quill and slowly rose, pushing back from the table. She was nothing more than his servant. For the past two days she'd worked endless hours in this small airless chamber, and for what?

For the joy of wearing an ill-fitting gown belonging to his long-dead first wife? For the joy of helping him, the man who'd lain atop of her, his finger easing into her body, making her hot and frantic and . . .

"Stop it, you stupid wench!"

"I thought your name was Philippa."

She could have gladly removed her own tongue at that moment. Dienwald stood in the doorway, amusement lighting his eyes.

" 'Twas a private exhortation," she said. "It had naught to do with you."

"As you will, wench. How goes the work?" He waved toward the stacks of foolscap on the table.

"It is an abominable mess."

"I imagined as much."

"You do not read," she said, and unknowingly, her voice softened just a bit.

"Nay, not very much. 'Twas not deemed important by my sire. Few read or cipher—you know that. Why ask you?"

She shrugged. "I merely wondered. You insist upon Edmund's learning from Father Cramdle."

"Aye. The world changes, and men must change with it. It is something Edmund must know if he is to make his way."

Philippa had seen no sign of change in her brief lifetime, but she didn't disagree. She realized belatedly that she was staring at him, hunger in her look, and that he was already aware of it.

He grinned at her. "Come have your dinner. That is why I am here, to fetch you."

She nodded and rounded the table. He caught

her hand and pulled her against him. "You miss me, wench?"

She more than missed him. She lay awake at night, thinking of how much she wanted him lying beside her.

"Of course not. You are arrogant and filled with conceit, my lord."

"You don't miss my hands stroking you?"

One arm kept her pressed against his chest. She felt his other arm lower, his fingers parting her, pressing inward. She tried to draw away—a paltry effort, they both knew.

Her breathing hitched. She felt the heat of his fingers, the heat of herself, and there was only the thin wool of her gown between the two.

Then he released her, turned, saying over his shoulder, "Come and have your dinner now, wench."

"I'm not a—" she yelled, then stopped. He was gone, the door closed quietly behind him.

That evening she learned from Northbert that the cistern keeper had escaped but that several men were out searching for him.

"Alain worked not by himself, so thinks the master," Northbert said, then wiped his bread in the thick beef gravy on his trencher.

" 'Tis a varmint named de Grasse the cistern keeper has run to," Crooky announced, his mouth bulging with boiled capon.

Philippa grew instantly still. "Walter de Grasse?" she asked slowly. Her heart was pounding, her hand squeezing a honey-and-almond tart.

Dienwald heard her and turned, saying, "What know you of de Grasse?"

"Why, he's my cousin," she said without thinking.

12

Dienwald's face was pale, his eyes dark and wild. "Your *cousin*? Lord Henry's *nephew*?"

He didn't sound angry, merely incredulous, and Philippa felt emboldened to add freely, "Nay, Walter is my mother's nephew. My father doesn't like him, but I do." She raised her chin, knowing that Dienwald wouldn't be able to keep his opinion to himself, and that it would be contrary to hers.

"I don't believe this," was all he said. He rose, slamming his chair back, and left the great hall.

Crooky looked at Philippa and shook his head.

"He is always slamming out of here like a sulking child!"

"Nay," Gorkel said. "He leaves because he is angry and he doesn't wish to strike you."

"Strike me? I have done nothing. What is

wrong with him this time? I cannot help that Sir Walter is my kin."

"It matters not," Crooky said. "You, mistress, you say that you like this serpent, this vicious brute . . . well, what do you expect the master to do?"

"But—"

Crooky cleared his throat, and Philippa closed her eyes against the discordant sounds that emerged loud and clear from the fool's mouth:

> A villain, a coward,
> A knave without shame.
> De Grasse maims and he destroys
> And takes no blame.
> He lies and he steals
> And he slithers out to kill.
> My sweet master will slay him,
> Come what will.

"Why do you keep calling him 'sweet master'?" Philippa asked, irritated and frightened and wondering all the while what her cousin had done to earn such enmity.

Crooky gave her a small salute with a dirty hand and said with a wink, "Think you not that he is a sweet master? The females hereabouts think him more than sweet. They like him to bed them, to push apart their thighs and—"

"Hush!"

"Forgive me, mistress. I forget you are yet a maid and unknowing of the ways of men and women."

Edmund, hearing this outpouring from Crooky, frowned at Philippa and said, "Are you truly a maid? Still? I know you were before, but . . . You still aren't my father's mistress, even after all the times he's carried you off to his chamber? You said that—"

"I'm not his mistress. I'm naught but his drudge, his captive . . ." Philippa ground to a halt. She was also St. Erth's steward. "Why aren't you wearing your new tunic? You don't like it? I know that it fits. Margot told me it did. 'Tis well made, and the color suits you. And the hose and shoes. Why don't—"

"I don't like them. Besides, my father doesn't wear anything new. Until he makes me, then I'll stay the way I am."

"You are such a stubborn little irkle."

" 'Tis better than being a maypole."

"Edmund, if you do not wear your new tunic on the morrow, I will come to your chamber, hold you down, and put it on you. Do you understand me?"

"You won't!"

She gave him a look to shrivel any male. He ducked his head, and she saw that he was quite dirty, his fingers and fingernails coated with grime. He looked like a villein's child; he looked like he'd been wallowing in mud with Tupper. She had to speak to Dienwald about this. He forced his son to learn to read and write and cipher but allowed him to look like a ragged little beggar.

"Yes," she said, "yes, I will. And you will bathe, Master Edmund. When was the last time your hands were in soap and water?"

"There ban't be any soap, mistress," Old Agnes shouted to Philippa. The old woman had amazing hearing when it suited her. "No one thought to make it," she added, quick to defend herself should the need arise. "The master said aught."

Philippa called back, "But that is absurd. I have used soap in the master's chamber."

"Aye, thass the last of it. The master likely didn't realize it was the last of it."

"We will make soap on the morrow," Philippa said. "And you, you pigsty of a boy, will be the first to use it."

"Nay, I won't!"

"We'll see."

Philippa had much to consider that night when she closed the door to her small chamber. She'd just pulled the frayed tunic over her head and laid it carefully over the back of the single chair when she heard his voice say softly, "Put it back on. I don't wish to enjoy you here. I want you in my bed, where you can warm me when it grows cold near dawn."

"I'm not your mistress! Go away, Dienwald!"

"I've already enjoyed a woman this night. I have no pressing need for another, be she even as soft and big and, in truth, as eager as you. Come along, now."

Her eyes had adjusted to the dimness of the chamber and she saw him now, holding her discarded gown, his hand stretched out to her. She was standing there quite naked, just staring at him. Philippa grabbed the gown and pulled it over her head. In the next moment he had her hand and was pulling her after him, out of the steward's chamber.

There were still a dozen or so people milling about the great hall, and two score more sleeping on pallets lining the walls. "Hush," he said, and pulled her after him. Everyone saw. No one said a thing. Not a single man yelled advice. Philippa wanted to kick him, kick *all* of them, hard.

She tugged and pulled and jerked, but it was no use. He turned on her then, frowning, and said, "No more carrying you. You come willingly or I will drag you by the hair."

"You will pay for this, Dienwald, you surely will." She gave him an evil smile. "I will send word to my dear cousin Sir Walter—aye, and I'll tell him what a cruel savage you are, a barbarian, a—"

"I'm already paying, wench. But I beg of you not to tell your precious cousin that I'm a ravisher of innocent maids. Nay, do not, even though it would please you mightily were I to take you." It was at that instant she realized he'd drunk more ale than usual. He didn't slur his words like Lord Henry did, nor was his nose flaming red. He walked very carefully, like a man who knows he's drunk but doesn't want anyone else to know. She wasn't at all afraid of him, drunk or sober. She found that she was rather anticipating what he would do.

Once inside his bedchamber, Dienwald went through the now-familiar routine of pushing her onto the bed. "Now," he said, looking down at her, "now you can remove the gown. It is ugly and offends me. Haven't you yet finished something for yourself?"

She lay there staring up at him, not moving, marshaling her strength. "I made you a tunic. 'Tis down in my chamber."

He paused. "Did you really finish it? It disappeared, and I believed you'd destroyed it in your ire at me."

"I should have." She began inching away to

the far side of the bed. "You have drunk too much ale."

"Philippa," he said quietly, "there are no more gowns, not another stitch of anything for you to wear. Take care of the only one you have, else you will be naked. Aye, I have drunk more than I usually do, but 'tis done. Take off the gown now."

"Blow out the candle first."

"All right." He snuffed the candle, throwing the chamber into gloom. Moonlight came through the one window, slivering clear light directly across the bed. There was nothing she could do about it. Still, she wasn't at all afraid of him or of what he could do to her if he so chose. Philippa eased out of the gown and laid it at the foot of the bed. Then she slid beneath the single blanket.

"It's deep spring now," Dienwald said, and she knew he was taking off his clothes as he spoke, even though she wasn't looking at him. His voice deepened, grew absent and thoughtful. He didn't sound at all drunk. "That's what we call it here. Deep spring. Very late April and early May. My grandmother told me of deep spring when I was but a boy, told me this was what men called it a very long time ago when priests ruled the land and everyone worshiped the endless force of spring, the timeless renewal of spring. She said they saw the wheat shoving upward, ever upward toward the blazing gold of the sun, all the while deepening its roots into the soil, into the darkness. Opposites, this light and darkness, yet bound together, eternal and endless.

"She called it by the old Celtic words, but I cannot remember them. Whenever I say 'deep spring' now, I think about how a woman takes in a man and holds him, then empties him and yet renews him and herself with his nourishment, just as spring is infinite yet predictable in its sameness, just as spring always renews the earth, and the light and the dark exist together and complement each other." He turned to face her now. "I like thinking about you in that way—how you would empty me and renew me and yourself with my seed.

"But you are Walter de Grasse's cousin, and that makes you my enemy, not just my slave or my captive or my mistress. Nay, my enemy. I loathe the very thought of the man. I wonder, wench, should I punish you for his evil? For his wickedness? Does the foulness of his blood run in you? In your soul?"

Philippa was shaken. He'd shown her another side of himself that drew her and made her want to weep, but it had also called forth his hatred, his bitterness. Was he speaking so freely only because he'd drunk too much to keep his thoughts to himself?

"What did he do to you that you hate him so?"

"I lost much with the burning of my crops. And not just the crops, but all the people who worked them, *my* people. All of them butchered, the women ravished, the children piked on swords, the huts destroyed, burned to the raw earth. And it was your cousin who ordered it done."

"But you are not certain? You could catch no one to tell you?"

"Sir Walter de Grasse was once a landless knight. He still is, though Lord Graelam de Moreton made him castellan of Crandall, one of his keeps to the southwest of St. Erth. It is not enough for Sir Walter; he believes it his right to

have more. The man hated me before I even knew
of his existence. My father won St. Erth from his
father in a tourney in Normandy when I was a
small boy. Walter screams of dishonor and trick-
ery. He demands back his supposed birthright.
King Edward wouldn't give him heed, yet he still
seeks my death and my ruin. He nearly suc-
ceeded once, not long ago, but I was saved by a
beautiful artless lady who holds my loyalty and
my heart, aye, even my soul. So there it is,
wench. Sir Walter will do anything to destroy me,
and you are his kin."

Philippa felt a lance of pain go through her. She
swallowed, and licked her dry lips. "Who is this
lady? How did she save you?"

Dienwald strode toward the bed then and
laughed, a drunken laugh, one that was sharp yet
empty, raw yet thick. She saw his body in the
shaft of clear moonlight and she thought him
beautiful—a strange word surely to describe a
being who was sharply planed and angled and
shadowed and hard, but it was so. He stood
straight and tall and lean, and still he laughed,
and it hurt her to listen.

Yet she wanted to hear his story, and he, free-
speaking from the ale, said, "You wish her name?
She is a lady, a sweet, loving, guileless lady, and
her name is Kassia. She hails from Brittany. I cannot have her, though I tried."

"Why can't you?"

"She is wedded to a powerful man who is also
my friend and a mighty warrior—the same overlord of your precious Walter, Lord Graelam de
Moreton."

"You . . . you love her, then?"

Dienwald eased down onto the bed, lifting the

blanket. She could feel the heat from his body, hear the steady rhythm of his breathing. She didn't move. He was silent for a very long time, and she believed him asleep, finally insensate from the ale he'd drunk.

"I know not of love," he said, his voice low and slurred now. "I just know of feelings and passions, and she took mine unto herself and holds them. Aye, she holds them gently and tenderly because she could do aught else. She is like that, you see. You are very different from her. She is small and delicate and fragile, yet her spirit is fierce and pure. Her smile is so sweet it makes you want to weep and protect her with your life. Aye, she came to womanhood, but she went to him—her body and her heart both went to Graelam. Go to sleep, wench. I grow weary of all this talk."

" 'Tis you who have done all the talking!"

"Go to sleep."

"I am not your enemy. I am merely your captive."

"Perhaps. Perhaps not. I will think about it. God knows, I think of little else. You are a problem that irritates like an itch that can't be reached. Perhaps I will send word to Lord Henry that I have you and will return you if I am given Sir Walter in your place. Perhaps I will demand his head upon a silver platter, like that of St. John, though Walter is about as righteous as a dung beetle. What think you? Would your esteemed father send me Sir Walter's head to have you returned?"

"My esteemed father won't even dower me. My esteemed father seeks to wed me with de Bridgport. My esteemed father probably doesn't even

care that I am gone. I have told you this before.
I didn't lie."

"It seems the answer is no, then. I am to be
cursed with the eternal itch. What am I to do with
you?"

"I am your steward."

He laughed again, low and deep, and she
wanted to strike him, but didn't move. Only then
did she realize she hadn't demanded that he
release her and let her go free.

"Well, I suppose you cannot do a worse job of
it than Alain. You will ruin me in your ignorance
and innocence just as he was doing in his dishonesty and thievery. Or will you cheat me as well
for your own revenge, since I stole from your
father?"

"I'm not ignorant. Nor will I cheat you."

"So you say. Come here, wench. I'm cold and
wish your big body to warm me."

When she didn't move, Dienwald rolled against
her, drawing her to his side. "Hush and sleep,"
he said, his breath warm against her temple as he
pressed her cheek against his chest. She smelled
the sweet ale on his breath as he said, his words
low and indistinct, "Do not berate me further. My
brain is calm for the moment."

Nay, she thought, there was nothing she had
to say now.

Philippa didn't sleep for a very long time. She
thought of a lady whose name was Kassia, a lady
who was small and delicate and sweet and loyal.
A lady who had saved Dienwald's life.

And Philippa was a naught but an irritant that
made his brain itch.

He, the drunken brute, was asleep almost at
once, his snores uneven rippling sounds, like his

dreams, she thought, aye, like his ale-filled dreams. She hoped monsters visited him that night. He deserved them.

Wolffeton Castle

Robert Burnell wrote industriously as Graelam de Moreton spoke of the man he believed would be the ideal husband for King Edward's bastard daughter.

"He is strong and young and healthy. He is comely and has excellent teeth and all his hair. He's an intelligent man who cares for his villeins and his lands. He was wedded once and has a son, Edmund, but his wife died many years ago. Is there aught else, Burnell?"

Robert accepted a flagon of milk from Lady Kassia, smiling up at her. "The day brightens now that you are here, my lady," he said, and nearly choked on his words, so unlike him they were. But something deep inside had leapt to speak to her poetically. Mayhap it was the sweetness of her look, the soft curve of her lips as she smiled. Burnell quickly recovered his wits and sent an agonized look to Lord Graelam, but that intimidating warrior merely cocked his head at him, his look ironic.

"I thank you, sir," Kassia said. She moved slowly because of her swollen stomach, and sat down. "You are telling Robert of Dienwald's excellent qualities?"

"Aye, but there are so many, my head buzzes with the sheer number of them. What say you, Kassia?"

"Dienwald de Fortenberry is loyal and trust-

worthy and kind. He enjoys a good jest and loud
talk, as do most men of spirit. He has wit and is
facile with words. He fights well and protects
what is his."

"He begins to sound like a possible saint," Burnell said, "and a man you perhaps praise more
than he deserves."

"Ha!" Graelam said. "I have many times wanted
to trounce him into the ground and crush his
stubborn head beneath my heel and give the
imbecile a kick in the ass—"

"But always," Kassia interrupted easily, "my
lord and Dienwald are grinning at each other and
slapping each other's shoulders in great friendship after they've decided not to kill each other.
We do not overpraise him, sir, for Dienwald is a
good man, sir, a very good man."

"Despite all his shortcomings," Graelam said.

"I must needs hear some of these shortcomings, my lord. Edward is sure to be suspicious if
I give him only this glowing praise."

Graelam grinned, and Burnell saw the answering smile on his lady's face.

"He is stubborn as a mule, grandiose in his gestures, poor in his material belongings, and doesn't
care. He revels in danger and enjoys treading the
narrow path. He is crafty and sly and cunning as
a fox. He isn't greedy, however, so Edward need
have no fear of his coffers. As I said, he doesn't
lust after earthly things. Further, there is no family, so Edward need have no worry that he will
be pressed for endless favors. Dienwald is also a
shrewd, ruthless, occasionally disgraceful man
who will do anything to gain what he wants."

"Ah," said Burnell, writing again. "He becomes
human at last, my lord."

"The lady, Philippa de Beauchamp," Kassia said. "Is she a pretty girl? Sweet-tempered?"

"I know not, save what I have been told, my lady. That is, she is a Plantagenet and thus must be considered beautiful. Since his majesty said that, it is a matter of close-held opinion and not be contested."

Kassia laughed. "And her disposition?"

"I know not. She was raised by Lord Henry and she still believes him her father. I know aught about the Lady Maude. The king, very young then, ordered that if the child survived her infancy, she be taught to read and write and cipher. She does these things well, I was told. She is perhaps too well-learned for Dienwald de Fortenberry—or mayhap for any man, no matter his rank or his leanings toward kindness and tolerance. She is possibly too set in her own ways of thinking to be content with a master's heavy hand, but truly, I know not for certain."

"Dienwald needs a woman of strong character," Graelam said. "A woman who can kick his groin one minute and salve his wounds the next."

"I travel to Beauchamp upon my return to London. I will see the girl then and report all to the king. De Fortenberry sounds like a man the king might wish for his daughter. Does the king know de Fortenberry?"

"I don't think so," Graelam said. "Edward hasn't been long in England yet, nor has he come to Cornwall to see his vassals. Dienwald is not a man to travel to London to wait upon his majesty. He is a man who holds to himself."

"I suppose that could show that he is not a leech. It is also true that his majesty has not long been home, but Edward is so overwhelmed with all the needs of England."

"Aye, and there are Wales and Scotland to be ground under the royal foot."

Robert Burnell gave Lord Graelam a thin smile. The lord was criticizing, though his tone was light and his sarcasm barely touched the ear, but Burnell wouldn't tolerate it. He harrumphed as his eyes narrowed, and said, "Did I tell you, my lord, that it was the queen herself who suggested that you be consulted? The *queen*! She advised him on his illegitimate daughter."

"The queen," Graelam said, "is a lady of honest and gracious ideals. Edward gained another part of himself when he wedded with her. Mayhap the best part."

At these last words, Lord Graelam smiled yet again at his wife as Burnell sipped his milk and looked on.

St. Erth Castle

Dienwald avoided his prisoner. He remembered, the next morning, what he'd said in his drunkenness. God's ribs, had he truly gone on and on about deep spring? What nonsense! Had he truly told her of Kassia and of his feelings for her? What idiocy! He despised himself so much that he'd welcomed the violent retching. He'd been a blockhead and a loose-mouth. The next thing he knew he'd be singing to her in rhyme like his fool.

Thinking of Crooky, Dienwald wondered where he was and went in search of him. He asked Hood, the porter, but he hadn't seen the fool. He

asked the armorer, who merely spat and
shrugged. It was Old Agnes who told him.

"Aye, the little mistress is fitting him for a
tunic, master. She told him she would have two
sewn for him if he would but promise not to sing
to her for a month."

"She's not little," Dienwald said, and strode
away. Damn the wench's eyes, he thought, interfering in everything, sticking her big feet in where
they didn't belong. If his fool's elbows stuck out
of his clothes, it wasn't her mission to give him
a new tunic. He looked down at his own nearly
worn-through tunic. He had yet to see the one
she'd made for him, sewed it herself, he remembered, and for an instant he softened. But only
for that brief moment. He'd told her about Kassia,
blathered on about a pagan belief that, in his
mind at least, fitted cleanly with Father Cramdle's
heaven and its multitude of saints. Then he'd
gone on and on about Walter de Grasse, a man
he'd sworn to kill, a man who'd given him no
choice but to try to kill him. He'd made an ass of
himself. It wasn't to be borne.

Everywhere he looked these days, the women
were sitting in small groups, gossiping whilst
they sewed. They'd see him and giggle, and he
wanted to bellow at them that Philippa wasn't
their damned mistress.

How had things gotten so twisted up? She'd
jumped out of the wool wagon looking like a
fright from hell itself, and then she'd proceeded
to take over. It wasn't to be tolerated, despite the
fact that she slept in his bed and he touched her
and caressed her whenever he wished to—but it
was harder now, because it was no longer the
game it had started out to be. He wanted her,

wanted her more than he'd ever wanted any of the women who'd always welcomed him when he'd had the need. But because the witch was still a maid and because he had somehow come to regard her as more than just another female to be treated according to his whims, he couldn't, wouldn't, suffer the obvious consequences of taking her maidenhead. He wasn't that great a fool.

His thoughts were interrupted by a shriek from his son, near the cistern by the weaving shed. Dienwald didn't worry about it until he heard Philippa yell, "Hold still or I'll break your ear! Edmund, hold still!"

Interfering again, and this time with his son. What was she doing now? He broke into a trot.

"You rancid little puffin! Hold still or I'll cuff you!"

Dienwald rounded the corner of the weaving outbuilding to see Philippa holding Edmund's arm and dousing him with a bucket of water. She quickly picked up a block of soap once she'd gotten him wet, and now she was scrubbing him with all her strength, which was considerable. Edmund was squirming and fighting and yelling, but he couldn't break away. He was also naked, his ragged clothes strewn on the ground.

Philippa wasn't unscathed, however. She was sopping wet, her hair loose from its tie at the nape of her neck and flying out in a wild nimbus around her head. Her frayed gown was plastered against her breasts. She and Edmund were standing in a growing mud puddle from all the water she was throwing on him.

Dienwald watched Philippa pull Edmund back against her, and now she scrubbed him with both hands—his face, his hair, even his elbows. He was shrieking about his burning eyes, but she just kept saying over and over, "Edmund, stop fighting me! It will go easier with you if you just hold still."

Edmund went on howling like a gutted hog.

Dienwald came closer but kept out of range of the deepening mud puddle. His people were wandering by, not paying much attention, but there was Father Cramdle, his arms crossed over his chest, looking pious and quite pleased. The pig, Tupper, was squealing near Philippa, coming close to her, then retreating quickly when threatened with flying streams of water from the bucket.

Dienwald kept quiet until Philippa had doused Edmund with another bucket of water to rinse him off. Then she wrapped him in a huge towel— one newly cut, he realized—and lifted him out of the mud and rubbed him until he was dry.

She kept him wrapped up, then lifted him onto a plank of pine and hunkered down to her knees in front of him. "Listen to me, you wretched little spittlecock. 'Tis done, and you're clean. Stay away from all this mud and filth. Now, you will go with Father Cramdle and garb yourself in your new clothes. Do you understand? And then you will have your lessons."

Dienwald heard a muffled shout of, "I hate you, Maypole!" coming from beneath the towel that covered Edmund's head.

"That's all right. At least you're clean and I don't have to watch you stuff food in your mouth with filth under your fingernails. Go, now."

Edmund's head emerged from the towel. He glowered at Philippa, but she didn't change expression. Edmund was about to retire from the field when he saw Dienwald.

"Father! Help me, look what the witch did to me!" And on and on it went as Dienwald just stood there, wanting to laugh, yet furious that Philippa had forced cleanliness upon his son, and wondering how she'd enlisted Father Cramdle in her task, for the priest was surely on her side.

Meanwhile Edmund kept shrieking and complaining, dancing about on his clean feet. Finally Dienwald, seeing that the result was to his liking, even if Philippa's pushing ways were not, said in a voice that brought his son to instant silence, "Edmund, I fancy that I hear your mother in you, which is distressing. You will go with Father Cramdle and clothe yourself. I had no idea you had become such a filthy little villein. Keep your shrieks behind your teeth or you will feel my hand."

Edmund, head down and silent as a pebble, trailed after Father Cramdle, the towel wrapped around him like a Roman toga.

"Thank you," Philippa said to Dienwald. He said nothing for a moment, just watched her try to straighten her hair, pulling it back, away from her face.

He strode up to her. "Hold still yourself, wench."

She did. He smoothed her hair and retied it with the bit of leather. He frowned at the dirty strip of hide. She needed a proper ribbon, a ribbon of bright color to complement her hair, something . . .

"You look worse than Edmund. Much worse. Like a dirty wet rag. Do something with your-

self." With those pleasing sentiments duly expressed, Dienwald turned on his heel. He heard
a loud whoosh, but not in time. A half-filled
bucket of water struck him squarely between the
shoulder blades and he went flying forward from
the force of it, hitting a goat. The goat reared back
and kicked Dienwald on the thigh. He cried out,
grabbing his leg, which caused him to lose his
balance and fell sideways into a deep patch of
black mud. He came up on his hands and knees,
but for a moment he didn't move. He had no
intention of moving until he'd regained complete
control of himself. Slowly, very slowly, he rose
and turned to see Philippa standing there like a
statue yet to be finished, a look of mingled horror
and defiance on her face. People had stopped
their conversations and were converging and staring. Then Gorkel, with a low rumbling noise,
came forward, stepped squarely into the mud,
and began to brush off his master.

" 'Twere an accident," Gorkel said as he grabbed
gobs of mud from Dienwald's clothing and flung
them away. "The mistress acts, then thinks—ye
know that, master. Aye, but she's—"

"You damnable monster, don't defend her! Be
still!"

Gorkel obligingly shut his mouth and continued
scraping off mud.

Dienwald shook himself free of his minion's
help and strode over to Philippa, who took one
step back, then stopped and faced him, squaring
her shoulders.

"You struck me!" The incredulity in his voice
equaled the outrage. "You're a *female*, and you
struck me. You threw that damned bucket at me."

"Actually," Philippa said, inching a bit further

back, "it was the bucket that struck you, not I. I didn't realize I was such a marksman, or rather, that the bucket was such a marksman." Then, to her own astonishment, she giggled.

Dienwald drew several very long, very deep breaths. "If I throw you into that mud, you will have nothing to wear. You haven't yet sewed anything for yourself, have you?"

She shook her head, not giggling quite so loudly now.

He looked at her nipples, taut against the wet tunic. The material also clung to her thighs.

He smiled at her, and Philippa felt herself shrivel with humiliation. "Throw me in the mud," she said. "Do that, but please don't do what you're thinking."

"And what is that, pray? Ripping off that rag and letting my people see the shrew beneath it?"

She nodded and tried to cover her breasts with her hands. "I'm not a shrew."

"All right," he said, and without another word, moving so quickly she had only time to squeak in surprise, Dienwald grabbed her about the hips, lifted her, and strode to the black puddle and dropped her. She landed on her bottom, arms and legs flying outward, and mud spewed out in thick waves, hitting him and Gorkel. She felt it squishing over her legs, felt it seep through the gown, and she wanted to laugh at the consequences that she'd brought upon herself, but she didn't. She now had nothing to wear, nothing save this now-ruined gown.

She looked up at Dienwald, who stood in front of her, his hands on his hips. He was laughing.

Philippa saw red. Tears clogged her throat, but her fury was stronger by far. She managed to come to her feet, the mud clinging and making loud sucking noises. She flung herself at him, clutching his arms and yanking him toward her. She locked her foot behind his calf and he fell toward her, laughing all the while. Together they went down, Dienwald on top of her, Philippa flat on her back, the mud flying everywhere.

Dienwald raised himself on his hands, his fingers clenching deep into the muck. He slowly raised one mud-filled hand and opened it against her face and rubbed. She gasped and spat, but then he felt her knees against his back and he was falling sideways as she rolled against him, knocking him onto his back, pounding her fists at him, her muddy hands sliding over his face, slapping him with it.

He dimly heard people laughing and shouting and cheering for him, cheering for Philippa. Wagers were screamed out, and even the animals were dinning, for once louder than the children. Then Tupper leaped into the mud, not three inches from Dienwald's head, snorting loudly, poking his snout into Dienwald's face.

It was too much for a man to suffer. Dienwald spread his arms in surrender and yelled at the bouncing fury astride him, "I yield, wench! I yield!"

Tupper snorted and squealed and kept the mud churning.

Philippa laughed, and as he looked up at her, he wanted her right then—muddy black face, filthy matted hair, and all.

"Master, pray forgive me." Northbert stood on the edge of the mud puddle, consternation writ on his ugly face.

Dienwald cocked an eye at him. "Aye? What is it?"

"We have visitors, master."

"There are visitors at St. Erth's gates?"

"Nay, master. The visitors are right here."

13

Philippa was shocked into numb silence. She didn't move, but of course, she had no drier place to move to. Dienwald looked behind Northbert and saw Graelam de Moreton striding toward them, tell and powerful and well-garbed and clean, and he was staring toward Dienwald as if he'd grown two heads. And then he was staring at Philippa.

"God give you grace, Graelam," Dienwald said easily. His eyes went to Kassia, standing now beside her husband, wrapped in a fine ermine-lined cloak of soft white wool. She looked beautiful, soft and sweet, her chestnut hair in loose braids atop her head. He saw she was trying very hard not to laugh. "Welcome to St. Erth, Kassia. I hope I see you well, sweet lady."

Kassia couldn't hold it back. She burst into laughter, hiccuping against her palm as she gasped out, "You sound like a courtier at the king's court, Dienwald, suave and confident, while you lie sprawled in the mud . . . Ah, Dienwald, your face . . ."

Dienwald looked up at Philippa, who'd turned into a mud statue astride him. "Move, wench," he said, grinning up at her. "As you see, we have visitors and must bestir ourselves to see to their comfort."

Kassia, Philippa was thinking, her mind nearly as muddy as her body. Kassia, the lady that Dienwald held so dear to his wretched heart. And Philippa could understand his feelings for the slight, utterly feminine confection who stood well out of range of the mud puddle. That exquisite example of womanhood would never, ever find herself sitting astride a man in a mud puddle. Philippa's eyes went to Lord Graelam de Moreton, and she saw a man who would never yield, a man both fierce and hard, a man who was Kassia's husband, bless his wondrous existence. She remembered now seeing him once at Beauchamp when she was very young. He'd been bellowing at her father about a tourney they were both to join near Taunton.

"Wench, move," Dienwald said again, and as he spoke, he laughed, circled her waist with his hands, and lifted her off him. He carefully set her beside him in the mud.

She felt the black ooze sliding up her bottom.

"Graelam, why don't you take your very clean wife into the hall. I will scrub myself and join you soon."

" 'Twill take all the water in your well," Graelam said, threw back his head, and laughed. "Nay, Dienwald, sling not mud at me. My lady just stitched me this fine tunic." He laughed and laughed as he took his wife's soft white hand in his and led her away, saying over his shoulder, "All right, but I begin to cherish that black face of yours. It grows closer to the color of your heart."

Dienwald didn't move until Graelam and Kassia, trailed by a half-dozen Wolffeton men-at-arms, had disappeared around the side of the weaving shed. He could hear Kassia's high giggles and Graelam's low rumbles of laughter.

Philippa hadn't said a single word. She hadn't made a sound, merely sat there in the mud, a study of silent misery.

Dienwald eyed her, then yelled for another bucket to be brought. "Get up, Philippa," he said, and when she did, he continued, "Now, step out of the mud," and when she did, he threw a bucket of cold water over her head. Philippa gasped and shivered and automatically rubbed the mud off her face. The late-April air was chill, but she hadn't realized it until now.

After three more buckets she was ready for the soap.

"You will have to remove the tunic soon," he said, then called for Old Agnes to fetch two blankets. He looked at the score of people staring at them, laughing behind their hands, and roared, "Out of here, all of you! If I see any of you in two seconds, you'll feel the flat of my sword on your buttocks!"

"Aye," Crooky yelled, "but the wenches would much enjoy that kind of play."

Dienwald bellowed again, and soon he and Philippa were alone standing on the plank of lumber, scrubbing themselves with the newly made soap. Dienwald had simply stripped off his clothes. He looked up at Philippa, his face clean and grinning. "I've dismissed everyone, wench— you heard and saw. Take off the gown now."

She did, without comment, seeing no hope for it, and together they washed and scrubbed and threw water on each other. At one point Dienwald paused, looking at her, beautifully naked in the April sunshine, and pulled her against him. He didn't kiss her, merely soaped his hands. Philippa felt his large hands soaping down her back and over her buttocks. She felt his soapy fingers sliding between her legs and tensed, but his touch seemed impersonal.

It wasn't, but Dienwald wasn't about to let her know that. When he'd finished, Philippa cleaned his back, her touch more tentative than his had been. He stared at the mud puddle, then thought of the eyes that were probably watching them at this very minute.

Once dry, they wrapped themselves in the blankets. Dienwald looked at Philippa, her face scrubbed pink, her hair plastered around her head, and he thought her exquisite. He said instead, looking once again toward the mud puddle, "You made me feel very young with our play. Do you wish to come into the hall and meet our guests?"

Speak to Lady Kassia, Philippa thought. She would feel like a great bumbling fool, like a huge ungainly blanket-wrapped beggar gawking next to a snow princess in her white cloak. She shook her head and swallowed her misery.

"They are my friends," Dienwald said, not seeing the misery, only the stubbornness.

"Not yet, if it pleases you."

"Very well," he said, her respectful tone softening him. "But if you wish to meet them, I would ask that you not tell them your name or that you're my prisoner."

"Then what am I?" she asked, irritation now writ clear in her voice.

Dienwald paused at that. So much for respect and deference from her. "My washerwoman?"

"No."

"My weaver?"

"Nay. I would be your steward."

"Graelam would burst his bladder laughing at that notion. No, you can be my mistress. You begin to look passable again, so that would not strain his credulity. Does that please you, wench?"

"Doesn't it worry you that I might beg Lord Graelam to return me to my father? That I might tell him you're naught but a miserable scoundrel and thief?"

"Why should it worry me? You'll not do that. You have no wish to return to your father. Don't forget that that toad William de Bridgport awaits you with widespread fat arms and foul breath."

That was true, damn him. She chewed on her lower lips. "I could ask him to send me to his vassal, Sir Walter, since I am his cousin and since that is where I was bound in the first place."

"Aye, you could do that, but it would displease me mightily. You know, Philippa, Sir Walter wouldn't treat you well. He is not the man you think him."

"Of course he would treat me well! I'm his cousin, his kin. I won't be your mistress."

He raised his hand and lightly touched his fingertips to her cheek. "You're a snare, Philippa. Of the devil? I wonder."

He said nothing more, merely turned on his

bare heel and strode away from her. He should have looked ridiculous, walking barefoot and wrapped in an ugly brown blanket, but he didn't.

Philippa followed more slowly, and she saw faces and heard laughter and knew that she and Dienwald had been observed whilst they bathed. Was there nothing private in this wretched castle? She knew the answer was no, just as it had been at Beauchamp.

How could Dienwald ask her to meet Kassia, the woman who was the most precious of all God's female flock? The woman who'd saved his life, the woman who was so lavishly guileless, the essence of purity and perfection?

Philippa wanted to be sick.

Instead, she walked up the solar stairs, the blanket wrapped close like a shroud, and locked herself in Dienwald's chamber. He'd already come and gone. His blanket was a heap on the rushes. She fretted about what he was wearing, wishing she'd given him the tunic she'd made for him. It looked every bit as fine as the one Lord Graelam was wearing, the one the beautiful Kassia had sewn for him.

In the great hall, Dienwald, garbed in a tunic and hose that were tattered and faded from their original gray to a dirty bile green, finally greeted his guests.

Graelam and Kassia were speaking with North-bert and Crooky, drinking ale and tasting the new St. Erth cheese that Dienwald had directed made from his own recipe, passed to him by his great-aunt Margarie, now long dead.

"Where is my wine, you whoreson?" Graelam asked without preamble upon Dienwald's appearance.

Dienwald looked at him blankly. "*Your* wine? What wine? That's not wine, it's ale, and made from my own recipe. I would have offered you wine had I some, but I don't. I have naught but ale, and no coin to purchase wine. God's bones, Graelam, I always bring myself to Wolffeton when I wish to reward my innards."

Graelam's dark eyes narrowed with suspicion. "You're a convincing liar when it pleases you to be so."

"What cursed wine?" Dienwald nearly shouted, flinging his arms wide.

Kassia laughed and placed her hand on his forearm. "You don't remember the wager between you and my lord? The Aquitaine wine my father was shipping to us? The ship was wrecked on the rocks and all the cargo disappeared. You didn't do it? You didn't steal the wine?"

Dienwald just shook his head. "Of course not. Are you sure, Kassia, that your wondrous lord didn't do it? He feared losing the wager to me, you know, and was at his wits' ends to find a way out of humiliating himself."

"Nay, don't try to win her to your side, you sly-lipped cockscomb."

Kassia laughed. "The both of you be still. 'Tis obvious that another rogue stole the wine, my lord. Drink your ale and forget your wager."

"But who?" Dienwald said as he accepted a flagon from Margot.

"Roland is in Cornwall," Graelam said.

"I don't believe it! Roland de Tournay! He's really here?"

"Aye, he's here. I heard it from a tinker who'd traveled the breadth of Cornwall."

"Aye, the tinker was here not long ago, but I was not." More's the pity, he thought, that the fellow hadn't as yet returned. He was seeing that strip of dirty leather tying Philippa's hair back. A narrow ribbon of pale yellow would be beautiful with her hair color. "He told you of Roland?"

"It seems that Roland stopped him, brought him to his camp in the forest of Fentonladock, and instructed him to tell me of his coming—not the why of it, but just that he would be at Wolffeton. I do wonder what he wants. You and Roland were boys fostering together, were you not? At Bauderleigh Castle with Earl Charles Massey?"

"Aye, we were. Old Charles was a proper devil, mean and evil and hard, but we both survived to become mean and evil and hard. I've not heard from Roland in five years."

"He went with Edward to go crusading, as did I. I didn't see him much in the Holy Land, but he survived, thankfully."

"I wonder how he does and what he wants with you."

"I am to meet him at Wolffeton in two weeks' time. He will tell me then. I was told that he used his talents spying for Edward whilst in the Holy Land. A Muslim he was, becoming so like them they never guessed he was an Englishman. He was an intimate of the sultan himself, so it was said."

"He's a dark-skinned bastard, looks like a heathen."

Graelam shrugged. "Aye, and his eyes are as black as a fanatical priest's and his tongue as smooth as an asp's."

Dienwald was thoughtful, then said without

thinking, "I should like to see him. Mayhap I
could bring the wench with me. She would
enjoy—" The instant it was out of his mouth,
Dienwald wanted to kick himself.

Graelam, a man of subtlety when he so wished,
inquired mildly, "Who is the wench, Dienwald?
She was the one astride you, I gather? Sporting
in the mud with you?"

"Aye."

"No more? No explanations? Is she clean?
Where is she now?"

"She has no clothes, not a stitch, the muddy
gown was old—it belonged to my first wife—and
it was the last one. The wench is wearing a blanket now, and is in my bedchamber."

Kassia cocked her head to one side. "Wench?
What is her name?"

"Morgan," Dienwald said without hesitation,
then nearly swallowed his tongue. Well, he'd said
it. He said it again, looking Graelam right in his
eye. "Her name's Morgan and she's my mistress."

"She's a villein?"

He shook his head vigorously, and said, "Yes."

Graelam snorted. "What goes on here, Dienwald? Don't try to lie to me, I'll know it. You're
clear as a spring pond."

"You said I was a fine liar just a moment ago."

"I exaggerated."

"Both of you relieve your minds and shut your
mouths! Now, the female we saw, her name is
Morgan, you say. An odd name, but no matter.
I shall go visit her. I have no extra clothing with
me, but I can have gowns and other things sent
to her."

"She is a maypole, a giant of a girl. Nothing
you own would fit her big body."

Kassia merely frowned at him, shook out the skirt of her finely woven pale pink gown, smoothed the sleeves of the delicate white over-tunic, and walked slowly from the great wall. It was then that Dienwald saw her big belly.

He was suddenly very afraid. He turned to Graelam and saw his friend nodding.

"I shield her as best I can. She is so small, and the child grows large in her belly. She insisted upon coming to St. Erth today. She grows bored and restless at Wolffeton—the women won't let her do a thing within the castle, and even my men hover about her when she is in the bailey—and I couldn't deny her. You should see Blount, my steward—he feels a quill is beyond her strength. She frets."

"How much longer before the babe comes?"

"Not until June. I die each day with the thought of it." Graelam then cursed luridly, and Dien-wald, looking hopeful and thoughtful, said, "She appears well and is beautiful and laughing."

"Aye," Graelam said, and drained his flagon. He eyed Dienwald. "I wish you wouldn't speak of my wife as though you were her lover. It irks me. Now, 'tis true you didn't steal the wine from Kassia's father? You didn't have the ship wrecked with false warning lights from the point?"

"I wish I'd thought of it," Dienwald said, his voice gloomy with regret.

"Roland, then," Graelam said, nodding in satis-faction at his conclusion. "I'll break two of his ribs for his impertinence."

"That I should like to see," Dienwald said.

Kassia slowly climbed the solar stairs. She held to the railing, careful, as always, of the babe she carried. She felt wonderful and healthy and very alive. If only Graelam would but believe her and stop his worrying and his endless agitation. It was driving her to distraction. And there was her father, now threatening to come to Wolffeton and watch over her. Between the two of them she'd go mad, she knew it.

She reached Dienwald's bedchamber and knocked softly on the solid door. Then she turned the handle. It was locked. She called out, "Please, Morgan, let me in. 'Tis Kassia de Moreton."

Philippa stared at the door from her huddled spot in the middle of Dienwald's bed.

Morgan!

Who in the name of St. Andrew was Morgan? She rose, wrapped the blanket securely about her, and padded on bare feet to the door. She opened it and smiled.

"Come in, my lady."

"Thank you. Oh, dear, I see Dienwald was speaking true. You have no clothes."

Philippa simply shook her head.

"You are no villein's daughter, are you? What prank does Dienwald play now?"

"What did he tell you?"

"That you are his mistress."

Philippa snorted and tossed her head. Her hair was nearly dry now, and curled wildly down her back.

"Your hair is beautiful," Kassia said. "I've always wished for hair such as yours. Not long ago I was very ill and my head was shaved. My hair has grown back thicker, but not like yours. Do you mind if I sit down? My burden is heavy."

Philippa realized as the small lady walked across Dienwald's bedchamber that this female was very nice and probably hadn't a mean bone in her very feminine body. She was also heavy with child. She was married to that huge warrior. For an instant Philippa imagined that huge man covering this very small female. It didn't seem possible. But it didn't matter. This Kassia was safely out of the way; Dienwald was safe from her perfection.

It was an unspeakable relief.

"Forgive me," Philippa said. "Would you care for some milk perhaps? I don't imagine that Dienwald thought of that."

"Nay, I am fine as I am, and no, he didn't. He is a man much like my dear lord. Tell me, what is your real name?"

Philippa wanted to spit it out, all of it, but she paused. She realized that she didn't want Dienwald to be put upon or doubted or questioned, even by his friends. Nor did she want to go to her cousin Walter. She wanted to stay right here. "Morgan *is* my name," she said, and her chin went up.

Kassia thought: You're a truly awful liar. She merely smiled at the tall, very lovely girl who sat on Dienwald's bed, a blanket wrapped around her. What was she doing here? It was a mystery, and Kassia was quickly fascinated. Then she thought of Robert Burnell's visit and of Dienwald as the husband of Edward's illegitimate daughter and how she and her husband had praised Dienwald's very eyebrows to Burnell. She felt a frisson of worry, but shook it off. If Dienwald loved this girl, then he would simply say no to Edward if he offered him his daughter's hand in marriage. Dienwald would say no to anybody, even the Pope. He would laugh in the king's face if it

pleased him to do so. No, Dienwald couldn't be
coerced into doing anything he didn't wish to do.
She wouldn't worry. Everything would work out
as it was meant to.

"I have come to offer you clothes, Morgan. I
have none with me, but if you will let me see
your size, then I can have some sent to St. Erth
on the morrow."

Philippa had sunk into guilt over the truly violent thoughts she'd harbored toward this elegant
lady. "I have woven wool. I merely haven't had
time to see to clothes for myself. There were
Edmund and Dienwald, even the fool, Crooky.
He was so worn and ragged and so . . . so *accepting* of it. I couldn't bear it. I will sew myself something this evening. But I thank you, truly. You
are kind."

"This is very interesting," Kassia said, cocking
her head to one side.

"What is, my lady?"

"You and Dienwald. He is not, in the usual
course of everyday events, a man in the habit of
giving much of his attention to ladies."

That's because he's thinking of you. "Is that true?"
Philippa said, noncommittal.

"Aye. Don't mistake my words. He has always
enjoyed women, that is true, but not for longer
than it takes him to relieve his needs with them.
He's a complicated man, and obstinate, yet loyal
and true. He is also a rogue, sometimes quite
a scoundrel, and he much enjoys being
unpredictable."

"I know."

"You do? Well, that is even more interesting.
Do you know him well, then? You've been at St.
Erth a long time?"

Philippa raised her chin. Was this lady toying
with her? Showing her that it was she, not Philippa, who held Dienwald? No covering it up with
fresh rushes, she thought, and said with the most
emotionless voice she could dredge up, " 'Tis
you, my lady, who holds Dienwald's interest, not
me. 'Tis you he worships and admires, not me.
'Tis you he bleats on about, not me. He finds me
unwomanly, ungainly, clumsy. But he speaks of
you as if you were a . . . a *shrine*, and he wishes
to fall on his face and worship at your feet."

"By all the saints' waggery, that is wondrous
stupid," Kassia said, and burst into laughter.
"And not at all like Dienwald."

"Dienwald is a man," Philippa said when Kassia had subsided into only an occasional giggle.

"Aye," Kassia said slowly, "he is, is he not? He
is just like my lord. A man who dominates, a man
who must rule, a man who yells and bellows
when one dares cross his will or challenge him,
and a man who will cherish and protect those
weaker then he with all his strength."

"I'm just barely weaker than Dienwald."

"I doubt that, Morgan."

"He doesn't cherish me at all. He knows not
what to do with me. I am a thorn in his flesh."
Philippa's chin went up yet another notch. "But
I am also his steward, though he doesn't wish to
tell anyone, the obstinate cockscomb. He said
were your husband to know, he would burst his
bladder with laughter."

"His steward? Tell me, please. What happened
to Alain?"

Philippa's dam burst, and words poured out of
her mouth. She didn't tell Kassia de Moreton who
she really was or how she came to be at St. Erth,

but she told her of Alain's perfidy and how he'd tried to kill her and how she had since taken his place because Dienwald had no one else of the *proper* sex to do it.

Kassia stared at this rush of confidences, but before she could speak, the door burst open and Dienwald catapulted into the chamber, yelling even before his two feet were firmly planted on the floor, "Don't believe a word she says!"

Philippa jumped to her feet. "Morgan!" she shouted. "Who the devil is this Morgan?"

Dienwald drew up, frowning. "I don't know. The name merely popped into my mind. I like it. It has a certain dignity."

"What is your name, then?" Kassia asked.

" 'Tis Mary," Dienwald said quickly. "Her name is Mary. A nice name, a simple name, a name without pretense or deceit."

"I wouldn't say that," Graelam de Moreton said as he came through the bedchamber door. He looked over at his grinning wife. "I once knew a Mary who was as cunning and devious as my former mistress, Nan. You remember, Kassia? Ah, perhaps you don't wish to. You wonder why I'm here, sweetling? Well, Dienwald feared what the girl was telling you and bolted out of the hall. What was I to do? All that was of interest was here, so I followed."

"This is the wench, Mary," Dienwald said, and he gave Philippa a look that would rot off her toes if she dared to disagree with him.

"You don't look like a Mary," Graelam said, coming closer. He studied Philippa, his dark eyes intent. Then he looked troubled, questioning. "You look familiar, though. Your eyes . . . aye, very familiar, the blue is brilliant, unique. I wish I could remember—"

"She doesn't look familiar," Dienwald said, stepping in front of Graelam. "She isn't at all unique. She looks only like herself. She looks like a Mary. Nothing more, just a simple Mary."

"She looks clean," Graelam said, and turned to his wife. "Kassia, have you learned all of Dienwald's secrets? Did he steal my Aquitaine wine?"

"Dienwald isn't a thief!" Philippa turned red the moment the words flew out of her mouth, but proceeded to make matters worse: "He isn't except when necessity forces him to be, and—"

"Ph . . . Mary, be quiet! I don't need you to plead my innocence before this hulking behemoth. I didn't steal your puking wine, Graelam."

Kassia rose slowly to her feet. "This is quite enough. Now, I suggest that we have our meal up here, since Mary can't come to the hall wearing naught but a blanket. What say you, Dienwald?"

What could he say? he wondered, both his brain and belly sour, even as he nodded.

The evening meal, all cozy in Dienwald's bedchamber, passed off more smoothly than Dienwald could have hoped. Philippa held her tongue for the most part, as did Kassia. The men spoke of men's things, and though Philippa would have liked to join in, because she was, no matter what Dienwald said, St. Erth's steward, she kept still. She was afraid she would inadvertently give something away. Neither Graelam de Moreton nor his lovely wife was stupid.

Why had Graelam looked at her so oddly? Could he believe she looked familiar because he remembered seeing her very briefly at Beauchamp some years before?

Graelam sat back in his chair, a flagon of ale between his large hands. "Kassia and I will return to Wolffeton on the morrow. She wished merely to see that you were all right."

"Why? Nay, Graelam, your lie contains more holes than a sieve. You wished to see if I was drinking your wine."

"That as well." Graelam paused a moment, then continued easily, "Let us go for a walk, Dienwald. I have something to discuss with you."

Kassia shot him a questioning look, but he only smiled and shook his head.

What was going on here? Philippa wondered. She watched the two men leave the bedchamber. On the threshold, Dienwald turned, saying, "Mary, we will give our bed over to Graelam and Kassia tonight. Tell Edmund that he is to sleep with Father Cramdle. No, wait—we will sleep in your small bed in the steward's chamber." That taken care of to the master's satisfaction, Philippa was left sitting on the bed, her face red with anger and embarrassment.

"I will surely kill him, the miserable bounder," she said to no one in particular.

To her surprise, Lady Kassia laughed.

Graelam made a decision as he and Dienwald walked down the solar stairs and into the inner bailey. He wouldn't tell Dienwald of Burnell's visit. Kassia was right: leave things alone. Dienwald delighted in doing precisely what he wanted to do, and King Edward at his most cajoling or his most threatening wouldn't change his mind once he'd set himself a course. The two men walked toward the ramparts and climbed the ladder to the eastern tower.

"Your steward stole everything?" Graelam asked, leaning his elbows on the rough stone.

Dienwald nodded. "Bastard. Gorkel the Hideous broke his neck. But Alain had a spy who managed to flee St. Erth. My fool, Crooky, somehow knows such things—his ways of finding out things both amaze and terrify me. He believes Alain was involved with Walter de Grasse and that one of the men who tried to kill Ph . . . Mary is even now at Crandall. He is the cistern keeper."

Graelam said nothing for several moments. Finally: "I know of the hatred between the two of you, needless to say! And yes, I heard about the burning of your crops on the southern border and the butchering of all your people. You have no proof that Sir Walter was behind it, though, do you?"

Dienwald admitted that he had none. Thus, he was surprised when Graelam said, "I have decided to remove Walter. I will tolerate no more discord. If we discover that he burned your crops and destroyed your people, I will kill him. Now, my friend, bring out my wine—I'm convinced you have it hidden."

Dienwald could but stare at Graelam; then he bellowed for Northbert. "Bring out the wine!"

It wasn't Aquitaine wine, but it wasn't vinegar either. There was but one cask, and it hailed from a Benedictine abbey near Penryn.

When Dienwald entered the steward's small chamber in the early hours of the morning, not at all drunk, for he hated wine, he smiled toward the lump on the narrow bed.

He walked silently to the bed and went down on his knees, setting his lit candle on the floor beside him. He said nothing, merely lifted the blanket that covered Philippa. She was naked, lying on her side facing away from him, one leg stretched out, the other bent, and all the beauty of her woman's flesh was there for him to see. He swallowed and didn't wait another moment. Lightly he touched his fingertips to her inner thighs, then moved them up slowly, very slowly, until he felt the warmth of her. He drew in his breath, aware that his sex was swollen and aching. Slowly, he eased his middle finger inside her. She was very tight and he loved the feeling of his finger stretching her and he imagined how it would feel to have her around his manhood, so tight, squeezing him until he wanted to die with the wonderful feelings. His finger deepened. Her body was responding, dampening, easing for his finger.

He leaned forward and kissed her hip even as he let his finger ease more deeply. He heard her moan and felt her tighten convulsively. He would spill his seed right here in this damned darkened room. He quickly withdrew his finger and tried to calm his frantic breathing. He rose and stripped off his clothes. He lay beside her, feeling her buttocks against his swelled sex. He began to knead her belly then let his fingers go once more where they ached to. He found her woman's flesh in the soft curls and moaned deep in his throat as he began to stroke her, gently exploring.

When her hips jerked and she moaned in her sleep, he rolled her onto her back and came over her.

14

Philippa was whimpering even as she opened her eyes. Then she shrieked into the shadowed face above her.

Dienwald cursed, bent down, and kissed her mouth. He gave her his full weight for an instant, then raised himself on his elbows, still kissing her wildly.

He was between her legs, his sex stiff and hot and hurting. He reared back onto his knees and parted her thighs with his hands, looking down at her. "You would make me debauch you," he said, his voice low and raw. "You're a witch, a siren, and you would take me and wring me out and make me feel things I don't want to feel."

Philippa's mind finally cleared. She was still throbbing, deep in her belly, but she saw him clearly now and heard his words and understood them and was enraged. All unwanted sensations quickly fled her body. "*I* make *you* debauch *me*? What about your grandmother's deep spring and all that religious nonsense of renewal and light and dark and how you thought of me as being deep and fulfilling and renewing you and . . . I am in my own bed, you insensate brute! 'Tis you who seek to dishonor me! I am a maid and not your wife. 'Tis you who make me feel things I shouldn't feel. 'Tis you who wish to desecrate me—a prisoner with no voice in anything, a wretched captive who has no clothing even!"

"A fine volley of words you fling at me—but naught but peevish rantings. You have no voice, you say? You beset me, wench, your mouth is nearly as bountiful as your ass!"

She saw red, fisted her hands, and smashed them against his chest even as he shouted, "You make yourself sound like a shrine, a relic to heedless virgins! Desecrate? You came to me through foul mischance, wench—that, or God sent you as my penance—" He was still holding her thighs when she hit him again as hard as she could.

Dienwald growled a half-dozen curses even as he teetered sideways and fell to the stone floor beside the bed. He didn't release her, and she came crashing down on top of him. When her head hit his as he was trying to rise, and he was plunged back, she heard the ugly thudding sound of his head against the leg of her steward's table.

His head lolled on the stone floor and he was still. Philippa was frozen for an instant, trying to comprehend what had happened; then she knew bone-deep fear, rolled off him, and flattened her palm against his chest. His heartbeat was slow and steady. She brought the single candle closer and examined his head. A lump was beginning to swell over his left temple. Well, it served the slavering ravisher right. He'd come to take her even as she slept, so she wouldn't fight him; then his wayward mouth had accused *her* of debauching *him*, or some such nonsense. She wanted to hit him again, but didn't. Instead she sat on the cold stone floor, crossed her legs, and eased his head onto her thighs. She didn't feel the chill of the stones against her flesh; rather she felt the heat from his shoulders, the warmth of him beneath her hands. She leaned against the bed and gently stroked his forehead. She was conscious only of him and her worry for him. After a while she also found that she was staring, and discovered he quite delighted her. His sex wasn't hard and throbbing now; quite the contrary. His long legs were sprawled out, slightly parted. She smiled and laid her hand on his belly. Slowly she traced the ridges of muscle, then let her fingers stray to the thick brush of dark hair at his groin.

"You are such a churlish knave," she said. "What am I to do with you?"

He didn't reply, nor did he stir. Philippa sang him a soft French ballad her mother had taught her when she was four years old. Then she stopped and sighed. More to the point of course was what *he* would do with *her*. She forced her fingers away from him. She couldn't begin to imagine how he would taunt her were he to know what she had done whilst he lay unconscious.

"St. Gregory's chilblains, wench, your voice sounds like a wet rag slapping against the side of a sleeping horse."

"You're awake," she said, her voice flat. "A minstrel who sojourned at Beauchamp just last

year told my parents that my voice was dulcet
and silvery, like a turtle dove's."

"Dulcet dove? The fellow lied, and is worse
with words than Crooky." Dienwald fell into melancholy silence, for he'd realized that his head lay
in her lap, that if he turned his face inward he
could kiss the soft flesh between her legs. He
didn't want to do that. Why must she offer him
such wondrous fodder for his weakness? It wasn't
to be borne. He turned his face against her, his
lips seeking.

Philippa sucked in her breath and shoved him
away. He moaned, and immediately she felt
guilty. "You shouldn't have done that. You'll hurt
yourself again."

He moaned again, dramatically, and Philippa
gritted her teeth against laughing. "Come, you
must get up now. You're naked."

"I'm pleased you noticed. So are you, wench."
Dienwald struggled to his feet, stood there weaving for a moment, then collapsed onto her narrow
bed.

Philippa looked down at him. He gave a loud
snore. She cursed and covered him with a
blanket.

"I'm cold and will die of watery lungs brought
on by your cruelty if you leave me."

"I like the sound of your snores better," Philippa said even as she eased down beside him.
"Nay, I shan't let you touch me again. It isn't
right you should do that, and well you know it.
I'm not your mistress. I shan't ever be your mistress." She grabbed another frayed blanket and
wrapped it about herself. "Go to sleep, master,
else I'll fling you off my bed again."

Dienwald sighed. "Big wenches are difficult."

"I know," she said, her voice nasty. "You'd much prefer your precious *little* Kassia, your so-perfect *little* princess who doubtless sighs and swoons all over you—a *big* warrior."

He laughed.

"Well, you can't have her, you ass! She's well-wedded and she's with child and she's not for you, so you might as well forget her."

"How well you extol her person," he said. "Mayhap you are right. I will think about it. Big wenches are even more difficult when they're jealous." He began snoring again and soon, much sooner than Philippa, he was truly asleep.

Jealous, was she? He turned onto his side away from her and soon she was snuggled against his back. She wondered what he'd do if she bit him. Probably just laugh at her again. She fell asleep finally, feeling warm and secure, damn him.

Graelam stood in the open doorway of the steward's chamber early the next morning, staring toward the narrow bed that held his host and the wench whose name wasn't Mary. The girl's face was pressed against Dienwald's naked back, but the rest of her was protected from him by an old blanket, a blanket that, he saw, separated the two of them. An eyebrow cocked upward. So the girl whose name wasn't Mary also wasn't Dienwald's mistress either. Kassia would find this fascinating.

Suddenly Dienwald groaned and turned onto his back, flinging his arm over his head. Philippa, jerked from a sound sleep, was nearly thrown off the narrow bed onto the floor. Dienwald groaned again, muttering, "My God, you've nearly killed me, wench. My head, it's swollen and hurts and—"

"And has put you in particularly good humor," Graelam said, stepping into the chamber.

Philippa's eyes flew open and fastened in consternation upon the intruder. He merely smiled. "God give you a good morrow, Mary. I am sorry to disturb your slumber, but my wife and I must take our leave soon. This door was open and I did tap my fist upon it, but there was no reply."

Dienwald opened an eye, and complaints issued rapidly from his mouth. "The wench nearly killed me. I've a lump on my skull the size of my foot."

Philippa was less than sympathetic. "You deserved it, you disgusting lout!"

"Lout? God's knees, you randy wench, all I did was think about letting you debauch me, nothing more." He smiled guilelessly up at her.

Philippa reared up, quickly jerked the blanket over her breasts, and sent her fist into his belly. "My lord," she said, turning immediately toward Graelam, "I cannot rise to see to you and your perfect wife's needs. But this attempted defiler of innocent maids can, and he will, once he stops acting like he's been flayed by a band of Saracens."

"I've never known him for a coward, thus it must be your superior strength and cunning, Mary. Dienwald, rise now, and pay your homage to my lady. Kassia wishes to bid you adieu." Graelam's eyes suddenly widened. "*Perfect* wife?" He guffawed. "I shall tell Kassia, it will amuse her. *Perfect!*" He shook his head. "The little witch—*perfect!*" Still laughing, Graelam left the steward's chamber, closing the door behind him.

"*You* think she's perfect," Philippa said.

"Feel the lump on my head. Tell me if I will survive rising from this bed."

Philippa leaned over and gently examined his head. "The lump will grow if you stay in this bed. You will survive it, so get thee gone, I tire of you."

He sighed and rolled over her, coming to his feet beside the bed. He was naked and quite unconcerned about it. He grinned down at her and said, "Don't stare, wench, else my manhood will rise like leavened bread." He gave a heartfelt sigh. "And 'twill make my hose uncomfortable. It will also bring the stares of all your gentle rivals— in short, most of the wenches here at St. Erth. What say you?"

"I grant you good morrow," Philippa said, then turned away from him and stared at the wall.

Dienwald knew well enough that his body pleased her. Although he wasn't a massive warrior like Graelam, he was big enough, well enough made, muscled and lean and hard, not a patch of fat on him. He leaned down and quickly kissed her cheek, then straightened, began whistling, and dressed himself. He was out of the steward's chamber in but a moment, still whistling.

Philippa spent her morning sewing herself a gown from soft wool dyed a light green that Old Agnes had brought to her; she hummed to herself as she sewed. She jumped at the knock on her door, then smiled when Edmund burst into the room. He drew to a halt, planted his hands on his hips, and said, "What think you, Maypole?"

She studied him silently for several minutes, until he began fidgeting about. "Very nice, Master Edmund. Come here and let me inspect you more closely."

Edmund swaggered over to where Philippa sat draped in her blanket. He was proud, that was clear to see, he'd even combed his fingers through his hair, and Philippa was pleased. "What says your father?"

"He just looked at me and rubbed his chin. Lord Graelam thought I would become a fine knight, and Lady Kassia asked that I carry her favors when I am in my first tourney."

Perfect Kassia had done it again, Philippa thought, had said just the right thing at the right time. Curse the woman.

"Father said that soon I will go to Wolffeton to foster with Lord Graelam. I will be his page, then, soon, his squire. I will prove myself and my loyalty."

"Do you wish to go to Wolffeton?"

Edmund nodded quickly, but then he fell silent. " 'Tis not far from St. Erth, no more than a half-day's hard ride. I shall go and I shall earn my spurs very soon."

"You will not, however, be an ignorant knight, Edmund. Few pages can read or write, but you will. Few men of any class can read or write, save priests and clerks. Lord Graelam will thank God the day you come to Wolffeton. Now, Father Cramdle awaits you. Go and leave the maypole to sew something to cover herself."

It wanted only Edmund's father, Philippa thought, watching Dienwald come into the small room after his son had left. She nearly filled it, and with him in here as well, it was suffocating. "What do you want?"

"I wish to tell you that my son is mightily pleased with himself."

Philippa merely nodded.

"Thank you, wench."

She swallowed a lump in her throat and said

in an offhand manner, "Shall you also be pleased
with your new tunic? 'Tis finished." Before he
could answer her, Philippa eased out of her chair,
her blanket firmly in place around her, and
handed him the tunic she'd sewn for him.

Dienwald took it from her outstretched hand
and stared down at it, running his fingers over
the tiny stitches, feeling the soft wool, marveling
that she had made it for him and that it was so
fine, the most excellent tunic he'd ever owned. It
was too special to wear on this ordinary day, but
he said nothing, merely pulled off his old tunic
and pulled this one over his head. It felt soft
against his flesh, and it fitted him perfectly. He
turned to face Philippa and she smiled at him.
" 'Tis very well you look, Dienwald, quite splen-
did." She reached out her hand and smoothed
the cloth over his chest. Her breathing quickened
and she suddenly stilled.

Dienwald stepped back quickly. "I'm leaving
and I wanted to tell you to stay close to St. Erth."

Her stomach cramped tight. "Where go you?
Not into danger?"

He heard the forlorn tone and the fear, and
frowned at it. "I go where I go, and 'tis none of
your affair. You will stay here and not move one
of your large feet from St. Erth. When I return, I
will decide what to do with you."

"You make me sound like entrails tossed out of
the cooking shed."

Dienwald merely smiled at that, touched his
fingertips to her cheek, then leaned down and
kissed her mouth. Still smiling, he jerked the
blanket from her breasts, gazed down at them,
kissed one nipple, then the other.

"Don't do that!"

He straightened, gave her a small salute, and strode from the room.

He began whistling again as the door closed firmly behind him. Philippa just stood there, the blanket bunched around her waist. He'd worn his new tunic.

Dienwald didn't think of her as anything remotely close to "entrails," but he didn't know what to do with her. What he wanted to do, in insane moments, was take her again and again until he was sated with her. And the insane moments seemed to be coming more and more often now; in fact, were he to count his errant thoughts, the moments would melt together.

He cursed and gave Philbo a stout kick in the sides. The destrier snorted and jumped forward. Northbert, surprised, kicked his own destrier into a canter, as did Eldwin, who rode on his left side.

Dienwald could remember the fragrance of her sweet woman's scent, and something else more elusive—perhaps 'twas the essence of gillyflowers, he thought, dredging the scent from his childhood memories.

The wench had bewitched him and beset him, curse her for the guileless siren she was. And somehow she'd made him like it and want more of it, more of her. He'd very nearly taken her maidenhead the previous night, and he hadn't even drunk enough ale to account for such stupidity. No, he'd just thought of her, seeing her in his mind's eye sleeping in her narrow bed in the steward's chamber, and he'd left Graelam to stare after him, their chess game still undecided. He would have taken her had she not awakened with that loud shriek in his face.

What was he to do with the damned wench?

He sighed, now picturing his son strutting about in his new clothes, bragging about the Maypole. His son, who just this morning hadn't carped and crabbed quite so much about being sacrificed to studies with Father Cramdle.

The wench was taking over St. Erth. Everywhere he saw her influence, her touch. It was irritating and disconcerting. He didn't know what to do about it.

It was Northbert who pulled him from his melancholy thoughts. "Master, what do you expect to find?"

"We didn't search before. We buried the dead and came back to St. Erth. I wish to find something to prove that Sir Walter ordered the burning and the killings. That or find someone who mayhap saw him or recognized one of his men."

Northbert chewed on that for several miles. Finally he said, "Why not just kill the malignant bastard? You know he's responsible, as do all the rest of us. Kill him."

Dienwald wanted to kill Walter, very much, but he shook his head. He wanted things done right. He wanted to keep Graelam's trust and his friendship. "Lord Graelam needs proof; then we will argue together to determine who gets to scatter the bastard's bowels."

"Ah," said Northbert, nodding his ugly head. "Lord Graelam includes himself now. 'Tis good, methinks."

They reached the southern acres of St. Erth late that afternoon. The desolation was shattering. There was naught but emptiness and black ruins. There was only the occasional caw of a rook. Curls of smoke still rose from some of the burned huts. There were a few peasants prodding the burned remains in leveled hovels, and Dienwald drew up and began to ask his questions.

Philippa was bored. More than bored, she'd discovered what Dienwald's errand was and she was worried, despite the fact that he was a trained fighter and no enemy was supposed to be where he was going.

She accepted without question that her cousin Sir Walter de Grasse was a black villain. She just wished there was something she could do.

She wore her new gown that afternoon and she looked proud and very pretty, so Old Agnes told her, very much the proper mistress. Then Agnes sought confirmation from Gorkel, who looked at Philippa and grunted, his hideous face achieving a repellent smile. She'd cut a narrow piece of wool and tied it around her hair. As for Crooky, he was feeling expansive in his own new clothes, which were still very clean, and praised her to her eyebrows. Philippa expected the worst and wasn't disappointed:

She sweetly sews for all of us, this lovely
maid whose name's not Mary.
Our sweet lord who stole her wool aches to
drink from her sweet dairy.
She made him a tunic and kissed it pure
Our sweet lord wonders what to do with her.

Philippa cheered loudly and the other servants in the hall quickly joined her. "It rhymed, truly," she said, wiping her eyes with the back of her hand. "Though your sentiments don't do the master justice."

Crooky, in a new mood of self-doubt, merely

said, "Nay, mistress, 'twas hideous. I must do
better, aye, I must tether my wayward thoughts
and bring them to smoothness and pleasure to
the ear. Aye, I will beg Father Cramdle to write
it down for me."

Philippa said, "You have lightened me for a few
moments, Crooky, and I thank you. Now, before
you go to the priest, tell me when the master will
return."

"No one knows," Gorkel said, stepping forward. "He's gone to the southern borders."

She knew that, and sat there worrying her
thumbnail. She paced the great hall. In a spate of
feverish activity to distract herself, she had lime
dumped down the privy hole in the guardroom.
She spaded the small garden near the cistern,
willing the few vegetables to grow. She watched
the women sewing, always sewing, and she
praised them, and joined in herself for an hour,
making another tunic for the master. Old Agnes
ran her arthritic fingers over it and gave her a sly
smile. Philippa went to the cooking shed and
spoke with Bennen, a stringy old man who knew
more of herbs than anyone she had ever known
and presided over the cooking with what Philippa's mother had called the "special touch." He
got along well with St. Erth's withered cook,
which was a good thing, because no one else
seemed to get along with him. She spoke of several dishes she herself liked, and Bennen committed them to memory, and called her "mistress"
and smiled at her, his toothless mouth wide. If
Dienwald wanted to feel trapped, he needed only
listen to his own people. She even visited Eleanor
the cat and her four kittens, all healthy and mew-
ing loudly.

The night was long, and Philippa wished Dien-wald were there, kissing her, fighting with her, trying to fit himself between her legs even as he fought himself.

The next morning, Edmund said to her after watching her crumble a particularly fine hunk of cheese and toss it to one of the castle dogs, "You didn't sleep well, Maypole. You look sour and your eyes are all dark-circled. My father has a nice palfrey that should be big enough for a female your size. Come riding, Philippa. You won't miss my father so much." He added after a little thought, "Aye, I miss him as well. We will both ride."

"I don't miss him, but I should like to ride."

The palfrey's name was Daisy and she was doc-ile and well-mannered. Philippa, her gown hiked up to her knees, her legs and feet bare, sat her horse, smiling down at Ogden, the head stable-man. He was wildly red-haired and so freckled she couldn't make out the tone of his flesh beneath.

Gorkel approached and said, "You'll want men with you, mistress. The master ordered me to . . ." He faltered, and Philippa could only stare, it was so unexpected of the man who'd without hesita-tion snapped the steward's neck.

"I understand," she said. "The master doesn't want me perchance to lose myself in the wilds of Cornwall."

Gorkel beamed at her. "Aye, mistress, thass it. I don't ride well, but I'll fetch men who will accompany you."

The afternoon was sunny, only a light breeze stirring the air, and the countryside was wild and hilly, trees bowed from the fierce winds and storms that blew from the Irish Sea just to the north—but not now, not during Dienwald's fanciful deep spring.

Edmund allowed that she looked less testy upon their return to St. Erth some three hours later.

"You must take care with your flattery, Master Edmund, else I may mistake your sweet words for affection."

To which Edmund snorted in disgust and said with a dignity that sat well on his boy's shoulders, "I am not a churl."

"Not today, at least," she said, and grinned at him.

Edmund didn't retort to that because they'd just crossed into the inner bailey and he was staring at a pack mule loaded with bundles, three men in Wolffeton colors lolling around the mule.

Perfect Kassia, the little princess, the glorious little lady, had sent clothing, just as she'd promised. An entire mule-load of clothing. Philippa gasped as she unwrapped the coarse-wool-wrapped garments. Gowns, overtunics, fine hose, shifts of the softest cotton and linen, ribbons of all colors, even soft leather slippers large enough for her, the toes pointed upward in the latest fashion from Eleanor's court. It was too much and it was wonderful and Philippa felt like the most sour-natured of wretches. She read the letter from Kassia, handed to her by one of the men. Mary was thanked for the hospitality of St. Erth, and Philippa could practically see Kassia smiling as she penned the words. The close of the letter made her frown a bit: ". . . do not worry if things transpire somewhat awry. Dienwald makes his own decisions and he is strong and unswerving.

Don't worry, please do not, for all will be as it should be."

Now, what did that mean? Philippa wondered as she rolled the sheet of foolscap and retied it. She looked at the clothing spread out on the trestle table in the great hall. So much, and all for her. Odd how she'd forgotten how much she'd owned at Beauchamp, and how dear one simple gown had now become to her.

She hummed and arranged the clothing in the steward's room. Then she began to work, quickly and happily, still humming. She sent Gorkel to direct the children to collect fresh rushes after she measured him for a new tunic. She asked Bennen for rosemary to scent it. More lime was dumped down the privy, for the easterly winds were strong.

The following morning, she and Edmund rode out from St. Erth again, this time with three men in attendance. Gorkel was master in Eldwin's absence, and he was directing the remaining men in the practice field. As they rode out, she could hear the men's shouts and yells and the dull thuds of the lances as they rode against the quintains. She wanted to see the cattle in the northern pastures, to make a count so she could be certain that her steward's ledgers were correct. She was garbed anew and felt like a very fine lady surrounded by her courtiers. Then it rained and she worried and fretted that her new clothing would be ruined. The cattle counted, they returned to St. Erth, Philippa to her steward's books.

On the third morning, she wore the gown she'd sewed for herself and left her legs bare. It didn't matter, for the day was warm and the master wasn't here to see her and perhaps smile at her

with lecherous intent. Ah, but she missed him
and his hands and his mouth and the feel of his
hard body. She missed his smile and his volley
of words. She missed arguing with him and baiting him. She thought suddenly that debauching
him was an interesting notion—folly, to be sure,
but seductive folly. Her fingers flexed as she
remembered holding his head on her lap that
morning and how he'd turned his face inward
and kissed her. She doubted she would have time
to debauch him before he'd already done the
debauching. She laughed aloud, and Edmund
stared at her.

As to her future, she refused to think about it.
As to St. Erth's future, it looked much brighter.
With luck, there would be some cattle to sell and
coins in Dienwald's coffers. She would need to
check on the pigs just as she had on the cattle.
She wanted nothing left to chance or hearsay. Her
entries in her steward's ledgers grew longer, by
the hour, it seemed, and she felt pleasure for St.
Erth's master as she worked. Repairs were needed
in St. Erth's eastern wall. Soon, perchance this
fall, there would be enough coin to hire them
done. She whistled and worked faster.

She turned her attention back to Edmund as he
demanded to know why she, a heedless maypole
of a girl, could read and write and cipher.
"Because my father wished it, I suppose," she
said, frowning as she spoke the words, the same
reply she'd given Edmund's father. "I do wonder,
though, why he wished it. My sister, Bernice, has
naught but space in her head, that and visions of
chivalrous knights singing praises to her eyebrows. Aye, she's a one, Master Edmund."

"Is she a maypole like you?"

Philippa shook her head. "She's short and plump and has a pointed chin and very red lips. She pouts most virtuously, having practiced before a mirror for the past six years."

"And she had all your suitors?"

"Must you keep asking me questions? All right, there was Ivo de Vescy, and he was wildly in love with me."

"His name sounds shiftless. Did he truly wish to wed with you? Was he a giant? You're almost as tall as my father." Edmund paused, then shook his head. "Mayhap not."

"You're naught but a little boy. How can you possibly tell from down there? I come nearly to your father's nose."

"He likes small women, *short* women. Just look at Alice and Ellen and Sybilla—"

"Who are Ellen and Sybilla?"

Edmund shrugged. "Oh, I forgot. Father married Ellen to a peasant when he got her with child, and Sybilla sickened with a fever and died. But Alice is small, not like you."

Philippa wanted to cuff his ears and stuff one of her new leather slippers into his mouth. She wanted to scream so loud that it would chase the cawing rooks away. Edmund's flowing child's candor had smitten her deep, very deep, with pain; she wanted to weep. Of course Dienwald had made no secret of his couplings. He'd said merely that they saved her maidenhead. And she'd not cared then because he was a stranger she hadn't come to know yet. But now she had and she wanted to send her fist into his belly and hear him bellow with pain. She wanted . . .

"Father will send you back to Lord Henry. He

has no choice. He doesn't want to wed, ever. Thass what he tells everyone."

"*That's*," Philippa said automatically. "Why do you believe that?"

Edmund shrugged. "I heard him tell Alain once that women were a man's folly, that if a man wished more than a vessel, he was naught but a windy fool and an ass."

"Your memory rivals a priest's discourse in its detail."

This was greeted with another shrug. "My father knows everything. Thass . . . *that's* why he doesn't use you as he does the others. He'd be ashamed, perchance worried that he would have to wed you. Is your father very powerful?"

"Very powerful," Philippa said. "And very mean and very strong and—"

It was then that Edmund grunted and jerked at his pony's reins. "Look yon, Philippa! Men, and they're coming toward us!"

15

Philippa saw the men and felt her heart sink to her toes. They were riding hard, and even from a distance they looked determined. Who were they?

"Your father, Edmund?"

"Nay, I don't recognize Father or Northbert or Eldwin, and they ride the most distinctive destriers. I don't know who they are. We must flee, Philippa."

The man-at-arms, Ellis, turned to Philippa, consternation writ clear on his face. "There are too many of them, mistress. Ride! Back to St. Erth. We can't fight them."

Philippa, without a word, jerked on her palfrey's reins and dug her bare heels into the mare's sides. She looked sideways at Edmund and realized that his pony didn't have the endurance to keep pace with the rest of them. Their pursuers' horses were pounding toward them, ever closer, their hooves kicking up whorls of dust into the clear air. Who were they?

It didn't matter. Philippa lowered her head and urged her palfrey faster. When Edmund's pony faltered, she'd simply bring him onto Daisy's back with her. Daisy was strong and stout of heart. Philippa gently tugged Daisy's reins to the right and drew closer to Edmund.

Sir Walter de Grasse looked toward the fleeing men, the girl and young boy protected in the midst of them. His destrier, a powerful blooded Arabian, couldn't be outrun, particularly by that muling mare Philippa was riding. He really didn't care about the others. Walter was pleased; he smiled and felt the wind tangle his hair and make his eyes tear. At last. He'd waited and planned and waited. Finally she'd ridden this way, and that whoreson peasant Dienwald wasn't with her. He was back scrounging about in his burned southern acres, finding nothing because Walter never left anything to find. Dead bodies were the only witnesses. Walter urged his destrier faster. If only Philippa knew that it was he, her own cousin, in pursuit, she would wave and flee from Dienwald's men. He noticed the little boy beside her on his laboring pony and wondered who he was.

He wished he could make out her face, but from this distance all he could see for certain was her wildly beautiful hair rippling out behind her head, atop the slenderness of her body. It was enough. If she had no teeth, he would still crave her above all women, this king's daughter who would shortly be his wife. He thought of St. Erth and how it would be his within the year, he doubted not. How could King Edward deny his son-in-law his own castle, stolen from his father by Dienwald's thieving sire?

Philippa could hear the pursuing horses. They were very close now. She knew all was lost. They were still a good two miles from St. Erth. The countryside around them held only a few peasants' huts, low pine trees and scrubby hawthorns and yews, and indifferent cattle. No one to help them. She saw the fierce look on Ellis' face, attesting to his impotent rage. Their pace was frantic and the horses were blowing hard, their flanks lathered white. She saw Edmund's pony stumble and she acted quickly, jerked Daisy close, dropped the knotted reins, and grabbed Edmund even as his pony went down. He was heavy, heavier than she'd imagined, but she pulled him onto Daisy's back. "My pony!" he yelled, nearly hurtling himself off Daisy's back.

Philippa fought to steady him. "The pony will make its way back to St. Erth. Worry not for the pony, but for us."

Edmund quieted, but he was breathing in quick sharp gasps, his small body shuddering.

"Your pony will go home," she said again, this time in his ear, hoping he heard her and understood.

He made no sign. His small face was white and grim.

She held him close and urged her mare faster.

Suddenly, without warning, Ellis screamed, a tearing raw-throated sound. Philippa saw an arrow bedded deep between his shoulder blades, its feathered shaft still vibrating from the force of its entry. Ellis lurched forward, gasping, then fell sideways, his foot catching in the stirrup. He was dragged along, blood spewing from his back onto

his maddened horse. Philippa tried to hide
Edmund's head, but he watched until Ellis' foot
worked free of the stirrup and he fell to the hard
ground, rolling over and over, the arrow's shaft
going deeper into his body.

Edmund made no sound; Philippa held him
tighter, swallowing convulsively.

The other two men closed around her, and one
of them yelled at her to keep down, to hug her
mare's neck, but even as the words left his mouth
he slumped forward against his horse's back, an
arrow through his neck.

Philippa knew it was no use. "Flee," she
shouted to the third man, whose name was
Silken. "Go whilst you can. 'Tis I the men want,
not you. Go! Get help. Get the master."

The man looked at her, his eyes sad and accepting. He drew his horse to a screaming halt,
whipped him about, and drew his sword. "I
won't die with a coward's arrow in my back," he
yelled at Philippa. "Nor will I die a coward's
death in my soul by escaping my fate. Ride hard,
mistress. I'll hold them as long as I can. Keep the
boy safe."

"Nay, Silken, nay!" Edmund shouted, and Philippa knew that she couldn't leave the man, knew
that even if she rode away, she would manage to
save neither herself nor Edmund. She pulled
Daisy to a halt. "Stay back behind me, Silken,"
she yelled at him. "Keep your sword to your
side!"

The men were upon them in moments. Dust
flew, blurring the air, making Philippa cough. She
couldn't have been more horrified or surprised
when one of the men yelled, "Philippa! My
dearest cousin, 'tis I, Walter, here to save you!"

Silken whirled on Philippa, his face gone white, his mouth ugly with sudden rage. "*You*, mistress! You brought this bastard cur upon us! You got word to him!"

"Find the master, Silken. Here, take Edmund with you, quickly!"

But Edmund wouldn't budge, shaking his head madly and clutching at the mare's mane. Silken waited not another moment, but rode away as only a desperate man can ride, and Walter, intent for the moment upon the object of his capture, allowed the man to gain distance. Then he yelled for two of his men to bring him down. Philippa prayed hard, as did, she imagined, Edmund. Silken was their only chance. He disappeared over a rise, the two men in pursuit.

"Philippa," Walter said as he rode up to her. "Ah, my dearest girl, you are safe, are you not?"

Philippa stared at her cousin Walter, a man she hadn't seen for some years. He wasn't a handsome man, but then, neither was he ill-looking. But he did look different to her. She had remembered him as very tall and thin. He wasn't thin now; he was gaunt and wiry, his face long, his cheekbones high and hollow, his eyes more prominent. She remembered thick dark brown hair fashionably clipped across his forehead. His hair was thinner now but still clipped across his forehead. She hadn't remembered his eyes. They were dark blue, and they looked hot with triumph, with success. She quickly assessed matters and got control of herself. He believed he'd rescued her, saved her. She whispered to Edmund, "Hold your peace, Edmund. Do as I do."

The boy was white with fear, but he nodded. She squeezed him comfortingly.

"Walter, 'tis you?"

"Aye, Philippa, 'tis I, your dearest cousin. You have changed and grown into a woman and a beautiful creature. You are most pleasing to mine eyes. And now you are safe from that knave." Walter paused a moment, noticing Edmund, it seemed, for the first time.

"Who is this? The bastard's whelp? Shall I dispatch him to heaven, Philippa? Surely that is where the angels would carry him, for he is yet too young to have gleaned the foul wickedness from his sire."

"No, leave him be, Walter. He is but a child, too young for heaven, unless God calls him. Leave him to me. He cares not for his sire, for he foully abuses him." She prayed Edmund would keep his small mouth firmly closed. He started, stiffening against her, but said nothing.

"Aye, that I can believe. The cruel traitor not only abused his own child, but you as well, I doubt not. You are both safe with me, Philippa, at least until I decide what to do with the boy. Aye, I'll ransom him. His father is coarse of spirit, but the boy is of his flesh and his heir. Aye, we'll all return to Crandall now."

"I'll tear out his lying tongue!"

"Shush, Edmund, please, say nothing untoward!"

Philippa turned Daisy about, saying as she did so, "What is the distance to your keep, Walter?"

"Two days hence, fair cousin."

"My palfrey is lathered and blowing."

"Leave the beast and take that one. Dienwald's man needs it no more." And Walter laughed, pointing to Ellis' body sprawled in a ditch beside the dusty road.

"Nay, leave me the mare, just keep our pace slow for a while."

Walter felt expansive. Everything had come about as he'd planned. Philippa was beautiful and she was gentle and yielding, her expressive eyes filled with gratitude for him. "I'll grant you that boon, Philippa." He rode forward to speak to one of his men. Philippa whispered in Edmund's ear, "We must pretend, Edmund, and we must think. We must exceed Crooky's most talented fabrications."

"I will kill him."

"Perhaps I shall be the quicker, but hold your tongue now, he returns. Say naught, Edmund."

"We will ride until it darkens, sweet cousin. I know you are tired, but we must have distance from St. Erth." He turned and looked behind them, and she knew he was at last worried that his men hadn't returned to report Silken's death. She prayed harder.

"We will do as you wish, Walter," she said, her voice soft and low. "You're right—we're too close to the tyrant's castle." He seemed to expand before her eyes, so pleased was he at her submissiveness.

"Shall I carry the boy before me?"

"Nay, he is afraid, Walter, for he knows you not. He can't abide me—he follows his sire's lead and insults me and abuses me—but at least I am a known adversary. Leave him with me for the moment, if it pleases you to do so."

It evidently suited Walter, and he turned to speak to a man who rode beside him.

"You act the flap-mouthed fool," Edmund said, his child's voice a high squeak. "He cannot believe you, 'tis absurd!"

"He doesn't know me," Philippa said. "He wants to believe me soft and biddable and as submissive as a cow. Fret not, at least not yet."

It wasn't until late that afternoon that the two men who had followed Silken caught up with them. Philippa held her breath as they pulled their mounts to a halt beside Walter. She waited, still with apprehension. To her wondrous relief, Walter exploded with rage. "Fools! Inept knaves!"

"Silken escaped," Philippa said into Edmund's ear. "Your father will come. He will save us."

Edmund frowned. "But he is your cousin, Philippa. He won't harm you."

"He's a bad man. Your father hates him, and for good reason, I think."

"But you mocked my father about him and—"

" 'Tis but our way—your father and I must rattle our tongues at each other, goad and taunt each other until one wants to smash the other's head."

Edmund said nothing to that, but he was confused, so Philippa just hugged him, whispering, "Trust me, and trust that your father will save us."

It came to dusk and the sky colored itself with vivid shades of pink. They rode inland a bit and stopped at the edge of a forest whose name Philippa didn't know. It was dark and deep, and she watched silently as two men immediately melted into the trees in search of game. Two other men went to collect wood.

Walter lifted Edmund down and paid him no more attention. Then he wrapped his hands around Philippa's waist and lifted her from Daisy's back. He grunted a bit because she wasn't a languid feather to be plucked lightly. She grinned. When her feet touched the ground he didn't release her, but held her, his hands lightly caressing her waist. "You please me, Philippa, very much."

"Thank you, Walter."

He frowned suddenly. "Your feet are bare. The gown you wear, it is all you have? That wretched bastard gave you nothing to wear?"

She lowered her head and shook her head. "It matters not," she said, her voice meek and accepting.

Walter cursed and ranted. To her horror, he turned on Edmund, and without warning, back-handed the boy. The blow sent Edmund sprawling onto his back on the hard ground, the breath knocked out of him.

"Foul spawn of the devil!"

"Nay, Walter, leave the boy be!" Philippa was trembling with rage, which she prayed her voice didn't give away. She quickly dropped to her knees beside Edmund. She felt his arms, his legs, pressed her hand against his chest. "Oh, God, Edmund, is there pain?"

The boy was white-faced, not with pain but with anger. "I'm all right. Get back to your precious cousin and show him your melting gratitude, Maypole."

Philippa gave him a long look. "Don't be a fool," she said very quietly. She got to her feet. Walter was standing there, absently rubbing his hands together.

"Come to the fire, Philippa. It will grow cool soon, and your rags will not protect you."

Her new gown wasn't a rag, she wanted to yell at him, but she held her peace. She gave Edmund another look and walked beside Walter. One of his men had spread a blanket on the ground, and she eased down, her muscles sore, her back aching from the long ride. "Let the boy warm himself as well," she said after some minutes had passed.

It was nearly dark before the two men returned with a pheasant and two rabbits. After they'd supped and the fire was burning low and orange, Philippa wrapped herself in a blanket, pulled Edmund down to the ground beside her, and waited. It took Walter not long to say, "I heard that de Fortenberry was holding you prisoner. I planned and schemed to get you free of him."

"Where did you hear that?"

Walter paused a moment, then said with a rush of dignity, "I am not without loyal servants, cousin. St. Erth's cistern keeper told me of your position." Walter paused a moment, then leaned over to take Philippa's hand in his. His was warm and dry. She said nothing, didn't move. "The man told me how his master had mistreated you, molesting you, holding you against your will in his bedchamber whilst he ravished you. He even told how Fortenberry had ripped your gown before all his people, then dragged you from the hall to rape you yet again. Then he told me how Alain, the steward, had wanted you killed and how he and another were to do it. He didn't realize that you, dearest heart, were mine own cousin. I killed him for you, Philippa. I slit his miserable throat even as the words gagged in his mouth. You need never fear him again."

The cistern keeper had deserved death, she would have killed him herself had she been able, but to hear of it done in so cold-blooded a fashion . . . And Walter believed she'd been abused, violated. It was, she supposed, a logical conclusion. "Does my father know?"

"You mean Lord Henry? Nay, not as yet."

"What else did he tell you?"

"That his master had stolen Lord Henry's wool and forced you to oversee the weaving and sewing, that he treated you as a servant and a whore. How was Alain found out?"

Philippa said this cautiously, not wanting Walter to realize that she'd discovered his treachery because she worried and fretted about St. Erth and its master. She said only, "He was a fool, and one of the master's men broke his miserable neck."

"Good," Walter said. "I just wish I could have done it for you, sweetling. Of course, I know why the steward feared you and wanted you dead. It was because you read and write and cipher and he knew you'd find him out. A pity he tried to kill you, for he was a good servant and bled St. Erth nearly dry of its wealth, and much of the knave's coin found its way to my coffers."

Philippa felt Edmund stir, felt fury in his small body, and she quickly laid a quieting hand on his shoulder. "Walter, will you return me to my father?"

"Not as yet, Philippa, not as yet. First I wish you to see Crandall, the keep I oversee. And you need clothes for your station, aye, soft ermine, mayhap scarlet for a tunic, and the softest linen for your shifts. I long to see you garbed as befits your position. Then we will speak of your father."

She frowned at him. What was going on here? Why was Walter acting loverlike? Her position? She was his cousin, that was all. Surely he didn't want her, since he believed she was no longer a maiden, since he believed Dienwald had kept her as his mistress. Had perchance her father gone to him? Promised him a dowry if he found her, thus promising her in marriage to her cousin? It seemed the only logical answer to Philippa. No man could possibly want her if he believed she lacked both a maidenhead and a dowry.

"Do we reach Crandall on the morrow?"

He nodded and yawned. He smiled upon her, seeing her weariness. "I will keep you safe, Philippa. You need have no more fear. I will make you . . . happy."

Philippa was terrified, but she nodded, her look as pleasingly sweet as she could muster it. *Happy!*

St. Erth Castle

"What say you, Silken? She what? That whoreson Walter killed both Ellis and Albe? *Both* of them? He took Edmund as well?"

"Aye, master. He took both the mistress and Master Edmund. We fetched Ellis' and Albe's bodies, and Father Cramdle buried them with God's sacred words."

Dienwald stood very still, weary from a long hard ride, his mind sluggish; he couldn't take it in. Two days had passed since Sir Walter de Grasse had taken his son and Philippa and killed Ellis and Albe. He himself had just ridden into St. Erth's inner bailey and learned what had happened from Silken. Dear God, what had Walter done to them? Had he taken them for ransom? Fear erased his fatigue.

Silken cleared his throat, his gnarled hand on Dienwald's arm. "Master, heed me. I have been filled with murderous spleen since my escape, but have wondered if what I first believed to be true was true or was the result of blind seeing."

"Make sense, Silken!"

"This Sir Walter greeted the mistress as if . . . as if she'd sent for him and he'd rescued her as she wished him to. As if he'd known she would be riding and he'd had but to wait for her to come in his direction. He was waving at her, smiling like a man filled with joy at the sight of her."

Dienwald stared blankly at the man, and his gut cramped viciously.

"Aye, she'd ridden out three days in a row, master, and that last day, only three men attended her and the young master."

"And was that her demand?"

"I know not," Silken said. "I know only that Ellis and Albe lie rotting in the earth."

The heavens at that moment opened and cold rain flooded down. Thunder rumbled and the sky darkened to night. Dienwald, his tired men at his heels, ran into the great hall. It was silent as a tomb. There were clumps of women standing about, but at the sight of him they became mute. Then Gorkel came to him, his hideous face working. With anger? With betrayal?

"Ale!" Dienwald bellowed. "Margot, quickly!"

He ignored Gorkel for the moment, his thought on his son, now a prisoner of Sir Walter de Grasse, his greatest enemy, his only avowed enemy. His blood ran cold. Would Walter run Edmund through with his sword simply because the boy was of his flesh and blood? Dienwald closed his eyes against the roiling pain of it, against the helplessness he felt. And Philippa . . . Had she betrayed him? Had she taken Edmund riding with her on purpose so that Dienwald wouldn't follow for fear his son would be killed?

He was tired, so tired that his mind went adrift with frantic chafing, with uncertainty. Philippa was gone . . . Edmund was gone, his only son . . . two of his men were dead . . .

Gorkel drew nearer to speak, but Dienwald said, "Nay, hold your peace, I would think."

It was Crooky who said in the face of his master's prohibition, "The mistress left her finery. Surely if she'd wanted to be rescued by her loathsome cousin, if somehow she'd managed to send him word, she would have taken the garments sent her by Lady Kassia, nay, she would have worn them to greet her savior."

"Mayhap, mayhap not."

"She knew you hate the man and that he hates you."

" 'Tis true, curse the proud-minded wench."

"She would not endanger Master Edmund."

"Would she not, fool? Why not, I ask you. Edmund calls her maypole and witch. She held him by his ear and scrubbed him with soap. He howled and scratched and cursed her. Surely she can bear him no affection. Why not, I ask you again."

"The mistress is a lady of steady nature. She has not a sour heart, master, nor did she allow herself to be vexed with Master Edmund. She laughed at his sulky humors and teased him and sewed him clothes, aye, and held him firm to bathe him, as a mother would. She would never seek to harm the boy."

"I don't understand women. Nor do you, so pretend not that you possess some great shrewdness about them. But I do know their blood sings with perversity. They become peevish and testy when they gain not what they want; they become treacherous when they believe a certain man to be the framer of their woes. They see only the ends they seek, and weigh not the means to achieve them. She could perceive Edmund as only a minor obstacle."

"You are the one who sees blindly, master."

"That is what Silken said. Oh, aye, I hear you. Get you gone, fool. Thank the heavens above that you did not sing your opinion to me. My head would have split open and my thoughts would have flowed into oblivion."

"I have known it to happen, master."

"Get out of my sight, fool!" Dienwald made a halfhearted effort to kick Crooky's ribs, but the fool neatly rolled out of reach.

"What will you do, master?"

"I will sleep and think, and think yet more, until the morrow. Then we will ride to Crandall to fetch my son and the wench."

"And if you find she deceived you?"

"I will beat her and tie her to my bed and berate her until she begs God's forgiveness and mine. And then . . ."

"And if you find she deceived you not?"

"I shall . . . Get out of my sight, fool!"

Windsor Castle

"Dienwald de Fortenberry," King Edward said, rubbing his jaw as he looked at his travel-stained chancellor. "I know of him, but he has never come to my court. Not that I have been much in evidence before I . . . But never mind that. I have

been on England's shores for nearly eight months
now and yet de Fortenberry disdains to pay his
homage to me. He did not attend my coronation,
did he?"

"Nay, he did not. But then again, sire, why
should he? If all your nobles—the minor barons
included—had attended your coronation, why
then London would have burst itself like a tunic
holding in a fat man."

The king waved that observation aside. "What
of his reputation?"

"His reputation is that of knave, scoundrel,
occasional rogue, and loyal friend."

"Graelam wishes an occasional rogue and a
scoundrel to be the king's son-in-law?"

Robert Burnell, tired to his mud-encrusted boots,
nodded. He'd returned from his travels but an
hour before, and already the king in his endless
energy wanted to wring him of all information.
"Aye, sire. Lord Graelam wasn't certain that you
knew Dienwald, and so he recited to me this
man's shortcomings as well as his virtues. He
claims Dienwald would never importune you for
royal favors and that since he has no family, there
are none to leech on your coffers. Lord Graelam
and his lady call him friend, nay, they call him
good friend. They say he would cease his outlaw
ways were he the king's son-in-law."

"Or he would continue them, knowing I could
not have my son-in-law's neck stretched by the
hangman's noose!"

"Lord Graelam does not allow that a possibility,
sire. I did question him closely. Dienwald de Fortenberry is a man of honor . . . and wickedness,
but his wickedness flows from his humors, which

flow from the wildness and independence of Cornwall itself."

"You turn from a shrewd chancellor into a honeyed poet, Robbie. It grieves me to see you babble, you a man of the church, a man of disciplined habits. De Fortenberry, hmmm. Graelam gave you not another name? You heard of no other man who would become me and my sweet Philippa?"

Burnell shook his head. "Shall I read you what I have writ as Lord Graelam spoke to me, sire?"

Edward shook his head, his thick golden hair swinging free about his shoulders. Plantagenet hair, Burnell thought, and wished he could have seen if Philippa was as gloriously endowed as her father.

"Tell me of my daughter," Edward said suddenly. "But be quick about it, Robbie. I must needs argue with some long-nosed Scots from Alexander's court, curse his impertinence and their barbaric tongue."

"I didn't see her," Burnell said quickly, then waited for the storm to rage over his head.

"Why?" Edward asked mildly.

"Lord Henry said she was ill with a bloody flux from her bowels, and thus I couldn't meet her."

"St. Gregory's teeth, will the girl live?"

"Lord Henry assures me the de Beauchamp physician worries not. The girl will live."

"I wish you had waited, Robbie, until you could have spoken with her."

Burnell merely nodded, but his soul was mournful. The king had abjured him to return as soon as he could. And he had obeyed his master, as he always did.

"Lord Henry showed me a miniature of the girl."

The king brightened as he took the small painting from Burnell's hand. He studied the stylized portrait, but saw beyond the white-faced expression of bland purity and the overly pointed chin to the sparkling Plantagenet eyes, eyes as blazing bright as a summer sky, eyes as blue as his own. As for her hair, it was nearly white, it was so blond, and her forehead was flawless, high and white with but thin eyebrows to intercede, but then again, an artist strove to please. He tried to remember the color of Constance's hair but couldn't bring it to mind. He couldn't recall that she'd had such flaxen white hair; no woman had hair that color. That much, he thought, was the artist's fancy. He placed the miniature in his tunic. "Let me think about this. I will speak to the queen. She will translate the artist's rendering, and her counsel rings true. I suppose if I agree, I must bring de Fortenberry here to Windsor to tell him of his good fortune." King Edward strode to the door, then turned back to say, "The damned Scots! Harangue me they will until my tongue swells in my mouth! You must needs rest, Robbie, 'twas a long journey for you, and wearying." The king turned again, his hand on the doorknob, then said absently over his shoulder, "Fetch your writing implements, Robbie. I must have you record faithfully their muling complaints. Then we shall discuss what is to be done with them."

Burnell sighed. He walked to a basin of cold water and liberally splashed his face. He was back in the royal harness, he thought, and smiled.

16

Crandall Keep

"You are beautiful, Philippa. The soft yellow gown becomes you."

"I thank you, Walter, for your gifts. The gowns and overtunics please me well." They were of the finest quality, and Philippa had wondered where her cousin had gotten them. Obviously from a woman who was short and had big breasts. Evidently she also had rather big feet for her height, for the soft leather slippers pinched Philippa's toes only slightly. Who and where was the woman? Surely she couldn't be pleased to have Philippa wearing her clothing.

"Crandall is a well-maintained keep, Walter, and since you are its castellan, it is to your credit alone. How many men-at-arms are there within the walls?"

"Twenty men, and they are finely trained. Lord Graelam does not stint on our protection, but of course 'tis I who have trained them and am responsible for their skills."

Philippa nodded, wishing there were only two, and those old and weak of limb. It didn't bode well for her and Edmund getting out or for Dienwald getting in. She hadn't spoken to any of the men, but she had spent a bit of time with several of the keep servants, and discovered that her cousin wasn't a particularly kindly master nor much beloved, but he did appear fair—when he wasn't brandishing his whip. "He's fast wi' t' whip," one of the servants, a bent old woman, had told her in a low voice. "Ye haf t' move fast when he's got blood in his eye and t' whip in his hand." Philippa had but stared at her. A whip! She remembered how several of the women had looked at her when they thought she wasn't paying heed, and they'd spoken behind their hands and looked worried, even frightened. Even now she could feel the female servants looking at her, judging her perhaps, and she wondered at it.

She said now to Walter as she accepted a hunk of bread from his hands, "These lovely garments, cousin—from whence did they come?"

" 'Tis not your concern, sweetling. I had them, and now they are yours. That is all you must needs know."

And Philippa could only wonder, and wonder yet more. He'd given her until yesterday to rest and be at her ease, and then he'd begun to woo her. Philippa couldn't be mistaken, particularly after enduring Ivo de Vescy's outpourings of affection. Walter was playing the besotted swain. Only he wasn't besotted; his words bespoke all the right sentiments, but his eyes remained cold and flat. At first Philippa couldn't credit it. There was no reason—no dowry, in short—for a man in Walter's position to be interested in marriage with her. And it was impossible that he could have fallen deliriously in love with her; he'd known her for but two days. No, her father was behind it; he had to be. But just how, Philippa couldn't imagine.

She toyed with the cabbage stuffed with hare and decided it was time to test the waters. "Walter, does my father know I am here?"

His eyes narrowed on her face, eyes that were always cold and flat when they looked at her. "Not as yet, Philippa. You care so much to return to Beauchamp?"

She shook her head, smiling at him, not chancing an argument because there was something in him that frightened her, something elusive, yet it was there, and she wanted to keep her distance from it.

Walter chewed thoughtfully on mashed chestnuts encrusted with boiled sugar, his favorite dish. Philippa wasn't what he'd expected. He saw flashes of contradiction in her, and although they surprised him, they didn't worry him unduly. Despite her hardy size, he could control her easily should the need arise. He would wed her by the end of the week. He had the time; he could afford to go gently with her, to bend her slowly to his will. Three days was enough time to bend the most rebellious woman to his will. He thought now that he could tell her some of the truth. Perhaps it would make her trust him all the more quickly, and it didn't really matter one way or the other to him.

"Your father was here, Philippa," he said, and watched her twist in her chair, her expression stunned. "He thought perhaps you had come to me when you escaped in the wool wagons, as you would have if that bastard hadn't captured you and taken you to St. Erth.

"At the time of Lord Henry's visit, I didn't know where you were. Lord Henry told me, Philippa, that he'd promised you to William de Bridgport in marriage. He was most adamant about it, even when I argued with him. I could not, nay, still cannot, imagine you wedded to that testy old lecher. But Lord Henry needs the coin de Bridgport will pay for you. You see, Philippa, as much as it hurts me to wound you, you must know the truth. Lord Henry holds his possessions more dear than he ever held you."

Philippa could only shake her head. So her father had come here. She'd shown surprise to Walter, guessing it was the correct response, but she'd already guessed her father's presence. Her insides felt cold and cramped. She wanted to scream that her father couldn't have told Walter that, he couldn't have, it wasn't true.

But it was true. Philippa had overheard him say it himself. It wasn't Walter's fault.

"You must still send a messenger to my father to tell him I am here. I would not wish you to be my father's enemy."

Walter started to shake his head, then thought better of it. He'd just been offered his best opportunity. "I think we still have some time, sweetling, before I do that. Three days, perhaps four." He saw her revulsion, her fear, and he moved swiftly to take advantage of it. He gently took her hand in his. There were calluses on the pads of

her fingers, attesting to the labors Dienwald had
forced her to, the mangy scoundrel. He felt her
tense, but she didn't pull away. "Listen, Philippa," he said, his voice low and soft, "if you
wed me, there is naught Lord Henry can do. You
cannot be forced to wed de Bridgport. You will
be safe as my wife, you will be secure. No one—
not even the king himself—could take you from
me."

There it was, Philippa thought, staring at her
cousin. He wanted to marry her, but it made no
sense. He believed her already ravished by Dienwald, so he couldn't expect a virgin's blood on
the wedding sheets. More important, there was
no coin forthcoming from her father. What was
going on? She must continue her deceit until she
discovered his plot. She kept her head modestly
lowered and let her fingers rest against his.

"You offer me much, Walter, more than I
deserve. You must allow me time to compose my
thoughts. All this comes as a surprise, and my
thoughts have gone awry." She raised her head
and saw the frown of impatience in his eyes. She
added quickly, "I am slow of reason, Walter,
being but a woman, and your generosity, though
a gift from God, leaves me tongue-tied, but just
for a brief time. Until tomorrow, dear cousin—
then I will speak to you of my feelings."

He gave her a grave nod and squeezed her fingers again before releasing her hand. Her tongue
was smooth, her words gently flowing, respectful, filled with deference, but something bothered
him. Perhaps it was that she hadn't asked of their
close kinship, thus requiring special permission
by the church. But she was but a woman and
probably ignorant of such things. Aye, just a

woman, but she could read and write and cipher.
He didn't wish to tell her that he shared not one
drop of her blood, that he knew her conceived of
another man's seed, a seed most royal, but he
wasn't at all certain of her reaction. No, he must
hold his tongue. She was biddable, soft and
comely, and she was endowed with beauty
aplenty. She was too tall for his taste, but then
again, there was Britta, hidden away now, but
waiting for him, and he would continue with her
when it pleased him to do so. Tonight, he
thought, his loins tightening at the thought of
her. He gave a small shudder. Were it not for
Philippa, he would leave this instant and go to
Britta. He saw that Philippa was looking about
the hall, and said, "What troubles you, sweet
cousin?"

"Naught, 'tis just that I see not the boy, Walter.
Although I do not hold him dear, I have a responsibility for him, since he was with me when you
rescued me. Have you yet sent a demand of ransom to Dienwald?"

Walter shook his head. He wouldn't send anything to anyone until he was her husband. Not
even to his overlord, Graelam de Moreton. "The
whelp keeps company with my stable lads. I do
him a good service. 'Twill humble him to see how
those beneath him live, and make him more
stouthearted. He will learn what it is like to
serve."

At least he wasn't locked away somewhere in
the keep, but she worried that the villeins would
abuse him. She said nothing, merely forced herself to eat another bite of the cabbage. It needed
some of the wild thyme she'd just planted in her
garden at St. Erth. *Her* garden. Philippa wanted

to cry, odd in itself, but it was true: St. Erth had become home to her in a very short length of time and its master had become the man she wanted. But he didn't want her, had never lied about it, had even kept his manhood out of her body because he feared having to keep her, having to take her to wive because she was too wellborn to use at his whim.

She pushed Dienwald and his perversity from her mind. She had to escape Walter, and she had to take Edmund with her. She had not many more days before Walter pushed her into wedlock. She doubted not that he would bed her to force her hand. She was sleeping by herself in a tiny chamber off the great hall, a chamber, from the smell of it, that had held winter grain but days before her arrival. It was airless, but she didn't mind; the stuffiness kept her awake, and that allowed her to think. And she thought of St. Erth and its master and wondered if he were close even now. But she knew she couldn't simply wait for Dienwald to do something; she had to act to save herself and Edmund.

Walter kept her with him that evening, playing draughts, and when she won, forgetting that she was but a woman and thus inferior to male stratagems, he was sharp with her.

"You were lucky," he said, his voice edged with anger. "I allowed you too much time with your moves because of your sex. You deceived me, cousin, but . . ." He paused, and the light changed in his eyes. He shook his head, wagging a playful finger in her face. "Ah, Philippa, you won because of your sweet nature and your softness. You took me in with your gentle presence, your glorious eyes. You see me slain at your dainty feet. All my thoughts were perforce of you, my dearest. Would you sleep now, sweetling?"

He wasn't stupid, Philippa thought as she rose from her chair. He'd been furious because she'd beaten him, but quickly adjusted himself to a more favorable position in her eyes. He was still her gallant suitor. But for how much longer? She shuddered as she walked beside him to the small room. Before he left her, he grasped her upper arms and pulled her against him. "Beautiful cousin," he said, and kissed her ear because she jerked her head to one side. It was a mistake. She felt his fingers dig into her flesh, heard his breath sharpen with anger.

"Please, Walter," she said softly, "I wish . . ." Words failed her. She wanted to scream at him to remove his slimy person.

He drew a false conclusion. "Ah, 'tis because he abused you, because he forced you. I won't hurt you, cousin, never will I touch you amiss. I will always be your gentle master. You must trust me, and I will make you forget the knave's violence toward you." He leaned down and lightly touched his mouth to her forehead and released her arms. "Sleep well, my heart."

Philippa nodded, her head down, but she couldn't prevent the words that came spilling from her mouth. "Walter, you know me so little. You met me only as a child. Why do you wish to wed with me? You know I am no longer a maid. You know that my father will not dower me. Tell me, dear cousin, tell me why you so wish me as your wife."

She raised her head and knew that she'd again jumped with her feet; she hadn't thought. What if he turned on her, what if . . . . ? She waited,

tense and still, hoping he would speak, yet fearful
that he would simply rant at her and perhaps beat
her with that whip of his.

Walter found himself at something of an im-
passe. Again he saw the contradiction in her. She
was but a woman, full of softness and gentle
smiles, and here she was questioning him, but,
ah, so sweetly she questioned. He'd thought to
slap her hard to show her that he wouldn't
always tolerate inquiries from her, but now he
thought better of it. That was doubtless how
Dienwald had treated her. Aye, Dienwald had
been violent and rough with her. Walter must
prove to her that he was different. He would
resort to more straightforward methods only if
she pushed him to them.

"I have loved you since I first saw you five
years ago, Philippa. I spoke to Lord Henry then,
but he only shook his head and laughed and
called me fool. I have corresponded with him over
the years, but had almost admitted failure of my
hopes when he came to me and admitted that
you'd fled to escape the marriage with de Bridgport. I am a simple man, Philippa, with simple
needs and only one desire that burns in my life,
and that is you, to earn you for my wife."

"But I am used," she said, and looked at him
straightly, wishing she could tell him his memory
was faulty. He'd last seen her more than five
years before. "He debauched me again and again.
He used me unnaturally."

If only Dienwald had done a bit more debauching than he had, she thought now, watching Walter. He wasn't stupid, this cousin of hers, so
when he leaned down and kissed her gently on
the mouth, she wasn't overly surprised. Dis-

mayed, but not surprised. "It matters not to me,"
he said in a richly sincere voice. He turned and
left her, locking the door behind him.

"But you must needs lock me in," she said after
him.

There was but one candle to light the chamber.
She felt the shadows surround her, and they were
comforting. She made her way to the narrow bed,
stripped off her soft yellow overtunic and the
gown beneath. She stretched out on her back,
staring up into the darkness.

What, after all, could he have said to her? she
wondered now. But why did he wish to wed her?
Why? Sir Walter was a dangerous man, and she
recognized the threat in him. She saw the intensity in him, the will to drive himself, to drive others. The last thing that would be his main desire
was a woman, any woman.

She must go very carefully. She must give him
false security. She must hang around his neck
until he wished her to leave him alone. Then,
perhaps, she would find a way for her and
Edmund to escape Crandall. If they didn't escape,
she feared what would happen to them. She
would refuse to wed Walter and he would rape
her endlessly. She knew it. But *why*?

She dared not wait for Dienwald, for the way
things were progressing, he might well be too
late. But why, she wondered again and again, did
Walter want to wed her so badly?

Over and over she tortured her brain with possible motives Walter could harbor. Had her father
changed his mind and offered Walter money if he
found her and wedded her? Land? She shook her
head on that possibility. Her father never changed

his mind. Never. There were no answers, only more questions that made her head ache badly.

Near Crandall Keep

Dienwald scratched his chest. He was hot and dirty and disliked the fact. He hated the waiting but knew there was naught else to be done. He rose and began pacing the perimeter of his camp. They were withdrawn into a copse of thick maple trees, well-hidden from the narrow winding road that led to Crandall. His men were lolling about, bored and restless, arguing, tossing dice, recounting heroics and tales of their male prowess.

Where were the fool and Gorkel?

What of Philippa and Edmund? Worry gnawed at him, paralyzed his brain. What was the truth? Had Philippa betrayed him, or had she been caught as certainly as Ellis and Albe had been slain?

Only she could give him the answer. She or that whoreson peasant, Walter. Dienwald sat down and leaned against an oak tree older than life itself, and closed his eyes. What he wanted, damn her soft hide, was Philippa. He saw her sprawled in the mud, laughing, her eyes a vivid blue in her blackened face; then he saw her naked as he threw buckets of water on her and soaped her body with his hands. His loins were instantly heavy, his rod hard and hurting. He knew in that moment that he would have to return her to her father the moment he got his hands on her again. If he kept her with him, he would take her, and he wouldn't allow himself to do that. If he did, it would be all over for him.

He wouldn't allow himself to be caught. Allying himself to de Beauchamp—he couldn't bear the thought of it. Lord Henry was a pompous ass, arrogant and secure in his own privilege, in his immense power and dignity. No, Dienwald would remain free, unencumbered, answerable to no one other than himself, responsible for no one but himself and his son. If he needed wool, he'd steal it. He wished now he hadn't forgotten about the wine arriving from Kassia's father. He would have gladly planned the shipwreck and the theft of every cask. He would have laughed in Graelam's face, and taken a pounding if Graelam had pushed him on it. He wanted to be free.

He wondered what was happening at Crandall, and he fretted, bawled complaints to the heavens, and paced.

Crandall Keep

In Crandall's inner bailey, Crooky smiled and sang and capered madly about, drawing everyone's attention. He held Gorkel on a chain leash fastened about his huge neck with a leather band, and tugged at him, carping and scolding at him as though he were a bear to be alternately baited and cajoled. "Nod your ugly head to that fair wench yon, Gorkel!"

Gorkel eyed the fair wench, who was staring at him, fear and excitement lighting her eyes. He nodded to her and smiled wide, showing the vast space between his front teeth. He felt the fool tugging madly at his leash and growled fearsomely, making the females in the growing crowd

scream with fear and the men step back a pace.
The bells on his cap tinkled wildly.

The fool laughed and pranced around Gorkel,
kicking out but not quite touching him. "Fret not,
fair maids. 'Tis a brute, and ugly as the devil's
own kin, but he's a gentle monster and he'll do
as I bid him. Hark now, yon comely maid with
the soft smile, what wish you to have the creature
do?"

The girl, Glenda by name and pert by nature,
angled forward, preening in the center of all
attention, and sang out, "I wish him to dance. A
jig. And I want him to raise his monstrous legs
high."

Crooky hissed between his teeth, "Canst thou
jig for the maid, Gorkel?"

Gorkel never let his wide grin slip. His expression vacuous, his eyes blank, he began to hop
and jump. He ponderously raised one leg and
then the other and clambered about gracelessly.
Quickly Crooky began to sing and clap his hands
to a beat Gorkel didn't need. His eyes scanned
the crowd as he bellowed as loudly as he could:

All come to see the beastie prance
He'll cavort and jump, he'll do a wild dance
He's a heathen and a savage, ugly and black,
But withal he's merry, no matter his lack.

Crooky wanted to shout with relief when he
saw Edmund slip between two men and gape at
Gorkel. The boy was ragged and bruised and
filthy, but at the sight of him and Gorkel, he
looked happy as a young stoat, his eyes gleaming.
Thank St. Andrew that he was alive. Where was
the mistress? Was she imprisoned? Had Sir Walter

harmed her? Crooky's blood ran cold at the thought.

Crooky jingled Gorkel's chain, and he ceased his clumsy movements and stood quietly beside the fool, breathing hard and still grinning his frightening grin. He eyed Edmund and nodded, his eyes holding a warning. "Ah," yelled Crooky suddenly, "methinks I see another fair wench. A big fair wench with enough hair on her head to stuff a mattress! Come hither, fair maid, and let my gargoyle behold your beauty. He'll not touch you, but let him behold what God created after he made a monster."

Philippa's heart was pounding madly. She'd watched Gorkel do his dance, not at first recognizing him in his wildly colorful and patched garments, the fool's cap on his head and the mangy beard that covered his jaws. It had been Crooky's bellowing verses that had brought her, nearly running, to the inner bailey. Dienwald was here, close, thank God. And she saw Edmund, filthy but well-looking, and quite alive, thank God yet again. "I come," she called out, voice filled with humor. "Let the monster gawk at the fair wench."

She picked up her skirts and raced toward them. She saw Crooky's relieved smile stiffen and go flat. She didn't understand. She drew to a halt, thinking frantically. "I am here. I bid you good morrow, monster." She curtsied. "Behold me, a maid who frets and who wishes for the moon but sees naught but a melting sun that holds her in bondage and gives her to chaff endlessly."

Crooky beheld her closely, all the while Gorkel loped in a clumsy gait around her, stroking his big bearded jaw.

She was beautiful, Crooky thought, finely dressed as a maid should be, as a *beloved* maid should be. She was no prisoner, Sir Walter no warden. Had he rescued her at her wish? He thought through her words, elegant words that twisted and intertwined about themselves. Had she meant that she wanted to escape her cousin? Crooky knew the matter wasn't his to decide. Since his tenth year, when the tree had broken and fallen on him, he knew that he wouldn't survive unless it was by his wits. He learned that his memory was his strength. He now committed her every word to his memory.

"Well, lovely maid," he said after a moment, "God grant you no ingratitude or bitter wrongs. If you will seek the moon, I will tell you that like the sun, the moon must hide in its hour, then burst forth, when least expected, to glow fairly yet in stark truth upon the face that seeks it forth. The moon awaits, maid, ever close as its habit, waits till tide and time issue it out."

"What is this, cousin? A cripple and a beast to be held by its leash?"

Philippa smiled at Walter, beckoning him to her side. "Aye, Walter, a team that brings shrewd humor and light laughter to Crandall. The little crooked one here tells me of the moon and the sun and how each must await its turn, and the monster there, he bellows and dances for all your fair maids."

Walter cared not a whit for the two who stood facing him. "If they please you, dearest heart, then so let them frolic and rattle their tongues to rhymes that bring good cheer."

Crooky said loudly, "Fair and hardy maid, what wish you for Gorkel the Hideous to do?"

"Why, I believe I wish to write him a love poem, not rhymed, for I have not your talent, but one to tell of beauty and love that ravaged the heart. What say you, beast? Wish you to have a love poem from me?"

Gorkel scratched his armpit, and Crooky, yanking hard at his leash, yelled, "Will you, monster? Nod aye, beast!"

Gorkel nodded and bellowed, and the crowd cheered.

Philippa nodded. "I shall hie me to my paper and write the poem for the monster. Give the crowd more laughter, then."

"I don't understand you," Walter said, and he sounded impatient and fretful.

"I amuse myself, Walter, as the beast has amused me. It pleases you not?"

She gave him that sweet, utterly diffident look that made him feel more powerful than a Palatine prince. It was on the tip of his tongue to tell her to write an immense tome, but he changed his mind. He mustn't give in to her female whims each and every time. "It doesn't please me this time, sweetling. Fret not." And before he left her, he raised his hand and lightly touched her cheek. As she looked at him, her smile frozen in place, his fingers fell to her throat, then to her breast, and before all of his people, he caressed her with his fingertips. He laughed and strode away.

Near Crandall Keep

"Tell me, and be quick about it."

Crooky, silent for once, looked at his master, uncertain how to begin.

"Did you see Edmund? The wench?"

"Aye, they're both alive," Gorkel said as he pulled off his belled cap. "The young master was dirty, his clothes rags, but he looked healthy."

"And the mistress?"

"She was finely garbed," Crooky said, looking over Dienwald's right shoulder. "Very finely garbed, a beautifully plumed peacock, a princess."

Dienwald felt his gut cramp. She'd betrayed him, damn her, betrayed him and stolen his son.

"Tell me everything. Leave nothing out or I'll kick in your ribs."

And Crooky related everything that had occurred. He recited faithfully what Philippa had said to him and to Gorkel. He paused, then ended, "She is no prisoner, at least it appeared not so. Sir Walter kissed her in full view of his people, and his hand caressed her breast."

Dienwald saw red and his fists bunched in savage fury. What had he expected, anyway? The wench had fled him, and that was that. "Tell me again her words." After Crooky had once more recited them, he said, "What meant she about the moon—am I the moon, silent and hidden, then bursting and malignant in her face? Bah! It makes no sense, the wench was playing with you, turning your own rhymes back on you, mocking you."

"She asked Sir Walter if she could pen a love poem to Gorkel, but he refused her. Mayhap she would have written of her plight, master."

Dienwald cursed with specific relish, saying in disgust, "She fooled you yet again! She would have penned her request for me to keep away, else she'd see Edmund hurt!"

Gorkel said, "Nay, master."

"What know you of anything!"

"Why did she keep the boy with her?"

"For protection, fool, what else? She isn't stupid, after all, for all that she's a female." He shook his fist in disgust at both of them, ignored his other men who looked ready to speak their opinions, and strode away from them all, disappearing into the maze of maple trees.

"He is sorely tried," Galen said, shaking his head. "He knows not what to think."

"The mistress wants rescuing," said Crooky, "despite all the plumage and display."

"And the boy," Gorkel added. "I fear what that whoreson will do to the boy, for he sorely hates the father."

17

Crandall Keep

Late that night Philippa lay in her bed thinking furiously, an occupation that hadn't paled since Walter had brought her to Crandall. She thought of her excitement, her hope, when she'd burst into the inner bailey to see Gorkel cavorting about like a mad buffoon and Crooky twirling Gorkel's leash while singing at the top of his lungs. But what good had any of it done? Her attempt to tell Crooky of her plight, her plea to write Gorkel a love poem, all had been dashed when Walter had shown his possession of her in front of everyone by kissing her and caressing her breast. Crooky would tell Dienwald, of a certainty. But still they would attempt a rescue, if not for her, then for Edmund. But how? What could Dienwald do? He couldn't very well storm Crandall Keep. Walter would kill Edmund without blinking an eye. No, Dienwald would use guile and cunning; she doubted not that he would succeed, but still, the thought of him being hurt terrified her. She knew well enough that Walter would kill him if but given a chance.

She had to do something, and she had to do it early on the morrow. She fell asleep, and her dreams, oddly enough, were of her first riding lessons at six years old on a mare named Cottie, a gentle animal Bernice had urged over a fence two years later, breaking the mare's leg.

Philippa came awake suddenly, tears still in her mind for the mare. She hadn't really heard anything, it was just a feeling that something wasn't right and she must pay attention now and wake up fully or she wouldn't like what happened to her.

Slowly, very slowly, Philippa turned her head toward the door. Walter had locked it as usual when he'd left her earlier, yet a key was turning in the lock and the door was opening slowly but surely.

It had to be Walter. He'd tired of waiting. He'd come to ravish her and be done with it. He didn't play the besotted swain very well.

So be it, Philippa thought, her muscles flexing to make her ready. She didn't move, just thought of what she would do to him to protect herself. She would fight him, and at the very least she would hurt him badly. She still wore her shift, one of soft linen that came to her thighs and left her arms bare. She wished now she had on every article of clothing Walter had given her, to make his task of ravishing her all the more difficult. She listened and strained her eyes toward the door.

Walter wasn't making any noise. Why? That made no particular sense. He wouldn't care, would he? He wouldn't care if she screamed or yelled. His men would do naught to help her.

The door widened, making no sound, the hinges not even creaking. From the dim light in the passage without, Philippa could at last make out the outline of the person.

It wasn't Walter. It was a woman.

Philippa didn't act immediately, as her nature urged her to. No, she held herself perfectly still, waiting to see what the woman would do, waiting to see what the woman wanted. Perhaps she wanted to free her. But how had the woman gotten the key to her chamber?

From Walter, of course. Walter was far too careful, far too possessive a man to allow others to keep something as important as the key to her chamber. So the woman must know him very well, must know him intimately. . . . Philippa gathered herself together and waited.

The woman was creeping across the narrow chamber now, and Philippa saw that she held a knife in her raised hand. The woman had come to kill her, not free her.

Philippa's astonishment was replaced by rage, and she jumped to her feet, yelling at the top of her lungs, "What do you want? Get away from me! Help! *A moi!* Walter . . . *A moi!*"

The woman lunged at her, extending her arm, bringing the knife down toward her chest. Philippa grabbed the woman's wrist, wrenching her arm back, but the woman was stronger than her meager inches would indicate. She was panting, gasping, fury making her as strong as Philippa, and she said, her voice vicious, filled with hatred,

"You damnable slut! You devil's spawn! You'll not have him! Do you hear me? Nay, never! I'll kill you!" And she jerked away from Philippa, her breasts heaving, staring at Philippa with hatred. Philippa slowly backed away from the furious woman and that very sharp knife.

She held up her hand in supplication. "Who are you? I've done nothing to you. What are you talking about? You're mad, wanting to kill me for no reason!"

"No reason!" the woman hissed, the words so harsh that spittle flew out of her mouth. "You damnable trollop, Walter is mine, only mine, and he'll stay mine. You'll not get him. He'll not wed you, no matter what you bring him! He loves me, wants me more than all the filthy riches you would bring him!"

But I wouldn't bring him anything, Philippa started to say, just as the woman lunged again, bringing the knife down in a brutal arc, sure and fast, and Philippa whirled to the side, away from the mad-dened woman, but she wasn't fast enough and she felt the tip of the knife slice through the flesh of her upper arm. She felt the coldness of it, then a quick numbness.

"You won't escape me, whore!"

Philippa, knowing there was no choice now, jerked about and struck out, backhanding the woman, her palm flat, ringing hard against her cheek. The woman yelled in pain and rage but didn't falter. She flew toward Philippa, the knife extended to the fullest.

Philippa saw the knife coming into her heart, stabbing deep, killing her, before she'd known what it was to really live, to love and be loved, and she whispered, "Dienwald . . ."

She could hear the air hiss as the knife sliced through it, and she dashed frantically toward the open door and into the arms of Walter de Grasse.

"What in God's name goes on here?"

Walter was shaking Philippa hard until he saw the blood flowing from her upper arm. He paled in the dim light, not wanting to credit it. Then he stared at the woman, half-crouched, the bloody knife dangling in her hand, and he whispered, "Britta . . . oh, no, why?" He pushed Philippa away from him and was at the woman's side, lifting her up, pulling her against him.

"Britta?"

She shook her head, her breath coming in painful gasps, her huge breasts heaving.

"She tried to kill me," Philippa said, watching with benumbed fascination as he caressed the woman. "Who is she? Why does she want me dead?"

She watched, silent now, as pain crossed Walter's face and it whitened, and she understood at last that this was the woman whose garments she wore, this was the woman who was her cousin's mistress, a woman who, incredibly, loved her cousin, and who couldn't, perforce, abide her. Philippa's mind clogged and she could but stare silently as Walter held the woman even more tightly, clutching her against him, speaking softly, so softly that Philippa couldn't make out his words.

Without further hesitation Philippa picked up a small three-legged stool, held it high over her head, and brought it down with all her strength on Walter's head. The woman cried out as Walter slumped against her, bearing her to the floor with his weight.

"Don't yell, you stupid fool!" Philippa hissed at the woman. "Just stay where you are and hold your peace and your lover. I'm leaving you and him and this cursed keep forever. He's yours until the devil takes him." Before Britta could push her lover off her, Philippa had grabbed the knife from her hand and jerked the keys from the pocket in her tunic.

"Just be quiet, you silly bitch, if you want him here and me gone!"

Philippa grabbed her gown and pulled it over her head even as she dashed toward the door. She locked it, then froze on the spot. Just around the corner, not three feet from where she stood, she heard two men in argument.

"I'll tell ye, thass trouble! I heard them wenches yelling and t' master runs in."

"Leave t' master be an' get back to yer bed."

"Oh, aye, there's trouble and it's yer ears he'll slice off, that, or he'll take his whip to yer back."

"Ye go back and I'll look."

Philippa flattened herself against the cold stone wall. She heard the one man still grumbling as he shuffled away. As for the other man, in the next instant he came around the corner to see a wild-eyed female with a knife in her hand and blood running in rivulets down her arm. He had time only to suck in his breath before the knife handle slammed into his temple and he crashed to the floor.

Slowly Philippa got enough nerve to peer around the corner. She saw sleeping men and women spread over the floor in the hall, and snores rose to the blackened rafters above. She crept as quietly as she could, inching slowly along the wall toward the large oak doors. Slowly, ever so slowly, she moved, knowing at any second a man or woman could rise up and shriek at her and it would be all over and perhaps Walter would kill her if his mistress didn't do it first. A dog suddenly appeared from nowhere and sniffed at her bare feet.

She didn't move, her heart pounding, letting the dog tire of her scent, then move on, praying the animal wouldn't bark. Then, without warning, she felt a spurt of pain in her arm and looked at it. So much blood, and it was hers. She had to slow it or she would faint. She slipped outside into the inner bailey and looked heavenward. There was no moon this night, and the sky was overcast, with no stars, no light whatsoever. She flattened herself against the wooden railing and ripped off a goodly section of the lower part of the gown. She wrapped it around her arm, using her teeth to tie the knot tightly. She felt the pain, felt it deeply, but it didn't matter. She had to find Edmund and they had to escape this wretched keep. She couldn't allow the wound to slow her. She had to be strong.

Fortune turned, and Philippa found Edmund close to the stable door, atop a heap of hay, sleeping on his side, his legs drawn up to his chest, his face resting on his folded hands. Philippa knelt beside him. "Edmund, love, come wake up." She shook him gently, ready to slap her hand over his mouth if he awoke afraid and cried out.

But Edmund awoke quickly and completely and simply stared up at her. "Philippa?"

"Aye, I'm here, and now we must leave. We'll need horses, Edmund. What think you?"

"Is my father here to save us?"

Philippa shook her head. "No, 'tis just us, but we can do it. Now, about those horses."

Edmund scrambled to his feet, excitement and a goodly dose of fear churning in his belly, and he grinned up at her. Then he was thoughtful, and Philippa waited. "We need to croak the two stable lads. We need—"

Philippa raised the knife handle. "It works," she said.

Edmund's eyes glistened and Philippa wondered if all men were born with the battle cry of war in their blood, with the love of violence and battle bred into their bones. "Show me where they are and then I'll . . ." She paused, then added, "You get the horses, Edmund. Pick well, for they must carry us to your father. He awaits out there somewhere."

"He can't be far away," Edmund said. "But we will come to him and not have to lie like helpless babes for him to rescue us. There is a difficulty, though, Philippa. I can't get the horses for us."

She stared down at him and saw the chain and thick leather manacle clamped about his right ankle. Those miserable whoresons! She wanted to yell in rage, but she said calmly, "Who has the key to that thing?"

"One of the stable lads you're going to croak," he said, and gave her an impudent smile.

They were good together, Philippa thought with surprised pleasure a few minutes later. She'd quickly found the key and released Edmund. She hadn't even paused before coshing the two stable lads on the head. They'd probably given Edmund his bruises, the malignant little brutes, and tethered him like an animal. No, she had no regrets that the both of them would have vile head pains on the morrow.

Edmund had brought out Daisy and the destrier that belonged to Walter. Should she dare? she wondered, then tossed her head. She dared. Her arm was paining fiercely now, and they weren't yet out of Crandall. She couldn't succumb to the pain, not yet, not for a very long while.

Edmund held the reins of the two horses, staying back in the shadows whilst Philippa sauntered like a whore in full heat and in need of coin toward the one guard who stood in a near-stupor near Crandall's gates. Three other sentries were patrolling, but they were distant now. She'd watched them, counting.

"Ho! Who are . . . ? Why, 'tis Sir Walter's mistress! What want you? Wh—"

She poked out her breasts and threw her arms around the man. He gaped and gawked and quickly grabbed her buttocks in his big hands, dropping his sword to fill his hands with her, and Philippa whipped out the knife and, leaning back, slammed the handle down on his head. He looked at her in mournful surprise but didn't fall. "You shouldn't ought to a done that," he said, and brought his hands up to her throat. He squeezed, saying all the while, "Ye're a handful, wench, but I'll show ye not to play wi' me." He squeezed harder and harder, and Philippa saw the world blackening before her eyes as the knife dropped from her slack fingers.

Then, as if from afar, she heard a voice saying, "You're a bloody coward, hurting a female like that . . . you whoreson, stupid lout with a mother who slept with infidels . . ." The fingers left her throat and she sagged to her knees, clutching her throat, gulping in air. She looked up to see the man turning, as if in a dream, turning toward Edmund, but Edmund was astride Daisy, and he was higher than the guard and brought a thick metal spade down as hard as he could on the guard's head. Philippa watched the man stare up at Edmund and shake his head as if to clear it. Then he made a small sound in his throat and fell in a heap to the ground.

Philippa staggered to her feet, grabbing the knife. Her throat felt on fire, and she croaked out, "Excellent, Edmund. Now we must go, quickly. The sentries will be returning in but moments now."

She raced to the keep gates and jerked at the thick beam levered from side to side of the large gate. It was heavy and she was getting weaker by the moment. She cursed and heaved, and finally the beam began to ease slowly upward until finally she managed to bring it fully vertical. "Now," she whispered, and pushed the gate open.

Philippa quickly mounted, grunting with effort, for there was no saddle and her right arm was now nearly useless. Suddenly she felt Edmund heaving her up, and she landed facedown against the destrier's neck, panting with exertion and pain.

Then Edmund was astride Daisy again and she cried, "Away, Edmund!"

The destrier was huge and fast and mean, and he quickly ate distance from Crandall. They needed to be fast. Philippa could imagine that Walter was already after them, unless she'd hit him so very hard that he was still unconscious and unable to give orders. The destrier pulled away even further, quickly outstripping Daisy. Philippa tried to pull him back, but her one strong hand wasn't enough. The destrier was in control.

"Edmund!" She turned back, her hair flying madly in her face.

"Hold, Philippa. I'm coming!"

But it wasn't Edmund who stopped the great destrier. It was a man flying out of the darkness astride a huge stallion, his head bare, his face averted, all his attention on the frantically galloping horse.

Other men appeared, shouting out, and she heard Edmund yell, "Father! Father, quickly, help Philippa!"

And she felt the reins jerked from her hand and then the destrier lurched up on his hind legs, whinnying frantically, his front hooves flailing, and she hard Dienwald's voice, soothing, calming the frenzied animal.

Then it was over and Philippa was weaving on the horse's back, her gown torn and pulled to her thighs, and she smiled at the man who turned to face her.

"The horse was maddened because of my smell," Philippa said, just content to stare at his face.

"You make no sense, wench."

"The blood . . . the smell of blood," she said. "It maddens animals to smell a human's blood." She slumped forward against the animal's neck. Before she fell unconscious, his arms were around her, drawing her close, and she sighed deeply, content now to give it up.

The burning pain brought her back. She tried to jerk away from it, cursing it in her mind, begging the pain to release her for just a few minutes longer, just a moment longer, but it was there and it was worse and she moaned and opened her eyes.

"Hold still."

She focused on Dienwald, leaning over her. He wasn't looking at her face, but looking grimly down at her arm. "Hello," she said. "I'm glad to see you. We knew you had to be close."

"Hold still and keep your tongue behind your teeth."

But she couldn't. There was too much to be said, too much to be explained. "Am I going to die?"

"Of course you're not going to die, you heedless wench!"

"Is Edmund all right?"

"Yes. Now, be quiet, you try me sorely with your babble."

"I fainted, I suppose, and I've never before fainted in my whole life. I was scared until I saw you, and then it was all right."

"Be still. Why is your voice so rough?"

"The guard tried to strangle me after I struck him with the knife handle. His head was powerfully hard, but Edmund told him his mother bedded infidels to get his attention from me, and then hit him with a spade and he finally fell. We got away from him, we got away from all of them. I counted the minutes, you know, and the other sentries were elsewhere. You knew we were at Crandall. Silken reached you safely."

"Aye, be quiet now."

"I prayed he would reach you. It was our only hope. Walter was stupid—he gave Silken time to outrun his men. I knew he would reach you, knew you would come."

"Wench, shut your irritating mouth."

"Walter's mistress tried to kill me, you know. Isn't that strange? And she kept screaming that she didn't care that I would bring him riches, 'twas she who would have him. I gave him to her freely, and I told her that. I also wanted to tell her that there were no riches, nay, not even a single coin. And he came in when I yelled my head off and he saw the blood on my arm, yet he went to her and held her and her name was Britta and it was her clothes he'd given me to wear. I struck him with a stool and he went down like a stone. It was a wonderful sound and he pinned the woman beneath him. I got her knife and the keys and locked them in."

"Philippa, you're weak from loss of blood and you're babbling. Now, be still."

"She has huge breasts," Philippa said, then closed her eyes at a particularly sharp jab in her arm. "Walter had given me her clothes and they were much too short for me and much too loose in the chest. Her breasts are of a mighty size. Gorkel and Crooky were wondrous funny." Dienwald drew in a deep breath at that moment and poured ale over the wound. Philippa lurched up, crying out softly, then fell back unconscious.

Dienwald stilled for a moment, then quickly placed his palm over her heart. The beat was slow and steady. He bound up her arm, then turned to see Northbert's legs. He didn't rise, just looked up at his man and said, "She's unconscious again, but the wound is clean, and if there is no poisoning, she will be all right."

Northbert nodded. "Master Edmund is overexcited, master, his tongue rattling about. Gorkel told him to go to sleep, but he can't close his mouth."

"She was the same."

Crooky hobbled up then. "The mistress wasn't a betrayer wi' her cousin, master."

"I suppose she wasn't, yet it strikes an odd chord."

"Aye, it does," said Gorkel in his low, terrifying rumble. "The boy refuses to sleep until he sees that the mistress is all right."

Dienwald looked surprised at that. "He *what*? Oh, the devil! Nothing is aright here, nothing! I let the two of them out of my sight for the space of a week, and everything goes topsy turvy. Bring Edmund and let him see the wench, I don't care."

Gorkel and Crooky exchanged looks, and Northbert merely shrugged.

Edmund knelt next to Philippa, and said softly as he stared down at her face, "She was very angry when she saw the manacle around my ankle. Her face turned all red and her hands shook. She'll be all right, truly?"

"Aye, she's too hardy to let this bring her down," Dienwald said. "You must sleep now, Edmund. At dawn we'll ride."

"You're not worried that the whoreson will come upon us tonight?"

His father grinned. "He'd never find us in this dark. There's not even a single star to guide him."

It was the middle of the night when Philippa awoke again. Her arm hurt, but not too badly. She was surrounded by darkness, which she'd become accustomed to in the small chamber at Crandall, but this was different. Sweet air touched her face and filled her nostrils, and she could hear the rustle of tree leaves in the gentle night breezes, and the deep breathing of a man. She opened her eyes and saw Dienwald stretched out next to her, his hand holding her wrist. He was snoring lightly.

She smiled and said, "Edmund and I escaped. Are you not pleased?"

His hand on her wrist tightened. Dienwald was dreaming of an explicitly passionate scene in which Philippa was naked, lying pliant in his arms, her hand was stroking down his belly, closing around his swelled rod and she was kissing him, her tongue thrust deep in his mouth and she was moaning as she kissed him and her fingers were caressing him and . . .

"Are you not pleased?"

He opened his eyes, startled, disoriented, and saw her beside him, not naked as he'd believed, but lying on her back, a blanket pulled to her waist. She was speaking of pleasure, but a pleasure different from the one of his dream. Philippa was really there with him, and he hurt with need for her, hurt with the urgency of it, and the reality melded into his dream and he didn't question it or the dark night or her beside him on the floor of a copse of maple trees.

"Philippa . . ." he said, his voice low as he rolled over until he half-covered her with his body.

"I'm so glad to see you, Dienwald," she said, and raised her hand to stroke his hair, to touch his jaw, his mouth. His tongue stroked over her finger, and she shivered. "Dienwald," she said again, and parted her lips, staring up at him as if he were the only man on earth, and she was so close to him, but a breath away from his mouth, and he couldn't bear it and leaned down and kissed her, gently at first, then more deeply because it was what she wanted and what he'd done in his dream, yet now the dream was real and his tongue was stroking her mouth. He didn't think, didn't consider his actions. He wanted her, wanted her more than he ever had.

He'd been terrified that Walter would kill her, and at the same time he'd hated her because she had perhaps betrayed him. He couldn't have borne that, but now she was here and it was all that mattered, and she was his at last.

The night was still and she was here, beneath him, and she wanted him. Her dream was his, and they were together. He stroked her face with urgent fingers, easing himself over her. He felt her part her legs, and he lay between them, hard against her woman's flesh, and she was making soft noises deep in her throat and her arm was around his neck, pulling him down, bringing him closer and closer.

She'd been hurt. God, she'd been hurt. Dienwald, his senses restored for an instant, drew back, saying, "Philippa, your arm, I can't hurt you. If your arm . . ."

She simply smiled up at him and said, "I will hurt more if you leave me. Don't leave me now. Please, Dienwald, debauch me. I've wanted you to for so long."

He laughed, he couldn't help himself. Then his laugh turned to pain as she said, "I didn't want to die, because if I did I would never have you, never know what it was like to have you come inside me."

He groaned now, her words burning deep, and he was drawn back into the intense feelings that

were conquering all of him. But he realized even
in his delirious state that she was a maid and he
didn't want to hurt her more than was necessary.
He saw his sex tearing through her maidenhead,
and he moaned with the excitement of it, the triumph in claiming her, of possessing her, finally.
He eased himself up until he grasped the hem of
her gown, and he pulled it up and felt her naked
flesh beneath his hand. Until he reached her
upper thighs. She wore a shift, and it stymied
him for a moment, for in his dream she'd been
freely naked and open for him. He worked in
growing impatience until she was naked to the
waist, then came over her again, wanting only to
feel her body against his, but he couldn't, for he
was still dressed. He cursed, softly and foully,
and came up onto his knees.

She was watching him, her eyes large and vivid
as he clumsily jerked off his tunic, his cross garters, his hose, and then he was finally naked and
she found him beautiful.

He was covering her again, his male flesh
against her, and she was kissing him wildly, her
tongue probing until she found his. He held her
head between his hands and kissed her face, his
words fast and frantic between kisses, telling her
of his need for her, how he loved the feel of her,
how he was happy she was still a maid and he
would be easy with her, and how he wanted to
come into her and meld into her flesh and stay
there even as he spilled his seed in her.

She watched his face as he looked down at her,
and she felt his fingers parting her flesh, then his
sex pressing against her.

He threw back his head, his eyes closed. "Don't
move," he said, and his voice trembled, for he

was coming very slowly into her, and despite his instruction, she was lifting her hips for him, wanting to feel all of him, now, this very moment. He came deeper and she whimpered as he stretched her and it hurt, but it was what she wanted because he was what she wanted. She could feel him so exquisitely, the hard smoothness of his member easing so gently, just a bit of himself at a time, pressing into her.

In the next instant he felt her maidenhead stretched against his sex. "Philippa," he said, his eyes on her face, "look at me!" He had wanted to be gentle at this moment, but he found he could not. He thrust deep. She cried out at the wrenching tear inside her. He fell over her, his mouth covering hers, and he soothed her with his tongue, even as he held himself still and deep inside her, saying again and again, "No more pain, my sweet Philippa, no more. Hold me and feel me and let me lie deep inside you. 'Tis where I belong."

Then slowly he began to move, his breath soft and warm against her mouth. "Nay, love, accept me now and hold me tight inside you. Aye, that's it, lift your hips for me and bring me deeper . . . ah, Philippa . . . no, don't move, I can't bear it, and—"

She watched his beloved face distort with the pain of his need, and he was heaving, delving deep, his breath sharp and raw and her body burned as he thrust again and again, his hands drawing her up to meet him. She couldn't help herself and cried out but he couldn't stop, wouldn't stop. He threw back his head and she felt his release, felt the wetness of his seed as he emptied himself deep inside her body.

He was limp and weak, torpid in mind and drained in body, and he came over her and she welcomed his weight and he lay with his head beside hers and he was still deep within her.

He said, his voice echoing from the dream, "I'm sorry, Philippa. I wanted you badly. Hold still and the pain will fade."

Philippa regained her breath and her equilibrium. He was still inside her but there was only stinging now, not the tearing pain of before. It was strange, this lovemaking. She'd wanted him, very much, felt desire for him that overcame the pain in her arm, that, actually, made the pain as nothing, and she'd been whipped about with wild, urgent feelings, wanting to touch him, feel him, urge him to come to her, but the incredible feelings had fallen away when he'd come into her and ridden her so wildly. She'd been left stunned, bewildered, and hurting.

Not hurting now, she thought, smiling as she lightly stroked her hand over his naked back. His flesh was smooth and warm and she felt the muscle beneath and she said quietly, "I love you." And she said it again and again and she knew he didn't hear her for he slept soundly. She felt his member sliding out of her, and the wet of his seed and her wetness as well, she supposed.

She kissed his ear and settled herself beneath his weight. Soon she slept.

It was nearly dawn when Dienwald opened his eyes and came abruptly and horrifyingly awake. He was lying naked, half covering Philippa and he was cold and shivering in the night air, and his rod was swelled again and pressing against her. He cursed his randy sex, and gently and

slowly eased himself off her, his mind still not
accepting what had happened, for the dream was
still strong in his mind, and it had become more,
that vivid dream. He shook his head. What he'd
done he'd done and it hadn't been a dream, but
it had been in the dark of the night and he'd
cleanly lost his wits. The early morning in the
copse was an eerie grey and thick white mist hovered overhead. He could see her clearly though,
her beautiful body bare from the waist down and
her parted legs, parted for him when he pushed
them apart to come over her, and there was her
virgin's blood mixed with his man's seed smeared
on her thighs, and he closed his eyes and
swallowed.

He'd done himself in. He cursed softly, then
smiled, feeling yet again the tightness of her, her
urging hand, how she'd lifted her hips to him,
how he'd driven into the depths of her, touching
her womb. He wouldn't worry about it now. He
looked down at her and wanted her again, powerfully, but he saw her wounded arm and the
wound he himself had inflicted inside her. He
would wait. He pulled a blanket over both of
them and pulled Philippa into his arms. He would
think soon, once the sun was shining down on
his face, warming his brain. He would think of
something, he would save himself and somehow
he would at the same time protect her from dishonor. How, he didn't know, but an idea would
come to him; it was still very early, his brain
foggy with sleep. He slept again, holding her
close, breathing in the scent that was uniquely
hers, but only for a few moments.

He was brought painfully and abruptly to his
senses by his son's outraged voice.

"Father!"

Dienwald opened an eye and saw Edmund standing over him and Philippa, his hands on his narrow hips, his eyes wide and disapproving.

"Father, you've taken Philippa."

"Well, perhaps . . . but perhaps not. Perhaps I am simply holding her, for she is hurt, Edmund—aye, very hurt and cold in the night and—"

"I won't allow you to dishonor her. You are holding her too close to just warm her, Father. And just look at her! She's hurt and yet she's asleep and she's smiling!"

Dienwald, startled, looked at the still-sleeping Philippa. She *was* smiling, her lips slightly parted, and the sight made him feel wonderful.

"Edmund, get you gone for a time. I am weary and the wench here will awaken soon and I must think—"

"You will wed her, Father. Aye, you must wed her. You've no choice now."

Dienwald looked with horror at his son and forgot that his men were all within hearing distance. "Wed her! God grant me death instead. 'Tis possible that she betrayed me, Edmund, aye, that she told her cousin to save her from me and took you as a hostage."

Edmund just shook his head and looked disgusted.

"You don't even *like* her! She bullies you and corrects your every word. You call her witch and maypole and you stick out your tongue at her and—"

"Father," Edmund said with great patience, "Philippa is a lady and you have taken her virtue. You must wed her."

Dienwald cursed and looked back down at Philippa. She was awake and staring up at him, and there where tears in her eyes.

18

"Why are you crying? For God's sake, cease your wailing this minute! I hate a woman's tears. Stop it, wench. Do you hear me?"

"She's not making a sound," Edmund said, peering down at Philippa.

Dienwald made no reply to this, simply kept staring down at Philippa.

Her tears didn't immediately do his bidding, and he turned further onto his side and leaned over her, his nose nearly touching hers. "Why are you crying? Did you hear Edmund and me, curse the boy's interfering habits?"

She shook her head and wiped her eyes with the back of her hand.

"Then why are you crying?"

"My arm hurts."

"Oh." Dienwald frowned at that. Her revelation was believable, yet somehow he felt insulted, and perversely he said, "Well, did you hear what my son demanded we do?"

Philippa lay on her back, looking up at the man she'd willingly given her innocence to during the night. His jaw was dark with whiskers, his hair tousled, and his naked chest made her heartbeat quicken. He looked beautiful and harried and vastly annoyed. He also looked worried, hopefully about her, which pleased her.

She smiled up at him then and raised her hand to touch his cheek. He froze, then jerked back.

"You're besotted," he said, his voice low, "and you've no reason to be. For God's sake, wench, I took your maidenhead but three hours ago, and you're smiling at me as if I'd just conferred the world and all its riches upon you. You got no pleasure from our coupling, I hurt you, and . . . ah, Edmund, you are still here, then?"

"Will you marry Philippa?"

"You know but one song, and its words more tedious than Crooky's. By St. Anne's knees, boy, the wench couldn't wish to wed with me, for—"

That was such an obvious falsehood that Philippa laughed. "Good morrow, Master Edmund," she said, facing him for the first time, her tears dry now.

The boy grinned down at her. "We must soon be on our way back to St. Erth," he said. "Northbert sent me to awaken you. *Both* of you," he added, meaning dripping from his voice. "Philippa, does your arm pain you sorely?"

She shook her head. "Nay, 'tis bearable, and thus so am I, unlike your father here, who must bring himself to the morning with foul words."

Dienwald said nothing, merely stared off into

the thick maple trees. "Go, Edmund, and strive to keep your opinions beneath your tongue."

Edmund frowned down at his father. "We are close to Crandall. Sir Walter could come this very very soon. Shouldn't we—"

Dienwald's expression changed suddenly. It was austere now, cold and forbidding, his eyes narrowed, and he said very softly, in such a deadly voice that Philippa could but stare at him, "I want the whoreson to come out from the safety of his walls. I owe him much, and the time has come to repay the debt. I've men carefully watching the road from Crandall. Aye, I want the bastard to come after you and Philippa, and 'tis I who will greet him."

Edmund grinned suddenly. "But Philippa struck him hard, Father. Perhaps he still lies in a heap."

Dienwald's expression lost its cruelty and he shook his head. "We'll see, but I doubt it. We will leave soon, Edmund, for St. Erth. The wench here needs to rest, and I can't very well wed her here in a forest. Search out Northbert and tell him that if Sir Walter hasn't shown his weedy hide within the next hour, we'll ride to St. Erth."

Edmund, swaggering with importance, took his leave. Dienwald stared after him, shaking his head, seemingly all thoughts of Sir Walter and his hatred of the man gone from his mind, for he said to Philippa, "I can't believe that my own son, a boy of good sense, would yell at me, and carp and bellow."

Philippa said nothing to that, and Dienwald, in a spate of ill-humor, flung back the blanket and jumped to his feet. For a moment it appeared he didn't realize he was naked, but not for a single instant was Philippa unaware of it. She stared at him in the gray light of dawn and was pleased with what she saw, very pleased. Before, she'd admired him, but this morning, now that she understood how men used their bodies to attach themselves to women . . . well, now she had a different way of looking at him, a softer way, a more intimate way.

He scratched his belly, stretched, looked down at himself and saw her blood on his member. He cursed then turned to frown down at her. "Open your legs."

"What?"

"Open your legs," he repeated, then dropped down to his knees beside her. He pulled the blanket to her ankles, then without asking her again, pulled her shift to her waist and pried her thighs open. His seed and her maiden's blood were on her inner thighs. Soft flesh, he saw, very soft, and he wanted to touch her, to ease his finger into her, feel her tighten about him. Curse her and curse his member that hadn't the good sense to remain calm and uninterested. Well, soon he wouldn't have to deny himself. He could have her again and again, as much as he wished and whenever he wished it until his member stayed quiet in exhaustion and his heartbeat stayed slow and steady. He drew in his breath and said, "By St. Peter's toes, there's no choice for me now. We'll wed upon our return to St. Erth."

His duty done, at least in his mind, Dienwald rose again and began pulling on his clothes. He frowned and said, turning to look down at her, "Don't fret about the blood, Philippa, 'tis your virgin's blood and all females are so afflicted their first time with a man. It won't happen again. Now, pull down your clothes else I'll be tempted to think you wish my rod between your thighs again."

She thought it was a fine idea but jerked down her clothes. She could hear Dienwald's men moving about in the woods, very close to them. "Wouldn't you at least like me to tell you what happened at Crandall?"

"You did," he said shortly. "I couldn't force you to keep your woman's mouth closed last night and you babbled until you finally slept. I learned everything, finally. Are you very sore?"

"But I didn't get to sleep all that long, did I? You didn't wish me to! Sore where?"

He shook his head, giving her a sour look. "Nay, it wasn't all my doing. You wanted me and you had me, curse my man's weaknesses. Your soreness is in your female brain and between your female thighs. You are small, Philippa, at least inside you are." He paused a moment, frowning toward her. "I was dreaming about you, wench, empty-headed dreams they were, and then there you were, beside me, and holding out your arm to me, making me want to debauch you, and making all those whimpering noises in your throat—" He stopped, finished fastening his cross-garters and took his leave of her, not looking back.

"Well," Philippa said aloud as she slowly got to her feet. "He will wed me and he won't mind, once 'tis done." She could still see the appalled look on his face when his nine-year-old son had demanded that he marry her. Truth to tell, that had surprised her as much as it had Edmund's father.

The boy didn't seem to mind that she would be his stepmother. So be it. She clutched her arm and gently began to massage it. The pain was a steady throbbing now, but she could bear it. She looked down at herself and shook her head. Her single garment, the once beautiful yellow gown, was now fatally wrinkled, and rents parted its folds, material torn off to make a bandage for her wounded arm. But she had become so used to wearing rough clothing, even rags, that she gave it not much thought.

She was standing there wondering where she could go to relieve herself when Crooky appeared.

"God gi' you grace, mistress," he said, and sketched her a bow. "I hear from the lad that you will soon wed the master. 'Tis well done. I knew his lust for you would plant his body in his brain, and so it has. Strange that it struck him so swiftly and here in a wild forest, and with you hurt and all, but perhaps that's what pushed him, fear for you and seeing you hurt.

"But the master holds strong feelings for you and missed you, though he cursed you more than he sang of your bountiful beauty. Father Cramdle will speak wondrous fine words for your ceremony." He paused and added, "Don't mind the master. He'll get used to the idea once it seeps into that thick head of his. Aye, 'twill be fine." Crooky gave her another bow and took himself off. She was left standing alone in the small clearing.

Crooky's words had sounded to her like an attempt to convince himself. Well, perhaps Crooky's master didn't love her, but at the moment Philippa didn't care. But she did feel discomfort that she was nothing more than a waif, not a coin in her possession, her only clothes those Lady Kassia had sent her. Once she and Dienwald were wedded, she would dispatch a message to her father. He would have no choice but to send her possessions to her. She knew little about marriage contracts, dowries, and the like, but it seemed that there had been none for her, so how could her father complain? He'd had no intention of forming a grand alliance with another house of Beauchamp's stature. She no longer brooded on his reasons. Indeed, she no longer cared. Beauchamp seemed a lifetime ago, and surely that was another girl who'd had servants attending her every whim and clothes to suit her every mood. That girl had had a mother who didn't like her and a sister who carped constantly at her. Both the pleasant and the unpleasant were gone, forever.

St. Erth. She liked the sound of it on her tongue, the feel of it in her blood. St. Erth would be her home and Dienwald would be her husband. Her father could bellow until all Beauchamp trembled and his nose turned purple, but it wouldn't matter. Sir Walter had told her that her father had needed coin. She didn't believe it for a moment. However, she didn't know what to believe, so she left off all thought about it and consoled herself with the fact that even that repellent toad de Bridgport wouldn't want a bride who'd been bedded by another man. She smiled and sang a tuneless song as she prepared to return to her home with the man who would be her husband.

Her smile remained bright even when she faced all Dienwald's men, for they knew now that she would be the lady of St. Erth and there would be no more vile cursing from the master because he wanted to bed the maid. Now that he had, he would do what was right. She smiled until she was riding in front of Dienwald. She didn't turn to face him, not because she didn't want to but because his destrier, Philbo, took exception whenever she moved, cavorting and prancing, sending shafts of pain up her arm. The miles passed slowly and her arm throbbed.

"You cry again and I'll kick you off my horse. God's teeth, wench, you have me now. What more do you wish?"

"I'm not crying," she said, and stuffed her fist into her mouth.

"Then what are you doing? A new mime for Crooky's benefit? I suppose you'll tell me your arm pains you again?"

"Aye, it hurts. Your horse likes not my weight."

He snorted and stared over her shoulder between Philbo's twitching ears. "It's true you're a hardy wench and an armful. Still, Philbo hasn't bitten you—aye, methinks even he approves you for the mistress—so cease your plaints. You wanted me and now you've got me. I suppose your woman's ears beg to hear rhyming verses to the beauty of your eyes? That's why you're crying."

She shook her head.

" 'Tis too late to woo you, wench. You'll be a wife before you can congratulate yourself on your tactics, and then 'tis I who will show you that I am master at St. Erth and your master as well. I will do just as I please with you, and there will be none to gainsay me."

"You've always done precisely as you wished with me."

That was true, but Dienwald said nothing. His ill humor mounted and he sang out his own grievances. "Aye, I will wed you, and with naught to your name or your body save the clothes that Lady Kassia sent you. Your damnable father will likely come to St. Erth and demand my manhood for the insult to the de Beauchamps, since I am not of his importance or yours. You'll cry and carp and wail, and he'll lay siege, and soon—"

"Be quiet!"

Dienwald was so startled that he shut his mouth. Then he grinned at the back of her head. He fought against raising his hand to smooth down her wildly curling hair, and merely waited to see if she would continue. She did, and in a very loud voice, right in his face as she whirled about.

"I never cried, never, until I met you, you wretched knave! You are naught but an arrogant cockscomb!"

"Aye," he said mildly, and tightened his arms about her to keep her steady, "but you want to bed the cockscomb, so you cannot continue to carp so shrewishly.

"Should you prefer to be my mistress rather than my wife? Would you prefer being my chattel and my slave and my drudge?"

She jerked back against the circle of his arms and slammed her fist into his belly. Philbo snorted and reared on his hind legs. Dienwald grabbed Philippa, pulling her hard against him. He was laughing so hard that he nearly fell sideways, bringing her with him. He felt Northbert pushing against him, righting him once again.

"Take care, master," Northbert said. "The mistress isn't well. You don't wish her wound to open."

"God's bones, I know that. But the wound isn't in her arm, 'tis in her brain." He leaned against her temple and whispered, "Aye, and between those soft thighs of yours, deep inside, where I'll come to you again tonight. Think about that, wench."

She lowered her head, not in defeat at his words, but because she wanted to strike him again, but both of them would probably crash to the ground if she did so.

Dienwald said nothing more. He enjoyed baiting her, he admitted to himself. For the first time in his adult male life, he enjoyed talking, fighting, arguing—all those things—with a woman. Well, it was a good thing, since he would be bound to her until he shucked off his mortal coil.

He looked sideways at Northbert and saw that his man was frowning at him. Curse his interference! He said curtly, "No sign of de Grasse?"

Northbert shook his head.

Dienwald cursed. "You've got the men in a line behind us? At intervals, and hidden?" At his man's nod, Dienwald looked fit to spit. "The man's a coward." He cursed again. "I've wanted him for a long time now."

"Why?"

"Ah, you deign to speak to me again, wench?"

"Why?"

"I got a letter supposedly written to me by Kassia, but 'twas from him. He captured me when I went to see her, and I ended up in Wolffeton's dungeons. Kassia saved me, but not before the bastard had broken several of my ribs and killed three of my men. I owe him much. More than enough, since he took my son. Soon now I will repay him."

"And he took me."

"Aye, and you, wench."

So Kassia—perfect *small* Kassia—had saved him. Hadn't she other things to do? Like saving her own husband every once in a while? Curse the woman, she was a thorn in her side, nay, a veritable bush of thorns.

Well, there were those who'd wanted her as well, and she said now, "Why did Walter want to marry me?"

"Are you certain that he did?"

"Unlike you," Philippa said, her voice as bitter as the coarse green goat grass that grew beside the road, "he was most desirous of it. Indeed, he would have ravished me to ensure it, had I not escaped from him when I did. But it makes no sense to me."

"The man's mad."

Her elbow trembled, wanting to fling itself back into his belly. Finally she could bear it no longer and allowed her elbow to have its way.

He said nothing, merely grunted; then he closed his arms more tightly around her, higher now, his forearms resting under her breasts. He raised them a bit until they were pushing up her breasts, very high.

"Stop it, your men will see!"

"Then bait me not, wench."

She chewed thoughtfully on her lower lip, then said suddenly, "When the woman came to kill me, she screamed at me, something about how he—Walter—didn't want me, really, but the riches I would bring him. What could she have meant? My father must have visited Walter and promised him coin if he found me. I can think of no other reason."

"I don't know. We will find out soon enough. Your family must be told, once it is over."

"Then my father will come and cut off your manhood."

"Don't sound so vicious. 'Tis my manhood that endears me to you." To her surprise and to Dienwald's own astonishment, he leaned forward and kissed her ear. "I will give you pleasure, Philippa. And not only my manhood. The pain last night was necessary—'twas your rite of passage into womanhood, 'tis said."

"Who says?"

"Women. Who else?"

"Some arrogant male."

"Acquit me, wench. I want only to give you pleasure and to teach you how to pleasure me."

"I didn't give you pleasure last night?"

He grinned at the hurt tone of her voice. "A bit, I suppose. Aye, a bit. At least you were willing enough."

He felt her stiffen, and very slowly he eased his hand upward to cup her right breast. He caressed her, his fingers circling her nipple until he could feel the slamming of her heartbeat beneath his palm. "Shall I call a halt and tell my men that my bride wishes to have me here and now? Would you like that, wench? Shall I slip my hand inside your gown to touch your warm flesh and feel your nipple tighten against my palm?"

Her breathing was ragged, her breasts heaving. She wanted to feel his hands caressing her body. She wanted his mouth too, and his manhood, and so, without thinking, she said on a soft sigh as she leaned back against his chest, "Aye, if you will, Dienwald, 'twould please me very much, I think."

He forgot all his baiting, forgot everything save his desire for her, his seemingly endless need for her. The more she yielded to him, the more he seemed to want her. It was disconcerting and it was vastly annoying and it was so enjoyable his brain reeled.

He very gently eased his hand into her gown and cupped her breast. He could feel her breathing hitch beneath his palm. He saw her lips part, and her eyes never left his face. He knew it was ridiculous, what he was doing. Any of his men could come upon the mat any time. Northbert could draw alongside to tell him something . . . his son . . . St. Peter's toenails!

He pulled his hand out of her gown and slapped the wool back over her. "There'll be time for this later," he said, and turned her away from him. "Watch the trees and the hawthorns and the yew bushes. Colors are coming out now. Life is renewing." His words stopped abruptly, for he suddenly realized that he'd spilled his seed deep inside her but hours before—a new life could have already begun. An image flashed in his mind: a girl child with wildly curling hair streaked with many shades of brown and ash colors, tall and hardy, filled with laughter, her eyes a vivid summer blue.

He growled into Philippa's ear, "I suppose you'll give me more children than I can feed."

She just turned and gave him a beautiful smile.

Windsor Castle

King Edward nodded decisively. "Aye, Robbie, you must needs go and inform de Fortenberry of his immense good fortune. The fellow probably has gaps in his castle walls, he's so poor. His sire had not a coin to bless himself with either. Aye, I'll have St. Erth repaired. I don't want my sweet daughter in any danger, so mayhap I'll have more men sent."

Robert Burnell said, "But I thought you didn't wish to acquire a son-in-law who would drain your coffers, sire."

"Nay, not drain them, but we're speaking of my daughter, Robbie, the product of my youth, the outpouring of my young man's . . ." The king grinned. "He has but a young son? All Plantagenet ladies love children. She will take to the boy, doubtless, so we need have no worries there. After you've gotten de Fortenberry's consent and endured all his endless thanks and listened to all his outpourings of gratitude, have Lord Henry bring our sweet daughter here to Windsor. My queen insists that my daughter be wedded here. Philippa's nuptials will take place in a fortnight, no longer, mind you, Robbie."

The king moved away from his chancellor, flexing his shoulders as he paced. "Aye, you must go now, for there is much else to be done. God's teeth, so much else. It never ceases. Aye, we'll soon finish this business, and it will end happily."

Robert Burnell, accompanied by twenty of the king's finest soldiers, left the following morning for Cornwall.

Not two days later, the king was sitting with Accursi, plotting ways of wringing funds from his nobles' coffers for all the castles he wanted to build in Wales. Accursi, the son of a famous Italian jurist, was saying in his high voice, "Sire, 'tis

naught to worry you. Simply tell the nobles to
open their hearts and thus their coffers to you.
Your need is greater than theirs. 'Tis *their* need
you seek to meet! They are your subjects and 'tis
to your will they must bow."

Edward looked sour. He stroked his jaw. Accursi
would never understand the English nobleman
despite all his years in service with him. He
thought them weak and despicable, sheep to be
told firmly to shed their very wool. Edward was
on the point of saying something that would
likely send Accursi into a sulk when he heard a
throat clear loudly, and looked up.

"Sire, forgive me for disturbing you," his cham-
berlain, Aleric, said quickly, "but Roland de Tournay has come and he awaits your majesty's
pleasure. You gave orders that you wished to see
him immediately."

"De Tournay!" Edward laughed aloud, rising
quickly. A respite from Accursi. "Send him hence.
I wish to see that handsome face of his."

Roland de Tournay paused a moment on the
threshold of the king's chamber, taking it all in, as
was his wont, and Edward knew he was assessing
the occupants, specifically Accursi. Edward saw
the very brief flash of contempt in Roland's eyes,
an instinctual Englishman's reaction to any
foreigner.

Edward said, grinning widely, "Come bow
before me, de Tournay, you evil infidel. So our
gracious Lord saw fit to save you to return to
serve me again, eh?"

Roland strolled into the chamber as if he were
its master, but it didn't offend Edward. It was de
Tournay's way. It did, however, offend Accursi,

who said in his high, accented voice, "See you to your manners, sirrah!"

"Who is this heathen, sire? I can't recall his face or his irritating manners. You haven't told the fellow of my importance?"

Edward shook his head. "Accursi, hold your peace. De Tournay is my man, doubt you not, and I'll not have him abused, save by me. 'Tis about time we see you in England, Roland."

"That is what I heard said of you, sire, you who wandered the world for two years before claiming your crown."

"Impudent dog. Come and sit with me, and we will drink to our days in Acre and Jerusalem and your nights spent wallowing in the Moslims' gifts. I hear Barbars gave you six women to start your own harem."

It was some two hours later when the king said to the man who'd done him great and loyal service in the Holy Land, "Why did you not come to my coronation October last? Eleanor spoke of your desertion."

Roland de Tournay merely smiled and drank more of the king's fine Brittany wine. "I doubt not the beautiful and gracious queen spoke of me," he said. "But, sire, I was naught but a captive in a deep prison, held by that sweetest of men, the Duke of Brabant. He, in short, demanded ransom for my poor body. My brother paid it, afraid not to, for he knew that you would hear of it if he didn't." Roland grinned wickedly. "Actually, I think it was his fair wife, lusty Blanche, who forced him to ransom me."

It took Edward only another hour before he slapped his knee and shouted, "You shall marry my daughter! Aye, the perfect solution!"

"Your daughter!" Roland repeated, staring blankly at the king. "A royal princess? You have drunk too much of this fine wine, sire."

The king just shook his head and told de Tournay about Philippa de Beauchamp. ". . . so you see, Roland, Robbie is on his way, as we speak, to de Fortenberry. I would rather it be you. You're a known scoundrel and de Fortenberry is an unknown one. What say you?"

"De Fortenberry, eh? He's a tough rascal, sire, a rogue, and worthy withal. I know naught ill of him as a man. But he's wily and likes not to bow to anyone, even his king. Why did you select him?"

" 'Twas Graelam de Moreton who suggested him. He's a force in Cornwall, a savage place still. I need good men, strong men, men I can trust. As a son-in-law I could trust his arm to wield sword for me. But you too could settle there, Roland. I would deed you property and a fine castle. What say you?"

"Will you make me a duke, sire?"

"Impudent cock! An earl you'll be, and nothing more."

Roland fell silent. It felt strange to be back in his own land, sitting with his king, discussing marriage to a royal bastard. He wanted no wife, truth be told, yet the truth hesitated on his tongue. Doubtless the king would regret his hastiness. The flagon of wine lay nearly empty between them. Roland would wait until the morrow.

" 'Twould enrage your brother, I vow," the king mused. "Himself the Earl of Blackheath, and to have his troublesome young brother be made an earl also and the king's son-in-law? Aye, 'twould make him livid."

That it would, Roland thought. But he didn't particularly like to rub his brother's nose in dung, so he slowly shook his head.

" 'Tis a generous offer, sire, and one that must be considered conscientiously and in absence of your good drink."

"So be it, Roland. Tell me of your harem," King Edward said, "before my beautiful Eleanor comes to pluck us away."

19

St. Erth Castle

On the last day of April, under the flowering
apple trees in the St. Erth orchard, Father Cramdle performed a marriage ceremony crowned with
enough ritual to please even the Archbishop of
Canterbury himself. The sweet scent of the apple
blossoms, musk roses, and violets filled the air,
the bride looked more beautiful than the yellow-
and-purple-patterned butterflies that hovered over
the scores of trestle tables laden with food and
ale, and the bridegroom and master of St. Erth
looked like he wanted to frown himself into the
ground. Father Cramdle ignored the bridegroom.
The ceremony was right and proper. All the people of St. Erth were happy. The master was doing
his duty by the maid.

The soon-to-be-mistress of St. Erth looked as

excited as any other girl at her own wedding, Old
Agnes thought as she watched Philippa de Beauchamp become Philippa de Fortenberry, the master's helpmeet and steward and keeper of the
castle. Aye, she was lovely in her soft pink gown
with a dark pink overtunic—both garments among
those sent to her by Lady Kassia de Moreton, a
fact that had seemed, for some unknown reason,
to annoy the mistress.

She wore her richly curling hair long and thick
down her back, with flowers twined together into
a crown on her brow. She was a maiden bride,
and if anyone thought differently, he was wise
enough to keep silent.

The master looked a magnificent animal as well,
clothed in the new bright blue tunic the mistress
had sewn for him, his long lean body straight and
tall. But he also looked uncommonly severe and
forbidding, something Old Agnes didn't understand but hadn't the courage to ask about. As for
the young master, he was grinning like a fatuous
little puppy after a big meal.

Since they were wedded here at St. Erth, no
dowry or bridal gifts involved, Dienwald spared
himself and his bride the ceremonial stripping.
He knew his bride was very nicely formed and
he knew that she thought well of his body as
well. He chewed his thumbnail and wished Father
Cramdle would finish with his array of Latin,
words spoken so slowly that Dienwald didn't
know where one word began and another left off.
Nor did he understand any of the words, so it
really didn't matter.

Neither did Philippa. She just wanted it over
with. She wanted to turn and smile at her new
husband and watch him smile back at her. They'd

returned the evening before, and to Philippa's surprise and chagrin, Dienwald hadn't come near his own bedchamber. She'd slept alone, wondering at his sudden bout of nobility—if, indeed, it were a case of nobility.

Perhaps, she thought, as Father Cramdle droned on, he'd not found her particularly to his liking that first time. Perhaps he didn't . . .

The ceremony was over, and there was suddenly loud, nearly riotous cheering from all the people of St. Erth. Gorkel had set Crooky on his massive shoulders and the fool was leading the people in shouts and yells and howls of glee.

" 'Tis done."

Philippa, her brilliant smile in place, turned to her new husband, but she didn't get a smile in return. He was staring beyond her at nothing in particular as far as she could tell.

"Aye," she said with great satisfaction, "you are now my husband. What is it? Is something the matter? Something offends you?"

"All my people," Dienwald said, still staring about him, "are shouting their heads off. And it is because they believe you to be good for their well-being. They make me feel I've been a rotten tyrant in my treatment of them."

"Mayhap," she said with a grin, "they believe I'll temper you rottenness and make you as sweet and ripe as summer strawberries. As for me, husband, I shall try to be good for our people. Mayhap they also believe I'll be good for their master. I had much food prepared. Indeed, everyone wished to help. Look at the tables, I vow they are creaking with the weight of it. There are hare and pork and herring and beef and even some young lamb—"

"Aye, I know." He struck his fingers through his hair. "Edmund," he bellowed. "Come hither!"

The boy was still grinning even as he came to a halt in front of his father and announced with glee, "You are wedded to the maypole."

Philippa laughed and cuffed his shoulder. "You weedy little spallkin! Come, give me a kiss."

Edmund came up to his tiptoes and hugged her, then raised his face, his lips pursed. She kissed him soundly. "Can you call me something a bit more pleasing, Edmund?"

Edmund struck a thoughtful pose. Crooky came up then and Edmund said, "A name, Crooky, I must have a comely name for my father's wife."

"Ah, a name." Crooky slewed a look at his master. "Mayhap Morgan? Or Mary?"

"Shut your teeth!" Dienwald bellowed, and cuffed Crooky, sending the fool tumbling head over arse to the ground in a well-performed roll.

"I think," Edmund said slowly, "that I wish to think about it. Is that all right?"

"That is just fine. Now, husband, would you like to partake of your wedding feast?"

There was enough feasting and consumption of ale to keep the people of St. Erth sick for a week. And that, Philippa thought, smiling, was probably the reason they'd cheered her so vigorously— enough food and drink and dancing to make the most sullen villein smile. Even the blacksmith, a man of morose habits, was laughing, his mouth stuffed with stewed hare and cabbage. Everyone was frolicking.

All but the master.

He danced with her; he picked at the roasted hare and pork Philippa served on his trencher, but he didn't try to pull her away to kiss her or fondle her on his lap. And that, she knew, wasn't at all like Dienwald. His hand should have been on her knee, moving upward, or caressing her breast, a wicked gleam in his eyes. She wished she had the courage to stroke her hand up his leg, but she didn't.

When the time came, Philippa allowed Old Agnes and the other women to see her to the master's bedchamber. Margot combed her hair and the women took off her clothes and placed her in Dienwald's big bed. Then, with much giggling and advice that Philippa found interesting but quite unnecessary, they left.

"Aye," Old Agnes called back, "we'll send up the master soon, if he isn't too sodden to move!"

Margot laughed and shouted, "We'll tell him stories to stiffen his rod! Right now 'tis too full of ale to do more than flop about!"

Now that, Philippa thought, was an interesting image to picture.

The night was dark, and but one candle flickered in the bedchamber. Philippa waited naked under the thin cover, for it was warm this night, her wedding night. Her arm was still bound in a soft wool bandage, but it scarce bothered her. She wanted her husband to come to her, she wanted him to touch her with his hands, with his mouth, and she wanted his rod to come inside her and fill her. She wanted desperately to hold him to her as he moved inside her. She loved him and she wanted to give him everything that she was, everything that she had, which, admittedly, were only her love and her goodwill for him, his son, and his castle.

Time passed and the candle gutted. She fell

asleep finally, huddled onto her side, her hands beneath her cheek.

The door crashed open and Philippa came instantly awake and lurched upright. Her new husband was standing in the open doorway holding a candle in his right hand. He was scowling toward her, and she saw that he wasn't happy.

He stepped into the chamber and kicked the door shut with his heel, then strode across the chamber and came to a halt beside the bed. He looked down at her. She pulled the blanket over her breast to her chin.

"Good," he said.

"Good what?"

"You're naked, wench—at least you had better be under that flimsy cover. The women were giggling enough about your fair and willing body, ready for me. Now that I've enslaved myself and all I own for you, now that you've gotten everything you wanted, I think I will take advantage of the one benefit you bring me."

He was pulling off his clothes as he spoke. Philippa stared at him, realizing that he was drunk. He wasn't sodden, but he was drunk.

She just looked at him. She wasn't afraid of him, but still she said, "Will you hurt me, Dienwald?"

That brought him upright. He was naked, standing with his arms at his sides, his legs slightly spread, and he was staring down at her. "Hurt you, wench?"

"I am not a wench, I'm your wife, I'm Philippa de Fortenberry, and—"

"Aye, I know it well . . . too well. Come, lie down and shut your woman's mouth and open your legs. I wish to take you, and if there is much more talk, I doubt I'll be able. Nay, I'll not hurt you if you obey me."

She didn't move for a very long time. Finally she said slowly, "You said you would give me pleasure."

He frowned. He had said that, it was true, but that was before he'd drunk so much ale he felt he'd float away with the Penthlow River. He felt ill-used, but he supposed it wasn't her fault, not really. No matter how he railed and brawled, he had taken her, and all because of that cursed dream of her he'd been having. That and the fact that he'd wanted her for longer than he could remember.

And so he said in a voice that was fast becoming sober, "I'll try, by all the saints' sweet voices, I'll try to bring you pleasure."

She smiled at that, all the while looking at him. He was tall and lean and hard, and so beautiful she wanted to cry. Her body was taut with excitement and soft with a need she knew lay buried within her, a need he would nurture into being. " 'Twill be fine, then, my husband."

She lay on her back and lifted her arms to him.

"Why must you yield to me so sweetly?" he asked as he lay down and pulled the blanket to her waist. He came over her naked breasts, and the feel of her so soft and giving beneath him made him shiver. "Ah, Philippa," he said, and kissed her. It was a gentle kiss until he felt her respond to him, and then he lightly probed with his tongue until she parted her lips and he slipped his tongue in her mouth. He felt her start of surprise and said into her mouth, "Touch your tongue to mine."

She did, shyly, as if she were afraid of what

would happen. Then she gasped with the wonder of it and threw her arms—both of them—around his back. He laughed at that, both amazed and pleased to his male soul at her yielding reaction. He taught her how to kiss and how to enjoy all the small movements he made with his tongue. He rubbed his chest over her breasts, and her response was beyond what he'd expected. She was panting and arching up against him, her hands fluttering over him.

"The feel of you," Philippa said, rubbing herself against his hairy chest. "I love the feel of you," and he felt her trying to open her legs for him. He fitted himself there, his sex against her belly, then raised himself and said, "Touch me, Philippa. I can't bear it anymore. Touch me."

She reached between their bodies and instantly clasped her fingers about him. "Oh," she said, and her fingers grew still. "I hadn't thought . . . 'tis wondrous how you feel . . . your strength." And she began to caress him, to stroke him, to learn him, and then she closed both hands about him and fondled him, and soon he couldn't bear it. He pulled back up onto his knees between her widespread thighs and looked down at her. Her sleek long legs were beautifully shaped and white and soft, and he wanted them around his flanks and wanted to come inside her, and he said only, "Now, Philippa, now."

There was in her expression only sweetness and anticipation, and it seeped slowly through his brain that he had become infinitely more sober than when he entered the room.

"Pleasure," he repeated slowly as he paused before guiding himself into her. "Pleasure." He stopped, drew a deep shuddering breath, and frowned down at her. "You're my wife." He eased down then between her legs, and his lips were on her stomach, his hands stroking her, his tongue wet and hot against her flesh. He was moving lower and lower, and Philippa, so surprised that she hadn't the chance to be shocked by what he was doing, yelled when his mouth closed over her.

He raised his head, staring at her in consternation. "Pleasure," he said. " 'Tis for your pleasure."

"Oh."

"Be quiet, wench. This is good."

And so it was, but it was also more, much more. When his mouth took her this time, she lurched upward but didn't yell. She felt the sensation of his mouth into the very depths of her, sensations she'd never before even guessed could exist. She whimpered, her fist in her mouth. His hands slipped beneath her buttocks, and he lifted her, his tongue wild on her and inside her, delving and probing, and she cried out, unable to keep still any longer. And it went on and on, gaining in urgency until she gave herself to it.

Dienwald felt the stiffening of her legs, the convulsions that tightened her muscles, and in those moments his mind was as clear as a cloudless summer day, and he saw her, really saw her, and felt her even as she stared at him, her eyes wide and wild, filled with surprise and passion, and she cried out and arched upward, giving herself to him fully. It was a woman's pleasure swamping her, and he was giving it to her and felt himself sharing it, deeply, and it dazed him. He wanted to shy away from it, to escape it, but he

couldn't because he was held firm and close, a
part of her, even though he had never known it
could be so. Nothing had prepared him for this
joining. When she quieted, he raced back, taut
and wild and fierce, lifted her hips even higher—
but again he looked down at her, and slowed
himself. He came into her very slowly, for she
was small. It was almost too much for him. She
was wet from the pleasure he'd brought her, and
the feel of her, the feel of himself inside her,
made him shudder and moan until he couldn't
bear it and he drove into her, coming over her
then, even as he felt her womb. And he exploded
then and groaned loudly, heaving into her as his
seed filled her.

He didn't want to think, didn't want to feel
anymore. It was all too new and too urgent. His
head was spinning and he felt ripped apart, for
she would see his soul and know that she'd taken
him, all of him, and so he escaped her and slept.

Philippa stared at her husband's face beside
hers on the pillow. He was breathing slowly and
deeply, his fingers splayed over her breast, one
muscled leg covering hers. She raised her hand
and stroked his hair. He'd promised pleasure, but
this had exceeded pleasure. Pleasure was a new
gown whose color suited one perfectly. What he'd
made her feel . . . It could make one mad, it
was madness. And she wanted it every day of
her life.

Light streamed onto Philippa's face and she
opened her eyes and smiled even before she saw
her husband's face. Dienwald was on his side,
balanced over her, and he was looking very seri-

ous and intent. He appeared to be playing with her hair.

"What are you doing?"

"Counting the different shades in your hair. Here is a strand as dark a brown as my own, and next to it is one so pale I can scarce see it against my arm."

"My father once frowned at me and told me my hair wasn't golden."

"He's right. It isn't. It's far more interesting. Here's a strand that's an ash color. So far, I've counted ten different colors. Why did your father want you to have golden hair?"

"I don't know. I just remember that he was shaking his head about it. I was hurt, but then he didn't say anything more. Indeed, he seemed to forget about it."

He went on as if she hadn't spoken, "And the hair covering your mound—"

Instinctively Philippa closed her legs, and he laughed. "Nay, you're my wife now. I'll look my fill and you'll not gainsay me." He laid his open palm over her, cupping her. "You feel warm beneath my hand."

He closed his eyes as he spoke, and Philippa felt a surge of something much stronger than mere warmth beneath his palm. It was desire, and it felt powerful and compelling. Unconsciously she lifted her hips against his hand.

He opened his eyes and looked into hers. "I thought you'd be a greedy wench," he said, a good deal of male satisfaction in his voice, and leaned down to kiss her. She felt his long finger glide over her, slip between her thighs, and enter her slowly. She gasped, and he took the sound into his mouth and kissed her more deeply. Then his tongue moved into her mouth just as his finger was moving into the depths of her and she lurched up, crying out, so overwhelmed by the feelings his actions brought that she was helpless against them. He pressed her down. "Hush," he said. "Lie quietly and enjoy what I'm doing to you."

"It's too much," she said, and began kissing him urgently, frantically, his chin, his nose, his mouth. He laughed into her mouth but it turned quickly into a groan as her tongue touched his.

In a sudden move he rolled onto his back and brought her over him. He arranged her over him, saying, "Sit up, wife, come astride me." He lifted her, his hands around her waist. "Guide me into you."

Philippa was eager and more than willing, and she brought him into her and felt him slowly ease her down over him. She stared at him, not moving.

He smiled painfully and moved his hands upward to cup her breasts. "Move," he managed to say. "Move as you wish to."

She was uncertain and tentative at first, then realized that she could make him insane with lust, moving quickly, then slowing until he thought he would die from sensations of it. She watched his face and quickly learned how far she could push him before drawing back. Then she drew back her head and thrust her breasts forward, her hands splayed on his chest and when his fingers found her, she yelled and jerked, beyond herself, seeking her climax and when it overwhelmed her it overwhelmed him as well.

"It's too much," she whispered a few moments later. She lay with her cheek on his shoulder, her legs stretched over him, his member still inside her.

Dienwald couldn't have said anything if the Saracens had been attacking St. Erth at that moment.

He was barren of wit. He heard Philippa's breath even into sleep. He'd worn her to a bone and he was pleased. He discounted his own feelings of utter contentment. He cupped her hips in his hands. Aye, his wife was a bountiful wench, her flesh soft and firm, and perchance 'twas a fine thing to have her here, at St. Erth, in his bed, for a very long time.

Windsor Castle
May 1275

"Well, what say you, Roland? Do you wish to wed with my daughter? My sweet Philippa?"

Roland chewed slowly on the honey bread. He didn't want to anger his king by saying frankly that the last thing he wanted in his life was a wife to hang around his neck.

The king frowned. "My man Cedric told me of two wenches who visited your chamber last night. I told him to keep his rattling tongue in his mouth."

"Two wenches," Roland repeated, his eyes widening in surprise. "Nay, sire, 'twas three, but I was too fatigued to do much with the third one. I let her assist."

The king stared at Roland de Tournay, his face darkening. Then he burst into laughter. "You make me a flap-eared ass, Roland. Aye, I will tell Cedric he miscounted your wenches. 'Twill serve the beetle-headed clod right. Now, what will you? Have you decided?"

Roland decided to postpone the inevitable anger that would take the king when he knew himself thwarted. "Why do I not travel to see this daughter, sire? Mayhap she will look at my churl's ugly face and shriek in despair."

"Aye, 'tis possible," the king said, stroking his chin as was his habit. "Very well, Roland, go to Cornwall and give the sweet maid your countenance and tell her to behold it with shrewdness. Tell her you are my trusted man. Nay, tell Lord Henry that."

Roland nodded. He didn't mind going to Cornwall. He needed to see Graelam de Moreton. He also trusted that something would happen to save him the fate of being wedded. He was lucky; his luck would hold without his having to insult the king or his bastard daughter. He doubted not that being a Plantagenet, she was beautiful. Edward sired only beautiful daughters, as had his father before him. But whenever Roland envisioned a beautiful face, it was Joan of Tenesby he saw, and he knew it would remain so until the day he died—the beautiful face of treachery that mirrored his folly.

St. Erth Castle

"Aye, 'tis besotted she is, and it's good." Old Agnes spat out a cherry seed, continuing to Gorkel, who was plaiting strips of leather into a whip, "I doubt t' mistress will be able to walk if t' master doesn't let her out of his bed."

Gorkel blushed and missed his rhythm with the plaiting.

Old Agnes brayed with laughter and wagged a gnarled finger at him. "Oh, aye, a beast like you turning red as a cherry pip! Aye, 'tis a wondrous thing to see. Look not sour, Gorkel, 'tis no pain t' master gives the mistress. Aye, 'tis she who plunders his manhood, I'll vow, and wrings him dry and limp."

She cackled until Gorkel, furious at himself, threw the half-plaited whip aside and strode to the well to drink. And there was the master himself, drinking from the well in the inner bailey.

Gorkel watched him straighten, then stretch profoundly. There was a smile on the master's face, a look of vanity perhaps, but in a man of the master's position, Gorkel forgave it.

"Aye, t' master has t' look of a man wrung out of all his seed," Old Agnes chortled close to Gorkel's ear, coming to a halt behind him.

Dienwald heard the old woman laughing and wondered at the jest. The sun was bright overhead, the air warm, and it was nearing midmorning. He became aware of all his people around him, looking at him from the corners of their eyes, smirking—one fellow, a shepherd, was slapping his hands over his heart and sighing loudly. Dienwald decided to sigh too. Then he saw Philippa in his mind's eye stretched on her back, her white thighs parted, her arms flung over her head. He felt a bolt of lust so great it made him reel. It vexed him to realize this effect she had on him, just thinking of her lying in his bed, naked and soft and warm. He cursed, turned on his heel, and rushed back up the solar stairs.

He heard laughter from behind him, but didn't slow. When he flung open the bedchamber door, it was to see his wife standing in the copper tub, naked.

Philippa, startled, brought the linen cloth over her breasts and covered her woman's mound with her hand. Her husband stood in the middle of the room and stared at her.

"You're too plentiful for such a small square of cloth, wench."

When she just stood there returning his stare, Dienwald strode to her, pulled the cloth from her fingers, leaned down, and took her nipple in his mouth. At her gasp, he straightened again and washed the cloth over her tautened nipple. "I think of you and my manhood is cock-sore for your attention. Now, stand still and I will finish your bath for you." He began to whistle as if he hadn't a care, bending over now, the cloth gliding down her belly and between her legs. "Wider, wench, part your legs for me." She opened her legs, her hands on his shoulders to balance herself. She threw her head back when she felt the cloth pressing against her, then his hands, slick with soap, stroking her buttocks. His whistling stopped. He was breathing heavily, and suddenly he was cupping water in his hands and pouring it over her, rinsing away the soap.

"Dienwald," she said, her fists pounding on his shoulders, "you make me frantic."

He looked at her. "Aye, wench? Is that true? This?" And his middle finger slipped inside her.

She looked at his mouth and he felt his blood churn and his member harden. She kissed him, moving against him, shuddering when his fin-

ger eased out of her, then plunged in deeply
again.

"You're mine," he said into her mouth, and she
moaned, kissing him frantically, biting him, her
fingers digging into his back. His finger left her
and he shoved his clothes aside, freeing his member. He looked at her and said, "I want you to
come to me now. Clasp your legs around my
flanks."

She stared at him, not understanding, but he
just shook his head and lifted her. Her legs went
around him and then she felt his fingers on her,
stroking and caressing her and parting her, and
her breath caught sharply in her throat as he slid
upward into her.

She gasped and wrapped her legs more tightly
around him. Then he carried her to the bed and
eased her down, not leaving her, driving furiously into her until she was crying out, nearly
bucking him off her in her frenzy. When his climax overcame him, he yelled, his head thrown
back, so deep inside her that he no longer
thought of her as separate from him, as a vessel
for his pleasure, as a wife to bear his children.
She was his and a part of him and he accepted it
and fell atop her, kissing her as she cried softly
into his mouth.

Late that afternoon, as Dienwald was sitting in
his chair drinking a flagon of ale, he looked up
to see Northbert run into the great hall, shouting at the top of his lungs. "Someone comes,
master!"

Dienwald rose immediately. "That peasant
whoreson Sir Walter?"

"Nay, 'tis Lord Henry de Beauchamp. He has

a dozen men, master," Northbert added. "All armed."

Dienwald straightened his clothes, mentally girded his loins, and went to greet his father-in-law. It hadn't taken Lord Henry long to reply to his message.

20

Dienwald watched two stout men-at-arms assist Lord Henry de Beauchamp from his powerful Arabian destrier. He was a portly man, not tall, but strongly built even in his late years.

He was huffing about, wheezing and cursing, and Dienwald soon realized it was with rage, not the result of his exertions. No sooner had Lord Henry seen him than he yelled to the four corners of St. Erth, "You lie, you filthy whoreson! You must lie! You cannot have wedded my daughter! 'Tis a lie!"

For a father who had planned to give his daughter to William de Bridgport without a dowry, Lord Henry seemed unaccountably incensed. Dienwald motioned him into the great hall. "It is not much more private, but the entire population of St. Erth will be spared your rage." He preceded him, saying nothing more. He could hear Lord Henry's furious breathing close to his back, and wondered if he should give Philippa's father such a good target for a dagger.

He motioned Lord Henry to his own chair, but his father-in-law wasn't having any niceties. He stood there facing his son-in-law, his hands on his hips. "Tell me you lied!"

" 'Twould be a lie to tell you that I lied. I wedded Philippa two days past."

Lord Henry actually spat in his fury. "I will have the ceremony proclaimed invalid! I will have it annulled! She had not her father's permission, 'tis a disgrace! Aye, 'twill be annulled quickly!"

"It is very possible that Philippa even now is carrying my babe. There will be no annulment."

Lord Henry's face, already red, now became purple. "Where is she? Where is that insolent, ungrateful—"

"Father! What do you here? I don't understand—why are you angry?" Philippa broke off. So Dienwald had written to her father telling him of their marriage, probably the very day of their wedding, to bring him here so quickly, and he had come and he wasn't pleased. But what matter was it to him? Why should he care?

Philippa walked quickly to her father and made to embrace him. To her surprise, he took several steps back, as if he couldn't bear the sight of her, much less her touch. "You spiteful little wretch! You wedded this . . . this scoundrel?"

Philippa grew very still. She made no more moves toward her father. She saw Dienwald looking at Lord Henry, his expression ironic, and said simply, "I love him and I have wedded him. He is my husband, my lord, and I'll not allow you to insult him."

" 'Tis no insult," Dienwald said with a sudden grin. "I *am* a scoundrel."

Lord Henry turned on Dienwald. "You make jests about your foul deeds! You ravished her, didn't you? You forced her into your bed and then to a priest!"

"Nay, but you will doubtless believe what you wish to believe. However, if you believe any man could ravish Philippa and not sport a year's worth of bruises and broken limbs for it, you are wide of your mark."

"And you, you female viper, what know you of love? You who have been protected all your life from curs of this sort? How long have you known this poor and ragged cur? Days, only days! And you say you love him! Ha! He seduced you, and being a witless fool, you let him!"

"I do love him," Philippa repeated quietly. She laid her hand on her father's arm when he would have erupted further. "Listen to me, sir. He did not ravish me. He is chivalrous. He is kind and good. He saved me from Walter, and I love him. 'Twas *he* who finally consented to marry *me*."

Lord Henry shook off her hand as if it were something abhorrent. He stared hard at her. "You little harlot," he said slowly. "Just look at you, your hair wild down your back like a peasant girl's, your feet bare! I can even smell him on you. You little whore!" He pulled back his arm and struck her a blow hard across the cheek with the palm of his hand. The blow was unexpected, and Philippa went careening backward. She cried out as her hip struck a chair and she went sprawling onto the reed-strewn floor.

Dienwald was on his knees beside her, his face

white with rage. "Are you all right?" He grabbed
her arm and shook it. "Philippa, answer me!"

"Aye, I'm all right. I wasn't expecting a blow.
It surprised me." She felt Dienwald's long fingers
stroke over the bright red mark on her cheek. She
watched him rise and stride to her father. Lord
Henry's men stood still as statues, staring at their
master and at their master's daughter and husband. They would, Philippa knew, protect Lord
Henry with their lives, but they were uncertain
now, afraid to move. It was a family matter and
thus more dangerous than fighting a band of Irish
thieves.

Dienwald stopped six inches from Lord Henry's
nose. "You will listen to me, old man, and listen
well. I sent you a message telling you of my marriage to your daughter as a courtesy. I didn't particularly wish to, but I deemed it proper to inform
you. You didn't want her; you held her in no
esteem; you planned to give her no dowry. You
were going to wed her to de Bridgport! Now you
have no more say in her life. Philippa is now
mine. What is mine I protect. Because you happen to share her blood, I will not kill you, but be
warned. My dagger is sharp and my rage grows
stronger by the moment. You touch her again in
anger and I will tear your worthless heart from
your fat body. Heed me, old man, for I mean my
words."

Lord Henry doubted not that this man meant
what he'd said. He took a step back and dashed
his fingers through his grizzled hair. He looked
toward Philippa, standing now, her hand pressed
against her side. She was very still, her face pale
with shock. He'd never struck her in her life. "I
am sorry to have clouted you, Philippa, but you

have sorely tried me. You ran away, leaving me to believe you dead or murdered or—"

"You know I ran away because I heard you tell Ivo that I was going to be wedded to William de Bridgport. I knew it must be the truth, because my mother was there as well. What would you expect me to do? Roll my eyes in thankfulness and joy and go willingly to that filthy old man?"

Lord Henry collapsed onto a bench, all bluster gone from him. He looked toward Dienwald—his treacherous son-in-law—and managed a bit more anger. "You stole my wool! You killed my men!"

"Aye, I did steal your wool. As for the other, acquit me. I am no murderer. 'Twas one of my people who killed your farmers without my knowledge, something that displeased me. The man responsible is dead. There is naught more I can do to avenge your people. As for the wool, this tunic I wear is a result of your daughter's fine skills. She sewed it, and many others for my people."

Philippa drew closer to her father. "Do you know naught of Sir Walter, sir? He kidnapped me and Dienwald's son and took us to Crandall. He wanted to marry me, Father, and I could find no reason for his ardor. I am a stranger to him, and beyond that, he had a mistress who . . . Never mind that. Did you perchance offer him a reward if he found me for you? Is that what made him want me for his wife?"

Lord Henry's eyes gave a brief renewed flash of rage. "That traitorous slug! Aye, I know why he took you, Philippa, and he would have wedded you . . . but why did he not? You are wedded to this man, are you not?"

"Edmund—'tis Dienwald's son—he and I managed to escape Crandall and Walter."

"Ah. Well, no matter now. I offered Walter no
reward, at least not in the way you think. I spoke
truth to him, and the malignant wretch planned
to gain his own ends. Ah, 'tis over for me. It
matters not now. One husband is much the same
as another, given that both are calamity to me. If
you prefer this man to your cousin, so be it. At
least this man wedded you without knowing
about you. But I am dead, no matter your choice.
'Tis this man, then, this rogue, who will comfort
you whilst you pray over your dead father's
body. Will you strew sweet ox-lips on my grave,
Philippa?"

Philippa wanted to shake him, but she held to
her patience. "But, sir, this makes no sense. Why
would Walter de Grasse want to marry me?
Why?"

Lord Henry shook his head, mumbling, pulling
at his hair. "It matters not; nothing matters now.
I'm a dead man now, Philippa. There is no hope
for me. My head will be severed from my body.
I will be lashed until my back is but blood and
bones. I will be drawn and quartered and the
crows will peck at my guts."

"Crows? Guts? What is he babbling about?"
Dienwald asked his bride. "Who would wish to
kill him?"

Philippa again approached her father, but she
didn't touch him. "What is it, Father? You fear
reprisals from de Bridgport? He's an old man full
of spleen, but he has no spine. You needn't fear
him. My husband won't allow him to harm you."

Lord Henry groaned. He dropped his head in
his hands and pulled his hair all the harder. He

weaved back and forth on the bench, distraught, and wailed, "I am undone and spent, and my remains will be fodder for the fields. Beauchamp will be stripped from me and mine. Maude will be cast out to die in poverty, probably in a convent somewhere, and you know, Philippa, she hates that sort of thing, despite all her pious ravings. Bernice will not wed, for she will have no dowry, and the saints know that her humors are uncertain. She will become more sour-hearted and wasp-tongued—"

"You weren't going to give me a dowry."

Lord Henry paid no attention. "Dead, all because I tried to discourage that silly young peacock de Vescy. I lost my wits, and my tongue ran into the mire with lies."

"What lies? Tell me, Father. What does Ivo de Vescy have to do with this?"

"He is to wed Bernice. Rather, he was. Now he won't. He'll run back to York and seek an heiress elsewhere."

Philippa looked at Dienwald. She was no longer pale, but she was confused. He nodded at her silent plea for help.

"You make no sense, old man," Dienwald said. "Speak words with meaning!" It was the tone he used with Crooky, and it usually worked. But it didn't this time, not with Lord Henry. He merely shook his head and moaned, rocking more violently back and forth.

Northbert came into the hall and motioned to his master. He was panting from running and his face was alight with excitement and anticipation. "Master! There is another party here at our gates. The man claims to be Robert Burnell, Chancellor of England, here to see you, master, as a personal emissary from the king himself! Master, he has twenty men with him and they carry the king's standard! The Chancellor of England, here! From King Edward!"

Dienwald exploded in Northbert's face, "Chancellor, indeed! By St. Paul's blessed fingers, your brain becomes as flat as your ugly nose! More likely 'tis Lord Henry's precious nephew, Sir Walter, come to carp to his uncle."

Lord Henry was staring in horror at Northbert. His face had gone gray and his chin sagged to his chest. "It is the chancellor, I know it is. Accept it, Dienwald. 'Tis over now." He clasped his hands in prayer and raised his eyes to the St. Erth rafters. "Receive me into heaven and thy bosom, O Lord. I know it is too soon for my reception. I am not ready to be received, but what can I do? 'Tis not my fault that I spoke stupidly and Philippa was listening. Perhaps some of the blame can lie on her shoulders for creeping about and hearing things not meant for her ears. Must all the blame be mine alone? Nay, 'tis not well done of me. Aye, I will go to my death. I will perish with my dignity intact and will carry no blame for my sweet Philippa, who was always so bright and ready to make me smile. Many times she acted stupidly, but she is but a female, and who am I to correct her? 'Tis done and over, and I am nearly fodder for Maude's musk roses."

"A soldier carries the king's banner!" Edmund shrieked, flying into the hall. He stopped in front of his father's visitor and stared. Lord Henry had raised his head at Edmund's noise, and his face was white with fear. Edmund looked from Philippa to his father, then back to the old man, and said, "Who are you, sir?"

"Eh? Ah, you're the villain's brat. Get thee away from me, boy. I am on my way to die. A sword will sever my gullet, and my tongue will fall limp from my mouth. Aye, a lance will spike through my ribs and . . ." He rose slowly to his feet, shaking his head, mumbling now. Philippa ran to him. "Father, what is the matter? What say you? Do you know the king's chancellor? Why are you so afraid?"

He shook her off. "Boy, take me away. Take me to your stepmother's solar, aye, take me there to wait for my sentence of torture and death. Aye, I'll be thrown into a dungeon, my fingernails drawn out slowly, the hairs snatched from my groin, my eyeballs plucked from their sockets."

Edmund, wide-eyed, said, "Philippa, is this man your sire?"

"Aye, Edmund. Take him to your father's bed-chamber. He seems not to be himself. Quickly."

"He pays homage to witlessness," Dienwald said, staring after his father-in-law. "What does this Burnell want, I wonder."

"The king's chancellor . . ." Philippa said, her voice filled with awe and fear. "You haven't done anything terribly atrocious, have you, husband?"

"Do you wonder if the king has discovered my plans to invade France?" Dienwald shook his head and patted her cheek, for he could see she was white with fear. "I shall go greet the fellow," he said. "I bid you to remain here until I discover what he wants. No, go to your father and let him continue his nonsense in your ears. Perhaps he will say something that will make sense to you. I want you kept safe until this matter is clear to me. Heed me in this, Philippa."

She frowned at his back as he strode from the

great hall. He was her lord and master and she loved him beyond question, but for her to hide away whilst he faced an unknown danger alone?

"Come away from here, as the master bids, mistress."

"Gorkel, you shan't tell me what to do!"

"The master told me you would try to come after him. He says your loyalty is dangerous to yourself, for you're but a female with crooked sense. He told me to take you to your steward's room and keep you there until he was certain all was well and safe. He decided he doesn't want you near your father. He believes him mired in folly."

"I won't go! No, Gorkel, don't you dare! No!"

Philippa was an armful for her husband, but for Gorkel she was naught but an insignificant wisp, to be slung over his massive shoulder and carried off. She pounded his back, shrieking at him, but he didn't hesitate. Philippa gave it up for the moment, since there was nothing else for her to do.

In the inner bailey Dienwald waited, his arms crossed negligently over his chest as he watched England's chancellor ride through the portcullis into St. Erth's inner bailey. The man wasn't much of a rider; indeed, he was bouncing up and down like a drunken loon in the saddle. Suddenly the chancellor looked up and saw Dienwald. The man's eyes were intense, and Dienwald felt himself being studied as closely as the archbishop would study a holy relic.

Burnell let his destrier come apace, then turned to an armored soldier beside him and said something that Dienwald couldn't make out. He stiffened, ready to fight, but held his outward calm. He watched Burnell shake his head at the soldier.

Robert Burnell was tired, his buttocks so sore he felt as though he were sitting on his backbone, but seeing St. Erth, seeing this man who was its lord, he felt a relief so deep that he wanted to fall from the horse and onto his knees and give his thanks to the Lord. Dienwald de Fortenberry was young, strong, healthy, a man of fine parts and good mien. His castle was in need of repairs and many of the people he'd seen were ragged, but it wasn't a place of misery or cruelty. Burnell straightened in his saddle. His journey was over, thank the good Lord above. He felt hope rise in his blood and energy flow anew through his body. He was pleased. He was happy.

He said to the man standing before him, "You are Dienwald de Fortenberry, master of St. Erth, Baron St. Erth?"

"Aye, I am he."

"I am Robert Burnell, Chancellor of England. I come to you from our mighty and just king, Edward I. I come in peace to speak with you. May I be welcomed into your keep?"

Dienwald nodded. The day, begun promisingly with lust and passion and a bride who seemed to believe the sun rose upon his head and set with his decision, had become increasingly mysterious with an irate and mumbling father-in-law, and now a messenger from the King of England. He watched Robert Burnell dismount clumsily from the mighty destrier, then nodded for the man to precede him into the great hall.

He was aware that all his men and all his people were hanging back, staring and gossiping, and he prayed that no one would take anything amiss. He told Margot in the quietest voice she'd ever heard from the master to bring ale and bread and cheese. She stared at him, and Dienwald was annoyed with himself and with her.

"Where is the mistress?" Margot asked.

Dienwald wanted to cuff her, but he merely frowned and said, "Do as I bid you and don't sputter at me. The mistress is reposing and is not to be disturbed for any reason." He turned back to Burnell, praying that Margot wouldn't go searching for Philippa, and cursing the fact that the servants appeared more eager to serve his wife than him. If it was so after but two days of marriage, what would be his position a week from now?

"I have looked forward to this day, sir," Robert Burnell said as he eased himself down into the master's chair. "My cramped bones praise your generosity."

Dienwald smiled. "Take your rest for so long as it pleases you."

"You are kind, sir, but my duty is urgent and cannot be delayed longer."

"I pray the king doesn't want money from his barons, for I have none and my few men aren't meant to swell the ranks of his army."

Burnell merely shook his head, forgiving the presumption of the speaker. "Nay, the king wishes no coin from you. Indeed, he wishes to present you with a gift."

Dienwald felt something prickle on the back of his neck. He was instantly alert and very wary. A gift from the king? Impossible! An inconsistency, a contradiction. Surely a danger. He cocked his head to the side in question, already certain he wasn't going to like what Burnell said.

"Let me peel back the bark and get to the pith, sir. I'm here to offer you a gift to surpass any other gift of your life."

"The king wishes me to assassinate the King of France? The Duke of Burgundy? Has the Pope displeased him?"

Burnell's indulgent smile faltered just a bit at the blatant cynicism. "I see I must speed myself to the point. The king, sir, is blessed with a daughter, not one of his royal daughters, not a princess, but, frankly, sir, a bastard daughter. He wishes to give her to you in marriage. She is nonetheless a Plantagenet, greatly endowed with beauty, and will bring you a dowry worthy of any heiress of England to—"

Dienwald was reeling with surprise at this, but he still managed to remain outwardly calm. He held up his hand. "I must beg you to stop now, Lord Chancellor. You see, I am wedded two days now. You will thank the king, and tell him that as much as I wish I could hang myself for being unable to accept his wondrous offer, I am no longer available to do his bidding. I am already magnificently blessed." He hadn't realized that he would ever be blessing Philippa as his wife with such profound gratitude.

Wed the king's bastard? He wanted to howl aloud. It was too much. Such an offer was enough to make his hair fall out. But he was safe, bless Philippa and her escape from Beauchamp in a wool wagon.

Burnell looked aghast. He looked disbelieving. He looked vexed. "You're wedded! But Lord Graelam assured me that you were not, that you had no interest, that—"

"Lord Graelam de Moreton?"

"Naturally I spoke to men who know you. One cannot give the daughter of the King of England to anyone, sirrah!"

"I am already wedded," Dienwald repeated. He sounded calm, but now he had a target—Graelam—he wanted to spit on his lance. So Graelam would make *him* the sacrifice to the king's bastard daughter, would he! "Will you wish to stay the night, sir? You are most welcome. St. Erth has never boasted such an inspiring and important guest before. And do not beset yourself further, sir. I doubt this will gravely disappoint the king when he is told his first choice of son-in-law is not to be. Indeed, I venture to say that his second choice will doubtless be more to his liking."

Robert Burnell got slowly to his feet. He ran his tongue over his lips. This was a circumstance he hadn't foreseen, an event he hadn't considered as remotely possible. He felt weary and frustrated, bludgeoned by an unkind fate.

Margot made a timely entrance with ale, bread, and cheese. "Please," Dienwald said, and poured ale into a flagon, handing it to Burnell, who drank deeply. He needed it. He needed more ale to make his brain function anew. So much work, and all for naught. It wasn't just or fair. He couldn't begin to imagine the king's reaction. The idea made him shudder. He started to think of a curse, then firmly took himself in hand. He was a man of God, a man to whom devoutness wasn't a simple set of precepts or rules, but a way of life. But neither was he a man to rejoice when providence had done him in. He looked at the man he'd hoped would become the king's son-in-law and asked, "May I inquire the name of our lady wife?"

" 'Tis no secret. She is formerly Philippa de Beauchamp, her father Lord Henry de Beauchamp."

To Dienwald's astonishment, the chancellor's mouth dropped open; his cheeks turned bright red. He dropped the flagon, threw back his head, and gasped with laughter. It was a rusty sound, Dienwald thought, staring at the man, a sound the fellow wasn't used to making. Was the king so grim a taskmaster? What was so keen a jest? What had he said to bring forth this abundance of humor?

Dienwald waited. He had no choice. What in the name of the devil was going on?

Burnell finally wiped his eyes on the cuff of his wide sleeve and sat back down. He ignored the fallen flagon and poured himself more ale, taking Dienwald's flagon. He drank deeply, then looked at his host and gave him a fat, genial smile. He felt ripe and ready for life again. Fate was kind; fate gave justice to God's loyal subjects after all.

"You have saved me a great deal of trouble, Dienwald de Fortenberry. Oh, aye, sir, a great deal of trouble. You have made my life a living testimony to the beneficence of our glorious God."

"I have? I doubt that sincerely. What mean you, sir?"

Burnell hiccuped. He was so delighted, so relieved that God still loved him, still protected him. "I mean, sir, that the Lord has moved shrewdly and quite neatly, mocking us mere men and our stratagems and our little fancies, and all has come to pass as it was intended." And he began to laugh again. He swallowed when he saw that his host was growing testy. "I will tell you,

sir," Burnell said simply, "and I tell you true—
you have wedded the king's daughter. I know not
how it came about, but come about it did, and
all is well now, all is as it should be, praise the
Lord."

"You're mad, sir."

"Nay, Philippa de Beauchamp is the bastard
daughter of the King of England, and somehow
you have come to wed her. Will you tell me how
it chanced to happen?" Burnell smiled a moment,
and added under his breath, "So Lord Henry lied
about her bloody flux. The girl wasn't at Beauchamp. Ah, this tempts me, this ingenious story
he will soon tell me."

Dienwald's brain was a frozen wasteland. His
belly was twisted with cramps. He couldn't feel
his tongue moving in his mouth. He couldn't hear
his own heartbeat in his breast. Philippa, the
king's bastard? Philippa, who didn't have the
golden hair of the Plantagenets but instead a
streaked blond that was uniquely hers? Philippa,
whose vivid blue eyes were as bright as a summer's sky—like the king's, like all the Plantagenets' . . . He shook his head. It was inconceivable,
impossible. She'd leapt from a wool wagon and
into his life, and now she was his wife. She
couldn't be the king's daughter. She couldn't. She
wasn't to be dowered by her father—by Lord
Henry. Oh, God.

"How came it about, you ask? She fled from
her father—from *Lord Henry*—because she heard
him say that he wasn't going to dower her and
was going to wed her to William de Bridgport, a
man of sour nature and repellent character."

Burnell waved an impatient hand. "Of course
Lord Henry wouldn't dower her, 'twas not his

responsibility to do so. The king would. The king, who is in fact her father."

"She ran away, hiding in a wagon of wool bound for St. Ives Fair. She came here quite by accident. We were wedded, as I told you, two days ago."

"God's ways are miraculous to behold," Burnell said in a marveling voice. "I cannot wait to tell Accursi of this. He will not believe it." Burnell then shook his head and gazed at St. Erth's smoke-darkened beams high above, just as Lord Henry had done. Dienwald looked up too, hopeful of inspiration, but there was none, only Burnell saying complacently, "Well, now there need to be no agreements from you, sir. You have taken unto yourself the right wife. All is well. All has transpired according to God's plan."

"Don't you mean the king's plan?"

Burnell simply smiled as if the king and God were close enough so that it didn't matter.

Dienwald opened his mouth and bellowed, "Philippa! Come here. Now!"

She heard him yelling and lowered her brows at Gorkel. She walked past him, head high, into the great hall, and came to a halt, staring from her husband to the man seated in her husband's chair. "Aye?"

"Philippa," Dienwald bellowed, higher and louder, even though she stood not four feet away from him, "this man claims you are the king's bastard daughter, not the daughter of that damned fool Lord Henry. He convinces me, though I fought it. No wonder Lord Henry wouldn't dower you. 'Twas not his duty to do so. He lied about de Bridgport just to keep Ivo de Vescy away from you. Don't you see, you're the king's daughter and thus his responsibility. Damn you for a lying, deceitful wench!"

She continued to stare at him a moment, then transferred her gaze to the other man, who was nodding at her like a wooden puppet. "But this makes no sense. I don't understand. Lord Henry isn't my father?"

Burnell had no chance to reply, for Dienwald howled, "I do have a father-in-law, curse you, wench, but it isn't that fat whining creature in my bedchamber. Nay, him I could have tolerated. Him I could have threatened and intimidated until he did as I wished him to do.

"Nay, my father-in-law has to be the cursed King of England! Did you hear me, Philippa? He is the *King of England*. I, a scoundrel and a rogue, a man happily lacking in wealth and duty and responsibility, have the wretched king for a father-in-law! You have ruined me, wench! You have destroyed me! You are a thorn to be plucked from my flesh. Foul mischance brought you to me, and the devil wove you into my mind and body until I was forced to seduce you!"

Burnell gaped at him. A tirade such as this was unthinkable and completely astonishing. He said in his most reasoned churchman's voice, "But, sir, you will be made an earl, the king has commanded it. You will be a peer of the realm. You will be the Earl of St. Erth, the first of a mighty line to hold power and land and influence in Cornwall. The king will dower your wife handsomely. She is an heiress. You will be able to make repairs to your castle, swell your herds, grow more crops. You will know no want, no lacks. Your lands will prosper and extend themselves. Life will be better. Your people will live longer. Your priest will save more souls, all of St. Erth will show bounty and plenty and—"

Dienwald raised his voice to the beams above, yelling in misery, "I repudiate this wretched woman! Before God, I won't have the king's daughter as my wife. I won't be bound to the damned king or to his damned bastard! I want to be left alone. I demand to be left to my humble castle and my crumbling walls! I demand to be left to my blessedly profligate life and sinful deeds! Give me ragged serfs and frayed tunics! Save me from this foul penance! Damnation, my people don't *want* to live longer. My priest doesn't *want* to save more souls!"

He turned on his speechless wife, snarled something beneath his breath—the only thing he'd snarled that no one hadn't clearly heard—and strode from the great hall.

"Your father, our gracious king, bids you good grace, my lady," said Burnell, for want of anything better. He rose and took her limp hand. Her face was white and she looked uncomprehending.

He sought words to comfort her, to bring her understanding, for he imagined it wasn't a daily occurrence to be told you were the offspring of the king. "Lady Philippa, 'tis a surprise, I know it, this news has shaken you about, but all is known now and all is explained. The king . . . Naturally, he couldn't have acknowledged you before—he was wedded to his queen, even though at the time she was a very young girl. He wanted no hurt to come to her. But neither did he want to turn his back on you, for you were his dear daughter. He gave you for raising to Lord Henry. It was always his plan to come into your life when it was time for you to be married."

Philippa looked at him and said the most unlikely thing to him: "Why did the king wish me—a girl—to be taught to read and write?"

Burnell found his mouth open again. Had the girl vague and token wits? "I . . . ah, really, my lady, I'm not at all certain."

"I suppose I had a mother?"

"Aye, my lady. Her name is Constance and she is wedded to a nobleman of her station. She was very young when she birthed you, the king told me. Perhaps someday you will wish to know her."

"I see," Philippa said. At least Lady Maude's dislike of her was now explained. The king's bastard had been foisted upon a woman who hadn't wanted her. It was more to take in than she could manage at the moment, for in truth it was her husband who now filled her thoughts. Her husband and his outrage at what had happened to him.

"My husband doesn't want me," she said, looking away from the chancellor. She saw Old Agnes, Margot, Gorkel, Crooky, and a host of other St. Erth people staring at her, marveling at what she'd suddenly become, chewing it over, and wondering what to do. Would they mock her for being a bastard? Despise her or curtsy to her until their knees locked?

"Your husband is merely confused, my lady. His behavior and his unmeasured words demonstrate that he has no real understanding of what has happened. He must be confusing his new status with that of someone else; he must not comprehend his good fortune."

"My husband," Philippa said patiently, shaking her head at him, "comprehends everything per-

fectly. Understand, sir, he is not like most men."
That is why I love him and no other. "He doesn't
appreciate the sort of power and wealth some
men crave, nay, even covet unto death. He has
never sought it, never desired it. He enjoys his
freedom, and that means to him that he can do
just as he pleases without others interfering in his
life. Now all that has changed because of what I
am. He would never have wedded the king's bastard daughter, sir. Offers of an earldom, offers of
coin, offers of power and influence would have
driven him away, not seduced him. You would
never have convinced him otherwise. You could
not have even threatened him otherwise. But fate
arranged things differently for him, and for me.
He wedded me and now he doesn't want what
I've suddenly become. I don't know what to do."

Philippa turned away from the Chancellor of
England and walked out of the hall.

In the inner bailey she came to an appalled halt.
There was her father running toward Dienwald,
Edmund on his heels, trying to catch the tail of
his tunic. Her erstwhile father was shouting, "My
precious boy! My honorable lord, my savior!"

He caught Dienwald and threw his arms around
his neck and kissed him on each cheek.

Philippa shuddered at the sight.

Crooky came out of the Great Hall, observed
the spectacle, and shouted to the blue sky,

My poor master is now under the king's
    thumb
He wants to weep but his brain's gone numb
He's wed to a princess and will never be free
But he can't do a thing but accept it and be
—the king's proud son-in-law.

Philippa turned on the fool, cuffed him with all her strength, and watched him flail to keep his balance, then roll down the steps of the Great Hall, yelling loudly, "Kilt by a princess! The good king save me!"

21

Dienwald froze to the spot. Lord Henry had grabbed him firmly and was weeping copiously on his neck, kissing his ear, squeezing him so tightly Dienwald feared his ribs would crack, so great was Lord Henry's relief. "You're a fine, honorable lad, my lord. I knew it all the time, but I was just concerned and . . . well . . . Aye, 'tis God who has saved me and given me his blessing! I shall never again question the heavenly course of things, even though the course be a maze of blind turns."

Dienwald suffered Lord Henry for another moment, his mind still confused, when he looked up and saw Philippa cuff Crooky and send the fool flying. He grinned, then felt his face stiffen.

He pushed Lord Henry away. "Get thee gone, my lord! Take your *daughter* with you! I want her not. Just look at her—she even abuses my servants!"

"But, my precious boy, my dearest lord, wait! She's most desirable as a wife, Dienwald, she's quite comely—"

"Ha! Comely be damned! She's the king's daughter—that's her claim to comeliness!"

"Nay, not all of it. 'Twas I who raised her, I through my clerks and priests who taught her all she knows—and I saw to her lessons and to her prayers . . ."

"That certainly adds to her value." Dienwald didn't say another word. He just shook his head and broke into a run toward the St. Erth stables. Philippa walked slowly to where her father stood, looking in incredulous dismay after her retreating new husband.

"What ails him, Philippa? He's been given the earth and all its bounty. His father-in-law is the King of England! Oh, and you *are* comely, doubt it not, Philippa, truly. It matters not that you haven't the golden Plantagenet hair." Lord Henry looked upon his former daughter. "I don't understand him. He howls like a wounded hound and slinks off to hide. He acts as though he were to be hunted down and slain."

Philippa merely shook her head. She wasn't capable of more. Tears clogged her throat, and she swallowed.

Edmund tugged on her sleeve. "Are you truly the king's daughter?"

"It appears that I am."

Edmund fell silent, simply peering up at her, as if to observe some magical change in her.

"What, Edmund, you hate me too?"

"Don't be stupid, Philippa." Edmund stared

after his father. "Father's always boasted that his life was his own, you see. He's told me many times, since I was a very little boy, to be what I chose to be, not what someone else chose for me. He said that life was too rife with chance, too uncertain in measuring out its punishments and rewards, to be what someone else wished. He said he wanted no overlord, no authority to hold sway over him and to keep and hold what was his."

"Aye, I can hear him saying that. It's true, you know. It's what he believes, it's what he is." Philippa turned back to Lord Henry. "I wondered why I was so tall. The king is very tall, I hear. Is he not called Longshanks?"

Lord Henry nodded. "Listen to me, girl. I did my best by you."

"I know it well, and I thank you. It could not have been easy for Lady Maude. She always hated me, but she tried to hide it." At least in the beginning she'd tried.

Lord Henry tried his best to dissuade Philippa from this conclusion, but it was lame going, for Lady Maude had always resented the king's bastard being foisted upon her household. He stopped, unequal to the task.

Philippa looked thoughtful and said, "My hair— 'tis not Plantagenet gold, as you just said, but streaked and common."

"Nay, I simply spouted nonsense, that is all. Nothing about you is common. And your eyes, Philippa, they are the blue of the Plantagenets, a striking blue as vivid as an August sky." Philippa rolled her eyes at his effluence. "Aye," Lord Henry continued, rubbing his hands. "Aye, that is bound to please the king mightily when he finally meets you."

To meet the king. Her *father*. It held only mild interest for her now. All babes had to be born of someone. She was a royal indiscretion, nothing more, and that fact was going to ruin her life. "Please excuse me now, sir," she said. "I must decide what to do. If you wish to stay, you will use Edmund's chamber. If the chancellor wishes to stay, then he will sleep—" She broke off, shrugged, and walked away.

"Philippa's not happy," said Edmund to the old man who wasn't Philippa's father. Just imagine, Philippa was the king's get! It frayed the thoughts, such a happening. Did that make the King of England his step-grandfather?

"Your father, young Edmund, will make haste back to reason once he's had a chance to think things through. He's not acting like a man should act, given this heavenly gift."

"You don't know my father," said Edmund. "But Philippa does." Edmund left Lord Henry and walked to Crooky who was still sitting on the ground, rubbing his jaw.

"Aye, I was cuffed by a royal princess," said Crooky, his face alight with reverence and awe. "A real princess of the realm and she wanted to cuff me! Her fist touched me. *Me*, who's naught but a bungling ass and so common I am below common and thus uncommon."

"Nay, Crooky, she's the king's bastard and her fist did more than just touch you. I thought she was going to knock your head from your neck."

"Split you not facts into petty parts, little master. Your stepmother is of royal blood and that makes you . . . hmmmm, what does that make you?"

"Perchance almost as uncommon as you, Crooky." Edmund caught Gorkel's eyes and skipped away.

"The mistress is beset with confusion," Gorkel announced, "and so is the master."

"Aye."

Gorkel ground his teeth and stroked his jaw. "You must speak to the master. You're his flesh. He must heed you."

Edmund agreed this was true, but he knew his father well enough to realize he could say nothing to change his thinking. In any case, there was no opportunity. Dienwald, astride Philbo, was riding out of the inner bailey, alone, a blind look in his eyes. Men called after him, but he didn't respond, just kept riding, looking straight ahead.

In her bedchamber, Philippa sat on the bed and folded her hands in her lap. The situation was too much to absorb, so she simply sat there and let all that had occurred flow over her. Words, only words out of men's mouths, yet they'd changed her life. She didn't particularly care that she was the king's bastard. She didn't particularly care that now the facts of her life had become quite clear to her. She didn't care that Lady Maude had made much of her life a misery. And finally, she didn't care that she now knew why Walter had wished so much to wed her. She could only begin to imagine what prizes he believed would become his upon marrying her.

What she cared about was her husband. She saw his pale face, heard his infuriated words ringing in her ears, blanched anew at his rage over his betrayal. Betrayal in which she had played no part, but he didn't believe that. Or perhaps he did, only his outrage was so great, it simply didn't matter to him who had done what.

If King Edward had been in the bedchamber at this very moment, Philippa would have cuffed him as hard as she'd cuffed Crooky. She would have yelled at him for his damned perfidy—but then she would have crushed him with embraces for selecting Dienwald to be her husband. What was one to do, then?

Life had become as treacherous as Tregollis Swamp. She rose and began to pace. What to do?

Would Dienwald return? Of course he would. He had to, for he had no place else to go and he also had a son he wouldn't desert.

She knew she should give the women instructions; she should speak to Northbert about the lord chancellor's men as well as her fa . . . nay, Lord Henry's men-at-arms. She knew she should find out what Robert Burnell wished to do, and Lord Henry as well, for that matter. Thus, she finally left the bedchamber, duty overcoming loss and fear.

Lord Henry and Robert Burnell were drinking Dienwald's fine ale and chatting amiably. They would stay until the morning, they told her, both of them so ecstatic in drink that she doubted whether Burnell, that devout churchman who never flagged in his labors for his king, could stay upright for much longer. She sought out Margot.

The woman curtsied to her until Philippa thought she would fall on her face.

"You will cease such things, Margot. I am nothing more than I was before. Please, you mustn't . . ." Philippa broke off, stared blindly into space, and burst into tears.

She felt a small hand clasp hers and looked down to see Edmund through her tears.

"Father will come back, Philippa. He must come back. He'll soften, mayhap."

She could only nod. She retired to her bedchamber, rudely, she knew, but she couldn't bear to be with either Lord Henry or Robert Burnell, her *father's* chancellor.

Dienwald didn't return. Not that night or the following day.

Late the next day following, another man arrived at St. Erth, a man alone, astride a magnificent black barb, and he was searching for Robert Burnell. The chancellor had planned to depart that morning, but another long evening spent swilling ale with Lord Henry had kept him in bed—rather, the former steward's bed—until late that morning. Even now he was pale and of greenish hue.

For an instant Philippa thought it was Dienwald, finally come home, but it wasn't, and she wanted to kill the stranger for her disappointment.

His name was Roland de Tournay. She greeted him, not seeing him, not caring who he was, saying nothing, and merely led him to where Burnell and Lord Henry were sitting before a sluggish fire, trying to ignore their pounding heads.

Burnell leapt to his feet, his aching head forgotten. "De Tournay! What do you here? Is the king all right? Does he need to—"

"I am here on the king's orders," Roland said, waving his hand for Burnell to take his seat again. "I promised him to come speak to you about the heiress—the king's bastard daughter. He wants me to look her over."

Lord Henry bounded to his feet. "De Fortenberry is already the king's son-in-law, sirrah!"

Roland merely lifted a black brow. "The heiress is already dispatched, you say?"

"Aye, to the man the king intended her to have!"

Roland laughed. "A journey crowned with a neat escape for me. So that knave won her, eh?"

Philippa, who'd been listening to this talk, now stepped forward and said, "The king sent you?"

Roland stilled all humor as he looked at the king's daughter. He hadn't known who she was before. But as he looked at her closely now, he realized she had the look of Edward, with her clear blue eyes and her well-sculptured features. She was lovely and she was tall and well-formed, and her hair—ah, it was thick and curling down her back, framing her face. Then, for a brief instant Roland knew a sharp flicker of disappointment that he was too late. But only for an instant. He assumed a bland expression and said, "The king—your esteemed father—simply asked me to see you."

"I am already wedded," Philippa said in a remote voice. "However, it is uncertain whether or not my husband still will claim me for his wife. He left me, you see, when he learned my father is the King of England."

Roland's black brow shot up a good inch.

Lord Henry inserted himself. "You needn't tell this stranger all these things, Philippa. 'Tis none of his affair."

"Why not? The king sent him. Perhaps next he will send William de Bridgport when this man says he doesn't want me. Who knows?" Philippa turned to Robert Burnell and added, her voice hard, "Even if my husband dissolves our union, I don't want this man. Do you hear me? I don't want any other man, ever. Do you understand me, sir?"

"Aye, madam, I understand you well, for you speak clearly and to the point."

By God, Roland thought, staring at the young woman, she was in love with de Fortenberry. How had this come about, and so quickly? There was a mystery here, and he liked unraveling mysteries above all things.

Lord Henry snorted. "It matters not what he understands or doesn't understand. Look you, Roland de Tournay, my daughter was wedded to de Fortenberry before either of them knew who her real sire was. All is over and done with. You can leave with good conscience."

And Lord Henry stared at him as though he'd like to shoot an arrow through his neck. Well, it mattered not. Nor was it such a mystery after all.

"Don't be rude, Fa . . . my lord," Philippa said. "I care not if he remains at St. Erth. There is room, and there is more ale. Why not? Indeed, if he plans to return to London, he can tell the king what has transpired and . . ."

She stopped suddenly and just stared at Roland—not really at him, Roland thought, but through him and beyond him. There was a pain in her fine eyes, a very deep pain that made him flinch. Suddenly she turned and left the hall, simply walked away, saying nothing more.

"Damnable churl," Lord Henry said. "I'd slit his throat if he weren't already her husband."

Roland shook his head. "You mean that her husband left when he discovered she was the king's daughter?"

"Aye, that's the meat of it," Lord Henry said. "I'd like to smash the pea-brained young cockscomb into a dung heap."

Roland smiled at blessed fate. His luck had held him through this brief foray into possible disaster. He could not understand de Fortenberry's actions. Was the man mad? His own motives for not wishing to marry—even the king's bastard daughter— were different; they meant something. Roland decided to stay the night at St. Erth and on the morrow pay his visit to Graelam de Moreton at Wolffeton. The king's bastard daughter was no longer any of his concern. He'd done his duty by his king, and all, for him at least, had resolved itself right and tight. The heiress was already wedded and he had no more part to play.

He remarked upon the political situation with the Scots, the intractability of King Alexander and his minions, and forgot the purpose of his visit. The three men, without the presence of either the master or the mistress of St. Erth, ate their fill and consumed more of the castle's fine ale and kept watch and company until late into the night, talking, arguing, and yelling at each other, all in high good humor.

The master of St. Erth, the soon-to-be Earl of St. Erth, didn't appear. Nor did his discarded wife.

Wolffeton Castle

"Hold him down, Rolfe! Hellfire, grab his other leg, quickly, he nearly sent his foot into my manhood! You, Osbert, keep his arms behind him! Nay, don't break his elbow! Just keep him quiet."

Lord Graelam de Moreton rubbed his hand over his throbbing jaw and watched as two of his men held Dienwald down, another sitting on his legs and a fourth on his chest. Dienwald was panting and yelling and now he was gasping for breath, for Osbert was not a lightweight. His blow had been strong and knocked Graelam off his feet and flat on his back onto the sharp cobblestones of the inner bailey.

Of course, Dienwald had caught him off-guard. Aye, he'd taken Graelam by complete surprise. His so-called friend had ridden through Wolffeton's gates, welcomed by the men because he was a known ally. No one could have guessed that the instant Dienwald dismounted his destrier, he would attack him. Graelam looked down at his red-faced enraged friend. "What ails you, Dienwald? Kassia, don't fret, I'm all right. It's our neighbor here who's gone quite mad. He attacked me like a fevered fiend from hell."

"Let me up, you stinking whoreson, and you'll see how I split you with my sword!"

"Nay, sir," Rolfe said kindly. "Move you not, or I will have to twist your arm."

Kassia stared from Dienwald to her husband. "Ah," she said, "Dienwald has discovered what you did, my lord. He's come to express his disapproval of your interference."

"Aye, loose me, you coward, and I'll debone you, you lame-assed cur!"

Graelam hunkered down beside his friend, his face only inches from Dienwald's. "Listen to me, fool, and listen well. You needn't marry the king's daughter, and you know it well. Both Kassia and I saw Morgan or Mary or whatever her name is and knew it was she you wanted. We decided if you wanted to wed her, you would have her, and the king be damned. There was no reason for us to say anything. We knew you wouldn't bend to any man, be he king or sultan or God. Isn't that the truth?"

Dienwald howled. "I had already wedded her when Burnell came! She was already my wife!"

"So what is the matter? You're acting half-crazed. Speak sense and I will let you free."

"Her name isn't Morgan or Mary, damn you! Her name is Philippa de Beauchamp and she is our blessed king's cursed daughter!"

Graelam looked up at his wife. They simply stared at each other, then back at Dienwald. "Well," Graelam said finally, "this is a most curious turn of events."

Kassia knelt beside Dienwald and gently laid her hand on his cheek. "You're obstinate beyond all reason, my friend. You wedded the girl who was intended for you. And she was the girl you wished to wed. All worked out as it was intended to. Everyone is content, or should be. So you're now the king's son-in-law. Does it really matter all that much? You will perhaps have to become more, er, respectable, Dienwald, in your dealings, less eager to strip fat merchants of their goods, possibly a bit more deferential, particularly when you are in the king's presence, but surely it isn't too much to ask. We did it for your own good, you know—"

"Good be damned!" Dienwald howled, his eyes red. "Your mangy husband did it because he thought I'd stolen the wine your father sent you! Admit it, you hulking whoreson! You did it to revenge yourself upon me—I know it as I know you and your shifty ways!"

"You won't insult my lord," Kassia said in a tone of voice Dienwald had never heard from her before. It was low and it was mean. It drew him up short, and he said, his voice now sulky and defensive, "Well, 'tis true. He did me in, he did it to spite me."

Kassia smiled down at him. "You reason with your spleen and your bile, not with your wits. Hush now and behave yourself. Release him, Rolfe, he won't act the stupid lout again. At least," she added, giving a meaningful look to Dienwald, "he had better not. Yes, Dienwald, you will now rise and you won't attempt to strike Graelam again. If you even try it, you will have to deal with me."

Dienwald looked at the very delicate, very pregnant lady and grinned reluctantly. "I don't want to have to deal with you, Kassia. Cannot you turn your back for just a moment? I just want to smash your husband into the ground. Just one more blow, just a small one."

"No, you may not even spit at him, so be quiet. Now, come in and I will give you some ale. Where is Philippa? Where is your lovely bride?"

"Doubtless she is singing and dancing and playing a fine tune for the damned Chancellor of England and her fa . . . nay, that idiot Lord Henry de Beauchamp."

"You believe her wallowing in pleasure that you left St. Erth? That is what you did, isn't it, Dienwald? You shouted and bellowed at her and then ran away to sulk?"

Dienwald looked at the gentle, sweet, pure lady at his side, and growled at her husband, "Put your hand over her mouth, Graelam. She grows impertinent. She vexes me as much as the wench does."

Graelam laughed. "She speaks the truth. You've a wife, and truly, Dienwald, it matters not who her family is. You didn't wed her for a family or lack of one, did you? You wedded her because you love her."

"Nay! Cut off your rattling tongue! I wedded her because I took her and she was a damned virgin and I had no choice but to wed her since my son—my demented nine-year-old son—demanded that I do so!"

"You would have wedded her anyway," Kassia said, "Edmund or no Edmund."

"Aye," Dienwald agreed, shaking his head mournfully. "I will beget no bastard off a lady."

"Then why do you act the persecuted victim?" Graelam said. "The heedless brute who cares for no one?"

"Oh, I care for her, but I believed her father to be naught but a fool, and so it bothered me not. But no, her father must needs be the King of England. The *King of England*, Graelam! It is too much. I will not abide it. I will set her aside. She took me in and made a mockery of me. Aye, I will send her to a convent and annul her and she will forget all her besotted feelings for me. She smothered me with her sweet yielding, her soft smiles and her passion. She will hate me and it will be what we both deserve."

Kassia swept a cat off the seat of a chair and motioned Dienwald to it. "You will do nothing of the sort. Sit you down, my friend, and eat. You've eaten naught, have you? . . . I thought not. Here are some fresh bread and honey."

Dienwald ate.

Graelam and Kassia allowed him to vent his rage and sulk and carp and curse luridly, until, upon the third morning after his unexpected arrival at Wolffeton, Roland de Tournay rode into the inner bailey.

When Roland saw Dienwald, he simply stared at him silently for a very long time. The man looked to Roland's sharp eye to be at the very edge. His eyes were hollow and dark-circled for want of sleep, and he had not the look of a man remotely content with himself or with his lot. "Well," Roland said, "I wondered where you'd fled. Your wife is not a happy lady, my soon-to-be lord Earl of St. Erth."

"I don't want to be a damned earl! What did you say? Philippa isn't happy? Is she ill? What's wrong?"

"You yourself said she was besotted with you, Dienwald," Kassia said. "Would you not expect her to be unhappy in your absence?"

Roland marveled aloud at de Fortenberry's outpouring of stupidity. He said patiently, "Your lovely wife happens to care about you, something none understand, but there it is. As you say, she is besotted with you. Thus, in your unexpected absence, she is miserable; all your servants are miserable because she is; your son hangs to her skirts trying to raise her spirits, but it does little good. The chancellor and Lord Henry finally left because life at St. Erth had become so grim and bleak. No one had any spirit for jests, even your fool, Crooky. He simply lay about in the rushes mumbling something about the lapses of God's grace. I could be in the wrong of it, but it would seem to me that you are very stupid, my lord earl."

"I am not a damned earl! I don't recall having required your opinion, de Tournay!"

"Nay, you did not, but I choose to give it to you, freely offered. Your wife is a lovely lady. She doesn't deserve to be treated so meanly."

Dienwald appeared ready to attack Roland, and Graelam quickly intervened. "I expected you sooner, Roland. Dienwald, go lick your wounds elsewhere and look not to bash Roland. He isn't your enemy. And if you spit on him, Kassia won't like it."

Dienwald, still muttering, strode to Wolffeton's training field, there to besport himself with Rolfe and the other men.

As for Roland, he turned to Graelam and smiled. "It has been a very long time, my friend, but I am here at last. This is your wife, Graelam? This beautiful creature who looks like a fairy princess? She calls you, a scarred hairy warrior, husband? Willingly?"

"Aye," Kassia said, and gave her hand to Roland. He touched his fingers to her palm and smiled down at her. "You carry a babe, my lady."

"Your vision is sharper than a falcon's, Roland! Aye, she will give me a beautiful daughter very soon now."

"A son, my lord. 'Tis a son I carry."

Roland looked at the two of them. He had known Graelam de Moreton for many years and called him friend. But he'd known him as a hard man, unyielding and implacable, a valued man to fight at your side, strong and valiant, but no show of tenderness or gentleness in his character to please such a fragile lady as this. But he did please her—that was evident. Roland marveled at it and thought it excellent, but didn't choose to see such changes in himself. No, never. He didn't understand such feelings and had no desire to, none.

Graelam said, "Come, Roland, I assume you have something of import to tell me. Kassia, I wish you to rest now, sweetling. Nay, argue not with me, for rest you will, even if I have to tie you to our bed." He leaned down, his palm gentle against his wife's cheek, and lightly kissed her mouth. "Go, love."

And Roland marveled anew. The two men sat in Wolffeton's great hall, flagons of wine between them.

Roland said without preamble, "I must go to Wales and I mustn't be Roland de Tournay there. You have friends amongst the Marcher Barons. I need you to give me an introduction to one of them. Mayhap I will need to pay a surprise visit."

Graelam said, "You play spy again, Roland? I have no doubt, my friend, that you could dupe God into accepting you as one of his angels. Aye, I have friends there. If you must, you can go to Lord Richard de Avenell. He is the father of Lady Chandra de Vernon. You know her husband, Jerval, do you not?"

Roland nodded. "Aye, I met both of them in Acre."

"It's done, then, Roland. I will have my steward, Blount, write a letter for you to Lord Richard. He will welcome you to his keep. Will you leave for Wales immediately?"

Roland sat back in his chair and crossed his arms over his chest, his eyes sparkling with mischief. "If I may, Graelam, I should like to remain just for a while longer to see what transpires

between Dienwald and his wife and his wife's
father-in-law."

Graelam laughed. "Aye, I too would like to see
Edward's face were he to be told that Dienwald
cursed and fled when he discovered the king was
now related to him! He would surely be speechless for once in his life."

Near St. Erth

Walter de Grasse wanted to spit, and he did,
often. It relieved his bile. He'd argued fiercely
with Britta, who'd clung to him and wept bitter
tears and begged him to stay with her and not go
after Philippa. But he'd dragged himself and his
aching head away.

He would have Philippa, no matter the cost. He
would have her and he would kill Dienwald de
Fortenberry at last. Damned scoundrel! And he
would keep Britta, no matter what either female
wanted.

He'd cursed his men roundly, railing at them
for allowing one lone women with a little boy to
escape Crandall. But it had happened and they
had escaped and now he had to devise another
way of catching her again.

He and six of his most skilled and ruthless men
camped in a scraggly wood not a mile from the
castle of St. Erth. One man kept watch at all
times. It was reported to Walter that the master
of St. Erth himself had ridden off, no one with
him, and as yet he hadn't returned. Walter knew
of the chancellor's visit and of Lord Henry's visit
as well. The fat was now in the fire, and Philippa

as well as Dienwald had been told who she really
was.

Why, then, had Dienwald ridden away from
his keep alone? It made no sense to Walter.

He saw the chancellor and all his men leave,
which was a relief, for Walter had no wish to
tangle with the king's soldiers. Then Lord Henry
and his men left St. Erth. Walter sat back,
chewed on a blackened piece of rabbit, and
waited.

Wolffeton Castle

"The wench is what she is, and nothing can
change that."

"That is true," Graelam agreed.

"Do you love her, Dienwald?" Kassia asked
now, setting her embroidery on her knee, for the
babe was big in her belly.

"You women and your silly talk of love! Love
is naught but a fabrication that dissolves when
you but look closely at it."

"You begin to sound more the fool than your
Crooky." Kassia sighed. "You must face up to
things, Dienwald. You must go home to your wife
and your son. Perhaps, if you are very careful,
you could still raid on your western borders. Aye,
I think my lord would wish to accompany you.
He chafes for adventure now that there is naught
but boring peace."

"She's right, Dienwald. There would be no reason for the king to find out. You could be most
discreet in your looting and raiding. You would
simply have to select your quarry wisely. Aye,

Kassia speaks true. I should like a bit of sport myself, on occasion."

Dienwald brightened. "Philippa likes adventure as well," he said slowly. "I think she would much enjoy raiding."

"It is certainly something for the two of you to speak together about," Kassia said, lowering her head so Dienwald wouldn't see the smile on her lips.

Roland de Tournay, much to both Graelam's and his wife's appalled surprise, said suddenly, "Nay, I don't agree with Graelam. I agree with you, Dienwald. I think you should travel to Canterbury and explain to the archbishop what happened to you. I think he would annul his marriage. After all, the wench wasn't honest about her heritage. She's a bastard when all's said and done. What man would wish to be wedded to a bastard? Aye, rid yourself of her, Dienwald. It matters not if she carries your babe in her belly. Let the king, her father, see to it. You will be happy again and your keep will resume its normal workings. You can return to your mistresses with a free heart and without guilt."

To Graelam's and Kassia's further surprise, Dienwald bounded to his feet and stared at Roland as though he'd suddenly become a toad that had just hopped onto the trestle table and into the pigeon pie.

"Shut your foul mouth, Roland! Philippa knew not that she was a bastard! None of it was her fault, none of it her doing. She is honest and pure and sweet and . . ." He broke off, saw that he'd been trapped in a cage of his own creation, and turned red all the way to his hairline.

"You damnable whoreson, I hope you rot!" he bellowed as he strode with churning step from Wolffeton's great hall, leaving its three remaining occupants to explode with laughter.

22

St. Erth Castle

Philippa stood in the inner bailey, her hands on her hips, facing Dienwald's master-of-arms. "I care not what you say, Eldwin. I won't remain here for another day, nay, not even another hour! Don't you understand? Your master is at Wolffeton—he must be there—licking his imagined wounds and whining to Graelam and his *perfect* little Kassia about what his treacherous wife has done to him."

"And you wish to go to Wolffeton, mistress? If the master is there, you want to berate him in front of Lord Graelam? Rebuke him in front of the men? Mistress, he is your lord and master and your husband. You mustn't do anything that would reflect badly on him. Above all, surely you wouldn't wish to leave St. Erth! Why, 'tis your

duty to remain here until the master decides what
he will do and—"

Philippa was at the end of her tether. Crooky,
who stood beside her, looked knowingly at Eldwin and said, "You are naught but a stringy bit
of offal, sirrah! Don't pretend to rise above what
you are to tell *her* what she must and mustn't
do. She is a princess, Eldwin, so bite your churl's
tongue! A princess does what she wishes to do,
and if she wishes to fetch the master, well then,
all of us will go with her and fetch the master.
And the master will be well-fetched, and that's
an end to it!"

"Aye, I will go as well," said Edmund, "for he
is my father."

"And I!"

"And I!"

Eldwin, routed, looked about at the two score
of St. Erth people, who had obviously sided with
the mistress. Old Agnes was grinning her toothless grin and flapping her skinny arms at him as
if he were a fox in her henhouse. He gave over,
but not completely. "But, mistress, all of us can't
leave the castle! Old Agnes, you must stay and
see to the weaving and sewing! Gorkel, you must
keep the villeins at their tasks and see to the
keep's safety."

"Aye, and what will ye do, Eldwin of the
mighty arm?" Old Agnes said.

"I go with the mistress," Eldwin said, rose to
his full height, and stared down at Old Agnes,
who promptly moved back a few steps.

Philippa grinned, and Eldwin, pleased that he'd
made her smile, and equally pleased that Old
Agnes had retreated a bit, felt his chest expand.
Perhaps they *should* fetch the master. Perhaps it

was the best thing to do. Wasn't there more to his duty than to remain at St. Erth and command and protect the keep?

"Aye, mistress, it will be as our brave Eldwin says," Old Agnes shouted. "I'll keep all these rattling tongues at their tasks! I just hope Prink—the faithless cretin—gives me some difficulties. If Mordrid doesn't smack him down, then I'll have Gorkel flail off his wormy hide."

"Aye," said Gorkel the Hideous, "I'll keep everything and everyone in his place. You aren't to fret yourself, mistress. No one will fall into lazy stupor."

It was too much. Philippa looked from one beloved face to another and felt her smile crack. The past three days had been beyond wretched, and all of them had tried so diligently to make her feel better about her husband's defection. She swallowed her tears, and found herself nodding at Crooky with approval even as he cleared his throat and looked fit to burst with song.

> We go to fetch the master
> We go to bring him home.
> We'll not take a nay from him
> Unless he's torn limb from limb.

Crooky stopped, clapping his hands over his mouth, aghast at the shocking words that had come pouring forth. Philippa stared at him. Everyone stared at him. Then Philippa giggled; several nervous giggles followed. Finally Philippa sobered and turned to Eldwin. "Pick fifteen men and arm them well. We ride to Wolffeton within the hour. As for the rest of you, prepare the keep for your master's return. We will feast as we did the day of our wedding!"

Near St. Erth

Walter was livid. He saw her there, at the head of the men, riding away from St. Erth. Fifteen men—he counted them. Well-armed they were. Too many for him to attempt to capture her, damn their hides.

Where was she going? Perhaps, he thought, smiling, she was leaving her husband. Aye, that was it. She was leaving the perfidious lout.

At last he'd have her. Walter roused his men, mounted his destrier, and waved all of them to follow him. He would follow her all the way to Ireland if need be. He would find her alone at some point along the way. She would have to relieve herself or bathe. Aye, he'd get her.

Between Wolffeton and St. Erth

Dienwald patted Philbo's neck. His destrier was lathering a bit, beginning to blow hard now, but he plowed forward, ever forward, as if guessing they were homeward-bound.

Dienwald would soon have his wench again and he would kiss her and hold her and tell her he forgave all her multitudinous sins, even if she chose not to remember them. He would love her until he was insensate and she as well.

"Ah, Philippa," he said, looking between Philbo's twitching ears. "Soon all will be well again. Even though I'll be an earl, I shan't carp overly.

I will bend my knee to your cursed father when I must, and will show him that I am a man of honor and a man who cares more for his daughter than the world and all its bounty.

"I'll learn to write so that I can extol her beauty in love poems, and recite aloud what I have written to her." Dienwald paused at those outflowing words. Philbo snorted. Dienwald's vow rang foolish, so he quickly shook his head. "Nay, not poetry," he added quickly, "but I will show her how much I desire her and adore her by my actions toward her. I will whisper in her ear of my desire for her and wring her sweet heart with my tender tongue. I will never, ever yell at her in anger again." He smiled at that. Aye, 'twas good, that vow. It was a vow with meat and meaning, and he could hold to it; he was a reasonable man, he was controlled. It wouldn't be difficult.

Aye, he would tease her and love her and bend her gently to his will. He worried not about his own peculiar will, for he was not a tyrant to demand subservience. Nay, his was a beneficient will, a mellow will, a will to which she would submit eagerly, her beautiful eyes filled with pleasure at pleasing him, for she adored him and wanted above all things to delight him.

His brow lowered suddenly, and he added loudly, "I won't promise to become a shorn lamb in the king's damned flock!" He moaned, seeing himself in a royal antechamber, clothed like a mincing buffoon, waiting for the king to grant him audience. It was a hideous vision. It curled his toes and made his heart lurch.

Philbo snorted, and Dienwald ceased his flowing monologue and his dismal imaginings, which, after all, needn't necessarily come to pass. In the distance he saw a tight group of men riding toward him. He counted them, sixteen men in all. What could they want? Where were they going? And then he recognized Philippa's mare and Eldwin's huge black gelding and his son's pony.

What was happening here? Where was Philippa going with his men? There she was, riding right there in the fore, leading them, commanding them. Where was she taking his son? Then he froze in his saddle.

She was leaving him. She'd decided she didn't want him. She'd decided that she was too far above him to belittle herself with him further. She'd left St. Erth—her home—where she belonged. She was going to London, to her father's court, to wear precious jewels and fine clothes and never again worry about being naked and having only a blanket to wear.

His fury mounted and he cursed loudly, raising his voice to the heavens. Aye, and he couldn't begin to imagine all the men who would be at court, wanting her, damn her beautiful face and body, not just because of who her father was, but because of how she—

"Damnation!" he bellowed, and urged Philbo to a furious gallop. He saw Edmund riding close to Philippa, Eldwin on his other side. And there was Northbert, his loyal Northbert, riding just behind her. She was stealing his son from him, and his men were helping her. Rage poured through his body.

"By God," Eldwin said, coming closer to Philippa's side. "That's the master! See, 'tis Philbo he rides! He rides right for us, as if he comes from hell."

"Or he rides toward heaven," Philippa said, smiling.

"Aye," Edmund said from her other side, " 'tis Papa!"

"At last," Philippa said, drawing her mare to a halt. Her eyes sparkled for the first time in three days and her back straightened.

Philippa forgot her anger at her husband at the sight of him galloping toward her. He'd come to terms with matters and realized that he wanted her, only her, and she was his wife, no matter who her sire was. How fast he was riding! She felt warmth pouring through her, knowing that soon he would be kissing her and holding her, not caring that his men were watching, that his son would be tugging at his tunic for his own hug. He would probably pull her in front of him on Philbo so he could fondle her all the way back to St. Erth. Philippa closed her eyes a moment and let the sweet feelings flow through her. He would love her and there would be naught but smiles and laughter between them again. No more arguments, no more boiling tempers, no more shouting down the keep.

She opened her eyes, hearing his pounding destrier, and now she could see his face, and she urged her mare forward, wanting to reach him, wanting to lean into his arms when he drew close.

Dienwald jerked up on Philbo's reins, and the powerful destrier reared on his hind legs, snorting loudly.

"Philippa!"

"Aye, husband. I am here, as is your son, as you can see, and your men with us. We were coming to—"

He allowed Philbo to come only a few feet closer to his men and his wife. He needed some distance from her. He'd stoked the fire and now he was ready to blaze. "You damnable bitch! How dare you steal my son! How dare you steal yourself! Aye, I know where you're going, you malignant female—'tis to your father's court you were traveling with my treacherous men, to bask in the king's favor and gleam riches from him. Perfidious wench! Get thee out of my sight! I don't want you, I never wanted you, and I will whip you if you leave not this very instant, this second that follows the end of my words! Hear me, wench?"

"Papa . . ."

"You'll soon be safe from her, Edmund. We'll return to St. Erth and all will be restored to the way it was before she blighted us with her presence. You were right, Edmund: she was a witch, a curse from the devil, rising out of the wool wagon like a creature from Hades, criticizing you, scorching all of us with her tongue with the first words from her mouth. You won't have to suffer her further, none of us will. You, Eldwin, Galen, Northbert! all of you, leave her side. Ride away from her. She's naught but the most treacherous of beings!" He paused, breathing hard.

"Master," Galen said quickly in the moment of respite, though he was awed by his master's flawed fluency. He waved his hand to gain Dienwald's attention, for the master was staring straight at the mistress, blind with anger. The master was confused; he didn't understand. Galen looked toward the mistress, but she was simply staring back at the master, white-faced and still. "What you think isn't what is true, master. You mustn't believe those absurd words you spout—"

"We return to St. Erth at once!" Dienwald roared. "Get thee gone, wench. No more will you torment me with your lies and tempt me with your sweet body."

Philippa hadn't said a word. She'd stared at him, at his mouth, as if she could actually see the venomous words flowing out. He truly thought she was leaving him, taking his son with her to London, to her father's court? She felt a hollowness inside, an emptiness that at the same time overflowed with pain and fury. She stared at him as he yelled and bellowed and insulted her. It was all over now. So much for her silly dreams of his love.

He was exhorting his men now, calling them faithless hounds and churlish knaves. Then he stopped and stared at them, and his men were silent beneath his volley of fury. A spasm of pain crossed his face. They'd all betrayed him. They'd gone over to her side. He felt blinding grief and anger. Without a thought, he galloped through them. He would return to St. Erth. They could do as they pleased; if they chose to follow her, then they could, curse them. His men fell back from him, scattering, their destriers whinnying in surprise. He heard Galen shouting, Northbert bellowing something he didn't understand or care to. He wanted only to get away from her and the misery she'd brought him. He whipped Philbo into a mad gallop away from her, away from his men, straight through them, back to St. Erth. Away from his son, who'd also chosen the damnable wench.

" 'Tis over now," Philippa said. Her lips felt numb, her brain emptied of feeling and thought. She felt utter and complete defeat. Nothing mattered now. It was better so. Then suddenly she felt the blood pounding through her, felt the heat of fury roil and churn within her, felt such black rage at his stupidity that she couldn't bear it. How dare he, the disbelieving fool!

"No!" Philippa yelled after him. She whipped her mare about and raced after her husband. She yelled back over her shoulder, "Eldwin, remain here! None of you do anything! I'll be back soon! Edmund, don't worry. Your father but needs a sound thrashing!"

Dienwald's men, their ranks already split by the master's wild ride, let her go through as well. She rode straight after her husband, her eyes narrowed on his back, her hands fisted over the mare's reins. She saw Dienwald twist in his saddle at the sound of her mare closing on him, saw the surprise on his face, the brief uncertainty, the renewal of rage.

Philbo was tired and the mare was fresh. Just as her mare came beside Philbo, Philippa, not for the last time in her life, thought with her feet. Without hesitation, she jumped from the mare's back straight at her husband, her arms flying around his back. He stared at her in that wild instant, then knew what was going to happen. He lurched around in the saddle, clutched her against his chest even as both of them hurtled from Philbo's back to the ground. Dienwald twisted and landed first, managing to spare Philippa the brunt of the fall. His arms tightened, and he grunted, the breath momentarily knocked out of him.

The road was narrow and curved, alongside it the terrain sloped sharply downward. They rolled over and over, locked together, down the grassy incline, coming finally to a stop in the middle of a patch of eglantine and violets.

Dienwald lay on his back, Philippa atop him. They were both breathing hard. Dienwald wondered if his body was intact or strewn in bits amongst the eglantine. Then Philippa reared back, looking down at him. She, he saw, was just fine. He felt her belly against him and his sex responded instantly, and he knew, at least, that this part of him had survived the fall, and further, would never be immune from her. Her thick glorious hair had come loose of its ribbon and was a riot of wild curls around her face. Her eyes sparkled with fierceness and he found himself waiting eagerly for her outpouring of rage.

"You stupid lout," she shouted three inches from his face. "I should break both your arms and your head! You ignorant clod! Aye, I'll break you into small pieces!"

"You already have," he said. "Ridiculous woman, I tried to protect you, take the brunt of the fall, but your weight flying at me was enough to crush my spleen and pulverize my liver. When we smashed to the ground, my breath died, as did all feeling in my chest."

" 'Tis the loss of your brains that should concern you," Philippa said, and began to pound him. "You had few to begin with, rattling around in that fat head of yours, and now you have none, my lord husband."

Dienwald grabbed her flailing fists—not an easy task—and finally managed to roll her beneath him. He jerked her arms over her head, clasped her wrists together, and came up to straddle her so she couldn't rear up and kick him.

"Now," he said, looking down at her, his chest heaving. "Now."

"Now what, you buffoon?"

He felt words stick in his throat. Something was decidedly wrong here. She seemed unaware of his mastery over her, whereas he was aware of nothing but the maddening effect she had on him.

"I suppose you've been licking your false wounds, with your perfect little Kassia giving you her sweet, tender succor. Is that it, you wretched ass? Have you spent the past three days bemoaning your hideous fate? Cursing me and all the saints for the misery that has befallen you? And did your perfect little Kassia agree with you and cry with you as you smote your feckless brow? Answer me!"

"Not really," he said, and frowned.

She jerked, trying to free her hands, but he only tightened his grip. He wanted to kiss her and thrust inside her and throttle her all at the same time. Instead, he said in his most commanding voice, "I am your master, wench. Only I, no one else. You came to me and seduced me and I wedded you and that is that. Now, hold still and keep your tongue quiet, for I must think."

"Think! Ha!"

"Where were you going with my men and my son? You were escaping me, 'twas plain to see. You were going to London, weren't you? You were taking my son and going to your cursed father. Tell me the truth!"

She sneered at him and tried to kick him, but he held her securely and all she gained was the pressure of his sex, hard and demanding, against her. It drove her mad and enraged her at the same time. "Aye," she shouted so loudly she hurt his ears, "aye, we were all going to London! To my father—to cover myself with jewels and cavort and frolic and dance with all the fine courtiers."

"That's all you can think about? Gallants and jewels? And what would Edmund have done whilst you were cavorting and frolicking and flirting with these frivolous clotheheads?"

That stumped her, for her brain had fallen into wayward paths. He was astride her, his legs tight against her sides, and he was panting, so close she could nearly feel the texture of his mouth on her. She wanted desperately to hit him and then kiss him until he was breathless and so hungry for her that he forget everything.

"Don't look at me like that, Philippa. It will do you no good. I won't give in to you. It won't spare you my wrath. Don't deny it—you're trying to seduce me again. No, you've been disloyal to me, you've—"

She suddenly heaved upward with all her strength, taking him off-guard. He fell sideways, not releasing her wrists, and they were lying there with naught but thick clumps of purple violets between them, face-to-face, their noses nearly pressed together. He couldn't help himself. He kissed her, then lurched back as if stung by a hornet.

"Dienwald . . ." she whispered, and hurled herself toward him, trying to kiss him back.

"Nay, I shan't let you debauch me again, wench. Stay away from me." Blood pounded in her head and with a furious cry she pulled free of his hands and smashed down on him, rolling him again onto his back. She was lying atop him once more, and then she was kissing him, even

as he tried to duck away. She gripped his hair
and yanked hard, holding his head between her
hands, and she kissed him again and again, licking his chin, nipping at his nose, rubbing her
cheek against his ear. He felt her belly hard
against his sex and knew it was nearly the finish.
The finish for him. He didn't understand her. She
was yielding and taking both at the same time,
and it astonished him and pleased him. He stilled
his body, letting her have her way with him.

"Wench," he said finally when she'd momentarily left his mouth. "Wench, listen to me."

Eyes vague, heart pounding, Philippa heard his
soft voice and raised her head to look down at
him.

"You're my husband, you peevish fool," she
said, and kissed him again. "You're mine. I
would never leave you, never, no matter how
great my anger at you and your crazy thinking.
Do you understand me?" And she pounded his
head against the violets. "Do you? I was coming
to fetch you, to bring you home to me, where
you belong. Do you understand?"

"Stop it for but a moment! By the saints, my
head! You're breaking my head! There, stop! Aye,
I understand you. But now you heed me. You're
my wife and you won't ever leave me again, do
you understand me? You will remain at St. Erth
or wherever it is I wish you to remain. You won't
ever go haring off to London to see your father
without me. I won't have it, do you hear me?"

"Me leave you?" That made her stop her kisses
and clear her brain just a bit. "You left me! For
three days I didn't know where you were or what
you were doing. Then I realized you would go to

your beloved perfect little Kassia, so I was coming after you, your men and your son with me!"

In her indignation, she tugged at his hair all the harder and pounded his head several more times against the ground. He groaned loudly, and she stopped. "Your head is crushing the violets. How dare you think those awful things about me? You are impossible and I can't imagine why I love you more than I love—" She broke off, staring down at him, knowing that she'd left herself open to him, open to his scorn, his baiting, his insults.

He suddenly smiled, a beautiful crooked smile that made her want to kiss him until he couldn't think. "Were you really coming after me, to fetch me home?"

"Of course! I wasn't going to London. You honestly believe I would steal your son, leave my home? Command your men to attend me? Ah, Dienwald, you deserve this!" She reared back, her arm raised, yet at the last moment her fist stilled in midair. She stared down at him and saw the gleam of challenge in his eyes, the twist of a smile on his mouth. She cursed him softly, then leaned down and kissed him thoroughly. He parted his lips and let her tongue enter his mouth. It was wonderful. She was wonderful and she was his.

"Aye," he said into her warm mouth, "I deserve all of you, wench."

She felt his hands stroke down her back and pulled her flat against him. His fingers were parting her legs, pressing inward through her gown, to touch her. "Dienwald," she said against his mouth.

He jerked up her gown and his fingers were now caressing the bare skin of her inner thighs, working slowly upward, until they found her woman's flesh and then he paused, his fingers quiet now, not moving, merely feeling her warmth and softness. He sighed deeply. "I've missed you."

"Nay, 'tis my body you've missed," she whispered between urgent kisses. "Any female would suit you, 'tis just that you are a lusty cockscomb and a man who is randy all his waking hours. I have heard of all your other women, I even know all their cursed names for Edmund recited them."

"You would surely make me the most miserable of men were I to take another woman to my bed. Do you know that I dream of coming inside you, deep and deeper still, and all the while you're telling me how it makes you feel when I push into you—"

She kissed him again, wild for him now, unheeding of their surroundings. Dienwald was very nearly removed in spirit as well until he heard Eldwin's soft voice, "Master."

Dienwald wanted nothing more than to let Philippa debauch him right here, in the nest of violets and eglantine, the soft warm air swirling about them. He cocked open an eye even as he pulled down her gown.

"What want you, Eldwin? There is an army bearing down on you and you must know where to flee?"

"No, master, 'tis worse."

"What in the name of St. Andrew could possible be worse?"

"It will rain soon, master—a heavy rain, Northbert says, a deluge that could fill this ditch in which you lie. Northbert reads well the clouds and the other signs, you know that."

Dienwald looked up. It was true, the soft warm

air swirling about them was also dark and heavy and gray. But it didn't matter, not one whit. "Excellent, my thanks. You and the men take Edmund back to St. Erth. The wench—my wife and I will return shortly. Go now. Wait not another minute. Hurry. Be gone."

Eldwin wasn't blind to what he'd interrupted. He turned on his heel and hurried back to the waiting men. Soon Dienwald heard pounding hooves going away from them.

"Now, wench."

"Now what?"

"Now I shall have my way with you in the midst of the violets and the eglantine."

When the first rain drop landed on Philippa's forehead, she was glad for it for she felt fevered and so urgent she felt ready to burst. Dienwald brought her closer to his mouth and caressed her until she screamed, arching her back, wild with wanting and with the mounting feelings that filled her. Overflowing now. And when he left her, she lurched upward and pressed him back and he fell, laughing and moaning, for she was kissing his throat, his chest, her hands splayed over him, and soon she was crouched between his legs and her mouth was on his belly, her hair flowing over him, and she was caressing him with her mouth and her hands. When she took him into her mouth, tentatively, wonderingly, he thought he would spill his seed then so urgent did he feel, but it was as if she guessed, and left him, easing him gently with her fingers, before caressing him again until he cried out with it and pulled her off him. Then he was covering her, and his manhood was thrusting into her, deep and hard, and so sweet that she cried with the wonder of it. And when he spilled his seed within her, he tasted her tears on her lips.

Dienwald said as he kissed the raindrops away, "I love you, Philippa, and I will never cease loving you and wanting you. We are joined, you and I, and it is for always. Never, ever, will I speak to you in anger again. You are mine forever."

And she said only, "Yes."

He was heavy on her, but she didn't care. She wrapped her arms about his back and hugged him all the more tightly. The rain thickened and it was only then they realized that they were lying in the open, sheets of rain pouring down on them, in the gray light. And then Dienwald saw there was something else beside the rain.

There was Walter de Grasse standing at the top of the incline, staring down at them, his face twisted with rage.

23

Dienwald slowly eased away from Philippa and pulled her gown down her legs, pretending not to see Walter.

"Love . . ." she said, her voice soft and drowsy despite the rain battering down on her. "Love, don't leave me."

"Philippa," he said as he straightened his clothes, "come, you must awaken now."

Sir Walter's voice cracked through the silence. "Are you certain you are through plowing her belly, you whoreson? If the little slut wants more, I shall take her and give her pleasure she's never known with you."

Walter! Philippa sat up quickly, staring at her cousin, who still stood at the top of the incline, his hands on his hips, rain long since soaked through his clothes. He'd *watched* them. She felt at once sick to her stomach and blindly furious. She scrambled to her feet.

Dienwald took one of her hands in his and squeezed it. When he spoke, his tone was almost impersonal. "What do you want, de Grasse?"

"I want what is mine. I want her, despite what you've done to her."

Dienwald squeezed her hand tightly now, and said in the same detached way, "You can't have her, de Grasse. She was never yours to have, save in your fantasies. She's mine. As you have observed, she is completely mine."

"Nay, you bastard! She'll wed me! She'll have no choice, for I'll hold you to ensure her compliance!"

Dienwald stared at him. "Too late, de Grasse, you are far too late. Philippa is already wedded to me with her father's—the king's—blessing."

"You lie!"

"Why should I?"

That drew Walter up for a moment. He eyed his enemy of so many years that he'd lost count. De Fortenberry had been an enemy before Walter had even seen his face, his very name a litany of vengeance. So long ago Dienwald's father had beaten Walter's, but it hadn't been fair, it hadn't been unprejudiced. No, his father had been cheated, cheated of everything, his only son disinherited. "I should have killed you when I had you at Wolffeton. I broke your ribs, but it wasn't enough, though I enjoyed it. I should have tortured you until I tired of hearing your screams, and then I should have sent my sword into your belly. Ah, but no, I waited, like a fool I waited for Graelam to return, certain that he would mete out justice, that he would right the wrongs done unto my father and unto me. I was a fool then, I admit it. I didn't think that Lord Graelam's wife, that little bitch, Kassia—your lover—would dare rescue you. But she did, curse her. Hellfire, I should have killed her for saving you!"

"But you didn't," Dienwald said, bringing Philippa against his side. "And Graelam, not knowing the depths of your twisted hatred, made you castellan of Crandall. But you couldn't be satisfied with your overlord's trust. No, you couldn't dismiss your hatred and forget your imagined ills. You had to kill my people and burn their huts and their crops and put the sword to their animals. You went too far, de Grasse. Graelam knows what you did. He will not allow it to continue. He himself will kill you. I won't have to bother."

"Kill me? You? As for Graelam, you have no proof, de Fortenberry, of any burning or killing. Not a shred of proof do you have. Graelam would never act without proof. I know him well. He thinks he judges character like a god, when he is but a fool. And when he finds you dead, there will still be no proof, and he won't act against me."

"Then you stole Philippa and my son. You will die, Walter, and your enmity will die with you."

"Stole! Ha! I rescued my cousin! Your miserable brat just happened to be with her. I didn't harm him, the little vermin. Skewer not the truth for your own ends."

"Since there is no longer a rescue to be made, since Philippa is my wife with the king's blessing, then you intend now to take your leave of us? You intend to forget your plaints and return to Crandall?"

Even as he spoke, Dienwald saw Walter's men, in view now, yet blurred in the downpour. The shower was lessening a bit but they were still vague and gray. They looked miserable; they looked uncertain.

Philippa said, "Walter, I am wedded to Dienwald. I am his wife. Both Lord Henry and Robert Burnell, the king's chancellor, will attest to it. It is true. Leave us be."

Walter ground his teeth. He felt maddened with failure, his loss surrounding him, gashing into him, twisting him and taunting him. He'd not gained what was his by birthright. He'd gained nothing, less than nothing. Life hadn't meted out justice to him. There would be no retribution unless he gained it for himself. And now he'd stood watching his enemy enjoy the girl intended for him. He raised his face to the skies and howled his fury.

It was a grim sound, terrifying and haunting. Philippa clutched Dienwald against her side, turning her face inward to his chest. It was a howl of pain and defeat and ruin; a cry of loss of faith, loss of self.

Then Walter was silent; all his men were silent, though several were crossing themselves. The silence dragged on. It was frightening and eerie. The rain pounded down and the curving piece of ground upon which Dienwald and Philippa stood began to fill with water. The violets sagged beneath the weight of the rain.

Then Walter, without warning, drew his sword and leapt down the incline, his full weight landing against Dienwald's chest, battering him backward. Philippa was thrown to the side, splashing onto her knees into the water. She scrambled to her feet, flailing about to gain purchase in the swirling torrent.

Walter's sword was drawn, and in a smooth arc aimed toward Dienwald's chest. Dienwald had naught but a knife and he held it in his right hand, then tossed it to his left, back and forth, taunting Walter.

He said softly, "Well, you sodden fool? Come, let's see if you understand the uses for your sword! Or will you just stand there?"

Walter gave a roar of sheer rage and rushed toward Dienwald, his sword straight out in front of him. Dienwald sidestepped him easily, but his foot slipped on the slick grass and he twisted about, falling on his back.

Philippa picked up a rock and threw it with all her strength at Walter. It hit him square in the chest. He looked at her, surprise writ on his face. "Philippa? Why do you that? I am come to save you. You mustn't pretend you don't want to come with me, wed with me, there is no more need. I will kill him and then you will come with me."

Walter turned, but Dienwald was on his feet again, feinting to the right, away from Walter's sword thrust.

On and on it went, and Philippa knew Dienwald must fail eventually. His knife was no contest against Walter's sword. Suddenly there came shouts from the road above.

The men paid no heed.

Philippa paid no heed either. She had grasped another stone and was waiting for the chance to strike Walter with it, but the men were close, too close, and she feared hitting Dienwald instead.

"Philippa! Stand clear!"

She whirled about and looked upward. It was

Graelam de Moreton and he was standing on the road above them. Beside him stood the man Roland de Tournay. She watched through the now gentle fall of rain. Roland drew a narrow dagger from his belt, its shaft silver and bright even in the gray light, aimed it, and released it. It slit through the air so quickly, Philippa didn't see it. She heard a suddenly gurgling sound, then turned to see the dagger embedded deep in Walter's chest. He dropped the sword and clutched at the dagger's ivory handle. He pulled it out and stared at the crimson blade. Then he looked upward at Roland de Tournay.

He looked confused and said, "Do I know you? Why do you kill me?"

He said nothing more, merely looked once again at Philippa, gave a tiny shake of his head, and collapsed onto his face in the water.

Dienwald stood panting over him. He frowned down at Walter's lifeless body. " 'Twas a good throw." Then he looked up at Roland. "I was very nearly the victor. You acted too quickly."

"Next time I'll let your wife hit your adversary with rocks," Roland shouted.

"By all the saints above," Graelam shouted, "enough! Come up now and let us ride to St. Erth. Dienwald, thank Roland for saving your hide. But hurry, for I am so sodden my tongue molds in my mouth!"

Within minutes Philippa was huddled in the circle of her husband's arms atop Philbo. One of Graelam's men was leading her mare. Walter's men hadn't fought, for Lord Graelam de Moreton was, after all, Sir Walter's overlord, and thus they, his men-at-arms, also owed allegiance to Lord Graelam.

Dienwald looked at Graelam. "How came you by so unexpectedly? I was praying, but 'twas not for your company in particular."

"We came by design," Graelam said. "Roland wanted to see the final act of the play he'd helped to write."

"What does he mean?" Philippa asked, twisting about to face her husband.

"Hush, wench. 'Tis not important. Roland is loose-tongued, but he does throw a dagger well."

"But—"

"Hush," he repeated, then said, "Will you continue to welcome me as sweetly as did gentle, perfect Kassia?"

She stiffened, as he'd expected, her thoughts turned, and he grinned over her head.

They were shivering, their teeth chattering, when they finally rode into St. Erth's inner bailey. Once in the great hall, they were overwhelmed with cheers and shouts and blessed warmth and trestle tables covered with mounds of food. All of St. Erth's people were gathered in the huge chamber, and it was noisy and hot and the smells of food mingled with the smells of sweat and wet wool and it was wonderful.

"Welcome," Philippa said, her wet face radiant as she turned to her guests. "We're home!"

She sneezed suddenly, and Dienwald swooped down upon her and picked her up in his arms. He pretended to stagger under her weight, saying, "My poor back, wench! I'm nearly beyond my abilities, with you so weighty with wet wool."

Graelam and Roland watched Dienwald carry her from the great hall, grinning at the wild cheering from all St. Erth's people. "The king's son-in-law is a fine man," Graelam said.

"Aye, and no longer a fool," Roland said. He fell silent, frowning. "I do find it passing odd, though."

"What do you find odd?"

"That Philippa, a girl of remarkable taste and refinement, preferred him to me. I am incredulous. 'Tis not normal in my experience. Why, the harem I kept in Acre, Graelam—you wouldn't believe the appetites of my women! And it was my duty, naturally, to satisfy appetites each night. And they never complained that I shirked my duty to them. But Philippa gives me not a look."

Graelam merely laughed, grabbed a hunk of well-roasted rabbit, and waved it in Roland's face. "You braying ass! Lying dog! Harem? I believe you not, not for an instant. What harem? How came you by a harem? How many women? You satisfied more than one woman each night?"

Crooky chortled and waved his hands toward all the food. "A feast, my lords. A feast worthy of a king or a king's daughter and her friends!" And he jumped upon Dienwald's chair and burst into song.

A wedding feast lies here untasted
The lord and lady care not it's wasted.
They're frolic and gambol without a yawn
They'll play through the night 'til the dawn.

In their bedchamber, warm and dry beneath three blankets, the master and mistress of St. Erth lay together listening to the rain and enjoying each other's kisses. They heard a sudden shout of loud laughter and guffawing from below in the great hall, and wondered at it, but not for long, for Philippa nuzzled Dienwald's throat, saying, "Have you restocked your seed?"

"What?" Dienwald said, and pulled back to look at his wife's laughing mouth.

" 'Tis what Old Agnes said, that I would fetch you home and keep you in my bed until you begged me to let you sleep and restock your seed."

"Aye, all is in readiness for you, greedy wench. I ask for nothing more in this sweet life than to be debauched by you each night."

"A promise easily made and more than easily kept."

Epilogue

Windsor Castle
October 1275

Dienwald quickly closed the door to the opulent chamber, locked it, drew a deep breath, then let it out slowly as he sagged against the door, his eyes closed.

"My lord husband, you did well. My father thinks you nearly as wonderful as do I."

Dienwald opened his eyes at that. "He does, does he? Ha! I'll wager you he still thinks Roland de Tournay would have made the better husband and the better son-in-law. And I have to call Roland, that damned brute, friend! It passes all bounds, Philippa."

She wanted to laugh, but managed to keep her mouth from quivering, her eyes slightly lowered. "Roland is just a common fellow, husband, of little account to my life and of no account at all to my heart. And since my father no longer has any say in the matter, it's not important. What did you think of Queen Eleanor?"

"A beautiful lady," Dienwald said somewhat absently, then frowned, moaned, and closed his eyes again. "The king looked at me and knew, Philippa—he knew I'd raided that merchant's goods near Penrith."

Philippa laughed. "Aye, he knew. He was amused, he told me so, but he also hinted to me that I should scold you just a bit—'never be a testy nag, my daughter,' he said—and somehow keep you from plundering about the countryside. I truly believe he said nothing to you because he doesn't want to break your spirit."

"He doesn't want to break my spirit! I don't suppose you told him that you were with me, riding at my side, dressed like a lad, laughing at how easily we sidetracked that merchant who'd cheated us?"

Philippa straightened her shoulders and looked down her nose at him. "Naturally not. I am part Plantagenet, thus part of the very highest nobility. Besides, do you think me an utter fool?"

"Next time we will take greater care," Dienwald said. He pushed away from the door and walked to the middle of their chamber and stopped. The room was dazzling in the elegance of its furnishings, and the overwhelming luxury of it stifled him. The bed was hung with rich velvet draperies, their thick crimson folds held with golden rope and ties. The velvet was so thick, so voluminous, one could suffocate if the hangings were drawn at night.

"The ceremony was moving, Dienwald, and you looked as royal as my father and his family."

Dienwald grunted. He looked down at his flamboyant crimson tunic, belted with a wide leather affair studded with gems. A ceremonial sword was strapped to his waist. He looked well enough, he supposed, but one couldn't scratch in such clothing, one couldn't really stretch. One couldn't grab one's wife and caress her and fondle her and fling her onto the bed and wrestle with her, tearing off clothing and laughing together and tumbling about.

" 'Dienwald de Fortenberry, Earl of St. Erth.' Or perhaps I prefer 'Lord St. Erth.' Ah, that has a sound of proud consequence and arrogant privilege. It fits you well, my lord earl. And Edmund will grow nicely into that appellation, for already he scowls like you do when displeased, and orders me about as if I were his wench."

Dienwald was silent. He sat down in an ornately carved high-backed chair, stretched out his legs, and looked morosely into the fireplace.

Philippa, her humor fled, knelt in front of him and gazed up at his distracted face. "What troubles you, husband? Do you wish now that you weren't tied to me?"

He stretched out his hand and lightly touched his fingers to her hair. It was arranged artfully, with many pins and ribbons and fastenings, and he feared to dislodge such perfection. He dropped his hand.

Philippa snorted and flung away the pins and ribbons, shaking her head until her hair hung free, framing her smiling face.

"There, now do what you will. As you always do when we are home."

Dienwald sat back, his fingers absently sliding through strands of her hair, his eyes still melancholy, as he gazed at the orange flames in the fireplace.

"I'm no longer just me," he said at last.

"True," Philippa agreed, leaning her cheek against his knee. "I'm part of you now, as is the child I carry."

His fingers stilled abruptly and his dulled expression vanished in a flash. "The *what*?"

"The child I now carry. Our babe."

"You didn't tell me." She heard the beginnings of outrage in his voice and smiled.

"Why didn't you tell me? I am the father, after all!" He was ready for an argument, a banging loud fight, but she didn't plan to give him what he wished just yet.

In a voice as calm as a moonless night she said, "I wanted to wait until after you'd met my father and dealt with your honors and position. Now that you've survived all your new privileges and awards and tributes, all the banquets and fawning courtiers, we can return to Cornwall, to our real life. Tomorrow we leave London, and we'll look back on this and know it was but a fragment of something not really part of us, Dienwald, something like a dream that scarce touches us."

"Save that I'm now a peer of the realm and have my coffers filled with royal coin. Royal coin I never sought."

"Aye, I know," she said, gently rubbing her palm on his thigh. And, she thought, grinning, you're spoiling for a fight. You can't bear that I'm being so quiet, so reasonable. Not just yet, my husband.

His fingers tightened in her hair. "Aye, none

of this I wanted. I have been made to feel guilt over a bit of honest thievery, and that from a man who'd cheated me! I won't have it, wench! And now you deign to tell me you are with child! *You* decide it is time that *I* know of *my* babe. You have deceived me, and I shall make you very sorry that you did."

"Just what will you do?"

She was teasing him! He stared down at her laughing face, saw the dimples deepening in her cheeks, and wanted to throttle her. "I will think of something, and don't you doubt it."

Her voice was as demure as a virgin's. "Something worthy of an earl? Worthy of Lord St. Erth, that scoundrel and knave?"

He sought for words but couldn't find a single one, so instead he leaned down, grasped her face between his palms, and kissed her hard.

He pulled away and saw the darkening of her eyes, the sheen of passion building, the soft yielding to him. It was always so, and it always made him feel boundless satisfaction and immense male pleasure. He smiled and kissed her again. His hands left her face and stroked downward until they held her breasts. When she moaned softly, coming up on her knees to get closer to him, to come between his legs, he pulled back and grinned evilly down at her. "There, I have my revenge and it's worthy of any man in the realm who's worth his salt. I started to debauch you, and when you were reach to beg me for it, I stopped."

Philippa stared at him silently for a very long time. He fidgeted, but she didn't move, didn't speak. Then, as he looked at her, two tears seeped from her eyes and trailed down her cheeks. She didn't make a sound. Tears continued to gather and fall.

"Philippa, don't cry. I . . ."

He gathered her against him, wanting to pet her and fondle her and make her forget her tears. When he leaned forward to draw her up, she suddenly jerked back and smashed her fists against his chest. He lurched sideways, and the chair tipped and fell, sending them both flailing to the floor. But he didn't release his wife. They lay in front of the fire, facing each other, and she was grinning at him.

"You give over, husband?"

"I'll give you anything you want, wench."

"Will you love me here, on this soft Flanders carpet, in front of the fire?"

"Aye, I'll make you moan with pleasure before I'm done with you."

"Proceed, husband. I await your pleasure."

He laughed and drew her to him. She was his wife, this king's daughter, and he would wear his earl's laurels as would his sons and his sons' sons after them. And he would repair St. Erth and it would become a renowned and mighty castle, a bastion to defend the king's honor, a protector of those in his domain, in all Cornwall. And his wife would birth him a daughter who would likely marry the small son delivered earlier that summer at Wolffeton.

He knew himself unworthy. He prayed he would become more worthy as time passed.

He prayed also that worthiness had nothing to do with an occasional raid, an occasional theft, an occasional assault on some knave, who would, after all, deserve the fate that would befall him.

Philippa's hands stroked his face, and he kissed

her neck. "I love you," he said, nipping at her earlobe. "As do my son and all the people at St. Erth."

"You don't mind that Edmund chooses to call me Mama?"

"Nay, why should I? 'Witch' and 'Cursed Maypole' don't go well with your new dignities. Now, enough of this nonsense that has nothing to do with what I want to do to your body."

"And what is that?"

"If you will close your lips against your silly female words, I will show you."

About the Author

CATHERINE COULTER is the bestselling author of numerous historical romances as well as two contemporary novels. She lives in Northern California with her husband, Anton, and her cat, Gilly.

D0051896

Also available from
DIANA PALMER

Coming Summer 2015

Untamed

DIANA PALMER

INVINCIBLE

HQN™

ISBN-13: 978-0-373-77949-9

Recycling programs
for this product may
not exist in your area.

Invincible

This edition published by arrangement with Harlequin Books S.A.

For questions and comments about the quality of this book,
please contact us at CustomerService@Harlequin.com.

® and TM are trademarks of Harlequin Enterprises Limited or its
corporate affiliates. Trademarks indicated with ® are registered in the
United States Patent and Trademark Office, the Canadian Intellectual
Property Office and in other countries.

www.HQNBooks.com

Printed in U.S.A.

In Memoriam

For my friend Verna Jane Clayton; wife of Danny,
sister of Nancy, mother of Christina and Daniel,
grandmother of Selena Marie and Donovan Kyle

Your smile burns bright in our memories

Where you will live on, forever young, forever loved.

Never forgotten.

Dear Reader,

Carson, the hero of *Invincible*, is one of the Oglala Lakota people. For many years, the Lakota have had a special place in my heart. During World War II our mother dated a Lakota man and spoke of marrying him. Our father came along before that could happen. But my sister and I grew up hearing stories about the Plains tribes, especially the Lakota (whom most people outside the tribe refer to as Sioux).

I wrote a book once called *Paper Rose*, whose hero had Lakota blood. I thought at the time how nice it would be to do something useful for the nation I held in such esteem. I contacted the Oglala Lakota College in Kyle, South Dakota, and asked about founding a nursing scholarship there in the name of our mother, who was a nurse. So the Eloise Cliatt Spaeth Nursing Scholarship was born.

Over the years, the scholarship has helped a great many people with families afford to go back to school. My friend Marilyn sends me letters from them, which I keep and treasure. I can't tell you how proud I am to be contributing, even in a small way, to such a grand cause. I grew up poor. I can tell you that education makes all the difference in the world.

One other thing about this book that is special is the dedication. Last year, I lost a friend. She was my daughter-in-law's mother, Jane Clayton. Since Christina was seventeen years old, she and her mother, Jane, her father, Danny, and her brother, Daniel, have been part of my family. Of all my memories of Jane, there is this special one: at the kids' wedding rehearsal in Atlanta, she sat with my sister, Dannis, and my son, Blayne, her husband, Danny, and son, Daniel, and daughter, Christina, and my niece Maggie and me, shooting down enemy aircraft in an arcade game. I remember her laughing as if she were a kid. She did have the most beautiful laugh.

Oh, what fun that was! Jane, laughing, with stars in her eyes.

This book is for you, Jane, so that your name will be remembered as long as the book stays in print anywhere in the world. Good night, my friend.

Thank you for reading *Invincible*. As always, I am your fan.

Love,

Diana Palmer

INVINCIBLE

CHAPTER ONE

It was a rainy Friday morning.

Carlie Blair, who was running late for her job as secretary to Jacobsville, Texas police chief Cash Grier, only had time for a piece of toast and a sip of coffee before she rushed out the door to persuade her ten-year-old red pickup truck to start. It had gone on grinding seemingly forever before it finally caught up and started.

Her father, a Methodist minister, was out of town on business for the day. So there was nobody to help her get it running. Luck was with her. It did, at least, start.

She envied her friend Michelle Godfrey, whose guardian and his sister had given her a Jaguar for Christmas. Michelle was away at college now, and she and Carlie still spoke on the phone, but they no longer shared rides to town and the cost of gas on a daily basis.

The old clunker ate gas like candy and Carlie's salary only stretched so far. She wished she had more than a couple pairs of jeans, a few T-shirts, a coat and one good pair of shoes. It must be nice, she thought, not to have to count pennies. But her father was always optimistic about their status. *God loved the*

poor, because they gave away so much, he was fond
of saying. He was probably right.

Right now, though, her rain-wet jeans were uncomfortable, and she'd stepped in a mud puddle with her
only pair of good shoes while she was knocking cor-
rosion off the battery terminals with the hammer she
kept under the front seat for that purpose. All this in
January weather, which was wet and cold and miserable, even in South Texas.

Consequently, when she parked her car in the small
lot next to the chief's office, she looked like a be-
draggled rat. Her dark, short, wavy hair was curling
like crazy, as it always did in a rainstorm. Her coat
was soaked. Her green eyes, full of silent resignation,
didn't smile as she opened the office door.

Her worst nightmare was standing just inside.

Carson.

He glared at her. He was so much taller than she
that she had to look up at him. There was a lot to look
at, although she tried not to show her interest.

He was all muscle, but it wasn't overly obvious.
He had a rodeo rider's physique, lean and powerful.
Like her, he wore jeans, but his were obviously designer ones, like those hand-tooled leather boots on
his big feet and the elaborately scrolled leather holster
in which he kept his .45 automatic. He was wearing
a jacket that partially concealed the gun, but he was
intimidating enough without it.

He was Lakota Sioux. He had jet-black hair that
fell to his waist in back, although he wore it in a ponytail usually. He had large black eyes that seemed to
see everything with one sweep of his head. He had
high cheekbones and a light olive complexion. There

were faint scars on the knuckles of his big hands. She noticed because he was holding a file in one of them.

Her file.

Well, really, the chief's file, that had been lying on her desk, waiting to be typed up. It referenced an attack on her father a few weeks earlier that had resulted in Carlie being stabbed. Involuntarily, her hand went to the scar that ran from her shoulder down to the beginning of her small breasts. She flushed when she saw where he was looking.

"Those are confidential files," she said shortly.

He looked around. "There was nobody here to tell me that," he said, his deep voice clear as a bell in the silent room.

She flushed at the implied criticism. "Damned truck wouldn't start and I got soaked trying to start it," she muttered. She slid her weather-beaten old purse under her desk, ran a hand through her wet hair, took off her ratty coat and hung it up before she sat down at her desk. "Did you need something?" she asked with crushing politeness. She even managed a smile. Sort of.

"I need to see the chief," he replied.

She frowned. "There's this thing called a door. He's got one," she said patiently. "You knock on it, and he comes out."

He gave her a look that could have stopped traffic. "There's somebody in there with him," he said with equal patience. "I didn't want to interrupt."

"I see." She moved things around on her desk, muttering to herself.

"Bad sign."

She looked up. "Huh?"

"Talking to yourself."

She glared at him. It had been a bad morning altogether and he wasn't helping. "Don't listen, if it bothers you."

He gave her a long look and laughed hollowly. "Listen, kid, nothing about you bothers me. Or ever will."

There were the sounds of chairs scraping wood, as if the men in Cash's office had stood up and pushed back their seats. She figured it was safe to interrupt him.

Well, safer than listening to Mr. Original American here run her down.

She pushed the intercom button. "You have a visitor, sir," she announced.

There was a murmur. "Who is it?"

She looked at Carson. "The gentleman who starts fires with hand grenades," she said sweetly.

Carson stared at her with icy black eyes.

Cash's door opened, and there was Carlie's father, a man in a very expensive suit and Cash.

That explained why her father had left home so early. He was out of town, as he'd said he would be; out of Comanche Wells, where they lived, anyway. Not that Jacobsville was more than a five-minute drive from home.

"Carson," Cash said, nodding. "I think you know Reverend Blair and my brother, Garon?"

"Yes." Carson shook hands with them.

Carlie was doing mental shorthand. Garon Grier was senior special agent in charge of the Jacobsville branch of the FBI. He'd moved to Jacobsville some time ago, but the FBI branch office hadn't been here quite as long. Garon had been with the bureau for a number of years.

Carlie wondered what was going on that involved both the FBI and her father. But she knew that question would go unanswered. Her father was remarkably silent on issues that concerned law enforcement, although he knew quite a few people in that profession.

She recalled with a chill the telephone conversation she'd had recently with someone who called and said, "Tell your father he's next." She couldn't get anybody to tell her what they thought it meant. It was disturbing, like the news she'd overheard that the man who'd put a knife in her, trying to kill her father, had been poisoned and died.

Something big was going on, linked to that Wyoming murder and involving some politician who had ties to a drug cartel. But nobody told Carlie anything.

"WELL, I'LL BE OFF. I have a meeting in San Antonio," Reverend Blair said, taking his leave. He paused at Carlie's desk. "Don't do anything fancy for supper, okay?" he asked, smiling. "I may be very late."

"Okay, Dad." She grinned up at him.

He ruffled her hair and walked out.

Carson was watching the interplay with cynical eyes.

"Doesn't your dad ruffle your hair?" she asked sarcastically.

"No. He did lay a chair across it once." He averted his eyes at once, as if the comment had slipped out against his will and embarrassed him.

Carlie tried not to stare. What in the world sort of background did he come from? The violence struck a chord in her. She had secrets of her own from years past.

"Carson," Garon Grier said, pausing at the door. "We may need you at some point."

Carson nodded. "I'll be around."

"Thanks."

Garon waved at his brother, smiled at Carlie and let himself out the door.

"Something perking?" Carson asked Cash.

"Quite a lot, in fact. Carlie, hold my calls until I tell you," he instructed.

"Sure thing, Boss."

"Come on in." Cash went ahead into his office.

Carson paused by Carlie's desk and glared at her.

She glared back. "If you don't stop scowling at me, I'm going to ask the chief to frisk you for hand grenades," she muttered.

"Frisk me yourself," he dared softly.

The flush deepened, darkened.

His black eyes narrowed, because he knew innocence when he saw it; it was that rare in his world. "Clueless, aren't you?" he chided.

She lifted her chin and glared back. "My father is a minister," she said with quiet pride.

"Really?"

She frowned, cocking her head. "Excuse me?"

"Are you coming in or not?" Cash asked suddenly, and there was a bite in his voice.

Carson seemed faintly surprised. He followed Cash into the office. The door closed. There were words spoken in a harsh tone, followed by a pause and a suddenly apologetic voice.

Carlie paid little attention. Carson had upset her

nerves. She wished her boss would find someone else to talk to. Her job had been wonderful and satisfying until Carson started hanging around the office all the time. Something was going on, something big. It involved local and federal law enforcement—she was fairly certain that the chief's brother didn't just happen by to visit—and somehow, it also involved her father.

She wondered if she could dig any information out of her parent if she went about it in the right way. She'd have to work on that.

Then she recalled that phone call that she'd told her father about, just recently. A male voice had said, simply, "Tell your father, he's next." It had been a chilling experience, one she'd forced to the back of her mind. Now she wondered if all the traffic through her boss's office involved her in some way, as well as her father. The man who'd tried to kill him had died, mysteriously poisoned.

She still wondered why anybody would attack a minister. That remark of Carson's made her curious. She'd said her father was a minister and he'd said, "Really?" in that sarcastic, cold tone of voice. Why?

"I'm a mushroom," she said to herself. "They keep me in the dark and feed me manure." She sighed and went back to work.

SHE WAS ON the phone with the sheriff's office when Carson left. He went by her desk with only a cursory glance at her, and it was, of all things, placid. Almost apologetic. She lowered her eyes and refused to even look at him.

Even if she'd found him irresistible—and she was

trying not to—his reputation with women made her wary of him.

Sure, it was a new century, but Carlie was a small-town girl and raised religiously. She didn't share the casual attitude of many of her former classmates about physical passion.

She grimaced. It was hard to be a nice girl when people treated her like a disease on legs. In school, they'd made fun of her, whispered about her. One pretty, popular girl said that she didn't know what she was missing and that she should live it up.

Carlie just stared at her and smiled. She didn't say anything. Apparently the smile wore the other girl down because she shrugged, turned her back and walked off to whisper to the girls in her circle. They all looked at Carlie and laughed.

She was used to it. Her father said that adversity was like grit, it honed metal to a fine edge. She'd have liked to be honed a little less.

They were right about one thing; she really didn't know what she was missing. It seemed appropriate, because she'd read about sensations she was supposed to feel with men around, and she didn't feel any of them.

She chided herself silently. That was a lie. She felt them when she was close to Carson. She knew that he was aware of it, which made it worse. He laughed at her, just the way her classmates had laughed at her in school. She was the odd one out, the misfit. She had a reason for her ironclad morals. Many local people knew them, too. Episodes in her childhood had hardened her.

Well, people tended to be products of their upbringing. That was life. Unless she wanted to throw away her ideals and give up religion, she was pretty much settled in her beliefs. Maybe it wasn't so bad being a misfit. Her late grandfather had said that civilizations rested on the bedrock of faith and law and the arts. Some people had to be conventional to keep the mechanism going.

"What was that?" Sheriff Hayes's receptionist asked.

"Sorry." Carlie cleared her throat. She'd been on hold. "I was just mumbling to myself. What were you saying?"

The woman laughed and gave her the information the chief had asked for, about an upcoming criminal case.

SHE COOKED A light supper, just creamed chicken and rice, with green peas, and made a nice apple pie for dessert.

Her father came in, looking harassed. Then he saw the spread and grinned from ear to ear. "What a nice surprise!"

"I know, something light. But I was hungry," she added.

He made a face. "Shame. Telling lies."

She shrugged. "I went to church Sunday. God won't mind a little lie, in a good cause."

He smiled. "You know, some people have actually asked me how to talk to God."

"I just do it while I'm cooking, or working in the yard," Carlie said. "Just like I'm talking to you."

He laughed. "Me, too. But there are people who make hard work of it."

"Why were you in the chief's office today?" she asked suddenly.

He paused in the act of putting a napkin in his lap. His expression went blank for an instant, then it came back to life. "He wanted me to talk to a prisoner for him," he said finally.

She raised both eyebrows.

"Sorry," he said, smoothing out the napkin. "Some things are confidential."

"Okay."

"Let's say grace," he added.

LATER, HE WATCHED the news while she cleaned up the kitchen. She sat down with him and watched a nature special for a while. Then she excused herself and went upstairs to read. She wasn't really interested in much television programming, except for history specials and anything about mining. She loved rocks.

She sat down on the side of her bed and thumbed through her bookshelf. Most titles were digital as well as physical these days, but she still loved the feel and smell of an actual book in her hands.

She pulled out a well-worn copy of a book on the Little Bighorn fight, one that was written by members of various tribes who'd actually been present. It irritated her that many of the soldiers had said there were no living witnesses to the battle. That was not true. There were plenty of them: Lakota, Cheyenne, Crow and a host of other men from different tribes who were at the battle and saw exactly what happened.

She smiled as she read about how many of them ended up in Buffalo Bill Cody's famous traveling Wild West show. They played before the crowned heads of Europe. They learned high society manners and how to drink tea from fancy china cups. They laughed among themselves at the irony of it. Sitting Bull himself worked for Cody for a time, before he was killed.

She loved most to read about Crazy Horse. Like Carson, he was Lakota, which white people referred to as Sioux. Crazy Horse was Oglala, which was one of the subclasses of the tribe. He was light-skinned and a great tactician. There was only one verified photograph of him, which was disputed by some, accepted by others. It showed a rather handsome man with pigtails, wearing a breastplate. There was also a sketch. He had led a war party against General Crook at the Battle of the Rosebud and won it. He led another party against Custer at the Little Bighorn.

Until his death, by treachery at the hands of a soldier, he was the most famous war leader of the Lakota.

Sitting Bull did not fight; he was not a warrior. He was a holy man who made medicine and had visions of a great battle that was won by the native tribes.

Crazy Horse fascinated Carlie. She bought book after book, looking for all she could find in his history.

She also had books about Alexander the Third, called the Great, who conquered most of the civilized world by the age of thirty. His ability as a strategist was unequaled in the ancient past. Hannibal, who fought the Romans under Scipio Africanus in the Second Punic War at Carthage, was another favorite. Scipio fascinated her, as well.

The ability of some leaders to inspire a small group

of men to conquer much larger armies was what drew her to military history. It was the generals who led from the front, who ate and slept and suffered with their men, who won the greatest battles and the greatest honor.

She knew about battles because her secret vice was an online video game, "World of Warcraft." A number of people in Jacobsville and Comanche Wells played. She knew the gamer tags, the names in-game, of only a very few. Probably she'd partnered with some of them in raid groups. But mostly she ran battlegrounds, in player-versus-player matches, but only on weekends, when she had more free time.

Gaming took the place of dates she never got. Even if she'd been less moral, she rarely got asked on dates. She could be attractive when she tried, but she wasn't really pretty and she was painfully shy around people she didn't know. She'd only gone out a couple of times in high school, once with a boy who was getting even with his girlfriend by dating her—although she hadn't known until later—and another with a boy who'd hurt another girl badly and saw Carlie as an easy mark. He got a big surprise.

From time to time she thought about how nice it would be to marry and have children. She loved spending time in the baby section of department stores when she went to San Antonio with her father occasionally. She liked to look at knitted booties and lacy little dresses. Once a saleswoman had asked if she had children. She said no, she wasn't married. The saleswoman had laughed and asked what that had to do with it. It was a new world, indeed.

She put away her book on the Little Bighorn fight,

and settled in with her new copy of a book on Alexander the Great. The phone rang. She got up, but she was hesitant to answer it. She recalled the threat from the unknown man and wondered if that was him.

She went to the staircase and hesitated. Her father had answered and was on the phone.

"Yes, I know," he said in a tone he'd never used with her. "If you think you can do better, you're welcome to try." He paused and a huge sigh left his chest. "Listen, she's all I've got in the world. I know I don't deserve her, but I will never let anyone harm her. This place may not look secure, but I assure you, it is…"

He leaned against the wall near the phone table, with the phone in his hand. He looked world-weary. "That's what I thought, too, at first," he said quietly. "I still have enemies. But it isn't me he's after. It's Carlie! It has to have something to do with the man she saw in Grier's office. I know that the man who killed Joey and masqueraded as a DEA agent is dead. But if he put out a contract before he died… Yes, that's what I'm telling you." He shook his head. "I know you don't have the funds. It's okay. I have plenty of people who owe me favors. I'll call in a few. Yes. I do appreciate your help. It's just…it's worrying me, that's all. Sure. I'll call you. Thanks." He hung up.

Carlie moved back into the shadows. Her father looked like a stranger, like someone she'd never seen before. She wondered who he'd been speaking to, and if the conversation was about her. It sounded that way; he'd used her name. What was a contract? A contract to kill someone? She bit her lower lip. Something to do with the man she saw in the chief's office, the man she'd tried to describe for the artist, the DEA agent who wasn't an agent.

She frowned. But he was dead, her father had said. Then he'd mentioned that contract, that the man might have put it out before he died. Of course, if some unknown person had been paid in advance to kill her...

She swallowed down the fear. She could be killed by mistake, by a dead man. How ironic. Her father had said the house was safe. She wondered why he'd said that, what he knew. For the first time in her life, she wondered who her father really was.

SHE FIXED HIM a nice breakfast. While they were eating it she said, "Why do you think that man came to kill me?"

His coffee cup paused halfway to his mouth. "What?"

"The man with the knife."

"We agreed that he was after me, didn't we?" he said, avoiding her face.

She lifted her eyes and stared at him. "I work for the police. It's impossible not to learn a little something about law enforcement in the process. That man wasn't after you at all, was he? The man who was poisoned so he couldn't tell what he knew?"

He let out a breath and put the coffee cup down. "Well, Carlie, you're more perceptive than I gave you credit for." He smiled faintly. "Must be my genes. Your mother, God rest her soul, didn't have that gift. She saw everything in black and white."

"Yes, she did." Talk of her mother made her sad. It had just been Carlie and Mary for a long time, until Mary got sick. Then Mary's mother, and her hophead boyfriend, had shown up and ransacked the place. Carlie had tried to stop them... She shivered.

It had been several days later, after the hospital visit and the arrests, when her father had come back to town, wearing khaki pants and shirt, and carrying a pistol.

There had been no money for doctors, but her father had taken charge and got Mary into treatment. Mary's mother and her boyfriend went to jail. Sadly, it had been hopeless from the start. Mary died within weeks. During those weeks, Carlie got to know her absent father. He became protective of her. She liked him very much. He was gone for a day after the funeral. When he came home, he seemed very different.

Carlie's father spoke to someone on the phone then, too, and when he hung up he'd made a decision. He took Carlie with him to Atlanta, where he enrolled in a seminary and became a Methodist minister. He said it was the hardest and the easiest thing he'd ever done, and that it was a good thing that God forgave people for horrible acts. She asked what they were. Her father said some things were best left buried in the past.

"We're still not sure he didn't come after me," her father said, interrupting her reverie.

"I heard you talking on the phone last night," she said.

He grimaced. "Bad timing on my part," he said, sighing.

"Very bad. So now I know. Tell me what's going on."

"That phone call you had came from a San Antonio number. We traced it, but it led to a throwaway phone," he replied. "That's bad news."

"Why?"

"Because a few people who use those phones are connected to the underworld in some fashion or other, to escape detection by the authorities. They use the phone once to connect with people who might be wiretapped, then they dispose of the phone. Drug lords buy them by the cartload," he added.

"Well, I didn't do anybody in over a drug deal, and the guy I gave the artist the description of died in Wyoming. So why is somebody still after me?" she concluded.

He smiled. "Smart. Very smart. The guy died. That's the bottom line. If he hired somebody to go after you, to keep you from recognizing him in a future lineup, and paid in advance, it's too late to call him off. Get the picture?"

"In living color," she said. She felt very adult, having her father give her the truth instead of a sweet lie to calm her.

"I have a couple of friends watching you," he said. "I don't think it's a big threat, but we'd be insane not to take it seriously, especially after what's already happened."

"That was weeks ago," she began.

"Yes, at the beginning of a long chain of growing evidence." He sipped coffee. "I still can't believe how many people's lives have been impacted by this man and whoever he was working for."

"You have some idea who his boss is…was?"

He nodded. "I can't tell you, so don't ask. I will say that several law enforcement agencies are involved."

"I still don't understand why you're having meetings with my boss and that...that man Carson."

He studied her flushed face. "I've heard about Carson's attitude toward you. If he keeps it up, I'll have a talk with him."

"Don't," she asked softly. "With any luck, he won't be around long. He doesn't strike me as a man who likes small towns or staying in one place for any length of time."

"You never know. He likes working for Cy Parks. And he has a few projects going with locals."

She groaned.

"I can talk to him nicely."

"Sure, Dad, and then he'll accuse me of running to Daddy for protection." She lifted her chin. "I can take whatever he can hand out."

He smiled at her stubbornness. "Okay."

She made a face. "He just doesn't like me, that's all. Maybe I remind him of someone he doesn't care for."

"That's possible." He stared into his coffee cup. "Or it could have something to do with asking him for a grenade to start a fire..."

"Aww, now, I wasn't trying to start anything," she protested.

He chuckled. "Sure." He studied her face. "I just want to mention one thing," he added gently. "He's not housebroken. And he never will be. Just so you know."

"I have never wanted to housebreak a wolf, I assure you."

"There's also his attitude about women. He makes

no secret of it." His face hardened. "He likens them to party favors. Disposable. You understand?"

"I understand. But honestly, that's not the sort of man I'd be seriously interested in. You don't have to worry."

"I do worry. You're not street-smart, pumpkin," he added, with the pet name that he almost never used. "You're unworldly. A man like that could be dangerous to you..."

She held up a hand. "I have weapons."

He blinked. "Excuse me?"

"If he starts showing any interest in me, I'll give him my most simpering smile and start talking about how I'd love to move in with him that very day and start having children at once." She wiggled her eyebrows. "Works like a charm. They actually leave skid marks..."

He threw back his head and laughed. "So that's what happened to the visiting police chief...?"

"He was very persistent. The chief offered to punt him through the door, but I had a better idea. It worked very nicely. Now, when he comes to see the chief, he doesn't even look my way."

"Just as well. He has a wife, God help her."

"What a nasty man."

"Exactly." He looked at his watch. "Well, I have a meeting with the church officials. We're working on an outreach program for the poor. Something I really want to do."

She smiled. "You know, you really are the nicest minister I know."

He bent and kissed her forehead before he left.

"Thanks, sweetheart. Be sure to check your truck, okay?"

She laughed. "I always do. Don't worry."

He hesitated. He wanted to tell her that he did worry, and the whole reason why. But it was the wrong time.

She was already halfway in love with Carson. He knew things about the man that he'd been told in confidence. He couldn't repeat them. But if Carlie got too close to that prowling wolf, he'd leave scars that would cripple her for life. He had to prevent that, if he could. The thing was, he didn't know how. It was like seeing a wire break and being too far away to fix it.

He could talk to Carson, of course. But that would only make matters worse. He had to wait and hope that Carlie could hang on to her beliefs and ignore the man's practiced charm if he ever used it on her.

Carson seemed to hate her. But it was an act. He knew it, because it was an act he'd put on himself, with Carlie's late mother. Mary had been a saint. He'd tried to coax her into bed, but she'd refused him at every turn. Finally, in desperation, he'd proposed. She'd refused. She wasn't marrying a man because he couldn't have her any other way.

So he'd gone away. And come back. And tried the soft approach. It had backfired. He'd fallen in love for the first time in his life. Mary had tied him to her with strings of icy steel, and leaving her even for a few weeks at a time had been agonizing. He'd only lived to finish the mission and get home, get back to Mary.

But over the years, the missions had come closer together, taken longer, provoked lengthy absences. He'd tried to make sure Mary had enough money to cover her bills and incidentals, but one job had resulted in no pay and during that time, Mary had gotten sick. By the time he knew and came home, it was too late.

He blamed himself for that, and for a lot more. He'd thought an old enemy had targeted him and got Carlie by mistake. But it wasn't a mistake. Someone wanted Carlie dead, apparently because of a face she remembered. There might be another reason. Something they didn't know, something she didn't remember seeing. Even the death of the man hadn't stopped the threat.

But he was going to. Somehow.

CHAPTER TWO

CARLIE LOVED THE WEEKENDS. At work she was just plain old Carlie, dull and boring and not very pretty at all.

But in this video game, on her game server, she was Cadzminea, an Alliance night elf death knight, invincible and deadly with a two-handed great sword. She had top-level gear and a bad attitude, and she was known even in battlegrounds with players from multiple servers. She was a tank, an offensive player who protected less well-geared comrades. She loved it.

Above the sounds of battle, clashing swords and flashing spells thrown by magic-users, she heard her father's voice.

"Just a minute, Dad! I'm in a battleground!"

"Okay. Never mind."

There were footsteps coming up. She laughed as she heard them behind her. Odd, they sounded lighter than her father's....

"Sorry, we're almost through. We're taking out the enemy commander...."

She stopped while she fought, planting her guild's battle flag to increase her strength and pulling up her Army of the Dead spell. "Gosh, the heals in this battleground are great, I've hardly even needed to use a potion… Okay!" she laughed, as the panel came up displaying an Alliance win, that of her faction.

"Sorry about that…" She turned and looked up into a pair of liquid black eyes in a surprised face.

"A gamer," he said in a tone, for once, without sarcasm. "Put up your stats."

She was too startled not to obey. She left the battleground and brought up the character screen.

He shook his head. "Not bad. Why an NE?" he asked, the abbreviation for a night elf.

"They're beautiful," she blurted out.

He laughed deep in his throat. "So they are."

"How do you know about stats?"

He pulled out his iPhone and went to the game's remote app. He pulled up the Armory and showed her a character sheet.

"Level 90 Horde Tauren druid," she read, indicating that the player was from the Alliance's deadly counter faction, the Horde. "Arbiter." She frowned. "Arbiter?" She caught her breath. "He killed me five times in one battleground!" she exclaimed. "He stealthed up to me, hit me from behind, then he just… killed me. I couldn't even fight back."

"Don't you have a medallion that interrupts spells?"

"Yes, but it was on cooldown," she said, glowering. "And you know this guy?" she asked.

He put up the iPhone. "I am this guy."

She was stunned.

"It's a small world, isn't it?" he asked, studying her face.

Too small, she thought, but she didn't say it. She just nodded.

"Your father asked a couple of us to take turns doing a walk-around when he's not here. He had to go out, so I've got first watch."

She frowned. "A what?"

"We're going to patrol around the house."

"Carrying a Horde flag?" she asked, tongue-in-cheek.

He smiled with real amusement. "We'll be concealed. You won't even know we're on the place."

She was disconcerted. "What's going on?"

"Just a tip we got," he replied. "Nothing to worry about."

Her green eyes narrowed. "My father can pull that stunt. You can't. Give it to me straight."

His eyebrows arched.

"If it concerns me, I have the right to know. My father is overprotective. I love him, but it's not fair that I have to be kept in the dark. I'm not a mushroom."

"No. You're Alliance." He seemed really amused.

"Proudly Alliance," she muttered. "Darn the Horde!"

He smiled. "Better rune that two-hander before you fight me again," he advised, referring to a special weapons buff used only by death knights.

"It's brand-new. I haven't had time," she said defensively. "Don't change the subject."

"There may be an attempt. That's all we could find out."

"Why? The guy I recognized is dead!"

"We're pretty sure that he paid the contract out before he died," he replied. "And we don't know who has it. We tried backtracking known associates of the man who made the first attempt, the one who was poisoned awaiting trial. No luck whatsoever. But an informant needed a favor, so he gave up some information. Not much. There's more at stake than just your memory of a counterfeit DEA agent. Much more."

"And that's all I'm getting, right?"

He nodded.

She glared.

"So much frustration," he mused, studying her. "Why don't you go win a few battles for the Alliance? It might help."

"Not unless you're in one of them." Her eyes twinkled. "Better watch your back next time. I'm getting the hang of it."

He shrugged. "I don't want to live forever." He glanced around the room. It was Spartan. No lace anywhere. He eyed the title of a book on the desk next to her computer and frowned. "Hannibal?"

"Learn from the best, I always think."

He looked at her. He didn't look away.

Her eyes met his and she felt her body melting, tingling. There was a sudden ache in the middle of her body, a jolt of pure electricity. She couldn't even manage to look away.

"Wolves bite," he said in a soft, gruff whisper.

She flushed and dragged her eyes back to the computer. Somebody sold her out. She wondered if it was the chief. She'd only called Carson a wolf to two people and her father would never have betrayed her.

He chuckled softly. "Be careful what you say when you think people aren't listening," he added. He turned and left her staring after him.

LATER, SHE ASKED her father if he'd ratted her out.

He chuckled. "No. But the house is bugged like a messy kitchen," he confessed. "Be careful what you say."

"Gee, thanks for telling me after I said all sorts of things about Carson," she murmured.

He laughed. "He's got a thick skin. It won't bother him."

She studied him quietly. "Why are they after me?"

He drew in a long breath. "There are some political maneuvers going on. You have a photographic memory. Maybe you saw someone other than the murder victim, and the man behind the plot is afraid you'll remember who it is."

"Shades of Dalton Kirk," she said, recalling that the Wyoming rancher had been warned by the woman who became his wife about a vision of him being attacked for something he didn't even remember he'd seen.

"Exactly."

She poured them second cups of coffee. "So I guess it's back to checking under the truck every time I drive it."

"Oh, that never stopped," her father said with a chuckle. "I've just been doing it for you."

She smiled at him. "That's my dad, looking out for me," she said with real affection.

His pale blue eyes were sad. "There was a long period of time when I didn't look out for anybody except myself," he said quietly. "Your mother wouldn't even let anybody tell me how sick she was until it was too late." He lowered his gaze to the coffee. "I made a lot of mistakes out of selfishness. I hope that someday I'll be able to make up for a little of it."

She sipped coffee. "You never talk about your life before you went to the seminary," she pointed out.

He smiled sadly. "I'm ashamed to."

"You were overseas a lot."

He nodded. "In a number of dangerous foreign places, where life is dirt cheap."

She pursed her lips and stared at him. "You know, Michelle's guardian, Gabriel Brandon, spent a lot of time overseas also."

He lifted an eyebrow and smiled placidly. "Are you fishing?"

She shrugged. But she didn't look away.

He finished his coffee. "Let's just say that I had connections that aren't obvious ones, and I made my living in a shadow world."

She frowned. "You aren't wanted in some country whose name I can't pronounce?"

He laughed. "Nothing like that."

"Okay."

He stood up. "But I do have enemies who know where I live. In a general sense. So it's smart to take precautions." He smiled gently. "I wasn't always a minister, pumpkin."

She was remembering Carson's sarcastic comment when she'd mentioned that her father was a minister. She hadn't known that he was aware of things about her parent that she wasn't.

"I feel like a mushroom," she muttered.

He bent and kissed her hair. "Believe me, you're better off being one. See you later. I have some phone calls to make."

HE LOCKED HIMSELF in his study and she went to watch the news on television. It was mostly boring, the same rehashed subjects over and over again, interspersed with more commercials than she could stomach. She turned it off and went upstairs.

"No wonder people stopped watching television," she grumbled as she wandered back to her bedroom. "Why don't you just stop showing any programs and show wall-to-wall commercials, for heaven's sake!"

She pulled up her game and tried to load it when she noticed that the internet wasn't working.

Muttering, she went downstairs to reset the router, which usually solved the problem. Except the router was in the study, and her father was locked in there.

She started to knock, just as she heard her father's raised voice in a tone she'd rarely ever heard.

"I told you," he gritted, "I am not coming back! You can't say anything, threaten anything, that will make me change my mind. And don't you say one more word about my daughter's safety, or I will re-port you to the obvious people. I understand that," he continued, less belligerently. "Trust me when I say that nobody short of a ghost could get in here after dark. The line is secure and I've scrambled impor-tant conversations, like this one. I appreciate the tip, I really do. But I can handle this. I haven't forgotten anything you taught me." He laughed shortly. "Yes, I remember. They were good times."

There was another pause. "No. But we did find out who his enforcer is, and our local law enforcement people are keeping him under covert surveillance. That's right. No, I didn't realize there were two. When did he hire the other? Wait a minute—blond hair, one eye, South African accent?" He burst out laughing. "He hired Rourke as an enforcer?"

There was another pause. "Yes, please, tell him to come see me. I'd enjoy that. Like old times, yes. Okay. Thanks again. I'll be in touch."

Totally confused, Carlie softly retraced her steps, made a racket coming down the staircase and went directly to the study. She rapped on the door.

"Dad? The internet's out! Can you reset the router?"

There was the sound of a chair scraping the floor, but she never heard his footsteps. The door suddenly opened.

He pursed his lips and studied her flushed face. "Okay. How much did you hear?"

"Nothing, Mr. Gandalf, sir, I swear, except something about the end of the world," she paraphrased Sam from *Lord of the Rings*.

Her father laughed. "Well, it wasn't really anything you didn't already know."

"Who's Rourke?" she wondered.

"A man of many talents. You'll like him." He frowned. "Just don't like him too much, okay? He has a way with women, and you're a little lamb."

She gave him a blithe look. "If I could get around Barry Mathers, I can get around Rourke."

Her father understood the reference. Barry, a classmate, had caused one of Carlie's friends a world of hurt by getting her into bed and bragging about it. The girl had been as innocent as Carlie. He wasn't even punished.

So then he'd bet his friends that he could get Carlie into bed. She heard about it from an acquaintance, led him around by the nose, and when he showed up at her house for the date, she had two girlfriends and their boyfriends all ready to go along. He was stunned. But he couldn't call off the date, or he'd have to face the razzing of his clique.

So he took all of them out to dinner and the movies, dutch treat, and delivered Carlie and the others back to her house where her friends' cars were parked.

She waited until the others left and she was certain that her father was in the living room before she spoke to Barry. She gave him such a tongue-lashing that he literally turned around and walked the other way every time he saw her after that. He never asked her out again. Of course, neither did anybody else, for the rest of her senior year.

Barry, on the other hand, was censured so much that his wealthy parents sent him to a school out of state. He died there soon afterward in a skiing accident.

"You had a hard time in school," her father said gently.

"No harder than most other people with principles do," she replied. "There are more of us than you might think."

"I reset the router," he added. "Go try your game."

"I promised to meet Robin for a quest," she said. "I'd hate to let him down."

Her father just smiled. They knew about Robin's situation. He was in love with a girl whose family hated his family. It was a feud that went back two generations, over a land deal. Even the principals didn't really remember what started it. But when Robin expressed interest in Lucy and tried to date her, the hidden daggers came out.

It was a tragic story in many ways. Two people in love who weren't even allowed to see each other because of their parents. They were grown now, but Lucy still lived at home and was terrified of her father. So even if Robin insisted, Lucy wouldn't go against her kin.

Robin worked in his dad's real estate office, where he wasn't harassed, and he was a whiz with figures. He was going to night classes, studying real estate up in San Antonio, where he hoped to learn enough to eventually become a full-fledged real estate broker. Carlie liked him. So did her father, who respected a parent's rights but also felt sympathy for young people denied the right to love whom they pleased.

CARLIE WENT ONLINE and loaded the game, then looked for Robin, who played a shaman in the virtual world. His was a healing spec, so it went well with Carlie's DK, who couldn't heal.

I have a problem, he whispered to her, a form of typed private communication in-game.

She typed, How can I help?

He made a big smiley face. I need a date for the Valentine's Day dance.

Should I ask why? she typed.

There was a smiley face. Lucy's going to the dance with some rich rancher her father knows from out of town. If you'll go with me, her dad won't suspect anything and I can at least dance with her.

She shook her head. One day the two of them were going to have to decide if the sneaking around was less traumatic than just getting together and daring their parents to say anything. But she just typed, I'll buy a dress.

There was a bigger smiley face. It's so nice to have a friend like you, he replied.

That works both ways.

LATER, SHE TOLD her father she had a date. He asked who, and she explained.

"You're both hiding, Carlie," he said, surprising her. His eyes narrowed. "You need to think about finding someone you can have a good relationship with, someone to marry and have children with. And Robin and Lucy need to stand up and behave like adults."

She smiled sadly. "Chance would be a fine thing," she replied. "You might not have noticed, but men aren't exactly beating a path to my door. And you know why."

"Young men look at what's outside," he said wisely. "When they're more mature, men look for what's inside. You're just at the wrong period of your life. That will change."

She drew in a long breath. "You know, not everybody marries..."

He glared at her.

She held up both hands. "I'm not talking about moving in with somebody," she said hastily. "I mean, not everybody gets married. Look at Old Man Barlow, he never did."

"He never bathed," he pointed out.

She glowered at him. "Beside the point. How about

the Miller brothers? They never married. Their sister was widowed and moved back in with them, and they're all single now. They seem perfectly happy."

He looked down his nose at her. "Who spends half her time in department stores, ogling baby booties and little gowns?"

She flushed and averted her eyes.

"Just what I thought," he added.

"Listen, there really aren't many communities in Texas smaller than Comanche Wells, or even Jacobsville. Most of the men my age are either married or living with somebody."

"I see your point."

"The others are having so much fun partying that they don't want to do either," she continued. "Come on, Dad, I like my life. I really do. I enjoy working for the chief and having lunch at Barbara's Café and playing my game at night and taking care of you." She gave him a close scrutiny. "You know, you might think about marrying somebody."

"Bite your tongue," he said shortly. "There was your mother. I don't want anybody else. Ever."

She stared at him with consternation. "She'd want you to be happy."

"I am happy," he insisted. "I'm married to my church, pumpkin. I love what I do now." He smiled. "You know, in the sixteenth century, all priests were expected to be single. It wasn't until Henry VIII changed the laws that they could even marry, and when his daughter Mary came to the throne, she threw out all the married priests. Then when her half sister Elizabeth became Queen, she permitted them to marry, but she didn't want married ministers preaching before her. She didn't approve of it, either."

"This is the twenty-first century," she pointed out. "And why are you hanging out with McKuen Kilraven?" she added, naming one of the federal agents who sometimes came to Jacobsville.

He laughed. "Does it show?"

"I don't know of anybody else who can hold forth for an hour on sixteenth-century British politics and never tell the same story twice."

"Guilty," he replied. "He was in your boss's office the last time I was there."

"When was that? I didn't see him."

"You were at lunch."

"Oh."

He didn't volunteer any more information.

"I need to go buy a new dress," she said. "I think I'll drive up to San Antonio after work, since it's Saturday and I get off at 1 p.m."

"Okay. I'll let you borrow the Cobra." He laughed at her astonished look. "I'm not sure your truck would make it even halfway to the city, pumpkin."

She just shook her head.

IT WAS A CONCESSION of some magnitude. Her father loved that car. He washed and waxed it by hand, bought things for it. She was only allowed to drive it on very special occasions, and usually only when she went to the big city.

San Antonio wasn't a huge city, but there was a lot to see. Carlie liked to stop by the Alamo and look at it, but El Mercado was her port of call. It had everything, including unique shops and music and restaurants. She usually spent half a day just walking around it. But today she was in a hurry.

She went from store to store, but she couldn't find exactly what she was looking for. She was ready to give up when she pulled, on impulse, into a small strip mall where a sale sign was out in front of a small boutique.

She found a bargain dress, just her size, in green velvet. It was ankle length, with a discreet rounded neckline and long sleeves. It fit like a glove, but it wasn't overly sensual. And it suited her. It was so beautiful that she carried it like a child as she walked to the counter to pay for it.

"That was the only size we got in this particular design," the saleslady told her as she packaged it on its hangar. "I wish it was my size," she added with a sigh. "You really are lucky."

Carlie laughed. "It's for a dance. I don't go out much."

"Me, either," the saleslady said. "My husband sits and watches the Western Channel on satellite when he gets off work and then he goes to bed." She shook her head. "Not what I thought marriage would be like. But he's good to me and he doesn't cheat. I guess I'm lucky."

"I'd say you are."

Carlie was in the Jacobs County limits on a long, deserted stretch of road. The Cobra growled as if it had been on the leash too long and wanted off. Badly.

With a big grin on her face, Carlie floored the accelerator. "Okay, Big Red," she said, using her father's affectionate nickname for the car, "let's run!"

The engine cycled, seemed to hesitate, and then the car took off with a growl that would have done a hungry mountain lion proud.

"Woo-hoo!" she exclaimed.

She was going eighty, eighty-five, ninety, ninety-six and then one hundred. She felt an exhilaration she couldn't remember ever feeling before. The road was completely open up ahead, no traffic anywhere. Well, except for that car behind her...

Her heart skipped. At first she thought it was a police car, because she was exceeding the speed limit by double the posted signs. But then she realized that it wasn't a law enforcement car. It was a black sedan, and it was keeping pace with her.

She almost panicked. But she was close to Jacobsville, where she could get help if she needed it. Her father's admonition about checking the truck before she drove it made her heart skip. She knew he'd checked the car, but she hadn't counted on being followed. Someone was after her. She knew that her father's friends were watching her, but that was in Jacobsville.

Nobody was watching her now, and she was being chased. Her cell phone was in her purse on the floor by the passenger seat. She'd have to slow down or stop to get to it. She groaned. Lack of foresight. Why didn't she have it in the console?

Her heart was pumping faster as the car behind gained on her. What if it was the shadowy assassin come for a second try? What was she going to do? She couldn't outrun him, that was obvious, and when she slowed down, he'd catch her.

She saw the city-limit sign up ahead. She couldn't

continue at this rate of speed. She'd kill someone at the next crossroads.

Groaning, she slowed down. The black sedan was right on top of her. She turned without a signal into the first side street and headed for the police station. If she was lucky, she just might make it.

Yes! The traffic light stayed green. She shot through it, pulled up in front of the station and jumped out just as the sedan pulled in front of her, braked and cut her off.

"You damned little lunatic, what the hell were you thinking!" Carson raged at her as he slammed out of the black sedan and confronted her. "I clocked you at a hundred miles an hour!"

"Oh, yeah? Well, you were going a hundred, too, because you were right on my bumper. And how was I supposed to know it was you?" she told him, red-faced with embarrassment.

"I called your cell phone half a dozen times, didn't you hear it ring?"

"I had it turned off. And it was on the floor in my purse," she explained.

He put his hands on his slim hips and glared at her. "You shouldn't be allowed out by yourself, and especially not in a car with that sort of horsepower!" he persisted. "I should have the chief arrest you!"

"Go ahead, I'll have him arrest you, too!" she yelled back.

Two patrol officers were standing on the side-lines, spellbound. The chief came out and stopped, just watching the two antagonists, who hadn't noticed their audience.

"What if you'd hit something lying in the middle

of the road? You'd have gone straight off it and into a tree or a power pole, and you'd be dead!"

"Well, I didn't hit anything! I was scared because I saw a car following me. Who wouldn't be paranoid, with people watching you all the time and my father having secret phone calls…!"

"If you'd answered your damned cell phone, you'd have known who was following you!"

"It was in my purse and I was afraid to slow down and try to grab it out of my pocketbook!"

"Of all the stupid assignments I've ever had, this takes the prize," he muttered. "And why you had to go to San Antonio…?"

"I went to buy a dress for the Valentine's Day party!"

He gave her a cold smile. "Going alone, are we?"

"No, I'm not." She shot back. "I have a date!"

He looked oddly surprised. "Do you have to pay him when he takes you home?" he asked in a long, sarcastic drawl.

"I don't have to hire men to take me places!" she raged back. "And this man doesn't notch his bedpost and take in strays to have somebody to sleep with."

He took a quick step forward, and he looked dangerous. "That's enough," he snapped.

Carlie sucked in her breath and her face paled.

"It really is enough," Cash Grier said, interrupting them. He stepped between them and stared at Carson. "The time to tell somebody you're following them is not when you're actually in the car. Especially a nervous young woman whose life has been threatened."

Carson's jaw was set so firmly she wondered if his teeth would break. He was still glaring at Carlie.

"And you need to keep your phone within reach when you're driving," he told Carlie in a gentler tone and with a smile.

"Yes, sir," she said heavily. She let out a long sigh.

"She was doing a hundred miles an hour," Carson said angrily.

"If you could clock her, you had to be doing the same," Cash retorted. "You're both lucky that you weren't in the city limits at the time. Or that Hayes Carson or one of his deputies didn't catch you. Speeding fines are really painful."

"You'd know," Carson mused, relaxing a little as he glanced at the older man.

Cash glowered at him. "Well, I drive a Jaguar," he said defensively. "They don't like slow speeds."

"How many unpaid speeding tickets is it to date? Ten?" Carson persisted. "I hear you can't cross the county border up around Dallas. And you, a chief of police. Shame, shame."

Cash shrugged. "I sent the checks out yesterday," he informed the other man. "All ten."

"Threatening to put you under arrest, were they?"

"Only one of them," Cash chuckled. "And he was in Iraq with me, so he stretched the rules a bit."

"I have to get home," Carlie said. She was still shaking inside over the threat that turned out to be just Carson. And from Carson's sudden move toward her. Very few people knew what nightmares she endured from one very physical confrontation in the past.

"You keep under the speed limit, or I'm telling your father what you did to his car," Carson instructed.

"He wouldn't mind," she lied, glaring at him.

"Let's find out." He jerked out his cell phone and started punching in numbers.

"All right!" she surrendered, holding up both hands. "All right, I'll go under the speed limit." Her eyes narrowed. "I'm taking that sword to a rune forge tonight. So the next time you meet me on a battleground, Hordie, I'm going to wipe the ground with you."

He pursed his lips. "That would be a new experience for me, Alliance elf."

Cash groaned. "Not you, too," he said. "It's bad enough listening to Wofford Patterson brag about his weapons. He even has a dog named Hellscream. And every time Kilraven comes down here, he's got a new game he wants to tell me all about."

"You should play, too, Chief," Carlie said. She glanced at Carson. "It's a great way to work off frustration."

Carson raised an eyebrow. "I know a better one," he said with a mocking smile.

He might not mean what she thought he did. She flushed helplessly and looked away. "I'm leaving."

"Drive carefully. And buckle up," Cash told her.

"Yes, sir, Boss," she said, grinning.

She started the car, pulled it around and eased out of the parking lot.

She really hoped that her father wouldn't find out how she'd been driving his pet car. It would be like Carson to tell him, just for spite.

Odd, though, she thought, how angry he'd been that she'd taken such chances. It was almost as if he was concerned about her. She laughed to herself.

Sure. He was nursing a secret yen for her that he couldn't control.

Not that he ever would ask her out or anything, but she had grave misgivings about him. He was known for his success with women, and she was soft where he was concerned. He could push her into something that he'd just brush off as insignificant, but her life would be shattered. She couldn't let her helpless interest in him grow. Not even a little. She had to remember that he had no real respect for women and he didn't seem capable of settling down with just one.

She pulled into her driveway and cut off the engine. It was a relief to be home. Just as she got out of the car she saw the black sedan drive by. He didn't stop or wave. He just kept going. Her heart jumped up into her throat.

In spite of all the yelling, he'd shepherded her home and she hadn't even noticed. She hated the warm feeling it gave her, knowing that.

CHAPTER THREE

CARLIE HAD HOPED that her father wouldn't hear about her adventure. But when she got inside the house, he was waiting for her, his arms crossed over his chest.

"He lied," she blurted out, blushing, the dress in its plastic bag hanging over one arm.

He blinked. "Excuse me?"

She hesitated. He might not know after all. She cocked her head. "Are you…angry about something?"

"Should I be?"

He made her feel guilty. She drew in a breath and moved toward him. "I was speeding. I'm sorry. Big Red can really run…"

"A hundred miles an hour," he said, nodding. "You need special training to drive at those speeds safely, and you don't have it," he added patiently.

"I didn't know it was Carson behind me," she said heavily. "I thought it might be whoever still has me targeted."

"I understand that. I gave him…well, a talking-to," he amended. "It won't happen again. But you keep your cell phone where you can get to it in a hurry, whatever you're driving. Okay?"

"Okay, Dad," she promised.

"Got the dress, did you?" he asked, and smiled.

"Yes! It's beautiful! Green velvet. I'll wear Mama's

pearls with it, the ones you brought her from Japan when you first started dating."

He nodded. "They're very special. I bought them in Tokyo," he recalled, smiling. "She had the same skin tone that you inherited from her. Off-white pearls are just right for you."

She frowned. "You buy them for a skin color?"

"I always did. Pearls come in many colors, and many prices. Those are Mikimoto pearls. An armed guard stands in the room with them."

She lost a little color. "Maybe I should wear something else..."

"Nonsense. They need to be worn. That would be like getting a special dress and letting it hang in your closet for fear of spilling something on it. Life is what matters, child. Things are expendable."

"Most things," she agreed.

"I made supper, since I knew you were going to be late," he said.

Her eyebrows arched. "That was sweet of you, Dad," she said.

"It's just a macaroni and cheese casserole. Your mother taught me how to do it when we were first married. I never forgot."

"It's one of my favorite dishes. Let me hang up my dress and I'll be right down."

"Sure."

THE MEAL WAS DELICIOUS, even more so because she hadn't had to cook it. She noticed her father's somber expression.

"I'm really sorry about pushing Big Red," she began.

He leaned back in his chair. "It's not the car I was worried about." His pale eyes were narrow and thoughtful. "It might not be a bad idea to send you over to Eb Scott and let one of his guys teach you the finer points of defensive driving. Just in case."

Her heart jumped. "Dad, maybe there isn't a real threat," she said. "I mean, the guy who was afraid of what I remembered about him is dead."

He nodded. "Yes, but there are things going on that you don't know about."

"You were talking to somebody on the phone who wanted you to come back. Come back where?" she asked bluntly.

He grimaced. "I used to work for the feds. Sort of. It was a long time ago."

"Feds?" she repeated, trying to draw him out.

His chest rose and fell. "When you're young, you think you can do anything, be anything. You don't worry about consequences. You take the training and do the job. Nobody tells you that years down the line, you may have regrets." He studied her oval face. "I was away when your mother got sick. What happened to you, because nobody was at home, was my fault. I should have been there."

She glanced down. "They paid for it."

"Not enough," he said coldly, and his face was suddenly hard and merciless. "I don't wish harm to anyone as a rule, but when your grandmother left the world, I didn't shed a tear."

Carlie managed a smile. "Me, neither. I guess he's still around somewhere."

"No. He died in a prison riot last year."

"You didn't say," she faltered.

"I didn't know. My former boss and I were making connections. We looked for anyone dangerous who knew you in the past. I had someone do some checking. I only found out yesterday."

"It's a relief, sort of," she said heavily. She shook her head. "They were both crazy. She was the worst. My poor mother…"

He put his hand over hers and squeezed. "Mary was such a ray of light that nobody blamed her for what her mother did," he reminded her.

"I know, but people have long memories in small towns."

"You have your own spotless reputation," he said gently. "Don't worry about it."

"I guess you're right." She laughed. "Robin hired a limo for us, can you believe it?"

"I like Robin," he said. "I just wish he had more guts."

"Now, now, we can't all be real-life death knights with great swords."

"You and that game. You do need to get out more." He pursed his lips. "Maybe we need to organize some things for the young, single members of our church."

"All four of us?" she mused.

He rolled his eyes.

"I like my life," she declared. "Maybe it lacks excitement, but I'm happy. That should count for something, Dad."

He laughed softly. "Okay. I see your point."

THE CHIEF WAS UNHAPPY. He didn't come out and say so, but he was on a short fuse and it was difficult to get anything out of him past one-syllable words.

"Sir, what about the new patrolman's gear?" she asked gently. "You were supposed to give me a purchase order for it, weren't you?"

"New patrolman?" He frowned. "Oh, yes. Bartley. Okay. I'll do that today."

She bit her tongue so that she didn't remind him that he'd said the same thing the day before.

He caught her expression and laughed hollowly. "I know. I'm preoccupied. Want to know why?" He shoved a newspaper across his desk. "Read the headline."

It said, Matthew Helm to Fill Unexpired Term of U.S. Senator. She stared at Cash without understanding what he was upset about.

"There were three men in the running for the appointment," he said. "One was found by police in San Antonio, on the street, doped up by an apparent drug habit that nobody knew he had. A tip," he added. "The second withdrew from the nomination because his son was arrested for cocaine possession—a kid who'd never even used drugs, but apparently the glove compartment in his car was stuffed with the stuff. Another tip. The third contender, Helm, got the appointment."

"You think the others were set up," she began.

"Big-time," he replied. He glared at the headline. "If he wins the special election in May, we're in for some hard times in law enforcement. I can't prove it, but the prevailing theory is that Mr. Helm is in bed with Charro Mendez. Remember him?"

She nodded. "The enforcer who worked for the late El Ladrón," she said. "He was a cousin to the Fuentes brothers."

"The very same ones who used to run the distribution hub. He's now head of the drug cartel over the border in Cotillo. In fact, he's the mayor of that lovely little drug center."

"Oh, dear."

"I really wish somebody had furnished Carson with more than three hand grenades," he muttered.

"Shame!" she said.

He chuckled. "Okay. I'll get the purchase order filled out." He leaned forward. "Hell of a thing, to have a politician like this in Washington."

"He'll be a junior senator," she pointed out. "He won't have an important role in anything. He won't chair any important committees and he won't have powerful alliances."

"Yet."

"Surely, he won't win the special election," she ventured.

He looked at her. "Carlie, remember what I just told you about his rivals for the appointment?"

She whistled. "Oh, dear," she said again.

"Exactly."

The phone rang. She excused herself and went out to answer it.

CARSON WAS CONSPICUOUS by his absence for the next few days. Nobody said anything about him, but it was rumored that he was away on some job for Eb Scott. In the meantime, Carlie got her first look at the mysterious Rourke.

He stopped by her office during her lunch hour one day. He was wearing khakis with a sheepskin coat. He grinned at her where she sat at her desk eating hot soup out of a foam cup.

"Bad habit," he said, with a trace of a South African accent. "Eating on the job. You should be having that out of fine china in some exotic restaurant."

She was staring at the attractive man wearing an eye patch, with her spoon suspended halfway between the cup and her mouth. "Excuse me?" she faltered.

"An exotic restaurant," he repeated.

"Listen, the only exotic restaurant I know of is the Chinese place over on Madison, and I think their cook is from New York."

He chuckled. "It's the sentiment, you know, that counts."

"I'll take your word for it." She put down the cup. "How can I help you?"

"Is the boss in?" he asked.

She shook her head. "Sorry. He's at the exotic local café having a thick hamburger and fries with a beautiful ex-motion picture star."

"Ah, the lovely Tippy," he chuckled. "Lucky man, to have a wife who's both kind and beautiful. The combination is rare."

"I'll say."

"So, okay if I leave a message?"

She pushed a pad and pen across the desk and smiled. "Be my guest."

He scribbled a few words and signed with a flourish.

She glanced at it. "You're Rourke?"

He nodded. His one pale brown eye twinkled. "I guess my reputation has preceded me?"

"Something like that," she said with a grin.

"I hope you were told it by your boss and not Carson," he said.

She shook her head. "Nobody told me. I overheard my dad talking about you on the telephone."

"Your dad?"

She nodded. "Reverend Jake Blair."

His face softened. "You're his daughter, then." He nodded. "It came as a shock to know he had a child, let me tell you. Not the sort of guy I ever associated with family."

"Why?" she asked, all innocence.

He saw that innocence and his face closed up. "I spoke out of turn, there."

"I know he did other things before he came home," she said. "I don't know what they were."

"I see."

In that instant, his own past seemed to scroll across his hard face, leaving scars that were visible for a few seconds.

"You need to go to one of those exotic restaurants and have something to cheer you up," she pointed out.

He stared at her for a moment and then chuckled. "How about going with me?" he teased.

She shook her head. "Sorry. I've been warned about you."

"How so?" he asked, and seemed really interested in her answer.

She grinned. "I'm not in your league, Mr. Rourke," she said. "Small-town girl, never been anywhere, never dated much…" He looked puzzled. She gave him her best starstruck expression. "I want to get married and have lots of kids," she said enthusiastically. "In fact, I'm free today after five…!"

He glowered at her. "Damn! And I've got a meeting at five." He snapped his fingers. "What a shame!"

"Just my luck. There, there, I'm sure you'll find someone else who can't wait to marry you," she added.

"No plans to marry, I'm afraid," he replied. Then he seemed to get it, all at once. His eyebrows arched. "Are you having me on?"

She blinked. "Am I having you on what?"

He stuffed his hands in his pockets. "I can't marry you," he said. "It's against my religion."

"Which religion would that be?"

"I'm not sure," he said. "I'll have to find one that prohibits marriage…" He burst out laughing.

She grinned.

"I get it. I'm a bit slow today. Must stem from missing breakfast." He shook his head. "Damned weird food you Yanks serve for breakfast, let me tell you. Grits? What the hell is a grit?"

"If you have to ask, you shouldn't eat one," she returned, laughing.

"I reckon." He smiled. "Well, it was nice meeting you, Ms. Blair."

"Miss," she said. "I don't run a company and I'm not planning to start my own business."

He blinked. "Come again?"

She frowned. "How can I come again if I haven't left?"

He moved closer to the desk. "Confound it, woman, I need a dictionary to figure out what you're saying."

"You can pin a rose on that," she agreed. "Are you from England?"

He glared at her. "I'm South African."

"Oh! The Boer Wars. You had a very famous general named Christiaan de Wet. He was a genius at guerilla warfare and was never captured by the British, although his brother, Piet, was."

He gaped at her.

She smiled shyly. "I collect famous generals. Sort of. I have books on famous campaigns. My favorites were American, of course, like General Francis Marion of South Carolina, the soldier they called the 'Swamp Fox' because he was so good at escaping from the British in the swamps during the Revolutionary War," she laughed. "Then there was Colonel John Singleton Mosby, the Gray Ghost of the Confederacy. I also like to read about Crazy Horse," she added shyly. "He was Oglala Lakota, one of the most able of the indigenous leaders. He fought General Crook's troops to a standstill at the Battle of the Rosebud."

He was still gaping.

"But my favorite is Alexander the Great. Of all the great military heroes, he was the most incredible strategist…"

"I don't believe it." He perched himself on the edge of her desk. "I know South Africans who couldn't tell you who de Wet was!"

She shrugged. "I used to spend a lot of time in the library. They had these old newspapers from the turn of the twentieth century. They were full of the Boer Wars and that famous Boer General de Wet," she laughed. "I almost missed class a couple of times because I was so entranced by the microfilm."

He laughed. "Actually, I'm distantly related to one of the de Wets, not really sure if it was Christiaan, though. My people have been in South Africa for three generations. They were originally Dutch, or so my mother said."

"Rourke is not really a Dutch name, is it?" she asked.

He sighed. "No. Her name was Skipper, her maiden name."

"Was your father Irish?"

His face closed up. That one brown eye looked glittery.

"Sorry," she said at once. "That was clumsy. I have things in my past that I don't like to think about, either."

He was surprised at her perception. "I don't speak of my father," he said gently. "Didn't mean to unsettle you."

"No problem," she said, and smiled. "We're sort of the sum total of the tragedies of our lives."

"Well put." He nodded thoughtfully. "I might reconsider about that marriage thing…"

"Sorry. My lunch hour's over."

"Damn."

She laughed.

He studied her with real interest. "There's this do, called a Valentine's Day dance, I think. If you need a partner…?"

"Thanks, but I have a date," she said.

"Just my luck, being at the end of the line, and all," he chuckled.

"If you go, I'll dance with you," she promised.

"Will you, now? In that case, I'll dust off my tux."

"Just one dance, though," she added. "I mean, we wouldn't want to get you gossiped about or anything."

"Got it." He winked and got to his feet. "If you'll

pass that note along to the chief, I'll be grateful. See you around, I expect."

"I expect so," she replied.

WHAT A VERY strange man, she thought. He was charming. But she really didn't want to complicate her life. In his way, he seemed far more risky than even Carson, in a romantic sense.

When she got home, she mentioned his visit to her father.

"So now you know who Rourke is," he chuckled.

"He's very nice," she said. "But he's a sad sort of person."

"Rourke?" he asked, and seemed almost shocked.

"Yes. I mean, it doesn't show so much. But you can tell."

"Pumpkin, you really are perceptive."

"He said he'd take me to the Valentine's dance. That was after he reconsidered the wedding, but I told him my lunch hour was over…"

"What?" he blurted out.

"Nothing to worry about, he said he wasn't free today anyway."

"Listen here, you can't marry Rourke," he said firmly.

"Well, not today, at least," she began.

"Not any day," came an angry voice from the general direction of the front door. Carson came in, scowling. "And what did I tell you about keeping that cell phone with you?" he added, pulling it out of his pocket. "You left it on your desk at work!"

She grimaced. "I didn't notice."

"Too busy flirting with Rourke, were you?" Carson added harshly.

"That is none of your business," she said pertly.

"It really isn't," her father interjected, staring at Carson until he backed down. "What's going on?" he added, changing the subject.

Carson looked worn. "Dead ends. Lots of them."

"Were you at least able to ascertain if it was poison?"

He nodded. "A particularly nasty one that took three days to do its work." He glanced at Carlie, who looked pale. "Should you be listening to this?" he asked.

"I work for the police," she pointed out. She swallowed. "Photos of dead people, killed in various ways, are part of the files I have to keep for court appearances by our men and women."

Carson frowned. He hadn't considered that her job would involve things like that. "I thought you just typed reports."

She drew in a breath. "I type reports, I file investigative material, photos, I keep track of court appearances, call people to remind them of meetings, and from time to time I function as a shoulder for people who have to deal with unthinkable things."

Carson knew what she was talking about. His best friend, years ago, had been a reservation policeman. He'd gone with the man on runs a time or two during college vacation. In the service, overseas, he'd seen worse things. He was surprised that Carlie, the innocent, was able to deal with that aspect of police work.

"It's a good job," she added. "And I have the best boss around."

"I have to agree," her father said with a gentle smile. "For a hard case, he does extremely well as a police chief." He sighed. "I do miss seeing Judd Dunn around."

"Who's Judd Dunn?" Carson asked.

"He was a Texas Ranger who served on the force with Cash," Jake said. "He quit to be assistant chief here when he and Christabel had twins. But he was offered a job as police chief over in Centerville. It's still Jacobs County, just several miles away. He took it for the benefits package. And, maybe, to compete with Cash," he chuckled.

"They tell a lot of stories about the chief," Carlie said.

"Most of them are true," Reverend Blair replied. "The man has had a phenomenal life. I don't think there's much he hasn't done."

Carson put Carlie's phone on the table beside her and glanced at his watch with a grimace. "I have to get going. I'm still checking on the other thing," he added to Reverend Blair. "But I... Sorry."

Carson paused to take a call. "Yes, I know, I'm running late." He paused and smiled, gave Carlie a smug look. "It will be worth the wait. I like you in pink. Okay. See you in about thirty minutes. We'll make the curtain, I promise. Sure." He hung up. "I'm taking Lanette to see *The Firebird* in San Antonio. I have to go."

"Lanette?" Reverend Blair asked.

"She's a stewardess. I met her on the plane coming down with Dalton Kirk a few weeks ago." He paused. "There's still the matter of who sent a driver for him, you know. A man was holding a sign with his name on it. I tried to trace him, but I couldn't get any information."

"I'll mention it to Hayes," Reverend Blair said. "He's still hoping to find Joey's computer." Joey was the computer technician who'd been killed trying to recover files from Hayes's computer. The computer itself had disappeared, leading Hayes to reset all the department's sensitive information files and type most of his documentary evidence all over again.

Carson's expression was cold. "Joey didn't deserve to die like that. He was a sweet kid."

"I didn't know him," Reverend Blair said. "Eb said he was one of the finest techs he'd ever employed."

"One day," Carson said, "we'll find the person who killed him."

"Make sure you take a law enforcement officer with you if it's you who finds him," Reverend Blair said shortly. "You're very young to end up in federal prison on a murder charge."

Carson smiled, but his eyes didn't. "I'm not as young as I look. And age has more to do with experience than years," he said, and for a minute, the sadness Carlie had seen on Rourke's face was duplicated on Carson's.

"True," Reverend Blair said quietly.

Carlie was fiddling with her phone, not looking at Carson. She'd heard about the stewardess from one of the sheriff's deputies, who'd heard it from Dalton Kirk. The woman was blond and beautiful and all over Carson during the flight. It made Carlie sad, and she didn't want to be. She didn't want to care that he was going to a concert with the woman.

"Well, I'll be in touch." He glanced at Carlie. There

was that smug, taunting smile again. And he was
gone.

Her father looked at her with sympathy. "You can't
let it matter," he said after a minute. "You know that."

She hesitated for a second. Then she nodded. "I'm
going up. Need anything?"

He shook his head. He took her by the shoulders
and kissed her forehead. "Life is hard."

"Oh, yes," she said, and tried to smile. "Night,
Dad."

"Sleep well."

"You, too."

SHE PLUGGED IN her game and went looking for Robin
to run some battlegrounds. It would keep her mind
off what Carson was probably doing with that beautiful blond stewardess. She saw her reflection in the
computer screen and wished, not for the first time,
that she had some claim to beauty and charm.

Robin was waiting for her in the Alliance capital
city. They queued for a battleground and practiced
with their weapons on the target dummies while they
waited.

This is my life, she thought silently. A computer
screen in a dark room. I'm almost twenty-three years
old and nobody wants to marry me. Nobody even
wants to date me. But I have bright ideals and I'm
living the way I want to.

She made a face at her reflection. "Good girls
never made history," she told it. Then she hesitated.
Yes, they did. Joan of Arc was considered so holy
that her men never approached her in any physical
way. They followed her, a simple farm girl, into battle

without hesitation. She was armed with nothing except her flag and her faith. She crowned a king and saved a nation. Even today, centuries later, people know who she was. Joan was a good girl.

Carlie smiled to herself. So, she thought. There's my comeback to that!

SHE WAS TYPING up a grisly report the next day. A man had been found on the town's railroad tracks. He was a vagabond, apparently. He was carrying no identification and wearing a nice suit. There wasn't a lot left of him. Carlie tried not to glance at the crime scene photos as she dealt with the report.

Carson came in, looking weary and out of sorts.

She stared at him. "Well, it wasn't you, after all," she said enigmatically.

He blinked. "Excuse me?"

"We found a man in a nice suit, carrying no identification. Just for a few minutes, we wondered if it was you," she said, alluding to his habit of going everywhere without ID.

"Tough luck," he returned. He frowned as he glanced at the crime scene photos. He lifted one and looked at it with no apparent reaction. He put it back down. His black eyes narrowed on her face as he tried to reconcile her apparent sweetness with the ability it took to process that information without throwing up.

"Something you needed?" she asked, still typing.

"I want to speak to Grier," he said.

She buzzed the chief and announced the visitor. She went back to her typing without giving Carson the benefit of even a glance. "You can go in," she said, nodding toward the chief's office door.

Carson stared at her without meaning to. She wasn't pretty. She had nothing going for her. She had ironclad ideals and a smart mouth and a body that wasn't going to send any man running toward her. Still, she had grit. She could do a job like that. It would be hard even on a toughened police officer, which she wasn't.

She looked up, finally, intimidated by the silence. He captured her eyes, held them, probed them. The look was intense, biting, sensual. She felt her heart racing. Her hands on the keyboard were cold as ice. She wanted to look away but she couldn't. It was like holding a live electric wire...

"Carson?" the chief called from his open office door.

Carson dragged his gaze away from Carlie. "Coming."

He didn't look at her again. Not even as he left the office scant minutes later. She didn't know whether to be glad or not. The look had kindled a hunger in her that she'd never known until he walked into her life. She knew the danger. But it was like a moth's attraction to the flames.

She forced her mind back on the job at hand and stuffed Carson, bad attitude and blonde and all, into a locked door in the back of her mind.

CHAPTER FOUR

THINGS WERE HEATING UP. Reverend Blair went to San Antonio with Rourke. They seemed close, which fascinated Carlie.

Her dad didn't really have friends. He was a good minister, visiting the sick, officiating at weddings, leading the congregation on Sundays. But he stuck close to home. With Rourke, he was like another person, someone Carlie didn't know. Even the way they talked, in some sort of odd shorthand, stood out.

THE WEATHER WAS COLD. Carlie grimaced as she hung up the tattered coat, which was the only protection she had against the cold. In fact, she was worried about going to the dance with Robin because of the lack of a nice coat. The shoes she was going to wear with the green velvet dress were old and a little scuffed, but nobody would notice, she was sure. People in Jacobs County were kind.

She wondered if Carson might show up there. It was a hope and a worry because she knew it was going to hurt if she had to see him with that elegant, beautiful woman she'd heard about. The way he'd looked at her when he was talking to the woman on the phone was painful, too; his smug expression taunted her with his success with women. If she could keep that in mind, maybe she could avoid some heart-break.

But her stubborn mind kept going back to that look she'd shared with Carson in her boss's office. It had seemed to her as if he was as powerless to stop it as she was. He hadn't seemed arrogant about the way she reacted to him, that once. But if she couldn't get a grip on her feelings, she knew tragedy would ensue. He was, as her father had said, not tamed or able to be tamed. It really would be like trying to live with a wolf.

On her lunch hour, she drove to the cemetery. She'd bought a small plastic bouquet of flowers to put on her mother's neat grave. A marble vase was built into the headstone, just above the BLAIR name. Underneath it, on one side, was the headstone they'd put for her mother. It just said Mary Carter Blair, with her birth date and the day of her death.

She squatted down and smoothed the gravel near the headstone. She took out the faded plastic poinsettia she'd decorated the grave with at Christmas and put the new, bright red flowers, in their small base, inside the marble vase and arranged them just so.

She patted her mother's tombstone. "It isn't Valentine's Day yet, Mama, but I thought I'd bring these along while I had time," she said, looking around to make sure nobody was nearby to hear her talking to the grave. "Dad's gone to San Antonio with this wild South African man. He's pretty neat." She patted the tombstone again. "I miss you so much, Mama," she said softly. "I wish I could show you my pretty dress and talk to you. Life is just so hard sometimes," she whispered, fighting tears.

Her mother had suffered for a long time before she finally let go. Carlie had nursed her at home, until that last hospital stay, taken care of her, just as her mother had taken care of her when she was a baby.

"I know you blamed yourself for what happened. It was never your fault. You couldn't help it that your mother was a…well, what she was." She drew in a breath. "Daddy says they're both gone now. I shouldn't be glad, but I am."

She brushed away a leaf that had fallen onto the tombstone. "Things aren't any better with me," she continued quietly. "There's a man I…well, I could care a lot about him. But he isn't like us. He's too different. Besides, he likes beautiful women." She laughed hollowly. "Beautiful women with perfect bodies." Her hand went involuntarily to her coat over her shoulder. "I'm never going to be pretty, and I'm a long way from perfect. One day, though, I might find somebody who'd like me just the way I am. You did. You weren't beautiful or perfect, and you were an angel, and Daddy married you. So there's still hope, right?"

She moved the flowers a little bit so they were more visible, then sat down. "Robin's taking me to the Valentine's Day dance. You remember Robin, I know. He's such a sweet man. I bought this beautiful green velvet dress to wear. And Robin's rented us a limo for the night. Can you imagine, me, riding around in a limousine?" She laughed out loud at the irony. "I don't even have a decent coat to wear over my pretty dress. But I'll be going in style."

She caressed her hand over the smooth marble. "It's hard, not having anybody to talk to," she said after a minute. "I only ever had one real girlfriend, and she moved away years ago. She's married and has kids, and she's happy. I hear from her at Christmas." She sighed. "I know you're around, Mama, even if I can't see you.

"I won't ever forget you," she whispered softly. "And I'll always love you. I'll be back to see you on Mother's Day, with some pretty pink roses, like the ones you used to grow."

She patted the tombstone again, fighting tears. "Well…bye, Mama."

She got to her feet, feeling old and sad. She picked up the faded flowers and carried them back to her truck. As she was putting them on the passenger's side floor, she noticed a note on the seat.

Keep the damned cell phone with you! It does no good sitting in the truck!

It was signed with a big capital *C*.

She glared at it, looking around. She didn't see anybody. But he'd been here, watching her. He'd seen her talking to her mother. Great. Something else for him to hold against her. She started to crumple up the note, but it was the first one he'd ever written her. She liked the way he wrote, very legible, elegant longhand. With a sigh, she folded it and stuck it in the glove compartment.

"Mental illness must be contagious," she muttered to herself. "Maybe I got it from Rourke."

She got in under the wheel and started the engine. It didn't occur to her until much later that it seemed to matter to Carson if something happened to her. Of course, it could have just been pride in his work that she wouldn't get killed on his shift. Still, it felt nice. Unless he'd seen her talking to Mary and thought she needed to be committed.

HER FATHER CAME in with Rourke that night just as she was taking the cornbread out of the oven. She'd made a big pot of homemade chili to go with it.

"What a delightful smell," Rourke said in the kitchen doorway.

She grinned. "Pull up a chair. All you need is some butter for the cornbread. I have real butter. Homemade chili to go with it. There's always plenty."

"By all means," Reverend Blair chuckled. "Carlie always makes extra, in case I bring someone home with me."

"Do you do that often?" Rourke asked.

"Every other day," the reverend confessed. "She never complains."

"He only brings hungry people who like the way I cook," she amended, and laughed. Her face, although she didn't realize it, was very pretty when she smiled.

Rourke studied her with real appreciation. If his heart hadn't been torn, he might have found her fascinating.

He looked around the stove and the cabinets.

"Did I forget something?" she asked.

"I'm looking to see if you cooked a grit."

She and her father both laughed.

"It isn't a grit, it's grits. They're made with corn," she pointed out.

He shook his head. "Foreign fare."

"Yes, well, I expect you know how to cook a

springbok, but I'd have no idea," she said as she put the pot of chili on the table.

"And she knows about springboks!" Rourke groaned. He sat down and put his napkin in his lap. "She also knows the history of the Boer Wars," he said.

Her father shook his head. "She's a student of military history. A big fan of Hannibal," he confided.

"So am I. He was from Carthage. Africa," Rourke added.

There was silence while they ate. Rourke seemed fascinated with the simple meal.

"I've had cornbread before, but it's usually so dry that I can't eat it. My mother used to make it like this," he added quietly. "She was from the States. Maryland, I believe."

"How in the world did she end up in Africa?" Carlie exclaimed. She blushed. "I mean, if you don't mind my asking."

He put down his spoon. "I was very rude about my father. I'm sorry," he said, his brown eyes steady on her face. "You see, my birth certificate lists my mother's husband in that capacity. But a covert DNA profile tells a very different story." His face was hard. "I don't speak of it in company because it's painful, even now."

She was really blushing now. She didn't know what to say.

"But I wouldn't have hurt you deliberately just for asking an innocent question," Rourke continued gently. "You don't even know me."

She bit her lower lip. "Thanks," she said shyly.

"Now, if you'd been a *man*..." her father mused, emphasizing the last word.

Carlie looked at him inquisitively.

He exchanged a look with Rourke. "There was a bar in Nassau," her father said. "And a member of the group we were with made a sarcastic remark. Not to add that he did know Rourke, and he certainly knew better, but he'd had one too many Bahama mamas." He pursed his lips and studied Rourke's hard face. "I believe he made a very poetic dive into the swimming pool outside the bar."

"Deliberately?" Carlie asked.

"Well, if it had been deliberate, I don't think he'd have done it through the glass patio door," her father added.

Carlie sucked in a breath. She looked behind her.

"What are you looking for?" her father asked.

"Glass patio doors..."

Rourke chuckled. "It was a while back," he remarked. "I'm less hotheaded now."

"Lies," her father said. "Terrible lies."

"Watch it," Rourke cautioned, pointing his chili spoon at the reverend, "or I'll tell her about the Russian diplomat."

"Please do!" Carlie pleaded.

Her father glowered at Rourke. "It was a long time ago, in another life. Ministers don't hit people," he said firmly.

"Well, you weren't a minister then," Rourke teased, "and your embassy had to call in a lot of favors to keep you out of jail."

"What in the world did you people do in those days?" Carlie asked, shocked.

"Bad things," Reverend Blair said softly. "And it's time to change the subject."

"The things we don't know about our parents," Carlie mused, staring at her father.

"Some things are better not known," was the reply. "And isn't your chili getting cold, pumpkin?"

"Why do you call her 'pumpkin'?" Rourke wanted to know.

"Now that's a really long story…"

"And we can forget to tell it unless we want burned meat for a week," Carlie interjected.

The reverend just smiled.

HER FATHER WENT to answer a phone call while Carlie was clearing the dishes in the kitchen. Rourke sat at the kitchen table with a second cup of black coffee.

"You really don't know a lot about your dad, do you?" he asked her.

"Apparently not," she laughed, glancing at him with mischievous green eyes. "Do you take bribes? I can make almost any sort of pie or cake—"

"I don't like sweets," he interrupted. "And it's worth my life to tell you," he added with a laugh. "So don't ask."

She made a face and went back to the dishes in the sink.

"Don't you have a dishwasher?" he asked, surprised.

She shook her head. "Money is always tight. We get a little extra and there's a pregnant woman who can't afford a car seat, or an elderly man who needs dentures, or a child who needs glasses…" She smiled. "That's life."

He frowned. "You just give it away?"

She turned toward him, curious. "Well, can you take it with you when you go?" she asked.

He paused, sipping coffee.

"The Plains tribes had this philosophy," she began, "that the richest man in the village was the one who had the least because he gave it all away. It denoted a good character, which was far more important than wealth."

"I would ask why the interest in aboriginal culture," he began.

She turned, her hands around a soapy plate. "Oh, my best friend was briefly engaged to a Lakota man," she said. "We were juniors in high school. Her parents thought she was too young, and they made them wait a year."

"From your tone, I gather things didn't go well?"

She shook her head. She turned back to the sink to rinse the dish, aware of a pang in the region of her heart because the story hit close to home. "His parents talked him into breaking the engagement," she said. "He told her that his religion, his culture, everything was so different from hers that it would be almost impossible to make a life together. She'd have had to live on the reservation with him, and his parents already hated her. Then there was the problem of the children, because they would have been trapped between two cultures, belonging to neither."

"That's very sad," Rouke commented.

She turned to look at him, then lowered her eyes to the sink again. "I didn't realize how much difference there was, until I started reading about it." She smiled sadly. "Crazy Horse, Tashunka Witko in

his own tongue—although that's translated different ways in English—was one of my favorite subjects. He was Oglala Lakota. He said that one could
not sell the ground upon which the People—what the
Lakota called themselves—walked." She glanced at
him. "Things never mattered to them. Materialism
isn't really compatible with attitudes like that."

"You're one of the least materialistic people I
know, Carlie," her father said as he came back into
the room. "And I'd still say it even if I wasn't related
to you."

"Thanks, Dad," she said with a smile.

"I need to talk to you," he told Rourke. "Bring
your coffee into the office. Carlie, that new science
fiction movie you wanted to see is playing on the
movie channel."

"It's not new, it's four months old," she laughed.
"But you're right, I guess, it's new to me. I'll watch
it later. I promised Robin I'd help run one of his little
toons through a dungeon." She made a face. "I hate
dungeons."

"Dungeons?" Rourke asked.

"She plays an online video game," her father explained, naming it.

"Oh, I see. You're Horde, too, huh?" Rourke teased.

She glared at him. "I'm Alliance. Proudly Alliance."

"Sorry," Rourke chuckled. "Everyone I know is
in Horde."

She turned away. "It seems like it sometimes,
doesn't it?" She sighed. She turned at the staircase
and held up her hand as if it contained a sword. "For

the Alliance!" she yelled, and took off running up-stairs.

Her father and Rourke just laughed.

IT WAS FRIDAY. And not just any Friday. It was the Friday before the Saturday night when the Valentine's Day dance was being held at the Jacobsville Civic Center.

Carlie was all nerves. She was hoping that it would be warmer, so she could manage to go to the dance without wearing a coat, because she didn't have anything nice to go with her pretty dress. She had to search out a file for the chief, which she'd put in the wrong drawer, and then she hung up on a state senator by pushing the wrong button on her desk phone.

The chief just laughed after he'd returned the call. "Is it Robin that's got you in such a tizzy?" he teased.

She flushed. "Well, actually, it's the…"

Before she could finish the sentence and tell him it was her wardrobe that was the worry, the door opened and Carson came in. But he wasn't alone.

There was a beautiful blond woman with him. She was wearing a black suit with a red silk blouse, a black coat with silver fur on the collar, and her purse was the same shade of deep red as the high-heeled shoes she was wearing. Her platinum-blond hair was pulled back into an elegant chignon. She had a flawless complexion, pale blue eyes, and skin like a peach. Carlie felt like a cactus plant by comparison.

But she managed a smile for the woman just the same.

The blonde looked at her with veiled amusement and abruptly looked toward the chief.

"Chief Grier, this is Lanette Harris," Carson said.

"So charmed to meet you," the blonde gushed in an accent that sounded even more Southern than Carlie's Texas accent. She held out a perfectly manicured hand. "I've heard so much about you!"

Cash shook her hand, but he didn't respond to her flirting tone. He just nodded. His eyes went to Carson, who was giving Carlie a vicious, smug little smile.

"What can I do for you?" he asked Carson.

Carson shrugged. "I was at a loose end. I wondered if you'd heard anything more from your contact?"

Cash shook his head. Just that. He didn't say a thing.

Carson actually looked uncomfortable. "Well, I guess we'll get going. We're having supper in San Antonio."

He was wearing a dark suit with a spotless white shirt and a blue pinstriped tie. His long hair was pulled back into a neat ponytail. He was immaculate. Carlie had to force herself not to look at him too closely.

"That desk is a mess! Don't you know how to file things away?" Lanette asked Carlie with studied humor, moving closer. Her perfume was cloying. "However do you find anything?"

"I know where everything is," Carlie replied pleasantly.

"Sorry," Lanette said when she saw Cash Grier's narrow look. "I can't abide clutter." She smiled flirtatiously.

"Don't let us keep you," Cash replied in a tone that sounded as icy as his expression looked.

"Yes. We'd better go." Carson moved to the door and opened it.

"Nice to have met you, Chief Grier," Lanette purred. "If you ever want a competent secretary, I might be persuaded to come out of retirement. I used to work for a law firm. And I know how to file."

Cash didn't reply.

"Lanette," Carson said shortly.

"I'm coming." She smiled again at Cash. "Bye now." She didn't even look at Carlie.

She went to the door and through it. Carlie didn't look up from her computer screen. She hoped she wasn't going to bite through her tongue. Only when she heard the door close did she lift her eyes again and looked through the window.

Carson was striding along beside the blonde and not with his usual smooth gait. He was almost stomping toward his black sedan.

Carlie started coughing and almost couldn't stop.

"You okay?" Cash asked with concern.

"Got…choked on the air, I guess," she laughed. She could barely stop. "Gosh, do you think she bathes in that perfume?"

"Go outside and take a break. I'll turn the AC on for a few minutes to clear the room," Cash said abruptly. "Go on."

She wasn't about to go out front and risk running into Carson and his beautiful companion. "I'll just step out back," she managed, still coughing.

She got outside and leaned against the door, dragging in deep breaths until she was able to get her breath again. There must be something in that perfume that she was allergic to. Although, come to think

of it, she'd almost choked sitting next to a woman in
church the week before who'd been wearing a musky
sort of perfume. She'd learned long ago that she could
only manage the lightest of floral colognes, and not
very often. Funny, her lungs giving her so much trouble over scent, and she didn't even smoke.

She went back inside after a couple of minutes.
Cash was talking to two patrolmen who'd stopped by
with a legal question about a traffic stop.

She went back to her desk and sat down.

"You should see your doctor," Cash said when the
patrolmen went out.

She raised both eyebrows. "He's married."

He burst out laughing. "That's not what I meant,
Carlie. I think you had a reaction to Ms. Harris's
perfume."

"Too much perfume bothers me sometimes, it's
just allergies." She shrugged. "I have a problem with
pollen, too."

"Okay. If you say so."

"I'll get the files in better order," she offered.

"Don't let some outsider's comment worry you,"
he said curtly. "Women like that one tear holes in everything they touch."

"She was very beautiful."

"So are some snakes."

He turned and went back into his office. Carlie
tried not to mind that Carson's elegant girlfriend had
treated her like dirt. She tried to pretend that it didn't
bother her, that Carson hadn't brought her into the
office deliberately to flaunt her.

If only I was beautiful, she thought to herself. I'd
be twice as pretty as his friend there, and I'd have

oodles of money and the best clothes and drive an expensive car. And I'd stick my nose up at him!

Fine words. Now, if she could only manage to forget the miserable afternoon. She was going to a dance, with a nice man. There might be an eligible man there who'd want to dance with her when he saw her pretty dress.

She smiled. It was a gorgeous dress, and she was going to look very nice. Even if she wasn't blond.

THE LIMOUSINE WASN'T what she expected. It wasn't one of the long, elegant ones she'd seen in movies. It was just a sedan.

"Sorry," Robin said when they were underway, the glass partition raised between them and the driver. "I did order the stretch, but they only had one and somebody got there before I did. Some local guy, too, darn the luck."

"It's okay," she said, smiling. "I'm just happy I didn't have to bring my truck!"

He laughed. Then he frowned. "Carlie, why aren't you wearing a coat?" he asked. He moved quickly to turn up the heat. "It's freezing out!"

"I don't have a nice coat, Robin," she said, apologizing. "I didn't want to embarrass you by wearing something ratty…"

"Oh, for God's sake, Carlie," he muttered. "We've known each other since first grade. I don't care what the coat looks like, I just don't want you to get sick."

She smiled. "You really are the nicest man I know. Lucky Lucy!"

He laughed. "Well, at least she and I will get to dance together," he said, sighing. "You're so kind to do this for us." He shook his head. "I've tried everything I know to make her folks like me. They just can't get past who my grandfather was. Some grudge, huh?"

"I know." She searched his dark eyes. "You and Lucy should elope."

"Don't I wish." He grimaced. "When I get established in my own business, that's exactly what I have in mind. They're pushing Lucy at the guy who's bringing her tonight. He's old money from up around Fort Worth. She likes him but she doesn't want to marry him."

"They can't make her," she pointed out.

"No, they can't. She's as stubborn as I am."

THEY PULLED UP at the door to the civic center, just behind the stretch limousine that belonged to the same car service Robin had used.

"There's our car. At least, the car I wanted to order for us." He frowned. "Who is that?" he added.

Carlie didn't say, but she knew. It was Carson, resplendent in an immaculate dinner jacket. Getting out of the vehicle beside him was the blond woman, in a saucy black gown that hugged every curve from shoulder to ankle, and left a lot of bare skin in between. Her breasts were almost completely uncovered except for a bit of fabric in strategic places, and her long skirt had a split so far up the thigh that you could almost see her panty line.

"Well, that's going to go over big in conservative Jacobsville," Robin muttered as the driver opened the backseat door for them. "A half-naked woman at a dance benefiting the local church orphanage."

"Maybe she'll get cold and put more clothes on," Carlie mused, only half-jokingly.

"Let's get you inside before you freeze," he added, taking her hand to pull her toward the building.

There was a crowd. Carlie spotted the chief and his beautiful wife, Tippy, over in a corner talking over glasses of punch. Rourke was standing with them. He looked oddly handsome in his formal attire. Tippy was exquisite in a pale green silk gown, decked out in emeralds and diamonds. Her long, red-gold hair was up in a French twist, secured with an emerald and diamond clasp. She looked like the world-class model she'd once been.

Close at hand was Lucy Tims, wearing a long blue gown with a rounded neckline, her black hair hanging down her back like a curtain. She was standing with a tall, lean man who seemed far more interested in talking to two of the local cattlemen than with his date.

She waved to Robin, said something to the tall man, who nodded, and made a beeline for Carlie and Robin.

"You made it!" Lucy enthused. "Oh, Carlie, bless you!" she added, hugging the other woman.

"You may call me Cupid," Carlie whispered into her ear, laughing.

"I certainly will. You don't know how grateful we are."

"Yes, she does because I told her all the way over here," Robin chuckled. "Shall we get some punch?"

"Great idea." Carlie looked down at the spotless green velvet dress. "On second thought, the punch is purple and I'm clumsy. I think I'll just look for a bottle of water!"

They both laughed as she left them.

Well, at least she didn't see Carson and his new appendage, she thought, grateful for small blessings. She walked down the table with a small plate, studying the various delicacies and grateful that food was provided. She'd been too nervous to eat anything.

She was trying to decide between cheese straws and bacon-wrapped sausages when she felt the plate taken from her hand.

She started to protest, but Carson had her by the hand and he was leading her out toward the dance floor.

"You…didn't ask," she blurted out.

He turned her into his arms and slid his fingers into hers. "I didn't have to," he said at her forehead.

Her heart was beating so hard that she knew he had to feel it. He had her wrapped up against him, so close that she could almost taste his skin. He was wearing just a hint of a very masculine cologne. His shirtfront was spotless. His black tie was ruffled. Just above her eyes she could see the smooth tan of his jaw.

He moved with such grace that she felt as if she had two left feet. She was stiff because it disturbed her to be so close to him. Her hand, entwined with his, was cold as ice. She could just barely get enough air to breathe.

"Your boyfriend's dancing with someone else," he observed.

She could have told him that she didn't have a boyfriend, that she was only helping play Cupid, but it wasn't her secret to tell.

"Will you relax?" he said at her ear, shaking her gently. "It's like dancing with a board."

She swallowed. "I was getting something to eat."

"The food will still be there when you go back."

She stopped protesting. But it was impossible to relax. She followed him mechanically, vaguely aware that the song they were playing was from the musical *South Pacific* and that the evening actually did seem enchanted. Now.

"Whose tombstone were you talking to?" he asked after a minute.

She cleared her throat. "Nobody was around."

"I was."

"You weren't supposed to be there."

He shrugged.

She drew in a steadying breath and stared at his shirt. "I took my mother a bouquet," she said after a minute. "I go by the cemetery and talk to her sometimes." She looked up belligerently. "I know it's not normal."

He searched her soft green eyes. "Normal is subjective. I used to talk to my mother, too, after she was gone."

"Oh." She glanced down again because it was like a jolt of lightning to look into those black eyes.

His fingers became caressing in between her own where they rested on top of his dinner jacket. "I was six when she died," he said.

"I was fourteen."

"How did she die?"

"Of cancer," she said on a long breath. "It took months. At least, until she went into hospital. Then it was so fast…" She hesitated. "How did your mother die?"

He didn't answer.

She groaned inside. She'd done it again. She couldn't seem to stop asking stupid questions…!

His hand contracted. "My father was drunk. She'd burned the bread. She tried to get away. I got in front of him with a chair. He took it away and laid it across my head. When I came to, it was all over."

She stopped dancing and looked up at him, her eyes wide and soft.

"She was very beautiful," he said quietly. "She sang to me when I was little."

"I'm so sorry," she said, and meant every word.

He smoothed his fingers over hers. "They took him away. There was a trial. One of her brothers was in prison, serving a life sentence for murder. He had the bad luck to be sent to the same cell block."

She studied his hard, lean face. She didn't say anything. She didn't have to. Her eyes said it for her.

The hand that was holding hers let go. It went to her face and traced the tear down to the corner of her full, soft mouth. It lingered there, the knuckle of his forefinger moving lazily over the pretty line of her lips.

She felt on fire. Her legs were like rubber. She could feel her heart beating. She knew he could, because his eyes suddenly went down to the discreet rounded neckline, and lower, watching the fabric jump with every beat of her heart, with her strained breathing.

Her whole body felt tight, swollen. She shivered just a little from the intensity of a feeling she'd never experienced before. She swallowed. Her mouth was so dry…

"You'd be a pushover, little girl," he whispered in

a deep, gentle tone as he looked at her soft mouth. "It wouldn't even be a challenge."

"I...know," she managed in a broken tone.

His head bent. She felt his breath on her lips. She felt as if she were vibrating from the sensuous touch of his hand at her waist, pulling her close to the sudden, blunt hardness of his body.

He was burning. Hungry. Aching. On fire to touch her under that soft bodice, to feel her breasts under his lips. He wanted to push her down on the floor here, right here, and press himself full length against her and feel her wanting him. Her heartbeat was shaking them both. She was dying for him. He knew it. He could have her. She wouldn't even try to stop him. He could take her outside, into the night. He could feed on her soft mouth in the darkness, bend her to his will, back her up against the wall and...

"Carson!"

CHAPTER FIVE

"CARSON!" THE STRIDENT voice came again.

The second time, Carson heard it. He steeled himself to look away from Carlie's rapt, shocked face and slowly let her move away from him.

He turned to Lanette. She was glaring at them.

"You promised me the first dance," she accused, pouting.

He managed to look unperturbed. "So I did. If you'll excuse me?" he asked Carlie without actually meeting her eyes.

She nodded. "Of course."

He took Lanette's hand and moved to the other side of the room.

Carlie was almost shaking. She went back to the buffet table mechanically and picked up another plate.

"Might better calm down a little before you try to eat," Rourke murmured. He took the plate away from her, just as Carson had, and pulled her onto the dance floor. "Just as well to escape before complications arise," he added with a chuckle. "You seem to be the subject of some heated disagreement."

She tossed a covert glance toward the other side of the room where Carson and his date appeared to be exchanging terse comments.

"I was just trying to get something to eat," she began.

He studied her. "That's a nice young man you came in with. Very polite. Odd, how he's ignoring you."

She looked up at him. "Private matter," she said.

"Ah. So many things are, yes?"

The way he said it amused her. She laughed.

"That's better," he replied, smiling. "You were looking a bit like the hangman's next victim."

She lowered her eyes to his shirt. It had ruffles, and crimson edging. He had a red carnation in the lapel of the jacket. "You're not quite conventional," she blurted out.

"Never," he agreed. "I like to buck the odds. Our friend over there is Mr. Conservative," he added. "He doesn't like the assumption of ownership, so you can figure the beautiful companion will be gone quite soon."

She tried not to look pleased.

He tilted her face up to his and he wasn't smiling. "That being said, let me give you some sound advice. He's living on heartache and looking for temporary relief. Do you get me?"

She bit her lip. She nodded.

"Good. You remember that. I've seen him walk on hearts wearing hobnailed boots, and he enjoys it. He's getting even."

"But I haven't done anything to him," she began.

"Wrong assumption. He's paying back someone else. Don't ask," he said. "I'm not privy to his past. But I know the signs."

There was such bitterness in his voice that she just stared at him.

"Long story," he said finally. "And no, I won't share it. You just watch your step. Carson's big trouble for a little innocent like you."

"I'm the only one of my kind," she said a little sadly. "Everybody says I'm out of step with the world."

"Would you enjoy being used like a cocktail napkin and tossed in the bin after?" he asked bluntly.

She caught her breath at the imagery.

"I thought not." He drew her back into the dance. "That platinum-armored blond tank he's with doesn't care what she's asked to do if the price is right," he said with icy disdain. "She's for sale and she doesn't care who knows it."

"How do you know...?"

He looked down at her with weary cynicism. "This isn't my first walk round the park," he replied. "She's the sort to go on the attack if anything gets between her and something she wants."

"Well, he doesn't want me," she said, "but thanks for the warning."

He chuckled. "Not to worry, I'll be around."

"Thanks, Rourke."

"Stanton."

She pulled back and looked up at him with real interest. "Stanton?"

He smiled. "It's my first name. I only share it with friends."

She smiled back, shyly. "Thanks."

"And *Carlie?* Is it your name or a nickname?"

She looked around to make sure nobody was close enough to hear. "Carlotta," she whispered. "My mother thought it sounded elegant."

"Carlotta." He smiled gently. "It suits you."

"Just don't tell anyone," she pleaded.

"Your secret's safe with me," he promised.

She was remembering Lanette's nasty comment about her desk, right in front of her boss. She imagined the other woman was furious that she'd even danced with Carson. She just hoped there wouldn't be a price to pay.

APPARENTLY CARSON DIDN'T like possessive women, because Carlie had no sooner finished her small plate of canapés than he was back again. He stopped by the bandleader and made a request. Then he went straight to Carlie, took the punch out of her hand and led her to the dance floor.

"That's a tango," she protested. "I can't even do a two-step…!"

"I lead, you follow," he said quietly. He shot a look of pure malice at the blonde, who was standing across the room with an angry expression.

"You're getting even," she accused as the band began to play again.

"Count on it," he snarled.

He pulled her close and began to move with exquisite grace. He stopped abruptly, turned, and in a series of intricate steps, wound his legs around hers.

It shocked her that he was so easy to follow in such a hard dance. She laughed self-consciously. "This doesn't look like tangos in movies," she began.

"That's Hollywood," he mused. "This is how they do it in Argentina. People go to dance halls and do it with strangers. It's considered part of the culture. Strangers passing in the night."

"I see."

He pulled her close again, enjoying the soft feel of her slender young body in his arms. She smelled just faintly of roses. "Have you ever been to South America?"

"You're kidding, right?" She gasped as he pulled her suddenly closer and made a sharp turn, holding her so that she didn't stumble.

"Why would I be kidding?" he asked.

"I've never been any place in my life except San Antonio."

He frowned. "Never?"

"Never." She sighed. "I went up with Tommy Tyler once in his airplane when he bought it. It was one of those little Cessna planes. I threw up. I was so embarrassed that I never wanted to get on an airplane again."

He chuckled deeply. "I imagine he was unsettled, as well."

"He was so nice. That just made it worse. I apologized until we landed. He got somebody to come and clean it up. To his credit, he even offered me another ride. But I wouldn't go."

"Were you serious about him?"

"Oh, not that way. He was in his fifties, with grown children," she chuckled. "His wife and my mother were great friends."

"People around here are clannish."

"Yes. Most of us have been here for several generations. I had a teacher in grammar school who taught my grandfather and my mother."

He looked down at her curiously as he did another series of intricate steps, drawing her along with him.

The close contact was very disturbing. He loved it. He glanced at the blonde, who was steaming. He enjoyed that. He didn't like possessive women.

Carlie followed his glance. "She'll be out for blood soon," she murmured.

"Which is none of your business." He said it gently, but his tone didn't invite comment.

She clenched her teeth and tried not to give away how hungry the contact was making her. She was astonished at how easy a partner he was. The tango was one of the hardest dances to master, she'd heard. She'd always wanted to try it, but she'd never had a date who could actually dance.

Carson could. He was light on his feet for such a big man, and very skilled. She didn't let herself think about how many partners he must have had to be so good on the dance floor. She drew in a quick breath. She was getting winded already. It irritated her that she couldn't run or even walk fast for long without needing to stop and catch her breath.

She'd never have admitted it to Carson. The feel of his body against hers was intoxicating. She felt his hand firm at her waist, his fingers curled around hers, as he led her around the dance floor.

She was vaguely aware that they were being watched by more people than just the angry blonde, and that the police chief and his wife had taken the dance floor with them.

Cash was a master at the tango. He and Tippy moved like one person. He danced closer to them, and winked. "You're outclassed, kid," he told Carson. "But not bad. Not bad at all."

Carson laughed. "Don't rest on your laurels. I'm practicing."

"I noticed," Cash said with a grin at Carlie, and he danced Tippy, who also smiled at them, to the other part of the dance floor.

Several other couples came out, trying to keep up with the two accomplished couples on the floor. Their attempts ranged from amusing to disastrous.

Carson's chest rose and fell with deep, soft laughter. "I think square dancing has a larger following in this vicinity than the tango," he pointed out.

"Well, not many men can dance. Even square-dance," she added shyly.

He slowed his movements, and held her even closer, his head bent to hers so that she could feel his breath, smell its minty tang, on her mouth. "My mother danced," he whispered. "She was like a fairy on her feet. She usually won the women's dances at powwows."

She looked up into liquid black eyes. "The Lakota have powwows?"

He nodded. "It's what we call them. The first in is the drum. Several men sit around it and play, but it's always called the drum. There are men's dances and women's dances. They're very old."

She nodded. "I went to a powwow up near San Antonio once," she recalled. "There were Comanche people there."

His fingers moved sensuously against hers. "I have Comanche cousins."

"Your people are clannish, too," she remarked.

"Very. Both sides."

"Both sides?"

"One of my great-great-grandmothers was blond and blue-eyed," he said. "She married a Lakota man. He was a rather famous detective in Chicago at the turn of the twentieth century. He was at Wounded Knee. She nursed him back to health. Later, he was with Buffalo Bill's Wild West show for a time."

She wouldn't have mentioned it, but his skin was a light olive shade. She'd guessed that his blood was mixed.

"That must have been one interesting courtship," she said.

He chuckled. "So I'm told." He searched over her face. "Your father has Norwegian ancestors somewhere."

"Yes, from someplace with a name I can't even pronounce. I never met any of his people. He didn't come back here until I was thirteen…" Her voice trailed away. She didn't like thinking about that. "Mama had pictures of him, but I only saw him a few times when I was growing up. He'd stay for a day or two and go away again, and Mama would cry for weeks after."

He scowled. "Why didn't he stay with her?"

She stared at his shirtfront as the music began to wind down. "They argued once. I heard. He said that she trapped him into marrying her because I was on the way. I wouldn't speak to him after that when he came home. I never told him why. It wasn't until she was dying that he came home. He's…different now."

"That's what I've heard from other people who knew him. He seems to enjoy the life he has now."

"He says he has to do a lot of good to make up for the bad things he used to do," she replied. "He won't talk about them. At least, he wouldn't. Rourke had supper with us and he and Daddy talked about old times. It was fascinating."

"Rourke?"

She smiled. "He's really nice. He likes my cooking, too."

His hand on her waist contracted as if he were angry. "Rourke's more of a lobo wolf than I am. You'll break your heart on him."

She looked up at him with wide, shocked eyes. "What?"

He pulled her closer, bent her against his body in such a sensual way that she gasped. His head lowered until his mouth was almost touching hers as he twirled her around to the deepening throb of the music. "But better him than me, baby," he whispered at her soft mouth. "I don't do forever. Even a child on the way wouldn't change that."

She was barely hearing him. He'd called her "baby." No man had ever called her that, and certainly not in such a sexy, hungry sort of tone. She felt herself shiver as his hand smoothed up her rib cage, stopping just under her breast on the soft fabric. And she couldn't even protest.

She felt as if her body was going to explode from the tension he raised in it. She bit off a soft moan as she felt him drag her even closer, so that she was pressed against him from breasts to hips.

In all her life, she'd never felt a man become aroused, but he wanted her, and he couldn't hide it. She shivered again, her heart beating so hard that she thought it might break out of her chest.

"You…shouldn't," she choked.

His cheek rasped against hers. "You'd be the sweetest honey I ever had," he breathed at her ear. "I'd go so hard into you that you'd go up like a rocket."

She moaned and hid her face, shocked, embarrassed…excited. Her nails bit into his jacket. Her body moved against his helplessly as his long leg moved in and out between hers as the dance slowly wound down.

He arched her against him as it ended, positioning her so that her head was down and leaning back, his mouth poised just over hers.

She held on for dear life. Her eyes were locked into his, imprisoned, helpless. He pulled her up with exquisite slowness, held her against him while people clapped. Neither of them noticed.

He let her go, his cheeks ruddy, as if he were angry and unsettled by what had happened. He had to recite math problems in his mind to force his body to relax before he let her go. She wouldn't realize what was going on, but that blonde would see it immediately.

"You dance well," he said stiffly. "All you need is practice."

She swallowed. "Thanks. You're…amazing."

His eyes, narrow and wise, searched hers. "You have no idea how amazing, in the right circumstances," he whispered huskily, his eyes falling to her mouth. "And if you're very lucky, you won't find out."

She felt her heart shaking her. She knew he must be able to feel it, too. She could barely get her breath. Funny, it felt as if air could get in but couldn't get back out. She coughed slightly.

He frowned. "What's wrong?"

"Perfume," she faltered. "It bothers me sometimes."

He arched an eyebrow. "I don't wear perfume."

"Not you," she muttered. "Other women."

He sniffed the air and smiled. "Florals, musk, woodsy tones," he said. His eyes smoothed over her face. "You smell of roses."

"I love roses," she told him.

"Do you?"

She nodded. "I grow them at home. Antique roses. My mother used to plant them."

"My mother was an herbalist," he replied. "She could cure anything."

"The music has stopped," the blonde pointed out coldly.

Carlie and Carson turned and looked at her blankly.

"And I'd like some punch, if you please?" Lanette added icily.

Carson let Carlie go. He hadn't realized that the music had stopped, or that he and Carlie were standing so close together...alone on the dance floor.

"I'll be back in a minute," he told Lanette. He let go of Carlie's hand and moved toward the restrooms.

Carlie, left alone with the overperfumed blond wildcat, braced herself for what she knew to expect.

"WELL, THAT WAS an exhibition if I ever saw one!" Her pale blue eyes were like ice. "Don't you get any ideas about Carson, you little hick secretary. He's mine. Hands off. Do you understand me?"

Carlie just stared at her with equally cold green eyes. She was still shaking inside from Carson's sensual dance and the things he'd said to her. But she wasn't going to let the other woman cow her. "That's his choice."

"Well, he's not choosing you. I'm not kidding," the other woman persisted. She smiled coldly. "You think you're something, don't you?" She looked Carlie up and down. "Did your dress come from some bargain basement up in San Antonio?" she asked sarcastically. "Marked down 75 percent, perhaps?" she added and laughed when Carlie blushed. "And those shoes. My God, they must be ten years old! I'm surprised he wasn't embarrassed to be seen dancing with you in that dress…!"

"Got yours at a consignment sale, darling?" came a soft, purring voice from beside Carlie.

Tippy Grier moved closer, cradling a cup of punch in her hands. She looked elegant in her green silk gown, dripping diamonds and emeralds. She smiled at the blonde. "That particular dress was in a collection of only five gowns. I recognize it because I know the designer," she added, watching the blonde's eyes widen. "It isn't to my taste," she added, "because I don't sell myself."

"How dare you…I was on the runway!" Lanette almost spat at her, reddening.

"Honey, the only runway you've been on is at the airport," Tippy drawled. She looked down. "Those shoes are two seasons out of date, too, but I suppose you thought nobody would notice." She pursed her bow lips in a mock pout. "Shame."

Lanette's hands were clenched at her sides.

"Run along now, kitty cat," Tippy dismissed her. "Your saucer of cream's waiting outside the door." She smiled. "Do have a lovely evening."

Lanette was almost sputtering. She turned and went storming off toward Carson, who was just returning. She ran into his arms, making a big production of crying, wiping at her eyes, and gesturing toward Tippy and Carlie. The look Carson gave Carlie was livid before he took Lanette's arm and walked her toward the front door.

"Wow," Carlie said to Tippy. She shook her head. "You're just incredible! I didn't even have a comeback."

Tippy laughed. It sounded like silver bells. Her reddish-gold hair burned like fire in the lights from overhead. Her green eyes, lighter than Carlie's, twinkled. "I've seen her kind in modeling. They think they're so superior." Her smile was mischievous. "When I was new to the runway, there was this terrible woman from upstate New York who made fun of everything from my big feet to my accent. I cried a lot. Then I got tough." She pursed her lips. "You know, if you time it just right, you can trip someone on the runway and make it look like a terrible accident!"

"You wicked woman," Carlie gasped, laughing.

"She really did have it coming." She shook her head. "I almost felt sorry for her. She lost her contract with the designer. She didn't work for six months. When she finally got another job, she was a different person." Her green eyes glittered. "I hate people like that woman. I know what it is to be poor."

"Thanks," Carlie said. "I couldn't think of a thing to say. It is a sale dress, and my shoes are really old."

"Carlie, you look lovely," Tippy told her solemnly.

"It doesn't matter how much the dress cost if it flatters you. And it does." She smiled. "I hope she tells Carson what I said to her."

"If she does, he might have something to say to you."

Tippy laughed again. "He can take it up with my husband," she replied, and raised her cup of punch to her lips.

"How was the dance?" Reverend Blair asked when Carlie came in the front door.

"It was very nice," she said.

He moved closer, his eyes probing. "What happened?"

She drew in a breath. "Carson danced with me and his girlfriend got really angry. She said some really unpleasant things to me."

His pale blue eyes took on a glitter. "Perhaps I should speak to her."

She smiled. "Tippy Grier spoke to her."

"Say no more. I've heard about Mrs. Grier's temper."

"She was eloquent," Carlie said. She shook her head. "And she never said a single bad word the whole time."

"Good for her. You don't have to use bad words to express yourself. Well, unless you're trying to start a lawnmower," he amended.

She pursed her lips. "Daddy, you think 'horsefeathers' is a bad word."

He frowned. "It is!"

She laughed. "Well, I did enjoy the dancing. Rourke is really light on his feet."

"Yes." He gave her a concerned look.

She waved a hand at him. "No way I'd take on that South African wildcat," she said. "I have a good head on my shoulders."

He seemed relieved.

"I'm going on up. You sleep well, Daddy."

"You, too, pumpkin," he replied with a smile.

SHE WAS HALF-ASLEEP when her cell phone rang. She picked it up and punched the button. "Hello?" she asked drowsily.

There was a pause. "It will come when you least expect it," came an odd-sounding masculine voice. "And your father won't walk away." The connection was broken.

"Right." She turned off the phone and closed her eyes. She'd remember to tell her father in the morning, but the last threat about her father had never materialized, nor had any threat against herself. She was beginning to think that it was a campaign of terror. If so, it wasn't going to work. She refused to live her life afraid.

But she did say an extra prayer at church the next day. Just to be on the safe side.

HER FATHER WASN'T at the breakfast table Monday morning. She had a cup of coffee and two pieces of toast and paused to check the truck over before she started it. She wasn't afraid, but caution wasn't too high a price to pay for safety.

She got into the office, put her coat away and shoved her purse under the desk. She pushed her hair back. It was a damp morning, so her naturally wavy hair was curling like crazy because of the humidity.

She turned the mail out of its bag onto the desk. She'd stopped by the post office, as she did every morning on her way to work. There was a lot of it to go through before the chief came in. She made coffee and shared it with one of the patrolmen. He went out, leaving the office empty.

She sat down at her desk and picked up a letter opener. She'd just started on the first letter when the door opened and a cold wind came in.

Carson was furious. His black eyes were snapping like flames. He stopped in front of the desk.

"What the hell did you say to Lanette Saturday night?" he demanded.

She blinked. "I didn't—"

"She was so upset she couldn't even talk," he said angrily. "She cried all the way home. Then she phoned me this morning, still in tears, and said she was having to go to the doctor for anxiety meds because of the upset."

"I didn't say anything to her," she repeated.

His eyes narrowed. "Don't get ideas."

"Excuse me?"

"It was only two dances," he said in a mocking tone. "Not a marriage proposal. I've told you before, you're not the sort of woman who appeals to me. In any way."

She stood up. "Thank God."

He just stared at her. He didn't speak.

"Your girlfriend was showing more skin than a bikini model," she pointed out. "Obviously that's the sort of woman you like, one who advertises everything she's got in the front window, right? You know why you like her? Because she's temporary. She's a throwaway. She's not the sort of woman who'd want anything to do with a permanent relationship or children…"

His face went hard. His black eyes glittered. "That's enough."

She bit her lip. "You're right, it's none of my business. But just for the record," she added angrily, "you're the sort of man I'd run from as fast as my legs would carry me. You think you're irresistible? You, with your notched bedpost and years of one-night stands? God only knows what sorts of diseases you've exposed yourself to…!"

The insult put a fire under him. He started toward her with blood in his eye, bent on intimidation. The movement was quick, threatening, dangerous. The shock of it took her stumbling backward toward the wall. On the way, she grabbed a chair and held it, trembling, legs out, toward him while she cursed herself for her stupid runaway tongue.

He stopped suddenly. He realized, belatedly, that she was afraid of him. Her face was chalk-white. The chair she'd suspended in midair was shaking, like her slender young body. She was gasping for breath. Wheezing. Coughing.

He frowned.

"Don't…!" she choked, swallowing, coughing again.

The door opened. "What in the hell…?"

"Stay with her," Carson said curtly, running past Cash. He made a dash to his car, grabbed his medical kit and burst back in the door just as Cash was taking the chair from Carlie and putting her firmly down in it.

"Grab her driver's license," he ordered Cash as he unzipped the kit. He pulled a cell phone out of his slacks. "Who's her doctor?"

"Lou Coltrain," Cash replied.

Carlie couldn't speak. She couldn't even breathe.

She heard Carson talking to someone on the other end of the phone. She heard her boss relaying statistics. Why did they need her weight? She couldn't breathe. It felt as if the air was stuck inside her lungs and couldn't get out. She heard a weird whistling sound. Was that her?

Carson tore open packages. He swabbed the bend of her elbow and pulled up a liquid from a small bottle into a syringe. He squirted out a drop.

"This may hurt. I'm sorry." He drove the needle into her arm. His face was like stone. He was almost as pale as she was.

Her breathing began to ease, just a little. Tears sprung from her eyes and ran, hot, down her cheeks.

"Call the emergency room," Carson told Cash. "Tell them I'm bringing her in. She needs to be checked by a physician."

"All right," Cash said tightly. "Then we'll have a talk."

Carson nodded curtly. He handed Carlie her purse, picked her up in his arms and carried her out the door.

CHAPTER SIX

OUTSIDE, A PATROL car was waiting, its lights flashing like mad.

"Chief said for me to lead you to the emergency room," the patrolman called to Carson.

"Thanks," he said. He put Carlie in the passenger seat, strapped her in and threw himself behind the steering wheel.

He ran two red lights, right behind the police car. It was only a short drive to the hospital, but he wanted to get Carlie there as quickly as he could. Her color was still bad, although she was breathing a little easier.

"Damn...you," she cursed, sobbing.

"Yes," he rasped. He glanced at her as he pulled up at the emergency entrance. "God, I'm sorry!"

He got out, unfastened her seat belt and carried her right past the waiting gurney with its attendant, past the clerk, back into a waiting room, trailing irritated people.

"Dr. Coltrain is ready for her, we called ahead," he said over his shoulder.

"Is that Carlie?" the clerk exclaimed. "Is she all right?"

"Not really," Carson said in a rough tone. He carried her into a treatment room. Seconds later, a blond woman in a white lab coat came in, a stethoscope around her neck.

"Are you the one who called me from her office?" she asked, glancing at Carson. "You said that she was upset and having trouble breathing."

"Yes," Carson said quietly. "I'd bet my left arm on asthma."

"Asthma?" Dr. Lou Coltrain frowned at him.

She turned to Carlie, who was still gasping. "Epinephrine. You said on the phone that you were giving her epinephrine."

"Yes," Carson replied tersely. He reminded her of the dosage. "I checked her weight on her driver's license first."

She nodded. "Fran, bring me an inhaler," she said to a nurse nearby. She gave the name brand and the dosage. "Hurry."

"Yes, Doctor," the woman said, and went to get it.

Lou examined Carlie, aware that she was glaring at the man who'd brought her in. He had his hands shoved deep in his pockets and he looked as if somebody had cut the life out of him. She didn't have to guess what had prompted Carlie's attack. Guilt was written all over him.

"She has no history of asthma," Lou said.

"Allergies to perfume, difficulty breathing after exertion, coughing fits," Carson said.

Lou frowned as she glanced at him. "Sporadic?"

"Very. Difficult to diagnose without proper equipment. I'd recommend an allergist."

"Yes. So would I."

She finished her examination. Fran was back with

the inhaler. Lou instructed her in its use and waited until she'd taken several puffs.

"You're lucky that you had no underlying heart conditions, like a sinus node issue," Lou said as she watched Carlie suck in the meds. "Epinephrine can kill someone with a serious arrhythmia." She glanced at Carson. "You knew that."

He nodded. His face was solemn, still. He didn't add anything to the nod.

"One more puff, and then I want you to lie there and rest. I'll be back to check on you in a minute. Feeling better?" Lou asked Carlie, and smiled as she smoothed the ruffled wavy dark hair.

"Much. Thanks, Lou."

Lou turned to Carson. "Can I speak with you?"

He glanced at Carlie. She averted her eyes. He sighed and followed Lou into an empty treatment room nearby.

Lou turned, pinning him with pale eyes. "You know too much for a layman."

"Field medic in the military," he replied.

She pursed her lips. "Try again."

He drew in a breath. She was quick. Nobody else had ever questioned his skills. "I finished medical school and got my degree. I'd have gone into an internship after, but I quit."

"I thought so. Why did you quit?"

His face closed up. "Personal issues. Serious ones. I went off the deep end for a few years."

"I think you're still there," Lou replied. "Off the deep end, I mean." She jerked her head toward Carlie. "What do you know about her?"

"A hell of a lot more than I thought I did, after the

past few minutes," he said flatly. "We had an argument. My fault. I'm hotheaded and I was...frustrated. I started toward her..." He held up a hand when she looked ready to explode. "I've never hit a woman in my life," he interrupted, his black eyes flashing. "My father beat my mother to death in a drunken fit. He went to prison and he was killed by one of her relatives who was serving life on a murder charge. I know more about violence than you have time to hear."

Her face relaxed, just a little. "I'm sorry."

"I would never have struck her. I just went closer." He drew in a breath and leaned back against the block wall, his arms crossed over his chest, his eyes sad. "She backed away and picked up a chair to hold me at bay. That's when I noticed that she was barely able to breathe. I frightened her. I don't know why. Unless there's some violence in her past that I'm not aware of."

"There is," Lou said quietly. "But I don't discuss patients." She smiled to soften the words.

"I understand."

"You reacted very quickly. You may have saved her life." She studied him from across the cubicle. "You also treated Sheriff Hayes Carson when you rescued him and Minette, across the border. You know, doctors are getting thin on the ground. Except for specialists, there's just me and Copper," she added, referring to her husband, also a physician, "and Micah Steele."

His face tautened. "I'm doing a job I like."

"Really?"

He averted his eyes.

"I'm no psychologist," she said after a minute, "but

even I can see through the anger. You're hiding, inside yourself."

"Don't we all do that?" he asked.

"To some extent, yes." She smiled. "I'll stop. I just hate to see waste. You surely don't want to spend the rest of your life feeding people to crocodiles?" she added.

He groaned. "Does everybody know everything in this town?"

"Pretty much," she agreed. "We don't have secrets from each other. We're family," she explained. "We come from all backgrounds, all cultures, all religions. But there are so few of us in Jacobsville and Comanche Wells that we think of ourselves as just one big family."

"Not what I connected with small towns," he confessed. "And I don't share my secrets."

"You never carry ID with you," she began. "You work for Cy Parks, but Eb Scott sends you on assignments periodically. You have a very bad reputation for being a womanizer. You don't drink or smoke, you keep to yourself, and you and Rourke are friends."

"Damn," he muttered.

"See?" she added smugly. "Family."

He shouldered away from the wall. "Not for long. I'm moving on soon."

"Because of Carlie." She laughed softly.

He glared at her. "Because I don't stay in one place long. Ever."

She crossed her arms with a sigh. "You can't run away from the past," she said gently. "It's portable. No matter how far you go, it travels with you. Until you come to grips with it, face what you're running away from, you'll never be satisfied."

"Well, if it catches up with me, it had better be wearing track shoes," he replied. He stood erect. "I need to get Carlie home."

"She's more fragile than she looks," Lou said surprisingly. "Try not to hurt her too much."

He didn't say a word. He just walked by her.

CARLIE REFUSED TO be carried. She walked out the front door beside him, slowly, although her breathing was easier.

"I have to go to the pharmacy," she began.

"I'll drive you. Don't argue," he said heavily. "It's the least I can do."

She shrugged. "Okay. Thanks."

She got in and fastened her seat belt so that he wouldn't have to do it for her. She didn't want him any closer than necessary. He affected her too much, and her nerves were raw after what had happened.

HE DROVE HER to the pharmacy and went inside with her. Bonnie, at the counter, smiled at Carlie.

"How's it going?" she asked as Carlie handed her the prescription. She read it and grimaced. "Oh. I see how it's going."

"Can you fill it while I wait?" Carlie asked in a subdued tone.

"Sure. Let me see if we have this in stock." She went to talk to the pharmacist Nancy, who waved and smiled. Bonnie gave Carlie a thumbs-up and went to fill the order.

One of the other clerks, a new girl, who was returning from lunch, stopped by Carson and smiled. "Can I help you?" she asked in a very sweet tone.

He didn't even look at her. "I'm with her." He nodded toward Carlie.

"Oh. Okay." She gave him a hopeful look. He didn't even glance her way.

She went on to the pharmacy, smiling at Carlie.

Carlie was breathing much better, but the experience had shaken her badly. She hated showing weakness in front of the enemy. Because that's what Carson was, however much she tried to convince herself otherwise.

Filling the prescription didn't take long. Bonnie motioned her to the counter and smiled as Carlie handed her a debit card.

"Directions are on the box," Bonnie said. "I hope you feel better."

"Me, too." Carlie sighed. "Asthma. Bummer. I never even guessed I had it. Dr. Lou's sending me to an allergist, too."

"It will probably be Dr. Heinrich," Bonnie said. "He comes here every Friday to see patients. He's from San Antonio. It will save you that long drive." She looked at Carlie over her glasses as she finished ringing up the purchase, returned the card and handed Carlie the medicine in its white bag. "Especially after you were doing a hundred on the straightaway in your dad's Cobra," she added with pursed lips.

Carlie flushed. "Don't you start."

"I like you," Bonnie replied. "And I hate funerals."

"Same here!" Nancy called across the counter.

"Okay. I'll drive like an old lady," she muttered.

"Mrs. Allen is an old lady, and she pushes that Jaguar of hers over a hundred and twenty when the sheriff's deputies aren't looking," Nancy reminded her.

"I'll drive like a conventional old lady," Carlie corrected.

"Senior citizen," Bonnie whispered. "It's more politically correct!"

Carlie laughed, for the first time since the ordeal began.

THEY WERE BACK in the car. Carlie glanced at Carson, who still looked like a locked and boarded-up house. "Thanks for taking me to the pharmacy," she began.

He ignored her. He wasn't driving toward her house. He went down the highway until he spotted a roadside park by the Jacobs River. He stopped at a convenience store and parked the car.

"Come on," he said gently, helping her out.

"Where are we going?" she asked.

"Lunch." He led the way inside. She picked out a packaged ham and cheese sandwich, a bag of chips, and a soft drink. He got a roast beef sandwich and a soft drink. He paid for all of it and led her behind the store to a picnic area beside the river, complete with concrete table and benches.

The sound of the river, even in winter, was soothing. It was February, and her ratty old coat felt good, but she could have taken it off. It was warmer in the sun.

They ate in silence for several minutes. She liked being outside. When she was at home, she did all the yard work, planted a garden, tended flowers, raked leaves, did all the things she could to keep her out of the house. She loved the seasons, the rain and the rare snowfall. She was an outdoor girl at heart.

When they finished eating, he took the waste paper and put it in a container. There was a recycling bin for the soft drink cans, and he put them in it.

She started toward the car, but he caught her hand gently in his and led her down to the river. He leaned against a tree, still holding her hand.

"Your Dr. Coltrain said that I'm hiding from the past. She's right." He drew in a long breath. "I was married."

Carlie caught her breath. His hand tightened around her fingers.

"She was younger than me. Pretty, bright, full of fun. She teased me and provoked me. I loved her more than my life. We grew up together on the Wapiti Ridge Sioux Reservation in South Dakota. Our people had known each other for generations. She was several grades behind me, but we were always friends. I was in my final year of…graduate school—" he didn't want to say "medical school" "—when we went to a dance together and fell in love. Her parents thought she was too young, but we wouldn't listen. We were married by the local priest."

He hesitated, then went on. "It was a long commute for me, and expensive because I had to fly there. And I had to stay in the dorm during the week. I had a scholarship, or I could never have managed it. My people were poor." He watched the river, his eyes sad and quiet. "She got tired of staying in the little house all alone. She liked to party. She thought I was a real stick-in-the-mud because I didn't drink or smoke." He laughed hollowly. "I guess she understood the drinking part because my father was a drunkard. Everybody on the rez knew about him."

She swallowed. "They say that alcoholism is a problem in some Native American cultures…"

"My father was white," he said, and his voice was cold as ice. "He sold seed and fertilizer for a living. He met my mother at a feed store when he was restocking there. He flattered her, took her places, bought her flowers. She was crazy about him. They got married and he moved onto the rez to live with her. She didn't know he was an alcoholic until she was pregnant with me. He started beating her then, when he lost his temper." His eyes closed. "When I was six, and he was beating my mother, I tried to block him with a kitchen chair. He picked it up and laid it across my head. When I came to, she was lying on the floor, still and quiet, and he was gone. I ran for help. It was too late."

She held her breath, listening. He'd told her some of this before, but not in such detail. She could only imagine the terror he'd felt.

"He went to prison and I went to live with my mother's uncles, aunts and cousins in a small community on the rez. One of my uncles was a reservation cop. He formally adopted me in a tribal ceremony, so I call him Dad, even though he isn't really. He's great with livestock. He and my other relatives were good to me, but they were poor and we didn't have much. I wanted more. I knew the only way to get out was to get an education. So I studied like crazy. I worked at anything I could get paid for, on ranches, in stores, on the land, and I saved every penny. When I graduated from high school, I was second in my class.

I got scholarships and commuted back and forth. I graduated with honors and went on to grad school. But then, suddenly, there was Jessie. I couldn't really afford to get married, but I was conventional in those days. My people were religious." He let go of Carlie's hand and folded his arms across his broad chest. His eyes had a lost, faraway look. "Things were good the first two years. But we were drifting apart. I still had a long way to go to a profession and I was away a good deal of the time. There was a man on the rez who wanted her. He bought her stuff, took her to dances, while I was at school or working after classes to help pay for the tuition. I came home one weekend, just after finals, and she was gone. She'd moved in with him."

He drew in a breath. "I tried to get her to come home, but she said she loved him and she was carrying his child. She wasn't coming back. I was sick at heart, but I couldn't force her to leave him. I went back to school and gave up the house. No reason to keep renting it just for weekends, anyway.

"I was getting ready for the graduation exercises when one of my cousins came to see me at school. Another relative back home told him that she'd lied. The child she was carrying was mine. The man she was living with couldn't have children. And worse, he was beating her. She'd just come back from the hospital. He'd beaten her so badly that she had a concussion."

His face hardened. "So I went home. I had a beat-up old car parked in Rapid City that would hardly make the trips back and forth from my house to the airport, and there were heavy floods, but I made it home. I went to see her. I told her that I knew about the child and that if she wouldn't come back to me, I'd have her boyfriend put in jail for beating her. She looked ancient," he said, his face twisting. "What she'd endured was written all over her. But she loved him, she told me. She was very sorry, but she loved him. I could see the child when it came, but she wasn't leaving him, even if I refused to give her a divorce."

He swallowed. "He drove up. We exchanged words. He said no way was she leaving him. He grabbed her by the hand and dragged her out to his car. I tried to stop him, but he was a big guy and I had no combat skills at the time. He wiped the floor with me. He threw her into his car and took off. I picked myself up, got in my own car and chased after him."

He shook his head. "I don't know what I thought I could do. She wanted to stay with him and he wasn't going to give her up. But I knew if she stayed he'd kill her one day, just as my father had killed my mother. And my child would die with her.

"He speeded up and so did I. His car was all over the road." His eyes closed. "If I'd had any sense, I'd have stopped, right then, but I didn't. He went onto a bridge that was unsafe. There was even a sign, but he didn't pay it any attention." He looked away, hesitated. "The bridge collapsed. They fell down in the car, into the river below. It was deep and in full flood." His eyes closed. He shuddered. "They found the bodies almost two days later. If they'd been found sooner, the child might have lived." He bit his lower lip. "It was a boy…"

"I'm so sorry," she whispered. Her eyes were wet. "So sorry."

He turned, pulled her to him and held her. Just held her. Rocked her. "I've never spoken of it, except once. Dalton Kirk's wife, in Wyoming, sat at a table with me and told me all about it, and she'd never met me or heard anything about me. It was a shock."

"I heard about her." She savored the feel of his jacket. It was leather, but soft and warm from his body, fringed and beaded. She'd never seen anything so beautiful. She closed her eyes. He'd frightened her earlier. Now she began to understand him, just a little.

He smoothed over her dark, wavy hair. "I would never have hit you," he whispered at her ear. "I know too much about brutality and its result."

"You move so quickly," she faltered.

"And for all the wrong reasons sometimes." He sighed. "Dalton Kirk's wife told me that my wife's boyfriend was drinking at the time. I didn't really notice, but if you drink something like vodka, others may not be able to smell it on your breath. She said that was why he went off the bridge, not because of me. I checked the police report. She was right. But it didn't help much. Nothing does. I still feel like a murderer."

"It isn't fair, to blame yourself for something like that." She drew back and looked up at him. "You aren't a person of faith."

"No," he said stiffly. "I don't believe in anything anymore."

"I believe that things happen the way they're meant to," she said softly. "That sometimes God uses people to say things or do things that hurt us, so that we learn lessons from it. My dad says that we should always remember that events in our lives have a purpose. It's all lessons. We learn from adversity."

He searched her green eyes quietly. "You're such an innocent, Carlie," he said gently, and her heart leaped because it was the first time he'd ever called her by name. "You know nothing about the world, about life."

"And you know everything," she murmured with a flash of laughter.

"I do." He traced a line down her cheek. "We're total opposites."

"What happened," she asked. "After?"

He looked over her head. "I went to my own graduation, alone, and enlisted in the military the same week. I learned how to fight, how to kill. I took the most dangerous assignments I could find. For a long time, I avoided women like the plague. Then it became second nature to take what was offered and walk away." That wasn't quite true, but he'd shared enough secrets for one day. "I never got serious about anyone again. I met Cy Parks overseas. He and his group were doing a stint as private contractors for the military, teaching tactics to locals. I fell in with them and came back here to work for Cy and, occasionally, for Eb Scott. It's an interesting life. Dangerous. Unpredictable."

"Sort of like you," Carlie mused.

He looked down into her eyes. "Sort of like me," he agreed.

She drew in a breath. It was much easier to do that now.

"I am truly sorry for what happened this morning," he said, searching her eyes. "I had no right to frighten you."

"You're scary when you lose your temper," she replied.

"Sheltered little violet, under a stair," he said softly.

"Not so much," she replied. "It just seems that way." Her own eyes were sad and quiet.

"You know my secrets. Tell me yours."

She swallowed. "When I was thirteen, my mother was diagnosed with cancer. She was in and out of hospitals for a year. During one of those times, her mother showed up." Her face hardened. "My grandmother was a pig, and that's putting it mildly. She had a reputation locally for sleeping with anything in pants. She had a boyfriend with her, a man who used drugs and supplied them to her. I had the misfortune to come home while they were ransacking my mother's bedroom, looking for things they could sell. I'd hidden Mama's expensive pearls that Daddy brought her from Japan, just in case, but they were trashing the house. I tried to stop them."

She shivered.

He pulled her closer. "Keep talking," he said over her head.

Her small hand clenched on his jacket. "Her boyfriend picked up a beer bottle and started hitting me with it." She shivered again. "He kept on and on and on until I was on the floor. I fought until I was so numb that I just gave up." She laughed. "You think you can fight back, that you can save yourself in a desperate situation. But that's not how it works. You feel such…despair, such hopelessness. After a while, it seems more sensible to just lie down and die…"

"Go on."

"Our next-door neighbor heard me scream and called the police. They got there just in time to keep him from killing me. As it was, I had a concussion and broken ribs. I spent several days in the hospital. They took my grandmother and her boyfriend to jail. She testified against him and got off, but our police chief—one of the ones before Cash Grier—had a nice talk with her and she left town very quickly. She didn't even apologize or come to see me. I heard later that she died from a drug overdose. He was killed in a prison riot just recently." She shook her head. "I've been terrified of violent behavior ever since."

"I can see why."

"One of our patrolmen brought a man in handcuffs in the office once to ask the chief a question. The man grabbed a nightstick off the counter and came at me with it. I fainted." She sighed. "The chief turned that man upside down, they said, and shook him like a rat until he dropped the nightstick. Then he threw him into the patrol car and told the officer to get him to the county detention center right then. He took me to the emergency room himself. I had to tell him why I fainted." She shrugged. "He isn't what he seems, is he?" she asked, looking up. "I mean, criminals are terrified of him. Even some local men say he's dangerous. But he was like a big brother with me. He still is."

"I respect him more than any other man I know, with the possible exception of Cy Parks."

"Mr. Parks is pretty scary, too," she added.

He smiled. "Not when you get to know him. He's had a hard life. Really hard."

"I know a little about him. It's a sad story. But he and his wife seem to be very happy."

"They are."

She searched his serious eyes. "I didn't say anything to your...date," she said quietly. "She was making fun of my dress and my old shoes." She lowered her eyes. "I didn't have a comeback. It was a bargain dress, and my shoes are really old. I didn't wear a coat because this is the only one I have—" she fingered the frayed collar "—and I didn't want to embarrass Robin by showing up in it."

He was very still. "She said that you insulted her."

"Tippy Grier did," she replied. She tried not to smile at the memory. "She was eloquent. She said that my dress looked nice on me and it didn't matter where it came from."

He let out a long breath. "Damn."

"It's all right. You didn't know."

His hand smoothed over her dark hair as he stared down at the river below. For a minute, there was only the sound of the water running heavily over the rocks. "She didn't mention Tippy."

"I just stood there," she said. "I guess she was mad that I danced with you."

His hand caught her hair at her nape and turned her face up to his. Black eyes captured hers and held them. "She was mad that I wanted you," he said curtly.

"Wa...wanted me?" She hesitated.

He let out a rough breath. "God in heaven, can't you even tell when a man wants you?" he burst out.

"Well, I don't know a lot about men," she stammered.

His hand slid down her back and plastered her hips to his. His smile was smug and worldly as he let her feel the sudden hardness of his body. "Now you do."

She flushed and pulled away from him. "Stop that."

He actually laughed. "My God," he said heavily. "I'm dying and you're running for cover." He shook his head. "Just my luck."

She swallowed. It was embarrassing. She tried to draw away completely but he held her, gently but firmly.

"Doesn't your friend Robin ever touch you?" he asked sarcastically. "Or are you having a cerebral relationship with him?"

She wasn't about to admit the truth to him. Robin felt like protection right now, and she needed some.

"He reads poetry to me," she choked. Actually, he wrote poetry about Lucy and read it to Carlie, but that was beside the point.

"Does he now?" He brushed his nose against hers and began to quote. "When I am dead, and above me bright April shakes out her rain-drenched hair, though you should lean above me broken-hearted, I shall not care. I shall have peace, as leafy trees are peaceful when rain bends down the bough; and I shall be more silent and cold-hearted than you are now," he whispered deeply, reciting lines from a poem called "I Shall Not Care," by Sara Teasdale. "It was written in 1919," he added. "Long before either of us was born."

Her heart jumped, stopped and ran away. His voice was like velvet, deep and sexy and overwhelmingly sensual. Her nails curled against the soft leather of his jacket.

"Yes, I read poetry," he whispered, his mouth hovering just above hers. "That was one of my favorites. I learned it by heart just before Jessie died."

Her mouth felt swollen. Her whole body felt swollen. "D...did you?" she asked in a voice that wasn't quite steady.

His lips brushed like a whisper over hers. "Are you sure you don't know what desire is, Carlie?" he whispered huskily.

She was almost moaning. His mouth teased hers, without coming to rest on it. His body was close, warm, powerful. She felt the heat of it all the way down. She couldn't get her breath, and this time it wasn't because of the asthma. She knew he could feel her heartbeat. She could hear it.

"Your father is going to kill me," he said roughly.

"For...what?"

"For this." And his mouth went down against hers, hard enough to bruise, hard enough to possess.

CHAPTER SEVEN

CARLIE WAS DYING. Her whole body was pressing toward Carson's, pleading for something she didn't quite understand. She shivered as his mouth pressed harder against hers, insistent, parting her lips so that he could possess them.

Her arms reached up, around his neck. He lifted her, riveted her body to his, as the kiss went on and on and on. She moaned under his mouth, shivering, wanting something more, something to end the torment, to ease the tension that seemed bent on pulling her young body apart.

"Carlie," he whispered roughly as his fingers tightened in her hair and he paused to catch his breath. "This is not going to end well," he rasped.

She looked up at him, breathless, wordless, shivering with needs she hadn't even known she could feel.

"Oh, what the hell," he muttered. "I'm damned already!"

He kissed her as if he'd never felt a woman's mouth under his own, as if he'd never felt desire, never known hunger. He kissed her with utter desperation. She was an innocent. He couldn't have her. He wasn't going to marry her, and he couldn't seduce her. It was one hell of a dead end. But he couldn't stop kissing her.

Her mouth was soft and warm and sweetly innocent, accepting his, submitting, but not really responding. It occurred to him somewhere in the middle of it that she didn't even know how to kiss.

He lifted his mouth and searched her wide, soft, dreamy eyes. "You don't even know how," he whispered huskily.

Her lips were as swollen as her body. "Know how to what?" she began dazedly.

The sound of a car horn intruded just as he started to bend his head to her again. She jumped. He caught his breath and moved back from her just as Cash Grier got out of his patrol car and started down to the river where they were standing, now apart from each other.

"Dum dum de dum dum de dum da da de dum," Carson hummed Gounod's "Funeral March of a Marionette" as Cash approached. He smiled wryly, through the piercing agony of his unsatisfied need.

Carlie chuckled.

"Your father was concerned," Cash told Carlie. "He asked me to look for you."

"I'm okay," Carlie said, trying to disguise the signs that she'd been violently kissed. She pushed back her disheveled hair. "He bought me lunch." She nodded at Carson.

"Did you have it tested for various poisons first?" Cash asked blandly.

She laughed again.

"I was apologizing," Carson said heavily. "I jumped on her for something she didn't even do."

"Which was?" Cash asked, and he wasn't smiling.

"Lanette said that Carlie insulted her and made her cry," he returned.

"That wasn't Carlie. That was my wife." Cash smiled coldly. "I understand that she was eloquent."

"Quite," Carlie confirmed.

"Your friend has a rap sheet," he told Carson. He smiled again. This time it was even colder.

Carson scowled. "A rap sheet?"

"It appears that she wasn't always a stewardess. In fact, I don't know how she got to be accepted in that type of job. Probably her lawyer helped her out more than once," he said.

"What was she arrested for?" Carson asked.

"Assault with a deadly weapon. A smart lawyer got her off by pleading temporary insanity, acting in a fit of jealousy." He pursed his lips, enjoying Carson's discomfiture. "She went after another woman with a knife. Accused her of trying to steal her boyfriend."

Carson didn't show it, but he felt uneasy. Lanette had made some threats about Carlie, and he hadn't taken them seriously.

Carlie's face fell at the realization that the blonde might be more dangerous than she'd realized already.

"I'd watch my back if I were you," Carson told Carlie somberly. "The rest of us will help. It seems you've got more trouble than we realized."

"There was another phone call the other night, too," she said, suddenly recalling the cryptic message. "It was a male voice. He said to tell Dad he was coming soon. It didn't make sense."

"A male voice?" Cash asked at once.

"Yes." She frowned. "Odd-sounding voice. If I ever heard it again, I think I'd remember it. Why is somebody after Dad?"

"I don't know," Cash said tersely.

"Rourke and I are trying to dig that out," Carson said abruptly. "We have contacts in, shall we say, unusual places."

"So do I," Cash reminded him. "But mine were a dead end."

"One of my cousins is a U.S. senator," Carson said, surprisingly. "He's using some of his own sources for me."

"A senator." Cash grinned. "Not bad."

"Well, not quite in the same class with having a vice president or a state attorney general for a relative," Carson retorted, smiling back.

Cash shrugged. "We all have our little secrets." He glanced at Carlie, who'd reddened when he said "secrets." His eyes narrowed. "You told him?"

She nodded.

He looked at Carson and the smile was gone. "I'll tell you once. Don't ever do that again."

"I can promise you that I never will."

Cash jerked his head in a nod.

Carson glanced at Carlie. "I tried to take him once, in a fight." He grimaced. "It wasn't pretty."

"I was a master trainer in Tae Kwon Do," Cash explained. "Black belt."

Carson rubbed one arm. "Very black."

Cash laughed.

"I was going to take her home, but we hadn't had lunch," Carson explained.

"Or dessert," Carlie mused.

Carson glanced at her with warm, hungry eyes. "Oh, yes, we had dessert."

She blushed further, and he laughed.

"Come on," Cash told them. "It isn't wise to be out in the woods alone with crazy people on the loose."

"Did somebody escape from jail?"

"Nothing like that," Cash said. "I was remembering Carlie's phone call and your girlfriend's rap sheet."

"Oh." Carson didn't say another word. He helped Carlie into the passenger seat of his car and made sure her seat belt was fastened before he closed the door.

Cash drew him over to the patrol car, and he was somber. "You need to do something about that temper."

"I had anger management classes," Carson said quietly. "They helped, for a while." He shook his head. "It's the past. I can't deal with it. I can't live with what I did. I'm at war with myself and the world."

Cash put a heavy hand on the younger man's shoulder. He knew about Carson's past. The two were close. "I'll tell you again that it was her time. Nothing could have stopped it. Somewhere inside, you know that. You just won't accept it. Until you do, you're a walking time bomb."

"I would never hurt her," he assured Cash, nodding toward the car. "I've never hit a woman."

"The threat of force is as bad as the actual thing," Cash replied. "She hasn't gotten over what happened to her, either. We carry the past around like extra luggage, and it gets heavy from time to time."

"You'd know," Carson said gently.

Cash nodded. "I've killed men. I have to live with it. It's not easy, even now."

"For me, either." He shoved his hands into his pockets. "I didn't realize Lanette had started the trouble. She was so upset that it really got to me. She's just someone to take around. Something pretty to show off." He shrugged. "Maybe a little more than that. But nothing permanent."

"Your past in that respect isn't going to win you points with certain people around here," Cash said.

"I'm just beginning to realize that. When I was in Wyoming, Dalton Kirk's wife told me that my past was going to have a terrible impact on my future, that it was going to stand between me and something I want desperately."

"It wouldn't matter so much if you didn't flaunt it, son," Cash replied.

Carson drew in a breath. "I don't know why I taunt her," he said, and they both knew he meant Carlie. "She's a kind, generous woman. Innocent and sweet."

"Something to keep in mind," Cash added. "You'd walk away and forget about it. She'd throw herself off a cliff. You know what I'm talking about."

Carson seemed to pale. "Nothing so drastic…"

"You don't know anything about people of faith, do you?" he asked. "I didn't, until I came here and had to face living my life with what I'd done hanging over me like a cloud. I came to faith kicking and screaming, but it gave me the first peace I've ever known. Until that happened, I didn't understand the mindset of people like Carlie." His face tautened. "I'm not joking. Her faith teaches her that people get married, then they become intimate, then children come along. It doesn't matter if you agree, if you disagree, if you think she's living in prehistoric times. That's how she thinks."

"It's radical," Carson began. "She's totally out of step with the times. Everybody does it—"

"She doesn't," Cash interrupted. "And everybody around here knows it. It's why she doesn't date. Her grandmother was the town joke. She had sex with a department store manager in a closet and they got caught. He was married with three kids. She thought it was hilarious when his wife left him. In fact, that's why she did it. She was angry at the woman for making a remark about her morals."

"Good grief," Carson exclaimed.

"She was caught with men in back rooms, in parked cars, even once in a long-haul truck in the front seat at a truck stop with people walking by." He shook his head. "It was before I came here, but I heard about it. Carlie's mother was a saint, an absolutely good woman, who had to live with her mother's reputation. Carlie's had to live it down, as well. It's why she won't play around."

"I didn't realize that people knew about it."

"We know everything," Cash said simply. "If you don't care about gossip, it doesn't affect you. But Carlie's always going to care. And if something happens to her, it will show like a neon sign. Everybody will know. She won't be able to hide it or live with it in a small community like this."

"I get your point." He grimaced. "Life is never easy. I don't want to make it even harder for her," he added, glancing toward Carlie, who was watching them curiously.

"No." Cash studied the younger man. "The world is full of women like your pretty blonde, and they work for scale. Don't try to class Carlie with them."

He smiled coldly. "Or you'll have more trouble than you can handle. You do not want to make an enemy of Reverend Blair."

"I do have some idea about her father's past," Carson confessed.

"No, you don't," Cash replied. "Just take my word that you don't ever want to see him lose his temper. And you work on controlling yours."

"I'm reformed." Carson took his hands out of his pockets. "I suppose we all have memories that torment us."

"Count on it. Just try not to make more bad ones for Carlie."

"I'll drive her home." He hesitated. "Is her father there?"

Cash nodded.

Carson sighed. "There are a few unmarked places on me," he commented wryly. "I guess I can handle some more. Time to face the music."

Cash laughed. "Well, you've got guts, I'll give you that."

"Not going to arrest me?" he added.

"Not this time," Cash said.

"Just as well. You can't prove I'm me."

"Why in the hell don't you carry identification?" Cash asked. "Don't you realize that if you were ever injured, nobody would know anything about you, right down to your weight or your medical history?"

Carson smiled wryly. "When I was doing wet work overseas, it would have been fatal to carry any. I just got into the habit of leaving it behind."

"I know, but you're not in the same line of work now," Cash said.

"Certain of that, are you?" he asked with a vague smile.

"Yes."

Carson made a face. "All right," he said after a minute. "I'll think about it."

"Good man."

Carson went around the car and got in under the steering wheel. Cash drove off as Carson was starting up the car.

"Look in the glove compartment and hand me my wallet, will you?" he asked Carlie.

She rummaged around through the papers and produced it. "Do you have a last name?" she wondered aloud.

"Look at the license."

Curious, she opened the wallet. His driver's license read "Carson Allen Farwalker."

She handed it to him. He shoved it into his jacket while they were at a stoplight.

"No comment?" he asked.

"I'd be embarrassed," she replied softly.

He laughed. "On the morning I was born, a man came into our small rural community, walking. It was driving snow, almost a blizzard. He said he'd come from Rapid City, all the way on foot in his mukluks and heavy coat, hitching rides, to see a sick friend who lived near us. It was a far walk. So my mother named me Far Walker." He glanced at her. "Our names don't translate well into English sometimes, but this one did." His face tautened. "I refused to take my father's name, even as a child. So I was known on the rez as Far Walker. When I got my first driver's license, that's what I put on it, Anglicized into one word. It's my legal name now."

"It suits you," she said. "You walk like an out-doorsman."

He smiled.

"I read about how native people get their names. We tend to distort them. Like Crazy Horse. That wasn't his Lakota name, but it was what he was called by Wasichu—by white people," she said, and then flushed. She hadn't meant to give away her interest in his culture.

"Well," he said and chuckled. "Hannibal and Crazy Horse. You have wide interests. Do you know his Lakota name?" he added.

"Yes. It was Tashunka Witko." She laughed. "Although I've seen that spelled about four different ways."

"And do you know what it really means, in my tongue?" he asked.

She grinned. "'His horse is crazy,'" she replied. "I read somewhere that the day he was born, a man on a restless horse rode by and his people named him Crazy Horse."

"Close enough." He smiled gently as he met her eyes. "You're an eternal student, aren't you?"

"Oh, yes. I might have gone to college, but I didn't make high grades and we were always poor. I take free classes on the internet, though, sometimes. When I'm not grinding Horde into the ground," she added without looking at him.

"Runed that sword, did you? We'll find out how well it works on the next battleground we fight."

"I can't wait," she said smugly. "I've been practicing." She glanced at him. "What's a mukluk?"

"Heavy boots that come up to the knee, made of fur. I have some at home. I bought them in Alaska. They're made with beaver fur, with wolf fur trim and beadwork."

"Your jacket is beautiful," she remarked, glancing at it. "I've never even seen one that looks like that before."

"You never will. A cousin made it for me." He smiled. "He makes these from scratch, right down to the elk he hunts for them. He eats the meat and cures the hides. Not the wolves, however. It's illegal to kill them in the States, so he buys the fur from traders in Canada."

"I saw this movie with Steven Seagal, about Alaska. He was on a talk show wearing a jacket a lot like yours. He said the native people he worked with on the movie made it for him."

"Not a bad martial artist. I like Chuck Norris best, however, for that spinning heel kick. The chief does one just like it. Ask him sometime how he learned it," he teased.

"I already know," she laughed. "He says it's his claim to fame locally."

"Feeling better?"

She nodded. "I never dreamed it was asthma," she said heavily. She frowned and glanced at him. "But you knew right away," she said. "You even knew what to give me…"

"I was a field medic in the army," he said easily. "Emergencies were my specialty."

"You must have been very good at it," she said.

"I did what the job called for."

He pulled up in front of her house. Reverend Blair was waiting on the porch, wearing a leather bomber jacket and a black scowl.

He came down the steps and opened Carlie's door. He hugged her close. "You okay?" he asked tersely.

"I'm fine. Honest. I just overreacted."

He didn't reply. He was glaring at Carson, who came around the car to join them.

"It was my fault," Carson said bluntly. "I accused her of something she didn't do and I was overly aggressive."

The reverend seemed to relax, just a little. "You take it on the chin, don't you?" he asked half-admiringly.

"Always." He sighed. "If you want to hit me, I'll just stand here. I deserve it."

The reverend cocked his head. His blue eyes were glittery and dangerous, hinting at the man he might once have been.

"He treated me in the office, took me to the emergency room, then the pharmacy and bought me lunch after," Carlie said.

The reverend lifted an eyebrow and glanced at Carson. "Treated her?"

"I was a field medic in the army," Carson replied. "I recognized the symptoms. But if you're thinking I acted without a doctor's orders, you're wrong. I had her doctor on the phone before I opened my medical kit."

The reverend relaxed even more. "Okay."

"I was more aggressive than I meant to be, but I

would never have raised a hand to her," he added. "Violence is very rarely the answer to any problem."

"Rarely?"

Carson shrugged. "Well, there was this guy over in South America, in Carrera. Rourke and I sort of fed him to a crocodile."

The reverend glowered at him. "You're not helping your case."

"The guy cut up a young woman with his knife and left her scarred for life," Carson added. His black eyes glittered. "He bragged about it."

"I see."

"It was an act of mercy, anyway," Carson added doggedly. "The crocodile was plainly starving."

Reverend Blair couldn't suppress a laugh, although he tried. "I begin to see why you get along so well with Grier."

"Why, does he feed people to reptiles, too?"

"He's done things most men never dream of," the reverend said solemnly. "Lived when he should have died. He took lives, but he saved them, as well. A hard man with a hard past." The man's pale blue eyes pinned Carson's. "Like you."

Carson scowled. "How do you know anything about me?"

"You might be surprised," was the bland reply. He shook a finger at Carson. "You stop upsetting my daughter."

"Yes, sir," he said on a sigh.

"I'd invite you to supper but she might have some poisonous mushrooms concealed in the cupboard."

"I won't poison him," Carlie promised. She smiled.

"You can come to supper if you like. I'll make beef Stroganoff."

Carson looked torn, as if he really wanted to do it. "Sorry," he said. "I promised to take Lanette out to eat. I need to talk to her."

"That's okay," Carlie said, hiding the pain it caused her to hear that. "Rain check."

"Count on it," he said softly, and his eyes said more than his lips did. "You okay?"

She nodded. "I'll be fine."

"I'm really sorry," he said again.

"Stop apologizing, will you? You'll hurt your image," she said, grinning.

"I'll see you."

She nodded. He nodded to the reverend, got in the car and left.

"I HAVE TO see an allergist," Carlie said miserably. "Asthma, can you believe it? I couldn't get my breath, I felt like I was suffocating. Carson knew what it was, and what to do for it. He was amazing."

"He needs to work on his self-control," her father said tersely, sipping coffee while she dished up pound cake for dessert.

For just an instant she thought of Carson out of control at the river, hungry for her, and she flushed. Then she realized that he was talking about another sort of self-control.

The reverend wasn't slow. He had a good idea why she was blushing.

"Carlie," he said gently, "he goes through women like hungry people go through food."

"I know that, Dad."

"He isn't a person of faith. He works in a profession that thrives on the lack of it, in fact, and he's in almost constant danger." He hesitated. "What I'm trying to say is that he isn't going to settle down in a small town and become a family man."

"I know that, too," she replied. She put his cake down in front of him on the table and refilled his coffee cup.

"Knowing and walking away are two different things," he said curtly. "Your mother was like you, sweet and innocent, out of touch with the real world. I hurt her very badly because we married for the wrong reasons. I wasn't ready. Before I knew it, I was a father." He looked down at the uneaten cake. "I felt trapped, hog-tied, and I resented it. I made her pay for it." His lips made a grim line. "I stayed away, out of that resentment. She didn't deserve the life I gave her."

She was shocked to hear him say such things. She knew that they'd had to get married. She'd heard him say it. But even so, she'd thought her parents married for love, that her father was away because he was making a living for them.

He didn't seem to notice Carlie's surprise. He wasn't looking at her. "I didn't know she was sick. One of my friends had a cousin here, who told him, and he told me that she was in the hospital. I got back just after her mother and her drug-crazed boyfriend did a number on you." His teeth ground together. "That was when I realized what a mess I'd made of all our lives. I walked away from the old life that same day and never looked back. I only wish I'd been where

I was supposed to be so that you'd have been spared what happened to you."

"You're the one who's always saying that things happen to test us," she reminded him.

"I guess I am. But for someone who'd never hurt anybody in her life, you paid a high price," he added.

"Mama said that if she'd been a different sort of person, you would have been happy with her," she recalled. "She said her way of thinking ruined your life." She frowned. "I didn't understand what that meant at the time. But I think I'm beginning to." She did, because Carson was the same sort of person her father must have been.

"No. I ruined hers," he said. "I knew I couldn't settle down. I let my heart rule my head." He smiled sadly. "You see, pumpkin, despite how it must sound, I really loved your mother. Loved her desperately. But I loved my way of life, too, loved being on my own, working in a profession that gave me so much freedom. I was greedy and tried to have it all. In the process, I lost your mother. I will never get over what happened to her because of me. If I'd been here, taking care of her…"

"She would still have died," Carlie finished for him. "It was an aggressive cancer. They tried chemo and radiation, but it only made her sicker. Nothing you could have done would have stopped that, or changed a thing."

He studied her soft eyes. "You always make excuses for me." He shook his head. "Now you're making them for the wild man from South Dakota."

"He's wild for a reason," she said quietly.

"And you're not sharing it, right?"

"I'm not," she agreed. "It's his business."

"Nice to know you can keep a secret."

"For all the good it does me. You won't share any of yours," she pointed out.

"Why give you nightmares over a past I can't change?" he asked philosophically. He glanced at his watch and grimaced. "I'm late for a prayer meeting. You'll be okay here, right? Got the inhaler Lou prescribed?"

She pulled it out of her pocket and showed it to him.

"Okay." He shook his head. "I should have recognized the symptoms. My father had it."

"Your father? I never met him."

"He was dead by the time I married your mother," he said. He smiled. "You'd have liked him. He was a career officer in the navy, a chief petty officer."

"Wow."

"I've got photographs of him somewhere. I'll have to look them up."

"What was your mother like?"

"Fire," he chuckled. "She left trails of fire behind her when she lost her temper. She had red hair and an attitude. Tippy Grier reminds me of her, except that my mother wasn't really beautiful. She was a clerk in a hotel until she retired. She died of a stroke." He shook his head. "Dad was never the same after. He only outlived her by about two years."

"I'm sorry."

"Me, too."

"Mama said my grandfather was a kind man. He died when she was very small. He worked for the

sheriff's department. His wife was my crazy grandmother who couldn't control herself."

"I remember Mary speaking of him." He cocked
his head. "Your family goes back generations in this
community. I envy you that continuity. My folks
moved a lot, since Dad was in the service. I've lived
everywhere."

"And I've never been anywhere," she mused. "Except to San Antonio."

"Next time you go there, I'm driving," he said
flatly.

She made a face at him.

"I'll be home soon."

"Please be careful. Check your car before you start
it."

"Cash and Carson told me about the phone call,"
he replied. "Apparently I'm the target."

"I don't know why," she said. "I was the one who
could identify the man who was killed in Wyoming.
You never saw him."

"Pumpkin, you're not the only one with enemies,"
he said softly.

"Would this be connected with that past you won't
tell me about?"

"Dead right." He bent and kissed her forehead.
"Keep the door locked."

"I will. Drive safely."

He chuckled as he went out the door.

Carlie cleaned up the kitchen, played her video
game with Robin for an hour and went to bed. Her
dreams were vivid and vaguely embarrassing. And
of Carson.

CHAPTER EIGHT

ROURKE WAS SITTING with a worried politician in one of the best restaurants in San Antonio. Unknown to the man, Rourke was working with the feds. Rourke had managed to wiggle himself into the man's employ.

This particular politician, Matthew Helm, had been named the acting U.S. senator, and was hoping to be elected to a full term at the special election in a few months. Rourke was equally determined to find a way to connect him with the murder of a local assistant district attorney. All the evidence had been destroyed. But there were other ways to prove collusion.

Rourke had been in touch with Lieutenant Rick Marquez of the San Antonio Police Department and was keeping him informed through Cash Grier. This politician had also been responsible for the attempt on Dalton Kirk's life, and the one on Carlie Blair's father—or Carlie herself—the intended victim had never been determined—in Jacobsville.

His murdering henchman, Richard Martin, had been killed in Wyoming, but the man's evil deeds persisted. Word was that before he'd died, he'd hired someone to kill Carlie. Nobody knew who had the contract.

Rourke was hoping against hope that this man might provide answers to many questions. But Helm was secretive. So far he hadn't said one incriminating word. Rourke would have known. He was wearing a wire, courtesy of Rick Marquez.

"There are too many loose ends," Matthew Helm said after a minute. He glanced at his other enforcer, Fred Baldwin, and glared at him. "You take care of that problem up in Wyoming?"

"Oh, yes, sir," the big, brawny man assured him. "You can stop worrying."

"I always worry." Helm then glared at Rourke. "What have you found out about my competition for the job?"

"Both men are clean as a whistle," Rourke replied easily. "No past issues we can use against them."

Helm smiled secretly. "So far," he murmured.

"You thinking of planting some?" Rourke asked conversationally.

Helm just stared at him. "What the hell does that mean?"

"Just a comment."

"Well, keep your comments to yourself," Helm said angrily. "I don't fix elections, in case you wondered."

"Sorry. I'm new here," Rourke apologized.

"Too new," Helm said suspiciously. "I can't dig out any information on you. Any at all."

"I'm from South Africa, what do you expect?" he added.

"Well, that last name you gave, Stanton," Helm began, "is a dead end."

"I like to keep my past in the past," Rourke returned. "I'm a wanted man in some places."

"Is that it?" Helm studied him for a long moment.

"Then maybe you're not as suspicious as you seem, huh?" He snickered. "Just don't expect instant trust. I don't trust anybody."

"That's a good way to be," Rourke agreed.

Helm drew in a long breath. "Well, we need to get back to the office and work up some more ads and a few handouts for the campaign office. Not much time to bring this all together."

"Okay, Boss," Rourke said. "I'll see you there." He got up, nodded to both men, paid for his coffee and pie, and left.

Helm studied his other enforcer. "I don't trust him," he told the man. "You keep a close eye on him, hire extra men if you have to. See where he goes, who he associates with. I don't want any complications."

"Yes, Boss."

"And start checking out our sources. We'll need some more drugs planted. I can't afford competition for the job," he added. His face firmed. "You don't share that information with Rourke, got it? You don't tell him anything unless you clear it with me."

"I got it, Boss."

"You destroyed the watch, right?"

The other man nodded vigorously. "Oh, yeah, Boss, I smashed it into bits and tossed it into a trash bin."

"Good. Good."

The other man was hoping his uneasiness didn't show. He couldn't destroy the watch, he just couldn't. It was the most beautiful timepiece he'd ever seen, and it played that song he liked.

Fred Baldwin had envied Richard Martin, wearing that watch that cost as much as a sports car. He'd tried to borrow it once, but Martin had looked at him like he was a worm.

Well, Martin was dead now, and Baldwin had the watch. It was warm against his fingers, warm in his pocket where he kept it. He'd set the alarm so it wouldn't go off accidentally. Nobody was crazy enough to throw away a watch that cost so much money! Who knew, one day he might be desperate enough to pawn it. A man had to live, after all, and what Mr. Helm paid him was barely enough to afford his keep. His criminal record made him vulnerable. He couldn't get another job and Mr. Helm warned him that if he even tried to leave, he'd make sure Fred never worked again. It wasn't a threat. It was a promise. Fred knew better than to try to quit, although he hated the job.

Of course, that watch had a history, and Fred knew it. He might be desperate enough one day to talk to somebody in law enforcement about it. The watch could tie Mr. Helm to a murder. So, no, Fred wasn't about to throw it away. That didn't mean he didn't have to keep it hidden, of course. And he did.

ROURKE STOPPED BY Carlie's house that evening to talk to Reverend Blair. He was amused that Helm's men had tried to follow him. He'd had Carson take his car to San Antonio and park it at a bar. The trackers were sitting out in the parking lot in the freezing cold, waiting for Rourke to come out. He laughed. It was going to be a long night for them.

"Well, you look happy," Carlie remarked when she let him in.

"I've discovered that misdirection is one of my

greater talents," he mused, grinning. "Got any more of that wonderful cornbread?"

She shook her head. "But I just took a nice enchilada casserole out of the oven, and I have sour cream and tortilla chips to top it with," she said.

"Be still my heart," Rourke enthused. "Listen, are you sure you wouldn't like to marry me tomorrow?"

"Sorry," she said, "I'm having my truck waxed."

"Ah, well," he sighed in mock sorrow.

"Stop trying to marry my daughter," Jake Blair muttered, his ice-blue eyes penetrating, as Rourke joined him at the kitchen table. "You are definitely not son-in-law material."

"Spoilsport," Rourke told him. "It's hard to find a nice woman who can also cook and play video games."

"You don't play video games," Jake pointed out.

"A lot you know! The police chief is teaching me."

"Cash Grier?" Carlie exclaimed. "My boss doesn't play."

"Apparently that's why he thinks it's a good idea if he does the teaching. His young brother-in-law has forced him into it," he laughed, "because he can't get any friends to play with him. Cash is always up for anything new and exciting."

Jake shook his head. "I just don't get it. Running around a cartoon world on dragons and fighting people with two-handed swords. It's...medieval."

"Teaches combat skills, strategy, social interaction and how to deal with trolls," Carlie retorted, pouring coffee for all of them.

"Trolls?" Rourke asked. "Those great Norwegian things...?"

"Internet trolls," she clarified with a glower. "People who start fights and stand back and watch. They're really a pain sometimes, especially if somebody new to the game makes the mistake of asking for help on trade chat." She started laughing.

"What's so funny?" her father asked.

"Well, this guy wanted a mage port—that's a portal they can make to the major cities. He didn't know what class could do ports, so he asked if anybody could send him to the capital. This warlock comes on and offers to port him for fifty gold." She was laughing heartily. "Warlocks can't port, you see. They can summon, but that's a whole other thing." She shook her head. "I've spent months wondering how that came out."

"Probably about like the death knight your boss told me about, who offered to heal for a dungeon group," Rourke replied, tongue-in-cheek.

Carlie looked shocked. "DKs can't heal!"

"I'm sure the dungeon group knows that now," he quipped, and he was rakishly handsome when he smiled.

"I guess I'm missing a lot," Jake Blair said.

"You should come and play with us," Carlie said.

He shook his head. "I'm too old to play, pumpkin."

"You're kidding, right? One of the best raid leaders on our server is seventy-three years old."

His eyebrows arched. "Say what?"

"Not only that, there's a whole guild that plays from a nursing home."

"I met them," Rourke said. "Cash and I were in a dungeon with several of them. Along with a ten-year-old Paladin who kicked butt, and a sixty-eight-year-old grandmother who was almost able to kill the big boss single-handed."

"I suppose my whole concept of gaming is wrong," Jake laughed. "I had no idea so many age groups played together."

"That's what makes it so much fun," Carlie replied. "You meet people from all over the world in-game, and you learn that even total strangers can work together with a little patience."

"Maybe I'll get online one of these days and try it," Jake conceded.

"That would be great, Dad!" Carlie exclaimed. "You can be in our guild. Robin and I have one of our own," she explained. "We'll gear you and teach you."

"Maybe in the summer, when things are a little less hectic," Jake suggested.

"Oh. The building committee again," Carlie recalled.

"One group wants brick. The other wants wood. We have a carpenter in our congregation who wants the contract and doesn't understand that it has to be bid. The choir wants a loft, but the organist doesn't like heights. Some people don't want carpet, others think padded benches are a total sellout... Why are you laughing?" he asked, because Rourke was almost rolling on the floor.

"Church," Rourke choked. "It's where people get along and never argue...?"

"Not in my town," Reverend Blair said, sighing. He smiled. "We'll get it together. And we argue nicely." He frowned. "Except for Old Man Barlow. He uses some pretty colorful language."

"I only used one colorful word," Carlie remarked

as she served up the casserole, "and he—" she pointed at her father "—grounded me for a month and took away my library card."

He shrugged. "It was a very bad word." He glowered at her. "And Robin should never have taught it to you without explaining what it meant!"

"Robin got in trouble, too," she told Rourke. "But his parents took away his computer for two weeks." She shook her head. "I thought withdrawal was going to kill him."

"He uses drugs?" Rourke asked curiously.

"No, withdrawal from the video game we play together," she chuckled. She glanced at her father. "So I had to do battlegrounds in pugs for those two weeks. It was awful."

"What's a pug?" Reverend Blair asked.

"A pickup group," Rourke replied. "Cash taught me." He glared. "There was a tank in the last one that had a real attitude problem. Cash had him for lunch."

"Our police chief is awesome when he gets going," Carlie laughed. "We had one guy up for speeding, and when he came in to pay the ticket he was almost shaking. He just wanted to give me the fine and get out before he had to see the chief. He said he'd never speed in our town again!"

"What did Cash do?" Jake asked.

"I asked. He didn't really do anything. He just glared at the man while he wrote out the ticket."

"I know that glare." Rourke shook his head. "Having been on the receiving end of it, I can tell you truly that I'd rather he hit me."

"No, you wouldn't," Carlie mused. "I wasn't work-

ing for him then, but I heard about it. He and Judd
Dunn were briefly interested in the same woman,
Christabel, who eventually married Judd. But it came
to blows in the chief's office at lunch one day. They
said it was such a close match that both men came
out with matching bruises and cuts, and nobody declared victory. You see, the chief taught Judd Dunn
to fight Tae Kwon Do–style."

"Wasn't he going to teach you and Michelle Godfrey how to do that?" Jake asked suddenly.

"He was, but it was sort of embarrassing, if you
recall, Dad," she replied. She glanced at Rourke, who
was watching her curiously. "I tripped over my own
feet, slid under another student, knocked him into
another student on the mat, and they had to go to
the emergency room for pulled tendons." She grimaced. "I was too ashamed to try it again, and Michelle wouldn't go without me. The chief wanted us
to try again, but I'm just too clumsy for martial arts."

Rourke's eyes twinkled. "I can sympathize. On
my first foray into martial arts, I put my instructor
through a window."

"What?" she exclaimed.

"We were standing near it. He threw a kick, I
caught his foot and flipped him. The momentum took
him right into a backward summersault, right out the
window. Fortunately for him it was a low one, raised,
and very close to the ground."

"Well!" she laughed.

"I've improved since then." He shared an amused
look with Jake.

"Shall we say grace?" Jake replied, bowing his head.

"YOU DIDN'T TELL me that it was the police chief's wife, not Carlie, who insulted you," Carson said as they shared coffee during intermission at the theater in San Antonio.

Lanette looked at him under her long lashes. "I was very upset," she remarked. "Perhaps I was confused. Honestly, that girl is so naïve. And she isn't even pretty! I don't understand why you were dancing with her in the first place!"

He studied her covertly. She was getting more possessive by the day, and she was full of questions about Carlie. It bothered him. He kept thinking of her rap sheet, too.

"Several of us are watching her," he said after a minute. "There was an attempt on her father's life, and she was injured. We think there may be another one."

"On a minister?" she exclaimed, laughing loudly. "Who'd want to kill a preacher?"

His black eyes narrowed. "I don't recall telling you that her father was a man of the cloth," he said.

Her face was blank for just an instant and then she smiled prettily. "I was asking about her at the dance. Someone told me who her father was."

"I see."

"She's just a backward little hick," she muttered irritably. "Let's talk about something else. Are we going to see the symphony Friday night? I bought a new dress, specially!"

He was thoughtful. He didn't like the way Lanette had started to assume that he was always available to take her out. She was beautiful to look at, to show off in public. The poor reservation kid in him enjoyed the envious looks he got from other men when he escorted his striking blond companion in the evenings. But she was shallow and mean-spirited. He forgave a lot because she eased the ache in him that Carlie provoked.

Funny thing, though. Although he enjoyed the physical aspects of their relationship, he couldn't quite manage to go all the way with his gorgeous blonde. It unsettled him, and irritated and insulted her, but expensive presents seemed to pacify her.

He didn't understand his reticence. Lanette was eager and accomplished, but her talents were wasted on him. Deep down, he knew why. It didn't help the situation. Carlie was never going to fall into bed with him. And if she did, her father would kill him and Cash Grier would help.

"I'll be very happy when you're finished with this dumb assignment and you don't have to be around that little hick," Lanette was saying. She brushed back her long, thick, blond hair.

"People in Jacobs County are very protective of her," was all he said.

"She's probably not even in trouble," she muttered. "I expect people are just overreacting because of that attack on her father. For goodness sake, maybe whoever's after her isn't even after her, maybe it's her father!" She glanced at him. "Isn't that what you said about that knife attack, that he was trying to kill her father and she tried to stop him?"

"That's what they said."

She shook her head. "Well, it was a really stupid job," she murmured. "Imagine a man going to the victim's house in the middle of the day, in broad daylight, and attacking a minister in his own house!"

Carson frowned as he listened. "I didn't know it was in broad daylight."

"Everybody knows," she said quickly. "They were even talking about it at that silly dance you took me to."

"Oh."

She glanced away, smiling to herself. "They also said that the man who tried to kill the preacher ended up dead himself."

"Yes, poisoned. A very nasty, slow poison. Something the late Mr. Martin was quite well-known for in intelligence circles."

"I hate poison," she said under her breath. "So unpredictable."

"Have you been poisoning people, then?" he mused.

She laughed. "No. I like to watch true crime shows on television. I know all about poisons and stuff." She moved very close to him. "Not to worry, handsome, I'd never want to hurt you!" she added, and lifted her arms toward his neck.

He raised an eyebrow and stepped back.

"Oh, you and your hang-ups," she muttered. "What's wrong with a hug in public?"

"It would take too long to tell you," he said, not offering the information that in his culture, such public displays were considered taboo by the elders.

"All right," she said with mock despair. "Are we going to the theater Friday?"

"Yes," he said. It would keep his mind off Carlie.

"Wonderful!" She smiled secretly to herself. "I'm

sure we'll have a lovely time." She paused. "That mad South African man you know, he isn't coming to the theater, is he?"

"Rourke?" He laughed to himself. "Not likely on a Friday night."

"Why not on a Friday?" she asked.

He almost bit his tongue. Rourke played poker with Cash Grier. He didn't dare let that slip, just in case Lanette knew anyone who had contact with Matthew Helm. "Rourke drinks on weekends," he lied.

"I see." She thought for a minute. "What about your friend the police chief?" she asked, laughing. "I'll bet he takes that prissy wife of his to the theater."

"Not on a Friday night," he chuckled. "The police chief and several other men get together at the chief's house and play poker after supper."

"Exciting game, poker. Especially the strip kind," she purred.

He sighed. "I don't gamble. Sorry."

"Your loss, sweetie," she said with pursed red lips. "Your loss."

FRIDAY NIGHT, REVEREND BLAIR had a call from a visitor to the community who was staying in a local motel outside town.

"I just want to die," the man wailed. Jake couldn't quite place the accent, but it definitely wasn't local. "I hate my life! They said you were a kind man who would try to help people. They gave me your number, here at this motel—" he named it "—so I said I'd call you. Before I did it, you know. Will God forgive me for killing myself? I got some rat poison…"

"Wait," Jake Blair said softly. "Just wait. I'll come to see you. We'll talk."

"You'd come all this way, just to talk to me?" The man sounded shocked.

"I know the motel you mentioned you were staying at," Jake said. "It's just a few minutes from here. I'll be on my way in a jiffy. What's your room number?"

The man told him. "Thank you. Thank you!" he sobbed. "I just don't want to live no more!" He hung up.

"Pumpkin, I have to go out," he informed his daughter as he shrugged into his bomber jacket. "I've been contacted by a suicidal man in a motel. I'm going to try and talk him down before he does something desperate."

She smiled. "That's my dad, saving the world."

He shrugged. "Trying to, anyway. You stay inside and keep the doors locked," he added. "And keep that cell phone close, you hear me?"

"I'll put it in my pocket, I swear."

"Good girl." He kissed her forehead. "Don't wait up. This may take a while."

"Good luck," she called after him.

He waved at her, left and closed the door behind him.

Carlie finished cleaning up the kitchen and went upstairs to play her game. On the kitchen table, forgotten, was the cell phone she'd promised to keep with her. The only other phone in the house was a fixed one, in her father's office...

"GOODNESS, COFFEE JUST goes right through me," Lanette whispered into Carson's ear. "Be right back."

He just nodded, aware of irritated glances from other theatergoers nearby. He wasn't really thrilled with the play. It was modern and witty, but not his sort of entertainment at all, despite the evident skill of the actors.

His mind went back to Carlie on the riverbank, standing so close that he could feel every soft line of her body, kissing him so hungrily that his mind spun like a top. Carlie, who was as innocent as a newborn, completely clueless about the hungers that drove men.

He wanted her until he couldn't sleep for wanting her. And he knew he could never have her. He wasn't going to settle down, as Cash Grier had, with a wife and child and a job in a small town. He liked adventure, excitement. He wasn't willing to give those up for some sort of middle-class dream life in a cottage or a condo, mowing the grass on weekends. The thought of it turned his stomach.

He brushed away a spec on his immaculate trousers and frowned. He didn't understand why Carlie appealed to his senses so strongly. She wasn't really pretty, although her mouth was soft and beautiful and tasted as sweet as honey. Her body was slender and she was small-breasted. But she had long, elegant legs and her waist was tiny. He could feel her small breasts swelling against his hard chest when he kissed her, feel the tips biting into his flesh even through layers of fabric.

He groaned silently. His adventures with women had always been with beautiful, practiced, elegant women. He'd never been with an innocent. And he wasn't about to break that record now, he assured himself firmly.

He'd been vulnerable with Carlie because he felt guilty about sending her to the hospital when he lost his temper. That was all. It was a physical reaction, prompted only by guilt. He was never going to forgive himself for frightening her like that. Her white face haunted him still. He'd only moved closer to make his point, it hadn't been a true aggression. But it must have seemed that way to a young girl who'd been beaten, and then later stabbed by an assassin.

But he hadn't hurt her at the dance, when they'd moved together like one person, when he'd felt the hunger so deeply that he could have laid her down on the dance floor right then. What the hell was he going to do? It was impossible. Impossible!

While he was brooding, Lanette returned. She slid her hand into his and just smiled at him, without saying a word. He glanced at her. She really was beautiful. He'd never seen a woman who was quite this exquisite. If it hadn't been for her attitude, and her other flaws, she might have seemed the perfect woman. That made it all the more inexplicable that he couldn't force himself to sleep with her; not even to relieve the ache Carlie gave him.

CARLIE WAS FIGHTING two Horde in the battleground. Sadly, neither of them was Carson. She flailed away with her two-handed sword, pulled out her minions, used every trick she could think of to vanquish them, but they killed her. She grimaced. She had the best gear honor points could buy, but there were these things called conquest points that only came from doing arenas. Carlie couldn't do arena. She was too slow and too clumsy.

So there were people far better geared than she was. Which was just an excuse, because the playing field was level in battlegrounds, regardless of how good your armor was.

The painful truth was that there were a lot of players who were much better at it than Carlie was. She comforted herself with the knowledge that there was always somebody better at the game, and eventually everybody got killed once or twice during a battle. She was just glad that she didn't have to do it in real life.

"Ah, well," she said, and sighed.

She resurrected at the battleground cemetery, got on her mount and rode back off to war. Before she got to either her home base or the enemy's, the end screen came up. The Alliance had lost to the Horde. But it had been an epic battle, the sort that you really didn't mind losing so much because it was fought by great players on both sides.

"Next time," she told the screen. "Next time, we'll own you, Hordies!"

She was about to queue for the battleground again when she heard a knock at the door downstairs.

She logged out of her character, although not out of the game, mildly irritated by the interruption, and went down the staircase. She wondered if maybe her father had forgotten to take his house key with him. He was so forgetful sometimes, it was funny. Twice now, he'd had to wake Carlie up when he came back from a committee meeting that lasted longer than expected, or when he returned from visiting and comforting congregation members at hospitals.

She peered through the safety window and

frowned. There was a big man in a suit outside. He looked uneasy.

"Is there something you want?" she asked through the door.

"Yeah," he said after a minute. "I need help."

"What sort of help?" she answered.

He paused for a minute. He looked through the small window at the suspicious young woman who was obviously not about to open that door to a man she didn't know.

He thought for a minute. He was slow when it came to improvisation. Maybe he could fool her if he was smart. Yeah. Smart. Who would she open the door for?

"I, uh, came to tell you about your dad," he called through the door. "There's been an accident. I was passing by and stopped. He asked me to come and get you and drive you to the hospital where they're taking him."

"Dad's been in a wreck?" she exclaimed. "Why didn't the police come?"

What did she mean? Did police notify people about wrecks here? He supposed they did. He'd done that once, long ago. He paused.

"Well, they were coming, but I told them your dad wanted me to bring you, and they said it was okay."

She still hesitated. Perhaps it was one of the new patrolmen, and her father had been impatient about getting word to her. A kind stranger might have been imposed upon to fetch Carlie.

"He's hurt pretty bad, Miss," he called again. "We should go."

She couldn't bear to think of her father injured. She

had to go to him. She grabbed her coat off the rack near the door. Her pocketbook was upstairs, but she couldn't think why she'd need it. Her father would have money in his wallet and a house key.

"Okay, I'm coming," she said, and opened the door.

He smiled. "I'll take you to him," he promised.

She closed and locked the door behind her. Too late, she remembered her cell phone lying on the kitchen table.

"Have you got a cell phone?" she asked abruptly.

"Yeah, I got one," he said, leading the way to his late model sedan. "Why?"

"In case we have to call somebody," she explained.

"You can call anybody you like, Miss," he said. "Just get right in."

She bent down to slide into the open passenger side when she felt a cloth pressed against her mouth and pressure behind it. She took a breath. The whole world went black.

THE BIG MAN cuffed her hands together behind her before he slid her onto the backseat. She was breathing sort of funny, so he didn't gag her. He hoped that would be okay with the boss. After all, where they were going, nobody was likely to hear her.

Before he got into the car, he dropped a piece of paper on the ground deliberately. Then he got in the car, started it and drove away.

CHAPTER NINE

REVEREND JAKE BLAIR knocked at the motel door, but there was no answer. He immediately thought the worst, that the man had actually attempted suicide before his arrival. He might be inside, fatally wounded.

He ran to the motel office, explained the situation, showed his ID and pleaded with the man to open the door.

The manager ran with him to the room, slid home the key and threw open the door.

"Is this some sort of joke?" the manager asked.

Jake shook his head. "He phoned me at home and begged me to come and speak with him. He said that someone locally had recommended that he call me and gave him the number. He said he was suicidal, that he was going to take poison." He turned to the man. "Did you rent this room tonight?"

"Yes. To some big guy with a Northern accent," he replied. "He didn't have any luggage, though, and he didn't look suicidal to me." He glowered. "He just left without paying the bill or handing back the key," he muttered.

"Isn't that the key?" Jake asked, nodding toward the bedside table.

It was. There was a fifty-dollar bill under it.

"Well," the manager chuckled drily. "A man with a sense of honor, at least. Sort of."

"Sort of." Jake shook his head. "I can't imagine why he'd fake something like this." Then he remembered. Carson had a date. Rourke was playing poker with Cash Grier. Jake was here. Carlie was alone. At home.

He bit off a bad word, chided himself for the slip and ran for his car. On the way he dialed Carlie's cell phone, but there was no answer. He was referred to her voice mail. He'd told her to keep that phone with her. She never remembered. He dialed the home phone. The answering machine picked up after four rings. Now, that was unusual. Carlie would hear it, even if she was playing, and she'd pick it up before the message finished playing.

He was very concerned. He wasn't certain that someone was after him because of his past, despite the threatening phone call Carlie had taken. The man with the knife went for Carlie deliberately, it had seemed to Jake. He groaned as he pictured it, recalled her pain and terror. She'd had so much misery in her short life, so much violence. He hated what she'd gone through. Some of it was his fault.

He burned rubber getting home. He ran up the porch steps, put his key in the lock and went in like a storming army. But the house was empty. Carlie's computer was still on. And, although she'd logged out temporarily, her character screen was still up and the game was still running. That meant she'd been interrupted while she was playing. He checked every room. In the kitchen he found her cell phone, lying on the table.

He backtracked out the front door and, with a flashlight in addition to the porch light, searched around. He noticed tire tracks that weren't his. He also noted a piece of paper. It was a rough drawing, a map of sorts. It was a clue that the police would want undisturbed. He had no idea what the map depicted. But he knew what to do at once. He pulled out his cell phone and called Cash Grier.

"I HAD TO call Hayes," Cash apologized when he was on the scene. "You don't live in the city limits."

"That's okay." Jake clapped him on the back. "You're forgiven."

"Don't worry. Hayes has an investigator who dines out on forensics. He even has membership in several professional societies that do nothing else except discuss new techniques. Zack's good at his job."

"Okay." Jake shoved his hands into his pockets. He felt as if it was the end of the world. "I should have realized it was a ruse. Why didn't I think?"

"We'll find her," Cash promised.

"I know that. It's what condition we'll find her in that concerns me," Jake said tautly.

"I don't think they'll harm her," Cash said. "They want something. Maybe it's you."

"They can have me, if they'll let my daughter go," he rasped.

"I phoned my brother," Cash added. "It's a kidnapping. That makes it a federal crime. He'll be over as soon as he gets dressed."

Cash's brother, Garon Grier, was the senior special agent at the Jacobsville FBI office. He was formerly with the FBI's Hostage Rescue Team, and one of the best people to call in on the case. But Jake was concerned that the police presence might cause the kidnapper to panic and kill Carlie in order to get away.

"Where's Rourke?" Jake asked. "Was he playing poker with you?"

"He was, but he had a call from the politician he's supposedly the enforcer for," came the reply. "It seems the other enforcer was indisposed and he needed Rourke to run an errand for him."

"Interesting timing," Jake said.

Cash knew that. He could only imagine how he'd feel if it was his little girl, his Tris, who was missing. He drew in a breath and patted Jake on the back. "Don't worry," he said again. "It's going to be all right."

"Yes," Jake said and managed a smile. "I know that."

JAKE BLAIR EXCUSED himself in the early hours of the morning by saying that he had to visit a sick member of his congregation at the hospital. He left his cell phone number with Cash and asked him to please call if there was any word from the kidnapper.

He went inside and put on jeans and a pair of high-topped moccasins with no soles and his bomber jacket, along with a concealed knife in a scabbard, a .45 magnum in a Velcro holster and a pair of handcuffs.

With his equipment carefully hidden under the roomy bomber jacket, he waved to local law enforcement and spun out of the yard in the Cobra.

Unknown to the others, he'd had time to process the crude drawing on that map. He didn't for a moment think it had been dropped accidentally. No, this was a setup. They wanted Jake to come after Carlie. Which meant that, in his opinion, Jake was the real target.

He assumed that someone in his past was out to get him. He didn't know why. But there were plenty of reasons. His former life had been one of violence. He'd never expected that he would ever revisit it. Until now. His old skills were still sharp. Nobody was hurting Carlie. And as the Good Book said, God helps those who help themselves.

Probably, he amended, God didn't mean with guns. But then, he rationalized, they hadn't had guns in Biblical days, either. He was winging it. He wouldn't kill anybody. Unless it came to a choice between that and watching Carlie die. He couldn't do that. He couldn't live with it.

He followed the highway to a dirt road leading off to a deserted area with just the beginnings of scrubland, with cactus and sand. He parked the car, got out, checked his weapon, stuck it back in the holster and belted it around his waist. He strapped the bottom of the holster to his thigh with the Velcro tabs. He pulled out his knife in its sheath from under the jacket and fixed it on the other side of the belt buckle. Then he started off, with uncanny stealth, down the road.

CARLIE REGAINED CONSCIOUSNESS slowly. Her mind felt as if it was encased in molasses. She couldn't imagine why she was so sluggish, or why it was so hard to breathe.

She tried to move and realized, quite suddenly, that it was because her hands were tied behind her. She was lying on her side on a makeshift pallet. A big, worried man was standing nearby, wearing a business suit and a big gun. He wasn't holding it on her. It was on his belt, inside his open jacket.

"You okay?" he asked. "You was breathing awful jerkylike."

"I'm okay." She tried to take small breaths. She was scared to death, but she was trying not to let it show. "What am I doing here?" She swallowed. "Are you going to kill me?"

"No!" he said, and looked shocked. "Look, I don't do women. Ever." He blinked. "Well, there was one, once, but she shot me first." He flushed a little.

He was the oddest sort of kidnapper she'd ever seen. He was as big as a house and he seemed oddly sympathetic for a man who meant her harm.

"Then why did you bring me here? You said my father was hurt...!" she remembered, almost hysterical.

"Not yet," he said. "We had to get him out of the house so we could get to you," he explained. "It takes time to do these things right, you know. First we get you. Then he comes out here, all alone, and we get him. Real easy."

"Why do you want my father?" she asked, relieved that her dad was all right, but nervous because the man was making threats.

"Not me," he said with a shrug. "Somebody else."

"Why?"

"Lady, I don't know," he muttered. "Nobody tells me nothing. They just say go do something and I go do it. I don't get paid to ask questions."

"Please don't hurt my dad," she said plaintively.

He made a face. "Look, I'm not going to do anything to him," he promised. "Honest. I don't kill people for money. I just had to get him out here. There's two guys outside...they'll do it."

Her heart jumped up into her throat. Her father would be lured here because she was under threat. He'd walk right up to the door and they'd kill him. She felt sick all over. "Couldn't you stop them?" she asked. "Don't you have a father? Would you like to see that done to him?"

His face closed up. "Yeah, I had a father. He put me in the hospital twice. I wouldn't care if somebody did it to him. No way."

Her eyes were soft with sadness. "I'm so sorry," she said gently.

He looked uncomfortable. "Maybe you should try to sleep, huh?"

"My wrists hurt."

"I can do something about that." He went around behind her and fiddled with the handcuffs. They were less tight. "So funny, I got kicked off the force five years ago, and here I am using cuffs again," he mused.

"The force?"

"I was a cop. I knocked this guy down a staircase. Big guy, like me. He was trying to kill his kid. They said I used excessive force. There was a review and all, but I got canned anyway." He didn't add that it was really because he'd ruffled his partner's feathers when he wouldn't take bribes or kickbacks. That was sort of blowing his own horn. He'd been set up, but that was ancient history now. The bad thing was that it had given Mr. Helm a stick to hit him with, because he'd been honest about losing his job. He hadn't known at the time that Mr. Helm was even more crooked than his old partner.

"I work for the police chief, here," she said. "He'd use excessive force with a guy who was trying to kill his kid, too, but nobody would fire him for it."

He moved back around in front of her. He smiled faintly. He had dark eyes and a broad face with scars all over it. He had thick black wavy hair. He was an odd sort of gangster, she thought.

"Maybe he knows the right people," he told her. "I didn't."

She studied him curiously. "You aren't from Texas," she said.

He shrugged. "From Italy, way back," he said.

Her eyes widened. "Are you in the Mafia?" she asked.

He burst out laughing. He had perfect white teeth. "If I was, they'd kill me for telling people about it."

"Oh. I get it."

"Your wrists okay now? That feel better?"

"Yes. Thanks." She made a face. "What did you do to me?"

"Chloroform," he said. "Put it on a handkerchief, see, and it works quick."

She drew in another breath. Her chest felt tight.

"You ain't breathing good," he remarked, frowning.

"I have asthma."

"You got something to use for it?"

"Sure. It's back at my house. Want to take me there to pick it up?" she asked. She wasn't really afraid of him. Odd, because he looked frightening.

He smiled back. "Not really, no. I'd get fired."

"Not a bad idea, you could do something honest for a living before your bosses get you locked up for life," she returned.

He seemed disturbed by that. He checked his watch. It was an oddly expensive-looking one, she thought. He'd said they didn't pay well, but if he could afford a timepiece like that, perhaps he'd just been joking about his salary.

He drew in a long breath. "I have to make a phone call," he said. "You just stay there and be quiet so I don't have to gag you, okay?"

"I can't let them kill my father," she said. "If I hear him coming, I'm going to warn him."

"You're an honest kid, ain't you?" he asked admiringly. "Okay. I'll try not to make it too tight, so you can breathe."

He took out a clean handkerchief and rolled it up, tied it around her mouth. "That okay?" he asked.

She groaned.

"Come on, don't make me feel no worse than I do. You're just a kid. I wouldn't hurt you. Not even if they told me to."

She made a face under the gag. Reluctantly, she nodded.

"Okay. I won't be long."

She heard him go to the door. Just as he started to open it, she thought she must be hallucinating, because she heard a chiming rock song. It went away almost at once, followed by a mild curse. The door opened and closed. She heard voices outside.

What could she possibly do that would save her father? She squirmed her way to the edge of the bed and wiggled so that her feet made it to the floor. She was still a little dizzy, but she managed to get to her feet.

She moved to the door and listened. She heard distant voices. She looked around. The room had no windows. There was a pallet on the floor, nothing else. There wasn't even a table, much less anything she could try to use to untie herself.

Well, she could at least listen and try to hear her father's voice. She might be able to warn him before they shot him. She groaned inwardly. It was going to be on her conscience forever if he died because she'd opened the door to a stranger. When she recalled what the big man had told her, it was so obviously a ruse that she couldn't imagine why she hadn't questioned his story. He'd said her father was hurt. After that, her brain had gone into panic mode. That was why she'd agreed to leave with him.

But it was going to make a really lousy epitaph for her father. If she was lucky, the FBI would involve itself because it was a kidnapping. There was also her boss, who'd come looking for her. Maybe Carson would, too. Her heart jumped. Sure he would. He was probably up in San Antonio with that gorgeous blonde, out on a date. He wouldn't even know she was missing and probably wouldn't mind unless somebody asked him to help find her. That made her even more depressed.

But how would they ever find her in time to save her father? She hoped he had no idea where to find her, that they hadn't left some sort of clue that would lead him here. But there were armed guards at the door, and they were waiting for him, her kidnapper had said. That meant they had to have left some clue to help him find this place.

She closed her eyes and began to pray silently, the last hope of the doomed...

CARSON HAD JUST walked back into his apartment, after insistently leaving Lanette at hers, when his cell phone went off.

He locked himself in and answered it, tired and out of sorts. "Carson," he said shortly.

"It's Cash. I thought you might want to know that we've had some developments down here."

He grimaced as he went into the kitchen to make coffee. "Somebody confessed to trying to off the preacher?"

There was a pause. "Someone's kidnapped Carlie..."

"What the hell! Who? When?"

Cash wanted to tell him to calm down, but he had some idea about Carson's feelings for the woman, so he bit his tongue. "We don't know who. Her father was hoaxed into going to a motel to counsel a suicidal man, who conveniently disappeared before he showed up. Rourke and I were playing poker. We had no idea Carlie was going to be home alone. Somehow she was lured out. Her father said that he found her telephone on the kitchen table and her purse upstairs."

"That damned phone..."

"I know, she's always forgetting it," Cash replied heavily. "It seems that Carlie was the target all along. There was one clue, a crude drawing of a building in the area, but nobody knows where it is. The map isn't very helpful."

"Where's her father?"

"Funny thing," Cash mused. "He says he has to visit a sick member of his congregation at the hospital. The timing strikes me as a bit odd."

"I'll be there in fifteen minutes."

"You won't help her if you die on the way."

"Thanks for the tip." He hung up.

"JAKE BLAIR'S ONLY been gone a few minutes," Cash told Carson when he arrived.

Carson glanced past him. "Crime scene guys at work already, I gather."

"Yes."

Carson went inside and looked at the map lying on the table in a protective cover. It had already been dusted for prints—none found—and cataloged in position. He also saw Carlie's cell phone.

"May I?" he asked.

"It's been dusted. Only prints are hers," Zack, Sheriff Hayes Carson's chief investigator, told him with a smile. "We checked her calls, too. Nothing." He went back to work.

Carson's fingers smoothed over the phone absently. It might have been one of the last things she touched. It was comforting, in some odd way. He thought of her being held, terrified, maybe smothering because the asthma would be worsened by the fear and confusion. His face mirrored his own fear.

He stuck the phone in his pocket absentmindedly as he studied the map once more. His black eyes narrowed. The drawing was amateurish, but he recognized two features on that map because they were on the way to Cy Parks's ranch. He drove the road almost every day. There was a ranch house that had burned down some time back, leaving only a ramshackle barn standing. It had to be where they had Carlie.

He was careful not to let his recognition show, because if the gangbusters here went shoving in, they'd probably shock the kidnappers into killing her quickly so they could escape. He couldn't risk that.

"Any idea where this place is?" he asked Cash with a convincing frown.

"Not a clue," Cash said tautly, "and I've been here for years."

"It's a pretty bad map," Carson replied.

"Yes."

"You said her father just left?" Carson asked in a low voice, incredulous. "His daughter's been kidnapped, and he's visiting the sick?"

Cash motioned him aside, away from his brother and the sheriff's department. "He was carrying a .45 magnum in his belt. Nicely hidden, but I got a glimpse of it." He pursed his lips. "Can you still track?"

"Not on pavement," he returned.

"He drives a red Cobra," he pointed out. "Not the easiest ride to conceal. And this is a small community."

"I'll have a look around."

"I'd go with you, but I can't leave." He hesitated. "Don't try to sneak up on him," he advised tersely, lowering his voice. "He's a minister now, but you don't ever lose survival instincts."

"What do you know that I don't?" Carson asked.

"Things I can't tell. Go find him."

"I'll do my best." He glanced past Cash at the other law enforcement people. "Why aren't they looking?"

"Forensics first, then action," Cash explained. His face hardened. "I know. I never really got the hang of it, either." His dark eyes met Carson's. "Her father knows where she is, I'm sure of it. Find him, you find her. Try to keep them both alive."

Carson nodded. He turned and went out the door.

JAKE SLOWED AS he neared the turnoff that led, eventually, to Cy Parks's ranch. Carlie, if the map was accurate, was being held at an old cattle ranch. The ranch house was long since burned down and deserted, but there was a barn still standing. He got around to the back of the building without being detected and observed two men standing guard in front of the door.

They were obviously armed, judging from the bulges under their cheap jackets. Apparently whoever hired them didn't pay much.

Jake had spent years perfecting his craft as a mercenary. He could move in shadow, in light, in snow or sleet, without leaving a trace of himself. He was going to have to take down two men at once. He would also have to do it with exquisite care, so as not to alert what might be a third man inside the structure holding Carlie.

It would seem impossible to survive a frontal assault against armed men. He only smiled.

He was able to get very close before he moved out into the open with both arms up. He approached the men who belatedly drew their weapons and pointed them at him. The element of surprise had confused them just enough, he hoped.

"Stop there," one of them said.

He kept walking until he was close to them.

"I said stop!" the other threatened.

"Here?" Jake asked, looking down at his feet. "Next to this snake?"

They looked down at his feet immediately. Big mistake. He ducked under them, hit one in the diaphragm to momentarily paralyze him while he put pressure to the carotid artery of the other man and watched him go down, unconscious. The second one, with his gun drawn, bent over, was easy to knock out with the .45.

Very quiet. Very precise. Not a sound came after. And he hadn't had to kill them. He drew out two lengths of rawhide from his bomber jacket and got busy trussing up the gunmen.

He knew he'd have to work fast. If someone had Carlie at gunpoint inside, they might have heard the men ordering him to stop. It was a long shot, though. He wasn't that close to the barn.

He secured them by their thumbs, on their bellies with their hands behind them, and moved quickly toward the shed.

On the way, he had company, quite suddenly, but not from ambush. The man, moving quickly, seemed to deliberately make a sound. He'd been warned, Jake thought and smiled. He turned to the newcomer with the knife still in his hand. When he recognized the man, he slid it quickly into its sheath.

The action wasn't lost on Carson, who was remembering what Cash had told him about this enigmatic man.

"Good thing you came with a little noise," the minister said softly. His glittering blue eyes were those of a different person altogether. "I wouldn't have hesitated, under the circumstances."

Carson stared at him with open curiosity. "I've never seen an action carried out more efficiently."

"Son, you haven't seen anything yet," Jake told him. "You get behind me. And you don't move unless I tell you to. Got it?"

Carson just nodded.

They got to the door. Jake pulled a device out of his pocket and pressed it to the old wood. His jaw tautened.

He drew back and kicked the door in, an action that is much easier in movies with balsa wood props than in real life with real wood. It flung back on its hinges. Jake had the automatic leveled before it even moved, and he walked in professionally, checking corners and dark places on his way to an inner room.

Carlie was, fortunately, on her feet about a yard away from the door her father had just broken down. She cried out through the gag as she saw him.

"Dear God," Jake whispered, holstering the gun as he ran to her. "Honey, are you okay?"

"Dad!" she managed through the gag. She hugged him with her cuffed hands around his neck, sobbing. She was breathing roughly.

Carson dug an inhaler out of his pocket and handed it to her while he took off the gag. "Two puffs, separated," he instructed. He touched her hair. "What did they do to you?" he asked angrily.

"Nothing," she choked. "I mean, he brought me in here and tied me up, but he promised he wouldn't hurt me and he didn't. Except for keeping me tied up all night, I mean," she stammered between puffs of the inhaler. "Thanks," she told Carson. "I forgot mine."

"And your damned phone," Carson muttered, digging it out of his jacket pocket. He handed it to her.

"They had armed men at the door," she exclaimed, gaping at her father. "He said the idea of taking me was to lure you here. He wasn't going to hurt you. But he said the two men, they were going to do it! They were supposed to kill you…!"

He shrugged. "They're not a threat anymore, pumpkin." He pulled a tool from his pocket and very efficiently unlocked her cuffs, touching only the chain. He turned to Carson. "You wouldn't happen to have an evidence bag on you?" he mused.

Carson pursed his lips, produced one from his jacket pocket and handed it to Jake. "I had a feeling," he replied.

Carlie watched her father slide the cuffs, gently and still without touching the parts that had locked her wrists, into the evidence bag. He laid them on the table and took a quick shot with his smartphone's camera. "Just in case," he told them.

"Someday, you have to tell me about your past," Carlie said.

"I don't, pumpkin. There are things that should never be spoken of." He smoothed over her hair. "Let's get out of here."

"I couldn't agree more," she said.

Carson took her arm. "Can you walk?" he asked softly, his eyes darker with concern.

"Sure," she said, moving a little stiffly. "I'm fine. Honest." It delighted her that he'd come with her father to rescue her. She hadn't expected it. She imagined his girlfriend was livid.

Her father led the way out. He had the automatic in his hand and he didn't apologize or explain why.

Carson let him lead, Carlie moving stiffly at his side.

The two previously armed men were still lying on the ground where Jake had left them. "Did one of these guys kidnap you?" her father asked.

She was staring almost openmouthed at them. Two automatic weapons lay in the dirt near them. They weren't moving. But they were certainly vocal.

"No," she said. "I didn't see these ones. Just the man who tied me up."

"You'll pay for this!" one of the captives raged.

"Damned straight!" the other one agreed. "The boss will get you!"

"Well, not if he's as efficient as you two," Jake replied blithely. "And I expect you're going to have a little trouble with the feds. Kidnapping is a felony."

"Hey, we didn't kidnap nobody! We was just guarding her!" the small man protested.

"Yeah. Just guarding her. So she didn't get hurt or nothing," the other man agreed.

As he spoke, several cars came into view along the road. Two of them had flashing blue lights.

Jake turned to Carson with a sigh. They'd figured out the map and now he was going to be in the soup for jumping the gun and leaving them out of the loop. He just shook his head. "You can bring Carlie to visit me in the local jail tonight. I hope they have somebody who can cook."

For the first time, Carson grinned.

BUT JAKE WASN'T ARRESTED. Cash Grier had already briefed his brother, who was in charge of the operation. A man with Jake's background couldn't convincingly be excluded from a mission that involved saving his child from kidnappers. So no charges were pressed. It would have been unlikely anyway, since Jake knew one of the top men at the agency and several government cabinet members, as well. Carlie hadn't known that, until she overheard her dad talking to Garon Grier.

"How did you get past the men with guns?" Carlie asked Carson while she was being checked out at the emergency room. Her father had insisted that Carson take her there, just in case, while he tried to explain his part in her liberation.

"I didn't," he mused. "Your father took them down." He shook his head. "I never saw it coming, and I was watching."

She signed herself out, smiled at the clerk and followed Carson out the front door. "My father is a mystery."

"He's very accomplished," he remarked.

"I noticed."

He stopped at his car and turned to her on the passenger side. "Are you sure you're all right?" he asked.

"Don't you start," she muttered. "I'm fine. Just a little bruised."

He caught her face in his big, warm hands and tilted it up to his eyes. "I thought they might kill you," he said with involuntary concern.

"And you'd miss killing me in battlegrounds online?" she asked, trying to lighten the tension, which was growing exponentially.

"Yes. I'd miss that. And other…things," he whispered as he bent and kissed her with a tenderness that was overwhelming. Then, just as suddenly, he whipped her body completely against his and kissed her with almost bruising intensity. He jerked his mouth away before she could even respond. "Next time, if there is a next time, don't open the door to anybody you don't know!"

"He said Daddy was in a wreck," she faltered. The kiss had shaken her.

"Next time, call Daddy and see if he answers," he retorted.

She searched his angry eyes. "Okay," she whispered softly.

"And for the last time, keep that damned cell phone with you!"

She nodded. "Okay," she said again, without an argument.

The tenderness in her face, the soft, involuntary hunger, the unexpected obedience almost brought him to his knees.

He'd been out of his mind when he'd heard she'd been taken; he couldn't rest until he'd got to her. After Cash had called him, he'd gone crazy on the way down from San Antonio as his mind haunted him with all the things that could have happened to her. The thought of a world without Carlie was frightening to him. He was only just beginning to realize what an impact she had on him. He didn't like it, either.

He fought for self-control. People were walking around nearby, going to and from cars. He let her go and moved away. He felt as if he were vibrating with feeling. "I need to get you home," he said stiffly.

"Okay," she said.

He helped her inside the car, started it and drove her home. He didn't say a word the whole way.

When he let her out at the front door, she ran to her father and hugged him tightly.

"I'm okay," she promised.

He smoothed her hair, looking over her head at Carson. "Thanks."

Carson shrugged. "No problem. Lock her in a closet and lose the key, will you?" he added, not completely facetiously.

Jake chuckled. "She'd just bang on the door until I let her out," he said, giving her an affectionate smile.

"Where's local law enforcement?" Carson asked.

"Packed up all the vital clues and left. They were just a little late backtracking the kidnapper to a lonely barn over near your boss's house," Jake said with biting criticism.

"You did that quite neatly yourself," Carson replied. "I'm reliably informed that local law enforcement followed you there after being tipped off."

"Did you tip them off?" Jake asked with a knowing smile.

Carson sighed. "Yes. I didn't want to have to bury both of you."

Jake became less hostile. "Carson," he said softly, "I wasn't always a minister. I can handle myself."

"And now I know that." Carson managed a smile, glanced at Carlie with painfully mixed feelings and left.

LATER, IN THE corner table at the local café, Carson cornered Rourke. "Okay, let's have it," he demanded.

"Have what?" Rourke asked with a smile.

"That mild-mannered minister—" he meant Jake Blair "—took down two armed men with a speed I've never seen in my life. I didn't even hear him walk toward them, and I was out of my car and heading that way at the time."

"Oh, Jake was always something special," Rourke replied with a smile of remembrance. "He could move so silently that the enemy never knew he was around. They called him 'Snake,' because he could get in and out of places that an army couldn't. He had a rare talent with a knife. Sort of like you," he added, indicating the big bowie knife that Carson was never without. "He'd go in, do every fourth man in a camp, get out without even being heard. The next morning, when the enemy awoke, there would be pandemonium." He hesitated. "Don't you ever tell her," he added coldly, "or you'll find out a few more things about the reverend Blair."

"I never would," Carson assured. "There are things in my past just as unsavory."

Rourke nodded. "His specialty was covert assassination, but he didn't work with a spotter or use a sniper kit. He went in alone, with just a knife, at night." He shook his head. "We tried one night to hear him leave. None of us, not even those with sensitive hearing, could ever spot him. The government begged him to come back when he left for the seminary. He told them he was through with the old life and he was never doing it again. Carlie's his life, now. Her, and his church." He glanced at Carson. "He says she's the only reason he didn't commit suicide after her mother died. You know, I don't really understand religion, but I guess it has its place."

"I guess it does," Carson replied thoughtfully.

"How was your date?" Rourke asked.

Carson made a face. "Tedious."

"She's a looker."

Carson stared at him with cool, cynical eyes. "They all look alike, smell alike, sound alike," he said. "And they don't last long. I don't like possession."

Rourke toyed with his coffee cup. "I don't, either," he said slowly, thinking of Tat. The last he'd heard, she went into a small, war-torn African nation, named Ngawa in Swahili, for a species of civet cat found there, to cover the agony of the survivors. She wouldn't answer his phone calls. She wouldn't return his messages. She might as well have vanished off the face of the earth. He had…feelings for her, that he could never, ever express. He, like Carson, had placated the ache with other women. Nothing did much good.

Carson finished his coffee. "I have to get back up to San Antonio. I may have an offer soon."

Rourke studied him. "Tired of working for Cy?"

Carson's lips made a thin line. "Tired of aching for something I can never have."

"Boy, do I understand that feeling," Rourke said tersely.

Carson laughed, but it had a hollow sound.

He was supposed to take Lanette dancing tonight. He wasn't looking forward to it, but he'd given his word, so he'd go. The job offer would involve travel to some South American nation for a covert op with some ex-military people, on the QT. They needed a field medic, and Carson's reputation had gotten around.

It was a good job, paid well, and it would get him away from Carlie. Suddenly that had become of earth-shaking importance. He didn't want to pursue that line of thought, so he called Lanette before he left Jacobsville and told her he'd pick her up at six.

CHAPTER TEN

CARLIE DESCRIBED THE kidnapper to Zack the next day, with her boss and the FBI special agent in charge, Garon Grier, listening in Cash's office.

"He sounded just like one of those gangsters in the old black-and-white movies," she said. "He was big as a house and a little clumsy. He was kind to me. He didn't say a thing out of the way or even threaten me."

"Except by kidnapping you," Garon Grier mused.

"Well, yes, there was that," she agreed. "But he didn't hurt me. He said he was supposed to take me out there to lure my dad to come get me. I suppose that meant they wanted to get him out of town to someplace deserted. I was so scared," she recalled. "I managed to get to my feet, to the door. I listened really hard, so if I heard Dad's voice, I might have time to warn him."

"You weren't afraid for yourself?" Cash asked.

"Not really. He didn't want to hurt me. I was just afraid for Dad. He's absentminded and he forgets things, like his house keys," she said with a smile. Then the smile faded. "But he took down these two huge guys. They had guns, too." She frowned worriedly. "I don't know how he did it. He even kicked in the door! I only just managed to get out of the way in time! And Dad had a gun…"

"He didn't use it," Cash reminded her.

"No. Of course not." She rubbed her wrists. "The kidnapper apologized for the handcuffs. He knew how to loosen them. He said he was a cop once. He knocked a man down a staircase for roughing up a child and they fired him." She looked up. They were all staring at her.

"What else did he say?" Garon asked. He was taking notes on his cell phone.

"I asked why he wanted my dad hurt and he said his bosses didn't pay him to ask questions," she recalled. She was going to add that he was wearing an expensive watch, and about that funny chiming sound she thought she'd heard, but she wasn't certain that she hadn't been confused by the chloroform the kidnapper had used on her. No use making wild statements. She needed to stick to the facts.

"That's not much to go on, but it's more than we had," Garon said a few minutes later. "Thanks, Carlie."

"You're very welcome." She got up. "I'll just get the mail caught up," she told her boss, rolling her eyes. "I expect that will last me a few hours."

Cash chuckled. "No doubt. Hey," he added when she reached the door. She turned. "I'm glad you're okay, kid," he said gently.

She grinned. "Me, too, Chief. Where would you ever get another secretary who didn't hide in the closet every time you lost your temper?"

She went out before he could come back with a reply.

"Isn't this lovely?" Lanette asked Carson as they did a lazy two-step on the dance floor.

"Lovely," he said without feeling it.

"You're very distracted tonight," she said. She moved a little away so that he could see how nicely her red sequined cocktail dress suited her, exposing most of her breasts and a lot of her thigh in a side split. Her exquisite hair was put up in a nice French twist with a jeweled clasp that matched the dress and her shoes. She looked beautiful and very expensive. He wondered vaguely how she managed to afford clothes like that on a stewardess salary. And she never seemed to go on any trips.

"Do you work?" he asked, curious.

"I work very hard," she said. She smiled secretively. "I was a stewardess, but I have a new job now. I work in…personnel," she concluded. "For a big corporation."

"I see."

"What do you do?" she asked.

He smiled enigmatically. "I work for a rancher in Jacobsville mostly, but I'm also a field medic."

"A medic? Really?" she exclaimed. "That's such a…well, I know it's noble and all that, but it sounds just really boring."

Boring. He was recalling several incidents, trying to treat men under fire and get them evacuated by helicopter or ambulance in trouble spots all over the world. Saving lives. "Maybe not as boring as it sounds," he concluded.

She shrugged. "If you say so." She looked up at him as they danced. "I heard on the news that there was a kidnapping in that town where your rancher boss lives. Was anybody hurt?"

"Carlie was frightened, but they didn't hurt her."

"Shame."

He stopped dancing. "Excuse me?"

"Well, she's a little prude, isn't she?" she said cattily. "Doesn't know how to dance properly, wears cheap clothes. My God, I'll bet she's still a virgin." She laughed heartily at the other woman's stupidity. This woman was annoying. He was beginning, just beginning, to understand how Carlie saw the world. She was blunt and unassuming, never coy, never shallow like this beautiful hothouse flower. Carlie was like a sunflower, open and honest and pretty. The fact that she didn't sleep around was suddenly appealing to him. He hated the implication of that thought. He wasn't going to get trapped. Not by some small-town girl with hang-ups.

"They say her father rescued her," Lanette purred.

"Yes. That's what I heard, too," he said, without adding that he'd been in on the rescue. Not that he'd had much work to do. Jake Blair had done it all.

"One guy against two armed men," she said, almost to herself. "It sounds...incredible. I mean, they were really tough guys. That's what I heard, anyway."

"Not so tough," Carson corrected her. "Blair had them trussed up like holiday turkeys."

She let out a rough breath. "Idiots," she murmured. She saw Carson's sudden scrutiny and laughed. "I mean, whoever planned that kidnapping was obviously not intended for a life of crime. Wouldn't you say?"

"I'd say they'd better be on a plane out of the country pretty soon," he replied. "The FBI got called in."

She stopped dancing. "The FBI? That's no threat. Those people are always in the news for doing dumb things—"

"The local FBI," he interrupted. "Garon Grier. He was formerly with the Hostage Rescue Team. His brother is Jacobsville's police chief Cash Grier. You met him at the dance."

She nodded slowly. "I see."

"So the kidnapper will not be sleeping well anytime soon," he concluded.

"Maybe he'll just have to step up his plans while the local FBI get their marbles together," she laughed.

"That's what bothers me," he replied. "What nobody understands is why someone would try to kill a minister."

"Loads of reasons," she said. "Maybe he's one of those radicals who wants everybody to take vows of chastity or something."

"A political opinion shouldn't result in murder," he pointed out.

"Well, no, but maybe the people who want him dead aren't interested in his opinions. Maybe it's just a job to them. Somebody big calling the shots, you know?"

Somebody big. Big. Like the politician who was finishing out the Texas U.S. senator's term and was campaigning for the May special election to earn his own term.

"What are you thinking so hard about?" Lanette asked.

"Work," he said.

"Oh, work." She threw a hand up. "We're here to have fun. We could dance some more," she said, sliding close to him. "Or we could go back to my apartment…?"

He felt like a stone wall. The thought of sleeping with her had once appealed, but now he felt uncomfortable even discussing it. He thought of all the men Lanette had bragged to him about, the men she'd had. Of course men bragged about their conquests. It was just…when she did that, he thought of Carlie. Carlie!

"Ow," Lanette complained softly. "That's my hand you're crushing, honey."

He loosened his hold. "Sorry," he snapped.

"You are really tense. Please. Let me soothe that ache," she whispered sensually.

"I want to dance." He pulled her back onto the dance floor.

THE NEXT MORNING, just before daylight, he drove back down to Cy Parks's place. He couldn't sleep. He and Lanette had argued, again, about his coldness to her and about Carlie. She was venomous about the small-town girl.

Carson was angry and couldn't hide it. He didn't like hearing her bad-mouth Carlie. He was tired of the city anyway. He just wanted to get back to work.

Cy was working on a broken hoof on one of the big Santa Gertrudis bulls. He filed the broken part down while a tall African-American cowboy gently held the animal in place, soothing it with an uncanny gift.

"That's good, Diamond," the other cowboy murmured softly, using part of the pedigree bull's full name, which was Parks's Red Diamond. "Good old fellow."

Cy grinned. "I don't know what I'd do without you, Eddie," he chuckled. "That bull's just like a dog when you talk to him. He follows you around like one, anyway. Nice of Luke to let me borrow you." He glanced up at Carson. "You've been AWOL," he accused. "Couldn't find anybody to hold Diamond while I filed the hoof down, so I had to call Luke Craig and ask him to lend a hand. He sent Eddie Kells here. Eddie, this is Carson."

Carson nodded politely.

Kells just grinned.

"Kells came down here to a summer camp some years ago that Luke Craig's wife, Belinda, started for city kids in trouble with the law. Didn't know one end of a horse from another. Now he's bossing cowboys over at Luke's place," Cy chuckled.

"Yeah, Mr. Parks here saved my life," Kells replied. "I was in trouble with the law in Houston when I was younger," he said honestly. "I was on Mr. Parks's place trying to learn roping with his cattle, trespassing, and he caught me." He let out a whistle. "Thought I was a goner. But when he saw how crazy I was about cattle, he didn't press charges and Mr. Craig hired me on as a cowboy when I graduated from high school." He smiled. "I got no plans to ever leave, either. This is a good place to live. Fine people."

Carson studied the tall young man. He'd have thought that a place like this would have a lot of prejudice. It didn't seem to be the case at all, not if Kells wanted to stay here.

"You Indian?" Kells asked, and held up a hand

when Carson bristled. "No, man, it's cool, I got this friend, Juanito, he's Apache. Some of his ancestors ran with Geronimo. He's hired on at Mr. Scott's place. He's been trying to teach me to speak his language. Man, it's hard!"

Carson relaxed a little. "I'm Oglala Lakota."

"I guess you couldn't speak to Juanito and have him understand you, huh?"

Carson smiled. "No. The languages are completely different."

"Only thing I can manage is enough Spanish to talk to some of the new cowboys. But I guess that's what I need to be studying, anyway."

"You do very well, too," Cy told the young man, clapping him on the shoulder. "That's it, then. You go down to the hardware and get yourself a new pocket-knife, and put it on my account," he told Kells. "I'll call and okay it before you get there. Don't argue. I know Luke sent you, but you should have something. That knife's pretty old, you know," he added. Kells was using it to clean under his fingernails.

"Only one I had," Kells said, smiling. "Okay, then, I'll do it. Thanks, Mr. Parks."

They shook hands.

"Nice to meet you," Kells told Carson before he left.

"I had a different concept of life here," Carson told Cy quietly.

Cy chuckled. "So did I. Blew all my notions of it when I moved here. You will never find a place with kinder, more tolerant people, anywhere in the world."

Carson was thinking of some of the places he had been which were far less than that.

"Sorry I didn't get back in time to help," he told Cy. "There's a new complication. I need to talk to Jake Blair. I think I've made a connection, of sorts. I just want to sound him out on it."

"If you dig anything out, tell Garon Grier," Cy replied.

"Certainly." He hesitated. "I'm going to be moving on, soon," he said. "I've enjoyed my time here."

"I've enjoyed having you around." Cy gave him a cynical smile. "I was like you, you know," he said. "Same fire for action, same distaste for marriage, kids. I went all over the world with a gun. Killed a lot of people. But in the end, it was the loneliness that got me. It will eat you up like acid."

"I like my own company."

Cy put a hand on his shoulder. His green eyes narrowed. "Son," he said gently, "there's a difference between being alone and being lonely."

"I'm not lonely," Carson said doggedly.

Cy just chuckled. "Go see Jake. He'll be up. He never was a late sleeper."

"You knew him before?" he asked slowly.

Cy nodded. "He was on special duty, assigned to support troops. We ended up in the same black ops group." He shook his head. "The only person I've ever known who comes close to him is Cash Grier. Jake was…gifted. And not in a way you'd ever share with civilians."

"I heard that from Rourke."

Cy pursed his lips. "Make sure you never share that information with Carlie," he cautioned. "You do not want to see Jake Blair lose his temper. Ever."

"I'm getting that impression," Carson said with a mild chuckle.

It was barely daylight. Carson knew it was early to be visiting, but he was certain Jake would be up, and he needed to tell him what he thought might be going on. Lanette had, without realizing it, pointed him in a new direction on the attempted kidnapping.

When he got to Reverend Blair's house, he was surprised to find Carlie there alone. She seemed equally surprised to find him at her door.

She was wearing a T-shirt and jeans. It was late February and still cold outside. In fact, it was cold in the house. Heat was expensive, and Carlie was always trying to save money. The cold had become familiar, so that she hardly noticed it now.

"What can I do for you?" she asked quietly.

He shrugged. "I came to see your father," he told her.

Her eyebrows arched over wide green eyes. "He didn't mention anything..."

"He doesn't know." He smiled slowly, liking the way her face flushed when he did that. "Is he here?"

"No, but he'll be back...soon," she faltered. She bit her lower lip. "You can come in and wait for him, if you like."

The invitation was reluctant, but at least she made one.

"Okay. Thanks."

She opened the door and let him in. Why did she feel as if she were walking into quicksand?

He closed the door behind him and followed her into the living room. On the sofa was a mass of yarn.

Apparently she was making some sort of afghan in soft shades of blue and purple.

"You crochet?" he asked, surprised.

"Yes," she replied. She sat down beside the skeins of yarn and moved them aside. Carson dropped into the armchair just to her left.

"My mother used to do handwork," he murmured. He could remember her sewing quilts when he was very small. She did it to keep her hands busy. Maybe she did it to stop thinking about how violent and angry his father was when he drank. And he never seemed to stop drinking…

Carlie toyed with the yarn, but her hands were nervous. The silence grew more tense by the minute. He didn't speak. He just looked at her.

"Would you mind…not doing that, please?" she asked in a haunted tone.

"Doing what exactly?" he asked with a slow, sensuous smile.

"Staring at me," she blurted out. "I know you think I'm ugly. Couldn't you stare at the— Oh!"

He was sitting beside her the next minute, his hands on her face, cupping it while he looked straight into her eyes. "I don't think you're ugly," he said huskily. He looked at her mouth.

She was confused and nervous. "You said once that you liked your women more…physically perfect," she accused in a throaty voice.

He drew in a breath. "Yes. But I didn't mean it."

His thumb rubbed gently over her bow mouth, liking the way it felt. It was swollen and very soft. She caught his wrist, but not to pull his hand away.

She hadn't felt such sensations. It was new and exciting. He was exciting. She wanted to hide her reaction from him, but he knew too much about women. She felt like a rabbit walking into a snare.

She should get up right now and go into the kitchen. She should…

His mouth lowered to her lips. He touched them softly, tenderly, smoothing her lips apart so that he could feel the softness underneath the top one. He traced it delicately with his tongue. His hands on her face were big and warm. His thumbs stroked her cheekbones while he toyed with her lips in a silence that accentuated her quick breathing.

He hadn't expected his own reaction to her. This was explosive. Sweet. Dangerous. He opened his mouth and pushed her lips apart. He let go of her face and lifted her across his lap while he kissed her as if her mouth was the source of such sweetness that he couldn't bear to let it go.

Helplessly, her arms went around his neck and she kissed him back, with more enthusiasm than expertise.

He could feel that lack of experience. It made him feel taller, stronger. She had nothing to compare this with, he could tell. He nibbled her lower lip while one big hand shifted down to her T-shirt and teased under the sleeve.

She caught his wrist and stayed it. "No," she protested weakly.

But it was too late. His long fingers were under the sleeve, and he could feel the scars.

She bit her lip. "Don't," she pleaded, turning her face away.

He drew in a harsh breath. "Do you think a scar

matters?" he asked roughly. He turned her face up to his. "It doesn't."

Her eyes were eloquent, stinging with tears.

"Trust me," he whispered as his mouth lowered to hers again. "I won't hurt you. I promise."

His mouth became slowly insistent, so hungry and demanding that she forgot to protest, and let go of his wrist. He slid it under the hem of her T-shirt while he kissed her and lifted it, sliding his hand possessively over her small breast and up to the scar.

"You mustn't!" she whispered frantically.

He nibbled her upper lip. "Shh," he whispered back, and quickly lifted the shirt over her head and tossed it aside.

She was wearing a delicate little white lacy bra that fastened in front. Just above the lacy cup was a scar, a long one running from her collarbone down just to the beginning of the swell of her breast.

Tears stung her eyes. She hadn't shown the wound to anyone except the doctor and a woman police officer. She tried to cover it with her hand, but he lifted it gently away and unfastened the bra.

"Beautiful," he whispered when he saw the delicate pink and mauve mound that he'd uncovered.

"Wh…what?" she stammered.

His hand smoothed boldly over her delicate flesh, teasing the nipple so that it became immediately hard. "Your breasts are beautiful," he said softly, bending. "I wonder if I can fit one into my mouth…?"

As he spoke, he did it. His tongue rubbed abrasively over the sensitive nipple while his mouth covered and possessed the pert little mound.

Her reaction was unexpected and violent. She shivered and cried out, and then suddenly arched up toward his lips as he made a slow suction that caused unspeakable responses in her untried body.

"No...nooooo!" she groaned as she felt the tension grow to almost painful depths and then, suddenly, snap. The pleasure was unlike anything she'd ever known in her life. She shivered and shivered, her short nails digging into his shoulders as she held on and convulsed with ecstasy.

He felt her body contort, felt the shudders run through her as he satisfied her with nothing more than his mouth on her breast. His hand went to her hip and ground it into his while he continued the warm pressure of his mouth on her damp flesh. He wanted her. He'd never wanted anything so much!

She was lost. She couldn't even protest. The pleasure swept over her in waves, like breakers on the ocean, on the beach. She arched her back and shuddered as her body gave in to him, hungered for him, ached to have more than this, something more, anything....

Finally, he lifted his head and looked down at her. She lay shivering in the aftermath, tears running down her cheeks. She wept silently, her eyes wide and wet and accusing.

"It's all right," he whispered. He kissed away the tears. "There's no reason to be embarrassed."

She sobbed. She felt as if she'd betrayed everything she believed in. If he hadn't stopped, she wouldn't have been able to. She was embarrassed and humiliated by her own easy acceptance of his ardor. He was a womanizer. God only knew how many women he'd had. And she was so easy...

She pushed gently at his chest.

He let her go, very slowly, his eyes riveted to her taut breasts, to the red marks on the one he'd suckled so hard.

She tried to pull the bra over them, but he prevented her with a gentle movement of his hand. He wasn't looking at her breasts. He was looking at the scar. He traced it, noting the ridge that was forming.

She drew in a sharp breath.

"It was deep, wasn't it?" he asked softly.

She swallowed. He didn't seem repulsed. "Yes."

He traced it tenderly. His finger moved down over her breast to the hard nipple and caressed it. He loved touching her. It was surprising.

"I've never had a virgin," he whispered. "I didn't realize how exciting it would be."

She flushed. "I'm...not perfect physically," she choked, remembering the hurtful things he'd said in her boss's office.

He looked into her eyes with regret darkening his own. "Here," he said quietly. "Show-and-tell."

He unbuttoned his shirt and pulled it away from his broad, muscular chest. He pulled her up into a sitting position on his lap and drew her fingers to the worst scar, where a long, deep wound went just below his rib cage on the side near his heart.

"This was deep, too," she said softly, tracing it.

He nodded. "He came at me with a sword, of all things. I drew him in and guided the blade where it would do the least damage, before I killed him." His eyes were narrow and cold.

She shivered. She could never kill anyone.

"He'd just raped a young woman. A pregnant woman," he said quietly.

Her expression changed. Her eyes went back to the scars. "These are...strange," she said, tracing several small round scars below his collarbone.

"Cigarette burns," he said with a faint smile. "I was captured once. They tortured me for information." He chuckled. "They got my name, rank and serial number. Eventually they got tired of listening to it, but my squad came and rescued me before they killed me."

"Wow," she whispered.

He cocked his head and studied her. "You are... unexpected."

Her eyebrows lifted. "I am?"

His eyes went down to her bare breasts. He drew her against him, very gently, and moved her breasts against his bare chest. She moaned. He bent and kissed her, hungrily, urgently.

"I want you," he murmured.

His hands were on her breasts again, and she was dying for him. She wanted that pleasure again, that he'd given her so easily, so sensually, with just his mouth. But with a harsh moan, she dragged herself away from him and pulled her T-shirt across her bare breasts like a shield.

"Please," she whispered when he started to draw her back into his arms. "Please. I'm sorry. I can't. I just...can't!"

She looked as if he'd asked her to go through the entire catalog of sins at once. Probably she felt that way. She was a person of faith. She didn't believe in quick rolls in the hay. She was innocent.

He felt oddly ashamed. He buttoned his shirt while

she fumbled her bra closed and put her shirt back on with tattered pride. As cold reality set in, she was horrified by what she'd let him do. All her principles had flown out the window the minute he touched her.

"I see," he said quietly. "You believe it's the road to hell. And I don't believe in anything," he added coldly.

She met his eyes. "You don't really even like women, do you?" she asked perceptively.

His smile was icy. "She said she loved me," he replied. "We were married for all of a year when she became pregnant. But by then there was another man." His eyes closed, and his brows drew together in pain at the memory while Carlie listened.

"It was almost two days after the wreck before they found the bodies. They thought they could have saved the child, a boy, if they'd found them just a little sooner." His face contorted. "I killed them all..."

"No, you didn't," she said. "You couldn't hurt a woman if you tried."

He looked at her with narrow, intent eyes. "Really? I scared you to death in your boss's office," he reminded her tautly.

"Yes, but you wouldn't have hurt me. It was the association with the past that frightened me, not you," she repeated softly. She touched his cheek, drew her soft fingers down it. "Some things are meant to be. We don't make those decisions. We can't. God takes people away sometimes for reasons we can't understand. But there's a reason, even if we don't know what it was."

His face hardened. "God," he scoffed.

She smiled gently. "You don't believe in anything."

"I used to. Before she destroyed my life." His eyes were dark with confusion and pain.

"You have to accept the fact that you can't control the world, or the people in it," she continued quietly. "Control is just an illusion."

"Like love?" he laughed coldly.

"Love is everywhere," she countered. "You aren't looking. You're living inside yourself, in the past, locked up in pain and loss and guilt. You can't forgive anything until you can forgive yourself."

He glared at her.

"The key to it all is faith," she said gently.

"Faith." He nodded. His eyes were hostile. "Yours took a hike when I started kissing your breasts, didn't it? All those shiny ideals, that proud innocence, would have been gone in a flash if I'd insisted."

She blushed. Her hand left his face. "Yes. That's true. I never realized how easy it would be to fall from grace." Her wide, soft eyes, wounded and wet, met his. "Is that why you did it? To show me how vulnerable I am?"

He wanted to say yes, to hurt her again. But suddenly it gave him no pleasure. No woman had ever reacted to him that way, been so tender with him, so patient, so willing to listen.

"No," he confessed curtly.

That one word took the pain away. She just looked at him.

He drew her hand to his mouth and kissed the palm hungrily. "I've never told anyone about my wife, except Grier and you, and one other person."

"I never tell anything I know," she replied huskily. She searched his dark eyes. "Ever."

He managed a smile. "You have a gift for listening."

"I learned it from my father. He's very patient."

He touched her soft mouth. "The angle of that wound is odd," he said after a minute, staring at the T-shirt. "Was the attacker very tall?"

"Not really," she confessed. "He reached around my father to do it." She shivered. She could still feel the pain of the knife.

"He'll never do it to anyone else," he assured her.

"I know. He died. They said it took a long time." She touched the scar involuntarily. "I'm sorry that his life took such a turn that he felt he was justified in killing people."

"He was an addict and they offered him product," Carson said coldly. "It works, most of the time."

"I'm sorry for him, for the way it happened. But I'm not sorry he's gone." She grimaced. "My dad wouldn't like hearing me say that."

"I won't tell him," he said gently. He looked down at her with faint possession. "Don't beat your conscience to death over what happened," he said quietly. "Any experienced man can overcome an innocent woman's scruples if he tries hard enough. And if she's attracted to him," he added gently.

She colored even more. "Yes, well, I…I didn't mean…I don't…"

He put a finger across her mouth. "It's an intimate memory. For the two of us. No one else will ever know. All right?"

She nodded. "All right."

He brought her hand to his mouth and kissed the

palm. "Keep your doors locked when your father isn't here," he said.

The tone of his voice was disturbing. "Why?"

"I can't tell you."

She just sighed. As she started to speak, there was a terrible rapping sound against the side of the house.

Carson was on his feet at once, his hand on the hilt of the big bowie knife.

"That's just George."

He scowled. "Who?"

"George. He's my red-bellied woodpecker." She grimaced. "I put nuts out for him at daylight every day. He's telling me he's hungry and I'm late." She laughed. "Listen." There was another sound, like something small bounding across the roof. "That's one of the squirrels. They let George do the reminding, and then they queue for the nuts." She listened again. There was a loud cacophony of bird calls. "And those are the blue jays. They fight George for the nuts…"

"You know them by sound?" he asked, surprised.

"Of course." She got up, frowning slightly. "Can't everybody identify them from the songs they sing?"

He shook his head. "I don't believe this."

"You can help me feed them if you want to. I mean, if you don't have something else to do," she added quickly, not wanting him to feel pressured.

But he wasn't looking for a way out. He just smiled. "Put on a coat," he said.

She pulled her ratty one out of the closet and grimaced. "This is what it's best for," she sighed. "Feeding birds."

"You should buy a new one."

She gave him a world-weary glance. "With what?" she asked. "We just had to fill up the propane tank again because winter doesn't appear to be leaving anytime soon. New things are a luxury around here."

He was estimating the age of her shoes and jeans. The T-shirt appeared new. He cocked his head. It was black with writing—it had a picture of a big black bird on it. Underneath it read, "Hey, you in the house, bring more birdseed!"

He chuckled. "Cool shirt."

"You like it? I designed it. There's this website. It has nice T-shirts for a reasonable price and you can design your own. This is one of the grackles that come every spring. I haven't seen one just yet."

She led the way, picking up a container of birdseed and one of shelled nuts on the way.

"The pecans came from our own trees," she said. "The farm produce store that sells them has a sheller you can run them through. I did enough to last several weeks."

"Back home, we have ravens," he told her, his hands in his jeans as he followed her out to the big backyard. Towering trees gave way to a small pasture beyond. "And crows." He pursed his lips and grinned. "Did you know that crows used to be white?"

"White?"

He nodded. "It's a Brulé Lakota legend. The crow was white, and he was brother to the buffalo. So he would warn the buffalo when the people came to hunt it. The warriors grew angry that they couldn't get close to the buffalo, so one of them put on a buffalo skin and waited for the crow to come and give its warning. When it did, he caught it by the feet.

Another warrior, very angry, took it from him and dashed it into the fire in revenge. The crow escaped, but its feathers were burned. So now the crow is black."

She laughed with pure delight. "I love stories."

"Our legends fill books," he mused. "That's one of my favorites."

That he'd shared something from his culture with her made her feel warm, welcome. She turned to look for the woodpecker. He was clinging to a nearby tree trunk making his usual lilting cry. "Okay, George, I'm here," she called. She went to a ledge on the fence and spread the nuts along it. She filled the bird feeder. Then she motioned to Carson and they moved away from the feeder.

A flash of striped feathers later, George was carting off the first pecan. He was followed by blue jays and cardinals, a tufted titmouse and a wren.

She identified them to Carson as they came in. Then she laughed suddenly as a new birdcall was heard, and started looking around. "That's a red-winged blackbird," she said. "I don't see him."

"I do know that call," he replied. He shook his head, smiling. "I've never known anyone who could listen to a birdsong and identify the bird without seeing it first."

"Oh, I can't do them all," she assured him. "Just a few. Listen. That one's a grackle!" she exclaimed. "Hear it? It sounds like a rusty hinge being moved… There he is!"

She indicated a point high in the bare limbs above. "They're so beautiful. They're so black that they have a faint purple tinge, sort of like your hair," she added, looking at it in its neat ponytail. Her eyes lingered there. He was so handsome that she thought she'd never tire of watching him.

He smiled knowingly and she flushed and averted her eyes. He was wearing that incredible fringed jacket that suited him so. Its paleness brought out the smooth olive tan of his complexion, made him look wild and free. She thought back to what her father had said, that Carson was a lobo wolf who could never be domesticated. The better she got to know him, the more certain she was of that. He'd never be able to stop picking up beautiful women, or looking for the next fight. Her heart felt sick.

She tossed seed onto the ground while the last of the nuts vanished from the fence. Carson reached into the bucket and pulled out a handful of his own and tossed it.

They stood very close, in the cold light of the morning, feeding the birds. Carlie thought it was a time she'd never forget, whatever came after. Just her and Carson, all alone in the world, without a word being spoken.

It felt…like coming home.

Carson was feeling something similar. He didn't want to think about it too much. His life was what it was. He wasn't going to get married again, settle down and have children. It was too tame for him, for his spirit. He'd lived wild for too long.

He knew she must have hopes. Her physical response to him was purely headlong. She would probably give in to him if he pushed her. He thought about doing that. He wanted her very badly. But no form of birth control was surefire. Carlie was an innocent, and she had strong beliefs. She'd never give up a child she conceived, especially his. It would lead to terrible complications…

He scowled. He was remembering some tidbit of gossip he'd heard. He glanced down at Carlie. She looked up, her eyes full of soft memory.

"Your father married your mother because you were on the way," he said gently. "True?"

She swallowed. "Well, yes. She was like me," she said, lowering her eyes to his chest. "She'd never put a foot out of line, never been…with a man. My father was dashing and exciting, well-traveled and smart. She just went in headfirst. She told me once," she recalled sadly, "that she'd ruined both their lives because she couldn't say no, the one time it really counted. She loved me," she added quickly. "She said I made everything worthwhile. But her love for my father, and his for her, never made up for the fact that he'd been pressured into marrying her."

"This isn't Victorian times," he pointed out.

"This is Jacobsville, Texas," she returned. "Or, in my case, Comanche Wells. I live among people who have known my people since the Civil War, when my family first came here from Georgia and settled on this land." She swept a hand toward it. "Generations of us know each other like family. And like family, there are some social pressures on people in terms of behavior."

"Prehistoric ones," he scoffed.

She looked up at him. "Is the world really a better place now that nothing is considered bad? People just do what they want, with anyone. How is that different from what animals do in the wild?"

He was lost for words.

"Everything goes. But the one thing that separates human beings from animals is a nobility of spirit, a sense of self-worth. I have ideals. I think they're what holds civilization together, and that if you cheapen yourself with careless encounters, you lose sight of the things that truly matter."

"Which would be…?" he prompted, stung by her reply.

"Family," she said simply. "Continuity. People get married, have children, raise children to be good people, give them a happy home life so that they grow up to be responsible and independent. Then the next generation comes along and does the same thing."

"Permissive people still have kids," he said drolly.

"They have them out of wedlock a lot, though," she pointed out. "So it's a one-parent family trying to raise the kids. I saw the result in school, with boys who had no fathers around to discipline them and teach them the things men need to know to get along in the world."

He averted his eyes. "Maybe my life would have been happier in a single-parent family."

She recalled what he'd told her, about his father's drinking problem, that he'd beat Carson's mother to death, and she grimaced. "I am so sorry for what happened to you," she said softly. "Except for my grandmother's evil boyfriend, nobody ever hurt me in my life, least of all my parents."

He drew in a long breath. His eyes were solemn as he stared off into the distance. "We attach the same importance to family that you do," he said quietly. "We live in small communities, people know each other for generations. Children are brought up not only by their parents, but by other parents, as well. It's a good way."

"But it isn't your style," she said without looking at him. "You have to be free."

He scowled and looked down at her, but she wouldn't meet his eyes.

"Here, spread the seeds over there, would you?" she asked, indicating another feeder. "I forgot to put up a seed cake for them." She pulled it out of her pocket and took the wrapper off.

In the house, unseen, Jake Blair was watching them with wide, shocked eyes. He turned. "Come here," he told Rourke. "You're not going to believe this."

Rourke followed his gaze out the window and let out a hoot of laughter. "You're having me on," he chuckled. "That can't be Carson, feeding the birds!"

"Oh, yes, it can." He pursed his lips. "I wonder…"

"I wouldn't even think it. Not yet. He's got a lot to work through before he's fit for any young woman, especially your daughter."

"Men can change. I did," Jake said quietly. "And in my day, I was a harder case than he is."

"You did change," Rourke agreed. "But you don't have the scars he's carrying."

"Tell me," Jake said.

Rourke shook his head and smiled sadly. "I won't do that. It's his story, his pain. He'll have to be the one to tell it."

Jake just nodded. He watched his daughter lead Carson around the yard, saw them laughing together as the birds came very close and they paused, very still, so that they came right up almost to their feet.

That jacket Carson wore was really gorgeous, he thought. Then he compared it to Carlie's old coat and he winced. He'd tried to give her all the necessities. He hadn't realized how difficult it was going to be, living on a minister's small salary in an equally small community. The days of big money were long gone. His conscience wouldn't let him go back to it. He did love his work, anyway.

He turned away from the window, leading Rourke back into his office.

CHAPTER ELEVEN

CARLIE WENT AHEAD of Carson into the house through the back door. Rourke and her father were just having coffee.

Jake held up the pot and raised his eyebrows.

"Please," Carson said. "I haven't had a cup this morning. Withdrawal symptoms are setting in," he added, deliberately making his hand shake.

The other men laughed.

"Breakfast?" Carlie asked, but she was looking at Carson. "I can make biscuits with scrambled eggs and sausage. Fresh sausage. One of our congregation brought it over yesterday."

"Sounds good to me, pumpkin," Jake said easily. "Make enough for everybody."

"You bet." She could almost float. It was one of the best days of her life so far. She had to make sure she didn't linger over Carson when she looked his way. She didn't want to embarrass him.

"Did you come over to help feed the local wildlife?" Rourke asked with a grin.

Carson chuckled. "No. I made a connection. Actually, I made it from something Lanette said. That whoever planned the kidnapping was sloppy, but that it must be somebody big. So I thought of the politician who's connected to the Cotillo drug cartel across the border."

"Why would he be after you, though?" Rourke asked Jake, frowning. "Have you had any contact with people who know things about the cartel?"

"None," Jake said. He sipped coffee and shook his head. "I have no idea at all why I've been targeted, or by whom." He smiled faintly. "Someone from the old life, possibly, after revenge. But if that's the case, they've waited a long time for it."

"I don't think it's that," Carson said quietly. "It just feels…I don't know, jagged."

The other two men stared at him.

"Jagged?" Rourke prompted.

"A man with a drug habit comes after Carlie, but tries to make it look like he was after you," Carson told Jake. "Now, a kidnapping attempt on Carlie to bring you into the line of fire so they could take you out. Why?"

"Jagged," Jake agreed. "Like someone jumped from one victim to another."

"It's just a thought," Carson continued, "but the man who hired the first assassin was on drugs."

"The man who died in the fire up in Wyoming, who was trying to kill Dalton Kirk for something he remembered," Rourke told Jake. "I mentioned it to you. The man, Richard Martin by name, was a former DEA agent, a mole who fed information to the drug cartel over in Cotillo. I'm pretty sure he hired the man who came after Carlie, to stop her from remembering what he looked like. With her photographic memory, she was giving out exact information about him. He didn't want that."

"Because he worked for Matthew Helm, a crooked politician who's just been named to the unexpired U.S. Senate seat in Texas," Carson concluded. "We know now why our computer expert Joey was killed and the computer was trashed, and why Carlie was targeted. You see, the killer had murdered an assistant D.A. in San Antonio who was investigating Helm for embezzlement and drug trafficking. He had files that mysteriously disappeared. Every bit of the evidence that could have been used against him is gone, and Lieutenant Rick Marquez of San Antonio PD told Cash Grier that two witnesses in the case have refused to testify. One just left the country, in fact."

"How convenient for Helm," Rourke commented.

"This is pretty big," Jake said, listening intently. "He didn't want his link to Helm to get out, obviously, but why kill a computer tech and try to kill Carlie?"

"Because of the watch and the shirt," Rourke said.

"Excuse me?" Jake asked, wide-eyed.

"The assistant D.A.'s wife was loaded," Carson said. "She'd just bought her husband a very expensive watch that played a song and chimed on the hour. She also bought him an exclusive, equally expensive, designer paisley shirt. Martin took a shine to both, so he stole them. He didn't want anyone to remember what he was wearing, because it linked his boss to the assistant D.A.'s murder."

Jake exchanged glances with his daughter. "You told me about this."

"Yes," Carlie said. She was deep in thought.

"What happened to the watch and the shirt?" Jake asked Carson.

"I assume whoever ransacked the room Richard

Martin was occupying at the local motel took both and destroyed them." Rourke sighed. "It would be insane to keep something so dangerous."

"The watch played a song, but nobody ever told me which song," Carlie said. She looked at Rourke.

He sang it, "I Love Rock 'n' Roll," and grinned because he was totally off-key. "It was a Joan Jett song from—"

"That's it," Carly cried. "I thought I was just reacting to the stuff he knocked me out with, so I didn't say anything. The kidnapper was wearing a cheap suit, but he had this expensive watch on his wrist. It was sort of like the one Calhoun Ballenger wears. You know, that Rolex."

"I know," Jake mused. "I told him once that he could feed a whole third-world country on the proceeds if he sold that thing. He just laughed and said it was two generations old and a family heirloom. He wouldn't sell it for the world." He glanced at Rourke. "He's going to run for that U.S. Senate seat against Helm. He told me yesterday. I ran into him in town."

"He'd be a wonderful senator," Carlie mused. "His brother Justin is dealing with the feedlot and the ranch anyway, since Calhoun's been a state senator for the past few years. He's done so much for our state…"

"He'll be a target, too," Jake said heavily.

"Yes," Carson said. "The other candidates for the temporary appointment ended up arrested on various drug charges. They swore the drugs were planted. I believe them."

"That politician needs to be taken down," Jake said shortly. "Once he has real power, he'll cause untold misery."

"I'm game," Rourke volunteered. "And since I'm officially his gofer, I have the inside track on what he's up to."

"You be careful," Jake told him.

"You know me," Rourke chuckled.

"I do. That's why I made the remark."

Carson was quiet. He was just remembering something. He didn't want to share it with the others. Lanette had excused herself at the theater the night Carlie had been kidnapped. It was a small, insignificant thing in itself and might be quite innocent. But Lanette hated Carlie. She wore expensive clothes, not the sort she could pay for on a meager salary working personnel for a company. A lot of things about her didn't quite add up.

"You're very quiet," Rourke prompted him.

"Sorry." He smiled faintly. "I was thinking about patterns." He glanced at Carlie. "The man who used the chloroform on you, he was wearing the watch?"

She nodded. "I thought I was hallucinating when it chimed. I mean, I've heard musical watches, but that was totally different."

"I'm reliably informed that the price of a new Jaguar convertible is in the same price range," Rourke commented wryly.

"The kidnapper is the connection," Carson said, frowning thoughtfully. "He can link Helm to the assistant D.A.'s murder."

"The watch by itself won't help a lot," Jake commented.

"Yes, but don't you see, the kidnapper has to be working for Matthew Helm. The fact that he has the watch connects him to Helm, through Helm's man,

Richard Martin, who killed the assistant D.A.," Carson emphasized. "It's a pattern, a chain of evidence."

"You're right!" Rourke said, drawing in a breath. "I didn't make the connection."

Carson gazed at Carlie quietly, his eyes dark and concerned. "You don't leave the house without the phone in the console of the truck, and not until it's been checked for devices," he told her.

She just nodded.

Jake hid a smile.

"Promise me," Carson added, staring her down.

She grimaced. "Okay. I promise."

Carson's gaze turned to Jake and became amused. "I've learned already that if she gives her word, she'll keep it. You just have to make sure she gives it."

Jake ruffled Carlie's hair. "That's my girl, all right." Carlie grinned.

"One of us needs to go up to San Antonio and talk to Rick Marquez," Rourke said, getting out of his chair. "This is a development he'll enjoy pursuing."

"If he needs to talk to me, I'll go up there, too," Carlie said.

"Not in the Cobra, you won't."

Jake and Carson stared at each other. They'd both said exactly the same thing at the same time, and they burst out laughing.

"Okay, okay," Carlie muttered. "If you're ganging up on me, I'll take the truck if I have to go. Just expect a call for help halfway there because my truck barely makes it to work every day. It won't make it to San Antonio without major engine failure!"

"I'll drive you," Jake told his daughter with a smile. "How's that?"

She grinned. "That's great, Dad."

"Carson, you're the best person to talk to Marquez," Rourke told the other man. "I can't be seen near anyone in law enforcement right now. You can ask if he needs a statement from Carlie," Rourke added. "But he lives in Jacobsville, you know. He could probably take a statement down here."

"I forgot. His mother is Barbara, who runs Barbara's Café," she told Carson, who looked puzzled.

"And his father-in-law runs the CIA," Jake added with a chuckle.

"Nice connections," Rourke said. He glanced at his watch. "I have to get back before Helm misses me. I'll be off, then."

"See you," Jake replied.

Rourke punched Carson on the shoulder and grinned as he walked out.

CARSON FINISHED HIS coffee. Carlie was clearing away breakfast. She glanced at Carson with her heart in her eyes. He looked at her as if she were a juicy steak and he was a starving man.

Jake turned his attention suddenly to Carson and jerked his head toward the office. Carson nodded.

"Breakfast was very good," Carson told her. "You have a way with food."

She smiled brightly. "Thanks!"

Carson followed her father into his study. "No calls for a few minutes, Carlie," Jake called before he shut the door. As an afterthought, he locked it.

Carson drew in a long breath as he studied the man across from him. Jake had been personable over breakfast, but at the moment he'd never looked less like a minister. His long, fit body was almost coiled. His pale blue eyes glittered with some inner fire.

"You're me, twenty-two years ago," Jake said without preamble. "And that child in there is my whole life. I'm seeing connections of my own," he added in a low tone. "I destroyed her mother. I'm not going to stand by and let you destroy her. She deserves better than a womanizing mercenary."

Carson sighed. He slid into a chair beside the desk where Jake sat down, and crossed his legs. "People are not what they seem to be," he began heavily. "You're thinking about the reputation I have with women. Carlie's already thrown it at me. It's why we argued the day I had to take her to the emergency room with the asthma attack."

"I thought as much," Jake replied.

"Six years ago," Carson began, "I was in the last two years of graduate school when I fell in love with a brash, outgoing, beautiful girl at a powwow on the reservation in South Dakota where I grew up. Her name was Jessica and I'd known her for years. I loved her insanely, so she married me. The first year was perfect. I thought it would never end. But my last year in college, she got tired of having me away so much at school. She took a lover. He was one of the most militant men on the reservation," he continued, his eyes cold and haunted. "He had a rap sheet, and the rez police knew him on sight. I tried to get her to come home, but she said she loved him, she wasn't coming back to a boring life as the wife of a college student. She didn't think much of higher education in the first place. So I let her go."

He shifted in the chair. "But I wouldn't give her

a divorce. I knew he was beating her. I heard it from my cousins. I talked to her on the phone, and tried to get her to press charges. She said he didn't mean it, he loved her, he'd never do it again." He met Jake's world-weary eyes. "My father gave my mother the same spiel after he beat her up, over and over again," he said coldly. "I was six years old when he hit her too hard and ran. He was prosecuted for murder and ended up in the same prison with one of my mother's brothers. He died not long after that. My uncle had nothing to lose, you see, and he loved my mother."

Jake's face was relaxing, just a little. He didn't interrupt.

"I went to live with cousins. One of my uncles, a rez cop, adopted me as his son since he had no children of his own. I was given all the necessities, but there's no substitute for loving, real parents. I missed my mother." He paused, took a breath and plowed ahead. "Jessie was pregnant and near her due date. She was living with her lover and she swore the child was his. But I had a visitor who knew one of my cousins. He said it was my child, that Jessie lied about it because she didn't want me to drag her into court for paternity tests."

He leaned forward, his eyes downcast. "I finished my last final and flew back to the rez to see her. She was alone at her house. She was afraid of me." He laughed coldly. "She said okay, it was my child, and I could see it when it was born, but she was staying with Jeff no matter what I did. I was about to tell her I'd let her get the divorce, when Jeff drove up. He stormed into the house and accused her of two-timing him. I tried to restrain him, but he blindsided me. While I was getting back up, he dragged Jessie out the door with him. I managed to get outside in time to watch him throw her into the passenger seat. She was screaming. She thought he was going to kill her. So did I."

Jake's pale eyes were riveted to him.

"So I got in my car and went after them. He saw me in the rearview mirror, I guess, because he sped up and started weaving all over the road. I didn't have a cell phone with me or I'd have called the police on the rez and had them pick him up. I followed them around the dirt roads. He started across a bridge that had been condemned. There were spring floods, huge ones, water coming right up over the wooden bridge."

He closed his eyes. "He went through the rotten boards on the side and right into the river. The car, with both of them inside, washed away." He lifted his head. His eyes were cold, dead. "They found the bodies almost two days later. The child was almost full-term, but they couldn't save him." He closed his eyes. "I graduated, joined the military, asked for combat because I wanted to die. That was almost eight years ago."

He felt a hand on his shoulder. He opened his eyes and looked into pale blue ones. "Listen, son," Jake said quietly, "you were trying to save her. In the process, a madman miscalculated his driving skills and wrecked his car. If it hadn't been that, he might have shot her and then shot himself. He might have died in a fight. She might have died from complications of childbirth. But, it would still have happened. When a life is meant to be over, it's over. That's God's business. You can't control life, Carson," he concluded.

"It's a fool's game to think you can even try. You're tormenting yourself over something that nobody could have prevented."

Carson averted his eyes. "Thanks," he said huskily.

"How did you end up with Cy?"

His eyes had a faraway look as he recalled that meeting. "I was doing black ops overseas," Carson said. "Political assassination, like Grier used to do." He drew in a long breath. "Cy and Eb Scott and Micah Steele were attached to the unit I was with as independent contractors. We went on missions together, discovered that we worked very well as a group. So I mustered out and signed on with them. It's been... interesting," he concluded with a mild laugh.

"I worked with mercs a time or two," Jake replied. He hesitated. "I also worked in covert assassination."

"I heard some gossip about that," Carson replied, without blowing the whistle on Rourke.

"She can't ever know," he said, nodding toward the other part of the house where Carlie was. "I gave it up for her. I had a crisis of conscience when her mother died. It took me to a bad place. A minister gave me the strength I needed to turn my life around, to do something productive with it." He leaned back with a sigh and a smile. "Of course, I'll starve doing it," he chuckled. "We're always broke, and there's always somebody who wants me fired because I say something offensive in a sermon. But I belong here now. Odd feeling, belonging. I never wanted it in the old days."

"Your wife," Carson said hesitantly. "Was she like Carlie?"

Jake's eyes narrowed with sorrow. "Exactly like

Carlie. I didn't believe in a damned thing. I had no faith, no understanding of how people lived in small towns. I wanted her. I took her. She got pregnant." His face was like stone. "I married her to stop gossip. Her mother was a slut. I mean, a real slut. She even tried to seduce me! So everybody locally would have said, 'like mother like daughter,' you know?" He leaned forward on his forearms. "I refused to stay here and be a tamed animal. I provided for her and the child when Carlie was born. I gave them everything except love. It wasn't until Mary was dying that I realized how much I had loved her, how much I had cost her with my indifference. You think you killed your wife? I know I killed mine. I've been trying ever since to find a way to live with it, to make up for some of the terrible things I've done. I'm still trying."

Carson was speechless. He just stared at the older man, with honest compassion.

"If you're wondering," Jake added softly, "this is a moral tale. I'm telling you about what happened to me so that you won't repeat it with my daughter. I think you have some idea of her feelings already."

Carson nodded solemnly. "I don't want to hurt her."

"That makes two of us. You've lived the way I used to. Women were like party favors to me, and I had my share…"

Carson held up a hand. "Slight misconception."

"About…?"

Carson let out a breath and laughed softly. "I pick up women. Beautiful women. I take them to the theater, the opera, out dancing, sailing on the lake, that sort of thing." He hesitated. "Then I take them home and leave them at the door," he said with a rueful smile.

Jake's confusion was evident.

"My wife was my first woman," Carson said with blunt honesty. "After she died, every woman I took out had her face, her body. I...couldn't," he choked out.

Jake put a firm hand on his shoulder, the only comfort he could offer.

"So other guys think I score every night, that I'm Don Juan." Carson laughed coolly. "I'm a counterfeit one. It makes me look heartless, so that honest women won't waste their time on me. But it backfired." He jerked his head toward the kitchen. "She thinks I'm dirty, because of my reputation. Funny thing, a visionary woman up in Wyoming told me that my past would threaten my future. She was very wise."

"Some obstacles can be overcome," Jake commented.

"So, you want me to go out and involve myself intimately with women...?"

"Shut up, or I'll put you down," Jake said in a mock growl. He laughed. "I could do it, too."

"I believe you," Carson said, with true admiration. "You haven't lost your edge."

"Where do you go from here?" Jake continued.

"When we wrap up this mess with Carlie's kidnapper, I don't know," Carson said honestly. "If I stay here, things will happen that will destroy her life, and maybe mine, too. I have to leave."

"For now, or for good?" Jake asked.

Carson drew in a breath. "I...don't know."

"If you graduated, then you got a degree, I take it?" Jake asked.

Carson pursed his lips. "Yes."

"You couldn't go into a normal profession?"

"It would mean a commitment I'm not sure I can make. I need time."

"Most life-changing decisions require it," Jake agreed. "What degree program were you pursuing?"

Carson smiled. "Medicine. I have my medical degree and I keep up my license. I just can't practice without doing the internship." He sighed. "I was going to specialize in internal medicine. I see so many heart patients with no resources, no money."

"On the reservation, you mean?"

"No. Here, in Jacobs County. I was talking to Lou Coltrain. She said they're short on physicians, not to mention physicians who specialize."

Jake searched the other man's face. He jerked his head toward the kitchen. "Going to tell her?"

Carson shook his head. "Not until I'm sure."

Jake smiled. "I knew I liked you."

Carson just laughed.

CARLIE WALKED HIM to the door. "Was Dad intimidating you?" she asked when they were outside on the front porch, with the door closed.

"No. He was listening. That's such a rare gift. Most people want to talk about themselves."

She nodded. "He's talked several people out of suicide over the years."

"He's a good man."

"He wasn't always," she replied. "I've heard a little

about his old life, although he won't tell me a thing himself." She looked up at him with raised eyebrows.

"It would be the end of my life to say a single word about it," he said firmly.

"Okay," she said, sighing.

He tilted her chin up and searched her green eyes. "What color were your mother's eyes?" he asked.

"They were brown," she said. "Like the center of a sunflower."

He traced her mouth with a long forefinger. "You're very like a sunflower yourself," he said softly. "Bright and cheerful, shining through storms."

Her lips parted on a surprised breath.

"I'm leaving, Carlie," he said softly.

She started to speak, but he put his fingers across her lips.

"You know how it is between us," he said bluntly. "I want you. If I stay here, I'll take you. And you'll let me," he said huskily.

She couldn't deny it.

"We'll be like your parents, one brokenhearted, one running away until tragedy strikes. I don't want to be the cause of that."

Her hand went up to his hard cheek. She stroked it gently, fighting tears. "You can't live a tame life. I understand."

It sounded harsh. Selfish. He scowled at the look on her face, dignity and courage mixed with heartbreak. It hurt him.

He drew her into his arms and held her, rocked her, in a tight embrace. "It wouldn't work. You know that."

She nodded against his chest.

He drew back finally and tilted her face up to his. It was streaked with hot tears that she couldn't help. He bent and kissed them away.

"I'll be around for a while," he promised. "Until we make sure we have the kidnapper in custody."

"Can they catch him, you think?"

"I believe so," he replied. "Just be careful."

She smiled. "I usually am."

"And if someone shows up and says your dad's been in a wreck…" he began.

She pulled her cell phone out of her jeans. "I'll call him up first."

He grinned. "That's my girl." He bent and brushed his mouth softly over hers, savoring the smile she couldn't help.

He left her on the porch and drove away. She stood there until she couldn't see the car anymore.

ROURKE HAD FINALLY convinced Matthew Helm that it was safe to trust him. He did a few discreet jobs— mostly by warning the people he was supposed to muscle first, and having them cooperate—and was finally handed something useful. Useful for the case against Helm, at least.

"I want you to go talk to Charro," Helm told Rourke. He pursed his lips, deep in thought. "That Ballenger man who's running against me has a fol- lowing. He's local. People know him and like him. He's got three sons. One of them, Terry, is still in high school. I want you two to find a way to plant some co- caine on him. Put it in his locker at school, in his car and tip off the cops, whatever. I don't care what you do, just make sure you do it. I'll handle the press. I'll have one of my campaign workers release the collar, to make sure it doesn't come directly from me and seem like I'm slinging mud. Got it?"

"Oh, yeah, Boss, I got it," Rourke said with a nod.

"Get going, then."

"You bet."

Rourke was too old a hand to go straight to Calhoun Ballenger or even to Cash Grier's office, much less up to San Antonio to see Rick Marquez. He wasn't trusting his cell phone, either, because Helm could very easily find out who he'd talked to recently.

So he went to Cotillo.

Charro Mendez gave him a careful scrutiny. "So Helm trusts you, does he?" he asked.

"He doesn't really trust anybody," Rourke replied. "Neither do I," he added, hands in his jeans pockets. "It doesn't pay, in this line of work. But he trusts me enough to relay messages, I believe."

"And what message does he wish you to bring me?" Mendez asked, propping his booted feet on his own desk in the mayor's office.

"He wants some product planted in a particular place," he replied, leaning back against the wall.

"Ah. Something to do with a rival in the political arena, *si?*"

"Exactly."

"This is not a problem. Who does he expect to perform this task, *señor,* you or me?"

"He didn't say," Rourke replied. "He told me you'd supply the product. I assume that means I'll have to plant it."

"I see." The man grinned, displaying gold-filled teeth. "I would assume that he would not expect a man in my position to perform such a menial chore, however."

"Exactly," Rourke said, nodding.

"Excellent! I will have the...product," he said, "delivered to you across the border. When?"

"He didn't tell me that, either. But it would be convenient to do two Saturdays from now," Rourke continued. "There's going to be a dance at the high school. I can sneak it into the glove compartment of the boy's vehicle while he's inside the building."

"I could almost feel sorry for his father. I also have sons." His face darkened. "I would kill someone who did that to me. But these rich men in Texas—" he waved a hand "—they can buy justice. I have no doubt the politician can have the charges dropped. The publicity, however, will be very damaging I think."

"I agree."

"Give me a cell phone number where my man can reach you," Charro said.

Rourke handed him a slip of paper. "It's a throwaway phone," he told the other man. "I'll answer it this once and then toss it in a trash bin somewhere. It will never be found or traced to me."

"A wise precaution."

"I try to be wise, always," Rourke replied.

"Then we agree. I will have my man contact you within the week."

"I'm certain my boss will express his appreciation for your help."

"Indeed he will," Charro returned thoughtfully. "Many, many times, whenever I ask." He smiled coldly. "I will have him, how do you say? Over a barrel."

"A big one," Rourke chuckled.

"Very big. Yes."

CHAPTER TWELVE

ROURKE COULDN'T RISK being seen with any law enforcement official, or overheard talking to one, not with things at this critical juncture. He called Carson.

"Have you been to see Marquez yet?" he asked quickly.

"Well, no," Carson replied. "Something came up over at Cy's ranch…"

"This is urgent. I want you to go see Marquez right now. I've got some news."

So Carson drove up to San Antonio to relay the information Rourke had transferred over to another throwaway phone, a pair he and Carson had arranged at an earlier time.

Rick Marquez did a double take when he saw Carson. The other man was almost his age, with the same olive complexion and long, black hair in a ponytail.

"Lieutenant Marquez?" Carson greeted the other man when the clerk showed him in.

"That would be me. Amazing," Rick mused. "We could almost be twins."

Carson smiled faintly. "Only if you turned out to be from South Dakota."

He shrugged. "Sorry. Mexico. Well, that's where my father was born. He's now president of a small

Latin American nation. Sit down." He offered his visitor a chair.

"I assume you have regular checks for bugs in here?" Carson asked, glancing around.

"My father-in-law runs the CIA," Rick told him as he dropped into his aging desk chair. "He might bug us, but nobody else would dare. What can I do for you?"

"There have been some new developments that you might not have heard about," Carson began.

"Jake Blair's daughter was kidnapped, you and her father freed her and took out two guards, the kidnapper got away," Rick rattled off. "I know everything."

"Not quite," Carson replied. He pursed his lips. "How about coffee?"

"We've got a pot right over there…"

Carson shook his head. "Real coffee. Come on."

Rick was puzzled, but he caught on pretty quickly that Carson didn't trust telling him in the office.

They drove to a specialty coffee shop and moved to a corner table.

"Sorry, I know you think it's secure in your office, but this information could get Rourke killed if it slips out somehow. He's working for Matthew Helm and there's a plot underway. But let me tell you this first. Carlie Blair's kidnapper was wearing a watch. An expensive watch that chimed an old Joan Jett rock tune—"

"You're kidding!" Rick exploded. "We thought the watch burned up with the man who was wearing it, in Wyoming!"

"No," Carson replied. "I was there when he died. There was no watch on him. The local police were trying to backtrack him to any motels he'd stayed at. I assume his boss's men got to the room first."

"What a stroke of luck," Rick said with a short laugh. "That watch, if we can get our hands on it, is the key to a murder and perhaps the end of a truly evil political career."

"The problem is that we don't know where the watch is. The kidnapper has vanished into thin air."

"We have to find him."

"I agree. Rourke's working on it. He's wormed his way into the political process. That's why I'm here."

"Okay. Shoot."

"Helm sent Rourke over the border today to arrange for the delivery of some cocaine. Enough to charge someone with intent to distribute. The idea is for Rourke to plant it in the glove compartment of Calhoun Ballenger's youngest son, Terry, at a school dance in two weeks."

Rick's face hardened. "What a low-down, dirty, mean…"

"All of the above," Carson agreed grimly. "But we know it's going down, and when, and where. Believe me, this is going to send Helm up the river. All we have to do is set a trap and spring it."

"Why isn't Rourke here?" Rick asked.

"Because he's being watched, and probably listened to, as well. We used throwaway phones to communicate, just to exchange this much information."

"And you think my own office isn't secure?" Rick sounded a little belligerent.

"This man has ex-cops working for him," Carson explained. "They'll know all the tricks. It isn't far-fetched to assume he has a pipeline into your office. The missing evidence the assistant D.A. had on Helm, for example, that was destroyed right here in impound?"

Rick let out a heavy sigh. "I get your point. I've been careless."

"Don't sell yourself short. Helm has some pros on his team. His main enforcer is gone, but he's got others. One is an ex-cop who got fired for using excessive violence. Carlie's kidnapper. He knocked a perp down the stairs when he caught him beating a child."

"Know where?" Rick asked suddenly.

"Carlie said the kidnapper had an accent, like you hear in those old gangster movies of the '30s and '40s."

"Chicago, maybe, New Jersey, New York…" Rick's eyes were thoughtful. "I can send out some feelers to people I know in departments there, ask around. Some of the veterans might remember something."

"Good idea. Meanwhile, Rourke's on the job."

"Should we warn Calhoun Ballenger?" Rick wondered aloud.

"If he knows, he'll warn his son, and his son might mention it to a classmate," Carson replied. "It's better to keep him in the dark. We'll make sure his son is watched and protected."

"Don't toss any hand grenades around," Rick warned.

Carson sighed as he stood up. "My past will haunt me."

"Actually, if it was up to me, you'd get a medal," Rick said. "So many dead kids because rich men want to make a profit off illegal drugs." He shook his head. "Crazy world."

"Getting crazier all the time."

"Thanks for the heads-up," Rick said, shaking hands with the other man. "By the way," he added, "nice hairstyle." He grinned. Carson grinned back.

FRED BALDWIN WAS WORRIED. Mr. Helm had promised that he was going to protect him, that he was in no danger of getting arrested for kidnapping Carlie Blair. But he knew from painful experience that Mr. Helm didn't keep many of the promises he made. That was, unless he promised to get you for crossing him. He kept all those promises.

He fingered the expensive watch that he still had, that Mr. Helm didn't know about. He knew why the watch was important. It had belonged to Richard Martin, who burned up in Wyoming after trying to kill two women. He'd killed an assistant prosecutor for that watch. But Martin was dead. And Fred had the watch.

Mr. Helm didn't know that he hadn't destroyed it. He liked the watch. That chime it sounded wasn't a song he knew, but it was okay. It was the two-tone gold on the timepiece, very expensive, and that made him feel good. His father had been a low-level worker at an automobile plant in Detroit. His mother had kept a day care in their home. There were four kids and never enough money. His father drank it up as fast as he got paid.

Two of his brothers were in jail. His oldest brother had died last year. His mother had finally left his father, and went to live with a sister in California. He hadn't heard from her in a long time. She'd loved her oldest child best, the one who died. She hadn't wanted the others. She thought they were too stupid to be her kids. She said so, often.

The only time she'd liked Fred was when he became a policeman. Finally, one of her kids besides her favorite might actually amount to something.

Then he got arrested and fired and she turned her back on him. Well, it was no surprise.

Fred didn't like women much. His mother was cold as ice, heartless. Maybe his father had made her that way. Maybe she was that way to begin with.

He liked that little woman he'd kidnapped, though. She should have hated him. He'd terrified her. But she'd been sorry for him when he told her about his father beating him up. He felt bad that he'd scared her. He was glad to know she'd escaped, that her father hadn't been killed.

Luckily for him, the two would-be assassins got blamed for the screwup. Mr. Helm hadn't hired them in person, so he wouldn't be connected with them.

On the other hand, Fred had hired them for the person who was contracted by Richard Martin to kill Reverend Blair, on Mr. Helm's orders. If they talked, Fred was going to be the one who'd go to prison.

Well, that little woman knew what he looked like, and he had no reason to believe she wouldn't have told the law about him. He knew from something Mr. Helm had let slip once that Carlie Blair had a photographic memory. Mr. Helm said not to worry about it, that he'd make sure Fred was okay. But Fred had seen what had happened to the man Richard Martin had hired to kill Carlie Blair, the same woman he'd kidnapped. Martin had poisoned the would-be killer, right under the cops' noses, and apparently on Mr. Helm's orders.

Funny, that he'd been ordered to kidnap Carlie, when Richard Martin had been ordered to hire somebody to kill her. Not only that, when the first killer failed, Martin had hired someone else to finish the job. But the person he was taking orders from had sent him to kidnap Carlie to draw the reverend out to be killed.

Why did Mr. Helm want the preacher dead? As far as Fred knew, the preacher didn't have anything on Mr. Helm at all. And what Carlie knew didn't matter before, because she remembered Richard Martin and he was dead.

She'd remember Fred now, though. That would be a motive. But they were trying to kill her father!

Well, his opinion was that Richard Martin had been so high on drugs that he hadn't made it clear who was supposed to be the victim. And his hire, to put it politely, was as crazy a person as Fred had ever met. He'd been sent to kidnap Carlie on that person's orders, to strike at a time when she was unprotected at her home. He shook his head. It was nuts. Worse, he was the one who was being set up to take the fall.

He looked at the watch again. He'd never been tempted to talk about it. But after what he'd just overheard Mr. Helm say to his new enforcer, that South African guy, he had to do something. The South African man was going to plant drugs on the son of a politician who was the only serious contender for the U.S. Senate seat. If the man had been a stranger, he might not have cared. But Fred knew Calhoun Ballenger.

He'd seen the cattleman a few months ago, coming out of a downtown hotel where some cattlemen's conference was being held. Two men were waiting in the shadows. One of them was armed. When Mr. Ballenger started down the street, they jumped him.

He was a big man, and he handled himself well, but the man with the gun struck him in the head.

Fred didn't like bullies. He'd never been one, for all his size, and he hated seeing anybody pick on an unarmed man. It was why he'd become a cop in the first place years ago. So without really thinking about it, he jumped in, subdued the man with the pistol and knocked out his accomplice.

He'd left them in the alley and dropped a dime on them while he took Mr. Ballenger down the street to the emergency room of a local hospital.

He didn't dare tell the cattleman who he was, but Mr. Ballenger had wanted to do something for him, to pay him back for the kindness. He'd looked at Fred with admiration, with respect. Those were things sadly lacking in his life. It had made him feel good about himself for the first time in years. He'd waved away the older man's thanks and left the hospital without identifying himself.

Mr. Ballenger's son was going to be targeted by Matthew Helm, and Fred didn't want to be any part of it. But how was he going to warn the man without incriminating himself and his boss? Mr. Helm would turn on him, make sure he went to prison for the kidnapping if he lifted a finger.

He couldn't go to the law, as much as he'd have liked to. But there was one other possibility. This watch was important. The right people could do good things with it. And suddenly, right in front of him, was the very girl he'd kidnapped…

CARLIE WAS PUTTING her groceries into the back of the pickup truck when she came face-to-face with the man who'd kidnapped her.

"Don't scream," Fred said gruffly, but he didn't threaten her. He was wearing a raincoat and a hat, looking around cautiously. "You got to help me."

"Help you? You kidnapped me!" she blurted out.

"Yeah, I'm sorry," he said heavily. "I got in over my head and I can't get out. I can't go to the law. They're always watching. Mr. Helm is going to plant drugs on Mr. Ballenger's youngest son," he said hastily, peering over the truck bed to make sure nobody was nearby. "He's going to try to get him out of that Senate race."

"Terry?" she exclaimed. "He's going to try to set Terry Ballenger up?"

"Yeah. That South African guy who works for him, he's going to plant the evidence," he said quickly. "You got to tell your boss."

She was absolutely dumbfounded. She couldn't even find words. He didn't know that Rourke was working with the authorities and she didn't dare tell him. But he was risking his very life to try and save Calhoun's son from prosecution. It really touched her.

His dark eyes narrowed. "I'm so sorry for what I done," he said, grimacing. "You're a nice girl."

Her face softened. "Why do you work for that rat?" she wondered.

"He's got stuff on me," he explained. "I can't ever get another job. But I can help you." He took off the watch, looked at it admiringly for just a few seconds and grimaced. "Never had nothing so fancy in my whole life," he said, putting it in her hands. "He told me to bust it up and throw it away. I couldn't. It was so special. Anyway, that watch belonged to some prosecutor that had evidence on Mr. Helm. Richard Martin killed him. It was his watch. Martin took the watch and then killed people who remembered he had it."

"He tried to have me killed," she told him.

"Yeah, and then he hired somebody to kill your dad." He shook his head. "See, Martin was high on drugs, out of his mind. I think he got confused, gave the contract out on the wrong person. I think it was supposed to be you, again, but we got sent after your dad."

"You know who's behind it," she said, surprised.

He nodded solemnly. "Mr. Helm's behind it. But the contract was given out by Martin."

"Who's got it?" Carlie asked. "Please?"

He searched her eyes. "Some pretty blond woman up in San Antonio. I didn't know until a day ago. Funny, she didn't even know about my connection to Mr. Helm. She asked around for some muscle to help with a hit, and the other guys got hired. One of them was a man I knew, he said I could do it on the side and Mr. Helm would never have to know." He laughed coldly. "Well, Mr. Helm knew already. He just didn't tell us."

"Blond woman…?"

"Yeah. She used to work for Mr. Helm, years ago, when he started out in the local rackets."

Blond woman. Hit woman. Contract killer. Somebody who knew that Carlie would be home alone on that Friday night. Somebody with ties to Jacobsville.

"Do you know her name?" Carlie asked.

He frowned. "Funny name. La...La...something."

Carlie's blood froze. "Lanette?"

"Yeah. That's it. How'd you know?"

Now wasn't the time to fill him in on personal information. But it meant that Carson could be in real danger if Lanette suspected that he might blow her cover. She'd be in jeopardy if her link to the kidnapper here was ever found out.

She slid the watch into her pocket, gnawed her lower lip. She looked up into his broad, swarthy face. "They'll kill you if they find out you gave me the watch."

His dark eyes were quiet and sad. "I don't care," he said. "I never done anything good in my whole life except for being a cop, and I even fouled that up. You were nice to me." He forced a smile. "Nobody ever liked me."

She put a small hand on his arm. "How do you feel about small towns?"

He frowned. "What do you mean?"

"You have to trust me," she said quickly.

"Why?"

"Because I'm going to do something that will seem crazy."

"Really? What?"

She threw back her head and screamed.

"JUST RELAX," CASH GRIER told his prisoner under his breath. "This isn't what it seems. You may think she

sold you out, but we're trying to save you. Your boss
will think you're being arrested for assault."

Fred Baldwin went along, stunned but willing to
cooperate on the off chance that he might not have to
spend his whole life in federal prison. "Okay, Boss,"
he said. "It's your play."

Cash marched him out to the police car, put Carlie
in front beside him, and left a patrolman to take her
truck home and explain things to her father.

ONCE THEY WERE in the police station, Cash took Fred
into his office and removed the handcuffs. He put
Fred's automatic in his desk drawer and locked it.
Carlie produced the watch out of her pocket.

"And I've got you filing," Cash said, shaking his
head at her. "You should be wearing a badge, kid."

"No, no," she protested. "He—" she pointed at
Fred "—just turned state's evidence. So to speak. He
can make the connections. But we have to get word
to Carson," she added quickly. "His girlfriend is the
woman who hired Fred and the other two guys to
kidnap me and kill my dad."

"Why did you give Carlie the watch?" Cash asked
Fred. "You had everything to lose!"

"She was nice to me," he murmured, glancing at
Carlie. "They tried to kill her dad, with my help. And
now they're trying to frame Mr. Ballenger's son. I
took down two hoods who jumped him in San Antonio. Never seen a rich man so grateful for just a little
help. I liked him. It's not right, to punish a man's son
because the father's just doing something good for
the community. I got tired of being on the wrong side
of the law, I guess. I thought if I gave her the watch,

she'd give it to you and maybe you could stop Mr. Helm before he hurts somebody else."

"I'll stop it, all right," Cash said. He frowned. "But it's suicide on your part. You think Helm wouldn't know who gave us the watch?"

Fred smiled sadly. "I ain't got no place to go, nobody who cares about me. I thought, maybe I could do one good thing before he took me out."

"You're not going anywhere," Cash told him firmly.

"And you do have somebody who cares about you," Carlie said firmly. She took the big man's hand in her own and held it. "Right here."

Incredibly, tears ran down his wide cheeks.

"Now, don't do that, you'll have me doing it, too," Carlie muttered. She pulled a tissue out of her pocket and wiped his eyes and then wiped her own.

"I'm Italian," Fred muttered, embarrassed. "We don't hide what we feel."

"You'd better let me get this on paper," Cash said, smiling. "Coffee?"

"Thanks."

"I'll make a pot," Carlie said. She glanced at Cash. "Carson…" she began.

"I'm two steps ahead of you," Cash promised, picking up the telephone.

CARSON HAD HIS phone turned off, which was a pity. Lanette had already heard from an informant that Fred Baldwin was in custody down in Jacobsville, Texas, for apparently confronting that pitiful little secretary that Carson was so crazy about.

She was livid. Fred was stupid. It was why she'd

hired him, because he was expendable and too dumb to realize she was setting him up to take the fall for her when she killed Jake Blair.

But somewhere along the line, he'd had a flash of genius. He was probably spilling his guts. They'd be after her in a heartbeat. That little secretary would be gloating, laughing, feeling so superior to the beautiful woman who was obviously her superior in every single department.

Fred had flubbed his assignment. His cohorts were in jail. Now he'd been arrested, too. She'd been paid for a job that she hadn't completed. Word would get around that she was incompetent. She'd never get another contract. Worse, Fred would implicate her to save himself. She'd be running from the law for the rest of her life. The perks of her profession, all that nice money, her spectacular wardrobe, everything would be lost because her own plan had backfired on her.

Even Matthew Helm had refused to help her. Oh, he made promises, but his back was to the wall right now, and he was trying to save his own skin. He had to know that Fred would rat on him.

Well, she reasoned, at least she was going to have one bit of satisfaction on the run. That stupid little hick in Jacobsville wasn't going to get to gloat. Her feelings for Carson were so apparent that a blind woman could see them. Carlie loved Carson. So Lanette would go to prison for kidnapping and assault and conspiracy, and little Carlie would end up with Carson.

No way. If she lost Carson, for whom she had a

real unrequited passion, Carlie wasn't going to have him. She'd make sure of it.

She reached into the purse she carried to make sure the automatic was where it was supposed to be.

"I can't stay long," she told Carson, who was impatient to be gone and seemed surprised and irritated to have found her at his apartment door when he arrived.

"Just as well," he said curtly, "because I have someplace to go and I'm already late."

"Couldn't we have just one cup of coffee first?" she asked, smiling softly. "I found out something about that attempt on the preacher."

"You did? How?" he asked, instantly suspicious.

"Well, let's just sit down and talk, and I'll tell you what I know," she purred.

CASH PHONED ROURKE, using the number Rourke had sent him. "Carson's in danger," he told the other man. "His blond girlfriend is the contract killer Richard Martin hired to take out Reverend Blair."

"What!" Rourke exploded.

"I don't have time to go into the particulars," Cash said. "Suffice it to say I have a witness," he glanced at Fred, who was smiling as Carlie handed him a mug of black coffee, "and no time to discuss it. Do you know where he is?"

"At the apartment he rented," Rourke said, shell-shocked. "In San Antonio."

"Can you get in touch with him?"

Rourke let out a breath. "No. Not unless I do it in the open."

"Rourke will have to blow his cover to call Carson, they're monitoring his phone," Cash said aloud.

"I'll do it," Carlie said urgently. "Give me the number."

"Rourke, give me the number," Cash said.

He did. Cash scribbled it down and handed it to Carlie.

"What's this written in, Sanskrit?" she exclaimed.

Cash glared at her, took it back and made modifications. "It's just numbers, for God's sake," he said irritably

"Sir, your handwriting is hands-down, without a doubt, the worst I ever saw in my life," she muttered as she pushed numbers into her cell phone.

"Hear, hear!" Rourke said over the phone. "I have to go. I'll let you know about Ballenger's son as soon as I have word." He hung up.

Carlie held her breath as the phone rang once, twice, three times...

"Hello?"

Carlie recognized the voice. It wasn't Carson's. It was hers. Lanette's.

She swallowed, hard. "I want to speak to Carson," she said.

"Oh, do you? I'm sorry," Lanette said in a silky sweet tone. "I'm afraid he's indisposed at the moment. Really indisposed." She laughed out loud. "I can't have him. But, now, neither can you, you little backward country hick! And you can spend hours, days, just watching him die!" She cut off the connection.

"She's with him," Carlie said with an economy of words. "You have to get someone to him, quick!"

Cash was already punching in numbers.

While her boss worked to get a medical team

to Carson, Carlie hovered, tears running down her cheeks.

"You sit down," Fred said softly. "They'll get there in time. It will be all right. Everything will be all right."

She just looked at him, her face that of a terrified child. It hit him in the heart so hard that he let out a breath, as if it had been a blow to his stomach.

He put down his coffee, got up, picked her up and sat down with her in his lap, wrapped up in his big arms, sobbing her heart out on his broad shoulder. He patted her back as if she were five years old, smiling. "It's okay, honey," he said softly. "It's okay."

Cash watched them and mentally shook his head. What a waste. That man had a heart as big as the world, and he was going to take the fall for that crooked politician unless Cash could find him a way out. That might just be possible. But first he had to save Carson. And that mission had a less hopeful outcome.

THE PARAMEDICS HAD to wait while San Antonio PD broke down a door to get inside, on Lieutenant Marquez's orders. Once the way was clear, they rushed in with a gurney. They found Carson in the kitchen, facedown on the floor. He was unconscious and bleeding from a wound in his chest. There was a lump on his head, as well.

One paramedic looked at the other and winced. This was not going to be an easy run. He keyed his mike and started relaying medical information. It was complicated by the fact that the victim apparently had no ID on him.

BECAUSE FRED BALDWIN could make all the right connections to Matthew Helm, and because they knew about the fate of the former failed hit man, Cash Grier refused to turn him over to the authorities in San Antonio, where Helm would have to be arrested and tried.

"You'll get him over my dead body," Cash assured Rick Marquez on the telephone. "I'm not risking his life. He's too valuable. You come down here and take a deposition, bring all the suits you need and add your district attorney to the list. I'll give you free access. But he is not, under any circumstances, leaving Jacobsville!"

Rick drew in a breath. "Cash, you're putting me in a tough spot."

"No, I'm not. My cousin is still the state attorney general. He'll pull some strings for me if I ask him," Cash added. "Besides that," he said with a whimsical smile, "I have a few important connections that I don't talk about."

"You and my father-in-law would get along," Marquez chuckled. "All right. I'll get the process started. But I'm going to need that watch."

"No way in hell," Cash said pleasantly.

"It's state's evidence!"

"Yes, it is. And evidence doesn't walk out of *my* property room," he added, emphasizing the "my."

"Rub it in," Rick muttered. "Carson already did, in fact." He sobered. "They have him in intensive care."

"I know. My secretary is up there with him. Or as close as she can get," Cash said heavily.

"So I heard. She's parked in the corridor next to the emergency room surgical suite and won't move."

"Stubborn."

"Yes, and very much in love, apparently," Rick replied solemnly. "It won't end well. I know the type, and so do you. Even if he makes it out of the hospital, he'll never settle down."

"Are you a betting man?" Cash mused.

"Why?"

"Because several years ago, you'd have laid better odds that I'd never marry and live in a small Texas town. Wouldn't you?"

Rick laughed. "Point taken." He hesitated. "Well, can we at least see the watch and photograph it?"

"Mi casa es su casa," Cash said smugly. "My house is your house."

"I'll bring an SUV full of people down. May I assume that the state crime lab has already dusted the watch for prints?"

"Our own Alice Jones Fowler did the job herself. She does still work as an investigator for state crime," Cash reminded him, "although she lives here with her husband, Harley, on their ranch. She's not only good, she's unforgettable."

"Nobody who ever met Alice would forget her," Rick agreed. "She even makes autopsies bearable."

"No argument there. Anyway, the watch is adequately documented, even for a rabid prosecutor. And you're going to need the best you've got for Helm," he added quietly. "The man is a maniac, and I don't mean that kindly. He'll sacrifice anybody to save himself. Even assistant district attorneys."

"You don't know how much I'd love to tie him to

that murder," Rick said. "The watch is the key to it all. Good luck for us that it wasn't destroyed."

"Even better luck that the man wearing it decided to also turn state's evidence. He can put Helm away for life."

"You've got him in the county jail, I hope?"

Cash hesitated. "Someplace a little safer."

"Safer than the lockup?" Rick burst out laughing. "What, is he living with you and Tippy and Tris?"

"Let's just say that he's got unique company. I'll give you access with the D.A. when you get down here."

"This is going to be an interesting trip," Rick predicted. "See you soon."

"Copy that."

THE HOSPITAL WAS very clean. Carlie noted that the floors must be mopped frequently, because when she got up to use the ladies' room, the back of her jeans didn't even have dust. She knew she was irritating the staff. Security had talked to her once. But she refused to move. They could throw her out, but that was the only way she was leaving. Her heart was in that intensive care emergency surgery unit, strapped to machines and tubes, fighting for his life. They could put her in jail, after, she didn't care. But she wasn't moving until they could assure her that Carson would live. And she told them so.

CHAPTER THIRTEEN

THE NEUROLOGIST ON Carson's case, Dr. Howard Deneth, paused at the nurses' station in ICU, where they'd taken Carson an hour ago, and glanced toward the cubicle where Carson was placed.

"She's still there?" he mused.

The nurse nodded. "She won't leave. The nurses called security, but she said they'd have to drag her out. She wasn't belligerent. She just stared them down, with tears rolling down her cheeks the whole time."

"Unusual in these days, devotion like that," the doctor remarked. "Are they married?"

"Not that we know. Of course, we don't know much, except what she was able to tell us. He doesn't carry identification."

"I noticed. Some sort of covert work, I imagine, classified stuff."

"That's what we thought."

Dr. Deneth looked down at the nurse over his glasses. "He's deteriorating," he said heavily. "The wound was superficial. There was minor head trauma, but really not enough to account for his condition. However, head injuries are tricky. Sometimes even minor ones can end fatally." He pursed his lips. "Let her in the room."

"Sir?"

"On my authority," he added. "I'll write it on the chart, in case you have any flak from upper echelons. They can talk to me if they don't like it."

The nurse didn't speak. She just smiled.

CARLIE HELD HIS HAND. She'd been shocked when the nurse came to tell her that she could have a comfortable chair beside Carson's bed. One of the other nurses had been curt to the point of rudeness when she tried to make Carlie leave the hall.

She guessed that nurses were like policemen. Some were kindhearted and personable, and some were rigorously by-the-book. She worked for a policeman who'd thrown the book away when he took the job. He believed in the rule of law, but he wasn't a fanatic for the letter of it. Case in point was big Fred Baldwin, who was now living in a safe but undisclosed location, so that he didn't end up dead before he could testify against his former boss.

No arrests had been made yet, that she was aware of. She did know that they had an all points bulletin out for the blond woman who'd left Carson in this condition. She really hoped the woman resisted arrest, and then she bit her tongue and said a silent apology. That wasn't really a wish that a religious person should make.

Her father had come to see Carson a few minutes ago. The nurses had at least let him into the room. But when he came out he was somber and although he tried to get Carlie to come home, he understood why she wouldn't. He'd done the same when her mother was in the hospital dying. He'd refused to leave, too.

Carlie supposed he'd seen cases like Carson's many times. Judging by the look on his face, the results had been fatal. He reminded Carlie that God's will had precedence over man's desires. He wanted to stay with his daughter, but she reminded him that having two people in the corridor to trip over would probably be the straw that broke the camel's back for the nursing staff. He went home, leaving Carlie's cell phone—which she'd forgotten—with her so that she could keep him posted.

Unknown to her, one of Rourke's buddies was nearby, posing as a family member in the intensive care waiting room. Just in case Helm had any ideas about hurting Carlie. It was a long shot, but nobody wanted to leave anything to chance.

Meanwhile, the forces of good were coalescing against Matthew Helm. He knew they had Baldwin in custody, and the man was probably spilling his guts. But his attorney could take Baldwin apart on the stand. The man had a criminal record, which is how he was pressured into taking Helm's jobs in the first place. He had a conviction for assault when he was a cop in Chicago. That could be used against his testimony.

After all, Helm's hands were clean. He'd never broken the law. They might have Baldwin and a lot of hearsay evidence, but there was nothing that could connect him to the murder of the assistant D.A. He'd made sure of it.

So now he was free of that worry, and he could concentrate on the Senate race. He was in Washington, D.C., of course, learning his way around, making contacts, making use of all the connections that

Charro Mendez had in the country's capital. He liked the power. He liked the privilege. He liked bumping elbows at cocktail parties with famous people. Yes, he was going to enjoy this job, and nobody was taking it away from him in that special election in May!

What he didn't know was that Fred, like Carlie, had an excellent memory for dates and places. With it, the authorities could check telephone records, check stubs, gas receipts, restaurant tickets, even motel logs to see where Helm was at particular times and with particular people. They could now connect him directly to the assistant district attorney's murder through Richard Martin because of the theft of the watch. It went from the assistant D.A.'s body to Richard Martin, who worked for Helm, to Fred Baldwin whom Helm had sent to retrieve it, right back to Helm himself.

The San Antonio D.A.'s office put together a network, a framework, that they were going to use to hang Matthew Helm from. The watch was going to put Helm away for a very long time. Added to Baldwin's testimony, it would be the trial of the century. It had all the elements: intrigue, murder, politics, kidnapping—it was almost a catalog of the deadly sins. And now, with Rourke ordered to set up Calhoun Ballenger's youngest son—with cocaine provided by Charro Mendez—a concrete link between the two men had been formed. The trap was about to spring shut.

Fred had been kept in the dark about Rourke's true allegiance. What he didn't know, he couldn't accidentally let slip.

"TONIGHT'S THE NIGHT," Rourke told Cash Grier on a secure line. "Seven o'clock. Helm himself ordered the plant and I have it on tape."

"Sheer genius," Cash announced. "We're going to catch you in the act." He groaned. "Calhoun Ballenger is going to use me for a mop when he finds out that his son was the bait."

"I'll save you," Rourke promised. "But it's what we need to make the case."

"Good thing we spoke to Blake Kemp about this before you agreed to do it," Cash added.

"Yes, the Jacobs County D.A. should be in on such matters. Just to keep yours truly out of the slammer," Rourke chuckled. "Don't be late, okay? I'm not absolutely sure that Helm won't assign backup in case I get cold feet or he suspects I'm not reliable."

"No worries. We've got one of Eb Scott's men watching you, and one with Carlie up in San Antonio."

"How is he?" Rourke asked.

"No change," Cash said heavily. "Well, one change. They finally let Carlie into the room with him."

"Probably because they got tired of tripping over her in the hall," Rourke remarked. "Stubborn girl."

"Very." Cash's voice lowered. "It doesn't look good. Head injuries...well, you know."

"Any luck turning up that deadly blonde?" Rourke added coldly.

"Not yet, but I'm told they have a lead. She ordered the kidnapping. That's a federal offense. It means my brother gets involved." There was real pride in his tone. "Nobody gets away from Garon."

"Maybe they'll hit her over the head and shoot her while she's lying helpless," Rourke said icily.

"In real life, it doesn't go down like that." Cash sighed. "Pity."

"Yeah. Okay, I'll see you later."

"Be careful," Cash cautioned.

"Always."

CARLIE HELD CARSON'S hand tightly in both of her small ones. He had beautiful hands, the skin smooth and firm, the nails immaculately clean and neatly trimmed. No jewelry. No marks where jewelry might ever have been. She remembered the feel of his hands on her skin, the tenderness, the strength of them. It seemed like an age ago.

The neurosurgeon had come in to check Carson's eyes, and how his pupils reacted to light. He was kind to Carlie, telling her that sometimes it took a little time for a patient to regain consciousness after a blow like the one Carson had sustained. If they were lucky, there wouldn't be too much impairment afterward. He didn't add that the head trauma didn't seem damaging enough to account for the continued unconsciousness. That bothered him.

The head trauma being the predominant condition, Carson was in the ICU on the neurological ward. The gunshot injury, by comparison, was far less dangerous and had a better prognosis. That damage had been quickly repaired by the trauma surgeon.

She only half heard him. She wanted him to tell her that Carson would wake up and get up and be all right. The doctor couldn't do that. Even he, with his long experience, had no guarantees. At the moment, they weren't certain why he was still unconscious.

Carson had been in shock when they transported him, but now he was still breathing well on his own, his levels were good, BP was satisfactory. In fact, he should be awake and aware. But he wasn't. They'd done a CT scan in the emergency room. It did not show extensive brain injury. There was some minor bruising, but nothing that should account for the continued unconsciousness.

Blood had been sent to the lab for analysis, but it was a busy day and a few patients in far worse shape were in the queue ahead of him.

The doctor asked, again, if Carson had any next of kin in the area. She shook her head. Carson was from the Wapiti Ridge Sioux Reservation in South Dakota, but she didn't know anything about that part of his life. Neither did anybody else locally.

He suggested that it might be wise to contact the authorities there and inquire about relatives who might know more about his health history. So Carlie phoned Cash Grier and asked him to do it. She was too upset to talk to anyone. His medical history would certainly be useful, but he was fighting for his life from a set of circumstances other than illness. She prayed and prayed. Please let him live, she asked reverently, even if he married some pretty sweet young woman from his hometown and Carlie never saw him again.

She whispered it while she was holding Carson's hand. Whispered it over and over again while tears ran hot and salty down her pale cheeks.

"You just can't die," she choked, squeezing his

hand very hard. "Not like this. Not because of that sick, stupid, beautiful blond female pit viper!" She swallowed, wiping tears away with the tips of her fingers. "Listen, you can go home and marry some nice, experienced girl who'll be everything you want, and it will be all right. I want you to be happy. I want you to live!" She sniffed. "I know I'm not what you need. I've always known it. I'm not asking for anything at all. I just want you to live until you're old and gray-headed and have a houseful of kids and grandkids." She managed a smile. "You can tell them stories about now, about all the exotic places you went, the things you saw and did. You'll be a local legend."

He shifted. Her heart jumped. For an instant she thought he might be regaining consciousness. But he made a soft sound and began to breathe more deeply. Her hands tightened around his. "You just have to live," she whispered. "You have to."

While she was whispering to him, the door opened and a woman with jet-black hair and black eyes came into the room. She was wearing a white jacket and had a stethoscope around her neck. She glanced at Carlie and smiled gently.

"No change, huh?" she asked softly.

Carlie swallowed. Her eyes were bloodshot. She shook her head.

The newcomer took something out of her pocket and removed Carlie's hand, just for a few seconds, long enough to press a small braided circle with a cross inside into Carson's palm.

"What is it?" Carlie asked in a whisper. "It looks like a prayer wheel…and those are Lakota colors…"

"You know that?" the visitor asked, and the smile

grew bigger. "It is a prayer wheel. Those are our colors," she added. "Red and yellow, black and white, the colors of the four directions."

"It may be just what he needs," Carlie replied, folding his hand back inside both of hers, with the prayer circle inside it. "Are you a *wicasa wakan?*" she added, her eyes wide with curiosity as she referenced a holy person in the tribe who could heal the sick.

"A *wasichu,* and you know that?" she laughed, using the Lakota word that referred to anyone outside the tribe. She grinned from ear to ear. "No. I'm not. But my grandfather is. He still lives on the rez in Wapiti Ridge Sioux Reservation. It's where I'm from. Somebody called the rez to find a relative who knew him, so my cousin answered their questions and then he called me. We've got family all over," she added with a twinkle in her eyes. "Even in South Texas."

Carlie smiled. "Nice to know. It's like where I live, in Comanche Wells. I know everybody, and everybody knows my family for generations."

She nodded. "It's that way back home, too." She looked at Carson. "Cousin Bob Tail is praying for him. Now he is a *wicasa wakan,*" she added.

"I believe in prayer," Carlie replied, looking back at Carson. "I think God comes in all colors and races and belief systems."

The visitor laid a hand on her shoulder and leaned down. "Cousin Bob Tail says he's going to wake up soon." She stood up and chuckled. "Don't you tell a soul I said that. They'll take back my medical degree!"

"You're a doctor," Carlie guessed, smiling.

"Neurologist," she said. "And I believe in modern

medicine. I just think no technology is so perfect that it won't be helped by a few prayers." She winked, glanced at Carson again, smiled, and went out.

"You hear that?" she asked Carson. "Now you have to get better so people won't think Cousin Bob Tail is a fraud."

EVEN SHE, WITH no medical training, could tell that Carson was getting worse. She got up and bent over him, brushing back the unruly long black hair that had escaped the neat ponytail he usually wore it in.

She leaned close to brush her mouth over his. She stopped. Frowned. There was a fleeting wisp of memory. Garlic. He smelled of garlic. She knew he hated it because he'd once told Rourke he couldn't abide it in Italian dishes and Rourke had told her, just in passing conversation.

Another flash of memory. Wyoming. Merissa Kirk. She'd been poisoned with the pesticide malathion disguised in capsules by Richard Martin, who'd substituted it in her migraine headache capsules. A cohort of Martin's, a woman, had tried again to poison Merissa when she was in the hospital. The woman, on Martin's orders, had put malathion in a beef dish that Merissa had for supper. It had smelled of overpowering garlic! Cash Grier had told her all about it. She let go of Carson's hand and rushed out the door. The doctor, the Lakota neurologist, was standing at the desk.

"Please, may I speak with you?" she asked hurriedly.

"Yes…"

Carlie pulled her into Carson's cubicle. While she

was walking, she was relaying the memories that had gone through her head. "Smell his breath," she asked softly.

Dr. Beaulieu caught her breath. "Poison?" She was thinking out loud. "It would account for the deterioration better than the slight head injury…"

"The woman who did it, she answered the phone when I called Carson. She said I'd get to watch him die slowly, over days!"

"Poison," the doctor agreed, black eyes narrowed. "That could explain it."

SHE WENT OUT. They came and took Carson out of the cubicle and wheeled him quickly back to the emergency surgical suite.

"It will be all right," Dr. Beaulieu assured her as she went by. "We're running a blood screen for poison right now, and I have a phone call in to the doctor whose name you gave me in Wyoming." She pressed Carlie's arm with her hand. "I think you may have saved his life."

"Cousin Bob Tail will be happy," Carlie said with just a hint of a smile.

"Oh, yes."

It seemed to take forever. Carlie sat in the waiting room this time, as close to the door as she could get, her legs pressed tightly together, her hands clenched in her lap, praying. She didn't have the presence of mind to call anyone. She was too involved in the moment.

She remembered Carson being so hostile to her in the beginning, antagonizing her with every breath, flaunting Lanette in front of her, insulting her. Then he'd frightened her, and with incredible skill, he'd treated her, taken her to the emergency room and then to have lunch by a flowing stream in the woods.

Afterward, in his arms, she'd felt things she'd never known in her young life. They'd fed the birds together and he'd told her the Brulé legend of the crow and how it became black. At the end, he'd told her it would never work out for the two of them and he was going to have to leave.

Now, there was the danger. She knew he wasn't tame. He would never be tame. He wouldn't marry her and settle down in Comanche Wells, Texas, and have children with her. He was like her father. Jake Blair had overcome his own past to change and transform himself into a man of God, into a minister. But Carson was different.

She looked at her hands, tightly clenched in her lap. Ringless. They'd be that way forever. She was never going to get married. She would have married Carson, if he'd asked. But nobody else. She'd be an old maid and fuss in her garden. She smiled sadly. Maybe one day Carson would marry someone and bring his children to visit her. Maybe they could at least remain friends. She hoped so.

The door to the surgical suite opened and Dr. Beaulieu came out. She sat beside Carlie and held her cold hands.

"We were in time," she said. "They've just finished washing out his stomach. They're giving him drugs to neutralize the effects of the poison. Your quick thinking saved his life."

Tears, hot and wet, rolled down Carlie's pale face. "Thank you."

"Oh, it wasn't me, honey," she laughed. "I just re-layed the message to the right people. I only do head injuries, although I've put in my time in emergency rooms." She smiled sadly. "Back home, there are so many sick people with no money, no way to afford decent health care. I tried to go back and work there, but I was just overwhelmed by the sheer volume of people. I decided I needed more training, so I special-ized and came here to do my residency. This is where my life is now. But one day, I'll go back to the rez and open a free clinic." She smiled, showing white teeth. "That's my dream."

"You're a nice person."

"You really love that man, don't you?" she asked with a piercing gaze.

Carlie smiled sadly. "It doesn't help much. He's a wolf. He isn't tameable."

"You know, that's what I said about my husband." She chuckled. "But he was. I have three kids."

"Lucky you."

"I am, truly." She cocked her head. "You know, Carson's great-great-grandfather rode with Crazy Horse. His family dates back far beyond the Little Big Horn."

The knowledge was surprising. Delightful. "Like mine in Comanche Wells," Carlie said softly.

"Yes. You both come from villages where families grow together. We aren't so very different, you know."

"He doesn't…love me," Carlie replied sadly. "If he did, I'd follow him around the world on my knees through broken glass."

"How do you know he doesn't?"

"He was leaving when this happened. He said it would never work out."

"I see." The other woman's face was sad. "I am truly sorry."

"I'm happy that he'll live," Carlie replied. "Even if he marries someone else and has ten kids and grows old, I'll still be happy."

Dr. Beaulieu nodded slowly. "And that is how love should be. To wish only the best for those we love, even if they choose someone else."

"When can I see him?"

"They'll take him out to a room very soon," she said, smiling. "We had him in ICU because he wasn't improving. But while they still had the tube down his throat he woke up and began cursing the technician." She chuckled. "I think they'll be very happy to release him to the poor nurses on the ward."

Carlie grinned. "He's conscious?"

"Oh, yes." She stood up. "Now will you relax?"

"I'll try." She stood up, too. *"Pilamaya ye,"* she said softly in Lakota. The feminine form of *thank you.*

Dr. Beaulieu's eyes widened. "You speak Lakota?"

"Only a few words. Those are my best ones, and I imagine my accent is atrocious."

"I've been here for two years and not one person has ever spoken even one word of Lakota to me," the other woman said with pursed lips. "However few, I appreciate the effort it took to learn them." She nodded toward the emergency suite. "Does he know you speak them?"

Carlie hesitated and then shook her head. "I was afraid he'd think I was, well, doing it just to impress him. I learned it when I was still in school. I loved reading about Crazy Horse. Of course, his mother was Miniconjou Lakota and his father was part Miniconjou, but he was raised Oglala Lakota…"

Dr. Beaulieu put her hand on Carlie's shoulder. "Okay, now you have to marry him," she said firmly. "Even on the rez, there are some people who don't know all that about Crazy Horse." And she laughed.

CARSON WAS MOVED into a room. Carlie had phoned her father and her boss to tell them Carson was out of danger.

She was allowed in when they got him settled in the bed and hooked up to a saline drip. He was sitting up, glaring, like a wolf in a trap.

"You look better," she said, hesitating in the doorway.

"Better," he scoffed. He was hoarse, from the tube. "If you agree that having your stomach pumped with a tube down your throat is better!"

"At least you're alive," she pointed out.

He glared at her. "What are you doing here?"

She froze in place. Flushed. She wasn't certain what to say. "I phoned you for Rourke and Lanette answered…"

"Lanette." He blinked. "We were having coffee. I was about to tell her that I'd never tasted worse coffee when she came up behind me and hit me in the head. A gun went off." He shifted uncomfortably. "She shot me!" He glanced at Carlie. "Where is she?"

"They have a BOLO for her," she replied, using the abbreviation for a "Be on the lookout." "She hasn't surfaced yet. Fred Baldwin, who kidnapped me, is in custody in Jacobsville, along with the watch that

Richard Martin stole from the assistant prosecutor he killed. He's turned state's evidence against Matthew Helm. They should be at his door pretty soon."

Carson was staring at her. "That doesn't answer the question. Why are you here?"

"Nobody else could be spared," she lied. "My father came by earlier. The others will be along soon, I'm sure."

His black eyes narrowed. He didn't speak. He didn't offer her a chair or ask her to sit down.

"There's a neurosurgeon here. A Dr. Beaulieu. She's Lakota. She said your cousin Bob Tail was praying for you, and that he said you'd live."

"Cousin Bob Tail usually can't even predict the weather," he scoffed.

"Well, he was right this time," she said, feeling uncomfortable. She twisted her small purse in her hands.

"Was there anything else?" he asked, his eyes unblinking and steady on her face.

She shook her head.

"Then I imagine visiting hours are over and you should go home before it gets dark."

"It's already dark," she murmured.

"All the more reason."

She nodded.

"They'll have someone watching you," he said.

"I guess."

"Don't go down any back roads and keep your phone with you."

"It's in my purse."

"Put it in your coat pocket so that you can get to it in a hurry if you have to," he continued curtly.

She grimaced, but she took it out and slid it into her coat pocket.

"Good night," he said.

She managed a faint smile. "Good night. I'm glad you're okay."

He didn't answer her.

She walked out, hesitated at the door. But she didn't look back when she left. She didn't want him to see the tears.

THEY'D GIVEN HIM something for pain. The gunshot wound, while nonfatal, was painful. So was his throat, where the tube had gone down. He was irritated that Carlie had come to see him out of some sort of obligation. Nobody else was available, she'd said. It was a chore. She hadn't come because she was terrified that he was going to die, because she cared. She'd come because nobody else was available.

Yet he was still concerned that she was driving home alone in the dark, when there had been attempts on her life. He'd wanted to phone Cash and ask him to watch out for her. Then he laughed inwardly at his own folly. Of course Cash would have her watched. He probably had somebody in the hospital the whole time, somebody who would keep her under surveillance even when she drove home.

He fell asleep, only to wake much later, feeling as if he had concrete in his side where the bullet had hit.

"Hurts, huh?"

He looked up into a face he knew. "Sunflower," he said, chuckling as he used the nickname he'd hung on her years ago. Dr. Beaulieu had been a childhood playmate. He knew her very well, knew her family for generations.

She grinned. "You're looking better."

"I feel as if a truck ran through my side," he said, grimacing. "They pumped my stomach."

"Yes. Apparently the woman who shot you also hit you on the head to show us an obvious head injury. But she poisoned you first. The poison was killing you. If it hadn't been for your friend from Comanche Wells, you'd be dead. We were treating the obvious injuries. None of us looked for poison because we didn't expect to see it." She hesitated. "We did blood work, but it was routine stuff."

"My friend?" He still felt foggy.

"Yes. The dark-headed girl who speaks Lakota," she replied. "She smelled garlic on your breath and recalled that you hated it and would never ingest it willingly. Then she remembered a poisoning case in Wyoming in a hospital there, a woman who was given malathion in a beef dish…"

"Merissa Kirk," Carson said heavily. "Yes."

"So we checked with the attending physician there for verification. I was involved only peripherally, of course, since my specialty is neurology. We thought you were unconscious because of the head wound."

"The coffee," Carson recalled. "The coffee tasted funny."

She nodded. "She told the dark-haired girl that she would get to watch you die slowly. When she smelled your breath, she remembered what the woman told her."

"Lanette." His face tautened. "I hope they hang

her. If they'll let me out, I'll track her down, wherever she goes."

Dr. Beaulieu was smiling. "She said you were like a wolf, that you could never be tame. She said it didn't matter, that she only wanted you to be happy, even if it was with some other woman." She shook her head. "She thanked me in Lakota. It was a shock. Most *wasicus* can't speak a word of our language."

"I know."

"She even knew that Crazy Horse's mother was Miniconjou," she said.

"Where's my cell phone?" he asked.

She raised both eyebrows. "Cell phone?"

"Yes. Wasn't it brought in with me?" he asked.

"Let me check." She phoned the clerk at the emergency room where he was brought in. They checked the records. She thanked them and hung up. "There was no cell phone with you when you were admitted," she said.

He grimaced. All his private numbers were there, including Carlie's, her father's and Rourke's. If Lanette had taken it...

"Will you hand me the phone, please? And tell me how to get an outside line...?"

CARLIE WAS NO sooner back home than her phone rang while she was opening the front door. She answered it.

There was nobody there. Only silence.

"Hello?" she persisted. "Look, tell me who you are or I'm calling the police."

There was a dial tone.

It worried her. She went inside to talk to her father,

But he wasn't there. A note on the hall table said that he'd been called to a meeting of the finance committee at the church. He wouldn't be long.

Carlie hung up her old coat. She started upstairs when she remembered that she'd left her cell phone in her coat. She went to get it just as there was a knock on the door.

CHAPTER FOURTEEN

"WHAT DO YOU MEAN, you can't get her on the phone?" Carson raged at Cash Grier. "Get somebody over there, for God's sake! Lanette has my cell phone. It has Carlie's number and Rourke's real number on it!"

"Will you slow down and calm down?" Cash asked softly. "I've got people watching Carlie's house. Believe me, nobody's touching her."

"Okay. How about her father?"

"At a church meeting. We have someone outside."

"Rourke?"

Cash laughed. "I arrested Rourke two hours ago in the act of placing cocaine in the glove compartment of Calhoun Ballenger's son's truck."

"Arrested?"

"You've been out of the loop," Cash told him. "Blake Kemp, our district attorney, was on the scene, along with agents from the DEA, ICE and several other agencies. We had to make it look good, in case Helm slips through our fingers and Rourke has to go undercover again."

"All right." Carson's head was throbbing. His wound hurt. "Carlie said she came because nobody else was available to sit with me—"

"Really? You should talk to the staff. She sat in

the corridor outside the E.R. and refused to budge. When they got you to ICU, she did the same thing. They even called security. She sat where she was and cried. Finally, the neurosurgeon on your case took pity on her and let her in."

"Dr. Beaulieu?" he asked.

"No, it was a man. Anyway, she smelled garlic on your breath. She connected you with the Wyoming case, told Dr. Beaulieu, and the rest is history. Saved your life, son," he added. "You were dying and they didn't know why. I assume your blond friend hit you on the head and shot you so that they wouldn't think of looking for poison until it was too late."

"I don't remember any of this."

"I guess not. I had Carlie call you at your apartment because Rourke couldn't risk having his number show up on your phone, assuming that it was bugged by Helm's men. Lanette answered it. She told Carlie that you'd be a long time dying and she'd have to watch you suffer. Almost came true."

"Almost." His heart lifted like a bird. Carlie had lied. She'd been with him all the way, all the time. She did care. Cared a lot.

"So just get well, will you? We've got everything covered down here."

"Okay." He drew in a breath. "Thanks, Cash."

"You'd do it for me."

"In a heartbeat."

He hung up the phone and closed his eyes. He should call Carlie. He wanted to. But that was when the pain meds they'd been shoveling into him took effect. He went to sleep.

CARLIE OPENED THE DOOR. Just as she did it, she re-alized that she shouldn't have done it. She had no weapon, her phone was in her coat, she was vulner-able. Just like when she'd answered the door and Fred Baldwin had carried her off.

Her father stared back at her with set lips. "How many times do I have to tell you to make sure who's at the door before you answer it?" he asked.

She smiled sheepishly. "Sorry, Dad." She stared at him. "Why did you knock?"

He grimaced. "Forgot my keys."

"See? It's genetic," she told him. "You lose your keys, I lose my phone. It's catching, and I got it from you!"

He chuckled. "Heard from Carson?"

"He's sitting up in bed yelling at people," she said.

He let out a relieved whistle. "I wouldn't have given a nickel for his chances when I saw him," he replied. He smiled. "I wouldn't have told you that. You still had hope. I guess they've got some super neurosurgeons in that hospital."

"It wasn't the head injury," she said. "Or the gun-shot wound. It was poison. She put malathion in his coffee."

"Good Lord!" he exclaimed. "That's diabolical!"

"Yes. I hope they catch her," she said doggedly. "I hope they lock her up for a hundred years!"

He hugged Carlie. "I can appreciate how you must feel."

She hugged him back. "Carson sent me home," she said, giving way to tears. "I think I made him mad by just going up there."

He grimaced. "Maybe he's trying to be kind, in

his way, Carlie. You know he's probably never going to be able to settle in some small town."

"I know. It doesn't help."

She drew back and wiped her eyes. "How about some coffee and cake?"

"That sounds nice."

"Did you just try to call me?" she added on the way.

"Me? No. Why?"

"Just a wrong number, I guess. Somebody phoned and hung up." She laughed. "I'm probably just getting paranoid, is all. I'll make a pot of coffee."

TWO DAYS LATER, Carson was out of the hospital. He was a little weak, but he felt well enough to drive. He went to his apartment first, looking for the missing cell phone. He knew he wouldn't find it. He hoped they could catch Lanette before she managed to get out of the country. She probably had several aliases that she could refer to if she was as competent at her job as he now believed she was.

A contract killer, and he'd been dating her. All the while she'd been hell-bent on killing Carlie's father. He felt like an idiot.

He drove down to Jacobsville to Cash Grier's office. As soon as he opened the door, he looked for Carlie, but she wasn't at her desk. He went on in and knocked at Cash's door.

"Come in."

He opened the door, expecting Carlie to be taking dictation or discussing the mail. She wasn't there, either.

"You look like hell," Cash said. "But at least you're still alive. Welcome back."

"Thanks. Where's Carlie?" he asked.

"Bahamas," he replied easily.

He frowned. "What's she doing in the Bahamas?"

"Haven't a clue," Cash said heavily. "She and Robin took off early yesterday on a red-eye flight out of San Antonio. She asked off for a couple of days and I told her to go ahead. She's had a rough time of it."

"I tried to call her. I didn't get an answer."

"Same here. I don't think her cell phone is working. Her father's still looking for it. She said she left it in her coat pocket, but then they noticed there's a hole in the pocket. Probably fell out somewhere and she didn't notice. She was pretty upset over you."

"I heard." He was feeling insecure. He thought Carlie cared. But she'd gone to the Bahamas with another man. He'd heard her speak of Robin with affection. Had he chased her into the arms of another man with his belligerent attitude? He should have called her father when he couldn't reach her, called the house phone. The damned drugs had kept him under for the better part of two days!

"Why did she go to the Bahamas with a man?" he asked shortly.

Cash frowned. "I don't know. She and Robin have always been close, from what I've heard. And he took her to the Valentine's Day dance." He hesitated. "It didn't seem like a love match to me. But…"

"Yes. But."

Cash could see the pain in the other man's face. "I'm sorry."

"So am I." He managed a smile. "I'm leaving."

"Today?"

He nodded. "I'm going home. I have some ghosts to lay."

Cash got up, went around the desk and extended his hand. "If you ever need help, you've got my number," he told the younger man.

Carson returned the pressure. He smiled. "Thanks."

"Keep in touch."

"I'll do that, too." He glanced out at the empty desk where Carlie usually sat.

"What do you want me to tell her?" Cash asked.

Carson's face set into hard lines. "Nothing. Nothing at all."

CARLIE STOOD UP with Robin and his fiancée, Lucy Tims, at their secret wedding in Nassau.

"I hope you'll be very happy," she told them, kissing both radiant faces.

"We will until we have to go home and face the music," Robin chuckled. "But that's not for a few days. We're going to live in paradise until then. Thanks so much for coming with us, Carlie."

"It was my pleasure. Thanks for my plane ticket," she added gently. "I sort of needed to get away for a little while."

"Stay for a couple of days anyway," Robin coaxed.

She shook her head. "Overnight was all I can manage. The chief won't even be able to deal with the mail without me," she joked. "I'm going back tonight. You two be happy, okay?"

"Okay." They kissed her again.

She didn't want to say, but she was hoping that

Carson might come to see her when he was out of the hospital. It was a long shot, after his antagonistic behavior, but hope died hard. She went home and wished for the best.

SHE MISSED HER cell phone. She knew it had probably fallen through the hole in her pocket and it was gone forever. It was no great loss. It was a cheap phone and it only had a couple of numbers in it, one was her father and the other was Cash Grier.

But it was like losing a friend, because Carson had carried it around with him before he brought it to her. It had echoes of his touch. Pathetic, she told herself, cherishing objects because they'd been held.

It had been several days. She was getting used to the idea that Carson was gone for good. Chief Grier had told her that Carson had come by the office on his way out of town. But he hadn't had a message for Carlie. That was all right. She hadn't really expected one.

She disguised the hurt on the job, but she went home and cried herself to sleep. Wolves couldn't be tamed, she reminded herself. It was useless to hope for a future that included Carson. Just useless.

ROURKE WAS BAILED out by Jake Blair. They had a good laugh about his imminent prosecution for breaking and entering, possession of narcotics and possible conspiracy.

They laughed because Rick Marquez and the San Antonio assistant D.A. working the case finally had enough evidence to arrest Matthew Helm. It made headlines all over the country, especially when

Rourke gave a statement to the effect that Mr. Helm had ordered him to plant narcotics on Calhoun Ballenger's son Terry and that Charro Mendez had supplied them.

There was an attempt to extradite Mendez to stand trial in the U.S. on drug charges, but he mysteriously vanished.

Helm wasn't so fortunate. He, his senior campaign staff and at least one San Antonio police officer were arrested and charged with crimes ranging from attempted murder to theft of police evidence and narcotics distribution.

It came as a shock when Marquez released a statement heralding Fred Baldwin as a material witness in the case. Fred, who was turning state's evidence, was being given a pardon by the governor of the state in return for his cooperation.

That news was pleasing to Eb Scott, whose kids had become great playmates of the big, gentle man who lived with them while Helm was under investigation. Eb wanted to give Fred a job, in fact, but Cash Grier beat him to it. Fred was wearing a uniform again, having been cleared of all charges against him in Chicago, his record restored, his reputation unstained, his former partner now under investigation for police corruption.

He was Jacobsville's newest patrol officer, and his first assignment was speaking to children in grammar school about the dangers of drugs. He was in his element. Children seemed to love him.

Carlie went about her business, working diligently, keeping up with correspondence for the chief. But the sadness in her was visible. She'd lost that impish

spark that had made her so much fun to be around.
Her father grieved for her, with her. He understood
what she was going through as she tried to adjust
to life without Carson, without even the occasional
glimpse of him in town. He was long gone, now.

AUTUMN CAME TO Jacobs County. The maples were
beautiful and bright, and Carlie was filling her bird
feeders for the second time, as the migrating birds
came from the north on their way to warmer climates.
Cardinals and blue jays were everywhere. The male
goldfinches were losing their bright gold color and
turning a dull green, donning their winter coats.

Carlie was still wearing her threadbare one with
the hole in the pocket sewn up. Her phone had mirac-
ulously reappeared, brought in by a street person who
found it and traded it to a soup kitchen worker for a
sandwich. The worker had turned it in to police, who
returned it to Carlie. She had the phone in her pocket
even now. It was safe enough with the hole mended.

The birds usually stayed nearby while she filled
the feeders, but they suddenly took off as if a preda-
tor was approaching. It was an odd thing, but she'd
observed it over the years many times. Sometimes,
for no apparent reason, birds just did that. Flew up
all together into the trees, when Carlie saw nothing
threatening.

This time, however, there was a threat. It was
standing just behind her.

She turned, slowly, and there he was.

She tried valiantly not to let her joy show. But tears
stung her eyes. It had been months. A lifetime. She

stood very still, the container of birdseed held tight in her hands, her eyes misting as she looked at him.

He seemed taller than ever. His hair wasn't in a ponytail. It was loose around his shoulders, long and thick and as black as a grackle's wing. He had something in a bag under one arm. He was wearing that exquisite beaded jacket that was so familiar to her.

"Hello," he said.

"Hello," she said back.

He gave her coat a speaking look. "Same coat."

She managed a smile. "I was going to say the same thing."

He moved closer. He took the seed canister out of her hands and placed it on the ground. He handed her the bag and nodded.

She opened it. Inside was the most exquisite coat she'd ever seen in her life, white buckskin with beading, Oglala Lakota colors of the four directions, in yellow, red, white and black patterns on it. She gasped as she pulled it out of the bag and just stared at it.

He held out his hand. She took off her ratty coat and gave it to him to hold while she tried on the new jacket. It was a perfect fit.

"It's the most beautiful thing in the world," she whispered, tears running down her cheeks.

"No, Carlie," he replied, dropping her old coat on top of the birdseed canister. "You're the most beautiful thing in the world. And I've missed you like hell! Come here…!"

He wrapped her up against him, half lifting her so that he could find her lips with his hard, cold mouth. He kissed her without a thought for whoever might see them. He didn't care.

He was home.

She held on for dear life and kissed him back with all the fear and sorrow and grief she'd felt in the months between when she thought she'd never see him again. Everything she felt was in that long, slow, sweet kiss.

"I love you," she choked.

"I know," he whispered into her mouth, the words almost a groan. "I've always known."

She gave up trying to talk. It was so sweet, to be in his arms. She was probably hallucinating and it wasn't real. She didn't care. If her mind had snapped, it could stay snapped. She'd never been so happy.

Eventually, he stood her back on her feet and held her away from him. "You've lost weight."

She nodded. She studied him. "You look…different."

He smiled slowly. "At peace," he explained. "I had to go home and face my demons. It wasn't easy."

She touched his hard face. "There was nothing you could have done to stop it," she said softly.

"That's what his own brother said. I made peace with his family, with her family."

"I'm glad."

"I had my cousin make the jacket. I'm glad it fits."

She smiled. "It's beautiful. I'll never take it off."

He pursed his lips. "Oh, I think you might want to do that in a week or so."

"I will? Why?"

He framed her face in his big, warm hands. "I'm not wearing clothes on my honeymoon. And neither are you."

"How do you know what I'll be wearing?" she asked, brightening.

"Because we'll be together." The smile faded. "Always. As long as we live. As long as the grass grows, and the wind blows, and the sun sets."

Tears rolled down her cheeks. "For so long?" she whispered brokenly.

"Longer." He bent and kissed away the tears. "I would have been here sooner, but I stopped by to talk to Micah Steele."

"Micah?"

He nodded. "I still have to do an internship. I'm arranging to do it here. Afterward, a year or two of residency in internal medicine, here if possible, San Antonio if not. Then I'll move into practice with Lou and Micah."

She was standing very still. She didn't understand. "You're going to medical school?"

He laughed softly. "I've already been to medical school. I got my medical license. But I never did an internship so I couldn't, technically, practice medicine." He smoothed her hand over his chest. "I did keep my medical license current. I guess I realized that I'd go back to it one day. I have some catching up to do, and I'll have to work late hours, but—"

"But you want to live here?" she asked, aghast.

"Of course," he said simply. "This is where your tribe lives, isn't it?" he teased.

Tears were falling hot and heavy now. "We're going to get married?"

He nodded. "I'm not asking, by the way," he said with pursed lips. "We're just doing it."

"Oh."

"And I don't have a ring yet. I thought we'd go together to pick them out. A set for you, and a band for me."

"You're going to wear a ring?" she asked.

"It seems to go with the position." He grinned.

She hesitated, just for a second.

"You're thinking of my reputation with women. I took them home, kissed them at the door and said good-night," he said, reading her apprehension. "It was a nice fiction, to keep homebodies like you from getting too interested in me." He shrugged. "I haven't had anybody since I was widowed."

She pressed close into his arms, held on for dear life. "I would have married you anyway."

"I know that."

"But it's nice that you don't know a lot more than I do…"

"And that's where you're wrong," he whispered into her ear. "I'm a doctor. I know where ALL the nerve endings are."

"Gosh!"

"And the minute your father pronounces us man and wife, I'll prove it to you. When we're alone, of course. We wouldn't want to embarrass your father."

"No. We wouldn't want to do that." She pressed close into his arms, felt them fold around her, comforting and loving and safe. She closed her eyes. "You didn't say goodbye."

His arms contracted. "You went to the Bahamas with another man."

She jerked back, lifting horrified eyes. "No! I went to be a witness at his wedding to Lucy Tims!" she exclaimed.

He grimaced. "I know that, now. I didn't at the time. I tried to call you, but I never got an answer."

"I lost my phone. Some kind person turned it in at a soup kitchen in San Antonio."

He sighed, tracing her mouth with a long forefinger. "A comedy of errors. I felt guilty, too. I'd sent you packing without realizing that you'd saved my life. I was still confused from the blow on the head and the drugs. I was worried that you'd be on the road alone in the dark." He leaned his forehead against hers. "Lanette was still on the loose. I was afraid for you. I should never have let you leave the hospital in the first place—"

"I was okay," she interrupted. "Cash Grier had people watching me all the time. Dad, too. Just in case."

"I hurt you. I never meant to." He closed his eyes as he rocked her in his arms. "I wasn't sure, Carlie. I had to be sure that I could settle down, that I could give up the wild ways. Until I was sure, I wasn't going to make promises."

She drew away. "And are you? Sure, I mean?"

He nodded. "That's why I went home." He smiled. "Cousin Bob Tail says we're going to have three sons. We have to name one for him."

"Okay," she said, without hesitation and with a big grin.

He laughed. "He wants us to name him Bob. Just Bob."

"I wouldn't mind." She searched his black eyes. "Our sons. Wow."

"Just what I was thinking. Wow." He chuckled. "I haven't been playing online for a while."

"Neither have I," he confessed. "I missed you so much that I really wanted to. But I had to be sure, first." He sighed. "I guess if push comes to shove I can make an Alliance toon and we can run battle-grounds on the same side."

"Funny, I was just thinking I could make a Horde toon for the same reason."

He smiled. "We're on the same side in real life. That's enough."

"So," she asked, her green eyes twinkling, "when are we getting married?"

"Let's go and ask your father when he's free," he said.

She slid her hand into his and walked back into the house with him. Her father didn't even have to ask. He just grinned.

THEY WENT TO Tangier for their honeymoon. Carlie was horrified at the expense, but Carson just laughed.

"Honey, I've got enough in foreign banks to keep us going into our nineties," he said complacently. "I work because I enjoy working. I could retire tomorrow if I felt like it. But I think practicing medicine will occupy me for many years to come. That, and our children."

"You told Rourke you wanted to be an attorney," she recalled.

"Yes, well, if you tell somebody you gave up law they don't care. If you tell them you gave up medicine, that's a whole other set of explanations I didn't want to make. As it happens, I did a double major in undergraduate school in biology and chemistry, but

I minored in history and anatomy. History and law do go together."

"I wouldn't know. Will it matter to you that I haven't been to college?"

"You're kidding, right?" he teased. "You can speak Lakota and you know who Crazy Horse's mother was. That's higher education enough to suit me."

"Okay. Just so you're sure," she laughed. "And you don't mind if I go on working for the chief?"

"He'd skin me if I tried to take you away," he said with a sigh. "He'd never find a stamp or a potato chip, and some new girl would surely find out about the alien files he's got locked up in his office and call the Air Force. So, no, you can go on working. I intend to."

She smiled. "Dr. Farwalker. Sounds very nice."

"I thought so myself."

TANGIER WAS AN amazing blend of old and new. There were high-rise apartment buildings near the centuries-old walled marketplace. Carlie found it fascinating as they drove through the city at night in the back of a taxicab.

It had been a very long flight, from San Antonio to Atlanta, Atlanta to Brussels, Brussels to Casablanca, Casablanca to Tangier. They'd arrived in the dead of night and Carlie was worried sick about being able to find a way to get into the city as they waited end-lessly to get through passport control and customs. But there were cabs sitting outside the main building.

"Told you so," he chuckled.

"Is there any foreign city you haven't been to?" she wondered.

"Not many," he confessed. "You'll love this one.

I'll take you around town tomorrow and show you where the pirates used to hang out."

"That's a deal."

CARLIE WAS SO tired by the time they got into the hotel, registered and were shown to their room that she almost wept.

"Now, now," he said softly. "We have our whole lives for what you're upset about missing. Sleep first. Then, we explore."

She smiled shyly. "Okay."

He watched her undress, with black eyes that appreciated every stitch that came off. But when she was down to her underwear, he moved close, pulled out a gown and handed it to her.

"First times are hard," he said gently. "Go put on your gown. I'll get into my pajamas while you're gone. Then we'll get some sleep before we do anything else. Deal?"

She smiled with relief. "Deal. I'm sorry," she started to add.

He put his fingers across her lips. "I like you just the way you are," he told her.

"Hang-ups and all?"

He smiled. "Hang-ups and all."

She let out the breath she'd been holding and darted into the bathroom, chiding herself for her wedding night nerves. It was natural, she supposed, despite the fact that most people had the wedding night long before the wedding. She and Carson must be throwbacks, she decided, because he'd wanted to wait as much as she had.

The lights were out when she came back into the room. The shutters were open, and moonlight filtered across the bed, where Carson was sprawled under the sheet. He held out his arm. She darted into bed and went close, pillowing her cheek on his hard, warm chest.

"Oh, that feels good," she whispered.

"I was about to say the same thing. Happy?"

"I could die of it."

"I know exactly what you mean." He closed his eyes, tucked her close and fell asleep almost at once. So did she. It had been a very long trip.

SHE WOKE THE next morning to the smell of coffee. She opened her eyes. Carson was sitting on the side of the bed in his pajama bottoms holding the cup just over her head.

"What a wonderful smell," she moaned.

"Sit up and have a sip. They serve a nice buffet breakfast downstairs, but I thought you might like coffee first."

"I would." She sat up, noticing at once how much of her small breasts were visible under the thin gown. He was looking at them with real interest, his eyes soft and hungry.

The way he looked at her made her feel beautiful. Exciting. Exotic.

"Tangier," she murmured, putting the cup down on the side table. "It makes me feel like I should be wearing a trenchcoat or something." Breathlessly, she slid the straps of the gown down her arms and let them fall.

Carson's expression was eloquent. He didn't even hesitate. He moved across the bed, putting her down on it, while his mouth opened and fed on her firm, soft breasts.

She arched up, shyness vanishing in the heat of sudden passion. She felt his hands go down her back, sliding fabric out of the way. She felt him move and then his body was moving on hers, bare and exciting.

He eased between her legs, his mouth poised over hers. He teased her lips while his body teased hers. He was smiling, but there was heat and passion in the smile. "Lift up," he whispered. "Seduce me."

"Gosh, I don't have…the slightest idea…I'm sorry…I…!" A tiny, helpless moan escaped her as his hand moved between them. "Carson, oh, gosh!"

"Yes, right there," he murmured at her lips. He chuckled softly. "It feels good, doesn't it? And this is just the beginning."

"Just the…?" She cried out again. Her body arched, shivering. What he was doing was shocking, inva-sive, she should be protesting or something, she should be… "Carson," she sobbed against his mouth. "Please…don't stop!"

"Never," he breathed against her lips. "Move this leg. Yes. Here. And that one. Now lift. Lift up, baby. Lift up…that's it…yes!"

There was a rhythm. She'd never known. In all her reading and covert watching of shocking movies, she'd never experienced anything like this.

It was one thing to read about it, quite another to do it. He knew more about her body than she did, apparently, and used that knowledge to take her to places she'd never dreamed about. The sensations piled upon themselves, growing and multiplying, until she felt as if she had the sun inside her and it was going to explode any second. The tension was so high that it was like being pulled apart in the sweet-est sort of way.

She dug her nails into his hips as he strained down toward her, his powerful body arched above her as he drove down one last time.

She heard herself sobbing as she fell and fell, into layers of sweet heat that burned and burned and burned. It was like tides, rippling and falling, over-whelming and falling, crushing and falling, until fi-nally she burst like fireworks and shuddered endlessly under the heavy, hard thrust of his body.

She heard him cry out at her ear, a husky sound that was so erotic, she shivered again when she felt his body cord and ripple and then, quite suddenly, relax.

He was heavy. His skin was hot, damp. She held him, smoothed the long, thick hair at his back, lov-ing him.

"Everybody says it hurts the first time," she mur-mured.

"Oh? Did it?"

She laughed secretly. "I don't know."

He chuckled, the sound rippling against her hard-tipped breasts. He moved on her, feeling her instant response. He lifted his head and looked into her wide, soft eyes. "You will never get away," he promised her. "No matter how far, how fast you run, I will find you."

"I will never run," she said with a sigh. "Every-thing I want or love in all the world is right here, in my arms."

He bent and kissed her eyes shut as he began to move. She shivered gently.

"How long do you want to wait?" he whispered at her mouth.

"How…long? For…what?" she gasped, moving with him.

"To make a baby," he whispered back.

Her eyes opened. She shivered again. The look on her face was all the answer he needed. He held her gaze as he moved, tenderly, enclosing her in his legs, bending them beside her, so that they were locked together in the most intimate position she'd ever experienced.

"Oh…my…goodness," she said, looking straight into his eyes.

His hands framed her face. His was strained, taut, as he moved expertly on her body.

"I can't bear it," she managed to say.

"Yes, you can," he whispered. His eyes held hers. "I love you. This is how much…"

He shifted, and she cried out. The pleasure was beyond words, beyond description. She held on and sobbed with each slow, deep, torturous movement of his hips as he built the tension and built it and built it until she exploded into a million tiny hot pieces of sheer joy.

He groaned, almost convulsing, as the pleasure bit into him. "Never," he whispered hoarsely. "Never, never like this!"

She couldn't even manage a word. She just clung to him, enjoying the sight of the pleasure in his face, in the corded muscles of his body, in the sweet agony that echoed in the helpless movements of his hips.

Long after they felt the last ripple of pleasure, they

clung to each other in the bright stillness of the morning, unable to let go.

"I think I dreamed you," he whispered finally.

"I know I dreamed you," she replied at his ear, still holding tight.

He rolled over so that she was beside him, but still joined to his body.

"I didn't know it felt like this," she confessed shyly. "I feel hungry now in a way I didn't before."

He smiled, brushing his mouth over hers. "You can't miss what you've never had."

"I guess so." She drew in a breath and looked down.

He smiled to himself and pulled away, letting her look. Her eyes were as wide as saucers when he moved away.

"Show-and-tell," he teased.

She blushed. "Men in racy magazines don't look like that," she whispered. "I only saw one and he was, well, he was…" She cleared her throat. "He wasn't that impressive."

He chuckled. He pulled her to her feet, enjoying her nudity. "I have an idea."

"You do? What?" she asked, looking up at him with a smile.

"Let's have a shower, and then breakfast and go look for pirates."

"I would like that very much."

He led her toward the bathroom.

She hesitated at the door.

He raised an eyebrow.

"What you said." She indicated the bed. "Was it just, I mean, did you really mean it?"

He pulled her close. "I want children very much, Carlie," he said softly. "They'll come when it's time for them to come." He smiled. "If it's this year, I don't mind at all. Do you?"

She laughed and hugged him close. "Oh, no, I don't mind!"

"Then let's have a shower and go eat. I'm starving!"

LIFE WITH CARSON was fascinating. They found more in common every day. They moved into a house of their own and Carson went to work at Jacobsville General as an intern. It was long hours and hard work. He never complained and when he got home, he told Carlie all the interesting things he'd learned that day. She never tired of listening.

Fred Baldwin had coffee with her when he started out on his patrols. He'd turned into a very good cop, and he'd have done anything for Cash Grier. He'd have done anything for Carlie, too. He told her that her father was going to have to share her with him because he didn't have a daughter of his own. She'd almost cried at the tenderness in his big brown eyes.

Lanette had been found, but not in a condition that would lead to trial. She took a flight to a small South American country that had no extradition treaty with the United States, but had the misfortune to run into the brother of a man she'd killed for money. Since she had no living family, they buried her in an unmarked grave in South America.

Matthew Helm was arrested, prosecuted and convicted on so many felony counts that he'd only get out of prison when he was around 185 years old. Or so the jury decided.

His cohorts went with him. The wife of the murdered assistant district attorney was in the courtroom when the sentence was pronounced.

Calhoun Ballenger won the special election and went to Washington, D.C., with his wife, Abby, as the junior United States senator from the grand state of Texas. Terry, having just graduated from high school, was off to college with his two brothers, Ed and Matt.

Calhoun had given Fred Baldwin a musical watch that played an Italian folk song when he learned about Fred's role in preventing the potential criminalization of his son Terry. Fred wore the watch to work every day.

Charro Mendez was still on the run. But people across the border were watching and waiting for his return.

Two months after Carlie and Carson were married, she was waiting for him at the front door when he came home from a long day at the hospital. She was holding a small plastic device in her hands. She handed it to him with an impish grin.

He looked at it, read it, picked her up and swung her around in his arms, kissing her the whole while and looking as if he'd won the lottery.

Seven months later, a little boy was born at Jacobsville General Hospital. They named him Jacob Allen Cassius Fred Farwalker, for his father, his grandfather and his two godfathers. Officer Fred Baldwin held him while he was baptized. He cried.

* * * * *

*Don't miss Diana Palmer's next
HQN in the summer of 2015—UNTAMED—
the romance of Rourke and the woman
who finally tames the rogue warrior!*

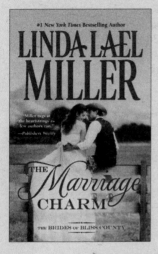

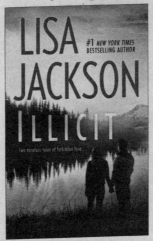

REQUEST YOUR
FREE BOOKS!

2 FREE NOVELS
FROM THE ROMANCE COLLECTION
PLUS 2 FREE GIFTS!

YES! Please send me 2 FREE novels from the Romance Collection and my 2 FREE gifts (gifts are worth about $10). After receiving them, if I don't wish to receive any more books, I can return the shipping statement marked "cancel." If I don't cancel, I will receive 4 brand-new novels every month and be billed just $6.24 per book in the U.S. or $6.74 per book in Canada. That's a savings of at least 22% off the cover price. It's quite a bargain! Shipping and handling is just 50¢ per book in the U.S. and 75¢ per book in Canada.* I understand that accepting the 2 free books and gifts places me under no obligation to buy anything. I can always return a shipment and cancel at any time. Even if I never buy another book, the two free books and gifts are mine to keep forever.

194/394 MDN F4XY

Name _____ (PLEASE PRINT) _____

Address _____ Apt. # _____

City _____ State/Prov. _____ Zip/Postal Code _____

Signature (if under 18, a parent or guardian must sign)

Mail to the Harlequin® Reader Service:
IN U.S.A.: P.O. Box 1867, Buffalo, NY 14240-1867
IN CANADA: P.O. Box 609, Fort Erie, Ontario L2A 5X3

Want to try two free books from another line?
Call 1-800-873-8635 or visit www.ReaderService.com.

* Terms and prices subject to change without notice. Prices do not include applicable taxes. Sales tax applicable in N.Y. Canadian residents will be charged applicable taxes. Offer not valid in Quebec. This offer is limited to one order per household. Not valid for current subscribers to the Romance Collection or the Romance/Suspense Collection. All orders subject to credit approval. Credit or debit balances in a customer's account(s) may be offset by any other outstanding balance owed by or to the customer. Please allow 4 to 6 weeks for delivery. Offer available while quantities last.

Your Privacy—The Harlequin® Reader Service is committed to protecting your privacy. Our Privacy Policy is available online at www.ReaderService.com or upon request from the Harlequin Reader Service.

We make a portion of our mailing list available to reputable third parties that offer products we believe may interest you. If you prefer that we not exchange your name with third parties, or if you wish to clarify or modify your communication preferences, please visit us at www.ReaderService.com/consumerschoice or write to us at Harlequin Reader Service Preference Service, P.O. Box 9062, Buffalo, NY 14269. Include your complete name and address.

ROM13R

DIANA PALMER

77977	LONG, TALL TEXANS VOLUME III: ETHAN & CONNAL	___ $7.99 U.S.	___ $8.99 CAN.
77976	LONG, TALL TEXANS VOLUME II: TYLER & SUTTON	___ $7.99 U.S.	___ $8.99 CAN.
77975	LONG, TALL TEXANS VOLUME I: CALHOUN & JUSTIN	___ $7.99 U.S.	___ $8.99 CAN.
77941	WYOMING TOUGH	___ $7.99 U.S.	___ $8.99 CAN.
77910	WYOMING STRONG	___ $7.99 U.S.	___ $8.99 CAN.
77854	PROTECTOR	___ $7.99 U.S.	___ $8.99 CAN.
77762	COURAGEOUS	___ $7.99 U.S.	___ $9.99 CAN.
77727	NOELLE	___ $7.99 U.S.	___ $9.99 CAN.
77724	WYOMING BOLD	___ $7.99 U.S.	___ $8.99 CAN.
77696	WYOMING FIERCE	___ $7.99 U.S.	___ $9.99 CAN.
77666	MERCILESS	___ $7.99 U.S.	___ $8.99 CAN.
77631	NORA	___ $7.99 U.S.	___ $9.99 CAN.
77570	DANGEROUS	___ $7.99 U.S.	___ $9.99 CAN.
77283	LAWMAN	___ $7.99 U.S.	___ $7.99 CAN.

(limited quantities available)

TOTAL AMOUNT	$_____
POSTAGE & HANDLING	$_____
($1.00 FOR 1 BOOK, 50¢ for each additional)	
APPLICABLE TAXES*	$_____
TOTAL PAYABLE	$_____

(check or money order—please do not send cash)

To order, complete this form and send it, along with a check or money order for the total above, payable to Harlequin HQN, to: **In the U.S.:** 3010 Walden Avenue, P.O. Box 9077, Buffalo, NY 14269-9077; **In Canada:** P.O. Box 636, Fort Erie, Ontario, L2A 5X3.

Name: _____
Address: _____ City: _____
State/Prov.: _____ Zip/Postal Code: _____
Account Number (if applicable): _____

075 CSAS

*New York residents remit applicable sales taxes.
*Canadian residents remit applicable GST and provincial taxes.

www.HQNBooks.com

PHDP0215BL